Desert Rites

Xuemo

Translated by Howard Goldblatt and Sylvia Li-chun Lin

First Edition 2018

ISBN 978-7-5202-0342-5

Published by Encyclopedia of China Publishing House

Fuchengmen Beidajie No.17, Xicheng District , Beijing, China

Tel:(86)10-88390739

http://www.ecph.com.cn

E-mail:limoyun2008@sina.com

Printed by Allied Fortune Industrial Limited (AF printing)

Contents

Chapter One

1

The rabbit-hawks come in late summer, around the time of Bailu, or White Dew, when the desert sand yellows, the grass grows tall, and the rabbits are plump. After a restive summer, they swoop down from the Qilian Mountains and wheel toward the Tengger Desert in Gansu.

Laoshun set his snare on the dry Dasha River bed.

Constructed of cotton thread on three sides, it formed a tripod over a tethered pigeon—the bait. A hawk, famished from failing to catch any of the increasingly elusive rabbits, flew headlong into it.

With eyes that can see for miles, it did not notice the snare right in front of it.

The usual morning task: "crush" a hawk.

Laoshun awoke early that morning, jolted out of a dream teeming with rabbits that descended on him with bloody mouths, so many they nearly blotted out the sky. A believer in retribution, he was sure they were animals that had died at his hands, now coming to claim his life. He had dreams like that all the time, and after the first time actually decided to stop flying hawks altogether.

"Nonsense!" Meng Eight had exclaimed. "Stop and the rabbits will ruin our crops. We'd be lucky if we didn't starve."

That comment persuaded Laoshun that flying hawks was in fact a moral act that accumulated good karma. Mostly, though, he grew restless and hated the idea of giving up the tasty rabbit meat after White Dew passed. And yet the killing of sentient beings cast a shadow on his mind, so the dream haunted his sleep, and he awoke in a cold sweat each time it visited him. The dream recurred, yet he kept flying his hawks. Rabbits ruined the crops, and that thought was the "broom" with which he managed to sweep the shadow off across the mountains.

The moment he turned on the light, the hawk named "Stubborn Yellow" flapped its wings to show its agitation. Obviously, it too was having visions, likely dreaming of soaring aloft. That must be it, Laoshun said to himself. Humans smack their lips when they dream of eating meat, and a hawk flaps its wings when it dreams of flying. He noticed that the bird's eyes were open. Those commanding eyes were always in motion; he loved eyes like that, true hawk eyes, the windows through which he could see what made a hawk a hawk.

Stubborn Yellow was an exasperating bird, hard to care for, with a violent temper; but that meant it was a good hawk, the way a fine steed is hard to tame, and a loyal minister is staunch and upright. The hotter the temper, the more likely that the bird will turn out to be a treasure. Once tamed, it will be an expert rabbit hunter and unfailingly dependable. A second-rate hawk like Indigo Widow, on the other hand, turns docile the moment it is trapped; it eats what it is given and allows itself to be touched. On the surface, it appears to have been subdued, but it will fly away the moment it is released. Catch a rabbit? Sniff a rabbit's rear end is more likely!

Laoshun preferred spirited hawks.

A thumb-sized ball of wool lay on the ground. He had forced it down Stubborn Yellow's craw the night before, and the bird had expelled it in the morning with a twist of its neck. He picked the ball up and examined it under the light; it was spotless, which meant that the bird had cleaned out its phlegm and was now ready to be flown over rabbits. This was the seventh ball. The previous six had gone in at night and come out the next morning covered with a viscous yellow substance called "tan," a term passed down by Laoshun's ancestors. Lingguan, his youngest son, said it was fat. It did not matter to Laoshun what it was called, only that it was the substance that made a hawk wild. Without removing it, he would lose the bird the moment he let it go. Swoosh—into the sky and out of sight by the time it went into its dive. Once the phlegm was cleared, the hawk would experience vertigo when it flew too high, and hunger would force it to pounce on the first rabbit it saw.

Laoshun decided that this was the day to let Yellow Stubborn hunt. Timing was critical. If he held off too long, it might be too tame to recall that it was a bird of prey. Everything was ready, and what he needed now was the proverbial east wind. All his training led to this singular act of setting it loose; Laoshun was as keyed up as a soldier before battle.

Fresh air greeted him when he opened the door. It was the cheering smell of a rural morning; his insides were washed clean with brisk air that filled his lungs and reminded him of cool water. It was not entirely light out yet, and a few stars twinkled playfully in the sky, like the shifty eyes of Maodan, the old bachelor of the village.

A deep, drawn-out, and powerful bellow from Handless Wei's bull rent the air. It was a huge animal, with a long, muscular body whose flesh and bones churned when it ran. When it mounted milk cows, the smaller animals crumpled under its weight. Laoshun laughed, amused by such thoughts at a moment like this.

Clearing his throat noisily, he knocked on his sons' door.

"Time to get up, young masters. The sun's high enough to bake your asses. Don't forget, it's thanks to your parents' gray hair that yours has remained black all these years."

"All right, enough," Lingguan grumbled. "Would your belly burst if you kept your complaints to yourself for a change?"

Laoshun smiled. He knew how to talk to his sons. If he went easy on them, nothing would happen, like pounding on water; they would sleep on and ignore him. But they talked back if he came down too hard, and getting hot under the collar so early in the morning would not bode well for the rest of the day.

"It's thanks to your parents' gray hair that yours has remained black all these years" sounded just right, stinging a bit but not too much; besides, it was the truth. Laoshun and his wife had toiled from dawn to dusk to raise four children, the family's "young masters," sons who don't act like sons, and sent them all to school. Mengzi had finished middle school, Lanlan, the girl, had completed one year of middle school, and Lingguan had gone all the way through high school. Hantou had fared the worst, with only a primary education. But that was not his fault. A family of six had depended solely on the labors of Laoshun and his wife until Hantou started work at the well. On this morning he was not back yet from his night shift.

Laoshun carried a basket of grass into the animal pen. The familiar smells of animal sweat and manure seemed to bathe his heart in warm water. This was his favorite daily chore. The black mule, sired by Handless Wei's donkey, had grown so fast it was nearly a full-sized animal at one year. Gimpy Five had his eyes on this mule, pestering Laoshun to sell it to him. Laoshun could not do that. He might be talked into selling another animal, but not this one, as close to him as an animal could be. He could not and would not part with it. Just look at that fine creature, with its long, slender legs, the essence of nobility. The young mule liked company, so when it saw Laoshun, it touched his hands with its soft, white lips. That felt as good as anything he could imagine. Look, here it comes. Patting its neck, Laoshun scolded tenderly:

"You're always hungry."

The mule brayed fawningly, and that made him smile. The warm spot in his heart stirred anew.

After laying out grass for the mule, Laoshun heard the camel growl in its shed, a voice that was full and a bit of a monotone, as if choking back a cry. While it was not as pleasing a sound as the mule's soft bray, the camel was his favorite animal. The largest and strongest of its kind anywhere in the village, it had a fine, smooth coat that was bright and glistened yellow. Its humps stood tall and straight, like mountain peaks, in contrast to Baigou's emaciated camel, with humps like sagging breasts. Its patchy coat was a sorry sight, matted and covered with straw and twigs, a camel's version of a slattern. So sad. It could not compare with Laoshun's camel, a voracious eater and a great farm animal that fattened up easily. When yoked to a plow, it could clear an acre of land with ruler-straight rows in no time. To be fair, Laoshun favored the camel in part because its molted hair fetched eight hundred or a thousand each year, providing the family with a steady income.

2

After slipping a leather gauntlet over his hand, Laoshun left the house with Indigo Widow on his wrist. A misty cloud drifted by as the sun started its climb. Distant trees and nearby houses were almost illusory, like a wash painting that has soaked up too much ink.

A dreary chill was borne on an air current that surged up from the heart of the desert. It carried early morning moisture and a sting that bored through clothes and skin, straight into the heart.

The village was waking up. The deep, drawn-out lows of cattle; the loud, eager brays of donkeys; and the gentle, lingering calls of sheep were suspended in cool breezes. Villagers left their houses in twos and threes, spiritedly leading farm animals or lugging buckets of water. Sleep had washed away the exhaustion from the day before, and everything was starting anew. Shawan villagers are never nostalgic for the past, nor do they ponder the future; they care only about the present; every morning generates a good beginning.

Laoshun was happiest in the morning, before troubling matters intruded.

Setting Indigo Widow down on the ground in front of his gate, he undid the leather thong on the opening of a plastic bag and extracted a strip of beef soaked in bloody water. He stepped away and shouted. The hawk flew over and landed on his wrist, stretched its neck, and the meat was gone.

Indigo Widow was a well-crushed hawk.

An expert in every step involved in training a hawk, Laoshun understood well why his ancestors called it "crushing," not "taming," a hawk. For it was like crushing a sheet of paper until it was creased and wrinkled; the hunters crushed a spirited, intractable, fearless hawk until it was a submissive ball of feathers.

It was a wretched process.

It started out with stuffing the wool ball down the craw. Then it was necessary to wear the hawk down, shouting at it day and night, not giving it a moment's peace or rest. Hunger and exhaustion forced it to peck at blood-leached meat, a fare not intended to bring out its wild nature. Taunted, humiliated, and denied sleep from early morning to late at night, it ultimately capitulated by perching passively on a gloved wrist, having been turned into a tool.

Indigo Widow was well contained; shorn of its wild nature and largely dispirited, no matter how it was touched, it never flapped its wings, shrieked, or fought back like a hawk worthy of the name. It was said that a good bird will never let you ruffle its feathers. Could a tamed creature that would not struggle to soar into the sky, but would perch on a human wrist to beg for food still be called a hawk? Laoshun could only smile.

He had trapped but two unyielding hawks. One had died the moment it was caught, before he'd had a chance to place bamboo guards over its talons. He would never forget the violent struggle it waged before dying. The snare, which he'd built on the dry riverbed, had collapsed, and a terrifying glint shot out of the bird's blood-red eyes, those of a true hawk.

The other one had died ten days into its captivity, soon after the training process had begun. With guards over its talons and a leather thong tied to its leg, it had fought all "crushing" attempts. Laoshun's every touch had provoked tempestuous resistance. It had thrashed its wings and screeched, a cry unlike that of most hawks, and had flailed about angrily until, exhausted, it had swayed listlessly on its perch, like a dishonored woman who has hanged herself.

This hawk had starved to death, refusing to look at the meat, even when it had been reduced to a ball of dull feathers that could seemingly be carried off by the wind. Its nobility made Laoshun feel loathsome and cruel. One morning, he'd found it dead, still on the perch, as if asleep. It had not fallen off, and he'd had to break its talons to remove it. "That was some hawk," he liked to say.

Laoshun did not care for his son's trick of letting go the hawk, quickly hiding from it, and then shouting, so the bird would follow the sound onto his wrist. Laoshun had no interest in a hawk like that; he much preferred Stubborn Yellow, whose wild eyes appeared to view the world with contempt. Its lethal beak terrified him.

After tossing a few strips of meat to Indigo Widow, he retied the thong and headed down the village dirt road.

By then the sun was up. Not yet bright, it rolled up to sand dunes in the east, its yellow rays tinged with red, like a young hen's first egg. But then the egg began to roll, shedding its yellow and its red and turning into a shiny Ping-Pong ball that floated atop the waves of sand.

3

He reached the Dasha River just as the dark clouds dispersed. Animals were grazing on the grassy sandbar where some men were talking excitedly.

"Hurry, there's a trapped hawk!" Baigou shouted when he spotted Laoshun.

"Whose snare?"

"Yours," Meng Eight said.

"I don't care whose it is," a young man named Beizhu complained, baring his teeth and cradling one hand in the other. "I'm going to kill this feathered monster. It just about tore my hand off." He snatched a whip from Baigou and snapped it at the hawk, drawing a shriek from the bird.

"Stop that, Beizhu, you dumb ass!" Laoshun shouted. "Who said you could touch it. You're too used to fondling your sister-in-law's breasts. You can't do that just because you feel like it. It's a hawk. No wonder it clawed you."

"Nobody touched it," Baigou said. "It looked so sad hanging there, he wanted to help it down."

"Who do you think you're kidding?" Laoshun said with a contemptuous smile. "You two are windbags with nothing worth boasting about, like butter in a dog's guts! Seeing my hawks catch rabbits has made you jealous, so you want to steal one. Have I got that right? You bring shame to your ancestors. Do you really think you can train a hawk?"

"He's right," Meng Eight said. "I've been a hunter all my life and I've never trained a hawk. I was born to fire a gun, not crush a bird. I either kill them or they fly off and refuse to catch rabbits. How many animal droppings have you licked up? No, you got exactly what you deserved. In fact, I think you got off easy; it should have snatched off your donkey balls. That'll show you what a hawk can do."

"Stop laughing at a man in agony," Beizhu said, looking downcast. "Anyone who doesn't help a man in pain will die a horrible death. Being clawed isn't serious, is it, Uncle Shun? Will it get infected?"

"No, it's not that bad. It'll heal in a few days." Laoshun turned to Meng Eight's grandson, Huaqiu. "Run to my house and have Lingguan bring the talon guards and some ointment."

Huaqiu did as he was told.

"Since you're such a great hunter, why don't you take it out of the snare?" Baigou mocked Meng. "It'll probably be as docile as a sparrow when it sees you."

"And get clawed? I'm not bragging when I say I can shoot a bird on the wing and an animal on the run. But taking a hawk out of a snare requires a special skill, if you want to keep your hand. Like tangled string around a chicken's neck, the more you try to free it, the tighter it gets."

"So there is something you can't do," Baigou jeered. "I thought you were so fucking good you could do anything."

"I can sure as hell do more than you." Meng laughed dryly. "What are you good at besides messing around with your sister-in-law? Ah, I nearly forgot. You also know how to add a second leg to the baby in her belly. Beizhu, since you added a leg to your nephew in the womb, it must have been Baigou who gave one to your son. Baigou, go home and tell your sister-in-law, 'Fengxiang, I haven't given a leg to my future niece, and we don't want her to come out a cripple.' Then you show her what you've got and deposit that leg."

Everyone had a good laugh over that, including Meng, who added:

"Do a good job, Baigou. Just follow Beizhu's example. Like they say, an eighteen-year-old is hot to trot, but a twenty-year-old does the trotting."

"You old skunk," Beizhu swore. "There's no need to drool. Pluck a turnip and the hole remains. What does the blind storyteller say? 'An old pear tree can mount a fresh begonia, but nothing will come of it.'"

"I never knew that Beizhu could be so generous with his wife," Meng said as he stroked his beard. "But I'm too old for that now. Like they say, all an old man is good for is shitting his pants when he meant to fart, spitting out more words than a dog has fleas, and wetting his shoes when he pees. I had a proud youth, but those days are gone. I'm old."

In the midst of this friendly banter, Huaqiu arrived with Lingguan, who was arguing with Mengzi.

"See?" his brother said. "I told you we'd bag one today, but you didn't believe me."

"You said the same thing yesterday and the day before," Lingguan retorted.

"But I repeated it three times last night."

"You repeated it seven times the night before."

"I said I'd give you a pig's foot if we didn't get one today."

"You already owe me for yesterday, but I haven't seen a single hog bristle."

"Why are you arguing with him?" Laoshun said to Lingguan. "Nothing ever comes out of him but empty words and empty gas."

Meng Eight laughed at the comment, his goatee quivering as he said:

"Listen to you, fighting so early in the morning. A trough can't feed three donkeys, you know. Say, Laoshun, how about crushing a hawk for me?"

"A man who neuters cats can't castrate a pig. Stick with your musket. What do you need a hawk for?"

"I want both, one for foxes and one for rabbits. Whenever I hunt foxes, I see rabbits, and I wish I had a hawk."

"Just shoot the damned things." Laoshun took bamboo guards out of the sack.

"I could do that, but it's not as much fun as flying a hawk.

Swoosh—into the air to engage the enemy. Those fights are better than the martial arts scenes you see on TV. I'm getting old. Who knows when I'll draw my last breath? I'll stick out my legs and ball up my fists as I head down to the underworld. Could I still fly a hawk down there? Hell, no."

"All right." Laoshun walked up to check on the hawk in the snare. "This is a red hawk, hot tempered and hard to raise. I can train it for you, but you'll have to teach Lingguan and his brothers how to shoot. Deal?"

"Hah! What a cunning old shit! You're so greedy you'd bend down to breathe in someone's farts. So that's what you have in mind. I'll tell you, Laoshun, you should help your sons find a better future and forget about muskets. It's not something to take up lightly. Sometimes I'll be hunting in the desert all day and not get a bite of hot food in me. Besides, it's not good to be killing all the time. Lingguan, are you still studying for next year's exam?"

"Not anymore. I guess I was born to live off the land."

"That's the idea. Martial arts can't cure a cold, and book learning won't fill your stomach. You've got to live whether you pass the exam or not. Soon you'll get yourself a wife and a son, then a grandson, and that's what life is all about."

"I think you ought to take the exam," Huaqiu cut in. "It'd be a shame to waste all that schooling."

"Why is that a shame?" Meng Eight said. 'I've never been inside a schoolroom, and I've had a good life. I don't believe officials or rich men live a more carefree or satisfying life than I do. Forget about carefree and focus on satisfaction, I mean a satisfied heart, what you youngsters call contentment. Can they match me on that? When I bag a fox or eat a rabbit, I feel con—tent—ment. Them? They scowl even when they're eating fine food."

"You're always saying things like that. You destroy my faith in life." Huaqiu frowned.

"It's for your own good. There'll never be enough of anything. When your belly's full, you want something nice to wear, and when you've got clothes on your back, you want to be rich. When you've got money, you want to go whoring. Where does it end? You conquer the world, but all you wind up with is four boards for a coffin."

"If you don't want to conquer the world, why hunt foxes?" Baigou asked.

"I have my use for them. I hunt when I need money. I don't hanker after two foxes when I get one just so I can put money in the bank. Why waste the effort? There are foxes in the desert so people can dig themselves out of tight spots, and it's against the laws of Nature to want more. Once you get greedy, you get restless, you're troubled, and your life won't be carefree and satisfying. Now that I think about it, having your sons learn to use a musket is probably a good idea, Laoshun. Anyone with a skill will survive a famine."

"That's what I'm talking about." Laoshun went up and gently shook the snare, making the hawk shriek and struggle violently. "You have to live no matter what. What kind of future is it if you don't have a son to give you a grandson? See those two young masters of mine—they're old enough now, and I can't have them stay bachelors forever. You have to shed a few layers of skin when you marry off a son. But how much money will my little slice of land bring in?"

"Foxes." Meng Eight sighed. "You think they're easy to hunt? Sometimes you can be down to skin and bones without seeing a single fox hair. Besides, no one has ever gotten rich from fox hunting. A lot of it is pure luck."

"You might be right." Laoshun carefully removed the threads from the hawk's legs. The screeches grew louder and the hawk's bloodshot eyes looked about to pop out of their sockets. There was rage in those eyes, and fright, but mostly there was exasperation over the humiliating experience, as if to say, "Who are you to handle me like that?"

As the hawk screeched on, Laoshun grabbed hold of its legs and secured them, while Lingguan put ointment into the bamboo guards and fitted them over the talons.

"You may be tough and you may be clever, but you're no match for me," Laoshun said.

"Okay, come on, claw me again." Beizhu walked up and held out his injured hand.

Ignoring him, the hawk exploded with another burst of shrieks, venting the outrage of the king of the sky over falling into a snare.

Laoshun was swift but cautious; the tangled threads around the bird's wings fell away wherever he touched them. It was a skill he had honed over many years. A newcomer at training hawks could follow the process, but would have trouble unraveling the mass of crisscrossing threads. As the bird fought wildly, every thread was like a restraining rope, and it was essential to quickly disentangle the mess and free the bird without damaging its feathers. A hawk depends on its feathers to display its dominance, which is decreased with the loss of even one.

"See that?" Meng Eight said to the young men, who were staring wide-eyed. "See how he did it? Don't try repairing porcelain pots if you don't have a diamond drill. Training a hawk isn't as easy as you think."

Laoshun proudly removed the hawk from the snare, and was caught off guard when it dug its beak into his hand. He cried out in pain. "Put on your gauntlet, Hantou, and get over here!"

Meng Eight chuckled. "I thought muskets were hard. Obviously, hawks are too."

"You can say that again." Laoshun handed the hawk to Hantou, who had come with Mengzi, and sucked in air. "No pain, no rabbit. That's what I say."

4

Potatoes with millet and flour slurry is traditional breakfast fare for the people of Liangzhou; it is a common dish they have eaten for thousands of years. They never tire of it. It is easy to make: combine millet and chopped potatoes, cook until soft, and then add the flour slurry. Obviously, it offers little nourishment, but this simple and not particularly nutritious dish has supported generations of Liangzhou residents, to the puzzlement of food experts.

By Laoshun's generation, the dish had been demoted from its role as a mainstay and had become a companion breakfast food to steamed rolls called *mantou*. But nothing could replace the unique texture and the sense of familiarity the dish instilled in their blood.

Meng Eight walked in when Laoshun's family was eating. Laoshun told his daughter-in-law, Ying'er, to bring Meng a bowl.

"Sounds good to me. I was born to be poor. I get restless if I go three days without the stuff." Meng took the bowl from Ying'er and, like a hawk devouring meat, slurped the contents down.

Ying'er was about to refill his bowl, but Meng waved her off and politely refused the offer by scraping his bowl against the rammed-earth wall, sending specks of dirt into it. "Do you really want your sons to learn how to shoot?" He wiped his mouth. "If so, tell them to get ready. After the first frost, the foxes have a nice coat. It will be better a month after the winter solstice, but what we get now will still fetch a decent price. I'm going out a little early this year. We can leave today or tomorrow if you scrape some provisions together."

"Let's do it." Laoshun smiled. "But I haven't found time to train a hawk for you yet. I cleared Stubborn Yellow's phlegm and am taking it out hunting today."

"You took me seriously?" Meng laughed heartily. "You're so tightfisted you're afraid rice will come out of your ass when you fart. I wouldn't take something that precious from you. Besides, dealing with a creature like that is too much trouble."

"That works, too." Laoshun smiled again. "I'll bring you a rabbit every once in a while. Training a hawk isn't for everybody. So, who do you want to take?"

"Makes no difference to me. I can take one or I can take three; the desert is open to everyone. This is a good time, when you think about it. The autumn harvest is almost in, and you only need a couple of men to dig potatoes. The storyteller wants to sell his musket. The dumb ass refused to give it up even after he blinded himself with it. He swore he'd never sell it. But I hear he fell in love with a musical instrument he can't afford. So he has to part with his weapon. It's a good piece. A hundred twenty, not bad, about the cost of a fox pelt. Go buy it tonight, before anyone else shows up."

Laoshun snorted a response.

After breakfast, Laoshun picked up Indigo Widow and told Lingguan to cut up a rabbit head. Laoshun dumped it into a metal container, shouted, and the bird devoured it, meat and bone, like swallowing soupy millet.

Laoshun was born to train hawks. When he saw the resolute look in their eyes, he felt something new pour into him, and whatever might be bothering him at the time melted away. Some people drown their sorrows in drink; Laoshun forced worries out of his heart with hawks. He and the majestic birds were friends; they communicated through their souls. Sometimes, when the burdens of life became intolerable, and he was on the verge of despair, his hawks could talk him around in their own language:

"What's there to be afraid of?" was the message. "The worst that can happen is you lose your head and leave a bowl-sized scar."

After feeding his hawks, Laoshun left for the desert with Lingguan, taking along Stubborn Yellow, canteens, *mantou*, and a rabbit's head.

Needle grass, noxious fleabane, camel thorn, and other vegetation, all with typically small, sand covered leaves, grew in the narrow strip of desert that separated the village from the rocky desert known as a gobi. That these plants could survive through long periods of drought was nothing short of miraculous.

The sun was high in the sky when father and son walked into the desert; it was not yet noontime, but the white hot sun was already spreading its punishing heat. There was no wind, nor any of the cool, watery currents from deep inside the desert. The sandy ridges blocked the flow of air, turning the desert into a steamer.

They spotted sand babies.

Sand babies look like geckos, which the Shawan residents call snaky rats; but sand babies are not snaky rats. They are true babies of the desert—born in the sand, they live, even swim in it. With head like toads, they have the bodies of tiny crocodiles, with speckled, sand-colored skin. A casual observer cannot conceive of the vast quantities of sand babies in the rocky desert.

They flourish in blistering heat. The hotter and more stifling the air, the greater their numbers and the happier they seem. At noon in the heart of summer, when there isn't a cloud in the sky, there will be what looks like drifting clouds atop the dunes—in reality, sand babies swimming merrily along.

Their legs are too weak to support their bodies, but they slither along at high speeds. Village children sometimes catch them and put them in the grass for the livestock to eat. Meng Eight said that animals grow fat after eating sand babies, but there were few village animals that actually looked the part. Sand babies worm their way out of danger, and instead of struggling against predators, they escape by shedding their tails. New tails grow back before long, and they continue to enjoy a carefree life.

After spending most of his life walking in sand, Laoshun was a lot like a sand baby; his scrawny legs moved at an astonishing speed. He was a superb desert walker, his tiny, rapid steps lessening the depth to which his feet sank into the sand. He avoided walking up the dunes and down the hollows in straight lines. Instead, he followed the lay of the land at a measured, even pace, leisurely and with no labored breathing. His son, on the other hand, strutted along with his head up and chest out, and was soon gasping for breath as his feet sank into the sand.

Laoshun stopped where he'd often seen rabbits, a spot with three characteristics: complex terrain dotted with holes and caves that is rich in shrubbery, and where wild hawks circle in the sky above.

Telling Lingguan to stay back, Laoshun moved up to flush out a rabbit, for he knew the kinds of plants rabbits liked to hide under and he needed to get close. Stubborn Yellow would face a critical test today; it could lose its confidence and half of its prowess if it failed its first attack. Taking a burlap bag from Lingguan's shoulder, he told his son:

"You're faster than me, so chase down the hawk as soon as it seizes a rabbit. Make sure to yell as you run. Don't give the rabbit a chance to kick. All the effort spent in training a hawk will be wasted if a rabbit lands a kick on it. When you reach the rabbit, stomp on its back and leave the rest to the hawk."

Lingguan bent down to tie his shoelaces. This is such an unfair contest, he said to himself. The king of the sky, with its sharp beak and talons and human help, pitted against small, defenseless rabbits. He felt sorry for the rabbits and worried he might not have it in him to break a rabbit's back.

Laoshun inched cautiously up to the shrubbery, Stubborn Yellow perched on his wrist. Obviously, the familiar surroundings awakened distant memories in the bird, which was aware of its mission. It had been a long time since it had experienced the excitement of catching prey. With its feathers tucked back and a terrifying glint in its eyes, it was ready.

Laoshun was tense, a common state for even the most confident hawk-flyer. There is no way of knowing how good a hawk is until it is turned loose. Sometimes a tamed bird will abruptly turn wild and fly off the moment it's let go. Or a fierce-looking bird will lose its nerve and shrink into itself when facing a rabbit. What emerges with the balls of wool is not just its phlegm, but its courage as well. For a "crushed" hawk, the first attack is a means of regaining the fierce nature it had lost during the training process.

Some people unfairly use domestic rabbits for this vital attack. Wild rabbits are no match for hawks, but at least they have powerful legs and a will to fight, plus an innate ability to deal with winged enemies. Domestic rabbits, by comparison, will not think of running away when let out of a bag, but will wait to die under a hawk's talons.

It was unthinkable for Laoshun to use a domestic rabbit, which was one reason why he believed he was better than all the others. That said, he still had to go through the steps of restoring the hawk's fearless nature. He would get as close to a wild rabbit as possible, ready to deliver the hawk the moment the rabbit tried to escape.

He took pride in his "delivery" technique, which required all the combined qualities of a skillful hunter—keen eyesight, speed, the right amount of force, and good judgment. Even an inferior rabbit-hawk was expected to do what it was trained for when it was flown over a rabbit.

Laoshun stopped and waved behind him. Lingguan knew his father had spotted a rabbit, so he rushed up on the balls of his feet.

"Pay attention," Laoshun said to his son. "Start running as soon as I let it go."

Following the direction his father was pointing, Lingguan spotted a rabbit under some Artemisia, a big, sandy-colored animal in a frozen crouch. Its long ears were like radar antennae, searching and scanning for noise and movement. Its eyes darted back and forth, evidence that it had detected its stalkers.

Rabbits are among the cleverest animals in the desert, with many surprising habits. They rarely set foot on unfamiliar places, always preferring routes they have used before and are proven to be danger-free. They are unusually calm and do not flee until they are about to be stepped on; they will not run the moment they spot a human. Adept at taking advantage of the terrain, they use Artemisia and desert rice plants as natural protection, since not even the most ferocious hawk will fly into these plants. An experienced rabbit can sometimes lure a hawk into the vegetation and punish it if does not manage to stop in time. A hawk, no matter how talented at hunting, cannot catch a wily rabbit without human help.

Now the rabbit had obviously spotted the men, and it knew they saw it too. Its head turned side to side, as if weighing the pros and cons of fleeing as Laoshun moved closer. If it ran, a hawk's talons would be waiting out there, but the enemy was approaching, so after a momentary hesitation, it shot out from under the shrub.

Lingguan finally understood the meaning of "nimble as a fleeing hare." The rabbit vanished before he even had a chance to follow its trajectory. Only a cliché can describe how he felt at that moment: it happened in the blink of an eye.

Laoshun had already delivered his hawk.

Following the bird's flight path, Lingguan spotted the yellow dot bounding across the dunes. It came in and out of view, like a shooting star. But Stubborn Yellow was faster; with a few quick beats of its wings, it was upon the rabbit and had buried its talons in its hindquarters.

"Go!" Laoshun yelled. Lingguan took off, but half-heartedly, as if he were enjoying the spectacle. "Go, I said!" his father roared angrily. "Hei—dai! Hei—dai!" His shouts bounced off the sand.

The talons slowed the rabbit down, but its hind legs remained powerful and fast as they kicked up columns of yellow sand. Pulled along by the rabbit, Stubborn Yellow cut a sorry sight, its wings dragging on the ground with a shushing sound.

"Its back, you stupid creature, get its back!" Laoshun screamed at the hawk.

A relatively powerful bird, Stubborn Yellow did not let go even as it was being dragged across the sand, which was now stained with the rabbit's blood.

Racing up and down the dunes, the rabbit could not shake the hawk, its natural enemy, nor could it flee the intensifying yells from the approaching humans, which gave it no chance to kick with its lethal hind legs.

Beating its wings violently, Stubborn Yellow strained to lift off the sandy ground, but the rabbit pulled it down each time. Finally, it landed on the animal's back when it jumped down from a ridge.

"Good," Laoshun said breathlessly. "It knows how to move to its back."

After a brief respite, Stubborn Yellow shifted its left leg and thrust its talons into the rabbit's midsection. With a pitiful screech, the rabbit kept moving forward, its front legs leaving gouges in the sand, now that its hind legs had been rendered virtually useless.

Stubborn Yellow proceeded to the second stage of its attack from the back: shifting its body forward, it freed its right talons and plunged them into the rabbit's head. It fell to the ground, its legs twitching. It cried pitifully, filling the trough with "keh-wa, keh-wa," like the yowl of a scalded baby.

A tremor shot through Lingguan's heart; the pores constricted. It was so cruel. A vibrant life abruptly ended, all because humans want to eat meat.

The sun seemed to be getting noisy, like the chirps of cicadas on a stifling hot day. The steady buzz mingled with the whimpers of the dying rabbit and turned into an eddying turbulence that surged and soared in Lingguan. He felt he might wet himself.

The rabbit died, having lost the fight when the hawk's talon pierced its brain. It was stared wide-eyed, as if unwilling to accept its fate. Stubborn Yellow was already pecking away, pausing after each bite to look around with a self-satisfied air.

Laoshun ran up. Breathing hard, he wiped his sweaty face.

"That was close. Damned close." He glared at his son, upset that

Lingguan hadn't tried harder to chase down the rabbit.

"If the rabbit drags the hawk along the ground, one kick can kill it. You should know that. Some hawks lose their nerve and never hunt again, others lose their minds, and some even die. The more fortunate ones. We're lucky this rabbit didn't have time for that."

Lingguan stood blankly, sensing a gulf between him and his father. Just because they want to eat meat, he said to himself.

"It was an old rabbit." Laoshun's tone betrayed a hint of smugness. "Cunning. Did you see how it didn't hesitate when it bounded out from under the shrub? And it didn't panic when it was caught. It even made Stubborn Yellow look bad. If we hadn't chased after it, the hawk could have been in trouble. But, Stubborn Yellow is a good bird. If it had been trained by one of those bunglers, it would have been lucky to sniff the rabbit's rear end."

Stubborn Yellow was also pleased, gazing around before giving the rabbit a few more savage pecks; tufts of rabbit fur fluttered in the air and were carried away on the wind. Soon the hawk, which had gone without food all night and that morning, stopped showing off, perhaps realizing that the master was no longer impressed. It shook its head listlessly before turning its attention to its prey. It tore off strips of furry meat.

"Take it away," Laoshun cautioned. "Don't let it eat any more. It can't hunt with a full stomach."

Lingguan took out the bloody rabbit's head from a plastic bag, drawing the hawk's attention away from the one it had just killed. With a red glint in its eyes, it swung its head side to side while devouring pieces of rabbit flesh like slurping soup. It finally loosened its grip on the killed rabbit.

"That's enough." Laoshun said, "Don't let it eat too much."

5

It was nearly noon by the time they stopped for some water and *mantou*. Breezes in the sand hollows were squeezed out by the sunlight raining down on them. They felt smothered in heat. The sun seemed to spew fire down on them. The cloudless blue sky was like a towering void that carried no sense of coolness; rather, it was like a sheet of silk spitting out blue flames. The sand was an ocean under the glaring sun, its waves surging toward the edge of the sky; a bright sheen, as if carrying moisture, flickered and glimmered.

Stubborn Yellow caught a few more rabbits that day. It did well with its first three kills. Without waiting for Laoshun's help, it knew to plunge its talons into the heads, making the prey's sad cries echo in the hollows. The fourth one did not go so well, and Laoshun had to run up to break the rabbit's spine as it wrestled with the hawk.

By then Lingguan was getting used to the savagery. Human sensitivity to cruelty has a tendency to dull, like the resistance to powerful medicine, over time. But he still could not stand his father's method. "It's so unfair," he muttered.

"Hogwash!" Laoshun shot back. "What do you know about fairness? Could a hawk catch that many rabbits without our help? All these years at school have made you stupid. What's fair? You tell me. The rabbits ruin our crops. Is that fair? What's fair in this world? Some people can afford a car, while others have to walk. Do you think that's fair? Some get to enjoy rare delicacies, but you survive on potatoes. Is that fair?"

Lingguan's guilt feelings lessened with the mention of ruined crops.

All they had to do after that was beat the shrubs and poke into burrows to drive out hidden rabbits. Stubborn Yellow got good enough that it never again suffered the sorry fate of being dragged along the sand. It learned to pick the right spot for its talons while still in the air, and, ignoring the hind quarters and legs, went straight for the back with its left talons and attacked from behind—shifting its right talons forward and aiming for the head, swift and clean, not giving the rabbit a chance to fight back.

Laoshun was so happy he could not stop grinning.

"Ha-ha! That idiot Goubao says things without thinking. He couldn't get his hawk to do a damn thing, but he shared his experience of spending forty or fifty days to finish the training. I told him he was a dope. He huffed and puffed. So I told him he could use my head as a football if he ever caught a rabbit. Know what happened? He trained one hawk that couldn't catch a rabbit, and then he trained another one—same thing. He wasted all that meat on his hawks, without a tuft of rabbit fur to show for it."

"And why is that?' Lingguan asked.

"Why? Who knows? If you ask people, they'll tell you to crush the bird for forty or fifty days. Actually, if you do that, the hawk will be too tame to catch anything. Goubao, that idiot, kept at it that long and got a tame hawk for his effort. It was used to eating out of his hand, but forgot that it could catch rabbits. And he wanted to share his experience. Ha!"

"Would it have worked if he'd flown the hawk earlier?"

"You can't do it too early either. If it's still wild, it won't come back. It would be like throwing a meaty bun at a dog."

"How long is best then?"

"Hard to say. It depends, but usually about three weeks, when the hawk has lost its wild nature, but still remembers to catch rabbits.

Don't share this with Goubao, Lingguan. That boy knows how to train a hawk; he just isn't good at flying one. And it's not up to us to teach him."

"Didn't you say that rabbits ruin our crops? Wouldn't it better if there were more hawks to catch them."

"What we do works precisely because there aren't many who are good at it." Laoshun crinkled his nose. "If everyone knew how to do it, there wouldn't be any rabbits left. Look, a wild hawk."

A black hawk sat like a statue on a sand dune by a giant Artemisia bush. It looked their way when it heard voices, but then turned away and ignored them. A few others were circling in the sky. A large pile of white material lay near the shrub. "That's wild hawk droppings," Laoshun said.

"Those birds up there may look ferocious, but they can't catch rabbits," he continued. "A wild hawk doesn't know what to do if a rabbit stays put under the shrub, so it often goes hungry. When it does catch one, it can't finish it all at once. So guess what it does. It sits by its catch and eats. It fills its stomach, digests the food, and relieves itself, before starting over again. That's why there's a large pile of dropping right next to it. Look, the hawks have spotted a pair of rabbits."

Sure enough, there were two rabbits under a large Artemisia shrub. One was big, the color of sand, clearly an old hand in desert battles, for it lay there, eyes shut, knowing full well that the hawks could not touch it. It looked to be sleeping, though its ears twitched from time to time. The other one, with gray fur, was staring wide-eyed, its head shifting uneasily as it looked around and then up at the sky, as if anticipating an enemy attack.

"See that?" Laoshun laughed. "See what I mean? The hawks can't do anything if the rabbits stay put. They can watch all they want, but nothing will happen. By nighttime, the hawks' eyes aren't good enough to see, and the rabbits will get away."

The big sandy rabbit jumped to its feet and called out anxiously, clearly aware of what the approaching humans meant to its existence.

The gray one shrank back into a small depression near the plant's roots. Maybe the threat from the approaching humans seemed more terrifying than death. Dying produced momentary pain, while the approaching threat was agonizing, grating on frail nerves like a dull saw. There was terror in its eyes, like a woman surrounded by men with evil intent.

The wild hawks began to wheel lower, a warm-up before their attack.

Oddly, the sandy rabbit quieted down, not looking at the people drawing closer; its ears twitched as it gathered information.

"Hei!" Laoshun yelled.

The gray rabbit sat up in fear, gazing at the approaching people, and then at its companion, which seemed resigned to whatever fate awaited it. Short, shrill calls emerged from the gray rabbit, a sign that it was starting to panic.

"Hei!" Laoshun yelled again.

The rabbit ran out from under the plant and down the sandy trough. The hawks dove. Stubborn Yellow flapped its wings and wanted to follow, but was held back by the tether tying it to Laoshun's wrist.

A flash of yellow and the big rabbit ran out behind. Lingguan heard hawk wings dice the air around him; Stubborn Yellow had taken off.

"Hei—" Father and son shouted as they gave chase.

In a flash the sandy rabbit reached a dune many meters away, while Stubborn Yellow filled the area with the sounds of its beating wings.

Running as fast as he could, Lingguan waved his arms as if swimming. But he wasn't fast enough for his father, who yelled unhappily,

"Hei—hurry!" Laoshun realized that the sandy rabbit was not going to be easy to deal with, and that their hawk might be in trouble.

Stubborn Yellow was nearly atop the rabbit; it had covered the distance so quickly it seemed to be a beam of light zeroing in on its prey. It got closer and closer, its talons nearly touching the rabbit's hindquarters.

The rabbit stopped in its tracks, the hawk flew right past, and by the time it doubled back, its quarry had disappeared down a sandy ditch and into cogon grass.

"Did it get it?" Laoshun was panting as he reached the dune.

"No." Lingguan was also breathing hard. "It got away. Hei, I've never seen a rabbit like that."

A crestfallen Stubborn Yellow landed, truly "crushed."

"It was tricked." Lingguan was still panting. "Our rabbit took advantage of the distraction, getting the gray rabbit to draw the wild hawks away so it could escape. Hei, that was one cunning rabbit." Lingguan was actually relieved; he admired the rabbit, a weaker animal that had defeated a hawk.

"It wasn't afraid of us," Laoshun said, "and Stubborn Yellow was inexperienced; otherwise, it never would have gotten away. But, who knows, maybe the rabbit could have landed a kick. Wow—what a rabbit. The gray one must have been caught by now."

"Carried off by a wild hawk," Lingguan said.

"No way. A rabbit is two or three times heavier than a hawk. How is one bird going to lift it? I'll bet they're feeding right now. Go get it."

Wild hawks were feasting on the rabbit in the trough. Lingguan threw his bag at them, and they rose into the air, where they wheeled and screeched. The rabbit had been pecked and torn into a bloody mess. Lingguan frowned as he scooped it up and tossed it away.

"Go get it. We'll feed it to our birds," Laoshun said.

6

When Laoshun walked in the door, his wife and Lanlan, his daughter, who had been married to a man in a neighboring village, were weeping. He learned that his son-in-law, Bai Fu, had been arrested for gambling and was being fined five hundred yuan. Lanlan's mother-in-law had sent her to borrow the money.

"No! I'm not paying that fine," Laoshun said angrily. "That good-for-nothing has to learn a lesson if he's ever going to change. Besides, I don't have that kind of money. All I've got are my twelve ribs. In any case, you wouldn't find me throwing my money into that pit even if I had it."

"Just because you don't have the money doesn't mean you have to scream at our daughter," his wife grumbled. "It's not her fault he gambles."

"I'm just doing what my mother-in-law told me to do," Lanlan said as she dried her eyes. "I couldn't say no, but I agree that we should make that lowlife suffer a bit. You have no idea how many times I've lost my temper over that evil habit of his. We can't keep fighting over it forever."

"I agree," Laoshun's daughter-in-law, Ying'er, said. "Since our parents can't control him, it might be good for the government to teach him a lesson."

"I didn't mean to lose my temper." Laoshun heaved a sigh. "For one thing, I really don't have the money. Second, gambling's addictive, and he won't be able to control himself if he's around other people who do. If he pays a fine one day, then goes out and loses more money the next, what are you going to live on? He'll never change if something isn't done."

"You're right, he has to suffer a bit," Lanlan said, as she got up to leave, despite her mother's effort to have her stay a while longer. Her in-laws were beside themselves over the mess, and she could not stay away too long.

Her mother wrapped up two rabbits and told Mengzi to see her home.

Tough talk aside, Laoshun could not get over the arrest of his son-in-law. He went to the well site after Lanlan left, without bothering to stay for dinner.

Drilling a well is not a complicated procedure. All one has to do is hire a drilling team, set up a derrick, pound a drill head into the ground up to a hundred meters deep, then build a cement wall around it, and you have a well.

There are two potential snags. One is a failure to find water, which amounts to spending as much as ten thousand yuan just to make a hole in the ground. A second is the danger of a wall collapse, filling in the hole after days of hard work, possibly burying the drill head as well. There is nothing worse than that.

So the blind storyteller entertained the workers with ballads that made them laugh and promised to bring them good luck. Laoshun loved the tunes and the mood among the drilling team, who kept up a steady stream of good-natured banter as they smoked and talked. Energized by dark, fermented Fu Tea, they talked freely about everything from ancient days to the present, as if they were all latter-day Zhuge Liangs, the sage who knew events of five hundred years in the past and could see events five hundred years into the future. Just thinking about what was happening at the well site intoxicated Laoshun before he'd even arrived.

The storyteller's three-string lute created rich, deep, familiar sounds that seemed to seep into his blood and bore into his bones, soothing his troubled heart the way the daily fare of potatoes, millet, and slurry did.

He parted the door curtain, and was met by the acrid smell of tobacco smoke. Women were a taboo at well sites. He had heard that wells at several Beixiang villages had collapsed midway through the drilling process owing to the presence of women, whose bodies, it was believed, were not clean, especially during their menstrual periods. That offended the earth god, who safeguarded the work of drilling wells. Having pooled their hard-earned money, the villagers hired three ritualists who slaughtered three pigs, three goats, and three large white roosters as sacrificial offerings. To be sure, the offerings found their way into human stomachs, but the men were sure that the gods were pleased. How did they know that? Because the humans were pleased. On the day of the sacrifices, the village men got drunk, but no one caused any trouble. Gimpy Five's eyes turned red, but before he had a chance to shed tears that would have ruined the fun, he smiled after a reminder from Meng Eight. Later, the team Leader, Big Head Sun, told the men to keep their "ladies" in check, insisting that none would be allowed at the site. "Anyone who violates my order will answer to me."

The absence of women kept the chatter and the noise volume down. The men sat on the straw-strewn ground to smoke, drink water, and listen to the storyteller sing in his raspy, tobacco-infused voice.

He had started out as a hunter, not a storyteller. He said he could shoot a fly on the wing, and that he had shot a wagonload of foxes.

No one really believed him, especially the village marksman, Meng Eight, who sneered at the claim. But ten years earlier, he had ignited the gunpowder while loading his weapon and taken out his eyes in the process. Having read broadly before losing his sight, he had a greater repertoire than other blind storytellers. He enjoyed high self-regard and turned up his nose when any of his peers were mentioned, so often, in fact, that a tiny flesh bump grew on the tip of his nose over time.

On this night, he was singing the lovers' tale *Red Lantern*, about an impoverished scholar named Sun Jigao and a young lady named Zhao Lanying. When Laoshun walked in, he was treated to the part where Lanying's stepmother tricks Sun up to the second floor to whip him with a ball of thorns before dousing him with black vinegar. Infusing his song with emotion, he bared his teeth as if he were enduring the punishment.

When Gimpy Five greeted Laoshun, the storyteller turned his dead eyes in Laoshun's direction and acknowledged the newcomer's presence. But he continued to play and sing, sprinkling beautiful notes over Laoshun's heart.

When he laid down his instrument, one of the drillers handed a cigarette to Meng Eight, who laid it in the man's hand. He sniffed at it before tucking it behind his ear and taking out his pipe, made from the wing bone of a black hawk. He stroked it a time or two and smacked his lips as he lit it; he took a puff, held it in for a moment, and then blew into the mouthpiece to expel the hot ashes.

Laoshun was so engrossed in the story he did not hear what Meng and the other men were talking about. He mumbled a few acknowledgments before Gimpy Five's voice finally penetrated:

"That's right. Ten thousand. I tell you, I couldn't even dream about that much. In the old days, a bushel of wheat could buy you a wife."

"There's no way out. Your belly hurts when you hit it with a hammer, and when you reach the proper age you have to get married, no matter how much it costs." That was from Beizhu's father.

Picking up Meng Eight's teacup, Laoshun let the liquid slide down over his lips and teeth with a pleasant slurping sound. "People get stupid as they grow older. You want a son when you don't have one, and once you have a son, you have to worry about finding him a wife. What's the point? Family planning is the way to go. It saves us all a lot of gray hair."

"That's like a new mother passing odorless gas." Meng Eight laughed roguishly. "What's the point of that? I've never seen anybody crush a baby boy, have you? It's only baby girls that wind up in dogs' stomachs."

"You're right there. Someone dropped off a newborn at the township office last night, a girl, of course. It cried its head off, but no one went to pick it up. I heard that a civil servant wanted to take her in, but the township chief stopped him, saying it would just encourage others. If you take this one in, anyone who has a baby girl from now on will simply drop her off at the township office, and there'll be no end of it, he said. So he didn't bring the baby in. Hei, I hear she froze to death. What's the world come to? Can anyone tell me?"

"Right. What has the world come to?" the men said, echoed by sighs all around.

"Human hearts are made of flesh. The township chief had his concerns too," Beizhu's father said. "I hear the the higher-ups reprimanded him over the grain tax. Hei—sometimes you just have to be tough."

"It's not any easier on them than it is on us," Meng Eight said. "Every line of work has its rules. They have to eat, too, you know."

"When we hand the grain over we won't have much left, so we'll just have to tighten our throats." Gimpy Five tugged at his yellow beard and sighed.

"Are you kidding? You'll stick your face up to someone's ass to draw out a fart. You eat potatoes with and flour slurry millet at every meal, no *mantou* for you. I can't believe you don't have any savings."

"Good point," Meng Eight said. "People say that Gimpy Five looks behind him after a fart to see if he's ejected a kernel of rice. Don't tell us you don't have any savings."

"Savings? Sure, I might save a little here, but it goes out there. Drilling a well, paying the electricity bill, fees here, and taxes there. I handed over several thousand catties of grain, and what did I wind up with? They deducted for everything. Now I have to worry about paying for next year's fertilizer, and I can't begin to think about my son Wuzi's marriage. That's what saving gets me. But I have to try, or else I couldn't afford even a pair of pants."

"Saving's impossible," Laoshun said. You could stop eating altogether and still wind up with nothing. You work the field, and all that gets you is some loose change, never gold ingots. How do you stop one government office from taking a bowlful from you and another following up with a spoon? There's never enough to get by."

"Life is getting harder, that's for sure," said Gimpy Five.

"According to a geomancer," the storyteller said, "the problem is with the bronze horse in Liangzhou Square. It's too big and its mouth faces west, draining all the water from the Xiying Reservoir. No wonder we don't have good harvests."

"You know what?" Meng Eight said. "People in Yongchang say the horse eats their grass but then shits in Wuwei, which makes Yongchang poor and Wuwei rich. So they came up with the idea of having a gold-plated bull face Wuwei to push back against the horse."

"That's true," said one of the drillers. "I've seen it. It looks like it can't wait to gore somebody."

"Come on now!" The storyteller shook his head. "You know what Yongchang is? It's a grassy lakeshore. And Wuwei? A so-called land of prosperity. Back when Niu Jian served as tutor to the Qing throne, the emperor asked him about Wuwei, and he said it was a land of prosperity. So the emperor said, Good. Have them turn in more grain. Then the emperor asked Grand Secretary Hu about Yongchang. Since Hu didn't want the people to suffer, he said it was a grassy lakeshore, where life was hard. So the emperor told him to reduce their grain tax. As a result, the residents of the so-called land of prosperity had it hard, while Yongchang actually turned into a grassy lakeshore, with needle grass everywhere."

"Land of prosperity, my ass! Pompous officials pluck men's pubic hair to make beards for themselves. All they care about is looking impressive, and to hell with the suffering commoners."

"It's the people's fault," the storyteller said. "Hei, all Liangzhou people know how to do is kiss officials' asses."

"That's what I don't understand," the driller said. "Liangzhou is poor, but then outsiders come in and make money as easily as sweeping up leaves. And I'm not talking about specialized work. Carpenters, tailors, and barbers are all outsiders. Even the guy who sells rat poison isn't local. Where are all the Liangzhou natives? They say they're poor, but then they hand over money to out-of-towners like fallen leaves. Isn't that weird?"

"It's our bad feng shui," said the storyteller. "I heard that Liangzhou was supposed to be located at a place called Forty-li Fortress. But one day a Taoist priest walked by and was alarmed. Oh, no, he said, people in other towns would have a hard time surviving if a city was built here. So he moved the city limit markers to the current location. Local officials thought that some god must have come down and moved them, so they built the city where it is now. And see what happened? Hei, the place is taken over by out-of-towners. The residents, who have nothing, perform all the hard labor. They can earn a little by going to Xikou or Xinjiang, but there's no way they can get any money from the outsiders."

7

Laoshun stuck around for more tales before going home. His wife brought out a pot of stir-fried wild rabbit with sliced potatoes. It was not an appetizing sight, with mushy potatoes covering the rabbit, which had turned nearly black in the pan. But it had an aroma and a taste unlike anything else. As they ate, Lingguan and his brothers gave their versions of why wild rabbit tasted best. Hantou, the eldest, believed that it was so tasty because the animals ate vegetation that absorbed the best essences of heaven and earth. Mengzi, the second brother, disagreed. He said it was because wild rabbits steal grain; he argued convincingly that domestic rabbits eat plants and don't taste as good because humans don't supply them with grain they can pilfer. Lingguan, the youngest son, thought that it had something to do with the way wild rabbits live. First, they're always on the move, which burns off the fat and leaves only lean meat, which is tender and delicious. Second, they live in constant fear, and their mental state affects their physical makeup. They ate and talked throughout the meal. Hantou had a measured manner, like taking sips of soupy millet, while Mengzi spit out his words like frying beans. Lingguan was articulate and clever, enjoying arguing for argument's sake. At some point, Laoshun's patience gave out.

"You jackasses. Even chunks of tasty rabbit can't shut those yaps. None of you knows shit."

"What do you think the reason is?" Lingguan asked softly.

Laoshun tossed down a bone and made as if to lecture them, but hemmed and hawed without coming up with anything. So he simply said that wild rabbits tasted best because, one, they ate vegetation, two, they stole grain, three, they moved a lot, and four, they were often scared. All that from three brothers who didn't know shit! Father and sons looked at each other and burst out laughing, nearly spitting out the food in their mouths. Ying'er was laughing so hard she nearly split her sides.

"Like they say, dragons beget little dragons, phoenixes give birth to little phoenixes, and a mouse has sons who are good at squirming through mouse holes. You're a goofy father with a bunch of foolish sons," Laoshun's wife said to end the conversation.

When the meal was over, Hantou told his father:

"The production team is collecting money again. The leader said the well isn't finished yet, and that we'd waste everything if we stopped half way."

"Didn't they say fifty yuan per person?" Laoshun asked.

"Big Head said that had been enough when they did the calculation, but the cost of everything has gone up."

"Goes up, and goes up again. Will it reach the sky one day?" Laoshun fumed. "How much more do they want?"

"Thirty."

"Another thirty?"

"That includes money for the motorized pump. Sooner or later they'll have to collect for that anyway."

Laoshun knitted his brow, but said nothing.

"And that's not all," Hantou said. "Everyone has to chip in fifty for repairs on the village school. That's due by year's end, so they can start work next spring. Big Head said it was important work that concerns generations. It's not safe to go in there now. Beams are broken and the walls are cracking."

"All right, enough already." His father seethed. "Why talk about this right after we enjoyed some delicious rabbit? Do you want me to get cancer?"

"That's what they said at the meeting. I'm just telling you what I heard," Hantou stammered.

"There's a time for everything." Laoshun snorted, unnerving Hantou. Not sure what to do or say, he glanced at his brothers, looking as if he'd done something wrong, and was pleading for them to come to his aid.

"Ai!" Their mother stepped in. "You're always talking about cancer. Don't put a curse on yourself. You don't get a fatal disease if it's not in the cards. I can't believe the Heaven is so blind it would make the poor suffer terrible diseases on top of everything else."

"Heaven is blind," Laoshun said. "Can't you see that the good die young, while bad people live forever?"

That was the last thing his wife hoped to hear; all she wanted was for everyone to be healthy, and not have to worry about official positions or wealth. Laoshun's frequent mention of cancer always sent shivers of fright down her spine. Her comment had been intended to erase the effects of what came out of Laoshun's damned mouth.

She was an ardent follower of Grannie Qi, the shaman, who said that people's responses determine good or evil, so they should avoid talking about death and disease. If someone did, then it was important to balance the bad aura with auspicious words. But on this day, Laoshun spewed more unpleasant comments before she'd even finished, and her mood darkened. And yet, what he said was undeniably true, so she pretended not to care, even though that too could be considered a bad response. She changed the subject.

"What are you going to do tomorrow?" she asked Hantou.

"Big Head told me to go into to the city to buy palm fiber for the work at the well." He glanced at his father, afraid he might have said something to get him started in on cancer again.

"Good. Then you can get a physical checkup. Lingguan, you go with him. You have a classmate who works at the hospital, and that will speed things up."

"Checkup?" Laoshun knit his brows again. "Why go looking for illness when you're healthy? If nothing's wrong, don't waste money." He felt his wife step on his foot, and a light flashed in his head when he saw Ying'er blush. "Oh, yeah, you need to go. Have Lingguan go with you, so you won't walk into the women's toilet when you're looking for the hospital."

"You go with him, too," Laoshun's wife said to Ying'er.

"Not me." Ying'er looked flustered. "There's no need for me to go. I don't want to. It's a waste of money."

"Why not? There's not much to do around the house. In a little while, you won't be able to go even if you want to."

"No, I don't feel like going," Ying'er said to her mother-in-law. "I mean it. He can go without me."

"All right, don't go." Her mother-in-law sighed.

8

After the family discussion, Hantou went to the team leader's house for the money to buy palm fiber, and Ying'er went to her room. Lingguan turned on the TV to see if the nightly news was on. Laoshun went up and turned it off. "There's nothing to watch now. We'll wait till the Judge Bao drama comes on."

"You don't understand," Lingguan said. "It's national news."

" Want to know what national news is? It's feeding and clothing the people, giving them a good life. The most important thing the country can do is make our lives easier. What's the point of having a meeting one day and celebrating some damned holiday the next? Nothing but a waste of electricity."

"I guess you're right. They're always reporting on some meeting or commenting on the latest celebration."

"Of course I'm right. How many Autumn Festivals have you celebrated so far? I've been around and seen plenty and I could care less what they say or how they sing it. I want action. You know, during the Republican Era, the farms around here only turned in a few dozen tons of grain. Now we've got mountains of the stuff, but they get us with fees and taxes, like they're trying to squeeze milk out of our dicks."

"The paper says our burden will be eased soon," Lingguan said. "It's just that the lesser monks are reciting the wrong sutras."

"You really think our burden will be eased just because they say so?" His father snorted as his mood soured. "We farmers never listen to those people's empty talk. All we know is our burden is as heavy as it ever was. Got anything more to say? I just enjoyed a nice rabbit meal, and now you're making me mad. Do you want me to get cancer? Woman, I need a bottle. Why do you bring these things up?"

"You're the one who brought it up. No one forced you to talk about it," Lingguan grumbled.

"No, you started it." He glared at his son.

"Don't blame Heaven when the wind knocks you down," Lingguan's mother said. "You're someone who likes to shake empty baskets just to have something to do. Cursing people gets you all worked up. It's not your son's fault."

Laoshun's frown turned into a smile, as she set a bottle on the table. "You've forgotten how to appreciate anything. You eat rabbit and drink your liquor while you curse the government. Without the Communist Party you wouldn't get to drink cat piss. Don't be greedy. Remember what they say, a greedy man is like a snake trying to swallow an elephant. In the old days, you didn't even have rags for pants. Now you've got a coat with fur and good leather shoes. So stop complaining."

"Why do you always compare things with the past, Mother?" Lingguan said. "The papers say how farmers in foreign countries work the fields for six months and spend the next half year traveling. When they want to go somewhere, they get on a plane and whoosh—they're there. And the work isn't hard; all they have to do is push a button—zip, the seeds are in, and then press another button, shaa—the field is weeded. Press a third button and the wheat rumbles its way into the storehouse. Here we toil like mules and get barely enough to fill our bellies."

"And you're always talking about what's in the newspaper," she said. "Don't you know anything else? They're them and you're you. Why envy people because they're lucky. Grass or chaff, it doesn't matter so long as we can fill our bellies. Why go around jabbering like a certain old man? Act your age."

Laoshun sipped his liquor and smiled at his wife. "Don't lump me in with them. I didn't say a word about foreign countries. But, you know what's weird? In the old days, I'd be so happy I'd be singing opera if you gave me a bowl of watery soup, but now I can eat noodles or dumplings anytime I want, and we have meat once in a while. But there's always something to complain about."

"You didn't know what was what back then, and now you do, that's all," Lingguan said.

"Right. No one knew anything about foreign countries then," Mengzi said.

"Would you two stop talking about foreign countries? Foreigners have to shit, just like us."

Mengzi shrugged and exchanged a glance with his brother.

"The only foreign thing I give a damn about is their liquor," Laoshun said with a chortle. "I'd like to know what it tastes like."

"I know one kind," Mengzi said. "Remy Martin."

"And whisky," Lingguan added.

"Not for me," Laoshun said. "I might fall over like a dead chicken."

They all laughed.

Lingguan turned on the TV. Chen Shimei, the heartless husband, was already on trial in Judge Bao's court. Laoshun complained that he'd missed some of the opening. He was a fan of the actor who played Judge Bao, a man with the voice and mannerisms of an incorruptible judge.

"Ying'er, Judge Bao is on," Laoshun's wife called out.

Claiming a headache, the younger woman stayed in her room, while her mother-in-law stole a glance at her husband, whose eyes were glued to the TV, his mouth hanging slack, exposing his tobacco-stained teeth. He was too engrossed in the drama to notice her, so she walked out, but quickly returned. Lingguan heard her sigh softly.

The episode had ended, and Laoshun noticed he'd been drooling. He wiped off the saliva with his sleeve and glanced at his sons, relieved to see that neither had noticed.

"Chen Shimei shouldn't have been executed," Mengzi said. "The princess was pretty, and she was from a rich and powerful family, a hell of a lot better than Chen's wife. I'd have chosen the princess for sure."

"You were born with the heart of an animal that shits donkey turds, so of course you would," his father said. "If they let him go instead of executing him, what about the rule of law? Just think how his wife worked to support him while he studied, then raised their children alone. And what does she wind up with? Nothing. He not only denies her everything, he even sends someone to kill her. There's the injustice."

"But she's not guilt free," Lingguan said. "She asked for it. Wouldn't they have been better off staying home, her doing housework while he worked the land? But no, she sent him to the capital for the imperial exam. Serves her right."

"When her husband's a scholar, a woman is the lady of the house. If he's a butcher, she's up to her elbows in pig's guts," their father said. "Who doesn't hope for a better life?"

"So she ends up with nothing, like a fly chasing a fart," Mengzi said.

"What's the matter with you two jackasses? Have dogs eaten your hearts?" Laoshun banged his cup on the table. "How can you mock someone who's suffered so much?"

"Why don't you rescue her, then?" his wife quipped. "She's young and pretty. If her husband doesn't want her, you take her."

Laoshun glared at her. "Be serious, why don't you?"

"In my view, his wife is the ruthless one. He doesn't love her anymore, but she won't let him go. She can do whatever she wants to keep him, but she shouldn't ask the judge to lop off his head just because he wants to leave her. She's mean and cold-hearted. What do books say about something like that?"

"They say that the fangs of a bamboo green snake and the sting of a hornet are full of venom, yet cannot compare with the heart of a woman."

"Watch your tongue, Lingguan. Does that include your mother? Haven't I always fed and clothed you?"

"I'm not talking about you."

"If I'd known I'd raise a bunch of ingrates, I'd have killed you all and tossed your bodies to the dogs," she joked.

Another episode started, so they stopped talking and watched the show. Hantou eased the door open and signaled to Lingguan.

"Will the hospital visit be expensive?" he asked.

"Hard to say. It could be a lot or it could be practically nothing."

"I only have thirty yuan. After the bus fare, that leaves about twenty. And that doesn't count food."

"Ask Father for some."

"I don't dare."

"I'll ask him later."

Lingguan waited until the show was over. Laoshun let out a cry: "You bloodsuckers, you're always wanting money. Not much can be squeezed out of these bones of mine, you know."

Hantou hung his head. "Forget it. I'll wait till next time."

"No, you can't keep putting it off," his mother said. "First it's tomorrow, then it's the next day. When does it end? Do it tomorrow. I have ten yuan here, from selling garlic."

Hantou looked up in alarm, glancing at his father and then his mother before lowering his head again, the roots of his ears turning red.

"If that's not enough, take some chickens to sell at the market," Laoshun said. "I'm so broke my farts sound like a weak fiddle. Oh, I forgot. I've got half a yuan here. That's better than nothing."

"I have one yuan and twenty *fen*," Mengzi said, "so there's no need to sell the chickens. Skin a couple of rabbits. City folks love gamy meat. You won't have any trouble selling them."

"He's right." Laoshun slapped his thigh. "They're tired of all that chicken and fish, so they hunger for game animals like a scrawny dog drooling over a bone."

Hantou hemmed and hawed. "I can't. I get all turned around when I'm in the city."

"I'll do it," Lingguan offered. "It's not illegal, so what's there to be afraid of?"

"He's right." Laoshun shot Hantou a look. "City folks may be cutthroat, but they can't lop off your dick or skin you alive."

9

After the episode finished, the three brothers left the room. Their mother sat lost in thought.

"Look at you," Laoshun said. "You're too old to be worrying about characters in a TV show."

She sighed. "Who's worrying about them? I'm afraid something's wrong with that boy."

"What makes you think so?"

"Have you seen how he blushes whenever I mention a checkup? Her, too. They've been married for a while now, but she keeps washing her underwear when she has her you-know-what. Obviously, no chance of getting pregnant."

"Having children is complicated. Some have them early and some late. Didn't Hantou come three years after we were married?"

"That's not the same. You heard Ying'er refuse to go into town with him. I think—I think something's wrong with the boy and she knows it. Otherwise, she'd have gone with him. She's not as wise as Zhuge Liang."

"So—what do we do?"

"We wait till he comes back and see what the checkup says. Make sure you don't let on anything. He's thin-skinned, so don't embarrass him."

Laoshun frowned as he stroked his pipe, not smoking, just picking at the bowl as if to rub something off it. A long time passed before he spoke up: "We can't go on like this. Too many depressing things. Who knows how much we'll have to spend this time? Nothing more can be squeezed out of these bones of mine."

"There you go again. You moan and groan whenever the topic comes up. You're getting old and have lost the ability to take what fate sends your way."

Laoshun packed in some tobacco and began smoking. "I'm the only wage-earner, and even working myself to death won't help anyone. The two young masters are old enough to get married, but we have nothing. How can I not worry? What do you expect me to do, laugh?"

"Worrying is a waste of time. There isn't a family anywhere that doesn't go into debt when they marry their sons off. Only fools try to save up money before they begin looking for a matchmaker."

Without replying, Laoshun blew hard on the pipe and sent sparks flying; they arced and fell to the floor. He added more tobacco, took a long puff, and held it in. Then, suddenly, he was coughing so hard his face turned red. When he caught his breath, he said, “Where are we going to borrow the money? In this day and age, plucking a single hair from a rich man is like taking his life. Anyone with a heart is dirt poor. Who’s going to lend us the money, the kitchen god? All you’d get is soot smeared over your hands and face.”

His wife heaved a series of soft sighs, as if afraid of disturbing her husband. In the end, she no longer cared how he’d react.

“A path opens up when the cart reaches the foothills, so what’s the point of worrying ourselves to death? I’ve always been concerned about Hantou. The boy was so timid he wouldn’t even flirt with a girl; he isn’t handsome, and would never have gotten married if not for his sister. I’m not worried about Lingguan and Mengzi. They’re clever enough to find wives on their own. We’ll have to figure something out, even if we have to pawn the pots and the bed, to get them married off. They can’t be bachelors forever… ah, if only Lanlan didn’t have to suffer.”

“Don’t get me started,” Laoshun said. “Mengzi gets angry every time I mention it.”

“What were we supposed to do?” She said. “Things like that happen all the time. It’s just that, well, the girl deserved better than that no-good husband.”

“I’m not so sure. She was all smiles when she was home last time.”

“It was an act. She didn’t want us to worry. Bai Fu hits her anytime he’s not pleased about something, and he’s addicted to gambling. She was sobbing under the blanket the last time she came home.” Her eyes reddened as she picked up an unfinished shoe sole and began to stitch, as if trying to sew away the unhappiness in her heart.

Laoshun squinted as he pinched some tobacco to put in his pipe, but he forgot to light it. "When you think about it, Huaqiu wouldn't have been half bad, except he was too young. Besides, Han—tou, ai. We couldn't let him be a bachelor forever. He was almost twenty-eight, so we had to do something. Sure, it was unfair to the girl, who'd always been so proud. But he'd have had to suffer if she didn't."

His wife did not reply as tears rolled down her cheeks.

"Enough," he grunted. "Let's not talk about it anymore. It's her fate. She was born to live off the land and work hard, not to sit on the dragon throne."

As she dried her tears, his wife stared blankly at a pattern Lanlan had sewn.

"Let's go to bed," said Laoshun. "We can muddle through if we stop talking about these things. It just depresses us, and it's pointless."

Chapter Two

1

Lingguan and Hantou slurped down two bowls of potatoes, millet, and slurry the next morning. Their mother handed them two sacks, one with *mantou* for lunch, the other with four skinned rabbits.

"Listen carefully to what the doctor says," she whispered to her youngest son. "But don't let on to your brother."

He asked why, but all she said was, "You'll know soon enough."

Team leader Sun arrived. He was a tall, heavyset man whose head was larger than a hog's, which is why he was called Big Head by many villagers. With a loud, choked voice, he sounded like he was quarrelling. "Be careful, Hantou. The palm fiber will be useless if it's too warm."

"If you're so worried, why don't you go buy it yourself?" Lingguan said.

"I'm too damned busy. I'm like a slingshot. You can only aim at one bird at a time. I can't get away." Sun cleared his throat noisily. "Being team leader is more trouble than it's worth. I have to take care of everything. It's going to shorten my life, that I can tell you."

"There you go again," Laoshun said. "I've heard you say that so many times calluses are growing in my ears. Quit if you don't like your job. Do you really think you're the only man in Shawan who knows how to do things?"

"I'll take over for you," Lingguan said. "You get to drink the people's blood and have all the say. Check yourself out in a mirror. See that fat? All acquired through the people's hard labor."

"Hogwash!" Big Head said with a laugh. "I can get fat drinking water, and there's nothing I can do about it. I'm not like your dad. He was born scrawny, with thin ears, a pointed mouth, and monkey cheeks. If he eats three rabbits, four of them come out the other end. What a waste. On the other hand, with such a nice little daughter-in-law, it makes sense for him to be skinny? Right, Laoshun?"

"Are there any more farts left in you, Big Head, you dumb ass? Don't compare me with your grandfather, the swine—"

Big Head waved to stop him. "That's enough, you old thief. You're like the donkey that hee-haws the second it opens its mouth. Be sure to pick the best fiber, Hantou." He rushed off.

2

Lingguan and Hantou caught a bus into town after Big Head left.

By then the sun was high in the sky. It looked different in the city, where it was more like a device that sprayed the world and people's heads with grime and racket. Vehicles, big and small, zigzagged like startled mules, and people on bicycles seemed to have gone mad, riding almost on top of each other. Pedestrians formed a mass of frenzied ants, shouting and cursing as they bumped into each other. All the moving heads and swaying hips made Hantou dizzy; he just walked in place for a while before crossing a street.

"Careful. You'll lose your eyeballs from all that staring," his brother quipped.

"Of course you're not afraid, after all those years in school here." Hantou blushed. "Why do they rush around like that?"

"They're going to work."

"Hei, they look like they're on the way to a fire. Why don't they slow down?"

"They'll have their wages docked if they're late."

"Then why don't they leave home earlier?"

"City folks don't have an easy life like us. We can sleep until the sun bakes our asses, but they can't. They have to take their kids to school before going to work. Some don't even have time for breakfast."

"That's so sad. I feel sorry for them."

"They feel sorry for you," Lingguan said with a smile. "What do we do first, buy the palm fiber or go to the hospital?"

Hantou's brow furrowed as he considered the choices. "What do you think?"

"The hospital's not busy now, and we might not get in later."

"Okay, we'll go there first."

They headed to the city hospital, Hantou reluctantly tailing his brother, like a nag on its way to the slaughterhouse. Lingguan decided not to say anything.

At the hospital, Lingguan looked up an old schoolmate by the name of Shi Wen. They exchanged some small talk and slapped one another on the back. Shi told Lingguan what he'd been up to and grumbled about all sorts of things, starting with his superiors at the hospital. Lingguan told him he'd brought his brother, so Shi asked which department. Hantou had disappeared. Lingguan looked around before spotting him on a corner bench, where he sat blankly, his head down. He blushed when his brother asked him what he wanted checked, but he wouldn't say. Lingguan was getting flustered.

"What exactly do you want them to look at?"

Hantou stammered, spraying the tip of his own nose with spittle. Eventually he pointed to the right side of his ribcage and said he had pain there.

"Internal medicine, then," Shi Wen said.

The duty doctor that day was a bespectacled young man who frowned as he felt the pulse of a pretty but talkative woman. He let her talk as he held her wrist, but she shut up when he gave her a cryptic look, thinking maybe he'd found something wrong.

Hantou staring warily at the doctor the same way he looked at his father when he was angry. His jaw hung slack, exposing a kernel of millet that had stuck between his teeth at breakfast. When the doctor let go of the woman's hand, Shi Wen pulled up a chair and told Hantou to sit down.

As he looked first at Lingguan and then at Shi Wen, Hantou's face reddened. He stammered for his brother to go buy him something to eat. Lingguan recalled what their mother had said and knew that Hantou wanted him to make himself scarce. He walked out.

Mantou in hand, Lingguan returned a little while later as Shi Wen was saying, "Go on, tell him. You're not the only with this problem."

"How long has it been?" another voice asked.

"I don't know," Hantou replied softly.

"Was it like this when you were young?"

"No."

"Are you married?"

"Yes."

"You haven't done it even once?"

Hantou mumbled something.

What their mother said that morning finally made sense to Lingguan. He felt his heart race. Damn, so that's what it is! He backed off and sat on a hallway bench, afraid he'd embarrass Hantou if he spotted him.

Twenty minutes later Hantou and Shi Wen walked out. Hantou's face was so red he looked drunk, and he didn't seem steady on his feet. Handing him a prescription, Shi Wen pointed to a window.

Shi Wen put his arm around Lingguan's shoulder and ushered him into his office after Hantou walked away. "Your brother's weird. He said he wanted his liver function checked, but changed his mind after the doctor ordered a test. He wanted to check something else, and was leaking sweat. But he refused to take off his pants. That was hilarious."

"What exactly does he have?"

"Nothing, really. Is your sister-in-law attractive?"

"Why do you ask that?"

"Why? Your bother's impotent. He said he's never had sex. So your sister-in-law is still a virgin, if she isn't seeing another man, that is."

Lingguan's heart skipped a beat, as Ying'er's delicate, sad face raced across his mind. Something had made him uneasy each time she looked at him; it was vague, like gossamer, fitful and uncertain. Now it made sense.

"You've got your work cut out for you." Shi patted his friend on the shoulder, but Lingguan was too preoccupied to joke with him.

"Can it be cured?" he asked anxiously.

"Hard to say. For some yes, but not everybody."

"Lingguan." Shi was barely finished when Lingguan heard his brother call him from the hallway. "Lingguan!"

He walked out and saw his brother looking distressed.

"What's wrong?"

"They told me how much it'll cost." Hantou waved the prescription. "So where do I pay?"

"That window over there," Shi said.

Stuffing the prescription and the money into Lingguan's hand, Hantou told his brother to pay while he went into Shi's office for a drink of water, or so he said.

Hantou came out after Lingguan paid and handed him the prescription. Shi Wen pointed at Hantou's receding back, held his index finger to his lips, and smiled. Lingguan nodded and shook his friend's hand.

The brothers left the hospital, and as they passed a trashcan, Hantou tossed in some scraps of paper that Lingguan knew his brother had peeled off of the pill bottles.

3

"I almost forget the rabbits," Lingguan said as he slapped his forehead.

"I didn't. But I don't know how to sell them. I'd be embarrassed to open my mouth."

"Why? What are you afraid of? I wouldn't mind seeing how it feels to be a peddler."

"How it feels?" Hantou laughed. "Mortifying, I'd say. You go ahead. I'm not interested."

"Don't worry, I'll be fine."

Lingguan nearly changed his mind at the sight of the bloody rabbits he took from his sack. But he'd been so cocksure he couldn't back out now.

"Wild rabbits!" he shouted.

Though the city could boast no tall mountains or long rivers, it had no shortage of people with time on their hands. They strolled, they looked around, they talked and they laughed; there was one tea stand after another to serve the human sea. Old women were drying their eyes over tales sung by a blind storyteller with a three-stringed instrument. A man with a skeletal face sitting at a mahjong table was shouting!

"You lucky jackass," the other man said.

"Of course I'm lucky. You have lousy luck because you keep reaching down between your sister-in-law's legs. That's sure to turn your luck bad."

The streets were festive with music, curses and arguments, smacking mahjong tiles, a din of people, of vehicles, and of screeching cassette tape players.

Lingguan's feeble shout was like a goose feather settling silently to the ground.

"What happened to your nerve? You sounded like a mosquito. You're not cut out for this either. Let's go home."

Bracing himself, Lingguan stepped out into the middle of the street, held up a rabbit carcass, and shouted, sounding almost combative, "Wild rabbit here!"

"What have you got?" A woman walked up.

"Wild rabbit." Lingguan gave it a little wave. "Authentic wild game."

"How much?"

Lingguan froze. It hadn't occurred to him to set a price.

"Ten yuan," Hantou answered for him.

"That's fair enough. It's cheaper than pork. I'll take one. But it's too messy to handle."

"It looks more like an aborted baby to me," a bearded man said.

"It sure does," a passerby said. "There's an epidemic of pregnant girls, you know. You can pick as many of those as you want at the hospital, and make a little money."

The onlookers laughed.

"It's not a baby, it's a rabbit," Hantou blushed as he said defensively.

"What if it was a baby?" Lingguan said. "People will eat anything these days, including other people."

Sounds of agreement were interrupted by a man with long hair who elbowed his way through the crowd and asked who the rabbits belonged to. Lingguan said they were his.

"Are you selling them?"

"Trying to."

"Do you have a license?"

"What for?"

"To sell these."

"No."

"Then I'll have to fine you ten yuan."

"Why?"

"Why? You're selling without a license, that's why, and you're outside the designated area. You're disrupting the market's orderly operation. You're getting off light at only ten."

"Hell! We haven't made a single sale—"

"I don't have all day." The man glared as he reached for the rabbit.

Lingguan's head swirled and his legs wobbled, something that always happened to him before a fight, even if he wasn't involved. He managed to pull himself together.

"How about waiting till I make the sale? I don't have any money on me."

"You refuse to pay the fine? Then I'll have to confiscate your rabbit."

"All right, that's enough." Hantou jumped in.

The fearful look on Hantou's face brought out something in Lingguan their mother had called an "unrelenting spirit," which was common to Lingguan and Mengzi. Mengzi got aggressive when that spirit rose up, while Lingguan took a more rational approach.

"On what grounds? Let's see proof that you're from the tax office."

Longhair took out a stack of ticket stubs and slapped Lingguan with them.

"How dare you!" Lingguan's legs stopped shaking, the blood rushed to his head.

"How? I've got these." Longhair flourished the stubs again. "I'll slap you again if you keep arguing."

"All right, that's enough." Hantou spread his arms like a hen protecting her chicks. "A man like you should be more forgiving." He took out ten yuan and thrust it at *the man*. "You can keep the rabbit too. Does that work for you? Or do you expect me to get down on my knees and beg."

Longhair puffed himself up, took a look around, and walked off grumbling.

Lingguan felt like flinging a rabbit at the man's back, but he knew that messing with the "law" was a bad idea.

"That tax guy does that all the time," the woman said.

The bearded man didn't think Hantou should have paid. "Would he bite off your dick if you didn't pay?"

"Didn't you see he was going to hit us?" Hantou murmured.

"That asshole's not the only one with fists. I'd have helped if you'd fought back. He loves to pick on peasants? Let's go get him."

Lingguan shook his head.

"Forget it. He'll have to spend it on medicine one day," Hantou said.

"Actually, he was pretty lenient," the woman said. "Here, I'll take one of those." She handed them a ten-yuan bill. Hantou gave her a rabbit. "Anyone else?"

When no one spoke up, an enraged Lingguan snatched the remaining rabbits away and hurled them into the air, where they described a bright red arc before landing in the middle of the street. They were quickly turned into rabbit pulp.

Hantou was unhappy that Lingguan had thrown them away. "We could have gotten another ten yuan at least," he said after they had walked awhile.

"Money, money," Lingguan raged. "All you can see is money."

"You can't survive without it."

"What's money worth without dignity?" Lingguan said as he breathed a sigh.

The brothers went into the farmers' market, bought the palm fiber, and rode the bus home.

4

The riverbank next to the village highway was a typical potters' field, crowded with graves under which lay people who had lived in the village, some known to Lingguan and some not. His anger disappeared when he saw the final resting place of all those people. Yes, everyone ended up as a pile of bones—the strong and the weak, assailants and victims. So what was the point of a meaningless fight?

Unaware of what was going through his brother's mind, Hantou tried to console him. "Let it go. We can pretend we gave the prick a gift, or that someone stole them. There's no need to be angry."

"Are you still thinking about that?" Lingguan laughed. "I've already forgotten it."

"I'm glad. It's only ten yuan." Hantou sighed. He seemed about to say more, but, after glancing around, he swallowed and said nothing. He walked on, seemingly lost in thought.

The once level riverbank was now dotted with craters and pits, caused by villagers taking the sand to grow peppers. Desert sand could last villagers a whole year. But they preferred to take what they needed from the sandbar, where the soil was more fertile from decomposing vegetation. So the sandbar suffered; during windstorms blowing sand blurred the line between sky and earth.

Hantou stopped when they walked by a hollowed-out spot.

Lingguan knew his brother had something to say, and he guessed it had to do with his condition. He did not want to start the conversation. Hantou was so shy and so sensitive that Lingguan could hurt his feelings if he wasn't careful. Hantou looked around, opened his mouth, but nothing emerged.

"If you have something to say, go ahead and say it. No one's going to yank your teeth out."

Hantou clenched his jaw, making his face muscles twitch. "Do you know what I've got?"

"No, I don't." Lingguan quickly added, "Something about your ribs, you said."

"Honest?" With an earnest look, Hantou said, "Didn't your schoolmate say anything?"

"He did."

"What did he say?" Hantou asked wide-eyed.

"He said his girlfriend wants three gold things—a gold ring, a gold necklace, and gold earrings, but he doesn't have the money, so he's very unhappy."

"Come on, what else did he say?"

"He also said they haven't been paid in two months."

"What else?"

"That's it."

"Really?" Hantou squinted into the distance, his lips moving unconsciously, like gumming a mouthful of beans. His typical pensive look, Lingguan knew. A moment later, Hantou said:

"It was nothing, actually. The doctor wanted me to have my liver functions checked, but I decided against that and got some medicine instead. Why waste the money? Besides, it doesn't hurt that much."

Lingguan felt terrible for his brother. For him, an unmarried man, what difference did it make? But poor Hantou was trying to conceal something that could not be hidden. Could he keep it from everyone for the rest of his life? Lingguan could understand how his brother felt, as he recalled a line from a tune called "Mrs. Wang Scolds a Chicken Thief": "A girl stole and ate my chicken, so she'll marry a man who can't get it up." Obviously, marrying a man who can't perform is like a death sentence. He wanted to say something to make Hantou feel better, but his brother was being evasive, so all he said was:

"Why not take the test if it bothers you? You have to know the cause before you can find a cure."

Without responding, Hantou squinted at a dark figure coming toward them.

"Mother wants a grandchild," he said. "She holds other people's babies and won't let go. She never says a word, but I know."

"She has Yindi."

"Yindi is the daughter of her daughter, an outsider no matter how you look at it. Mother wants one from her own son."

"That shouldn't be too hard."

"Of course not." Hantou glanced at his brother and sighed. Something unusual flashed in his eyes, which Lingguan found hard to interpret. But soon Hantou was gazing into the distance again and spat out angrily, "Life is so damned hard!"

A common phrase among the villagers, a simple grumble at times, it did not seem so common to Lingguan now. Hantou wasn't Mengzi, who rumbled like thunder, but when the eruption was over, everything was fine. Hantou, on the other hand, talked little and complained even less; but every word from him carried weight, solid as a wall. His complaint now was likely related to his illness, which bothered Lingguan. "Don't think unpleasant thoughts." That was all he could say, and he realized that he sounded as if he knew his brother's real illness. But Hantou did not seem to notice, as he continued staring into space.

The dark figure drew closer. It was Beizhu, on a rickety bicycle, his wife, Fengxiang, seated behind him, clink-clanking as they rode up.

"Where are you off to?" Lingguan asked.

Beizhu nudged his wife with his foot. They got off the bike, and the usually jovial Beizhu fumed.

"Where? Where else? Those goddamned people want to X-ray her to see the IUD. Why are they doing this to us? They'll take our land, fine us, even tear down our house if we say no. I can't let those people feel up my woman, can I? Damn them."

"You can go feel up other women if that's what's bothering you," Fengxiang said with a smile.

"You've got two kids already, why not have your tubes tied?" Lingguan said.

"Hell no!" Beizhu shook his head until he looked like a click-clack toy. "That would mean no one to continue the family line. Two good daughters are no match for a boy, even a blind one. Well, they can look if they want. We need to keep our land for now. I'm hearing they mean business this time. Over at Sangou, they confiscated someone's land over this. Did you get the palm fiber?"

Hantou shook the bag in his hand.

"Hurry back, then. They're waiting for you at the well site. Big Head has sent someone to your house to check on you several times already."

"That's enough." Fengxiang punched her husband. "Your tongue is like a foot-binding cloth, long and stinky. You never shut up."

"See that? She can't wait to have some other man feel her up," Beizhu said. "She doesn't know enough to be modest."

"What's to be modest about?" Fengxiang laughed. "Worst case, I open my legs and they shove something else up there." She giggled and climbed back onto the bike.

With his eyes on the couple clanking away, Hantou shook his head and said, "Even a cracked gong doesn't go unused."

"That woman is really—" Lingguan smiled. "I have to give it to them, though. After the township office carted away all their furniture, they're still going merrily on. All they've got left are some tattered blankets and bedding."

"No one will spare any effort to have a son," Hantou said as he cast a meaningful look at his brother.

5

Hantou took the fiber to the well site, while Lingguan headed home. Their mother rushed up when he walked in.

"What does he have?"

"Nothing serious. Some pain around his ribcage, that's all. The doctor prescribed something for it."

"That's all?" She was suspicious, her gaze like a fishhook trying to pry something out of his mouth.

"As far as I know. He made me get him something to eat while they were talking."

"I told you to pay attention. But you never listen," she complained with obvious disappointment. She handed him a glass of water. Lingguan took it, threw back his head, and drank, his Adam's apple jumping up and down. He choked and coughed when a careless swallow sent water down his windpipe.

"Take it easy. You're not out in the desert," she chided. "What do you want to eat?"

"How about some noodle soup?"

"Go in and rest if you're tired. If not, go help your sister-in-law clean the pigpen." She walked into the kitchen.

Lingguan mumbled a response and lay down on a leatherette sofa. He shut his eyes, but no sleep came; since it was pointless to keep lying there, he got up and changed his clothes before picking up a spade and walking outside.

It was a large yard, littered with corn stalks. He pushed open the pigpen door, startling the chickens into cackling noisily. The old sow grunted as she waddled over, looking for a handout.

Ying'er stopped and looked his way when he walked in, but she did not greet him; no "So you're back" or anything like that. He saw her in a different light, now that he was aware of his brother's affliction. Something in her eyes disturbed him.

"Has the manure turned hard?" he asked. He knew how stupid that sounded, and that made his face burn.

She smiled but said nothing, just looked at him. A moment later she asked, "Did he get his checkup?"

"Yes, he did." Lingguan added, "Nothing serious. A little discomfort around his ribcage, that's all. The doctor prescribed some medicine."

She looked away. Their rooster was chasing a hen, stirring up dust. Ying'er sighed and jammed her spade into the manure; soon she was breathing hard.

Lingguan slowly regained his composure, but was angry at himself for being so flustered. He knew his face showed it. That was an annoying trait of his. Their village was overrun with coarse men and women who did not blush easily, which was why women liked to tease him. Ying'er never did. They did not talk often, but sometimes, when they were out working together, village kids would taunt, "Hei, hei—a young man diddling his sister-in-law. A rare sight." That always made her blush, and she would race ahead.

She stopped what she was doing, but did not look at him. With a blank expression, she asked casually, "You really don't know?"

"What do you mean?" he asked, though he knew what she was referring to. "He sent me out to get him something to eat, so what was there to know?"

She gave him a perplexing look, and he felt she could see through him. "You must know something, so don't lie to me."

"It's really nothing." Now he had to come up with something. "The doctor said he'd be okay."

"This isn't the first time. Every time he goes into town he buys medicine, even secret formulas, but nothing works." She tried to sound matter-of-fact.

Recalling the conversation in the house, Lingguan realized that their mother did not know what was wrong with Hantou, which he himself had just learned. He was surprised that his brother had covered it up so successfully.

"Then why go to the hospital?"

"I don't know," she said as her face turn bright red.

Lingguan's throat was dry. To cover up his unease, he worked fast with his spade.

"Slow down." She smiled. "You're not used to working this hard. Keep it up and you'll be like a worn-out camel. Did he say anything on the way home?"

"Nothing special. He just asked me what my friend and I talked about."

"That's all?"

"Yes."

Ying'er turned to look at him as she gave the loosened manure a few gentle pokes. "Think harder."

Lingguan was about to mention Hantou's comment about their mother's desire for a grandchild, but when he realized how that might make her feel, he said instead, "It can be fixed, honest."

Ignoring his attempt to comfort her, she worked listlessly. A moment later, she wiped her sweaty face with a corner of her headscarf and said:

"Women are born to suffer, don't you think? Take Lanlan, for example. A wonderful girl like her forced to marry a hothead like my brother. There was nothing she could do. Your parents wanted her to marry my brother so your brother could marry me. Could she say no? She was born a girl, so she had no choice."

He knew what she was getting at, but could say nothing about the deal struck between the two families. Without it, Hantou might have remained a bachelor all his life. Lingguan's heart softened at the thought of his brother, who had opposed the arrangement. When he had too much to drink, he might cry like an old cow, saying he'd done his sister wrong.

"You're right, maybe it's fate." It was all he could say.

"Fate. Fate." She clenched her teeth. "It's so easy to say that, but it's a lifetime for someone. In a way, Lanlan has done better than me, because she at least has her daughter. I know what Mother is thinking. I do, even though she never says anything. She won't scold the hen that doesn't lay eggs, because she doesn't want to hurt my feelings." Her voice cracked and her face was soon streaked with sparkling tears.

That sent Lingguan into a panic. How would he explain himself if someone saw his sister-in-law crying like that? He didn't know what to say to comfort her, afraid that might make her cry even harder. Some women were like that—the more you tried to get them to stop, the harder they cried. So he threw himself into the work, grunting loudly to draw her out of the sadness that was making her cry.

It worked. She dried her tears with the headscarf and went back to work, keeping her head down. "Men are all the same," she said after a moment. "They're so thoughtless their hearts are filled with holes big enough to drive a camel through. I thought you were smart and sensitive, but you're as dumb as all the others."

His mind drifted. He sensed that she was insinuating something, but could not grasp the floating thought, like a silk thread gliding on a breeze. Her voice, soft and serene as still water, usually washed away the troubles in his heart. But the mellow voice seemed almost oppressive now.

"Don't you think so?" A smile danced around her lips. Obviously, she had sensed his unease. "Have you heard the ballad about Liang Shanbo? He's as dense as a pine pole trying to carry a willow bucket. I think that's the perfect description for you."

What she was hinting at seemed pretty clear. Feeling pressure build in his chest, he was getting breathless. He forced himself to calm down and breathe more evenly, but that only succeeded in making it worse.

"He must have said something else. Think harder," she said.

Lingguan was getting lightheaded and his face was hot. Ying'er was like the sun, drying up the moisture in him. Assaulted by an unusual thirst, he said, "I forget. I'll tell you if I think of it," and headed out of the yard.

"You're too young to have an old man's memory," she said with a laugh, and then let the strains of a ballad follow him:

The wood of a poplar, the heart of an apricot tree
Ruined a pair of cross-cut saws
Elder Brother has no interest in my heart
A waste of Little Sister's feelings.

6

Lingguan's mother was shocked when she saw him.

"What's wrong? Your face is red."

"I don't know," he stammered. "Maybe I'm coming down with something. I've got a terrible headache."

"There are pain pills on the table."

Grunting a reply, he got a glass of water.

"Cover your head and sleep it away."

"I'm not a child anymore," he said. "Don't worry about me."

Feeling better after drinking the water, he lay down to mull over what Ying'er had said. Every word was pregnant with implications, he discovered, and then again, with no special meaning at all. It all depended on how he interpreted it. Village women were known for flirtatious talk that sounded seductive only to men who fancied themselves as irresistible; most did not take it seriously. Ying'er was not like that; she did not talk much, and when she did, her words were gentle and soft, like whispers. But she had acted differently on this day. Lingguan did not let his thoughts go further, out of respect for Hantou. Poor Hantou.

In earlier days, Lingguan's fondest wish had been to escape the desert by taking the college exam. But that dream had gone unfulfilled. He was disappointed, but had to leave it behind, with the knowledge that he'd done as his father had asked—he'd given it his all. There was no need for regret, and he need not feel sorry for himself. He'd studied hard and had "spent enough money to pay for a wife." So what if he could not strut around like those city boys with a girl on his arm? He'd done his best, and that was enough.

Inevitably, he'd been on edge since returning home to work in the field. The sight of the collapsed sandbar and dry riverbed had formed a cloud over his heart. The prospect of spending the rest of his life in this sandy corner of the world, a lonely village folded into a curve of the legendary sand dragon, saddened him. Was this really his hometown? Was it the place that had sent warm currents through his heart whenever he thought about it during his student days in the city? The word hometown was comforting only when he was away from it; the real place was impoverished, backward, and mostly quiet. He sensed an oppressive, deathly stillness even amid the din of human shouts and horse whinnies.

Loneliness was unavoidable. But he knew he had to put on a smiling face for the sake of his father and mother. They smiled. Life was hard and exhausting, but still they smiled; so did Hantou, Mengzi, and Lanlan. So Lingguan smiled along with them.

Ying'er became a cool and refreshing dream.

Lanlan had left home, and Ying'er had arrived. An outgoing girl, Lanlan was lively and given to laughing. She had little schooling, but seemed content with her lot in life. When their father wanted her to marry so her brother could have a wife, she cried through the night, but agreed to it the next day. She had bartered herself so her twenty-seven-year-old brother could have Ying'er.

Lingguan had heard that Ying'er was a famous "Queen of Liangzhou Folk songs" in her hometown, where she had won every singing contest she'd entered. He loved the songs, which were unique to their Western region. Heavenly sounds, straight from the heart, simple and unaffected, perfect and natural, with no need for embellishment. One of them said it all: "The Liangzhou song has words from the heart/I cannot help wanting to sing it forever/You can chop off my head/But as long as I live I'll keep singing." In school he'd even written a short essay about the songs.

Ying'er rarely sang after marrying Hantou.

Lingguan roused himself and walked outside. The sun was slanting west above a sandy ridge, looking ghostly pale and pathetic. The herders were returning from the desert; camels, sheep, and mules entered his field of vision, each walking in its peculiar way. Camels had a deep, dragged-out, mournful call, as if weighed down by heavy burdens, even when they carried no load. The mules seemed so much more carefree, galloping along and kicking up columns of sand, braying loudly, as if wanting tear up the sky. One eager donkey was going after a pretty jenny that had run off, playing hard to get.

Lingguan liked the sheep calls best, sounds of nature devoid of bitterness, anger, complaint, or struggle, brushing through his heart like a spring breeze to bestow uncommon peace. To him, sheep were unfathomable beasts, always meek and silent. They never seemed angry; even when facing the knife, they seemed resigned to their fate, contented, never struggling to be free or cry. Instead, they gazed at the butcher with unbearably kind eyes, as if to console him, "Go ahead, kill me. I won't be angry." Lingguan did not like to look into those eyes.

Laoshun and Gimpy Five approached with their flocks. Lingguan saw that his father was looking old, dragging dry branches from a desert date tree behind him, his back bent. The setting sun etched his shadow in the sand and twisted it into a writhing old tree. He was aging fast. Lingguan felt an indescribable sorrow rise up, as he recalled a morning three years before, when Father, a sack of flour on his back, had left with him to hitch a ride. He'd always remember how Father had panted as he laid down the sack.

"Study hard, son, and don't let your mother and me down."

Two years later, when he failed to pass the exam, Father had said nothing. Now, Lingguan was besieged by a powerful sense of guilt and regret, as the pain of failure was dying away. How elated Father would have been if he'd gotten into a college.

"Eaten yet?" Laoshun asked when he saw his son.

"Who?" Lingguan was puzzled.

"The red hawk."

Now Lingguan recalled the hawk caught the day before; he'd completely forgotten about it. "I don't know."

Laoshun turned to Gimpy Five. "It's a terrific hawk, hot tempered. It refused to eat anything I tried to feed it. It ignored me and beat its wings as it hopped up and down. It will probably take a few more days for the anger to run its course before it will eat anything. A good bird does not let you touch its wings, so it fumes. Just think, why wouldn't it be upset over being captured? Oh, what does he have? Hantou, I mean."

Noticing that the topic of the hawk had come up before Hantou, Lingguan was miffed that their father seemed to value the bird over his own son, but he brushed that feeling off once he recalled that his father could sometimes be inattentive. Their mother had told him how not even a dangerously high fever he'd run as a child had interrupted his father's sleep.

"It's nothing."

"What's wrong?" Gimpy Five asked. "Is someone sick at your house?"

"It's nothing," said Lingguan. "No one's sick."

"Hei, that's good news, really good." Laoshun brightened up. "In this day and age, all anyone can hope for is good health. We can't afford to get sick. Your mother, that crone, is always worrying about something, turning a minor issue into a major event. It's great that nothing's wrong. Really great."

Gimpy Five snorted, but said nothing.

When they reached Laoshun's house, the two older men cried out at the same time, "Gao! – Gao! – Gao! – Gao!" It was a command for the sheep to separate into two groups, which they did, one entering Laoshun's yard, while the other followed Gimpy Five home.

After closing the pen, Laoshun took out some rabbit meat whose blood had been leached out in water, cut it into thin strips, and took them over to the red hawk. Hei! He shouted and shook the meat, but the hawk shrieked angrily and beat its wings, a fierce glint shooting out from its blood-red eyes, as if it would devour Laoshun if it could. Upon hearing the shout, Indigo Widow and Stubborn Yellow tried to bound over, but were held back by tethers and flipped off the perch; hanging upside, they noisily flapped their wings.

More shouts failed to get the red hawk to eat, so Laoshun gave up.

"This creature has a temper." He laughed. "I'll feed you turnips at night, and then we'll see how you feel about that."

He and Lingguan slipped on leather gauntlets, untied Stubborn Yellow and Indigo Widow, and went to the backyard after filling plastic sacks with the meat.

Ying'er was still cleaning the pigpen. She looked down after a quick glance at Lingguan, who felt the unease again. He tugged at Indigo Widow's feathers until he had smoothed out the creases in his heart.

Laoshun put Stubborn Yellow on the ground and walked to a spot about ten meters away, where he stopped, held up a strip of meat, and shouted – Hei! Stubborn Yellow flew to his wrist, stretched out its neck, and the meat vanished. Even after the act was repeated three times, the bird fixed its lively eyes on Laoshun, making him laugh. He rubbed its feathers. "That's enough, you greedy thing. You won't go after rabbits if you eat too much."

Following his father's example, Lingguan fed Indigo Widow two strips of meat. "Enough," Laoshun said. "It's time to clear its phlegm. Feed it a spool of wool tonight."

7

Before dinner, Hantou announced, "The drilling team is complaining about the food, saying it's little more than pig swill. So the leader told us to collect half a *jin* of chicken per person from every family. For us, rabbit will do, but it has to be one *jin* per person."

Mengzi spat. "Fuck. This is outrageous. We pay them to work and now we have to feed them chicken. They collected enough last time to feed a wolf."

"It's not all their fault," Hantou said. "When the village and township cadres come, they have to eat and drink too. The few drillers don't eat that much, but some of our villagers have no shame. They drop in to eat from time to time. Too many wolves and not enough meat."

"Then I'm going to go eat my share," Mengzi said. "Why not, if others are doing it?"

"Eat too much and you'll get the runs," their father said. "It's not like we never feed you, so don't say that. They can steal food if they want, but don't make me lose face."

"I was just saying." Mengzi replied. "Do you really think I'd do that?"

"Rub your lips against the wall if they itch, and stop the nonsense. You talk too much. It pisses people off."

Mengzi mumbled something incomprehensible in return.

Ying'er carried a pot of boiled potatoes into the living room, the sight of which set Mengzi off again. "Is that all you can cook?" He frowned. "Boiled potatoes, and more boiled potatoes. My scalp itches every time I see one of those."

"What's wrong with boiled potatoes?" Their mother walked in with some pickled vegetables. "I was born to be a beggar, and boiled potatoes are my favorite. Go eat fluffy *mantou* if you don't want potatoes. I steam rolls and your sister-in-law cleans out the pigpen while you do nothing. Today you'll have to make do."

Mengzi frowned.

"So what do you want to eat?" Laoshun shot Mengzi an angry look. "You too were born to be a beggar, but you think you've got a scholar's belly. Count yourself lucky to have this. In the old days, only landlords and rich people could afford to eat potatoes. I went to old Master Chen's house in Nantan to borrow grain one day. After giving me boiled potatoes, they watched me. If I'd peeled them, they'd have said I had plenty to eat and wouldn't lend me anything. Even someone like him, with all his property and money, ate potatoes, skin and all. Just who do you think you are? You'll know the value of potatoes when there's a bad harvest and your mouth stinks from hunger."

"All right, already." Mengzi frowned again. "Can't you talk about anything except old Chen and his potatoes? Always landlords and rich people. You're not one of them." He rose angrily to fetch a *mantou* from the kitchen to go with the pickled vegetables.

"What's wrong with landlords and rich people?" Laoshun asked when Mengzi returned. "In the spring, old Master Chen came to the village and swore at anyone who hadn't yet taken their manure out to the fields. But then he lent them animals for the job." He grabbed a potato, peeled it, and scowled. "Hei, woman. No matter what I just said, I was out in the sun all day and I'm still tied up in knots. Wouldn't it be nice to have some soup or something like that? This stuff—hei."

"I see you found the words while you were bawling him out." His wife laughed.

"He's all about Marxism-Leninism with others, but with himself—"

"That's enough!" Laoshun cut Mengzi off. "You think your old man can't handle a potato?" He took a savage bite, but spat it right out, yelping in pain. It was a very hot potato. They all laughed.

Lingguan ate quietly, feigning indifference while keeping an eye on Ying'er. Without looking his way, she quietly peeled a potato, sprinkled on salt, and picked up some pickled vegetables, aloof and yet approachable. He turned over in his mind what had happened earlier that day, like a dream, a very long dream. Everything seemed distant and hazy, as if it had taken place decades earlier. Strange. Was life really a dream, as they say? He shook his head, trying to sort out his jumbled thoughts, but that only made matters worse. Had he hurt her feelings by running off? What was he afraid of, he wondered. Rationally speaking, he had nothing to fear. She hadn't said anything out of the ordinary, and nothing had happened between them. But she seemed to have said something and something could have happened. Everything was blurry and yet clear—he just lacked the courage to stare at the clear picture. He wanted to look her way, but couldn't quite do it, for his guilty conscience made him feel that they all knew what he was thinking, and were keeping a watchful eye.

"When the meal was over, Hantou wiped his hands on a towel and said, "I have to go. It's my turn to guard the well tonight."

"Not tonight," Laoshun said. "You've been working too hard. Mengzi, you go."

"I'm busy tonight."

"What could you be busy with?" Laoshun reacted angrily. "You're always busy. You spend too much time with those hooligan friends of yours. Whatever you want to do, it can wait till tomorrow."

"I really do have something to do. Guarding the well isn't hard work. I wouldn't mind going if I wasn't busy."

Lingguan saw their father's face darken and knew he was about fly into a rage, so he quickly offered, "Let him do what he has to do. I'll go. It's just one night."

"Son, I know you won't like what I'm going to say, but I have to say it." Laoshun took a deep breath. "I don't care what else you do, but there's one thing you mustn't do, and that's gamble. That's my advice. Take it or leave it. You'll answer to yourself if you don't. You can be a dragon or a tiger, it's your choice."

"Aiya!" Mengzi laughed. "What do I have to gamble with? I'm so poor my farts sound like an out-of-tune fiddle. And no one wants my spirit money for the underworld."

"I don't care. Just remember what I said today."

8

What Mengzi had to do that night was quite simple; he had agreed to write a letter to Shuangfu for his wife.

Shuangfu was widely known in the village as "the chemist brain," someone with a dynamic mind, a good education, and the capacity for hard work. Several years earlier, he'd stolen some corn from the production team, and Big Head Sun had led a struggle session against him. Unable to stay in the village any longer, he'd run off to Lanzhou, where he'd opened a shop, become a skilled worker, taken on jobs big and small, and built a two-story house. He nearly wore himself out working, but eventually became a successful entrepreneur.

"Come over after dinner," Shuangfu's wife had said to Mengzi that afternoon. "I need you to write a letter to that no-good husband of mine."

So here he was.

He walked in when she was half naked, washing her hair; her breasts jiggled.

"Where's your daughter?"

"At her grannie's house," she said, and then ignored him as she scrubbed her head, making her breasts and buttocks jiggle and sway. His throat was dry.

When she finished with her hair, she oiled her face at a mirror, slowly and methodically. With that done, she brushed her hair and then opened a dresser to take out a blouse. He detected the smell of mothballs.

"Hungry?" She asked.

"No."

"I'll make you something."

"No need."

"I didn't think you'd come."

He didn't know what to say to that.

"Rest a moment. You can write the letter later." She sat on the edge of the bed with her eyes on him. He returned the look. Her blouse could not hide her bulging breasts. Her soft, pleasant voice tickled his heart like a feather.

"No, let's write it now."

"All right."

He didn't move. Shuangfu is an idiot, he said to himself. With a woman like her, why doesn't he stay home? He'd heard that Shuangfu was involved with some immoral women. It was truly a case of someone with a full belly ignoring the pangs of a hungry man. What was he looking for anyway?

"I'll write it now."

"Go ahead, if that's what you want."

Gazing at her open-mouthed, he looked quite foolish and experienced a vague loss of self-esteem, his usual cleverness gone. His mouth was drier than ever and he was slightly dizzy. "Shuangfu must be awfully busy if he only comes home a few times a year."

"I don't care if he ever comes home," she said. "You men are all the same. You eye the contents of the pot while your bowls are still full. You don't understand this, of course, but you will, once you're married."

Mengzi was tongue-tied. A cymbal clanged in his head —*kuang*—*kuang*—and his throat was on fire. He swallowed, sending his Adam's apple up and down, but his throat remained parched. "Let's write it, then."

"Go ahead." She brought him pen and paper. "If that's what you want."

"But, why write at all? You can ask someone to take a message."

"A letter is still best," she said. "Tell him the harvest is in, thanks to some hired help. He can come home if he feels like it, but it's okay if he doesn't. I'm out of money, but I'm fine if he doesn't want to send any more. Tell him to do what he wants. Don't worry about a thing, not his wife or his daughter. I'll have her take him food if he winds up in prison."

"Do you really want me to write that?"

"Sure."

"Anything else?"

"That's all."

He asked for an envelope, copied the address, sealed the letter, and, glancing at the woman, placed it on the bed. His heart raced when he saw her watching him.

"I'm not a man-eating tiger." She smiled. "Why do you look so scared?" She kept her gaze on him, something bright sparkling in her eyes.

"When he comes home I'll tell him you wrote the letter. And tomorrow, if anyone asks who was here, I'll tell them it was Mengzi."

His heart was beating so fast and so loud it sounded to him like a mountain torrent. He was getting short of breath.

"I'll tell everyone we didn't do anything, and they can ask you if they don't believe me." Her voice was as soft as water.

With a cry, he threw his arms around her and planted clumsy kisses on her face, like a chicken pecking at rice.

"Behave yourself, Mengzi," she said. "I asked you here to write a letter."

He was breathing hard as he groped around to untie her pants. She put up a weak resistance. "I'll tell your mother if you keep this up."

Her pants were so tight he struggled but failed to pull them down.

"You're getting out of hand, Mengzi," she said as she slipped out of her pants and lay back naked. "Let's see if you can eat me alive."

She was heavyset, with fair skin and big breasts, and her belly, bulging like a small hill, made her look like a beached whale. His mouth hanging slack, Mengzi was breathing hard and appeared frightened by her audacity.

"I don't believe you can do that." She laughed.

"I'll show you." He threw himself down on her, but she pushed him away. "Ouch, you're killing me! Your clothes are like armor."

"I'll take them off."

"That's up to you." He took off his clothes.

"I'm not in the mood," she said. He looked at her, but she kept her eyes shut.

"Your breasts are so—so—I want to suck them."

"Do whatever you want. I don't feel like it, anyway"

Her nipples were like on-off switches; she began to moan when he put his lips around one. "Does that hurt?" She just moaned, so he stopped.

"I'm really going to—" He touched her.

"Going to what? Don't be ridiculous."

He spread her legs and began to move. She was put off by his clumsy moves, and so, with a frown, she took hold and guided him. Then she moaned, loudly and melodiously.

"Does it hurt?" he asked.

"Not so fast," she said, but soon told him to move faster. She was like a wild beast, her face contorted. She bit his lips.

"Will you leave me alone now?" she said after they finished.

"Don't hold me so tight. I can't breathe." He was breathless.

"No, that would be too easy on you. You took advantage of me." She tightened her arms around him as if angry, and bit his lips. "I can't believe you actually did that. How am I supposed to face the world tomorrow?" she stopped biting him long enough to say.

Deflated, Mengzi quickly lost interest. She'd looked so appealing dressed, but now she seemed quite plain. "I should go."

"Go if you want. But there are people out and about. Aren't you afraid? When they ask you where you've been, just tell them Shuangfu wasn't home."

He didn't dare leave.

9

Lingguan felt he was entitled to sleep in after working the night shift. The sun was high in the sky when he got up, its light adding a brilliant sheen to everything in the yard. Mengzi had left with Father to hunt rabbits in the desert, while Hantou went to work his shift at the well site. Their mother was in the yard checking the grain, surrounded by a flock of cackling chickens that pecked at what she threw down. When she saw Lingguan, she said, "There's noodle soup on the stove. You can soak a *mantou* in it for breakfast."

With a mumbled reply, he washed up, rinsed his mouth, and had his breakfast.

"Get some rest if you're tired. If not, go clear the field. It's nearly time for winter irrigation, but the land is still lumpy and uneven."

"I hate that job. Just thinking about it galls me," Lingguan said.

"Who's going to work the land, if we hate this and are afraid of that? Go do as much as you can. Your sister-in-law left some time ago for Xihu Slope."

His heart raced, despite himself. His mother was picking pebbles out of the grain, so once he was breathing evenly, he picked up a shovel and walked out.

He spotted Xihu Slope as soon as he rounded the bend. The clear sky was like a sheet of blue satin that brightened the yellow ridge to the north. With the rolling waves of sand as a background, Ying'er looked irresistible in her red blouse. Why was she so fond of red? Blue fit her personality best, he thought, but she was captivating in red even so.

Maodan walked up to Lingguan with a bundle of wheat stalks under his arm.

"Didn't you work the night shift? he asked. "Why are you here instead of sleeping?"

"How about you?"

Maodan squawked again. "We're different. You can relax in the shade of a tree, but I have to work or I'll have nothing to eat but the wind." He took a furtive look around. "Handless Wei's wife had a baby," he whispered. "It died. Another girl." He patted the wheat stalks under his arm. Lingguan spotted a lump wrapped in cloth.

"The way I see it, Lingguan, he must have pulled some shenanigans with his scale on people. After shortchanging his customers, retribution has caught up with him. That's the only reason his cow bit him, and when that got infected, they had to saw his paw off. Weird, isn't it? Now, comes the ultimate retribution, all girls to end his family line."

"That's horseshit."

"That's what everybody says. If he'd been morally upright, why is he the only one whose family line is coming to an end, while every one else has a son?"

Maodan's logic displeased Lingguan, since neither his brother, Hantou, nor his sister, Lanlan, had a son. "I haven't seen any sons from you," he sputtered.

Maodan laughed with a wicked look on his face. "Don't lump me in with them. I—I don't want to get married—actually, women—hei. I know you can't wait to get something going with your sister-in-law. But I've got to go cremate this baby. I can't stop just because I don't want to disturb you two."

Lingguan ignored him and walked off.

With the bundled baby under his arm, Maodan hummed a tune as he fell in behind Lingguan. The soles of his shoes smacked the bottoms of his feet, like slaps in the face, as if to the beat of his tune. Judging by the smile on his face and his carefree attitude, sort of like Jigong, the Living Buddha, no one would believe that at that moment he was taking a tiny life off to burn it up.

Lingguan was disgusted.

He began shoveling soil onto a depression on the ground.

Maodan's eyes shifted when he saw Ying'er. He walked up with a cryptic look. "Look here! Ever seen one of these?" He parted the straw and peeled back the cloth wrap.

"Get away from there, Maodan!" Lingguan shouted.

But she'd seen it. With a frightened cry, she stumbled backward and fell on her tailbone.

Maodan grinned, pleased with the result of his prank. Ying'er's face was a ghostly white, her eyes glazed over, and tears gushed from her eyes. Lingguan flung a dirt clod at Maodan, hitting him in the rump. He grimaced and sprang away like a monkey. After running a ways, he turned around. "Lingguan is sweet on his sister-in-law." He was grinning.

With a curse, Lingguan threw another dirt clod. Seeing that Lingguan was seriously angry, Maodan ran off and disappeared.

Her face still ashen, Ying'er tried to stand with the help of her shovel, but could not manage. Lingguan didn't think it would be proper for him to help her up, but it felt wrong not to. He stood there, looking helpless.

She tried to catch her breath. "You think this is funny, don't you?" she chided, prompting him to come up and help her to her feet.

10

She patted her chest and sighed, before letting out a soft cry. "You know I'm even afraid of toads, so why did you let him show me a dead baby?"

"He was going to cremate it. I didn't think he'd use it to frighten you."

"You knew, all right. You just wanted to see how I'd react."

"It's no big deal," he said with a smile, seeing that she was regaining her composure. "The only difference between her and us is that she doesn't breathe any longer. What's there to be afraid of?"

"Be a woman in your next life and you'll know. Whose baby was it?"

"Handless Wei."

"Again? Ai! That wife of his has suffered enough. She used to have fair skin and a nice figure, and now, ai, she's skin and bones. Aiya! I'm still shaking. I'm afraid my soul has been scared off. I can't seem to focus. Do you know how to call a soul back?"

"No."

"It's easy. Just call out 'Soul and spirits return to the body.' That should do it."

"That's all? Really? Then I could be a shaman or a medium," Lingguan said. "All right, I'll try. Soul and spirits return to the body!"

"Who are you doing it for? A pig? A dog? You have to say a name."

"What should I say? Should I say sister-in-law or use your name?"

"My name, of course."

"All right, here I go. Ying'er's soul and spirits return to her body!"

"I can feel them coming back." She smiled. "Do it again."

"Ying'er's soul and spirits return to her body!"

"Again."

"Ying'er's soul and spirits return to her body!"

"They're back. Uh-oh! This means trouble." She looked both startled and nervous. "They went to you. How come?"

"Are you serious? That's ridiculous."

"Yes. The souls on the ground went to you, and so did my spirits. You didn't do it right. Ying'er—Ying'er—your voice was too soft, too sweet; anyone who heard it would think you were whispering tender nothings to me. No wonder they went to you." She was still smiling.

He blushed, and was tongue-tied.

"I always thought you were stiff, lifeless, but—but you sounded human just now. I couldn't tell if you were calling my soul back or casting a spell on me."

His face turned red. He knew he blushed too easily, an awareness that made him even more self-conscious. Ying'er was acting out of character. Ordinarily quiet, she could be as mischievous as the girls back at school. He liked the clever, impish Ying'er, despite the fact that she made him feel awkward.

Delighted to see him ill at ease, she teased him mercilessly. "Your face will burn and your heart will race if you have someone else's soul on you. Unless you're totally heartless, that is. Is your face burning? How about your heart? Oh, I see. You're a heartless man."

Clueless as to how to defend himself, he was sweating, as a drumbeat raged in his chest.

"Not burning? Oh, I know." She was persistent. "You don't have a heart."

Lingguan was helpless. But he enjoyed her relentless teasing, for he knew that she had to keep her real self under wraps at home. So he joined in on the fun. "So what if it burns? And so what if it doesn't? So what if I kidnapped your soul? And so what if I didn't? You seemed full of life when you lost your soul, but that's gone, now that you have it back."

"Is that so? That's a new one. So, do you like me to be spirited or spiritless?"

"How about you? Which one do you prefer?"

"Don't be so crafty."

"You should talk."

She looked at him with hooded eyes. "Do you recall what your brother said the other day? The day you went into town?"

"No." His heart raced.

"Yes, you do, Lingguan." She continued in a soft, sad voice. "You don't want to hurt my feelings, do you? He said your mother wanted a grandchild, didn't he? Actually I know everything. Your poor brother—I say that not because of his problem. That's no big deal, seriously; it's nothing. Everyone gets sick; all you have to do is find a cure. But not him, he cares too much about face and doesn't want anyone to know. So he moans and groans in private, worrying himself sick. What's he worrying about, if not his disorder? He doesn't want to lose face, for one thing. A man loses people's respect with something like that. For another, he's afraid of not having a son to continue the family line." She lowered her head.

His face was hot again.

All of a sudden, Maodan appeared on Xihu Slope. "Hei!" He called out. "A man diddling his sister-in-law. A rare sight."

Lingguan was alarmed, but quickly recovered. "Get over here and see what you've done! You scared her so much she can barely stand. I'll see you in court if anything happens to her."

Maodan's face betrayed a minor panic, but he retorted intractably, "All I did was let her see something she hadn't seen before. What law did I break?"

"You'll know soon enough. We'll see which is more powerful, the law or your swagger."

Maodan knew that Lingguan was bluffing, so he grinned. "I grew up on the five grains, not on your scare tactics. Go ahead, take me to court. If you do, I'll say you and she were—and when I discovered it, you turned around to accuse me. So go ahead."

Her spirits dampened, Ying'er shook her head, looking first at Maodan and then at Lingguan, signaling for him to send Maodan away.

"Enough," he said. "You can go now. Handless Wei is waiting to pay you."

"All right." Maodan winked and arched his brows. "I won't bother you. You can do what you want. Don't worry, I won't tell anyone. Lingguan, if you have it in you, worm your way in and see if you can bring out a little Lingguan." With his head flopping from side to side, he walked off, humming a tune to the beat of his soles smacking against the soles of his feet.

"You're smarter than me," Lingguan mumbled.

"Can't you see he was egging you on?"

Lingguan found, to his surprise, that a sort of understanding had formed between them, and that it had been violated with Maodan's arrival, which was why they wanted to get rid of him. But once Maodan was gone, he sensed something slightly ambiguous about that bond, which made him uncomfortable.

"He told you not to worry." She laughed softly, her bright eyes fixed on him.

"What's there to worry about? He responded mechanically, but regretted it the moment he said it. It was inappropriate and it spoiled the mood.

But it didn't bother her. "You should know." Her voice had always been soft, but now it seemed even more so, to the point that her words were more like air burrowing into him, where it turned into rippling water to melt his heart.

"Care for a tune? I'll sing one for you," she said tenderly, and started singing, without waiting for his reply:

Drops of rain fall on the rocks,
Flakes of snow fall on the water,
Love sickness falls on the heart,
A bloody scab falls on the mouth.

At midnight I watched the moon overtake the sky,
The door to my boudoir is half open.
Elder Brother, you're like a panacea,
Little Sister is in need of treatment.

A cow drinks on the bank of the Yellow River,
The water does not reach the tip of its nose.
When I pick up my bowl I think of you,
The noodles cannot reach my lips.

Again a cymbal reverberated in his head; his eardrums swelled and his mouth went dry. Even the sun raised the dizzying clamor of singing cicadas. His brain stopped functioning. He thought he heard what she sang, but could not bring himself to believe his ears. Did she really say all that? Really?

"Care to hear more?" she asked, still whispering.

A white peony fell into the river,
Fish it out quickly or it will float away.
Make sure to enjoy life in this world,
Hurry up, before you grow old.

The little chicks are chirping away,
Fighting over kernels of rice in a tray.
Do not be fooled by my silence among others,
I think of you no matter what they say.

Reputation is nothing but an empty word,
It all depends on how you wish.
Come to the room and we will
Talk to our hearts' content, free as fish.

"Are you willing?" she whispered with an unhappy glance. He knew what she was saying with that look: You call yourself a man? When a woman broaches a subject like this, do you not have the boldness to accept?

An unnatural thirst assaulted him again, worsening as his heart pounded wildly. He strained to say something, but could not utter a word.

The light in her eyes went out and a hint of shame and resentment emerged on her lowered face. He was sensitive enough to catch the change.

I've hurt her feelings. Heaven, help me, he pleaded silently.

"Of course I am," he managed to mutter.

11

They set out for home when the sun was directly overhead. It was a windless, stifling day; the sky felt suffused with sticky goo. A patch of something flashed in a distant field, so shiny that Ying'er felt she was dreaming. It truly did feel like a dream. How could those words have come so easily and naturally from her mouth, when she would normally have blushed if she'd even thought them? It did not feel forced at the time, more like being driven by a supernatural power. She was light-headed, but not the dizzy feeling that accompanies an illness; rather it was a euphoric sensation stirred by happiness. Her face was hot and her heartbeat quickened, as if she'd done something roguish. That is exactly how she felt, and she recalled the term the villagers used to revile women: "man-thief." That term had always disgusted her, but now it embodied a wicked happiness. In all fairness, she longed for something "wicked." Hantou was too nice, so good he might as well be an idol on an altar. She could not find any fault with him; he was just boring beyond words. She envied those women who could flirt with their own husbands in public. Women abhorred loose women, and yet they would all like to be wicked at least once if they had the chance. That included her, regardless of what others might think. To be sure, what she'd just said was nowhere near the kind of wicked behavior she had in mind; it was enough, however, to bring out a myriad of emotional reactions—unusual happiness, fear, shyness, and a sense of novelty. She wasn't sure if this was how it felt to be in love. In the dictionary of her life, love was a word covered in dust, hiding in a corner. Marriage had barged in before she'd had a chance to brush off the dust, and she became Hantou's wife, missing out on the one chapter that should never be passed up in the book of life—love.

"How could I have sung those words?" Covering her face, she stared at Lingguan's back. He walked with the carefree flair unique to those who have been to school. The sun disappeared, as did the cooling breeze and the flow of water in the ditch; there was nothing between heaven and earth but his back, and that brought her waves of happiness. Everything about him, his steps, his posture, even his dust-covered sneakers, seemed well balanced and perfect, wonderful beyond words, as if relaying sweet talk that nearly made her fall to pieces. "If—" A thought occurred to her. If it were him, and not "him," how wonderful the world would be. A fragmented dark shadow flitted across her mind at the thought of the other "him," but she forced herself to halt the thought, so as not to ruin her good mood of the moment.

As they neared the village, people were returning from work, creating chaos on the road. The villagers' noise, the dust, and the livestock returning from the pasture brought life to the stifling, gloomy noontime. A baby mule was having the time of its life, tossing its head and flicking its ears, kicking its hooves and breaking for the village before affectionately turning back to its mother. It was a captivating scene. Pretending to watch the mules, Ying'er slowed down to put some distance between her and Lingguan, while making a point not to look at him; yet she had a second pair of eyes—invisible eyes—that were trained on his back, as she continued to bathe in the swell of happiness emanating from his direction.

When Lingguan reached the road, he caught up with Baigou, but not before turning to look behind him. She managed to capture the instant of that gaze. That's odd, she said to herself, for she had not been looking at him; that realization enfolded her in a surge of joy and elation. He's thinking about me, she thought. Do you know that I'm thinking about you? She cast a quick glance his way. The two men were talking. Lingguan looked even more dashing alongside the coarse Baigou, with the ease and poise that graced only those with an education. It was an unaffected, innate comportment that seemed to emanate from deep inside, not something forced or enacted. Irredeemably uncouth Baigou looked like a pig alongside a gazelle. She smiled at the comparison, quickly sensing that even that was unfair to Lingguan. What was Baigou, anyway? A pig. He did not deserve to be anywhere near Lingguan. She strained to catch a few of his words carried on the wind, like pebbles dropping into the sea of her heart to create ripples of happiness. How incredible! Is this what it feels like to be in love? A smile danced around her lips when she thought of being in love, and her face turned hot again.

"Ai—Ying'er. What are you thinking about? Your face is so red."

Fengxiang, Beizhu's wife, startled Ying'er out of her reverie. "Were you out raking the field?" she asked.

"Mm," Fengxiang responded, her eyes glued to Ying'er's face. "Are you all right? Are you ill, running a fever?"

Deciding to pretend that was the case, Ying'er rubbed her temples.

"Get some rest. There isn't much you can do about a cold except drink lots of water and get plenty of rest. Beizhu learned that from a book."

"I'm not a little girl, like a walking stick made of crumbly flour."

"That's my advice. You can take it or leave it," Fengxiang said.

Sick? I am sick, but do you know what it is? Ying'er smiled secretly. It's lovesick. Fever? Of course I'm running a fever. I wouldn't be feverish if I weren't lovesick.

Ying'er looked first at Baigou and then at Fengxiang, trying to see if there might be something fishy going on between them. The villagers were always saying that there are plenty of young men who carry on with their sisters-in-law. That had not meant anything to Ying'er in the past, but it had taken on an intimate feel after what had just happened, as if it explained her behavior. In her view, Baigou and Fengxiang might—maybe even should—have a story like hers. But she was different, she thought; her feelings for Lingguan were pure, unspoiled, beyond human convention, without comparison. If Fengxiang had her own story, it would be disgusting—she even considered the word "sinful," but abandoned it. She smiled at how ridiculous her thoughts had gotten, and that confused Fengxiang. The two of you too? Ying'er indicated Baigou with her eyes.

Never the perceptive type, Fengxiang could not fathom the subtle change in Ying'er. "His mother went home to make lunch. See that one over there, the one who deserves to be eaten by wolves?" Fengxiang directed Ying'er's gaze to Fengxiang's sister-in-law, Yue'er, who had just washed her face in the ditch. She waved to Ying'er, who smiled back.

"A real fox fairy, that one," Fengxiang sneered. "I don't know how many times she washes her face a day. If you're born with a pig's face, no matter how often you wash it, you'll never become a lovely fairy. We were born here, we grew up in the fields, and we'll be buried in the ground one day, so how can we avoid dirt? If being clean means so much to her, she should go find a husband in the city. Too bad that's not in the stars for her."

"Young girls are all like that." Ying'er said.

"Are you kidding me?" Fengxiang said. "I wasn't particular about how I looked before I was married. Does she think she comes from a different place? She can wash all she wants, but she's still dirty inside—no cleansing detergent in there."

Ying'er just smiled. Though she did not respond, inside she was rebuking Fengxiang: What's wrong with washing her face? She likes to be clean, so let her. Do you want her to be like you, living in filth? Do you call that place of yours a house? More like a pigsty. It stinks, and there's no place to sit. Sure, she likes to be clean, which makes you look even dirtier. No wonder.

Footsteps sounded behind them. Fengxiang knew it was Yue'er

catching up, so she clamped her lips together and kept quiet.

"Wait up, Ying'er," Yue'er called out. "Afraid of missing lunch?"

Ying'er stopped and smiled sweetly; Fengxiang stormed off in a huff.

Yue'er caught up, put her arm around Ying'er affectionately, and gave her a peck on the cheek. "I'm so jealous. Your skin is always nice and fair no matter how long you spend under the sun. Just look at me. Ai—what kind of life is this? The same old sun blazing down on the same old desert every day."

"What's wrong with that? That's life. How would you like it to be?" Ying'er wasn't quite sure why Yue'er was complaining. To her, life was truly wonderful at that moment. The sky was unblemished, and so were the land, the sun, and the wind. A pool of warm water rippled in her heart, and everything between heaven and earth smiled cheerfully at her. Some women forget that even a momentary happiness can wash away the miseries of the past. Ying'er, who was in the midst of a giant eddy of bliss, naturally forgot she'd made the same sort of complaints herself.

"What's so good about it? You've been to school. You were the queen of folk songs once. Do you really want to live like this, not quite alive but still far from dying? There's nothing good about the life of a peasant."

"What would you prefer?" Ying'er asked. "Many people carry on with lives like this. There's nothing you can do about it, Yue'er. Remember physics class? It's called inertia, a powerful force. Nothing happens if you go along with it, but you'll meet with disaster if you try to oppose it. That's how people live their lives, and if you follow them, everything will be fine. In fact, when I think about it, being a peasant isn't all that bad. You get to admire the moon and the stars. What's the matter with that?"

"It's not for me. I'm not like you. You got a better deal; you look like a city girl. You'd have become a famous singer if you'd been born in the city. I'd have left to strike out on my own if I'd had your voice. Why did you—agree to—the exchange marriage?"

"My parents told me to. Besides, my brother was old enough, but he couldn't find a wife, and we couldn't just watch him—let him be a lifelong bachelor, could we?"

"Did you fight it?"

"What would have been the point? My parents had no choice. They felt worse than I did. My mother is always saying it wasn't a good match; she can't stop crying when she sees me, and I have to comfort her. Sometimes we have to think of others, don't you agree?"

"What a shame, Ying'er. It's a lifetime, don't you see that?"

"Actually it goes fast, a lifetime, I mean. It'll be over in the blink of an eye." Ying'er's eyes were half shut. She breathed an imperceptible sigh. This was an unhappy subject that touched a sore spot she would prefer to avoid. A veil fell over her heart, but her mood brightened when she thought of Lingguan. "Really. It goes fast, the blink of an eye."

"I couldn't do it if my life depended on it." Yue'er sighed. "Seriously. My mother wanted me to be part of an exchange marriage for my brother, but I'd have killed myself first."

"You mean Baigou? He's too young. Besides, he's clever enough to find his own wife. There's no reason to worry."

"But where are we going to get the money? We went into debt when both my brothers married. Baigou is always up to no good. People shake their heads when his name comes up. Even if someone were willing to marry him, we'd have no way of borrowing the money.

Most people can't take care of themselves, so why would they give us anything? Shuangfu's rich, but he's not about to lend us what we need."

Ying'er's mood darkened again, after hearing Yue'er say things that a girl her age should not be saying. She sighed softly. "It happens to every family."

"That's true. We can't pay my second brother's fine for exceeding the birth limit, so now he wants to divide up the family property. My father said we'll divide it up and let the government fine whoever they want. This kind of talk puts me in a bad mood. I want to ask you something." Yue'er sidled up close, pointed at Lingguan, and asked softly:

"Is that bookworm really going to quit school?"

Ying'er made a noncommittal sound, curious why Yue'er asked the question.

"He can't be a snob anymore. What does he have to be so stuck-up about? That he stayed in school longer than us? The more you study, the more bad ideas come out of your gut. Now see what happened to him? He's fallen. I thought he was going to fly high."

"Why are you saying that? You shouldn't gloat over other's failures."

"I know." The girl curled her lip. "But with him, I can't help it. He had his eyes fixed on the sky. No one expected him to end up like this. Now let's see him swagger!"

"I'm not going to talk to you anymore," Ying'er said with a frown.

"Aiyo!" Yue'er laughed. "What's with you? I wasn't criticizing your sweetheart, you know. Why get mad at me?"

"I am mad." Ying'er's face darkened. "No more talk like that."

Yue'er said nothing when she saw Ying'er's expression.

She was criticizing my sweetheart. But how would she know that? A happy smile appeared on her face when she recalled the earlier scene. She began to sing softly:

Corn stalks grow above,
Bean vines spread below.
A couple walks down the road,
One of them is my sweetheart.

On the limestone cliff is a lovebirds' nest,
My hands grab the railing to look down.
Elder Brother is a string in my heart,
It hurts if you tug at it.

12

Stubborn Yellow was missing.

Lingguan heard the news the moment he walked in.

Laoshun knit his brows as he sat stonily on the edge of the bed and smoked. Puffs of smoke rose into the air and tobacco ash fell to the floor. One look at his father told Lingguan that this was very bad news. He knew his father well; with a missing hawk, the old man would dredge up past complaints, leading to a major blowup.

Mengzi should have known better, but he mouthed off the moment he saw Lingguan. "Hei. Is this terrible, or what? We never expected the rabbit to run into the woods, damn it! The hawk gave chase, whoa—in it went, and the damned thing was gone. Dumb fuck."

Lingguan cast a worried glance at their father, who shot Mengzi an angry look, the tip of his nose crinkling, a sure sign that he was about to blow up. In fact, Mengzi had barely finished swearing when Laoshun roared:

"Watch your mouth, you dumb fucking ass. Who's the dumb fuck? The rabbit or the hawk?"

A muted cough escaped Mengzi's throat; the animated look froze on his face as he looked around, shifting his gaze from Laoshun to Lingguan to Ying'er. The awkwardness persisted until he mumbled:

"Don't blame me. I didn't let the hawk go until you told me to. I was actually worried the damned thing might head for the trees. I wanted to say so, but I didn't dare. Sure enough, hei – if it'd been me, I wouldn't have let it fly. It was so obvious, the trees nearby and all. That rabbit wasn't stupid. Did anyone think it would just lie there and wait for the hawk to tear into its back instead of running into the woods?" Mengzi was sending spittle flying, oblivious to the dark cloud over his father's face.

"You dumb fucking ass. If you knew it was going to do what it did, why did you fly it? Tell me that. Well, since you flew it, you go find it. Go now, and if you can't find it, you'll see what I'm capable of."

"What you're capable of?' Mengzi was losing his temper too. "You're going to chew me up and spit me out, is that it? The hawk wasn't my son; if it had been, it wouldn't have dared to fly west when I told it to go east. Who said you could curse me? It's always fucking this and fucking that when you open your mouth. I'm going to ask Mother how I'm a dumb fucking ass."

"How dare you talk back to me! You dumb ass!" Laoshun flung his pipe away, jumped off the bed, took off his shoe, and ran at Mengzi. Lingguan stepped in front of his brother while Ying'er nudged Mengzi to get him to leave.

"I'm staying. I want to see if he's going to chew me up." A crimson veil spread over Mengzi's face, which radiated stubborn anger; he seemed about to explode. "Would I have done it if you hadn't told me to? You're always right, aren't you?"

"You dumb fucking ass!" Laoshun's eyes bulged as he tried to get at his son. With Lingguan there to stop him, he could give his parental authority full play. "Your feathers are dry and your wings are stiff, so you're ready to fly the coop, is that it?" He flung the shoe.

It hit the door and fell to the floor. Mengzi picked it up and, with a flick of his wrist out the door, tossed it onto the roof. "So, you want to chew me up! Well, go ahead, do that, and see if you shit me out later" Mengzi was shouting, but with less bravado.

"What's going on here?" Their mother walked in with flour-covered hands. "What is going on? Look at you two; father not acting like a father and the son not like a son. It's only a bunch of feathers. So what if it's gone? It's no big deal. But you want to kill somebody over it. Lingguan, go get the cleaver and give it to your father. He can kill us all and live alone."

"It's your fault, you spoiled them. Ever since they were little, you stopped me every time I scolded them. And now, see what's happened? He thinks he's the head of the family."

"Won't you please stop it, Father?" Lingguan said. "It's just a hawk. You can train another one."

"Like hell!" Laoshun bellowed. "It's not just about the hawk. That's no big deal. But he's pushing me around and that is a big deal. You call yourself a man just because you can throw your father's shoe onto the roof."

Ying'er giggled, so did their mother. Lingguan managed to hold back and say, "That's nothing. I'll get it down for you. How's that?"

"Get it down? You think that'll do it? He thinks he can toss my shoe wherever he likes, and you think you can bring it down and everything will be fine. A couple of rebels!"

"What else do you want?"

"I'll tell you what I want. He can put it back on my foot."

Ying'er could not hold back any longer and burst out laughing, though she kept her hand over her mouth.

"I'm not the one who took it off," Mengzi grumbled. "So why should I put it back on?" Lingguan nudged him. "I'll do it," he said.

Mollified, Laoshun sat back down, picked up his pipe, and began puffing noisily.

Lingguan climbed onto the roof, got the shoe, and brought it down for his father, who by then did not care who put it on for him. He sat there scowling and raising a cloud of smoke. He laughed after a moment. "I've never seen such a dumb fucking ass, tossing his father's shoe onto the roof."

Finally Lingguan could laugh along with their mother. Ying'er's belly hurt from laughing so hard, while Mengzi, crouched on the threshold, shook his head and glared. But eventually, he joined the others.

After lunch, Laoshun, Lingguan, and Mengzi went around the village looking for the hawk. No one had seen the bird, so they gave up. Laoshun had to focus his efforts on Indigo Widow. He stuffed another roll of wool into the bird that night to release more phlegm.

13

Lingguan was in a quandary.

Hantou left to work the night shift at the well after dinner. Mengzi called Lingguan outside and whispered a request to leave the gate open early the next morning. He was going to play cards, and asked Lingguan not to tell their parents. Lingguan agreed to help. When he walked into the common room, Ying'er was just leaving; she gave him a stern look before returning to the room she shared with Hantou. The thud from the closing door felt like a hand squeezing his heart. He went to bed.

The TV show was over and their parents went to bed, while Lingguan went to the northern common room. He hadn't realized, until now, that what they called the common room was eerily large, with a dreary chill, though it was fairly warm inside. Late autumn nights were cold, but their mother had gotten a fire going under the *kang*, leaving enough heat around it to lessen the chill in the air. He was disconsolate, unbearably lonely, hollowed out.

His thoughts turned to Hantou. It's like he's running away from something, Lingguan said to himself. Maybe not running away, but— But what? He could not pinpoint what it was, but he could almost feel Hantou's sorrowful eyes on him. He wasn't entirely sure what was happening in his head, but he sensed that he and Ying'er had reached some sort of agreement. Tormented by guilt and shame, he felt like a man who has been stripped naked, and somehow that cooled his feverish emotions.

Father's thunderous snores emerged from the bedroom. Since his return to the village, Lingguan had gotten used to the noise; it reminded him that his parents were asleep, as were heaven and earth, and everything else in the yard, but he was not. And maybe not Ying'er either.

What is she thinking? Her sad eyes appeared before him. He was sure she was awake. She had to be. He could read her glance as she left the room, and he recalled a line from the drama *Romance of the West Chamber*: "Her parting glance was like autumn ripples." That fit perfectly. How better to describe her eyes? Is she waiting for me?

His heart stirred with thoughts of her, and he wondered how to approach her. She did not feel solid to him, more like surreal, ephemeral, crisp, clear air. As he recalled their bantering earlier that day, warm currents spread through his body. Go, don't worry, just go, he said to himself, to build up his courage. From where she lay, she could surely hear the snores. Her eyes must be staring into the empty night, her fair arms lying atop the blanket. He tried but could think of no other details, and was aroused by the image of her eyes sparkling in the darkness.

The yard was oppressively quiet. Gently folding back the blanket, he was alarmed by how it rustled, sounding in his ears like a raging torrent; his heart was pounding so hard his parents were sure to hear him. He took a deep breath and held it for as long as he could as he groped for his sandals. He stepped gingerly forward, as if on ice; the sound of his sandals scraping against the floor was like a cataract. His heartbeat filled the evening sky. Losing his nerve, he sat back down on the edge of his bed, discouraged. But he was bewitched by the eyes summoning him, and by the crystalline laughter that continued to ring in his ears. With bated breath, he took a few steps and opened the door, making a sound like tearing a piece of silk, but, undaunted, he walked into the yard.

The crescent moon was dim, but bright enough to see blurry outlines. He saw a faint light in his parents' room, and suspected that his mother might be watching him through the window. He sucked in cold air.

She was in the habit of spying on people. Back when he was a child and they lived in a large compound, he often saw her listening to neighbors' conversations through the cat door. She was a light sleeper. Has she heard me? Is she at the window? He thought he could "hear" her say under her breath, Aiyo, is my little boy really doing something like this? Has he thrown away all his schooling?

His fervor cooling, he backed up to his doorway, leaning against it so he was out of her sight line, but still able to survey his surroundings. He stayed there for some time, but noticed nothing unusual.

Mother must be asleep.

He tiptoed up to Ying'er's door. His footsteps continued to thunder in his ears, no matter how softly he walked. So he took off his sandals and held them as he inched toward his goal. He took a deep breath at her door to steady his racing heart, but that did no good. Before pushing it open, he lay down his sandals, rubbed his feet on top of them, and then put them back on so he would not soil her bed sheet when he took them off inside.

The door was not bolted.

The noise seemed to tear open the sky; that nearly drained his energy and crushed his willpower. That had to have awakened Mother. He backed out, ran through the yard, and was back in his room—no, that was just a thought, though he very nearly did that. He pushed open the door—the die was cast—slipped inside and shut the door behind him.

It was dark inside; the drawn curtain blocked out the moonlight. That suited him, for he would have been too shy to do anything were it light inside. With his hand on his chest, he looked around to see things more clearly. A rustle told him that Ying'er was sitting up. He could almost see the autumn ripples in her eyes.

"What are you doing here?" she asked softly.

He had not expected that. He had hoped she'd ask, "What took you so long?" and let her voice draw him to her. He would take her in his arms and kiss her under the cover of darkness, a daring act he believed he could carry out on a night like this. It was impossible to imagine his lips on hers in broad daylight; even the short distance between them at that moment would be an unbridgeable gulf. But on this night he found the courage, though her question unnerved him.

What should he say? He could not tell her the truth. Nor could he use Beizhu's clever excuse of giving a leg to his nephew. He hadn't imagined they'd be off to such an awkward start. Frozen in the darkness, he had no idea what to do next.

"Come up here if you want to talk." Ying'er said lightly. "The floor is cold."

Grateful for her use of the word "talk," he felt the unease vanish. With a smile, he took the sweaty hand reaching for him. He'd heard that a woman's palm sweated when she was aroused. He kicked off his sandals and climbed onto the bed, where he was enveloped in comforting warmth.

She held his hand so tight it hurt, but it was a pleasant pain. He was quiet because he still did not know what to say. Ying'er sighed softly. "What took you so long?" Holding her in his arms, he felt the two mounds of soft flesh through her thin chemise, which set his body on fire.

"With my hand on your willowy waist, like a ewe caring for a lamb." It was a line from a flower tune. She laughed softly.

She held him tight and began to murmur. Soon the murmur turned to sobs. Lingguan did not know how to console the lovely body in his arms.

"I've waited for so long," she said. "Kiss me."

Taking her face in his hands, he kissed her over and over, but clumsily, for he did not know if lips should be tender or wild. All he knew was to lay his lips on hers, heavily, over and over. A dizzy happiness overwhelmed him, and he was rendered defenseless. "This is how I want to die," he heard her say, as she bit his lip painfully.

"Your clothes are so cold."

She was breathing hard and fast as she undid his buttons, slowly, as if to savor the act, while he stroked her hair. Suddenly he thought of Hantou and reached out to stop her hand. "Will he be back soon?" Her hand trembled in his.

"No. And please don't mention him." She sighed; some time passed before the hand resumed its movements. She struggled with the buttons, so he took off his shirt. With a moan, she hugged him; taut breasts that had yet to suckle a child quivered against his chest, while her hand moved from his shoulder to his chest and abdomen, where it lingered before moving down.

"Why are you so stilted?" she murmured.

He did not know what he should be doing. With no prior experience in sex, he was rendered useless as he basked in the surprise and happiness. He felt her hand slide down, drawing an involuntary moan from him.

She smiled. Afraid she might have hurt him, she stopped and kissed his chest, biting him occasionally with careful, focused bites.

"Are you made of wood?"

Lingguan was pulled into an eddy of bliss, and then waves crashed against the shore. He touched her breast, followed by an exploration; he was entering unfamiliar territory. His hands felt the soft skin of her abdomen; an odd agitation swept over him when his hand reached the mound that seemed so full of life. Heaven help me! He felt himself sliding into an unknown world.

"Ah, so much…" he mumbled.

She was moaning; afraid she might wake up his parents, he put his mouth over hers and felt her lips greet his with violent abandonment.

"I don't know how. You'll have to teach me." He was breathing hard.

"I don't know either," she said softly.

14

Lingguan was in bed when Mengzi tiptoed into the house. He had the guilty look of someone who had tasted forbidden fruit. But Lingguan was not interested in his brother; he shut his eyes to savor and relive his first experience with a woman.

He had been the passive one. When they came down from the peak of their rapture, he'd found the way she'd clung to him afterward almost unbearable. He had fantasized many times about what happened between the sexes. Was it really supposed to be like that? He recalled the faint sense of loss he'd felt at the moment, but that had been replaced by desire when she'd aroused him again.

He could not forget her happy cry of pleasure when he entered her, the thought of which excited him.

He had been afraid that their parents might hear her, but it was her cries that puzzled him for days. His schoolmate had told him that Hantou was impotent and had been for at least ten years. Which meant that Ying'er ought to be a virgin. Since this was his first time, he could not tell if she was or not, and yet that cry of pleasure made him doubt that she was. He'd heard that a virgin feels pain her first time and that there would be blood. Lingguan did not know if she had bled; he'd wanted to look down to see the spot he had fantasized over. But she was too shy to let him. Disappointed by her refusal, he had thought her unreasonable.

"Why won't you let me see after what we've done?" he had whined. He recalled she had merely smiled. Now he wondered if she had been hiding something from him. He couldn't believe it hadn't hurt and that she had actually made such happy cries of pleasure. "Does it hurt?" he recalled asking. "No," she'd said. "Why are you crying?" "If feels so good." Now he was upset. It feels so good? How could it feel so good when it was her first time? Had she taken a lover in the past?

Something tightened in his heart when he thought of Hantou, whom he had betrayed. There had been pangs of guilt when he'd mounted Ying'er, and that had nearly cooled his passion. He'd had to force himself not to think about his brother, and he'd sighed when it was over. She'd asked why. When he told her why, she'd gone silent for a moment before saying, "Let's not talk about him."

Lingguan recalled how his brother had brought him food when he was a student in the city. Hantou would smile foolishly upon when he saw his younger brother; it was a smile devoid of deceit. Lingguan knew how proud Hantou was of him. Once, when he walked Hantou to the school gate, his brother had said:

"You have to work hard, Lingguan. There are people waiting for us to fail so they can laugh at us." Lingguan found the reference to "us" too weighty to bear, for he was taking the college entrance exam for "us." Failing the exam had meant there was no chance for "us" to go to college, and the smiling Hantou was who Lingguan had the most trouble facing.

Filled with remorse, Lingguan shook his head. What would he do if Hantou found out about this affair between his brother and his wife?

Would he give his silent assent just so he could have a son? If so, how would they face each other? Lingguan knew he would feel naked in front of his brother, no matter how normal he acted. He could deceive everyone but Hantou; he was ashamed.

Whatever I may think, I have betrayed my brother. He was mired in quilt, remorse, and self-reproach. What do I do after this night? Ying'er enchanted him not simply by the lure of her body or her pretty face, her intelligence, or her capacity for being fair and considerate, but also because of her relaxed airs, which would draw him to her over and over. He would never tire of her; she would always be a pleasantly cool dream, starting from when they became one. In fact, he wondered at one point if he had really possessed her.

He was enmeshed in a web of complex emotions. On the one hand, he was thrilled by his first time with a woman, an effervescent, serene woman no less; on the other hand, he was hounded by intense self-reproach and the awareness that he had betrayed his own brother. There was a shadow in his life now, one he could never shake off; he would always be dogged by it, even as he faced the sun.

Is this happiness? He asked himself. Yes, it is. It would have been hypocritical to deny this seductive happiness, but it was also a transgression, which diluted the pleasure. The notion of retribution occurred to him. Mother talked about it all the time, but he'd gained an understanding of the full meaning of the term only from Master Wu, the monk at Songtao Temple, who had said: "You reap what you sow. There is cause and effect for everything, and retribution is meted out for every action without exception." In accepting Buddhist books from Master Wu that day, he had also acquired a new worldview.

A dull pain below had him wondering if he was already experiencing retribution, a thought that made the soreness even more pronounced and spread through his body. If there was indeed retribution, then the sinful organ would likely grow malignant. He shuddered at the thought of cancer, as if he could actually feel the cells growing at the spot where it hurt. What did cancer look like? He had no idea, but it had to be terrifying, and he felt the onslaught of frightening possibilities.

He tried to defend his action with every excuse he could think of, including giving Hantou a son, but nothing worked. His justifications seemed feeble, because he truly liked (even loved) Ying'er. When they were in bed, the idea of continuing Hantou's line was the furthest thought from his mind; all he felt was her irresistible lure and an irrepressible desire to have her.

So it's a sin, he said to himself.

He felt repentant over what he'd done to his brother and to his parents, expressing remorse to all the deities he knew. Recalling what he'd read about eliminating sin by reciting the six-syllable Sanskrit mantra, he began, and it actually brought some peace of mind. Yet he could not keep up the mantra when he thought of Ying'er's smile and that rapturous scene. A monotonous chant was no match for the power of temptation.

His sin remained so long as he was unable to resist the temptation.

"Just this one time, I swear. Never again."

The promise lightened his mood and cleared his head.

Everyone makes mistakes. Anada, the Buddha's cousin, was once bewitched by a female demon from an unorthodox sect. He was saved only after the Buddha employed the Surangama Mantra. What about an ordinary man like Lingguan? He laughed at the word, "ordinary," as he had never considered himself ordinary. He had made a mistake, and that was that, he thought. He just had to make sure not to repeat it.

"I've recited the mantra a hundred times, so I should have washed away my sin by now." The soreness did seem to be lessening, and he was aware of his brother's snores.

He fell asleep at some point.

15

Lingguan woke up earlier than usual, after a sleepless night, which was strange. Even stranger was an unusual breeziness, a true feeling of casual comfort. His thoughts touched cheerfully upon what had happened the night before. It wasn't a dream, was it? He laughed, a happy, exuberant laugh. She was wonderful. He tried to recall what she'd looked like. I never imagined she could be so wild. Was it really her, that quiet, timid girl? Are all women like that when they show their true selves, acting with such abandon? Maybe she's the exception, since she always seems so repressed. Too much repression for too long can foster an explosion. Yes, an explosion. That's what it was.

He heard kitchen sounds. Who's cooking? Ying'er? Mother? He hoped it was Ying'er. The thought of seeing her aroused him. He wondered how she would react when she saw him. Bashful? Happy? Or awkward? It was hard to say. But he knew he would be excited, no matter how she reacted. He was sure of his own response, for his body was burning up. He pulled back the blanket.

Father's daily throat clearing ritual, followed by mutterings as he fed his hawk, were the next sounds Lingguan heard. He knew that Father would soon yell for him and Mengzi to get up, calling them his "young masters" and complaining about how it was thanks to their parents' gray hair that theirs had remained black all these years. Lingguan was amused. He thought they should get up on their own, so Father wouldn't scream his head off. The happiness of the morning was such a treasure he wanted to cherish it as long as possible, and not let Father's shouts destroy it.

"Get up." He kicked Mengzi. "Or Father will scream at us again."

Mengzi smacked his lips and snorted before going back to sleep.

Lingguan got dressed and went into his father's room, where he was feeding the red hawk. No longer angry or frightened, the hawk devoured the meat, but it still put up a fight whenever someone tried to touch it. When Laoshun reached out, it beat its wings in fear and protested with loud shrieks.

"You're looking spry this morning," Laoshun said when he saw his son.

Lingguan realized he'd made a mistake. Instead of getting up early, he should have been his usual self and waited for Father to wake him up. Has he sensed something unusual? His heart skipped a beat, but Laoshun had already turned his attention back to the hawk and was holding his hand out. The bird's eyes rolled before it gave Laoshun a surprising peck on the hand, making the old man bare his teeth and shake his arm. Lingguan laughed.

"What are you laughing at? Is Mengzi up? Get him up and go work on the new hawk."

Lingguan jerked the blanket off Mengzi and, imitating their father, smacked him on the rump. "Get up. The sun is baking your ass red."

Mengzi sat up, but then grumbled and lay back down when he saw it was Lingguan.

"Go ahead, sleep away, I don't care," Lingguan said. "Father's fuse is short this morning. He wants us to go work on the Hawk. I've done my duty by waking you."

Lingguan slipped on his gauntlet and walked out with Indigo

Widow on his wrist. It was a bright morning, a light fog in the air, as usual. To Lingguan, it felt like ice dust, which chilled every organ in his body with each breath.

Indigo Widow was fairly tame by now and needed little training. All Lingguan had to do was hold out his hand and shout "Hei" for it to fly over and land on the wrist. It no longer "objected" when or how it was touched.

As he touched the hawk, his mind returned to what had happened the night before, still speculating on how she would react when she saw him later that day. She could be bashful or try to be calm, he thought, but she would definitely look at him with a glow in her eyes. She might even smile. His heart stirred again when he thought of that smile, soundless, but tender and alluring. He was pleased with his imagination, which allowed him the possibility to digest and savor, like a cow with her cud, the bliss he had hastily gobbled up the night before.

The gate creaked as he was walking toward the village; it was probably his brother coming out with another hawk. And it was. Mengzi was making a racket clearing his throat. Lingguan did not want chatty Mengzi to catch up with him and spoil his mood, so he turned into a quiet side street.

As he savored his recollections of the night before, Lingguan alternatively smiled and shook his head; he came out of his reverie only when Indigo Widow screeched as it hung upside down from his wrist. Instead of putting the hawk back on his hand, he flicked his fist up over and over, like his father, until the bird regained its foothold.

On his way home for breakfast he ran into Ying'er to the yard. She was calm and detached, as if nothing had happened between them. I mean nothing to her; she doesn't care about me at all. He felt cheated.

Then he had a different idea. Maybe she regrets what she's done and is unhappy with me. To his chagrin, he realized that he had alienated both his brother and Ying'er; it had nearly escaped him that she was a married woman when she became his lover. How appalling. That would bring shame and ruin upon him. He tried not to think about Hantou's face and his foolish smile. She too must regret what we did. He watched her go into the kitchen.

16

After breakfast, Laoshun told Mengzi and Lingguan to go search for the missing hawk. He knew it had not gone far, because a hawk with its phlegm cleared cannot fly too high before its head begins to hurt. It must have settled somewhere. At sunset, it would grow anxious, and hungry. The worst outcome would be that someone ignorant of the situation might kill the bird, though the tether on its leg was a clear sign that it wasn't a wild bird. Or someone might catch it for his own use. "Take a rabbit head to lure it down if it's in a tree," he told his sons.

Mengzi went south, Lingguan headed north.

When Lingguan walked by Baigou's house, he saw Yue'er, Baigou's younger sister, washing clothes in the yard. He asked if she'd seen their hawk.

"Yes," she said with an animated look.

"Really?" He was delighted.

"Is that any way to ask a question? Standing at the gate? Are you a beggar?"

Lingguan stepped into the yard and sat on a stool she brought over.

"Where are Baigou and the others?" He realized that was the wrong thing to ask the moment he said it. Why had he asked about them when he should have asked about the hawk? It was as if he was hoping they weren't home.

"Out in the fields." She stopped scrubbing the clothes and stared at him so intently he felt his face begin to burn. "I want to ask you something. Have you really quit school?"

"Yes."

"Are you going to live the rest of your life like this?"

"What's wrong with this life? We have food to eat and clothes to wear. We're just ordinary people, and we can't expect anything magical."

"Not me." She sighed. "I can't stand it when people talk about nothing but food, clothes, clearing a field, and harvests. It bores me. It's like a donkey pushing a millstone round and round. I want to see the world."

"You can do that." He laughed. "You're pretty and smart, and you're capable of doing anything you want. You can marry someone in the city and enjoy good food, wear fancy clothes, and click-clack around in high heels. But not me. I was born to live off the land."

"Aiyo!" She smirked. "Listen to you. You sound like you're content with this life, but you're just pretending, like putting a leek on a pig's snout to make it look like an elephant. You think I don't know you? All day long, you—you and your poetic muse, you wanted to be poet, then a writer. How come you lost all that?"

"How about you? You were always talking about "youth" and "tomorrow" in your essays. But look what's happened. Only the sand is real; everything else is just an illusion. Don't you think so?"

"Ai." She shook her head with a soft sigh. "Girls are better off not going to school. I mean it." She picked up a piece of clothing and scrubbed it with a vengeance. “She can marry some guy and live an ordinary life. But if she goes to school she’ll learn so much she’ll be restless all her life.”

“That’s true,” Lingguan said. “Look at Fengxiang. She doesn’t know how to read, so she has no worries. Her heart and mind are uncomplicated. She’s happy raising pigs and being able to buy a pair of shoes. Unlike you, you’re always thinking about aspirations and a career. That can wear you out.”

The girl sneered at the mention of her sister-in-law. “Her heart and mind are uncomplicated because she has no conscience. We’re still paying off the debt from her marriage to my brother, and she’s already clamoring about dividing up family property. She raised hell again last night.”

“Enough of that. Women all love a good gossip.”

“All right, I won’t say any more. To tell the truth, I really want to do something else, like sell clothes or something. In any case, I can’t spend the rest of my life in this tiny village. My cousin sells clothes in the city, and she makes a lot of money. Would you ever do something like that?”

“Me? You have a cousin, who do I have? You can’t kill someone without a knife, as they say. My family, hei, we’re too poor to even buy a ladle for the well. Where would I get the money, when we don’t even have enough for Mengzi to get married?” His face darkened and he lost interest in the conversation. “Let’s not talk about that any more.”

“I didn’t mean to upset you. Mengzi and you will want to get married, and that takes money. The question is, do you want to do it or not?”

“We’ll talk about that some other time. Tell me, did you really see the hawk?”

“Sure I did.” She tossed the piece in her hand into the washbasin.

"See there? What's that up there in the sky?"

Lingguan shot an angry look at her before walking out the gate, trailed by her voice, "You make me mad, Lingguan. You don't appreciate it when people mean well." He ignored her and continued his search, but no one had seen the hawk.

17

Maodan walked into their yard with a broad smile the next morning. "I've got you now, Lingguan," he said as he stepped over the doorsill. "It'll cost you two packs of smokes."

That surprised Lingguan, who was readying the wagon for his father. Was the idiot going to say something about him and Ying'er? His father spoke up before Lingguan could respond.

"What rotten idea are you hatching in that mangy head of yours, Maodan? If you've got something to say, spit it out, if not, go fart in the outhouse. Show me what you've got. If it's worth something, I'll give you my dick on top of two packs of cigarettes. If it's worthless, you can buzz of and stop pestering us."

Maodan reacted to Laoshun's outburst by crossing his arms and shrugging his shoulders, with the brazen look of a donkey that does not fear a wolf's fangs. His face darkening, Laoshun continued, "Look at you. You sputter and pop off when I ignore you, but you back off like a donkey shitting when I talk to you. Get lost. I doubt that anything good could come out of that foul mouth anyway."

Maodan shrugged again, licked his lips, and rolled his eyes. "If you don't want to hear me out, then to hell with you. A cold bed greets hot cheeks, as they say. Why should I care if you've lost something?"

"Was it a hawk?" Laoshun jumped to his feet. "Maodan, something good might come out of your mouth, after all. Two packs, it is, then. Three even. How's that?"

Maodan shrugged again, but did not reply.

"Say something, will you?" Laoshun said impatiently. "Who has it? Out with it. You'll drive me crazy."

Maodan laughed. "I found it."

"You did?" Laoshun was elated.

"Yes, I found a piece of paper that fell out with Lingguan's handkerchief."

"Damn you, Maodan! I thought you might say something worthwhile for a change, but no, just hot air, like a new mother passing gas." A piece of paper. So what? Get out of here and stop causing trouble. I was feeling fine until you showed up."

Maodan thumped the dirt off his behind, and said in an affected tone, "I guess I kissed the wrong ass. Well, I'm out of here." He shuffled toward the gate, the soles of his shoes slapping noisily against his heels. He turned back. "No regrets, all right?" he said. "I did find a piece of paper, but someone else found a different thing."

"Ai—Maodan." Laoshun shouted. "Come back here. What's your hurry? Come, have a seat. Lingguan, bring a stool over."

"No need. I have nothing worthwhile to say, remember?"

"Of course you do." Laoshun said.

"That's more like it." Maodan happily arched his brows.

"Who found it?" Laoshun asked cautiously, as if afraid to insult him. "I'll give you three packs."

Maodan began cleaning his nails and studying his fingerprints.

"You're such an ass."

"All right, all right. I'll tell you."

"Who found it?"

"It's a deal, right?" He pointed at Lingguan. "I'll tell you for his sake, but two packs. Not one cigarette less."

"Aiyo." Laoshun cried. "What's all the fuss? It's just two packs of cigarettes."

"It's at Baldy Wang's house."

"The hawk?"

"The tether."

"Are you mocking me again?"

"There's a little hawkie on the end of the tether."

"Bullshit."

"Forget it if you don't believe me. I heard it from Baldy Wang's son. It was getting dark at dusk when that feathery creature pounced on a chicken and wouldn't let go, like a stubborn old goat. The tether was the only thing stopping them from killing it."

Laoshun exhaled. "It'll pounce on anything after dark. Hei—Maodan, you've done something decent this time." He went inside, groped under neatly folded bedding, and brought out some money, which he handed to Maodan. "Go buy your cigarettes."

"No. Didn't I say I'd tell you for Lingguan's sake? I don't want your money."

"Take it," Lingguan said. "Look at your eyes. They're about to pop out of their sockets."

"My eyes aren't me," Maodan said. "But I won't turn it down. I don't want your father saying I'm ungrateful."

18

A manmade berm in front of Baldy Wang's house shielded it from prying eyes. The compound was very remote. Laoshun rarely stepped foot in the place.

A pond on one side of the hill held enough water to last people and livestock a couple of months, though it turned slimy and rank after baking in the sun.

Frogs that had moved into the pond to escape the dryness croaked at dusk, creating a deafening din—a sort of love song, according to Huaqiu. With no family planning to worry about, they gloated over their ability to procreate. The surface was covered in what the villagers called "yi," dark, gossamer-like objects that spread out and drifted along the ripples. It took only a few days for tadpoles to appear; like miniature whales, but with long tails, they swam in water that was now black with the mass. Whoever came to get water had to bring along a sieve to filter out tadpoles that seemed to be always looking for an opportunity to jump into a ladle.

Baldy Wang's house backed up against a hill, where they had cut into the side and smoothed it out enough to create a yard. The wall they'd put up around it was squat and easy to jump over by using your hands. There were only three rooms in the yard, while the animal pen and hay storage were cut into the hill and secured with a gate made of latticed branches. It saved the trouble of building a wall and putting up a roof.

Baldy Wang wore a hat the year round. A taciturn man, he seemed to be wearing a hat over his heart also, and no one could ever guess what he was thinking. Laoshun always felt a cloud over his head when he saw the man's face.

After reaching the top of the hill, Laoshun spotted a truck outside Wang's house. A rare sight. Baldy Wang was as reclusive as a turtle that hides in its shell. How could he have visitors? What puzzled Laoshun was the crowd milling around in the yard, exuding an aggressive air.

Now Laoshun knew; they were there to coax Wang into turning in his grain.

It sounded civilized to say "coax," but these people were not there to cajole anyone, which was why the villagers preferred to use "plunder," a term reserved for predatory birds preying on small, weak animals. To the villagers, it was an apt term to describe the township officials who came for their grain.

Laoshun felt his head swell with concern.

19

Baldy Wang's head was swelling too, and his ears were buzzing. Big Head had said a few days before that if he didn't pay his grain tax, the township would send trucks. And now they were here, and he was scared witless. If he'd known this would happen, he'd have turned in his share even if the family had nothing to eat but the north wind. He probably had barely enough in his storehouse to pay the tax, but there were six people in his family with gaping mouths waiting to be filled. The two youngest girls, illegal births, had mouths but no assigned land. What could he do? Nothing would grow out of the bald top of his head. He couldn't club the girls to death and toss them into the stove, and he couldn't push them back where they came from, so he had to find a way. Beizhu said they'd fight it any way they could. Many of the villagers agreed; the law could not deal with the masses, so they should resist to the bitter end. No one had really expected them to come, especially not to hit his house first. The grain collection station paid less than market price, but that at least would have been better than having these people yelling and shouting at him.

His woman was sobbing. What are you crying about? Is that all you can do? Baldy Wang felt like slapping her. She was slight but felt solid under his hand. He beat her all the time, arcing his arm in a circle and, *pa*! It felt good. He might be quiet and easily pushed around, but he was more than her match when it came to a fight. I can't do anything else, and now I can't even beat my woman. Shit. He didn't dare hit her now because the arrogant township people had taken all the steam out of him. He had to watch himself.

"Go ahead, take it all" he grumbled.

Ordinarily a quiet woman, his wife muttered tearfully, but then she decided to fight, and her outburst surprised him. "How are we supposed to live with the little bit of grain we have if we turn it all over to you?" she said. He let her talk because that was exactly how he felt. "Do you expect us to eat the wind and shit gas?" She choked up, a bleak sound that darkened her husband's mood. She was right. They'd have to eat the wind if they turned everything over. He knew what they had left after selling some to a vendor in order to make a little more money: they could squeak by if they were extra careful. Even with the money from the sale, they would still be hard up if there were more expenses, such as fees at the kids' school. Baldy Wang was hoping his wife's complaint would make a difference.

"How are you supposed to live?" One of the officials echoed her question. "That's your problem. You have to turn in the required amount, no matter what."

She was sobbing more loudly now. "What's in the grain storage is all we have. The sprouts died in huge numbers this past spring. It's not like you didn't know that. Besides, we're not the only family that owes grain tax."

Wang was surprised. She's actually quite clever. She didn't breathe a word about selling that little bit of grain and focused instead on the dying sprouts. She even brought up other families. That's right. Didn't Beizhu say the law can't deal with the masses. Ours isn't the only family in the village. When the sky falls, tall people will have to hold it up, as the saying goes. Glancing at his wife, Wang felt bad about slapping her in the past; she might have been even cleverer if he hadn't boxed her around her so much. On the other hand, being clever only works on outsiders. She'd better not try it on him. He decided to let her go on.

"Don't you worry about that. No one's getting off without paying. They're doing the same thing in Beixiang. If you don't want to turn your grain in, we'll drive into your storehouse, load it up, and charge you for the transportation, and there's nothing you can do about it."

"You think it's up to you whether you turn in your grain or not, don't you?" A gruff man joined in. "We handled Chiang Kai-shek's eight million soldiers, so a few disruptive villagers don't concern us."

Baldy Wang felt a chill down his spine when he heard the threat, which he knew was real. As a child, he'd heard about how they'd routed eight million, a number too large to grasp. It was a lot, he knew, probably more than the kernels of grain in his storage, and they were not only dealt a crushing defeat, but their generalissimo was sent fleeing to Taiwan. How would he, a single bald man, dare to oppose the government? He was weakening, or, as Beizhu's would put it, his bottom was losing its grip. He couldn't let that happen, now that they'd planned to fight. At least his wife was sobbing, a powerful weapon that drew their fire power away; for the moment, no one paid him any attention, so he remained a human turtle with his head tucked in, shoulders up, neck down, as he squatted at a corner.

Keep it up, he said to himself, for he knew what she was capable of. We'll see what they decide do about her.

The fat official, the one called Township Chief Jiang, was talking to Big Head, who shook his head and pointed to Baldy. Wang knew that Big Head meant for him to load the grain himself. Big Head, you asshole, you're a traitor, a running dog, a turncoat. Why single me out? Sure enough, the gruff cadre walked over and touched his leg with the tip of his shoe. "Go on, load the truck."

Wang shut his eyes and stayed put, a trick he'd used for decades. He could sit on his haunches all day, and nothing could make him move, not the blistering sun, not blowing wind, not pouring rain, or thunder and lightning. It had helped him weather many storms, like the socialist education movement, the "Four Clean-ups" campaign, and the Cultural Revolution. Those who had made the loudest noise and wreaked the most havoc got their asses into big trouble, while no one touched him, Baldy Wang.

"Are you going or not?" the man roared.

Go on, shout all you want. It won't work. The only thing you'll accomplish is make yourself so hoarse you can't even scare a bird. You want me to load the grain? No way! I can hold out better than she can. So he let the gruff official kick his leg. I'm like a dead pig in boiling water, unafraid.

"Shameless!"

The man swore at him. So what if I'm shameless. Is that all you can do, call me names? Okay, I'm shameless, but so were your parents. They wouldn't have had you if they weren't. That thought nearly made him laugh out loud; he quickly tucked in his neck and swallowed the laugh. It was clear to him now; they weren't as scary as he'd thought. Their only trick was to kick him in the leg and call him shameless. He'd been intimidated by the menacing way they'd bored down on him earlier.

"I don't care who loads the truck, but I'm not going to do it," Wang heard Big Head say. "These are my people. How am I supposed to face them if I do that?"

"You're the team leader. If you don't do it, who will?" Township Chief Jiang said angrily.

"Then I'll quit. I'm not loading the truck, and that's final."

Wang felt a warm current course through his heart; Big Head was a good guy, after all. He forgave the man who had led these people to his house. Maybe he'd had no choice; probably the township office had forced him. No way to know. No matter what or why, Baldy Wang would not turn his wrath on Big Head now, not after what he'd just said.

"Then we'll do it ourselves," Jiang said as he looked at Wang, who felt the gaze trained on him even with his head down. Wang knew how badly the man wanted him to do the loading, since that would make it voluntary, not a predatory action on their part. What do I care who loads it? he said to himself. If you can come here to plunder, I can take it. Go ahead, do what you want, kill me, rob me. I don't care. Wang hung his head lower as these thoughts went through his mind.

Jiang waved two young men into the storeroom. Wang's wife was wailing now. She spread her arms to block them, like a hen protecting her chicks, but they shoved her aside. Noticing her frailty out of the corner of his eye, Wang reproached himself for mistreating her in the past, and he made up his mind to never again lay a hand on her. Why had he hit her? She was family. Only at a moment like this, with outsiders reaching into their family grain storage, did he feel the true meaning of the word, family.

The wheat was in sacks. There were also a few sacks of corn that had been reserved for the livestock or for the family when the wheat wasn't ready to harvest. "All corn does is turn your shit yellow," was the local saying, but it was still better than nothing. But now the wheat and the corn was all loaded onto the truck. The men, obviously well trained, finished in record time. Wang felt a strange sense of relief. He'd worry about the future tomorrow. You can't eat a goat's head till you pluck the hair. Go ahead, take it all. But his heart convulsed when he thought about the school fees that had to be paid in the spring.

All of sudden, he felt the urge to pick up a knife and use it on somebody.

20

Laoshun's head was swimming as he walked out of Baldy Wang's house. He was afraid of scenes like that. Government representatives are good at terrorizing people, the way a rooster flaps its wings to intimidate hens. His head swelled with concern, because his household had unpaid grain tax. He wondered what he'd have done if what had just occurred had happened at his house. For decades, he'd been a witness to such scenes; now he shuddered at the thought of others watching him. The fear was so intense it took away the delight over finding his hawk.

Clearly frightened, the unsettled bird looked this way and that. When he smoothed its feathers, it cried out a few times as if to tell him what it had been through. It looked different; it had lost weight and had a broken tail feather, a very important feather. He had searched all around Baldy Wang's shed before spotting the bird in the coal bin.

Baldy Wang's a good man, Laoshun said to himself, and not just because he found my hawk. Wang had signaled the bird's whereabouts with his chin. The dust from the departing trucks had yet to settle, and

Wang's wife was still sobbing breathlessly, so he had every right to ignore Laoshun, who, sensing he'd come at a bad time, was ready to walk off.

"I'll have Mengzi bring you a rabbit," Laoshun said before leaving with his hawk. Without a reply, Wang resumed his earlier stance, still as a rock.

Laoshun's wife was home alone. He did not feel like asking where their sons had gone, for he was preoccupied with other pressing thoughts. The return of the hawk did little to lighten his mood, and he knew why. Big Head had talked, wasting enough saliva to fill three carts, before he managed to get those young masters from the township office to give the village ten days of respite.

"Ten days. You're going to suffer if your village can't clear the owed tax in ten days," the fat official had said. Big Head had nodded like a chick pecking at food. Big Head's a good man, too, Laoshun said to himself. He's always yelling and screaming, but he does fine when it comes to important matters. When facing his superiors, Big Head knows how to put on an ingratiating smile, real sometimes and faking it at other times, to fight back; for those beneath him, he can be all bluster, making a fuss now or acting nice later. They could never do without people like him. After dealing with the township cadres, Big Head gave an ultimatum to families who still owed taxes. The township meant business this time and they should do what they were told or suffer the consequences.

A heavy weight landed on Laoshun's chest at the thought of grain tax. They had the grain, so that didn't worry him; he just couldn't stand any more worries. In his wife's words, he couldn't even handle a load of hot noodles. His heart was tied up in knots, and that put him out of sorts, even with the smallest problem. As soon as one matter was taken care of, there was another problem and another weighty rock. Luckily, he was blessed with the positive trait of forgetfulness, and he knew the art of distraction. When something bothered him, he found other things to do, like yoke the cattle or till the field, which usually relieved him of his emotional burden.

At this moment, the best distraction was to work on the hawk. His heart ached at the sorry sight. Stubborn Yellow was a different bird, its feathers disturbed by tree branches, and it had lost some of its fat, since Baldy Wang had not fed it. Worse yet, the hawk was fearful, whimpering like a baby. The only consolation was that it had not lost its appetite, devouring a rabbit's head as if swallowing soupy millet.

He trimmed the broken feather. Then he asked his wife to hold the bird down while he searched through its tail until he found the other half, which he also trimmed. He glued the two ends together and wound thread around it.

"It's just a feather," she said. "What's the big deal?"

"That shows how much you know," he said. "The tail feathers are what make a good bird. With even one missing, there's too little air for it to fly fast enough."

Meng Eight sent Huaqiu over with a message that night for them to be ready to go into the desert in a day or two. Laoshun and his sons had a discussion about who should go. Mengzi said he was born to be a hunter and had beaten everyone in target shooting. He was not exaggerating. Hantou said he worked indoors the year round, like a cow, and was in a perennial funk. It was time for him to go outside and limber up. That was not a lie either. Lingguan wanted more than anything to be a desert hunter, which to him was quite poetic. That was not much of a reason. Mengzi added that Lingguan had become a weakling from all the years in school, and he ought to stay home to toughen up. Then Laoshun spoke up. It was harvest time, and someone from the family had to work shifts at the well. Too much work and not enough manpower. Lingguan was a weakling, with no stamina for farm work, and was best suited to learn a skill from Meng, so he could earn a living. Mengzi wanted to argue his case, but opened his mouth without saying anything.

Laoshun went to get the musket from the storyteller that evening, agreeing to pay for it after selling the grain. When he returned, the family got busy preparing bedding, a pot and a bowl, water, flour and other dry goods, even frying two rabbits. Two mornings later, Lingguan went into the desert with Meng Eight and Huaqiu.

Chapter Three

1

Each year, after the harvest is in, the men of Shawan village pack up provisions and other necessities to travel three days with their camels east into the heart of the desert to fulfill interrupted dreams. The sand is a dull yellow as far as the eye can see, with dunes rising a hundred meters or more; encircled by mountain peaks, the desert is home to plants that crisscross the land in seeming disorder and yet form clearly discernible patterns. Like ships in a wave-tossed ocean, the camels weave their way between dunes that, under the sun's relentless rays, seem to roll and flicker, billowing furiously toward the edge of the sky.

The sky was dusty gray when Lingguan and the others set out in late autumn. The sun, its rays muted, hung in the air like a gigantic ping-pong ball, slicing the sky into two halves, one dark, the other bright. Smoky shadows spread above the ball, beneath which lay a white stratum infused with gray dust mites. They were barely on the road when a breeze slowly gathered enough force to send howling sand whipping against their faces. Rings from the camel's bell interwove with the shrieking wind before drifting into sand hollows.

As a child, Lingguan had gone with his father into the desert, where they had had lit a bonfire when darkness fell after they'd collected a load of the cactus-like plant shami, or desert rice. The crackling fire was a fitting ornament for a night cooled by a gentle breeze that got the men talking. They conjured up stories of Shawan's past, including a notorious affair between the collier and a village woman, and then sang Liangzhou songs, most with off-color lyrics. Lingguan had not understood the lyrics, but had blushed even so. The men had sung in gravelly voices that brimmed with emotion and blended with the wind-blown sand to produce sounds colored by the yellow hue of an arid landscape. What Lingguan wanted most was to see the chilled, lonely moon hang suspended in the sky. The desert exuded an unfathomable tranquility, like a fairy-tale world, by the time the moon emerged. Under its milky light, the dunes alternated between dark and bright. A languid breeze prompted the men to break into song again, which in turn drew fascinating echoes from the sand hollows and startled birds out of their roosts in the desert rice plants. Every time Lingguan heard the drawn-out calls, his body shook, and he shouted at the top of his lungs; a magical internal force compelled him to roll in the sand. Then he grew into adulthood. The sandy ocean remained unchanged, as did the desert winds, but he no longer felt the same joyful surprise; the child had disappeared into the stillness of the sand hollows and the wrinkles of the desert. The wind could continue to blow with all its might, and the bonfire could keep burning bright, but the adult Lingguan never could dislodge the emotional burden that frequently weighed him down.

They reached Magang in three days, when the sun had sunk into the sand, leaving a gaunt first-quarter moon suspended above the desert to sprinkle the area with its icy beams. Pale moonlight whitened the shifting hills to the south and darkened the steep ridges to the north, creating a mysterious haze with contrasting colors. Only Meng Eight knew how to read the enigmatic desert night. Soon they had gathered enough dry twigs and weeds to start a bonfire, which injected vitality and a poetic aura into the quiet desert; crackling Artemisia twigs sent flames whooping into the air and reawakened the child in Lingguan. A mysterious power churning inside drove away his fatigue and numbness. Late autumn nights in the desert are bone chilling cold; the night air seethes as it spreads wetly over the heaving waves of sand and seeps under the skin. Lingguan's sweat-soaked underwear was icy and as stiff as armor. The fire drenched him with warmth that reminded him of his mother, so he lay down near it, eyes shut and his mind clear, to let its softness soothe his weary body and mind.

With the aid of the firelight, Meng Eight and Huaqiu set up a "home" for themselves with a few wooden stakes, a tent, three sets of bedding, some simple cookware, and other basic necessities. Home, how cozy it sounded in this bleak spot. Meng had brought along his shaggy fur blanket, a prized possession woven from golden camel hair that protected him against moisture while keeping him warm. Over the days that followed, the feel of home would greet Lingguan whenever he saw the blanket.

The night was strangely quiet, but for the roaring bonfire; night seemed to have turned into a gigantic black pot, which, when gently overturned, cloaked the entire desert. Stars hung low above them, solidly three-dimensional, as if all the men had to do was reach up and pluck them out of the sky. Sandy hummocks came in and out of view in the firelight, like an ink-wash painting. Huge Artemisia plants curled into ghostly shadows, visible only when the flame burned brightly.

Meng Eight and Huaqiu were talking, but they sounded distant, almost unreal. In fact, everything appeared far away, all but the tranquility, a sensation Lingguan had not felt for a very long time. Turbulence had long filled his mind, both when he was at school in the city and back in the countryside, where people eked out a living. A restless mind was not a mind at all. To him, a real mind had to be an independent realm unaffected by outside factors. Yes, the mind and the outside world had to be distinct.

The crescent moon, hanging wormlike in the sky, hurled down pathetic beams of light unworthy of the name. More like diaphanous air, the wavelets of moonlight rippled before seeping into the uncanny depths of the desert; the moon shrank back in shame, quivering through the night to give Lingguan the impression that it was about to bury itself in the sand.

He lay awake in his makeshift bed, while the others fell asleep almost at once. Meng's stentorian snores were interrupted by great bursts of air blown from his mouth, reminding Lingguan of how the waves in Qiantang River roared in his imagination. Huaqiu was not as loud, faint, more like the gentle hum of a string instrument. Thoughts crowded into Lingguan's mind as he reflected on what had happened over the past few years. Then Ying'er came to mind and filled him with weary sadness. Was he going to live out his life like this? He found it hard to accept his lot.

2

Lingguan's first lesson from Meng Eight was learning to identify spoor.

Foxes searching for food attract hunters, who follow their tracks.

There are three types of tracks: nighttime, early morning, and daytime.

Nighttime tracks are virtually useless. Hunters say it takes three days to interpret the tracks of a fox laid in a single night. An experienced foxhunter never bothers with them.

Early morning tracks are useful, but hard to follow; if you are lucky, you might glimpse a fox by tracking from early morning to sunset.

Daytime tracks are the best, since foxes sleep during the day and hunt at night. According to Meng, a fox suffers headaches out in the sun, and must find a place to rest. It usually takes only a few hours to track a fox resting under desert shrubbery.

Tracks are easy to find but hard to interpret. A fox's prints resemble those of a dog, like a five-petal plum flower. Foxes seldom make turns, leaving prints in the fine sand in a straight line.

Many of Shawan's foxhunters knew how to find tracks, but only Meng Eight had the unerring knack of identifying them. For him, hunting was as easy as taking something out of a sack. He'd say with a grin, "I'm off to the bank for a withdrawal," meaning he was going into the desert with his musket to bring back as many foxes as he needed for his expenses.

"Some hunters are idiots," he said. "They're off on the chase as soon as they come across prints, but that's like a blind donkey trying to find a haystack. They won't even get a whiff of a fox's rear end after a day of tracking." He walked out with Lingguan, leaving Huaqiu to guard the campsite. Knowing that Huaqiu had a loose tongue and could not keep a secret, he revealed important details only when he was out of earshot.

"Most hunters can spot fox prints, but cannot tell when the fox left them. You can follow some of those, but not others. Many people spend half their lives hunting, but have little understanding of how it all works."

Lingguan's calves ached after trekking through the desert for days, with shooting pains at each step. Meng offered several times to let him ride the camel, but Lingguan could not bring himself to do that, not after lugging everything to their "home." Snorting heavily with slobber around the mouth, the camel was also straining, sweat flowing down its long coat and staining the sand.

The dogging ache in his calves and fatigue dulled Lingguan's mind, and he was too lazy to ask questions, though he knew that Meng was going to reveal secrets he had not shared with anyone before. Many masters hold back critical knowledge from apprentices, afraid that teaching them all they need to know could leave the master with no means of survival. Meng would tell him what he wanted him to learn, so there was no need to rush him. But Meng was surprised by his silence. "Why aren't you asking me how I tell the tracks apart?"

Lingguan knew that Meng was a child at heart, and that the more he pressed the old man, the more likely the chance that he would hold back; he would be eager to share what he knew only if Lingguan let him be. "What's there to ask? You have your reasons for not talking." Lingguan tried to sound nonchalant.

"My reasons?" The old man laughed. "You've been a student all these years, so how do you plan to make a living if you don't learn a skill? Actually, this is a good life. You're free to do what you want. I want to teach you things. Others have tried to get me drunk, bribed me with money, and treated me to fancy meals, but I've refused to tell them anything. It seems simple, but when dealing with foxes, everything is complicated. Fools who give chase the minute they see prints can manage to shoot a fox or two after running around for days. What would happen if they all learned the true secrets? There isn't an endless supply of foxes and we can't have everyone out here shooting them. Heaven would punish me if I turned out to be the cause of foxes going extinct. So, keep what I tell you to yourself."

"Don't tell me anything if you don't trust me."

"Ha! Do you think I don't know what goes on in that head of yours, Lingguan? Actually, I do want to tell you things. I'm old and I want to pass down my special skills. I wouldn't be able to shut my eyes if I took them to my grave." Meng sighed and continued, "It's actually very simple. Nothing is all that tricky once it's explained. True teaching can be summed up on a single sheet of paper, while phony transmissions come in ten thousand volumes. What does a fox eat? Rats. When are rats most active? You don't know? Hei, rats are out when there are no cats or other predators around. They come out late at night and return to their nests just before daybreak. Understand? No? Think about it. What happens if the foxes leave their prints before midnight?"

"There—will be—"

"Rats have prints too. Think."

"The rat prints will wipe out the fox prints."

"No, not wipe them out, but—but the fox prints will be disturbed, hard to evaluate. And that's a nighttime track. Now think about this. What will you see after the rats go back to their nests, that is, before daybreak? Right, the foxes will come out and leave clear prints in the sand. Those are the early morning tracks."

"So that's it. It's pretty simple."

"Early morning tracks aren't bad, but you'll have to chase the fox into the afternoon or even after dark. Why? Because it's run off. You'll be exhausted if you begin chasing one that started running just before daybreak. You might bag one, but by then you'll be worn out and far from camp."

Seeing that the old man was enjoying sharing his knowledge, Lingguan let him go on.

"Daytime tracks are the best. Now, think. Early morning and daytime tracks aren't disturbed by rat prints, and both are easy to see. So how do you tell which is which?" Meng stepped up onto a sand dune, where, trying to keep his breathing even, he looked at Lingguan with a triumphant gaze. He laughed when he noticed the sheen of moisture on Lingguan's forehead and heard the young man's labored breathing. "Maybe you should have stayed to guard the camp and let Huaqiu come with me."

Lingguan's thighs throbbed, while his calves cramped and tugged at his facial muscles with every step he took. He knew this was a "test" everyone had to pass in the desert, and that the symptoms would disappear in a few days. He wanted to take advantage of finding Meng in a rare talkative mood.

"I'm fine. Don't worry. I won't hold you back."

With the musket slung across his back, he crawled onto a dune and collapsed in a heap when he reached the top, barely able to catch his breath.

Meng sat down without looking at him, so he could get a bit of rest and wouldn't make Lingguan think he was rushing him.

"Go on, tell me more," Lingguan wheezed.

"What do you want to know?"

"How to tell daytime tracks from early morning tracks."

"Good for you. It's easy. What does a fox do at daybreak? It gets anxious. Why? Because it needs to find a place to sleep. So what does it do when it's anxious? It runs fast, taking big, frantic steps."

Lingguan got it.

3

They arrived at a low spot overgrown with Artemisia. Common vegetation in the desert, the woody plants are covered in tiny seeds, which, when ground into powder, aid in rolling dough out paper thin for thread-like noodles that remain intact and tasty.

Dense Artemisia also attracts a desert insect called *zhazha*, a stupid black bug with dark eyes, two long antennae, and many feet that slow them down and leave rows of tiny prints in the sand.

The abundant *zhazha* draw rats that thrive on the insects and in turn attract foxes that feed on them and the leaping mice the locals call *tiaotiao*. With long hind legs, *tiaotiao* look a bit like kangaroos, but with no marsupial pouches for their young.

Like the world beyond, the hollows are bloody battlefields for creatures trying to survive. Humans hunt the foxes that prey on rats that survive on *zhazha* that eat dirt, which swallows people in the end. A complete life cycle, a desert ecology. Shawan villagers say they are: "Born to the land, raised in the land, and buried in the land."

The first step in telling the tracks apart is finding a fox's hunting ground, where the nighttime tracks are as discernible as daytime tracks. By looking at the terrain alone, an experienced hunter can tell where a fox has been searching for food.

It did not take Meng Eight long to find tracks in a dense growth of Artemisia, a daytime track, no less, with clear prints showing large, frenzied steps. Obviously, it was a greedy animal that sought a place to rest only after it was already light out, leaving a row of prints in the direction of low ridges.

"I'm pretty sure this fox is in the hollow down there," Meng said, pointing to some low dunes. "What makes me say that? First, it's easy to find prey around here, and foxes don't stray far from their feeding ground. They aren't like humans with fixed domiciles. They go wherever they can find food. Second, foxes don't sleep just anywhere; they find a spot on the shady side of a hollow. In other words, they hide where they are shielded them from the wind. A fox gets dizzy from too much sun, so I'm betting it's over there."

Looking off to where Meng was pointing, Lingguan saw only a stretch of yellow sand that seemed to reach the horizon. It billowed like churning waves. Dunes sparkled in the sun, as if from the reflection of watery mists.

"Come up here, but lightly," Meng said. "Those creatures are canny. They sleep sprawled like a dog, and take off like the wind when they hear a noise, even a sound like this." Meng made a gesture of rubbing the butt of his musket against his lapel, "That faint rustle will alert it. Hei, a very shrewd animal." He walked toward the hollow.

Revived by the brief rest, Lingguan felt stronger, and his breathing was smoother; the desert wind blowing across his sweaty back was coolly refreshing.

Meng walked like a spotted deer, seemingly gliding across the surface. Most people sink into the sand with each step, leaving deep impressions in the sand, but Meng was uncommonly light-footed, and Lingguan wondered if it was a talent he was born with.

The plum-petal footprints headed straight to the low sandy ridge Meng had pointed out. As he had said, foxes rarely make turns when they're walking.

Meng waved for Lingguan to follow him more closely. The young man strained to catch up, earning him a stern look from the old man. "Are you hunting foxes or alerting them? Be quiet," Meng hissed.

Lingguan was facing a world of Artemisia when he reached the low ridge. With thick stems and twisted branches that spread in all directions, they dotted the desert.

Meng underwent an abrupt transformation. The crafty hint of a smile was gone, replaced by a chilling seriousness; his eyes were like those of a hawk. His body seemed to bulge with energy.

With one hand pointing at some Artemisia shrubs a short distance ahead, Meng laid his index finger over his lips. Lingguan looked, but failed to discern anything in the spot. Where was the fox?

Meng sat down and began moving forward, his legs serving as oars, his weapon trained directly ahead. Transported by the shifting sand, he slid forward and downward. Lingguan thought he heard the sound of flowing water, impossibly loud in his ears; his heartbeat seemed to rumble. Then he saw it. At first glance it was only a tiny, light yellow mound in the hollow under a shrub, curled up in the shade, just as Meng had said.

The old man floated over, like a weightless shadow, fifty steps, thirty, twenty, then he yelled out, startling the fox into leaping up at the very moment he fired. A muffled shot, more like popping corn.

"Ha! A fine beginning." Meng smiled.

Lingguan ran down to the hollow, making slow progress.

The fox was twitching and crying, fatally shot. The cry slowly weakened and soon it was quiet, its eyes staring angrily into the sky.

A vital creature had been rendered lifeless in an instant, all because humans were enamored of their pelts. Lingguan's heart ached; discomfited, he wondered why he had that feeling. Shouldn't he be elated?

"This one's fur isn't very good," Meng said. "We're a bit early this year. The fur will be shiny red in a few weeks, when they shed their base fur. But we can't help it; our needs in life can't wait that long."

Picking it up by the tail, Lingguan studied it. He'd have missed the gunshot wound if not for the slight trace of blood. "I can hardly tell where the bullet entered."

"That requires skill." Meng laughed merrily. "You can't hit the right spot if you're too far away, but you'll ruin the fur if you're too close. Imagine how ugly the fur would be if there was a big gaping hole. This was a head kill."

"A head—kill."

"Right. You aim at a sleeping fox, shout, and fire when it raises its paws. You can't miss. I don't miss with running shots either. Amateurs can only hit stationary targets, shooting at sleeping foxes. What fun is that? And it's not righteous. It's immoral to dispatch the fox to the King of Hell when it's in a dream world."

Lingguan had to laugh at the notion of morality and righteousness.

"That's good, enough for today. I know you're like a whipped gecko. Let's go get something hot to eat. I'm sick to death of water and *mantou*, *mantou* and water."

4

Meng told Huaqiu to start cooking, so he kicked the ground here and there to find a firm spot to dig a hole. After making a pit for firewood, he placed a pot over the hole and lit the Artemisia branches he'd collected. Soon smoke rose into the air.

The sun had slanted westward and hung above a broad ridge, fiercely red. In the windless open space cooking smoke rises not in a straight line, but in spirals, as if an invisible hand were gently lifting up gray threads. When reaching a certain height, they dissipate and turn into thin sheets of mist that fall shroud-like over the troughs and ridges. The setting sun, misty cooking smoke, sandy ridges in light and dark shades, and churning waves of sand create an illusory panorama.

Meng made a tripod and picked up the fox. "Come here," he said to Lingguan. "You have to learn everything, so pay attention. You'll likely end up in this work." He parted the fur around the fox's mouth and threaded a rope through the teeth to hang the animal over the tripod.

"We start from the head," Meng explained as he began skinning the fox. The knife in his right hand moved deftly while his left hand tore at the skin, loosening it as he went. "The hardest part is where the head meets the neck. The big bone makes it hard to get a handhold. Everywhere else is easy once you're done here."

Lingguan put his hands on the tripod to stop it from swaying, repelled by the pungent smell of blood. He abhorred bloody scenes like this; he could not even bring himself to watch a nurse give shots and fled whenever a chicken was slaughtered at home. Mengzi laughed at blood spatters, but not Lingguan. Humans and animals came in all sizes, but their lives weighed the same to him. Human or not, one has but a single life, and once it is lost, it is gone forever.

Meng agreed that taking a life was not a good deed, but he believed that everything in the human world was based on cause and effect. Some animals were born to be hunted and killed, while some people were born to do the killing; it was predestined, a fate none could escape. So he could carry on without qualms. When skinning the fox, he looked like a sculptor, with nimble, practiced hands, focused devotion, and a fine control of rhythm and sense of proportion; he seemed to enjoy the work. Only the blood on his hands and the emerging mess of a fox head highlighted the cruelty of the strong preying on the weak.

"Peeling from the top is the best way to do it." Holding the knife in his teeth, he pulled the skin down with his right hand and pointed to the joints where flesh and skin merged with his left. It made a sizzling sound.

"Pull hard here," Meng said. "You can't do any damage by putting some arm into it. But be careful around the bones," he cautioned. "A broken bone can tear the pelt. Avoid that at all costs." The tripod rocked back and forth.

A furless fox emerged before Lingguan's eyes. Was it still a fox, shorn of its pointed ears, its fur, and its cunning, or was it just a carcass that retained the animal's shape? In the light of the sun, the veins and the grain of flesh were clearly visible; the clots of dark blood seemed like a footnote to human savagery. Lingguan shuddered at the sight.

"Here's how you skin the tail," Meng said. "Don't worry, you'll get used to it." He broke off a pair of twigs from the shrub, scissored the tail between them, and pulled down. It took only a moment to free the tail of its splendid fur, leaving behind a string of bones, from large to small.

"What's the matter? Are you upset or are you afraid? This creature was born for our use. My only concern is that some people are simply too greedy. Greed ruins everything; it's the base of all evils. Liquor is good. It loosens the body up, but if you drink too much, you'll puke until your face turns green, and that's a problem. The same goes for foxes. You hunt a few when you need money to supplement your family income, and that's fine. But it's wrong to want two after you get one and ten after you bag two, with the idea of increasing the figure in your savings account book. Don't you agree? I don't put money in the bank. My bank is the desert. I'll come to withdraw two when I have the need, and that's enough for me. I'm not greedy. I was born to hunt, it's what I do. Is the food ready?"

"I'll dump the dough in as soon as the water boils," Huaqiu said.

Tossing the pelt to Lingguan, the old man told him to fill it with sand. "It's true. A hunter is born to take lives. Foxes are evildoers and murderers in a previous life who are reborn as animals. They have an outstanding debt for the lives they took, and must pay restitution. Once the debt is paid, they have a chance to be reborn as humans. How? I get them to pay, of course. Who knows, maybe they were in my debt in a previous life. Ha-ha."

Meng was in the middle of an animated talk, his beard flowing impressively in the wind, so Lingguan just smiled and continued to fill the pelt with sand.

"That's the truth." Meng's voice rose. "Years ago there was a hunter who spent his whole life hunting wolves. On his deathbed five wolves came to him at midnight. He thought they were seeking revenge, so he stuck his neck out for them to sink their teeth into. Hei, guess what happened? The wolves shook their heads and knelt before him to offer their heads. The old hunter knew they were there to pay off debts; if they didn't, they'd be reborn as wolves again, with no hope of becoming humans. Left with no choice, the old man had to shoot them, so he struggled to pick up his rifle. The wolves all went up to him. He could only shoot one at a time, so he'd need to reload, but there was no more ammo. What could he do? He killed one and the other four put their heads on the edge of his bed for him to shoot at. He managed to kill three with the butt of his rifle, sending blood flying. There was one left, but the hunter was too weak to do anything. The wolf jumped onto the bed for the old man to suffocate it with a blanket. Ha-ha, you see. A hunter is capable of good deeds, too. I'm accused of killing, but that isn't without karmic merit. Hei—there's a reason why the old man in the sky created this profession; he wouldn't have—I mean—ai—what about the food?"

"Hei, I almost forgot." Huaqiu jumped up and brought a basin over. "I think you must have been a wolf before," he said with a smile, "the one that was smothered. You'll say anything to make up for what you missed in a previous life. Nothing but boasting comes out of your mouth." He pinched off pieces of dough and lowered them into the pot.

"You're still wet behind the ears," Meng chided. "What do you know?"

Lingguan had filled the pelt with sand, turning it into a fox avatar sprawled on the ground. Tugging at its ear and nudging its paws, an indescribable emotion spread deep inside him.

"Go bury the meat," Meng told him.

"What?" Huaqiu continued dropping pieces of dough into the pot. "Aren't we going to eat it?"

"No one eats fox meat these days, though people did in the old days. It's like eating sawdust, and the gamy smell is overpowering. But it has curative powers. Any stomach problems, Lingguan?"

"Some."

"How about you, Huaqiu?"

Huaqiu was stuffing firewood into the makeshift stove. Thick smoke belched out when he blew on the fire, choking him until he teared up.

"Sometimes I get a touch of heartburn, especially after eating leftovers."

"What a stroke of luck for you both. Don't bury it then, Lingguan. Put it in that plastic bag and store it in a cool place, or it will start to stink."

"Come quick, Lingguan!" Huaqiu shouted. "The fire's too hot. It's going to boil over. I need another pair of hands here."

Meng went up and tossed sand onto the fire, immediately bringing the boiling water down. "See, that's another trick. When the heat's too high, toss sand on the fire. And if the water won't boil, pour in vinegar. It'll cook fast, and the noodles won't be mushy." Meng wiped his hands on a wet towel, picked up pieces of dough, and began turning them into long thin noodles.

5

Huaqiu ran off to relieve himself and quickly returned on tiptoes. "There's a rabbit under that big shrub," he whispered.

"You didn't scare it, I hope." Meng threw his noodles into the pot.

"I pretended I didn't see it."

"That's good." Meng took up his musket. "Today's the day to offer a sacrifice to the kitchen god, a good beginning."

"It must be long gone," Lingguan said. "What do you expect, that it's waiting for you to shoot it?"

"Gone? More like it doesn't think we've seen it. Besides, where's it going to run to? With all the sharp-eyed hawks up there, it won't dare make a move." Meng laid his finger over his lips to shush them, and, musket in hand, ambled over with feigned indifference, followed at a distance by an excited Huaqiu.

They were in the heart of the desert, encircled by towering sand dunes, in the middle of which was the basin where they'd set up camp. Around them velvety billows of sand spread like ripples. The basin was overgrown with Artemisia shrubs as tall as trees. No one came to collect their seeds, so the branches seemed to be draped in thick smoke.

Lingguan spotted the rabbit; it was light yellow, and its ears were twitching like probing radar. Obviously it had spotted Meng, but avoided looking at him, as if fearing that its line of sight would expose its location. Meng did the same, looking first at the distant dunes and then at hawks circling above, as if he just happened to be walking by the shrub.

A loud crack came from his musket when the rabbit finally gave up the pretense and vaulted out of the shrub; it flew into the air before dropping to the ground with a shriek. Huaqiu ran up and stepped on it. Meng laughed. "You thought you could outsmart us, didn't you?" Huaqiu gloated. He removed his foot when he sensed no more movement; blood had oozed from the rabbit's nose and mouth, and its red eyes stared into space, as if it was incredulous over what had just happened. "It wasn't heaven or earth that got you," Huaqiu taunted. "It was Master Meng."

"What are you mumbling about? I just helped it find peace. A rabbit lives in constant fear of humans and hawks. What's the point of living if it's scared all the time? My shot took its rabbit life, and maybe it will be reborn as human."

"It will come back to shoot you," Lingguan said.

"That's fine with me. It's the next life, anyway. I'm a good hunter, so I shot it. If it's holding a musket in the next life, well, it'll be my turn."

"Why did it wait so long to run?" Lingguan was puzzled.

"Those things are very clever. People say foxes are cunning, but the truly cunning ones are the rabbits. Our storyteller said he read somewhere about a fox smudging its footprints. Nonsense. Foxes don't have that kind of brain, but rabbits do. Isn't that weird? They get on the move once White Dew has passed, and they take the same route coming and going, not messing up even a single print. So humans set a trap on its path to add meat to their meal. But this creature is devious enough sometimes to go back and mess up the prints. Humans won't know where to set the traps or they'll assume it's returned to its burrow. Foxes aren't smart enough to do that."

"Then why is it so easy to shoot a rabbit?"

"Because sometimes they're too smart for their own good. Take this one. It thought we didn't see it, but it was just deceiving itself. It saw us, but it was probably too timid, and it hesitated, unsure of what to do next. Don't we say a timid person is as scared as a rabbit? Or maybe it didn't run because it was afraid of the hawks. Hard to say. Hiding under a shrub is safety for a rabbit—if there are no humans around, of course."

The food was ready. The steaming hot noodles made Lingguan and Huaqiu sweat. They had to put up with the sand in their food, which Lingguan knew was unavoidable in the desert. It sank to the bottom of the bowl if he didn't stir the contents and could be dumped out when he finished.

Huaqiu frowned, spitting out sand as he ate, annoying Meng, who chided, "What are you doing? Deal with it. We're lucky to have a hot meal today. You wouldn't have a fucking thing if it was windy or rainy."

"This is really weird," Huaqiu said. "I washed everything back at home, used clean water and flour, and there's no wind. So why is the food so sandy?"

Instead of picking up his bowl, Meng continued puffing on his pipe.

"Why don't you eat first and smoke later, "Lingguan said. "Would not smoking kill you?"

"Don't wait for me. You go ahead. I can do without the five grains, but not the sixth. Huaqiu, hurry up and finish so you can skin the rabbit. We'll have something tasty to celebrate our good beginning. Our cunning little rabbit. It's strange how it can think of blurring its tracks, but can't decide when to run and when not to. Foxes, on the other hand, run like the wind when they detect the slightest movement. So which one is smarter?"

The younger men buried their faces in their bowls, ignoring Meng, who didn't really care if they were listening. "Foxes may be smarter," he muttered, "but they don't know that they should smudge their tracks. If they did, then we hunters would never bag a single one. So rabbits are smarter, I guess. But they hunker down under a shrub, relying on luck and treating humans as fools. They don't believe we're smarter than they are. Foxes aren't smarter than rabbits, but they know we're smarter than they are. That must be it. We wouldn't be able to sniff a rabbit's rear end if it thought we were smarter and ran away at the slightest disturbance." He continued to mutter as if no one were around, exhaling thick puffs of smoke.

"Why don't you eat," Huaqiu said, "and stop worrying about who's smart and who's stupid?"

"I'm conducting—eh—scientific research," Meng said. "You don't know a thing about science; you're like a dog trying to catch a train. All you know is eating, and I sometimes wonder what's keeping you from turning into a pig." He wound his tobacco pouch around the pipe stem before putting it in his pocket, and picked up his bowl.

After sucking up three bowlfuls of noodles, Huaqiu poured water into his bowl to wash it. Meng jumped up. "What do you think you're doing? Don't squander water like that. It's the same as wasting life."

"So we don't clean our dishes?" Huaqiu grumbled.

"Of course we do." Meng put down his bowl. "Give it to me, I'll show you." He took Huaqiu's bowl, poured the water back into a basin, and scooped up a handful of sand to swish around in the bowl. When it was clean, he tossed it back. "There. It's clean. Can you do that with water?"

"You call that clean?"

"Don't be silly," Meng said. "Sand is cleaner than water. The sun kills the insects and worms—but if you're uncomfortable, you can rinse your bowl with a drop of water before we eat again."

6

The sun had reached the top of the dunes, bringing cool air to the hollows. Gusts of desert wind blew, but without enough force to send sand flying; it felt more like a gentle, surging liquid. With the burnt yellow of a hot sun gone from the desert, a hint of gray was discernible around them. Followed by long shadows, the vegetation crossed the threshold into dusk. The sun that had ruthlessly ruled the sky most of the day was now losing its strength, as a paleness seeped in. After eating its fill, the camel looked around in the fading sunlight. With the light now behind it, it lost its color and turned into a dark outline, encircled by a strange golden corona. Its shadow was like a toppled tree with gnarled branches.

Red clouds burned across the western sky and spread wildly

to form menacing shapes that made the desert seem drab. What Lingguan found most exhilarating were the sandy waves billowing under red clouds. They crested so high they nearly reached the sky and highlighted the boundless majesty of the desert, so powerful, so vast and masculine, and yet feminine at the same time. Yes, feminine. Small sand dunes between the cresting waves resembled sprays of sea foam, their lines soft and delicate, like ripples in the sea. Tiny insects crawled over the sand, leaving minute trails as they roamed the vast desert; their prints were so fine they were more like a suggestion, a sign of extreme caution. Were you afraid of disturbing the patterns of grain on the sand? Or did you not want to wake up the slumbering ocean of sand that yet seemed to seethe? Lingguan wondered. Have you found a place to rest? If so, where is it? The leaping mice, the gerbils, the foxes and the wild rabbits, where did they go? Did any of them take notice of the desert's tranquility at that moment? Or were they dreaming about evading predators? He felt terrible when he thought about all the lives sacrificed to hunters' bullets. Killing jarred manifestly with the desert at that moment—so quiet, peaceful, forgiving and generous; he felt the serenity seep into his body and soul, until he too became a bountiful desert.

Suspended at the crest of the sandy ocean, the sun arced downward fast. Gone were the threatening light and the scorching heat, leaving behind only a cool, lonely disk. It was perfectly round, large, calm, of course, and beautiful. It was a beauty born of a transition from splendid brilliance to tranquility, like the relaxed smile of someone achieving nirvana. At such a moment, the sun became a wise orb that nourished, not baked or parched, all the planet's creatures and vegetation.

The dunes seemed so much taller now, as if leaping up to take bites out of the sun, and then shifting in order to swallow it. Bursting with a thousand rays of white light, the sun sent its beams into the empty sky; it darkened the dunes, returning them to their original wavy shapes, as if they had switched tactics, gently squirming instead of biting madly, slowly submerging instead of aggressively devouring. A tide rose. Lingguan heard the sound of water, seemingly gentle and beguiling, but in fact laden with murderous intent.

As if possessed, the sun finally set, but reluctantly; it hopped a time or two before sinking into the sea of sand, when it could no longer forestall the tender summons. Submitting to the downward pull, and trailed by sighs, it strained to release a few more rays of lights. But all that accomplished was to instill increased brilliance in its celestial rival, offering no salvation to itself. It shut its eyes.

Dark shadows spread and unfurled toward them, immersing heaven, earth, the three of them, and their camel, as well as the desert, in its entirety.

7

They lit a bonfire.

After enjoying the quick-fried rabbit, Meng entertained them with outlandish tales as he sipped his liquor. Lingguan dumped some of the chopped fox meat, with its purported medicinal benefits, into a pot with white radishes and water. Instead of reusing the hole he'd dug to make dinner, Huaqiu collected some sticks formed out of sand and dirt, called donkey dicks by the locals, and stuck them into the sand around the fire to make a tripod. As he placed burning firewood under the pot, the flames leaped up between the sticks. Soon they heard the pot sizzle.

"Let it cook. The meat has to simmer a long time before the strong odor disappears. Nothing but radishes can rid it of its gamy taste.

Without them, hei, the smell alone will stink your guts off. Eating the meat is out of the question." Meng was slurring his words and sounded different, either because he'd had too much to drink or because he was still chewing rabbit. Seeing the old man's face, bright red in the firelight, Lingguan was gripped by a strange emotion. Meng was such an admirable man, always so upbeat, expansive, and witty, as if the word pessimism were missing in the dictionary of his life. Lingguan had admired Meng since childhood; it was more like worship, actually. In his youthful eyes, there was nothing Meng Eight could not do—catch rabbits, snare sparrows, hunt foxes, even weave lifelike animals like dogs and horses out of desert iris stalks of. After more than a decade, Meng was no longer his idol, but Lingguan's respect for him increased as time went by. At ease with himself, he lived a confident life, carefree as his beard, which flowed in the wind.

The water boiled noisily. Lingguan tossed a few more Artemisia twigs onto the fire.

"I think," Meng said, "that the fox must have been hot. I mean how it felt about itself. Otherwise, why had it slept in a shaded hollow, not a sunny one? That must have been its comfort zone."

"How long does a fox live?" Huaqiu asked.

"Hard to say. Ten years or so, in general, but no one knows how long once it becomes a fox fairy. Like humans, a fox can prolong its life through self-cultivation—haven't we all heard of immortals?"

"Foxes practicing self-cultivation? I don't believe you," Huaqiu jeered.

"Be serious, boy. All creatures can do that, like the snakes in the old story 'White Snake,' or dogs. I had a dog a few years back that howled at the moon on the fifteenth day of each lunar month. Foxes do that too. When they practice self-cultivation, they acquire supernatural energy, or maybe it's the other way around. In any case, an animal can prolong its life through self-cultivation. I've heard that a fox's fur turns white after a thousand years of self-cultivation, and black after ten thousand. But that's just what people say."

"Have you ever seen a white fox?"

"I have, but I didn't shoot it. Killing a creature like this brings disaster. In 1960, I once set a trap by the Dasha River. The next day, when I opened the gate, a white fox was waiting for me, caught by the leg. I freed it, bandaged its leg, and let it go. I knew not to shoot it, because that would have brought bad luck. I heard that the fool Bai Fu once shot a white fox—he didn't know. Maybe the fox was predestined to meet its end that way; otherwise, he wouldn't have gotten close enough to smell its farts. White foxes have supernatural intelligence and aren't easily caught. You have to use a castrated dog, the mortal enemy of the thousand-year old foxes. That's why we say that 'everything has its mortal enemy.' White foxes know transformation and invisibility magic, but when they meet a castrated dog, nothing works."

"Now you're getting absurd."

The heat from the fire was so high it made the pot lid clank as the water boiled. Lingguan lifted the lid with a pair of chopsticks, laid them across the top of the pot, and replaced the lid.

"Take it off altogether. There's no need for it," Meng said. "We want to let the gamy smell dissipate, so turn up the heat." Lingguan removed the lid and added firewood.

The campfire roared as accompaniment to the boiling water, creating a cozy, warm ambience for Lingguan, who realized that he was surrounded by profound silence only when he walked off to relieve himself. The sky was uncommonly dark as soon as he left the fire site;

it was black, so solid he could almost reach out and grab a handful. He felt the darkness seep into his body. Meng's voice was faint, which accentuated the solitude; the bonfire turned into a pathetic ball of light, looking feeble in the darkness. As if trying to regain the upper hand, the tongues of flame licked at the sky, but that only highlighted the indomitable force of the night. The bonfire was weak, and so were the humans in those surroundings.

Unable to stand the oppressive darkness and suffocating quiet, Lingguan hitched up his pants and hurried back to the bonfire, where the sound of crackling flames brought back the noise of the desert. The dreadful silence was gone and the solidified darkness receded into the distance; he now understood why people built bonfires at night—more than simply give warmth, they burn away the oppressive darkness and stillness and restored the clamor of life. Without a bonfire, the desert would be like a dead sea.

"That's good enough. You can dump the water now," Meng said.

Huaqiu poured it on the sand.

"Try it and see how it tastes," Meng said.

Lingguan tore off a piece and put it in his mouth; it felt more like sawdust than meat, and the odor was terrible. "Ai, it's nasty." He spat it out.

"It's not that strong. If it hadn't been cooked with radishes, the stench would take your breath away." Meng laughed at Lingguan's sorry face. "This is medicine, don't you know? Medicine never tastes good. It's bitter, but will make your better. You have to put up with it. Hei, it may taste awful, but it's good for you, with heat that is a sure cure for a stomach with too much cold *qi*. Now I'll show you a different way. Chop the meat finely and stir-fry it. Make sure to use plenty of oil. It will taste much better."

Following Meng's instruction, Lingguan stir-fried the meat and, sure enough, it did improve the taste. Meng and Huaqiu both had some as well.

8

Lingguan woke up early the next day, when he could no longer stand the dampness in the bedding.

They were sleeping on a "hot bed." First, cinders are spread over the sand to make it warm, and then covered with bedding to absorb the heat and make it comfortable. The only flaw is dampness from the sand, which slowly spreads through the blanket. That is what woke Lingguan up.

The stars were the first things he saw when he opened his eyes. In the desert stars look different than those seen from elsewhere; textured and low hanging, they seem lonely, like lanterns suspended in mid air. With his eyes on the night sky, he felt the bedding become a magic carpet, twirling him up into the sky to mingle with the stars. He was refreshed, transparently refreshed, his mind clear of confusion and distracting thoughts, translucent inside and out. Each breath had the quality of a cool, fresh liquid that cleansed his internal organs and every cell in his body. This is wonderful, he nearly shouted.

At some point he heard Meng waking Huaqiu up. The old man's voice traveled far on a morning breeze before echoing back, making it sound as if there were many old men calling out. Huaqiu yawned grandly, while Meng coughed, a loud, pleasant sound in the morning air and unexpectedly harmonious with the desert hollows. Lingguan was thrilled and intoxicated, a state he was afraid to disrupt. This is wonderful, he said again to himself. The desert is wonderful, life is wonderful, everything is wonderful. "Ah—" He cried out like a sentimental poet, but quickly changed the shout into a yawn when he realized that his emotional cry might draw mockery from the old man.

"What the hell are you ah-ing about? Get up," Meng scolded, though not harshly. Lingguan laughed and rolled over to rest on his pillow, so he could see the shadowy shrubs through morning fog that had thrown a veil over the plants and had given them a swaying beauty. Everything had an unreal quality, including the dunes, the hollows, and an unknown dark shadow on the distant ridges.

Lingguan and Huaqiu lacked the stamina to trek the desert because they came out so seldom, so Meng had them take turns guarding the campsite. This being the day for Huaqiu to go out with Meng, they left with their muskets and provisions. "Light a fire on a sand hill if we don't return before nightfall," Meng said to Lingguan. "You won't forget, will you?"

"Of course I won't forget. How could I?" Lingguan smiled and watched the two figures disappear into the desert, the old one light and agile, the younger one strong and solid. Soon they were on a ridge, where they seemed to freeze, as if deciding which direction to take. The moment produced a beautiful sight. The sky was turning from dusty gray to white, and with the dark ridge as a backdrop, the hunters created a freeze frame of incomparable beauty. He could find no words to describe the scene. Words paled when confronted with Nature.

His gaze shifted to the camel resting motionless nearby, its head raised, as if it, too, were captivated by the morning desert. To him, these ships of the desert were grand totems, so quiet and peaceful, devoid of emotion, uncomplaining and never contentious. Humans rarely sense their existence, for they quietly eat when hungry and lie down silently when tired, though they are always there by the humans.

Looking at the camel, Lingguan felt that he should become more like that. He got dressed and walked to the highest ridge.

The east was turning red, starting with a light swipe, like the blush on the face of a bashful girl, nearly imperceptible. Little by little, the sky took on a rosy hue, like rouge bleeding through rice paper, spreading quickly, turning darker, and looking like blood from the mother of dawn when giving birth to the sun.

An ocean of sand burst onto the rim of the sun—he could make out crashing waves. The shiny veneer looked like sunlight reflected off the surface of water.

Lingguan felt that he was melting into the whiteness of the sun. The desert woke up, as did everything around him as the morning fog slowly dissipated. The world was bathed in inebriating sunlight. Light and dark divided the ridges, the sunny side enveloped in a golden veil, while the shaded side remained inky black.

This was the desert's most beautiful moment. No chill, no harsh heat, no parching thirst or restlessness. Only beauty, vitality, and a surging life force.

Overcome by another tide of powerful emotions, he raised his arms and balled his fists, ready to jump and shout.

"Hei—dai—" he roared.

The shout traveled deep into the desert, where it was sent back to fill the hollow with echoes of "dai… dai."

9

The picturesque images vanished as the sun rose higher, and the desert could no longer hide its innate cruelty. Though it was late autumn, the sun seemed to be mindlessly clinging to a different season, splashing its heat and blazing light down on a place the locals jokingly called Scorched Donkey Bend. Had there been wind, it would have been bearable, but the more Lingguan longed for a breeze, the more the hot air turned the hollow into a steamer. No shelter from the wind existed once the temperature dropped and it turned cold. Even a circular bend in the sand that looked to be a haven would become a tunnel where gale-force winds came from all directions to rob you of your body heat.

Lingguan had taken water three times, a mouthful each time. Treasuring water in the heart of the desert meant survival, so he drank only enough to wet his throat. Strangely, however, the more he moistened his mouth the thirstier he got; his throat turned into dry potato skin the moment the cool liquid entered his belly. His pathetic mouth felt like it was stirring mud; his tongue reminded him of the trowel villagers used on plaster walls.

Standing atop the sandy rise, all he could see was a yellow expanse, devoid of even a trace of green, for autumn frost had dyed the plants gray. With the white sun above, the sky did not look as blue as usual. At the moment, it was the source of irritation and scorching heat, driving out all signs of coolness. Dry, unbearable heat everywhere. Unable to escape it, he went into the tent, where oilcloth blocked out the light, but he ran out as if fleeing for his life barely ten minutes later. He was convinced that Meng and Huaqiu would have returned to find a well cooked human if he hadn't.

He sought respite under Artemisia shrubs, but no coolness there either, nothing but choking dust. Left with no option, he sat on the ridge and covered his head with a white shirt. A hint of coolness rose up from his backside, for there was an air current from sand that had yet to be baked. The pleasant sensation served to remind him that the hottest moments were yet to come. In an hour or two, he would be like a fish on a grill.

All this he could endure.

But not the loneliness.

He tried to while away the time, the most difficult hours of his life. Loneliness tormented him more than the heat, for the only other living creature was the camel, which was grazing contentedly; mice and foxes slept in their burrows and dens. He wondered what happened to flies, insects, sand babies, and all those bugs and worms whose names he did not know. Where did they go? He longed to see another living thing. The camel, which was like a philosopher engrossed in thought or an ascetic silently meditating, only increased his sense of loneliness. How he wished to see a buzzing bee or a flitting butterfly. But he knew that these aristocratic insects seldom graced the sea of death with their presence.

The heat intensified. Covered in sweat from head to toe, he found the stickiness insufferable, as a powerful thirst assaulted him; but he refused to give in to the urge. To his surprise, the yearning for water took his mind off the loneliness, curing one affliction with another. But thirst was throbbing, like his beating heart, and the more focused he was, the stronger it came at him; the spastic sensation of thirst rippled through his body in waves, more visceral and irrepressible each time, until his head buzzed. At some point, thirst overpowered him, making him feel like a parched corpse.

He ran to the bucket and knelt down to drink water that smelled of plastic, but traveled coolly down his throat into his stomach, only to bring on an uncontrollable desire for more, making him even more acutely aware of his dehydrated body. No longer caring about conserving the water, he drank until his belly swelled like a drum.

Sighing with relief, he replaced the lid on the bucket and lay down on the hot sand to dry his sweaty back, savoring the wonderful sensation. After a while, he sat up to eat a *mantou* before tossing the shirt away and lying down again with his face baking in the sun.

He felt as if he'd spent a hundred years here alone, but the sun reminded him that it was barely noontime. How was he supposed to pass the long afternoon? He did not dare contemplate that. He was dying to be back home. Images of the village and the date trees by door of their house surfaced. The dates were ripe, their sweetness punctuated by a puckery taste, the memory of which made him smack his lips. How wonderful to have some of those thumb-sized dates with their tiny dark spots. Big, sweet, with thick meat, they were the finest in the village, and tasted best when sprinkled with liquor and fermented for a few days. His mouth watered, returning suppleness to his tongue. He thought about desert pears, which were soft and were dark ice orbs in the winter, but became balls of sweet juice when soaked in cool water. He smiled as he imagined himself biting into a pear and sucking gently, ah, the cool sweetness went straight to his heart. Refreshed by the vision, he felt more saliva in his mouth, so he abandoned himself to the fantasy, and the loneliness faded.

The hottest time of day finally arrived, when the sand seemed to howl. He sat up with the realization that he was drenched. His reverie quickly came to an end, and he was restless again. Scooping up his shirt, he climbed the ridge, where he was somewhat cooled by an air current, though unsettled by the burnt yellow all around him. He recalled reading about the color yellow, the most unnerving hue. The recollection made him fidget; greatly annoyed, he paced the ridge like a donkey crazed by sexual desire. He was reminded of lines from the folk song "Brother Wang Herding Sheep," so he sang at the top of his lungs:

Brother Wang — herding sheep — restless
Carelessly — he killed — a little — lamb
He planned to — pick it up — roast and eat it
What a shame — about — the pelt.

"Ha-ha." A burst of laughter. Now it made sense. With the yellow scenery, how could Brother Wang not be restless? Then he noticed a red dot at the tip of distant hill.

It was a woman. A woman in a red headscarf!

His heart began to beat wildly. Woman, how beautiful that sounded, so refreshingly cool, so endearingly sweet, so, so — he couldn't think of a better word.

There was no better word than this one — woman.

10

Lingguan had not known that a rock-and-dirt-covered stretch known as a "gobi" could exist in the vast ocean of sand. Obviously very old, it was pitch black, and he failed to understand how it could be preserved in the desert, just as he could not fathom how flying sand had not swallowed up the Crescent Spring in Dunhuang's soughing dunes over the centuries. Maybe overgrown vegetation had blunted the assault from wind and sand, he reasoned.

The woman in the red headscarf was standing on a high earthen mound, the sight of which alerted him to another she in a hollow below. He knew about the mound, called a beacon tower; it was where wolf dung had been burned as an alarm signal in ancient times. It was cone-shaped. There had once been one of those in his village, but the villagers had beaten it down to build a pigpen; the dirt, he'd heard, was prized fertilizer.

He heard giggles as he approached and saw the woman, the older one, wave her arms like a mother hen trying to get the young woman, a girl, actually, to come down. A man in a tattered straw hat, the type used on scarecrows, with a face like a walnut, glared at Lingguan with hostility-laden eyes.

"Are you here to gather hair moss?" he demanded in a gravelly voice with a Gulang accent.

"No, fox hunting."

"Are you sure?" A light shone in his muddy eyes. He exhaled when Lingguan nodded.

After much urging from her mother, the girl came down and wiped her face with a corner of her headscarf, slowly, over and over. Lingguan knew she was washing her face with her spit, a common practice among women in his village.

"That's odd," the old man said. "I've never seen a fox, not even a shadow, but people seem to be bagging them all the time."

"They're very clever. The slightest movement or tiniest noise will send them running like the wind," Lingguan said to the man, but his eyes were on the girl, who looked back at him with a surprised expression. Then she shrugged, lowered her head, and smiled.

Obviously displeased by the way Lingguan was looking at his daughter, the man—her father, he assumed—snarled at her, "What are you stopping for? Keep picking. Is that all you've got? Go back to bed if you're looking for comfort." She grumbled as she picked up a small twisted-wire rake and began combing the ground. Soon she'd gathered a black, hairy ball; after picking off weeds and dirt, she tossed it into a basket over her back.

Lingguan had eaten hair moss in egg rolls at banquets and found it bland; but he'd heard it was a favorite dish among merchants in the South, because it symbolized plenty. One *liang* could fetch nearly a hundred yuan, he'd been told.

"How much can you pick in a day?"

Her father ignored Lingguan and showed his animosity by scraping harder with his rake. The woman looked at Lingguan and then at her husband, but said nothing and kept her head down. The girl, however, looked at him and said, "One *liang*." Her reply earned an ugly look from her father. Ignoring Lingguan once again, the three of them carried on with their gleaning. He did not know whether he should leave or stay and, after a brief moment of indecision, he walked up to the beacon tower.

There he spotted the family's camp in a hollow among the desert rice and Artemisia shrubs, where his camel roamed and was now grazing leisurely. Steamy mist flashed and glared above sand ripples on the ridge, illusory and elusive, like a dream scene.

Poetic and romantic sentiments about the desert reappeared in Lingguan's mind as the sun turned westward and the temperature dipped. Standing on the beacon tower, he looked around and saw a very different vista open up. The dunes were not as tall, the sharp drops and steep rises now obscured; they spread out in a leisurely line, like water wrinkled by a breeze. Instead of waves crashing against the shore, there were only convulsive undercurrents that sent ripples to the horizon, toward eternity. Not a single dune, ridge, or valley was isolated or prominent; they all seemed to flow naturally, and a move by one affected all, but they formed a harmonious entity. Decorated by sand eddies, the ocean of sand swelled, charged with an imposing masculine vitality.

"Hey, they should be ready. I'm famished." The girl bounded over to a dark mound, where she dug up some objects, patted them from one hand to the other, and then blew on them. "Yes, they're done." Lingguan saw they were charred potatoes.

Her parents put down their rakes and walked over. She waved the potatoes at Lingguan. "Come have some with us," she said.

"No, thanks. I'm not hungry."

"They won't kill you," she insisted, tossing him a potato when he came down from the beacon tower.

"Go on, eat it," the old man said as he blew on the potato he was holding. "You don't look like the shy type to me.

"What about your lunch?" Lingguan asked.

"This is our lunch," the girl said with a smile.

"Really?"

"We're lucky to have this," her father remarked curtly. "Back in 1960, we couldn't sniff even a rotten potato."

"But it doesn't take long to cook a real meal."

"How would we do that? Potatoes and water are heavy enough on our backs. We came a long way." The girl took a bite; the burning hot potato made her suck in air.

"Can't you load it onto a draft animal?"

"A draft animal?" the old man snorted. "We come by bus. Where would a camel sit? Go ask a driver if he'd let a donkey on his bus, or a camel."

His argumentative tone shut Lingguan up, so he peeled his potato and took a bite. It had a wonderful, roasted taste. "You should eat a real meal every once in a while," he said, wanting to repay their kindness.

"That's true," she said. "But there's nothing we can do away from home."

"A mile from home is a trial unknown," the man said gruffly. "It's nice to lie in a bed at home, but you can't make a living that way."

"We've got everything you'd need over there, water, vegetables, flour. Come cook whatever you want. I haven't eaten yet either." Recalling that he'd said he'd already eaten, he felt his face turn red. They did not seem to notice.

"That sounds great." The girl jumped to her feet. "Even pinched noodle soup would be wonderful. I'm tired of roasted potatoes."

Her father frowned and glared at her through bloodshot eyes. "You'll eat anything, won't you? What they have belongs to them. You're not their friend or their family, so what makes you think you can eat their food?"

"It's no big deal. We don't mind sharing. Besides—"

"No." The man cut him off gruffly, an outburst that seemed filled with loathing. To hell with you if you don't want our food, Lingguan felt like saying. There's no need to get all worked up like that. But he swallowed the words when he noticed that the skin on the man's neck had turned white in the blazing sun.

The girl flashed an unhappy smile.

Picking up his frayed hat, which had turned flat by being sat on for who-knows-how-long, the man thumped it a few times and turned to Lingguan. "Go do what you came to do. We're busy here."

Lingguan had seldom been treated so shabbily. His face burned as he realized that the man was afraid he had designs on the girl. Put on the spot, he stood his ground until he recovered enough to laugh dryly. "I just came over to check on our camel."

11

It turned dark shortly after Lingguan tied the camel to an Artemisia shrub. The rosy evening sky turned inky black so fast it truly felt as if a night curtain had been pulled over the glorious sunset and everything before his eyes. He lit a lantern. Under dim yellow light that shone on a pot even darker than the night, he made some noodles and began to worry when he was done. On the day before, he and Meng had already been back by this time, so what was wrong today? Could they have gotten lost? The idea made him laugh, since Meng was always bragging how he knew more about the desert than about the lines on his palm. Besides, he'd said that an experienced hunter would never chase a fox that would prevent him from returning to the campsite before sunset, especially in the winter. If he forgot to take matches or a lighter along, the desert's cold night could turn anyone daring enough to go up against the rule of the land into frozen meat.

Naturally, Lingguan wasn't worried about that, for at this time of year, they would merely be cold, even sleeping out in the open desert. What put him on edge was what might have delayed the experienced hunter's return. Lingguan suspected that Huaqiu was the cause; maybe he was too tired to walk. Like an animal with little stamina, Huaqiu left full of energy and in high spirits, but that could have changed on the way back. He was the type who would moan and groan about a minor ache. Very likely he'd become a drag on Meng. Lingguan imagined Huaqiu baring his teeth and limping along, using his musket as a crutch, like a wounded Nationalist soldier in a war movie. His heart skipped a beat. Lingguan recalled a story his father had told him about a hunter who was walking uphill using his rifle as a crutch and accidentally shot himself. That was the kind of stupid thing Huaqiu was capable of. He'd do that; he'd be so tired he'd prop himself with his musket, and bang—he'd fall to the ground, mortally wounded, rolling around in his own blood—Lingguan felt his chest tighten as these thoughts raced through his mind.

They should be back by now. He gazed into the darkness. He could not tell time without a watch, but common sense told him it was still early, even though he felt as if years had gone by. A shooting star arced across the sky and fell in the direction of the beacon tower, which reminded him of the girl and sent a warm current through his heart. He tried to recall her face, but the screen of his brain remained dark, without a single image. Then it appeared, but with Ying'er's features. He recalled how carefully he'd looked at the girl, at her pleasant face and slightly upturned nose, and how she was given to laughing. But despite his effort, he could not recall either the way she'd laughed or her face. Instead, the stubborn old man's scowling face insinuated itself into his mind. He shook his head and managed to blur that image and turn it into an amorphous glare, like the reflection of the moon in water stirred by a breeze.

What's she doing now? He stood up to look in the direction of their camp, though he knew there was nothing to see. She must be sleeping. Maybe not, but there'd be no romance with her stubborn, knotty father around. He was a killjoy. Yes, kill joy. Lingguan laughed. The old man killed everyone's joy, even the joy of talking to someone. They hadn't really talked, and yet they seemed to have said quite a bit. He pondered her every word; her image was indistinct, but her words were clear, all etched on his mind. Particularly memorable was her rustic Gulang accent, which displayed a lilting softness as it fell on his heart like drops of water. She'd given him a potato, and it had smelled so good. He hadn't known that potatoes could smell like that. To her father it must have felt like the loss of a treasure. What had he said? "Go on, eat it." He recalled lines of poetry: "Nothing is higher than the sky or better than wine/nothing is sweeter than her tongue on mine." Lingguan felt a pang of guilt toward Ying'er. Am I being unfaithful? That would be terrible.

The vague hint of a memory flashed in his mind. There was something he had to do, but he couldn't recall what it was. Knitting his brows, he looked around with the help of the dim lantern light: their tent, which looked like a hut under the night sky; dinner, which had likely turned cold and mushy. The plastic bucket, the handbag, the string bag—his gaze fell at last on the pile of firewood. That's it! Before he left, Meng had told him to light a fire on a tall dune.

Aiya! Lingguan cried out as he slapped his head in exasperation. It was so dark outside they could never find the campsite. He must have eaten a pig's brain to be so dense. A good thing he remembered it; otherwise—hei! He ran up the dune with a bundle of firewood and lit it. Flames leaped up. He ran back down, picked up the lantern, and, even before he'd caught his breath, cut down more Artemisia branches. He had to have enough to keep the fire going, for he did not know when they'd reach the point where they could see it. If they stayed out all night, he'd keep the fire going till dawn.

It was getting cold, typical of the desert, where, as they said, you wore a leather jacket in the morning and a silk shirt at noon, and you ate a watermelon up near a burning brazier. With the temperature dropping, his back was cold, while the fire roasted his chest; but he was too occupied to put on more clothes. So when the chill grew unbearable, he simply turned around to let the fire warm his back.

Evening breezes blew over like icy water, making the fire roar. He turned to avoid choking on the smoke. It was too dark to choose only dry shrubs, so half the wood he'd cut was still damp; the wet firewood sizzled, a pleasant sound in the drab, lonely night. It did not catch fire easily, he discovered, but once it did, it burned more slowly than the dry, which quickly turned to ashes.

A long time passed before he heard human voices, still far away and faint. It's them, he said to himself. He moved to the side so the roar of the fire would not interfere with his hearing. Sure enough, he heard Meng's confident cough, and his heart settled back into place. After tossing more firewood onto the fire, he carried the lantern down the dune, put the pot on the cooking pit, and lit a fire. Soon the contents began to boil, and he heard Meng's voice.

"Eating pigs' brains again? We walked at least ten extra li, going off track and away from home. We'd still be out there walking at daybreak if not for your fire."

The old man sounded more happy than angry, which told Lingguan it had been a good hunt. He was right; they each had a fox over his shoulder.

"They haven't been skinned yet," Lingguan remarked.

"Didn't have time." Meng smiled. "We were about to turn back after shooting one, but then I saw another track, so I thought we ought to take that one too. We caught up with it as the sun dipped below the hilltops."

Huaqiu tossed down his fox without a word and sat down, as if he was about to collapse.

"Are you really that tired?" Meng laughed. "You're still a young man, but that little trip turned you into a scrawny mutt straining to pee. When I was your age, I could run miles with a ladder over my shoulder to visit women and still return at dawn to work in the field. Hei, you young men these days."

Huaqiu stretched out when he heard the comment.

Lingguan filled a bowl and handed it to Meng, who put it on the sand and took out his pipe. He took a few puffs, sending sparks into the distance.

After filling another bowl for Huaqiu, Lingguan called his friend over, but got no response. He was fast asleep.

Chapter Four

1

A major event in a peasant's life each year is grain collection, a way to pay agricultural taxes to the central government as well as local fees. The procedure is simple enough: inspect the grain, weigh it, settle the account, and cash out.

The grain station was a madhouse, crowded with people and animals and walking tractors, creating a din that made the large space seem much smaller. Laoshun never liked being there, repelled by the shouts of the station workers and the all-pervasive government presence. His sense of personal insignificance was heightened each time he entered the drying ground, which gave rise to stressful feelings of helplessness. What he found most oppressive were the mounds of grain, some loose, some in bags. His eyes glazed over at the sight of burlap bags piled dozens of feet high, and standing on the shifting planks atop the mountain of loose grain with his grain scoop reminded him of an ox that had died after rolling into a hollow at Xishan.

At some point he had concluded that the grain was pretty much worthless because there was so much of it. The rarer something is, the greater its value. The price of grain would rise if the peasants refused to sell, and he felt contempt for villagers who could not wait to come sell their grain, like donkeys in heat, though he overlooked the fact that he was not far behind.

"Hey, Uncle Shun, over here." It was Baigou and Beizhu.

"You've got space for me?"

"Sure."

Seeing that his donkey cart could not make it through to them, he tossed the reins aside, hoisted up a small sack of grain, and pushed his way through the crowd. Hantou hesitated before following suit.

Baigou had carved out a great spot, closer to the scale and to the mounds of grain, making it easy to weigh and drop off the sacks. Laying down his sack, Laoshun stopped to catch his breath. "That's enough for you," Baigou said. "We'll take care of the rest." He and Beizhu briskly lugged the sacks over.

"Is this all of it?" Beizhu asked Laoshun.

"No, there's another load."

"That's a lot. The price is too low, you know. Why not wait for it to go up? A knife-sharpener from Tiemen set up a stand a couple days ago and asked to be paid with grain, not money, but that's changed. He's going to wait till the price goes up to one yuan."

"That's what everyone says, but who knows? We have to survive whether or not it goes up. And we can't do that without money. Why didn't your father sell some of his grain to get you a wife, Baigou?"

"I need a few more years of freedom. A wife is a fetter and a son is a tether. Why would I want that?"

Hantou quietly left with their cart, and Laoshun sat down on a sack to rest his sore legs. He became aware of all the noise. Two men were wrangling over a weighing scoop, like fighting cocks. Stupid, Laoshun said to himself, really stupid. What difference does it make who gets the scoop first? No one's going lose any grain, so what's the point? Is the Angel of Death nipping at your heels? Ridiculous. Then he anxiously watched an old man and a girl carry a loaded scoop up the grain mountain, their feet bouncing dangerously on the wobbly planks. Elsewhere a man who looked like an official was cursing a youngster—"Fuck you and your mother too!"—and was immediately confronted by three husky men. "This isn't about you guys," he said. "We're his brothers, and we'll beat the shit out of you if we hear another word about our mother." Laoshun had to laugh.

When he heard Baigou snigger behind him, he turned to see the two brothers lay down a scoop of grain by his sacks. Beizhu winked conspiratorially, while Baigou kept a watchful eye on the man at the scale.

Laoshun knew they were up to no good. He'd heard of people carrying previously weighed and priced grain back into line a second, even a third time, earning far more than their grain was worth. He'd thought it was a tall tale, believing that the station workers weren't stupid enough to be fooled like that. But now he had to believe his eyes. Baigou tried to keep a straight face, but failed to mask how pleased he was.

Laoshun's feelings were more complicated than he could explain. He looked up at the sky, where the sun was a fiery ball, and he felt his face burn. He shut his eyes, recalling a day in 1960 when he'd stolen some unripe corn from the production team. He'd been discomfited by a mixture of shame, guilt, self-reproach, indignation, and despair, all combined to form a figurative noose around his neck for decades. He'd had to do it to survive, though he'd decided at the time that he would not live another day if someone, even a child, had discovered his deed; knife or rope, it would have made no difference. Decades had gone by, but he felt like hitting himself in the head each time he thought about it. And now these young men were actually doing something similar in broad daylight with no visible sense of shame.

With a sigh, he had to admit that the times had changed. In the old days, a man stealing or a woman selling her body would have brought such shame to the family that even the ancestors would have wanted to jump off the sacrificial altar. A man's life was essentially over if he was found stealing. How about a woman? According to the blind storyteller, a woman should cut off her arm if a man inadvertently touched it. But the world had changed, and thieving young men brazenly enjoyed a better life than anyone. Look at Baigou, how he was sniggering, as if he'd accomplished a great deed.

Reaping a harvest without sowing seeds galled Laoshun. A year's harvest required two years of backbreaking labor under a searing sun, with sweat pouring into the eyes and skin peeling from the palms. That was hard enough, but was child's play compared to the most aggravating part, the fertilizer. He'd to use the damned stuff, but could hardly afford it, for its price kept going up, rising higher and higher. And there were expenses for water and electricity. He worked hard to produce that little amount of grain for a bit of money, while these two picked up their scoop, walked around, and swaggered back, to be rewarded again. One orbit brought them several hundred yuan, and three or four brought them at least a thousand. Damn it, that's not fair. Laoshun was indignant. The world had been turned upside down; living a decent life led only to impoverishment.

The bright sunlight made his eyes water. Noise he'd managed to tune out while he was engrossed in his thoughts found its way back to his ears. Everything he saw upset him: people busily running around or lying on sacks and shooting the breeze; men arguing over scoops or leering at women; a man pulling a cart and hawking watermelons; and more. It was too much to take.

Baigou and Beizhu nudged the scoop that had made who-knows-how-many trips closer to the scale, where the worker was shouting and gesturing in a show of power. With ingratiating smiles, most of the villagers were bent nearly double, legs bowed and necks tucked in, to make themselves look more amiable to men who could undervalue their grain or subtract for "chaff." Baigou and Beizhu, however, looked smugly indifferent, cigarettes hanging from their lips as they talked, untroubled by a sense of shame.

They heaved their scoop up onto the scale. One worker checked their grain carefully, while another watched the markings on the scale. In the meantime, Baigou laughed and talked as he handed out cigarettes. He and Beizhu moved the scoop over to the mountain of loose grain once the worker had recorded the weight. They walked slowly, since Beizhu seemed to be having a problem with his feet; he staggered, looking as if he could not take another step. That made it easy to lay the scoop by the path to the grain mountain, where he stopped to empty grain from his shoes and push his scoop out of the way, clearing room for people to pass by.

Laoshun nervously witnessed their scheme and actually breathed a sigh of relief when they moved their scoop to a "safe zone." Why was he so concerned over a couple of thieves? He was irate. Damn you!

Then a different emotion rose up in his heart. "People cannot abide seeing a beggar holding an expensive bowl." That was how he felt. Life was tough for him. He'd brought no more than ten scoops of grain on that day, the result of his family tightening their belts for years. But Baigou could easily sell ten scoops each day. He could make a small fortune. Laoshun could not finish the thought.

Something stirred inside him—a sense of righteousness. Should I expose them? They aren't stealing from me, so why get so upset? Maybe I should just turn a blind eye. That, however, would not have been easy for him. An established equilibrium had been destroyed, and an anchorage that had supported his law-abiding lifestyle began to shift.

He glanced up at the bright sun. One thing was certain. Something shameful was developing in his guilt-laden heart, and that increased the guilt feelings. Once he became aware of its existence, it surged above all else—he had to stop them.

Laoshun searched every fiber of his being for something to justify a decision to report them. Maybe the workers will have to make up the shortfall. The notion of the state was never a powerful one to him, but the workers were real people. In particular, there was the station chief, Old Wang, a man with a perpetual smile, a good man, he thought. Can I stand by and watch them reap illegal gains while a good man suffers? No, I can't.

He walked off, buoyed by the belief that he was doing the right thing. Pretending to go to the toilet, he headed toward Old Wang's office.

2

Laoshun's pounding heart finally regained its rhythm when Hantou brought the second load to the ground and dumped a sack of wheat into a scoop. What had just occurred receded to the back of his mind, an instinct that made it possible to live in relative peace with himself. Those ripe, golden kernels of wheat in the scoop gradually filled his soul. Intoxicated by the familiar aroma, he was reluctant to give it up; this was his sweat and blood, he mused. He recalled what others were saying about the price going up. If the rumor was true, that meant that he would lose several hundred by selling it now.

Staring blankly at the throng of hectic people, he emerged from his inner world. Everyone else is selling, he told himself, so what if I lose a bit? I won't be alone. Besides, the boy can't be a bachelor forever; he'll be too old by the time the price reaches one yuan, and by then the cost for a bride will also go up. In the 1960s a single bushel of shriveled wheat brought in enough to get a man a wife, but that went up to hundreds, then thousands, then—it could be tens of thousands when the price reached one yuan. What the hell. Sell the damn stuff.

Moving along with the flow, Laoshun and Hantou carried their scoop toward the scale. The sun was tipping westward and the site was strangely hot. An electric fan nearby whirled at high speed, stirring up columns of dust and wheat husks and generating an unbearable annoyance. Laoshun was surprised by his ability to carry such a heavy scoop; that raised his spirits and wiped away unhappy thoughts, like an autumn wind sweeping away fallen leaves. He had felt old before this, and thoughts of aging were followed by an image of the grave. Now he was jubilant; the sky was a richer blue and the air had cleared; even the noise did not bother him so much. What he found especially satisfying was the surprised look in his son's eyes, one that would last Laoshun a long time, for Hantou had wanted to call Beizhu over to help them. Laoshun smirked.

As they moved closer to the scale, he watched the worker who examined and weighed the grain. He wore a frosty, menacing look as he thrust his hands into the wheat and came up with husks and chaff, then told the owner to run his wheat through the winnower or waving him off altogether. Laoshun's heart was pounding. Naturally, he believed his grain was clean, but dust was unavoidable after the threshing. Glancing at the sun in the western sky, he could tell that they would not be able to get the grain weighed on this day if they had to run it through the winnower. He took a furtive look around him before sticking his hand into his wheat the way the worker did. His palm emerged with a nearly non-existent film of dust, and he stopped worrying.

Suddenly he heard shouts of a fight nearby. He followed the sound and saw that station workers were beating someone; it drew a crowd. They were using belts and clubs, making noise that could only mean solid contact with human flesh. Then he heard a yell: "That one's getting away." A figure ran off and vanished. When Laoshun turned back, he saw the crowd part to let some men through. They were manhandling someone with swollen eyes and a bloody face. It took Laoshun a moment to realize that it was Beizhu.

He was shocked to see the shape Beizhu was in. His heart tightened as he began to question if what he'd done might have gone beyond the limits of moral behavior. No matter how he looked at it, Beizhu was beaten because he had informed on him, even though a thief deserved to be punished. His mood darkened as guilt and regret took over; he could almost sense people pointing at his back. His face burned. He looked around guiltily, only to see that everyone was watching Beizhu being dragged to the office; no one glanced his way.

"Those thieves are rotten," an old man said with a sigh. Another man intensified his sentiment: "Kill them! When enough are killed, we'll see if anyone dares cheat again."

That's right, Laoshun said to himself. I was reporting on bad people, helping to root out evildoers. That made him feel better, and yet something made the dark mood linger. He could not deny that his action had been partially motivated by the jealous notion of not wanting to see "a beggar holding a valuable bowl."

"Those asses live too good a life," a young man remarked.

"They sure do," another said. "They eat and drink what they like, and get to reap golden wheat every day. Not like us. Is this any way to live?"

"You hardly ever see one of them get a beating," an old man with a yellowed beard said. "I'll bet that hurt."

"You know it!"

Laoshun echoed their sentiments silently. But he detected something odd. With all those eyes on the drying ground, his had been keener than everyone else's. How strange. He had always minded his own business, or as the local saying went, he'd swept the snow around his house and paid no heed to a donkey knocking over somebody else's pot. Why had he acted out of character today? Was he unconcerned that Beizhu might take it out on his camel or that Beigou could burn down his house if they found out? They were capable of anything. The thought frightened him, and he was seized by an alarming terror. Sure, he could say he acted impulsively, but he still had to wonder what had made him do so. As a cautious man who was afraid a fart would hit his heel when he walked, where had the impulse come from? Why was he the only one who'd noticed the act, and how had he become so reckless? Damned weird. The more he thought about it, the stranger it seemed. He had been pushed into it, he reasoned. But by whom? Well, it had to be deities or ghosts. That being the case, they could not have escaped their fate. Maybe this was what people meant by retribution. Instant retribution.

The web of tangled thoughts melted away.

He had no time for those thoughts anyway, for his scoop had reached the scale. Like all the other peasants, he focused a worried gaze on the worker whose hand was in the wheat, his movements subtle and fast. Laoshun's heart skipped a beat, thumping so loud it seemed to drown out all the other noises. He couldn't help it. He had always been like that at critical moments, even though he had been selling his grain there for years. He hoped against hope that the wheat Hantou dumped into the scoop had not come from the last few sacks, which contained more dirt. That would surely affect the price of the other sacks. He watched the hand nervously while the man, who seemed to sense his anxiety, refused to remove it from the grain. With a hint of a smile dancing around his mouth, he appeared to savor the moment, like playing cat and mouse. But it was torture to Laoshun, whose forehead and nose were dotted with sweat. He heard his son breathing hard behind him. This was the dreaded moment of the process, and his nerves were shot.

Finally the man removed his hand. Laoshun detected a light film of dust between the man's fingers. He exhaled, realizing he'd been holding his breath. The worker grabbed a handful of wheat, examined it and then tossed a kernel into his mouth to check the dryness. The crunch told Laoshun it was not a bad kernel that could ruin the rest for him. He breathed another sigh of relief.

The man spat out the broken kernel and threw those in his hand back into the scoop. "Third grade," he said in a cold, steely voice.

What? Laoshun could not believe his ears. Third grade? How could that be? The man was crazy. Laoshun did a quick calculation. There was close to a hundred yuan difference between first and third grades. He could do a lot with that much money. Looking into the man's cold face. "Could you—"

"No." He cut Laoshun off and waved impatiently for them to move along.

His legs suddenly going weak under him, Laoshun felt his anger rise. "Third-grade?" He would not take this lying down. "Why is it third-grade? Give me a reason."

The worker cast an incredulous glance at this ordinary looking old man who dared to talk back. "Because I said so." His eyes bulged.

"Then show me what first-grade looks like. You can't push us peasants around!"

The man's face turned bright red as he pointed a finger at Laoshun; he was not used to being confronted like this and was too startled to know what to do. His finger shook, but he could not utter a word.

"Let me see your first-grade grain!" Laoshun refused to back down. He did not care if he provoked the man, for he believed he was in the right.

"It's third-grade because I say so," the man finally recovered enough to reply. "What are you going to do about it? How dare you defy me! Take this away if you don't want to sell it here. Go. The country doesn't need your pathetic bit of third-grade grain."

Now Laoshun was the one who did not know what to say. As if he were choking, his lips moved soundlessly, and his eyes turned red. Pointing at the man, he said, "You—you," but his quivering lips could not manage to finish the sentence.

"Take it away," the man said shrilly. "I didn't ask you to come here."

"So you say!" Laoshun struggled to continue. "There's always a temple if you have a pig's head. I don't believe I can't—there are other grain collection stations."

"What's that got to do with me?" The man was tense.

A crowd formed as the argument intensified. Someone grabbed a handful of Laoshun's wheat and examined it. "Aiya. How could such fine wheat be third-grade?"

No longer able to see or hear a thing, Laoshun felt a current billow up inside, making his lips, beard, and fingers shake uncontrollably, while tears welled in his eyes. It took a moment for him to finally shout shrilly, "Fuck you and your mother! I'm not selling it here, and there's nothing you can do about it. Maybe you can try to bite off our dicks!"

He wiped his eyes with a dusty, blackened hand and looked around. His gaze fell on a walking tractor. "Whose is this? Let me borrow it. I'll pay."

"Are you really going to take your grain home? Well, then, you can have it for nothing," a young man said.

Laoshun pushed his way through the crowd, picked up a sack and handed it to Hantou. He then plunged his shovel into the scoop.

When he passed the station entrance with his loaded tractor, he saw two men in long white gowns walk Beizhu out of the office.

He chided himself for being such a busybody.

3

By dinnertime, Laoshun's anger had abated somewhat. On the way home he'd inveighed against the official with all the nasty curses he could think of, the first real, complete venting in recent years. He felt as if the worries and dejection clogging his body had leaked out through his pores with every swear word out of his mouth; the shreds of depression in his chest also disappeared.

As he ate, he talked about what Baigou and Beizhu had done at the grain station, drawing sighs from his wife, who agreed that they had been reckless. Laoshun did not mention what he had done. He not only wished he hadn't done it, but felt that it had been a repugnant act. He realized, to his chagrin, that he too had his despicable qualities, and that soured his mood all over.

Juanjuan, Shuangfu's daughter, came to say her mother would like for Elder Brother Mengzi to come by to write a letter to her father. "She said it's okay if he's too busy," the girl added. Mengzi felt his face burn as, with a grunt, be lowered his head to shovel food into his mouth. Noticing Mengzi's ill manners, Ying'er covered for him:

"Sure. You go on home now. He'll be there after dinner."

Laoshun glared at Mengzi after Juanjuan left, but said nothing to break the silence.

"The team leader says Shuangfu is rich," Hantou said. "He donated tens of thousands to the school to buy desks and is setting up a scholarship. People always say the richer a man gets, the stingier he becomes. No one ever expected Shuangfu to be so generous."

"That's a piddling amount to him," Mengzi snorted. "I wonder how much he spends on women a year? He's trying to buy popular support. Who cares about his money?"

"That's unfair," Hantou objected. "No matter how you look at it, helping out the school makes him okay in my book."

"How do you know it's not dirty money? Maybe he earned it exploiting his workers."

"It's his money, no matter where it comes from. Just because he won't give you any doesn't give you the right to make him look bad,"

Hantou said.

"I hate the way he struts." Mengzi laid down his bowl. "They say he surrounds himself with young virgins."

"You'd do the same if you were good enough." Their father gave him a dirty look. Mengzi could find nothing to say, while Ying'er smiled with her hand over her mouth. "That's right. You think you're better, don't you? You sleep in till the sun shines on your dick, you lazybones. He can strut around if he feels like it."

"That's true," Hantou said softly. "What's the point in getting jealous? Virgins have no time for a penniless man like you. You could ask them to take pity on poor Mengzi, but they wouldn't give you a second look. They'd think you're crazy."

"Besides," Laoshun said, "bad food can still be eaten, but bad words are best left unspoken. He can do what he wants, and it's none of your business. So shut up and don't go around spreading gossip and causing trouble."

"What do you mean, spreading gossip? I'm not that stupid, and I'm not like you. You're afraid your farts will rot your pants."

"Eat your food and stop arguing," Mother said unhappily.

Mengzi sighed and went in to lie down.

"She asked you to write a letter," his mother said, "so what are you doing?"

"I worked hard all day. I don't feel like going."

"She sent her daughter, so you have to go, whether you feel like it or not. Asking favors doesn't come easily to that poor woman. Maybe Ying'er can go."

"I'm not the one she asked." Ying'er winked at Mengzi. "You won't find me volunteering to do things for people. Besides, she wouldn't want me there anyway."

Mengzi got up, reluctantly. Ying'er laughed. "You should be an actor." He left.

Shuangfu's wife greeted Mengzi coolly and sent her daughter out for cigarettes. He shut the door, grabbed her, and pressed her up against the door, covering her with frantic kisses. After a few moans, she pushed him away. "I thought you'd forgotten about me."

"I've been aching for you."

"I don't believe you."

"I don't care," Mengzi said as he wrapped his arms around her, bit her lips softly, and reached down to untie her pants.

"Not now. The girl will be back soon. Wait till she's in bed."

"I can't stay. They know I'm here, and will wonder why it took all night to write a letter."

"You're scared." She sneered. "Then why are you here? I think you don't want your brother's pretty wife to get jealous. No wonder—"

"Ai! No one has a body like yours." That made her smile.

They jumped when they heard a loud knock at the door during mid-flirtation. It was her daughter back with cigarettes.

"Stupid girl," she scolded her daughter, who tossed the cigarettes on the table wordlessly and took her schoolwork into her room. "Have some manners, you stupid girl." No response.

"She's older now, so we have to be careful," she whispered, then raised her voice: "That damned Shuangfu is all puffed up, giving money to the school for no reason. I hear the township is going to give him a plaque and a ceremony, complete with gongs and drums. Is that right, Juanjuan?"

"Do you mind not talking so much? I'm doing my homework."

"Silly girl. I need to find out if he still wants us or not. If he does, what'll he do about it? If not, he'll have to tell me what to use, a knife, a rope, or something else, to wrap things up. We can't go on like this, half dead and barely alive."

"What's the problem?" Mengzi asked. "He sends you money all the time. What else do you want from him?"

"What do I want? I don't care about that little bit of money."

"What do you care about?"

"I don't really know."

They heard the girl pound her desk. She knew her daughter was showing her displeasure over her mother flirting with another man, so she winked at Mengzi and murmured, "She's old enough that I shouldn't be doing this."

"That's true. Better behave yourself from now on. Go get a hundred coins and, when you can't sleep at night, toss them on the floor and then grope for them in the dark one by one. That should clear those ideas out of your head."

"I'm not some horny widow."

"Widow?" Meng smiled. "You're like the chaste Wang Baochuan, who knew her share of men while she waited for her husband's return."

That earned him a pinch on the face. She smiled.

"What's your name, by the way?" Mengzi asked.

"I can't believe this. You don't even know my name, after what we've done."

"I only know that people call you Shuangfu's wife. I'd like to know your real name. Actually, I don't know most of the village women's names."

She fixed her dark eyes on him and said, "You can call me Xiuxiu if you want."

"That's a pretty name for a slim girl, but it's wasted on you." Mengzi laughed.

"That's true." She laughed too. "No one's ever seen a fat Xiuxiu." She sighed. "I'm aging fast. I'll be old before I know what life's all about. Decades fly by while you're taking a nap."

"Quiet down, will you? I'm doing my homework," Juanjuan complained.

"We're not forcing our words into your ears," her mother scolded. "What is this? A first-grader acting like a college student."

"Let's cut the chat and work on the letter."

The woman laughed and whispered to Mengzi "What's the point? He's never written back. That girl—how about this? You go home now and come back later. There's something else I want to talk to you about. Will eleven work? Just tell them you're going to play cards."

When Mengzi got home and saw Ying'er, he said, "That petty woman was mad when she heard that Shuangfu had donated money to the school. She wanted me to write to show her anger."

"I didn't ask you why you went," Ying'er replied with a smile.

"I wasn't talking to you. I was talking to myself."

She giggled. Laoshun, on the other land, scowled and said, "I think she's up to no good. Why dress like that when her husband's away? Be careful not to pick up her stink."

"You won't get a crooked shadow if you stand up straight, " Mengzi said.

"It depends on how straight you stand," Ying'er said. Laoshun took two powerful puffs of his pipe, sending sparks into the air. "A fly won't touch an egg that isn't cracked," he said, drawing a confused look from Mengzi, who stared at his father foolishly before glancing at Ying'er and Hantou. Ying'er burst out laughing and Mengzi's sense of shame turned to anger. He felt like talking back, but didn't know what to say.

"Actually, it's not his fault," Ying'er said. "She sent her daughter, and Mother told him to go. It's just a letter, no big deal. People without stomach problems aren't afraid of eating watermelon, don't you think?"

Mengzi was grateful for the help. But she seemed to be insinuating something. Was he afraid of eating watermelon? Did he have a "stomach problem?" He fell silent for a moment before saying loudly: "Are you done? All this talk makes my head ache." With a dismissive wave, he walked out. He would not need an excuse to go out later. Too bad it was so early. Her daughter was probably still awake, which meant he could not go visit the woman called Xiuxiu. He chuckled at the ill-fitting name as he headed to Beizhu's house.

4

Fengxiang was sitting on the edge of the bed, noisily sewing shoe soles while she scolded her daughter in a voice that seemed to squeeze words through her teeth.

"What's wrong?" Mengzi asked. "Are you all right?"

Fengxiang smiled and offered him a seat, giving her daughter a chance to slink over to her grannie's house.

"Where's Beizhu?"

"You don't know?"

Recalling what his father had said about Beizhu's arrest at the grain station, Mengzi was amazed by her composure. She should have been wailing and cursing. "I'm surprised you can sit there so calmly."

"What else can I do? All you wind up with when your head is lopped off is a bowl-sized scar. What's there to be afraid of?"

"I guess you're right."

"He wouldn't have been caught if he'd been careful. Obviously, he's in for a beating."

"A beating? I don't think they'll stop there. They'll likely want to punish him more severely as a warning to others, like killing a chicken to scare the monkeys."

"They won't kill him, will they? They'll feed him if he goes to jail, and I'll be here when he gets out. But he can pay his own fine. This rag of a blanket and a few kids are all we have. They can have them. Look around. What else is there? Nothing but our lives."

Mengzi knew that the authorities had taken their furniture because they exceeded the birth quota, but his eyes followed her fingers around the dark, empty room anyway.

"There's nothing left." She turned shrill. "If they can rob us in broad daylight, why can't we steal a little something on the sly? We all have to live, don't we?" Her outcry turned to laughter that brought on tears, and she began to weep. Mengzi didn't know what to do. Fengxiang dried her tears and threw the shoe sole down on the bed.

"You've been to school, Mengzi, so tell me the truth. Who's responsible for having a boy or a girl?" Her question was met with silence, so she continued. "It's so strange. Why do I keep having girls? Beizhu complains about me giving him girls. But I say to myself, the seed decides everything. He gives me girl seed, so naturally I give him a baby girl. If he gave me some boy seed, he'd have a son. Women are like a plot of land, you know."

"Yes." He smiled. "Since you already know, why ask me?"

"It's complicated, like wrapping yarn around a chicken's neck. I'm getting confused. Just tell me, who decides, the man or the woman?"

"The man."

"There you go. Beizhu is an idiot. He keeps saying I'm the problem, while it's him all along. He blames me even though he doesn't give me good seed. How fair is that!"

“It’s not fair,” Mengzi said, and then quipped, “But you’re to blame too. Why not borrow some good seed since his is bad? If he can add a leg to the baby in his sister-in-law’s belly, why don’t you borrow his brother’s seed?”

“Baigou?” she sneered. “I can’t stand the sight of him.”

“Why’s that?”

“Why? You know why. In the past he and that damned mother of his made my life a living hell. He enjoyed it. That’s enough about him. It makes me mad just thinking about it.”

“No problem. People can grow to like each other. Like they say, one night together wins a life-time’s attachment.”

“Nonsense. You can go have a life-time’s attachment with a stray dog.”

Mengzi felt his body heating up as they bantered, and he realized that they were more or less flirting. Every time he came to their house, Beizhu and Fengxiang talked dirty to each other. Sometimes she’d be so blunt she made him blush. Before getting involved with Shuangfu’s wife, he’d whiled away lonely nights by relishing the sultry, slutty words from Fengxiang’s mouth. Now he was uncomfortable. Beizhu was his friend, and a man can get into his friend’s clothes but not his wife. He cast a guilty look at her and got up to leave after some more small talk. Fatigue had removed his earlier carnal desire, so he decided to forget his date and go home to sleep.

5

The beating of gongs and drums filled the village morning, which, as Mengzi knew, meant that students and teachers were delivering the plaque to Shuangfu’s house. He chuckled when he recalled the day before and wondered how she'd reacted to his non-show at night. She'd give him hell when she saw him. Muttering to himself uneasily, he followed the crowd to the show at Shuangfu's house.

The gongs and drums were quiet when he got there, having been replaced by a man with a neck like a duck who was giving a speech, mainly expressions of gratitude to Shuangfu, with phrases like "A contribution to the current generation but with beneficial effects reaching far into the future." Mengzi knew the man, a township official who was said to be in charge of education and often came to the school. He was a rousing speaker, his words oozing with bureaucratic bluster to dumbfound the villagers. Mengzi noticed how he punctuated his speech with constant glances at Shuangfu's wife, whose face glowed with a satisfied look. He hated that look and wondered if she was involved with him. Why else would he flatter Shuangfu like that? Even more upsetting was the absence of torment on the face of the woman called Xiuxiu after being stood up. She obviously didn't care about him, and her manner and appearance showed her approval of what her husband had been doing. Mengzi was not happy.

Two young teachers carried a plaque with the inscription, "Contribution To Native Place," and stood it by the door. The plaque, bright red with gold letters, added color to the ordinary door. He did not understand what "native place" referred to, and he was sure that neither Shuangfu, his wife, nor the villagers knew either. But it must mean something good, and she knew that. Just look at that stinking swagger. Mengzi felt resentment. She was putting on an act, parading her smug satisfaction. But who was she doing it for? Not him, obviously. Who, then? Like Meng Eight sniffing out traces of his prey, Mengzi searched her face, until he noticed that she was looking at women in the crowd out of the corner of her eye. Each time her eyes swept past them, a gloating smile emerged around her lips. Now he understood. She was covering her sadness with a display of superiority; deep down she was lonely and weak.

Big Head, the team leader, began speaking when the official was finished.

"Eh—Shuangfu is a decent man who remembered us after striking it rich, not like those ingrates who don't even know who we are after they make it big and turn greedy. You dicks don't recognize us, and we don't know you. You're all dicks, eh—just because you've made some stinking money. But Shuangfu's not like that. Who did he think of first? The school, the children, this mud hut. As the saying goes, a house made of gold or silver is no match for a mud hut back home. Hei—there's nothing wrong with a mud hut. Shuangfu is a decent man, with a good heart. Hei—it's good to have a good heart. That's all I have to say."

The villagers laughed at Big Head, filling the yard with guffaws. When Mengzi saw Shuangfu's wife laugh with him, he recalled her name and his heart stirred. He wished he hadn't stood her up the night before.

"That ass Shuangfu has done all right for himself. He gave fifty thousand without batting an eye. That's a big deal," Mengzi heard a villager say.

"He may be a stranger, the crafty ass," another volunteered, "but he's no miser. Fifty thousand! I get goose bumps just thinking about it."

"Yeah. I hear he gets a virgin every night, and each time it's eight thousand, maybe ten. So what's fifty thousand to him? A few less nights with women, that's all."

"A few less nights? You don't know what you're talking about. You really think he'd be poor after giving away this little bit of money?"

"But earning it wasn't easy. Doing business out on the street means you have to plead with Grandpa and beg from Grandma. That's not the carefree life we enjoy."

"You're right about that. And you can't take it with you."

The talk amused Mengzi, who wondered how Shuangfu would react if he heard it. He was probably convinced that the village was beyond grateful for his fifty thousand yuan, but in fact, people were saying all sorts of things about him. If you knew, you wouldn't be strutting around like a proud dick, Mengzi said to an invisible Shuangfu, and looked over at the woman again. She had spotted him and paused before sweeping the crowd with her eyes again. A hint of sorrow and anger had replaced the smug look.

"She still likes me," Mengzi said, buoyed by his discovery.

The gongs and drums started up again, after what needed to be said had been. The students banged with all their might, crowding the yard with their racket. The annoying din washed away the budding vanity in Mengzi's heart; he saw the township official chatting with Shuangfu's wife and thought she might turn to look at him. She didn't. Shit, Mengzi thought angrily, all she needs is a man, any man, one with a dick, to make her happy. With an irate stomp of his foot, he stormed out of the yard and went home.

Hantou was coming out of the house when Mengzi arrived.

"I'm glad you're home. Will you work my shift at the well tonight? Something's wrong here." He touched his ribcage.

"What happened? You look terrible." Mengzi was shocked by his brother's pallid face.

"Nothing. I think the night shifts have tired me out."

"Then take something."

"I'm not made of clay. Besides, medicine is too expensive. We can't afford it."

After a few attempts to console his brother, Mengzi left to work at the well.

Besides the dull pain in his ribcage, Hantou was exhausted, so he went to lie down in his room. Though his work at the well wasn't tiring, the rumbling drill and noisy machinery assaulted his ears daily. Now he found the quiet around him strange. The occasional rooster crow was sharp and shrill, head piercing and discordant. The noise his mother made in the kitchen similarly grated on his ears. His father had taken the sheep into the desert, Ying'er was out raking the field, and Mengzi was at the well; he was the only one idling at home, belly up. Embarrassed, he got up, drank a glass of water, and went into the kitchen.

"I'll go rake the field, Mother."

"Get some rest. You've been working too hard. They can handle that little bit."

"I'm not made of flour. No need to rest. Besides, I was born to toil like a donkey. I can't stand having nothing to do."

"Then go fix the pigpen."

He mumbled a response and walked out.

A sharp pain struck his ribcage as he worked, but he kept mixing the mud, trying to ignore it. His mother walked in with a bundle of straw and tossed it into the pit he'd dug to help him with the mixing. She noticed he was rubbing the area around his ribcage.

"What's wrong?" She cried out before he could answer. You look terrible; your face is yellow."

"It's nothing." He cracked a smile. "It just hurts a little."

She took the shovel from him and insisted that he go to the local pharmacy. He promised he'd go after they finished repairing the pigpen.

Alarmed shouts came through the opening on the newly finished pigpen wall. He and his mother saw a thick column of smoke.

"Fire!" He shouted as he ran toward the smoke, where Gimpy Five's son, Wuzi, was clapping and laughing at a flaming haystack. Women were shouting, but none dared come close, obviously fearful of him. Hantou knew that the young man was mentally deranged and loved to chase women. He must have set the fire. Hantou ran up with the half bucket of water left from his work and doused the fire, which sizzled, but then rose up again.

"Go get help," he shouted to the women, who were frozen with fear and shock. They ran off with a yelp, while he shook the bucket helplessly. He tossed it aside and picked up a spade to shovel dirt onto the fire. His mother went back to the yard to get another spade and shoveled alongside him. The fire died down until there was nothing but dense smoke.

Villagers who had heard the racket arrived with water to douse the embers, thickening the air with more smoke. Afraid that some embers remained and might flare up again, Hantou spread the wet, black and yellow hay out on the ground with his spade.

Now relieved, they finally heard Wuzi's giddy laughter. Hantou looked at him and shook his head, sighing wordlessly.

"Unbelievable. It would have burned the house down if you hadn't spotted it," his mother said.

"Beat the hell out of that ass," Goubao said. "Look, he's laughing."

"Why?" Hantou said. "He's not right in the head. Why hasn't his father taken him to see a doctor?"

"He has," Fengxiang said. "But they have to take him to Lanzhou.

Grannie Wu said they're still trying to find the money, and they'll go once they have enough."

They chatted as Wuzi, excited by women's voices, ran up to grab a woman and howled. The villagers dragged him off, and Goubao hit him in the back, but that had no effect; it was as if he were hitting a donkey.

"Take him back to Gimpy Five," Big Head Sun said, looking at Goubao. "Tell him to keep his son under guard or he'll be responsible if anything happens. And tell him I've got a little money if he needs more. He can come get it and take the boy to see a doctor."

With the help of others, Goubao bundled Wuzi off.

Chapter Five

1

Lingguan did not expect to find a shepherd in the heart of desert.

A man of indeterminate age from constant exposure to the baking sun, he had a young man's shape and was quick on his feet. Dust was etched into the bronzed furrows of his brow, and he wore a hat, blackened by rain and wind, that was more symbol than headwear, its tattered brim offering little protection from the sun. Wind swept his shaggy beard aside with each gust, giving him an air of easy grace.

His flock was spread across the desert hollow, grazing on grass touched by autumn frost. The occasional bleat lent the space around them an air of desolation. Fresh from the brutality of the hunt, Lingguan was captivated by the scenic beauty. His heart rippled, as if by a warm breeze. It was simply beautiful. The sky was blue, the clouds silvery white, all suspended above the yellow sand, the white sheep, and the old yet sprightly shepherd. Staff in hand, he calmly looked Lingguan over, a strange serenity stamped on his face.

"Bagged a fox, I take it," he said, noting the dead animal over Lingguan's shoulder.

"Tending sheep, I see." Lingguan echoed mimicked the man's tone.

Neither answered the other's question, since these were, in fact, mere greetings.

"Damned strange," the shepherd muttered. "We're out here all year, and I've never seen even the shadow of a fox, while you people shoot them almost daily."

"You scare them off. The slightest noise spooks them and they run off before you see them."

Meng Eight walked up, tying his trouser cord. "Hey!" he shouted. "I thought you were dead, you old scoundrel."

The shepherd laughed. "You're the scoundrel. After you feast on fox, the only place you can get rid of the stink is on your daughter in-law. Aiya. Is this your grandson?" he asked, an awkward smile showing his embarrassment over the inappropriate comment he'd made about the boy's mother.

"No."

"Oh, then don't pay any… got some tobacco? I've been out here eight days and I'm dying for a smoke. I can do without everything but grain number six. Being out in this forsaken place, not seeing a soul for ten days or more and nothing to smoke is killing me."

"Why don't you just pretend you're a donkey that doesn't smoke?" Meng wisecracked as he took out his pipe. The shepherd snatched it out of his hand, lit it, and took a satisfying puff, which he held in a long time. It emerged as a light mist. "Ai!" he exclaimed with obvious delight. “That went all the way to my brain. Don’t forget to pack tobacco, I told that beggar son of mine, not once, but twice. And that was the only thing he forgot!” He took another puff and let the smoke swirl around in his lungs.

Meng Eight looked at him with a twinkle in his eye, but said nothing so as not to spoil the mood. With no interest in whether Meng was listening to him or not, the shepherd smoked and talked, talked and smoked.

“I’ve got plenty of flour, but I haven’t got a donkey’s stomach. I don’t know if his head’s stuffed with paste or chaff. If my wife farts, it’s imprinted on his heart, but anything his old man says goes unnoticed, like hitting cold water with a stick.”

He smoked on, not looking at either of them, which Lingguan found amusing. Maybe he can’t stop talking because he has no one to talk to most of the time, Lingguan reckoned.

“Haven’t you got the balls to dress your son down, you old scoundrel?” Meng said with a chuckle. “I don’t think so. You’re out in the desert, because you were found in your daughter-in-law’s bed, a bad place to be. Am I right or not, you old scoundrel?”

“Bullshit,” the shepherd said with a smile. “I’m not like you, pretending to pick up your grandson so you can grab your daughter-in-law’s hand. Then you’ve got the nerve to say, ‘the baby’s hand is so nice and soft!’ Sure it is, but not as soft as her tits.” He giggled.

“You should know, you’ve done it yourself.” Meng joked in return. “It must be worth it. Tending sheep for a year to earn a little cash so you can cop a feel or two. A bargain. All you have to say is, ‘I’ve been out there a year already, and I can’t stop thinking about you, awake and asleep. Sucking on sheep’s teats is no match for a young mother’s breasts.”

Lingguan laughed. The lively banter swept away the bloody memories of the past few days. He was puzzled by why old men always joke about their daughters-in-law when they get together. Are they scratching an itch they can no longer find? Maybe. These thoughts were interrupted by a dark shadow, as he was reminded of Hantou's illness. It must be torture. Then came thoughts of Ying'er, and warm currents massaged his heart. Reminded of how he'd betrayed his own brother, he lifted the tail of the fox and let its dead eyes drive away these uncontrollable thoughts.

"Truth is," Meng said, "you should slow down. What has all these hard years brought you? You tended sheep for the agricultural co-op, and now that the land has been distributed, you're still tending sheep, alone in the desert spring, summer, fall, and winter. How much money is enough? When the immortal Iron Crutch Li tried to steal lamp oil from his neighbor, his plan was foiled, so he gave up on the mundane world. What did he say? Sons and grandsons have their own lot in life, so don't toil your life away for their sake. That's the truth. You can work yourself to death, but for what? As far as I'm concerned, you're throwing your life away here in the desert."

"I was born under an unlucky star, and there's nothing I can do about that." The old shepherd shook his head. "I can't stay cooped up at home. Toiling in the desert is my fate. Put me anywhere else, and I wouldn't know what to do with myself. That's just how it is. Besides, how else can I survive in times like this."

Meng Eight heaved a sigh. "I know what you mean," he said as his brow crinkled and he sucked on his pipe. "But why are you out here alone?" he asked after a moment.

"Huang Two went to Pig's Belly Well to pay off a debt."

"For what?"

"Water for his sheep. Harelip has made enough from the well to get himself a wife, a woman brought over by a wool merchant. It didn't cost him much." The shepherd squinted and turned to look at the sheep that were moving farther down the dune.

"He deserves it. He must be in his forties."

"Forty-two."

Meng Eight wound the tobacco pouch around his pipe, picked up his canteen, and drank. He held it out to the old fellow, who shook his head and patted the canteen on his hip. So Meng handed it to Lingguan, and then took up his musket, removed the buckshot pouch and loaded it. Lingguan drank a few mouthfuls and loaded his musket with buckshot too.

"Let's go," Meng said as he stood up.

"Hold up a minute," the shepherd said as he took a steamed roll out of a little canvas bag. He offered it to Lingguan, who was puzzled by the gesture.

"Take it," Meng smiled. "It's the custom, symbolizes good hunting. Ha-ha. I guess I can go without and help out an old chain smoker." He poured half the contents of his tobacco pouch into the shepherd's pouch. The gift was received with smiling eyes.

The plaintive bleats of his sheep reverberated in his heart. What a lonely old man. Out here with only the blazing sun, the wind, and the arid sand to keep him company, the only sound the bleating of his sheep. Those feeble, helpless bleats that sounded like pleas added to the bland nature of the desert, leading to feelings of helplessness and loneliness among the people in it. The old man, shepherd's crook in hand, saw them off, a small dot in the vast desert, his sheep scattered like crumbs across the dunes.

"Are there many shepherds in the desert?" Lingguan asked Meng

Eight.

"Lots of them, especially around Magang."

"Where do they live?"

"Live? Caves and places like that, anywhere they can stay out of the elements. Live? If they were looking for comfort, they'd be home in bed."

"How long do they stay out?"

"It depends. Some stay out for months, others are desert dwellers year round. They mainly travel in pairs, so when they run out of food, one of them can go for supplies."

Lingguan narrowed his eyes and sighed as he scanned the desert terrain. The dunes rose like angry ocean waves, each higher than the one before; the sharp drops between the crests and valleys created an air of vitality. His mind and body soaked up the sallow tones unique to the desert. Cruelty, silence, and death existed amid the collapsed hollows and dried riverbed. But there was more: abundance, power, and majesty that warmed the blood. In the midst of such magnificent scenery, a person is ashamed of pettiness and convinced that human disputes amount to nothing.

"That old guy leads a tough life," Meng Eight said. "Stuck out here in the desert, hollowing out spots to sleep at night on twigs and straw. Battered by winds, baked by the sun. So hard… and meaningless. Why does a man struggle to survive? You can't take it with you."

"It doesn't seem so bad," Lingguan said, intrigued by the peculiar lifestyle. He felt a sense of peace after several days involved in the bloody business of hunting. He had found a spot removed from fame and fortune, removed from trial and tribulation, removed from open strife and veiled struggle, where his sole companions were the desert, a flock of sheep, and his own soul. It was a haven of peace. Everything had faded into the distance to create a lonely beauty.

"Go over to Magang and have a look around. Maybe you'll find some daytime tracks," Meng said to Lingguan before sitting down on a sandy ridge, taking out his pipe, and enjoying a leisurely smoke.

Lingguan snorted a response, knowing that he was being given a chance to see what he'd learned.

By then he had learned how to distinguish daytime from nighttime tracks, but still could not tell what time of day or night, early or late, they had been left. He knew what he was supposed to be looking for, that predawn tracks were larger and tracks made in the light of day showed a sense of urgency and panic. But he only knew the principal behind that. He had not learned how to tell what a fox was feeling and thinking by examining its footprints; he could not tell the minute differences between them. The same was true for nighttime prints. He knew that the difference lay in how and when foxes preyed on rats: tracks laid early at night were covered by those left by rats, while those laid late at night covered the rat tracks, but those between the two confused him. He had not learned how to tell the time of night the tracks were laid, whether by male or female foxes, or the size and number, all easily managed by Meng.

The ability to discern differences in tracks was an essential quality of every hunter worthy of the name. It not only effectively conserved energy, but also was critical in rationing provisions for different stages of the hunt. A hunter had to absorb every drop of water he carried with him, and could go all day long without urinating. Often, their canteens would still be half full when they returned to their camp.

Meng Eight had yet another special talent. He could unerringly point out spots where a fox had slept the night before. He knew fox habits inside and out, and could tell you when and in what sort of weather one would come to a particular spot to feed. If you went there to see for yourself, you would find a knot of overlapping prints, signs that a savage feeding frenzy had occurred there the night before, involving a certain number of male and female foxes, some of them pregnant. Meng Eight hunted only male foxes, partly because their pelts were superior, but mainly because the females produce new generations of foxes. Meng Eight said that the females had supernatural powers and that most fox fairies were females. During the third or fourth months of the year, after the females had borne their litters, they pay homage to the moon and beseech the heavens not to rain; when it rained, the newborn kits would either drown or develop a fatal rash. It also drowned rats, eliminating a food source for the foxes. Rain created a natural disaster for foxes, and some believed that the dryness of the desert had evolved through homage paid to the moon by female foxes.

Killing female foxes brings bad luck, Meng Eight had said.

2

"Look there!" Meng Eight shouted.

An injured fox was staggering toward them, lurching from side to side, its equilibrium shattered. It didn't spot them until Meng Eight ran toward it, and it no sooner turned to run away than he fired.

"Hei, fallen fruit just waiting to be picked up." He laughed.

The fox struggled to its feet, took a couple more steps, and collapsed as Meng Eight rushed over and prodded it with the barrel of his musket. The fox attacked it with its teeth, crunching down as hard as it could.

"Hei, let's see which is harder, your teeth or my musket." He howled with laughter as he pushed down on it; the fox let go with its teeth and screeched in pain.

A red-faced man ran up onto the ridge, breathing hard, and saw Meng tormenting the screeching fox. He sat down, clearly dejected.

Lingguan did not have to be told that the man had shot badly, hitting but not killing the fox with a belly shot. Custom dictated that the pelt went to the one who actually killed the animal. "You wasted a bullet, didn't you?" Meng mocked the man. "This is the worst possible outcome, enough to upset anyone who has it happen to them."

The man looked up. "I know the custom, so I screwed up. What else do you want from me? Shit, four or five days without a single fox, and when one comes along, I miss the vital spot. Even so, I should have been able to catch up with it. Why did it have to land in your sights? Hei, my bad luck."

"Four or five days without seeing any? I see them every day."

"I searched till it got dark. Who knows where they were hiding?"

Meng Eight chortled as he winked at Lingguan. "What are you doing hunting foxes when you can't even follow their tracks? How many years have you been doing this?"

"Years? I just started."

"There's more than one road and more than one type of food in the world, so why force yourself to work at something you're not good at?"

"I've got no choice. I wouldn't spend my days taking animals' lives if I didn't have to. My son's old enough to get married, and I'd never see that day by scraping out a living in the field. It's up to me to make it happen. And this is the only way I can do that. My son nearly worked himself to death for a whole year, but had nothing to show for it. Why? The damned foreman ran off before he got paid, and no one's seen him since, that's why. This is what the world's come to."

Seeing that the fox was dead, Meng kicked it. "You're not cut out for this line of work," he said. "Trusting to blind luck won't get you anywhere. You'll be down feeling the King of Hell's crotch before you touch a single hair on any daughter-in-law."

The humiliated man shot an angry look at Meng."You've got yours," he said, "and you don't know what it's like to have nothing. I told you I've got no choice. I wouldn't take all this shit if I did."

"Go gather desert rice and sell it in town, eighty cents a cattie. Artemisia is worth even more, more than a yuan. It's hard work, but better than trying something you're not made for."

"How long do you think it would take to gather enough of the stuff to pay to get my son married? No, fox hunting's the way to go. At two or three hundred a pelt, a few dozen will fetch a nice daughter-in-law. Pick desert rice? My son would be an old man before I sold enough of it."

"What you've got there is a pipe dream," Meng Eight said. "A few dozen, you say, like picking fleas out of your crotch. Frankly, you're working in the dark, because if you can't make sense out of fox tracks, you're like a blind cat bumping into a dead mouse. You go after the first set of prints you see, and you'll never get close enough to a fox to smell its farts, even if it costs you an arm and a leg. If it's a night track, ten days won't be enough. Every track you find will take you three days to crack, and the animal will be long gone before you catch up with it. It goes where the food is, and isn't out there waiting for you to kill it. You don't believe me? Today you were like a blind donkey bumping into a haystack. You found a sick fox, you know that, don't you? Just look at its shabby coat. It was sleeping in a sunny spot, wasn't it? I'm telling you, only old and sick foxes do that."

The man's face fell. There was nothing he could say. Clearly dejected, he could only heave a sigh.

Meng prodded the carcass with his foot. "You know the custom," he said. "You wounded it, I killed it, which means it's mine. But if you'll take my advice to go home and give up this line of work, you can take it with you."

The man raised his head, wide-eyed, as if he couldn't believe it.

Meng turned to Lingguan. "Let's go." He walked off with his musket. The man stood there transfixed for a moment before running down the sandy ridge with a muffled whoop of joy and picking up the dead fox.

Without a word, Lingguan followed the man down. "It's all right," Meng said. "Let him have it, the poor guy. If he went home without a single fox he'd be ashamed to walk in the door."

Lingguan looked admiringly at Meng Eight. He knew from personal experience how hard it was to bag a fox for its pelt, so he could understand how miserable the man must have felt. He'd thought about suggesting exactly what Meng had done, but didn't know how to say it. Does it violate a taboo? he wondered. Was this the good luck bestowed upon them by the old shepherd's steamed roll? And could they give that luck away to the man along with the dead fox? No, it was better not to say anything, since he hadn't anticipated Meng's generosity.

There was a shout behind them. Lingguan turned to see the man running after them, musket in hand, dead fox slung over his shoulder. When he reached them he flung the fox to the ground at their feet. "I can't take this," he said. "If I ignored the custom, what would that make me?" His face was red and sweaty, his words came in gasps. The front of his shirt was stained with fox blood.

"What custom!" Meng Eight barked unhappily. "People decide what's a custom and what isn't. You didn't take that, I gave it to you. That's how you make friends. This'll get you in the door at home with no sense of shame. Take up another line of work. You don't have the knack for this one. Blind luck won't get you anywhere."

The man wiped his sweaty forehead, still slightly out of breath. He reached into his bag and retrieved a stack of pre-cut cigarette paper, out of which he removed a wrinkled banknote and stuffed it into Meng Eight's hand. "Buy yourself a pack of cigarettes," he said. Meng's face darkened as he snatched it away and threw the note down on the dead fox.

"Damn," he said. "Money! If I wanted money, why would I take this instead of going home with a pelt worth hundreds?" He stormed off.

The man just stood there, wringing his hands and looking for something to do. Then, as he watched Meng Eight's retreating back, he took something out of his pack and handed it to Lingguan. "Give him this," he said. "Made from the wing of a black hawk." Lingguan looked down at his hand. It was a beautifully carved pipe. He was going to hand it back until he saw that the man was already on the verge of tears, his face red. Lingguan mumbled his consent.

They'd walked a li or more before Lingguan took out the pipe, fully prepared to get an earful. To his surprise Meng's eyes lit up as he snatched it away. "Where'd you get this?" When Lingguan told him, he shook his head and laughed. He rubbed the dark red stem. "Fine work," he said. "It's alive, still alive. Just look, the wing of a real black hawk, not some dead bone."

Meng gazed at the lowering sun. "That's enough for today," he said. "Let's go back. We can't stay out till we're blind."

3

The sun was still fairly high when they approached the camp. Meng Eight handed his backpack to Lingguan and told him to go on ahead.

They had pitched their tent in a hollow that served as a windbreak and kept them warm. When it came into view, the sight warmed Lingguan's heart. He hadn't enjoyed a good night's sleep for days, getting up at four or five in the morning to head out and not returning till after dark. His strength was on the wane, and he had lost weight. Weight loss is common among hunters; no one who goes into the desert to hunt can escape it. Meng Eight called it shedding blubber, the process of sloughing off unnecessary fat, which, after a few days, made you nimble and increased your stamina. Lingguan was not there yet; all he wanted was to sleep. It was still early, plenty of sunlight left, and he did not want to disturb Huaqiu, who loved to sleep. So he ducked into the tent.

He heard a sound like a moan, and by the time he realized it was an unusual noise, he was already in the tent.

And there was Huaqiu, pants down, on top of a girl who was naked from the waist down. Since he was looking down at them, he could see her face, and a shocked look. Huaqiu's face was ghostly pale. He had never expected them to be back so early. But he grinned, looking quite foolish, and muttered something unintelligible.

Lingguan was stunned. His mouth opened and closed, as he tried, but failed, to say why he was back. He just stood there for a moment before sensing he should leave them be.

His head was still swimming after he was outside the tent, and his legs were like rubber. What the hell was he doing! Lingguan said to himself. While he and Meng Eight were nearly killing themselves out there, this is what he was up to, the bastard. Lingguan's anger lessened the embarrassment and fluster he'd felt at first. He knew he couldn't just wait outside in front of the tent opening, so he sputtered, "I'll go check on the camel." Back out to the dunes he went.

She must have been the girl who was gathering hair moss, he said to himself. It had to be her. The image of her frightened, twisted face stuck in his mind, and it gave him a bad feeling. As he thought back to her sweet smile, a strange feeling made him sink into an ugly mood. To hell with her! She doesn't belong to me. What kind of girl is she to do something like that only a few days after they'd met, giving herself to Huaqiu, who's no better? And in our camp. You'd put a coffin in camp before you'd let two people have sex in it. It's a taboo and, people say that if you violate it, your weapon will blow up in your face.

Lingguan was mad at himself for fleeing the scene in panic. I'm not the one who did that, so why get so flustered? What should I have done? Should I have stood there, stuck my finger in his face, and told him to get out? Make him go do it in the desert? This is a hunter's tent, not a whorehouse or a breeding farm. Go on, get out! Lingguan imagined himself venting his anger at the two of them, and that helped calm him down.

A few moments later he heard a rustling sound and knew that Huaqiu was coming out. Lingguan felt his face heat up; it was awkward to see him. That was odd, as if he'd been the guilty one.

"Elder Brother Lingguan."

Huaqiu sounded odd. He normally called him by his name only, wearing an easy, mischievous grin, but now he tacked on "elder brother" because he had been caught in the act. You were never willing to call me elder brother or acknowledge the fact that I'm older than you before, so why "elder brother" now? Lingguan stifled a laugh; somehow, hearing him called this way gave him a warm feeling. He turned to look at Huaqiu, who was smiling, trying to look unworried, proof that there was something wrong, and he knew it. His smile was forced, actually little more than the barest of parted lips. But even that was wrong, since one side was opened wider than the other, about as unattractive as humanly possible. Lingguan could tell how embarrassed he was, so he decided not to look him in the eye.

"We've already talked about it. I'm going to marry her," he said, as if to justify his actions. It had an immediate effect on Huaqiu himself, as he seemed to loosen up. He looked to see what effect it had on Lingguan, who shrugged his shoulders and felt a weight fall from him. "Does her father know?"

"We haven't told him yet. He's a headstrong old guy." He sighed. "But he's getting better. He's had a couple of meals here, and I expect him in a little while so she can cook for him."

"Aren't you something, making friends with our provisions so you can get a wife."

"Hei, you know what it's like for them, seven or eight days without a proper meal. It's tough. You've seen the girl, her lips are all chapped."

Lingguan had to laugh. How could he have seen her chapped lips? He never got that close. The laugh gave Huaqiu the lift he needed.

"Don't tell my granddad."

"What are you afraid of?" Lingguan teased. "He'll grin until his eyes are mere slits knowing his grandson has got himself a wife."

"Not yet. There's a long way to go; we've barely begun."

"Barely begun? The rice is cooked, so what else needs to begin? You aren't just having fun with her, are you? That would be unforgivable."

"No, what I mean is, we haven't told her father. Who knows if he'll let us go ahead? She's got a sister-in-law and a nephew back home. Her brother died when a gold mine at Shuanglonggou collapsed. So who knows what churns in the stubborn old guy's stomach? Will he want her to marry into my family or me to marry into hers? She can marry me, but I won't marry into hers, not to move to some wretched place where wolves won't shit. Poverty is bad enough, but there's nothing but mountains there."

Lingguan knitted his eyebrows and stared at Huaqiu, but said nothing for a moment. "Then why did you do that? If the old guy won't let her marry you, you've ruined the girl."

"Ruined? How? She said she'd marry me if he approved. If not, she'd run away with me. It would turn out the same, wouldn't it?"

"It's not been easy for them to raise a daughter, and you've got no right to do something immoral. If he says no, then try to talk him around. He's got a heart, just like everyone else."

"Okay, I've heard enough. When you reach the mountain a path will open up. Let's not talk about that anymore. She's too embarrassed to start cooking, but she's worried, knowing her folks will be here in a while, expecting to eat. She's ashamed to face you."

"Spit it out. Do you want me to leave, give you some space?"

"No, you can stay. When dinner's ready, she'll feel collected enough to face you." With a childish grin, Huaqiu walked down the ridge alone. A few moments later, the girl walked shyly out of the tent.

4

Huaqiu hadn't expected her to become his so easily. The day after Lingguan talked about them, he'd crossed the ridge and gone to the dark gobi. He was far more socially adept than Lingguan, forming a relationship with the old man after handing him a couple of cigarettes. Stubborn as always, but bombarded by his wife's nagging and his daughter's begging, he'd sent her over to cook lunch for them the next day. It was noon, the most unforgiving part of the day, the time when the deathly quiet, dull, insipid desert brought out the most passionate primitive impulses and soulful needs. And so, the moment she entered his world, he pounced on her.

She resisted tenaciously. The surprise, outrage, and fright had lessened her beauty, but her struggle invested her with a powerful attraction, which in turn fueled flames of desire in Huaqiu. The lively, young body under him was wonderful beyond words. Each time she struggled, the shifting movement of her breasts and belly nearly drove him crazy. To him, the only flaw in her beauty was the dryness of her lips. The softness he sought when he kissed her was replaced by a rough, chapped feeling. He later discovered that a week or more without nutritious food was the cause.

Huaqiu had no idea how long the struggle lasted, but it felt like a very long time, and he was exhausted. Strangely, the girl did not cry for help. If she had, even knowing there was no one around, he'd have backed off and let her be. But she didn't; she just put up a fight. Then she clenched her teeth and glared at him, an expression that made her look prettier than when he'd first set upon her. He smiled and bit down on her lips. The chapped feel bothered him, but he loved hearing her moan.

He stopped biting her and began fondling her breasts, which, given her position on the ground, were not prominent, but felt soft and substantial in his hand. It felt so good he squeezed again and again. Reminded that she had stopped struggling and was moaning, Huaqiu found her to be beautiful. Her lips were red from being bitten, unhealthy, damaged. To him it was the most beautiful red in the world.

The girl's moans turned to heavy breathing. The sun screamed, blood roared.

She stopped struggling at the critical moment. Huaqiu did not know why. He was worn out, his urges under control. He reached for her trouser sash, a tentative probe, ready to retreat if she resisted. She didn't.

As sunlight rained down, Huaqiu began exploring in the dark. His every move was ridiculously clumsy, like a bull crashing madly through weeds looking for a path. He was trying to find his way ahead without knowing what he was looking for. He was ashamed of himself not for what he was doing, but for what he wasn't doing, and if the girl had mocked him, he would have fled in panic. But she just kept her eyes shut and moaned.

All of a sudden, a warm current engulfed him.

He got up, as if awakened from a dream. Seeing the girl's naked lower body made him feel that he had done something terrible. He wiped his sweaty body. "Get dressed," he said. She lay there, eyes shut, without moving after crossing her legs. It took a few moments before Huaqiu heard her sob. Her face was tear-streaked.

"I can't go on living after this," she said, coldly enunciating each word.

Shit! Huaqiu's tongue felt like leather. He got down on his knees and banged his head against the sandy ground before her, over and over. "I'm not a man, I'm a beast," he said as sparks shot through his head. "The sky has fallen, my life is over!"

Huaqiu was in torment. What kind of man am I? I'm a filthy animal, an educated filthy animal. He pounded his head as hard as he could, as if to drive away his sins. I'm despicable, he told himself. How could I have done something so rotten? I'm doomed.

The thought that she might get pregnant terrified him. He wouldn't be able to hide it from anyone in the village, like trying to wrap fire in paper. People spit on men who seduce girls. Seduce, is that what it was? No, it was rape. Rape! The word alone called up the image of a name on a court bulletin board, with the word "rapist" and a red checkmark indicating execution underneath it. He broke out in a cold sweat, horrified.

Will she report me? He looked over at the girl, who was drying her tears. Yes. Yes, she will. A bullet in the head awaits anyone who rapes a girl. A bad deal! Run away, he said to himself. That was a way out. She did not know where he lived, didn't even know his name. He was just a hunter. It was a big desert, with lots of hunters, so who would know who the "rapist" was? Yes, it could work. He took a long look at the contents of the tent, which no longer mattered, not when his life was at stake.

His thoughts turned to his grandfather and to Lingguan. He knew his grandfather would never forgive him. The ancestors will be jumping off the altar out of shame. Granddad will hang me up from a rafter and whip me the way he whipped Huaqiu's father years ago. I deserve it. For someone who's done something so horrendous and shameful, a whipping is light punishment. The image of Meng Eight, with his head held high, nearly froze his heart.

"How am I supposed to go on?" the girl sobbed.

"What do you think we should do? Tell me." Huaqiu had no idea, but she had said something, and what he heard was embarrassment. What did that indicate? It indicated that she was not going to report him. That was certain. Yes, she was too mortified to do that. Good! He was relieved, feeling that his life had been returned to him. Everything would be easy to take care of if she did not report him. If it cost him money, fine with him. Or anything else, for that matter. "I'll go along with whatever you say. How about a couple of fox pelts?" he ventured. "Two hundred apiece, what do you say?"

"That's what I'm worth, two fox pelts?"

"How many then? You can have these. Will that work? I'll say they were lost, or stolen. The worst that can happen is I get chewed out. Will that work for you? Everything else is pretty much worthless—food, water, bedding, even the tent." He took a nervous look around, wishing he'd brought something more valuable with him.

She shook her head. "Fox pelts are all you can think about, aren't they? Nothing else. Don't you have anything valuable?"

"No, I honestly don't. You can look for yourself if you don't believe me."

"Are you worth nothing?" She looked down.

It took him a moment to realize what she was getting at, and he rejoiced. Why hadn't that occurred to him? Marry her, and my problems are over. How foolish he'd been to get all worked up. He took a good look at the girl. She was not the wife he'd imagined for himself, he discovered. What sort had he wanted? Someone like Lanlan. Of course, she was already married. "She" looked nothing like Lanlan. Lanlan had fair skin and wasn't as strong. He'd had trouble overpowering her earlier—Lanlan's lips weren't cracked and dry. Nothing was as he'd expected. He could see now that she wasn't nearly as pretty as she'd been when he'd forced her down, and a shadow fell across his heart. Now that he didn't have to worry about giving up his life, he tried to imagine if she'd work out as his wife.

"Are you really worth nothing?" she repeated.

Huaqiu muttered a response as he wondered if she'd had her eye on him all along. Had she in fact seduced him in order to get out of that mountain village? She hadn't struggled as he undid her sash, and there was no blood. Maybe… maybe she wasn't a virgin. Was it a trap? Shaking his head unhappily, he forced himself to smile, so she wouldn't guess that he was thinking, and strike back. He had to laugh at himself for his choice of words—strike back. For her that would mean saying he'd raped her, and that would be disastrous. The thought made him feel that his life was floating away in a bubble, and he took another look at her, smiling to hide his thoughts.

She smiled back. Apparently, she'd taken his smile as a promise. Her smile threw a scare into Huaqiu. Obviously, she was a homely girl who turned attractive when she smiled. It made her pretty in a hard to describe way. She was a girl well served by smiling, and that realization made him change his mind. Marrying her wasn't such a bad idea.

Half an hour later, when her parents showed up for a meal, she and Huaqiu were talking and laughing like a couple.

5

In the end, Huaqiu's escapade came to light.

That occurred three days after Lingguan found out about him. The stubborn old man and his gaunt wife had, by then, already eaten two meals at their camp. They feasted on rabbits Meng Eight had shot. Lingguan detected a sense of enmity by the old man toward Huaqiu, since he avoided talking to him. He looked elsewhere or cast his eyes down when he had to talk to Huaqiu, and Lingguan guessed that he knew what had happened. At the very least, he saw that his daughter was acting differently, and he stared at her with a look of malignant anger. She cowered under that look and constantly stole glances at him.

Huaqiu, meanwhile, smiled as if nothing were the matter, as if oblivious to the old man's malice. The smile never faded as he pinched off the dough, lit the stove, cooked the food, and served it to his guests, along with a bit of chitchat. Lingguan took note of how he observed the old man, with a feigned casualness. But as soon as he saw the dark expression on the old man's face, his smile became one of mockery. It was as if to say, "Be as angry as you want. I still slept with your daughter."

Lingguan knew this would not end well.

As expected, three days after they'd eaten a meal of wild rabbit, the headstrong old man burst into the tent and slapped Huaqiu's backside with the sole of his shoe. Huaqiu hitched up his pants and ran outside. Hearing the sound of slaps inside, he stood there trying to decide if he should go back in and rescue the girl, when the old came at him with a knife. He took off running, until he reached a distant hollow, where he was finally aware of the old man's curses.

In the meantime Meng Eight and Lingguan had bagged a fox that was nearly as tall as a grown man with a fiery red coat. As they neared the camp in high spirits, some bird shit landed on Meng's head.

"That's a bad omen," he said. When they reached the camp with the skinned fox, they saw the old man standing angrily in front of the tent alongside two sobbing women.

"Huaqiu's in trouble," Lingguan said.

Meng Eight knew instinctively what had happened. He handed his musket to Lingguan and said to the old man, "Let's go inside." He told Lingguan to boil some water. Ignoring Meng, the old man turned to the sobbing girl and bellowed, "What are you crying about? I'm going to report the son of a bitch! I don't believe… there are laws… he ran off? Where can he run to, the motherfucker!" Learning that Huaqiu had run away, Lingguan breathed a sigh of relief.

"What's wrong?" Meng Eight asked with an innocent smile. "The sky hasn't fallen, has it? Let's talk inside. Come in."

The old man stiffened his neck. "There's nothing to talk about. He deserves to be shot for what he did, and I'm not going to let him off. I'll trade this old hide of mine for his young one."

Meng Eight was relieved as he detected a bluff in the old man's angry words. It didn't worry him that he was shouting angrily. He'd have worried if he hadn't shouted. A barking dog won't bite. The same principle holds true for people; a man who shouts about killing someone won't actually do it. If he was really going to report the boy, he would not have waited till Meng Eight returned to say so. Meng, a man of wide experience, knew he would have little trouble with this fellow. If he'd just sat there stewing, Meng would not have known how to deal with him, but clamoring removed that doubt. Meng hunkered down, took out his pipe, and began to smoke.

As Lingguan filled the pelt with sand, he took notice of the sobbing mother and daughter. There was blood at the corner of the older woman's mouth, probably from being slapped by her husband, who blamed her for everything, obviously. That's what men do. But she just dried her tears and cried softly. The girl, on the other hand, was bawling. Lingguan knew this hadn't been the first time, and crying was one way to cover that fact up.

The old man obviously had a bad temper, but was not especially shrewd. He glared at his daughter, wishing that looks could kill, it seemed.

Meng Eight was making plans as he smoked his pipe. He knew the old man would not easily relent. What exactly did he have in mind? Meng assumed that he saw this as a chance to get some money out of them. The problem for Meng was how to keep the losses to a minimum. He wiped the stem of his pipe with his lapel, added tobacco, and handed it to the old man. "Take it," he said, "enjoy a smoke."

Already unhappy at how Meng was enjoying a carefree smoke, the old man now had a reason to vent. Taking the pipe, he stood up and flung it away. It landed on a nearby ridge. The tobacco pouch had broken loose and now dangled from a nearby Artemisia bush.

"You fuckers!" he bellowed shrilly, his voice cracking. "You're trying to push me around. What kind of people are you?"

"What's that?" Meng shot back as he jumped to his feet. "Who are you calling fuckers? What are you doing here, talking or passing gas? This is our camp, not yours, so why are you here? Did I invite you? Maybe planning to steal our camel or our fox pelts, is that it?"

The old man was stunned. His face paled, then darkened. A moment later, with a shake of his head, he said, "You people took advantage of my daughter."

"Us people? Was it me?" He pointed to Lingguan. "Was it him?"

"That other boy."

"You mean the passerby? I don't know where he came from. He hadn't eaten for a while, so we fed him."

The girl looked at Meng Eight with fear in her eyes. She was ghostly pale. "He said he was with you. He was watching the camp while you were away." She was too shocked to be embarrassed.

"Yes, I gave him five yuan a day to watch our camp for us. We settled with him yesterday."

"Liar!" She was crying again.

"Bullshit!" The old man glared at Meng. "You're trying to get out of this. Well, it won't work. I'm going to report him for rape. I'll see him get a bullet in the head for this. Like I said, I'm willing to trade this old hide of mine for his young one."

"Go ahead," Meng taunted with a chuckle. "You can slice Huaqiu into pieces, I don't care. Report him, put whatever you want in his head, I don't care. Don't ask me where that whirlwind came from. Not only that, who's to say who seduced whom?"

"Bullshit!" The old man spit in the direction of his sobbing daughter. "Why don't you go kill yourself!" he snarled. "Our ancestors are hanging their heads in shame." He sat down on the sand and wrapped his arms around his head.

Meng Eight signaled Lingguan with his eyes and tossed his cigarette lighter over, pointing at the pipe on the ridge. Lingguan retrieved it and the tobacco pouch, filled it, and handed it to the old man, expecting him to fly off the handle again. But all he did was exhale through his nose, take the pipe, and began smoking.

The girl's sobs turned to wails of despair. Lingguan could tell from Meng's look that he was clipping the old man's wings, so he said nothing.

"Let's talk," Meng said. "Yelling and cursing won't accomplish a thing. Anybody can spout nonsense and lose their temper. But what good does that do?"

The old man said nothing. He sat there smoking. Again he exhaled through his nose.

"You can't change what's already happened," Meng counseled amiably, "it's a solution we need, not legal action. Yelling and screaming won't do us any good. We didn't grow up being frightened, so let's talk this out. What do you think we should do?"

"What do you say?" The man was relentless. "She was unspoiled. Now what's she going to do?"

After a long sigh, Meng quietly picked up the pelt and slowly continued filling it with sand, free and easy. Soon, even Lingguan felt the silence had gone on too long. "There's a way out of this," Meng said at last. "But we'll have to wait till the boy returns. If the little bastard did what you say, I'll take the responsibility to make things right. But we don't have any money, nothing but a few fox pelts that will bring in two or three hundred each. You tell me how many you want. Then you go your way, he'll go his, and no one will owe anybody anything."

"No!" the girl cried out.

Her father glared at her. "Shut your mouth!"

With a whimper she said, "He promised to marry me."

"And there's the other solution," Meng smiled. "The girl said it. She can marry my grandson—heh-heh, the truth is, he's my grandson. He's a decent boy, a good match for the girl. They're about the same age. He likes to enjoy himself. Boys are usually fathers by his age, but not him; he shakes his head when we bring up the subject of marriage, so he hasn't found himself a woman yet. He got lucky this time. We live in a pretty good place that's certainly no worse than your mountain village. Let's just make them a couple. There'll be plenty of betrothal gifts."

The old man sucked in his breath as if suffering from a toothache, but said nothing.

Huaqiu did not return till late that night. He heard drinking games when he was still far from camp.

Chapter Six

1

A disaster struck Lingguan's village the day after he returned from the desert: a cave-in at the unfinished well site. "The well caved in, burying the drill bit and wasting the twenty or thirty thousand yuan spent so far," Hantou said. "In its cruelty, Heaven has piled one disaster upon another."

He explained the disaster to the family: "As team leader, Big Head set the rules and then he broke them. Other people can control their women, so why couldn't he keep that sow of his in check? I heard she was having her period. Talk about bad luck! As much as twenty or thirty thousand. What a dumb asshole."

"Who was it, his wife or his mother?" Lingguan asked to be clear.

"His wife, of course."

"He'll have to pay. That was the agreement," Laoshun said firmly.

"Pay? He couldn't make that up if he sold everything he owned, including his old lady. Think about it, all that shouting about their donkey not eating? Was that such a big deal that she had to come looking for Big Head? I knew something bad would happen when I saw her run up to the well flailing her arms and cackling. She knew that women have to stay away from a well site, but she… that afternoon, sure enough, with a thunderous bang, the whole thing collapsed."

"You saw her. Why didn't you stop her?" Laoshun asked him.

"I tried. I went up to her, but she jabbed me here…" Hantou pointed to his ribcage. "It hurt, almost knocked the wind out of me. Then she kept running over to the well site."

"Does it still hurt after taking the medicine?" his mother asked anxiously.

"Only a magic elixir could work that fast," Hantou said. "I took a couple pills and feel a lot better. It's no longer a sharp pain, more like a dull ache. It's much better. Nothing to worry about… Maodan's filthy mouth was partly to blame; when he spotted her he shouted, 'Bad news, there's a woman here, it's going to collapse'… Gimpy Five ran up and slapped him, then shut his eyes and began to pray… but it didn't do any good, the well collapsed anyway."

"It's the way he said it," Laoshun said. "It all depends on the tone. If Maodan had kept his mouth shut, maybe nothing would have happened. As soon as he popped off, that did it. The same thing happened back when Xu Si from the Third Brigade decided to build a house. Some old guy said, 'that's too many rooms. Who's going to live in them?' That sounded unlucky at the time, and people complained about his big mouth. Within a few years, everyone in the family was dead, and all the rooms were vacant. Hei, that's the way it is.

Auspicious talk leads to good luck. Inauspicious talk leads to bad luck. It's all in the tone."

"That's what Gimpy Five said, but Maodan refused to take responsibility. He said he didn't say anything about the well collapsing. No one believed him, so he tried to get out of it by saying, "I mentioned collapsed wells a lot of times when there were no women around, and no well collapsed. How come it only collapsed when she showed up? You're a bunch of donkey dicks, looking for soft places to enter.' Well, Baigou's father picked up a shovel. 'You son of a bitch,' he said, 'you think you're some kind of hero, don't you? That's all you know how to do, talk about wells collapsing. He smacked Maodan in the ass with the shovel and knocked him down."

"What the hell does that have to do with Maodan?" Lingguan asked. "He's not some supernatural being who can make things happen. He's just poor. That's why people pick on him."

"The well team said the collapse had nothing to do with any woman or with Maodan. They said the soil was too crumbly, but no one would listen. So now… next year… we'll have to cough up more money."

"What does Big Head say?" Laoshun asked.

"Him? Are you kidding? He was too busy taking his donkey to the vet's. He's probably not back yet."

"Make him pay!" said Laoshun. "He set the rules, so he has to pay."

"Go talk to him," Lingguan's mother said. "Talking behind his back won't make you look tough. I'm just afraid you'll back off when you see him."

"What's there to be afraid of? He can't do anything to me."

"Then go."

"I want to be a bigger man than him, so to hell with it. Besides, the well's supposed to belong to everyone. So what if it collapsed? I'll kick in the same as everyone else, so why do I want to provoke him?" He took out his pipe and began to smoke.

"See what I mean," she said, "talking behind his back gets nothing done. Keep quiet if you haven't got the guts to do something."

Lingguan laughed. "Liangzhou men are like that. They talk big in private, but are no-shows when it counts. Why do you think there are so many corrupt officials?"

"Are you all saying I should make it my business? That I don't have the guts to do anything? The worst that can happen is that they put me up against a wall and shoot me. What worries me is that the rest of you will cry like a bunch of women."

"Ah," said his wife as she crinkled her nose. "I see you think you're someone we can't live without. Well, you're wrong. We might actually be better off. You think peppers won't grow without dog shit for fertilizer, is that it?"

"You old crone… okay, I'll do it. That dumb asshole can't hurt me. The worst that can happen is I lose my head and leave a bowl-sized scar." He rolled up his sleeves.

"You're just looking for an excuse. See what you look like in a puddle of your own piss. You're a second-rate rooster, no matter how you shake your feathers. Everybody knows how much butter is in your gut. Go smoke that goat hoof pipe of yours. We listen when you scream at us, but you'd bring shame to your ancestors if you picked a fight with Big Head. You might wet yourself before you're even out the door," his wife jeered.

That made Ying'er giggle. The others laughed along with her.

"So you think I won't do it, you old crone." He stormed out the door. “Big Head Sun, you son of a bitch, I’m going to make you pay!”

His wife paled and shoved Mengzi out the door. “Go, stop him before he does something stupid.”

“Nah, let him have some fun.” Mengzi was still laughing.

“Don’t be silly. This isn’t his fight, and that man’s no one to make an enemy of. You go, Lingguan.”

Lingguan walked outside, and was back in seconds. “Guess what? He’s lying down in his room. Did you really think he was going to go after Big Head?”

They had a big laugh.

2

Lingguan and Mengzi went to the well site after dinner. The place was all lit up, with villagers crowding around to grieve over the loss of their hard-earned money and their dream, now nothing but a black hole. Big Head Sun was squatting atop the well platform, head bowed, looking as despondent as a condemned man. “Get out of here, all of you!” Meng Eight thundered at village kids. “There’s nothing to see. Everything’s drowned in mud, even the drill bit.” With the well gone, the taboo had left as well; women stood around chattering and occasionally pointing to the despondent Sun as an expression of their anger and a display of their dissatisfaction. Whenever the topic of next year’s costs for a new well came up, it was met with loud sighs.

The men were, in the main, silent, some squatting, others standing. From time to time one of them would walk up to the ruined well and groan.

Gimpy Five looked more crestfallen than ever. He had to sell off some grain every time he took his son to see a doctor. He had little left to sell, and the thought of kicking in next year for a new well was like stabbing him in the heart. "How are we going to live, I ask you, how? Is Heaven blind, or what?" He paced the area talking to himself.

"These things happen all the time," the leader of the drill team said. "Wells collapse if you're not careful. When one like this collapses, we lose too. That drill bit cost thousands and, poof, it's gone just like that."

"You work for the government!" Gimpy Five shouted, so loud he even scared himself and lowered his head. "We," he said sadly, "we're the big losers. Whip a gecko, it dies, it doesn't have a chance. Just like us." His voice weakened.

"What's the big deal? If a well collapses, drill another one, what's wrong with that?" one of the women said.

"Who said that?" Gimpy Five spun around, infuriated, looking like he was ready to fight.

"I did. Was I wrong?" It was Shuangfu's wife. "It's gone, but we still need one, and it won't get dug with complaints." She did not raise her voice.

"Sure, that's right," Gimpy Five said, his head still lower. "And you, you're the scrotum of the god of wealth, I suppose. But the rest… of us… have to tighten our throats."

"I know. Your son is sick, so don't worry, I'll kick in your share, how's that? However much they want you to come up with, all right?" This too she spoke calmly.

"We all heard that come out of your mouth." Gimpy looked up. "Did you hear her, Big Head? She made the offer."

"Of course. Everyone here heard me. Why lie to you over that little bit of money?"

"Little bit? There are three of us. This year it cost me two hundred."

She laughed. "I said however much. Wuzi's sick, I know that. Don't be so sensitive. I mean what I say."

Gimpy Five stared wide-eyed and tongue-tied at the woman for a long moment before holding his head in his hands and bursting into tears. "I'm worthless," he sobbed. "My pride, all gone… I don't… I don't want anything."

"You're getting it whether you want it or not," she said affably before turning and walking away.

"See how pleased she is with herself," Fengxiang commented.

"Why wouldn't she be, she's rich enough. One of her hairs is thicker than our waists."

"So what! She's still a grass widow."

"That's right. We may be poor, but we've got hold of our menfolk. They say… he's got a new one every night."

"You're got a point. But still, you have to feel sorry for her."

Gimpy Five stopped crying after venting his spleen. He felt like kicking himself over losing control when he heard the woman's offer to pay for him. Losing face is worse than a drink of cold water. Knowing that next year's contribution to the well project was taken care of compensated for his unhappiness with himself. "It's nothing. With the way life is, why worry about losing a bit of pride?"

"Aiyo!" Beizhu's shrill shout rent the air. Spending a few nights in custody and being fined several thousand yuan was like a donkey rolling in the mud to him. "What are we going to do? They fine us, they steal from us, until we're so poor we can't even hold a fart in. Forget the damned well. If we don't dig, each day is still just a morning and a night."

"He's right," said Maodan. "We'll get by. Who can say the next one won't do the same thing?"

"Horseshit!" Meng Eight roared. "The next time you put a curse on something, you dumb prick, I'll fling you down this black hole or know the reason why." He pointed his finger at Beizhu. "You think digging a well is as easy as poking your woman. You don't want to dig? All right. You don't have to, Beizhu. Don't irrigate your crop, and if it doesn't rain, you can just sew up your women's assholes and live off the wind."

Beizhu held his tongue.

"You can't stop good fortune and you can't escape bad," Meng Eight swept his gaze across the crowd and asked, as if demanding an answer. "What's wrong with sacrificing a bit to prevent a disaster? This well has already collapsed, and we can't keep pouring more into a black hole. No matter what, we have to go on living. You keep getting through the days, whether the Heaven tells you to or not. That's all you can do. This one collapsed, so we drill another. What's there to be afraid of? We tighten our throats again. Mix some coarse grain into your millet, or husks to your coarse grains if you have to, and add more water to the porridge. We have nothing to fear. What did we eat back in 1960? We fared worse than houseflies, and the Dasha River was piled high with dead bodies, but we made it through, didn't we? So what's there to be afraid of?"

"He's right," Gimpy Five said. "We keep going, even if we have to crawl. We do what we have to do. But… the money has to come from somewhere."

"Right, the money has to come from somewhere," Maodan agreed. "These workers won't let us pay them with spirit money, but if they did we'd still have to buy the paper to make it with. Damn, I don't even have money for that. I'm worse off than a hairless woman."

"No one buys that," Beizhu said. "You live alone, so your kitchen god is fed when you eat. And don't forget, you get paid every time you dig a grave or cremate a newborn baby."

"Sure, but how many dead are there each year? I don't dig holes or burn babies any time I want to. Every day I hope somebody in the village has died, so I could have a steady income."

"Ptui! Try hoping the next one will be you."

"No wonder no woman will have a wicked bastard like you."

The women spat their contempt for Maodan.

He could not have been happier. He sucked air in through his teeth. "Yeah? So what!" I can't wait to die. As soon as that happens, I'll be a ghost that can slip into your houses through the cracks and climb onto your beds. There'll be nothing you can do then."

More contemptuous spitting.

"What's so good about being alive anyway?" Maodan went on. "There's never enough to eat or decent clothes to wear. It's pointless. The government hits us up for money just about every day. I'm not digging any well. Whoever wants can keep digging. And I'm not working the field either. If I take in three of anything, the government wants five of them. Being a beggar in Liangzhou is better than wasting away here." Maodan was getting hoarse as his voice rose in anger.

"It's not worth it," Gimpy Five agreed. "It's really not. I don't want to work the field either. But what are you going to do if you don't plant crops?"

"I see," Beizhu said with a sarcastic laugh. "Everyone wants to become an immortal. No matter what you call it, a toad is still a toad. You can call it the God of Thunder but you still get a toad. You're better off keeping both your mouth and your asshole shut. A punch in the gut hurts. You just have to take what comes your way. You won't become an immortal otherwise."

"What are you talking about, Beizhu?" Maodan replied. "Do you think you're a toad that's gotten a magical breath from thunder, and now you're better than us?"

"How could I be better? You people may be in the eighteenth level of Hell," Beizhu said, "but I'm in the nineteenth. I'm always getting fined for something, and I have hardly anything left. What's there to be afraid of? Don't you see I'm still singing opera and enjoying myself? A crow's beak is still hard after it dies. I'm going to sing as long as I've got a mouth. What are you complaining about? Do you think you'll get something if you complain about hardships? Not on your life. Go steal or rob if you've got the guts. If not, sing some arias and swear at people. That's the way it is. As long as you're alive keep living, and that's what I'm going to do."

"That's enough!" Big Head laid down the law. "Getting mad accomplishes nothing, so go on home." Many of those milling around decided to take his advice, but within moments, several people were reminded that their reason for being there was the collapse of the well, which, according to Sun's earlier pronouncement, was caused by the presence of a woman. "Someone has to take responsibility for letting his woman onto the site." Without realizing it, they'd gotten sidetracked, and so had he.

"You think you've done something great and now you're teaching us a lesson,"Maodan said.

"Yeah, he's a real ass," someone echoed.

Big Head bowed his head, as if the truth had just hit him. He had abruptly fallen from the role of team leader to the accused. But almost immediately, he raised his head and bellowed, "Maodan, you prick, what did I do? I can't even talk now, is that it? You think you're hot shit, don't you? You blame me for the collapse of the well. I yell my head off all day, and what do I get out of it? You think I'm about to lay my head on the chopping block for you, just another dumb animal you can ride any time you want."

The crowd enjoyed hearing him scream at Maodan, at least for a while, until they realized that the "you" included them too. After exchanging looks, some drifted away.

He was, after all, the team leader, so he made an example of Maodan, the easiest target in sight, but his tirade included the rest of them at some point, to ease his own embarrassment. He refused to admit a mistake, flaunting his authority. Lingguan had to laugh at the man's behavior.

"Big Head," Meng Eight spoke up. "Who's been pushing you around? Who wants your head on the chopping block? Go ahead, yell at anyone you want, but go easy on the barbs."

"I was talking about Maodan, not you."

"We're not as stupid as you think." By now Meng was steamed.

"This wraps it up," Lingguan said to the head of the drill team. "People started out wanting Big Head to take responsibility, but instead they got a load of abuse from him and slinked away."

"Interesting," the driller said, smiling and shaking his head. "Very interesting."

3

The drilling team left the next morning, taking their machinery with them and leaving a terrible mess behind. After reprimanding Maodan the night before, Sun recaptured the authority of team leader and called all the males together at the well room, where they feasted on food and liquor left behind by the drill team. That effectively shut their mouths; no more talk about his wife being at the well site. Except from Maodan. The reason was clear. He was the only one Big Head "forgot" to summon. When he finally got out of bed late that morning, the food and drink had nearly passed through the men's bodies. He rushed to the site in an unforgiving mood, ready, it seemed, to have it out with the team leader.

"You prick, Big Head! How come you always include me when you collect money, but never when there's food. We're going to settle this with our fists if you can't come up with a good excuse."

"You just got here? I thought you were here all along," Sun remarked, feigning surprise. "It's your fault you're late. I went door to door. Whether people came or not was their business. I couldn't pick you up and carry you over here, could I? You're not my grandpa, but even if you had been, I wasn't about to carry you. See what I mean?"

"Bullshit!" Maodan sputtered. His eyes were bloodshot, either because he overslept or from anger. All the men were surprised to see that Maodan, who was usually insolent and took crap from every one, could be so assertive when he was mad. Showing the effects of the alcohol, they surrounded the two combatants, happily anticipating a fight.

"You never called me!" Maodan demanded, acting like a mad dog. "I know how much butter is in those dog guts of yours. Every organ in your body is full of filth. You show off like a peacock. You're someone who loves the rich and hates the poor. You think I'm poor, don't you? I'll tell you, jackass, I'm poor because I was born that way. Have I ever come to you for food? Or clothes? You've got no right to pick on people just because they're poor!" Sun could see how angry the cowardly Maodan was, and was surprised to see him develop some spine. That was a scary thought. A fight didn't bother him; he could handle two Maodans at the same time. What troubled him were all the possible entanglements with someone who knows no shame. Maodan was a master at causing a scene. He could lie down, cover himself with a blanket, and cry and shout. He could even wet himself or shit his pants. You couldn't hit him, because if you did, he'd get worse, threatening to hang himself, run headfirst into a wall, take poison, or jump down a well. Reason would not work. So Big Head decided to ignore him and instead told the man in charge to divide up all the palm fiber for the men to take home with them.

Seeing Sun ignore him only emboldened Maodan. Truth be told, Sun scared him. One punch by one of those huge fists would drive all the fluid from his stomach right out of his mouth. He'd acted differently from usual only because he'd been spurred on by his anger over missing out on a meal. But now that he'd vented his displeasure, his anger subsided. He was also fully aware that his reason for demanding an acknowledgment that the man had been wrong was weak. Villagers called this "fuming over one missed meal," so instead of concentrating on the food, he launched his attack on Sun's behavior. As soon as he realized he'd hit him where it hurt, he ratcheted up the angry tone.

"Don't think I give a damn about those pathetic droolings. Not a chance! It's the way you show off, how you love the rich and hate the poor. Who do you think you are, picking on people? A team leader is little more than a nit on a strand of pubic hair, so what does that make you? Tell me that. A tiger in the forest? You pick on people, you sink your teeth in them. Do you really think you could take my ribs if you were the township head?

Sun ignored him, now that the man in charge had divided up the palm fiber and told the men, "One portion per family, and that's all."

Maodan rushed over and picked up as many bundles as he could handle. "These are mine, all mine. I paid like everybody else, but didn't get to eat, so I'll take these instead. I've lived long enough, damn it, and I'll fight any of you who try to take this away from me. I'll trade this old sheepskin of mine for your lamb pelt, my life or yours."

"You have no use for those, Maodan," Hantou said. "Give them to me, and I'll give you a rabbit."

"No, I don't want that. This is what I want. I can't use this? I'll use it to warm myself." He took out a cigarette lighter, and lit the palm fiber after a look at Big Head Sun.

Sun saw the telltale pangs of contrition in Maodan's eyes and knew that the fury was spent. Now his act was all for show. So with a shout, he ran up and knocked Maodan to the ground, where he pounded his fists into his thigh. Maodan shrieked like a stuck pig.

"Damn you, you think you can do whatever you want to me. I go easy on you, and all you do is go wild. You think you can climb up over my head. Well, I'll show you what I can do and stain you red. Who does this stuff belong to? It belongs to everybody. Who told you that you could burn it up? You can get away with taking advantage of me, but try that with all the others, and I'll flay that lousy skin of yours. You've lived long enough? Well, so have I. I can trade this sheepskin of mine for your old pelt too. All this time, Sun kept punching Maodan on the leg.

"Ow… Big Head…Ow—you're hurting me—my leg—ow, you're breaking my… I was only joking—you—ow—you're hurting me." Maodan stopped screeching long enough to beg for mercy: "I'm sorry—ow—let me up—my fault—ow—please—"

Sun finally let up, but only after two hard punches to his backside.

"If I wasn't afraid of getting my hands so dirty, I'd kill you, you prick. All that swearing and bluster over a meal of leftovers! I put up with you, but you tried to climb over my head, you stupid son of a bitch."

Maodan got up and rubbed his bruised leg. "You… Big Head… love the rich and hate the poor… you even beat me up."

"Say that again, damn you, say it," Sun bellowed.

Maodan scrunched his head down and backed up. Then he turned and limped away. When he was some twenty meters away, he looked back. "Fuck you!" Big Head.

Sun took a step forward, making Maodan jump. He ran off. The men all laughed.

Chapter Seven

1

Shuangfu, who wore gold-rimmed eyeglasses, could tell that something was up the minute he walked into the compound.

He looked at his watch after sending the driver off. Two A.M. Just the right time. He had a special reason for choosing this time to return to the village.

He heard snores.

It was a nasal sound like rumbling thunder, with an occasional squawk. Snrkx—gugu—snrkx—gugu. Though he had prepared himself mentally, his head seemed to swell with anger. He knew his wife did not snore like that.

With a growl, he kicked open the door and snapped on the light.

The woman sat up with a jerk. Shuangfu saw someone else in bed with this woman he knew so well. The snoring continued unabated.

"Oh, no!" she croaked, eyes staring straight ahead, as if frozen in place. Time stopped. Then she gave the figure a vicious kick, and the snoring stopped.

"You whore!" Shuangfu rushed up, grabbed a handful of hair, and slapped her savagely.

She rolled out of bed, wrapped her arms around Shuangfu's legs, and snapped, "Get out of here! Go!"

Mengzi jumped out of bed and started to run. The sight of his nakedness disgusted Shuangfu. "You bastard!" He could not tell who it was. He was apoplectic; he saw stars.

Mengzi made it to the doorway before he stopped and turned back. He changed his mind about running away. A real man isn't afraid to face the music, he said to himself. He'd be a real bastard if he ran off and left her to suffer the consequences alone.

"So it's you… fuck you, Mengzi," Shuangfu snarled as he tried to rush Mengzi, but fell flat on his face, since the woman was holding on to his legs.

"Get out of here, you idiot," she said shrilly. "What are you waiting for? Just go!"

"I'm not going anywhere," Mengzi said. "I know what I did, and he can do what he wants to me."

"Go fuck yourself!" Shuangfu spat out as he got up and slapped Mengzi hard.

"Don't blame him," the woman sobbed. "It's my fault, so do what you want to me."

"You slut," Shuangfu said through clenched teeth. "You're actually protecting your lover. Whore! Slut!" He grabbed her by the hair with his left hand and slapped her twisted, ashen face with all his might.

"Don't hit her," Mengzi said. "Hit me, and leave her out of this."

"Don't you worry about that," Shuangfu said with a smirk. "You'll get yours." He struggled free of the woman's hold on his legs, picked up a glass from the night stand, and flung it across the room.

"Crash!" The impact smashed the TV screen resting on the cabinets.

Mengzi's scalp rippled. The woman had told him the set had cost them five thousand yuan. But he had no time to reflect on that, since Shuangfu was landing blows on him like a storm. He barely felt them, strangely enough. "He can do what he wants," was how he felt. Wrapping his arms around his head, he crouched down to protect his manhood and held his breath. All he could hear was the woman's heart-rending sobs.

Eventually, the pounding stopped. Mengzi opened his eyes. She had managed to drag her husband away. His eyeglasses were nowhere in sight, and with his twisted face, Shuangfu looked like a different man.

"Go on," she insisted, "get out of here."

Mengzi stood up and was nearly blinded by the painfully strong light. He did not quite know what to do, but he began to sense how unsightly it was to be standing there stark naked. So he walked over to the bed to retrieve his clothes, but while he was getting dressed, he fell to the floor from a painful kick to his leg.

"What are you waiting for, Mengzi? For him to kill you?" She grabbed Shuangfu's arm and shouted tearfully. Like a chained dog, Shuangfu dragged her across the floor, roaring in anger that was in danger of boiling over.

Mengzi walked out, carrying his clothes in his arms, and he could still hear the sound of slaps even after walking some distance.

He started dressing by the faint light of a crescent moon, and discovered that his underpants were missing. He came to his senses when he felt the cool evening air surging around him and realized that he'd done something shameful. Shit, that's it for me, he said to himself. When people get wind of this," he reflected as he shook his head regretfully, "I might as well kill myself.

Why not? The thought gave him a fright, but was liberating at the same time. Sure, do it, no big deal. One simple action will solve everything.

He started walking toward the well site at Xitan.

The moon hung in the sky, a lonely sight, while the enveloping darkness created a deathly silence. As he walked, the pounding of blood at his temples slowed. He stopped. Why should I do it? Who says I have to kill myself? Just because you got rich, you prick, you can bed all the women you want in the city. And I'm supposed to die because I relieved her of a bit of boredom? Hell no. He felt he was making too much of the whole affair. But the monologue continued: You bastard. You abandon your woman, leaving her at home to live like a widow. She's a human being, not some disposable object. Hell, she was dying of thirst like the desert, and I came along for a little irrigation. I'm supposed to die over something like that? Not me. What's there to be afraid of, losing my head?

Now he had a dilemma. Going ahead was a problem, but then so was turning back. As he backtracked, he knew that awaiting him was unbearable shame. His greatest fear? That his mother would find out. That thought amplified the immense loss of face over his despicable act. She would neither hit nor pile abuse on his head—that was the sort of thing his father would do, Mengzi knew—but he'd rather suffer a beating from his father than have his mother learn what he'd done.

He did not know how to put his feeling into words, but the thought of death resurfaced when he thought her, although weaker than before and less confounding.

Will Shuangfu tell people? I hope not… maybe not… not likely. He worries too much about face to want others to know that he'd been cuckolded. That thought opened up a sliver of light in the darkness ahead, and he felt much better.

But what about her, the poor woman? Shuangfu will never forgive her. So, should I go back? He shook his head. No, get someone else to go stop him from killing her. In his mind's eye he could see her rolling on the floor, trying to escape her husband's savage kicks, and leaving a trail of blood. Would he kill her? Probably not… but who can say… anything's possible. If one of his kicks lands on the wrong spot, that could do it, end it all… Mengzi shuddered.

He went straight to Meng Eight's house and pounded on the door. Half asleep, Meng asked who it was. "Shuangfu is killing his wife, Meng Eight, you have to go save her!"

"Is he in the village?" Meng asked. "Why's he here?"

"Who knows?" Mengzi muttered while going over to pound on Gimpy Five's door and repeating what he'd told Meng.

Before getting a response, he heard Meng Eight clearing his throat as he headed to Shuangfu's house, his sandals slapping loudly against the ground. Mengzi breathed a sigh of relief.

2

Afraid to go home, Mengzi went to see Maodan, who was sleeping like a dead pig. Mengzi tried to wake him up. That didn't work, so he slid under the lumpy comforter next to him. His nose was greeted by an unpleasant odor, but he couldn't let that bother him.

As he shut his eyes he could not help feeling fear over the incident, and wondered what might have happened if he'd stuck around. A beating for sure, though he'd have fought back at some point, and he knew that Shuangfu would be no match for him. But where would that lead? He surely would not turn a blind eye to what had happened, but what could he do to me? Mengzi mulled over Shuangfu's options and decided that the man could do nothing to him. He had to laugh at himself for being so anxious. He could report me to the authorities, but for what? Sleeping with his wife. That was no crime, and she wouldn't report it as rape, even if he told her to. Or would she?

Rape. The thought threw his mind into a whirl. He recalled the first time with the woman, when she'd fought him off and said she didn't want to do it. Could what he had done count as rape? If so, then he was a rapist—he nearly convinced himself that he had raped her—and he would be done for. Prison would be a foregone conclusion, and if Shuangfu put his money to good use, he could wind up getting shot. What he'd done did not seem worth it. Definitely not. Mengzi was wracked by regret.

What about her, would she try to get back at him? Who could say? Women are so unpredictable. What would she do if Shuangfu threatened her with divorce to get her to report him? He was rich and had all the advantages, and, staying with him, she'd have anything she wanted and could look as grand as she liked. Would she give all that up for Mengzi, who could offer her nothing? That was laughable. Mengzi felt a chill.

He thought back to how she'd grabbed hold of Shuangfu's legs and refused to let go while urging him to run away; that was heartwarming. She hadn't had a thought for her own safety at that moment. She must like me a lot, he was thinking. That was why she'd disregarded her own safety and held back her husband for him to escape. She would not report him just because her husband told her to. She's some woman! He had to laugh. He wouldn't have believed it if he hadn't seen it with his own eyes. Normally soft-spoken, she showed how tough she could be, soft as water and yet hard as fire. His thoughts returned to the happy escapade a few hours before Shuangfu showed up. Her shouts of pleasure aroused him, and he was surprised by how unyielding she could be. The useless Shuangfu was no match for her, not the way she fought him tooth and nail, dragging him this way and that. That lightened his mood.

Why had she shouted for me to run away? Afraid I'd be hurt? Or something else. Obviously, she was afraid it would get out of hand and end badly, no doubt about that. It's a good thing she did, or I'd still be standing there. And who knows how that would have turned out? But one thing was for certain: he would not have let that bastard pound away on him indefinitely. No, if he'd been backed into a corner, he'd have fought. He recalled the belly punch Baigou had taught him to use. One fist in the gut, and Shuangfu would have doubled over and curled up like a shrimp. Reverse the roles, and the punches from Shuangfu were like fly taps, like scratching an itch. Only the kick had had any effect. The more he reflected, the stronger he felt, and he began to wish he hadn't run off the way he had, half naked. It made him look like a mangy dog that's just been stepped on.

Worthless! He thumped himself in the head.

He recalled the disgraceful way he'd left her to deal with the situation alone. Shuangfu would vent all his anger on her, beating her bloody if he felt like it. What if he was so incensed he actually kicked her head bloody… then it had… fortunately, he'd sent Meng Eight and Gimpy Five to check… he wondered what was going on at that moment.

Mengzi shook Maodan, but he slept on. So he changed tactics by pulling back the bedding and holding a lit match to his feet. It was about to burn out beforeMaodan sputtered, "What the hell…"

"He's killing her!" Mengzi cried out.

"Who?"Maodan sat up.

"Shuangfu's killing his wife!"

"He's out of town on a job."

"He came back."

"Honest?"

"He stripped her naked and was going to carve her up!"

"Are you kidding me?" Maodan jumped out of bed and threw on some clothes.

"Go see what happened and then come back to tell me, all right? I'll pay you. Rush right back and I'll give you one yuan."

"It's a deal." Maodan vanished like a ghost.

Once he was out the door, the thought that concerned Mengzi the most rose to the surface. Would Shuangfu tell people what happened? He choked up when he thought about his parents finding out. Shuangfu mustn't be allowed to tell anyone, even if… his mind went blank and stayed that way for a moment. Then he broke out in a cold sweat when a fleeting thought surfaced after the blankness.

He had revealed everything himself.

Thoughts of her well being had driven out his concern over "secrecy." Now three uninvolved people knew—Meng Eight, Gimpy Five, and Maodan. Shuangfu would come up with an explanation for why he'd beaten his wife. Meng Eight would not say anything, but with Gimpy Five it was hard to say. He'd keep the secret as long as he was sober. But then there was loose-lipped Maodan, who couldn't keep a secret overnight. He would not hesitate to spread the word from one end of the village to the other, his words flowing like an old cow peeing while it's between the shafts. He wouldn't intentionally damage anyone's reputation, but Mengzi knew that he was capable of pounding his chest to swear allegiance one minute and disavowing it with the same measure of sincerity ten seconds later.

He thumped himself in the head over his foolishness.

But Mengzi, being Mengzi, foolish or not, had the ability to talk himself around when faced with an unpleasant reality. His attitude was, dying is the worst that can happen, so what's there to be afraid of? He'd deal with this head-on, and once he reached that decision, he relaxed. Suddenly overcome by exhaustion, he fell asleep.

He did not dream.

3

The sun was up when Maodan returned the favor by giving Mengzi a hotfoot. He could not figure out why he had been sleeping in a virtual pigsty as he gazed into Maodan's grinning face.

"Well, you're a piece of work," Maodan taunted. "You can sleep like a baby after having it on with another man's wife. You've messed up big time. It's a huge scandal."

As memories of what he'd done returned abruptly, a pall settled over Mengzi's heart. Speechless, he groaned as he squatted down on the edge of the bed.

"Your father kowtowed an apology and Shuangfu said he was divorcing his wife, all while you were asleep."

"How did he find out?" Mengzi was stunned.

"How? It's a huge scandal. Everybody knows. He swore he's going to kill you. When I whispered to Meng Eight where you are, he said for you to get out of here, go as far away as you can and stay there for a few days. Your life is at stake here, no kidding… you have to give it to that jackass, all that nice white flesh is now black and blue… how could he do that with his belt… 'I don't want her,' he said, 'and nothing she says will change my mind.' But she was too stubborn to admit doing anything wrong. 'Go ahead, say it, say you don't want me, but why did you have to sneak around? Everybody knows about that witch you're sleeping with.'" Maodan mimicked the woman's voice as he related the story. "Hei, that old lady isn't so old, after all, with her tender skin. Just thinking about it makes my heart melt."

"Was she still naked?"

"Not any more. Meng Eight told Shuangfu to let her get dressed. Finally he did, after he spent plenty of time ripping into her. Honestly I've never seen skin that fair. How could the jackass bear to use his belt on that?"

"Did my father really kowtow?"

"He did, and while he was doing it, he railed, 'How could I have raised someone who'd do that? Our family's pride is ruined. He might as well have killed us all!' He banged his head on the ground so many times he raised a welt on his forehead. It took both Meng Eight and Gimpy Five to get him to stop. I can't recall all that Meng Eight said, but there was something about even a great man cannot guarantee his wife's virtue or his son's obedience, and a lot of other stuff. Your father was crying, wailing, almost like a cow."

"Was my mother there?"

"No. They said she was home crying her eyes out."

Mengzi heaved a sad sigh and pounded his fist into his forehead a dozen times or more. Then he stepped down off the bed, slipped into his shoes, and said, “Any man worthy of the name faces his own actions. They can kill me if they want. It was all my fault. But why did he have to bring my father and mother into it. I’m going over there and see for myself. What can he do to me, chop off my dick? Skin me alive? Lop off my head?” With a stomp of his foot, he started out the door.

Maodan stopped him. “Are you serious, you idiot? There are lives on the line. Wait till he cools off a little. Don’t go stirring up more trouble.”

“Let go of me, I don’t care what happens. Whether he kills me or not is my business. I’m not going to let my parents suffer.” He flung his arms out, sending Maodan back onto the bed, and walked out the door.

“This is going to be good,” Maodan said as he got up and followed Mengzi out.

Mengzi tramped imperiously to Shuangfu’s house, not letting the whispered comments of people who knew what was happening distract him. They too fell in behind him. “Get ready for a spectacle!” Maodan shouted excitedly. The followers grew into what looked like a crowd on its way to a big show.

Shuangfu froze, too surprised by Mengzi’s daring move to know how to deal with the new development. People inside the house who were trying to smooth things over were equally dismayed. Laoshun, his eyes blazing and lips quivering, was speechless. The woman cowered in a corner, and when she saw Mengzi, her mouth fell open. He ignored them all, all but Shuangfu. “Here I am, you son of a bitch. Instead of dragging other people into this, take it out on me. Kill me if you have it in you.” Though he had composed himself after the shock, Shuangfu was cowed by Mengzi’s menacing demeanor. But when he looked outside and saw the excited crowd, he screwed up the courage to charge, and the fight was on.

"You damned monster!" Laoshun cursed as he bounded over and slapped his son as hard as he could, over and over. Meng Eight wrapped his arms around Laoshun and yelled, "Stop, everybody, stop! You have to talk, not fight." Shuangfu was first to let go, then Mengzi, who glowered at the other man.

"You've shamed us, damn you!" Laoshun slapped his own face over and over. "And you've brought so much shame to our ancestors they're jumping off the altar. I wish you were dead, you monster! You should go kill yourself. I didn't raise an animal for a son." His voice cracked.

"This is about me. I did it and I'll take full responsibility," Mengzi said as he stiffened his neck. "It's got nothing to do with you."

"What did you say? You smear dog shit all over my face, and it's got nothing to do with me? You're worse than an animal." Laoshun was getting angrier by the minute. He picked up a feather duster to use on his son. Mengzi stood his ground and let his father hit him a few times before grabbing the duster out of his hand and snapping it in two, making Laoshun choke on tears. "You've humiliated our ancestors, damn you." Meng Eight pulled him away.

"Humiliated, you say?" Mengzi shot back as he stamped his foot. "I did that, so what does it have to do with ancestors? Go ahead, hit me, kill me if you think that'll do any good, when you should be getting me a wife. Hitting me isn't going to make you look good!"

Laoshun stopped crying, paused, and ran out the door, pushing people aside. He bounded off like a marionette.

"You dumb shit!" Meng Eight swore at Mengzi, "How could you say that to your father?" He gave a signal to a seemingly paralyzed

Gimpy to go after Laoshun.

Mengzi wished he hadn't said those things, but that didn't lessen his truculence. "I did what I did," he stared daggers at Shuangfu, puffing himself, "so what are you going to do about it?"

Shuangfu glared at him, but said nothing as Meng Eight dragged Mengzi away. He snorted a time or two and shot a few angry looks at his wife. Then he turned and said to Meng Eight, "What can I say? What am I supposed to say after what he did? She's a bitch in heat, just waiting for a mutt to mount her. But who cares, I don't want the whore any longer."

His wife sneered. "What do you think you are? All you care about is making money. You don't give a damn about me or our daughter. I'm no less human than you are, but while you're out there having a good time, I'm supposed to suffocate here in the middle of nowhere. Tell me what you plan to do, and tell me straight. Okay, I slept with him. You can say I shamed myself, that I made a spectacle of myself, that doesn't change anything. If you want me to go slit my wrists or hang myself, say it, don't beat around the bush."

"You slut, you actually think you're the injured party here. Go kill yourself if you want; I don't give a damn how you die. Everyone will know I didn't force anything on you. If you think you can scare me with talk of death, you're sadly mistaken. You've disgraced yourself so much you might as well be dead anyway."

"Of course you'd like to see me dead, because that would make room for someone else. So go ahead, spit out what you want to say, no phony excuses."

"I'm not going to debate this with you. My mind's made up."

"Fine." She sneered. "You think being married to you is the good life. Hell, I might as well be a widow. Go on, have your fun, and I'll get by with what I have. You ride in your fancy car and I'll pull my wagon. You don't stop planting peppers just because you don't have dog shit."

"All right, then." Shuangfu snickered. "I'm glad you see the big picture. When do we file for divorce?"

"Anytime is fine with me."

"Don't be so uncompromising, Shuangfu," Meng Eight said. "Everyone makes mistakes. When all is said and done, the first batch of flour is always the best, like the original in everything. Don't think someone who styles her hair, wears high heels, and uses lipstick loves you. What she loves is your money, and when that runs out, then you'll see."

"Save your breath, Meng Eight," she said. "He's already made up his mind. He hasn't shown his face around here for years and he never answers my letters. He was supposed to be as hardworking as a mule, but who knows what he does? It's the hottest time of the year. My eyes sweat and my hands get calluses, while he's out there enjoying himself. Well, I'm human, and I can enjoy myself too, so let him go do what he wants. The two of us won't have to spend any more time worrying about what he's up to. I tell you, Meng Eight, he's been planning on getting rid of our daughter and me for a long time. It's been a matter of when, not if."

"I'm glad you figured that out." Shuangfu smiled coldly.

"Take it easy, both of you," Meng Eight counseled. "You can eat stale rice, but you can't take back angry words. No more talk of divorce. Calm down and talk it over. It's difficult, but you each have to give a little."

"Talk?" Shuangfu raised his voice. "What else can we talk about after it's gone this far? How do you expect me to face the world?

People will be talking about what my wife did behind my back. I've got my pride."

"What about you. Don't hold up a mirror only for other people. You should take a good look at yourself too. I may have done wrong, but how about you, are you perfect?"

"Men are supposed to make a name for themselves out in the world, don't you know that?" Shuangfu said with a sneer.

"So you have reason on your side, I suppose?"

"I can say it all with one word – divorce!"

"That's fine with me."

"What hogwash!" Meng Eight said with a stomp of his foot.

4

Laoshun was resting on his haunches on a sandy ridge east of the village. Gimpy was having no luck persuading him to go home.

A wind rose at midday, creating a howling sandstorm that had no effect on Laoshun. He did not move. His sunken eyes lent him a terrifying look.

The sun shrank and paled, seemingly quivering under the wind's violent assault. Sand filled the sky and in mad fashion stabbed people's skin like darts. The pain was excruciating, and the air was so thick with sand it was hard to even breathe, as if people's lungs were gummed up.

The most fearful aspect was the sound, like the bellowing of a thousand bulls, but worse. Some claimed it was the sound of wind blowing over sandy donkey dicks or through collapsed sand pits, but old timers knew it was the Yellow Dragon calling out for wind and sand. The desert was turning into a giant bellows. The wind even carried off the heat of the sun, which could not defend itself, like a sniveling young bachelor hugging himself for warmth in the depths of winter, unwilling to share body heat with anyone else. And yet, as long as the people stayed indoors, the icy stabs of wind could not hurt them. If they had to go outside, they wrapped themselves in their coats and cinched them with wide belts to hold in the heat. What about the face? No one worried about that during such times.

Laoshun had left Shuangfu's house like a sleepwalker. Fearing that his friend might be suicidal, Gimpy did not let him out of his sight as he floated out to the desert and sat on a sand ridge, immobilized.

"Don't let it get under your skin, Laoshun. As the old storyteller says, even a great man cannot guarantee his wife's virtue or his son's obedience."

Laoshun said nothing.

"It's no big deal. Things like this happen all the time. Mengzi's not the only one with no marriage prospects."

Still no reaction from Laoshun.

"The boy is too immature. He went off half-cocked, but he didn't mean what he said. You have to be bigger than him. You can't hold a grudge. If you let everything your son does bother you, you'll wind up with a heart attack."

Nothing.

Gimpy did not know what to say next, as he paced like a mule around a millstone, heaving a sigh with each turn. A long time passed before he went back to Laoshun's house.

Lingguan and Hantou ran out to the desert as soon as they heard what had happened. Gusting wind made sand fly. Lingguan spotted the dark figure on the ridge; naturally, he'd been told about the impact of Mengzi's outburst on his father. After hearing what Gimpy related, he realized it was serious.

The howling wind flung sand into Lingguan's face, numbing skin that burned as hot as when he'd heard the shameless thing Mengzi had done… as if he was the one who had been caught. But he couldn't blame Mengzi for bringing shame to the family. He understood his brother. What made him feel bad was the need for Mengzi to suffer embarrassment. No, in truth it was his parents who would suffer.

"Let's go, Father. The wind is getting stronger." Hantou nervously took hold of his father's sleeve. Lingguan saw that his father's face was covered with sand, and he looked gaunter than ever, as if the wind had sucked all the moisture out of him, turning him into a mummy.

"Come on," Hantou said. "Let's go home and get out of the wind."

Laoshun sat like a mute, a petrified figure.

"Say something," Hantou urged him. "Sitting out here won't do any good."

Lingguan poked his brother as he took hold of his father's left arm, a signal for Hantou to take the right one. Together they picked him up and started carrying him down the ridge. He did not resist, merely made gurgling sounds.

The brothers were winded before they'd walked very far, so they let go, and Laoshun went right back up onto the ridge, where he sat like a stone.

"What are you doing?" Hantou said anxiously. "Just what do you think you're doing like this? The wind is so strong." He had barely finished when his words were carried off to drift weakly toward a distant sand hollow.

The scene was repeated, with the same, fruitless result, the brothers breathing hard from the exhausting effort, except that Hantou ripped his father's sleeve.

"Stop what you're doing to me, would you?" he said at last, his voice cracking.

"Let's go home. You can say what you want there," Hantou said."

"Leave me alone for a while. Don't worry; I won't do anything foolish. I can't die as long as there is more to suffer for."

Lingguan shook his head with an unhappy smile. "You stay here with him."

Hantou volunteered. "I'll go get Meng Eight."

"Bring a wagon." Hantou left the scene.

Lingguan was besieged with sadness when he gazed at his father, who seemed to have aged a great deal. With a sigh, he went over and sat by him, his back to the wind, which beat like waves pounding against the shore.

Flying sand blurred everything.

Lingguan turned to look at Laoshun when he heard sobs. Turgid tears snaked past the side of his nostrils, washing away the dust on his face and streaming into the corners of his mouth.

Lingguan let him cry, happy to see him release pent-up emotions. But the sound of his sobs was miserable, like the moving teeth of a saw slicing through his heart to anguish him with grief.

A gust of wind sent sand swirling into the old man's face. It drowned out his sobs. Lingguan shut his eyes and squatted down by his father as resentment began to rise. It wasn't until he saw how pitiful their father looked that he realized that Mengzhi should have known better, especially the hurtful words.

The wind died down a bit. From deep in Laoshun's throat emerged sounds like those of an injured animal. He wore the dark face of death. It aged him, made him look pathetic. Lingguan felt sorry for a father who never gave an inch in a confrontation, and his eyes watered.

Meng Eight and Gimpy were on their way, and before they had

reached the ridge, Meng shouted, "What are you, a man or a woman? I didn't know you were capable of this. Where did you learn to do this, from your wife? Or maybe your daughter-in-law. Come on, let's go. Do you want women to laugh at you when I hogtie you like a dead piglet"

Hantou, who followed them with a handcart, had to laugh.

When Meng Eight walked up, he took a rope out of the cart pretending to tie his friend up. Laoshun stood up and walked down the ridge without a word.

"You succumb to pressure," Meng said, "so how can you call yourself a man?"

Expressionlessly, Laoshun headed back to the village like a sleepwalker. At that moment his clothes seemed too big for him. Every billowing gust of wind looked like it could carry him away.

The sun was about to set.

5

A dreary mood settled over the house after dinner. No one knew where Mengzi was hiding. Lao Shun and his wife lay on their bed ignoring the rice bowls that had been placed by their heads. Hantou sat on his haunches in the doorway, rubbing the right side of his ribcage, a worried look on his face. Ying'er walked in and out of the room quietly, almost as if she were guilty of something shameful. She turned red, lowered her eyes, and rushed by anyone she met on the way. Gimpy Five had walked in a couple of times, but merely sighed and said nothing.

Lingguan was depressed, feeling suffocated in the house, so he went outside. As he passed by Beizhu's house, his friend winked and gestured for him to come over. "Have you heard? Shuangfu is getting a divorce. That woman of his has her wits about her. 'You want a divorce,' she told him, 'that's fine by me.' They went to the township office, but there was no one there. She'd have gotten the divorce right then otherwise. What do you think… I hear Shuangfu agreed to give her two hundred thousand, but she turned him down. She said she can do just fine on her own, even if that meant scavenging trash, and he can keep his filthy money. She's weird, don't you think? I suppose she wants to hook up with Mengzi."

"Speaking of Mengzi, where is he?" Lingguan asked.

"He's at Maodan's place."

Lingguan heard Maodan's hoarse voice long before he reached his house: "What are you afraid of, huh? Shit, don't worry about it…"

Mengzi was there, all right, along with Baigou, Huaqiu, and others. Maodan greeted Lingguan with a goofy grin. He sniffled. "Good, you're here. You can be your brother's advisor. That way, you'll have a nice tit to suck on later." Lingguan ignored him.

Mengzi was obviously embarrassed to see his brother, but almost immediately was mad at himself for being embarrassed. His face reddened and he huffed angrily, about to say something, but stopped himself.

"What are you scared of?" Baigou said. "You didn't tell him to get a divorce. Is Shuangfu really that special?"

"That's true." Maodan agreed impishly. "What are you afraid of? Adultery doesn't harm a woman. It's like pulling out a turnip and leaving a hole. No big deal. But that SOB has probably had his head turned from spending so much time in town… he should stay clear of those dancehalls. What's that about this hand and that hand, Huaqiu? I forget."

Huaqiu laughed. "Hold her right wrist with your left hand and keep your right hand on her hip; press against the two mounds on her chest and beat the rhythm with your feet, that's how you get what you want."

"He's got money now," Maodan cut in, "so of course he goes for city girls. Hell, he's always got his arm around one of them, in her high heels, permed hair, soft tits, fair skin, and red lips. The prick's really got it made!"

"Jealous?" Baigou teased. "If so, then you go hug one of them."

"With what? What do I have?"Maodan said. "I've got nothing but these ribs, and she damned well wouldn't care for them. What does a woman want? Good looks, plenty of money, and power. Us? We're a sack of balls, and not good ones either."

"Says who?" Baigou retorted with a smile. "A city girl was getting it on with a randy official when they were caught in the act by a peasant collecting dung. She did it with him too to keep his mouth shut. And when she did, she shouted, my god, peasants are the best!"

Huaqiu sprayed the tea in his mouth, and Mengzi couldn't help but laugh. But he forced himself to stop when he looked at Lingguan.

"What's so good about being good?" Maodan argued. "All girls want these days is money. They don't give a damn who's soft and who's hard or who's long and who's short. It's all about money, the more the better. You're been around, Beizhu, am I right or aren't I?"

"How the hell would I know? You need to do it to know. Try it yourself if you're so eager to find out. Go to the square at night, and if you see one walking around with a bag over their shoulder and looking around, ask her if she's selling. Give it a try."

"Hard to say," Baigou said with a wink. "The thing about women is, if they don't have money, it's what they want. If they have it, they're looking for a good time. Take Shuangfu's woman. What's she looking for? Mengzi, what else?"

"I wonder how rough he was with her," Maodan said.

"Let's check it out and we'll know," Baigou taunted.

"Are you two itching for a fight?" Mengzi barked, a hard look on his face.

"Look here," Maodan said. "You're always in the right. How many times have you thrown your weight around with me? What did I say? We were just teasing you, why get mad? He needs to be punished. What do you say, Baigou, Huaqiu?"

The three men laughingly wrestled Mengzi to the ground. Lingguan stepped outside, so his brother wouldn't lose face in front of him. Raucous laughter and curses emerged from inside. Suddenly Maodan shouted, "Hey, he's got a flashlight here. No wonder…" "like a donkey's… so of course the woman… I've seen Shuangfu's, like a stump on a smooth riverbank, about the size of a silkworm…"

A crescent moon drove away the darkness. Seeing that his brother would be fine with the bunch clowning around, Lingguan felt reassured about going home. He hadn't gone far when he heard a conversation among some women up ahead. "That slut hasn't an ounce of self respect." "That's right, and with a growing daughter." "Is there anything Shuangfu doesn't have? He's rich enough not to have to worry about getting by, so what's she want? She's suffering from good fortune." "You're right there. What people won't do for you know what." When he turned the corner, he noted that one of the talkers was a woman people called the "public bus." What makes you think you can talk like that about people?

He thought about the depressing mood at home. Night had just fallen, and bedtime was a long way off. He was restless, and wanted someone to talk to. Meng Eight was the logical choice.

6

Meng Eight lived in a house with no outer wall on the northern edge of the village. Not one to be restricted by convention, he split the property with Huaqiu's father so he could live alone after his wife died. In a family of one, everyone leaves the table well fed.

He was sitting on a log in the yard, looking like a stone statue in the dark, his big, black dog beside him, another statue.

Stillness reigned all around, far from the noise and bustle of the village center. There was a desolate quality to the stillness, and a vague otherworldliness. The fields were visible though hazy in the moonlight, creating the illusion of great distance and vast space. The only sounds were the faint chirps of crickets and autumn winds rustling in the trees.

Lingguan stood there quietly for a moment, feeling cool, as if cleansed by water. He had left the uproar of the village behind and had entered a realm of unadorned solemnity. He did not want to disturb that.

Meng Eight wordlessly moved over to make room for Lingguan, who sat down and rubbed the dog's head; the dog licked his hand.

"It's getting cold," he murmured. "Another year about to end. The long-necked geese are calling, which means the winter will be brutal."

No response from Lingguan, who let Meng Eight's dreamy murmur, like soupy millet, slowly flow into his heart and untangle the knots there. Suffused in this ambience, Lingguan felt that no words were necessary.

"See how the leaves are turning," he said, "and how people are dying? It's interesting to ponder how everything changes and nothing is real. Yellow Beard died two years ago today. He was a man to reckon with. There was nothing he hadn't done – struggled against you, punched you, cheated you, and victimized you. He could also rescue you. There's nothing left of him now but bones. His widow, with her unbound feet, was a woman who could get things done. But she's dead too, and her grave mound has already settled. All gone. There used to be lots of trees, fast-flowing water, and foxes around the river. Now the trees are gone, the foxes have left, and there's only enough water for cats to drink. I wonder what it's going to be like a few years from now. Intriguing when you think about it. It's really fascinating."

Lingguan felt like saying something about the vagaries of life, but didn't know how, so he remained quiet. He sighed.

"The weather's changed too. It used to rain and snow a lot more. Coin-sized raindrops could fall for days, and snowflakes as big as sparrows' heads could bury your boots. No more. Now we have dry weather. What will we have next? With all these changes, what does the future hold? Can you tell me that?"

"If it changes it changes. Why worry about it?"

"You're right. But it is intriguing, it seems to me. I've seen and done a lot over the years, and I find it all fascinating. Liars get lied to. Cheaters get cheated. Those who struggled against others get wrestled down, and people who are a force to reckon with have nothing to show for it. Being rich doesn't help either. We're all alike; in the end, no one is different. An earthen mound takes care of everyone and all unfinished business."

"You're right. But people can't see that."

"They'd keep their sanity if they could. But of course they can't. Take a look around. Everybody's going crazy chasing money, power, this and that. But none of it is real. They're like dogs chasing a bladder that pops when they catch it. That ends their fun, their joy an illusion. They wind up with nothing, because it's not real. All you have to look forward to when you die is a pine box, and many people don't even have that. Just ashes in an urn. Tell me, don't you find it funny the way dogs chase bladders? Our pursuit is worse than that. Bladders at least have skins, but people have nothing. They shut their eyes and that's the end of it."

Meng stroked his dog's head. A low growl seemed to indicate that the dog understood what he was saying. The dog was old and was losing its fur in clumps. Lingguan had no idea just how old it was, but he recalled playing with it as a boy. Back then it was a powerful young animal that was always on the trail of good-looking bitches. When it caught one, it wasted no time. He recalled seeing boys beat and yell at the coupled dogs. There'll be no more of that for this old guy, and Lingguan wondered if it had any memory of the good times, and if it felt disconsolate, like people.

"Have you heard the story of the monkeys that tried to scoop the moon out of the water?" Meng asked. "The moon wasn't real, and if the monkeys had known that they would have stopped trying. But they thought it was, so they tried and tried to scoop it up. The smart ones knew it wasn't real, but not the stupid ones, who thought the moon was at the bottom of the pond; they fell in and drowned, without ever knowing that it wasn't real. Laughable, don't you think? There was nothing Yellow Beard didn't do. He was like an emperor during his heyday. He slept with anybody he wanted, married or not. But nothing was real when he died. And now? Just bones. And they'll be gone in a few years. That's how it is. Look at Beizhu's mother. She was so pretty when she was young, a rosy glow on her fair face, like a figure in a painting. Now? Where's the rosy glow and fair skin? All gone, nothing but coarse skin and gray hair. Everything else is the same. You're too young to realize this, but you will when you're old."

Lingguan's scalp itched. He felt a shock deep in his soul. Everything had changed, it seemed, and was like an old painting that gave off a stale odor, no matter how clear the image. That calmed him, and he felt like laughing at what Mengzi had done. Thoughts of Ying'er came and went, but with little effect on the indifference he was feeling.

The moon drifted amid clouds. Or were the clouds drifting? He did not know, but there was movement. The compound was still. Soft breezes rustled the yellow leaves. Meng Eight was staring into the distance. The old dog did not move, either because it was old or it had seen so much that there was nothing to move for.

Lingguan felt that he was withering away, body and mind.

A dog barked in the distance.

7

Mengzi was carried back home after Baigou beat him bloody that night.

The cause of the fight was remarkably simple. Wanting to see how virile Mengzi was, Baigou, Huaqiu, and Maodan forcibly examined his genitals, and if that weren't enough, pushed his head down into his crotch—what was usually called 'an old man checking on his melons.' It so infuriated Mengzi that he knocked Huaqiu and Maodan down, and then wrestled Baigou to the ground, where, according to Baigou he jabbed his genitals into Baigou's eyes. "Ever seen anything like that?" he demanded. "Well, take a good look." Baigou fought back, and they tangled up on the floor.

In the end, Baigou knocked Mengzi out with a bottle.

The sight of his bloodied head horrified his mother, who assumed that Shuangfu had done it. She sent Hantou for the doctor.

"Get him out of here!" Laoshun shouted. "Get him out. He deserved it; they ought to beat him to death. Even that would be too good for him after the shame he's brought down on this family. He'd be better off dead."

Mengzi moaned as he came to and struggled to get up.

"How dare you moan and groan after what you did!" Laoshun was hopping mad. "Why don't you go kill yourself? I'd rather you just die."

Mengzi's mother was quaking as she wiped off the blood with a hot towel, her tears flowing unchecked.

Hantou returned with the doctor, who examined Mengzi's wound, announced it wasn't serious, and put on a bandage. He wrote out a prescription when Mengzi complained about the pain.

Seeing that his friend was in no danger, Maodan explained what had happened. Lingguan's mother jumped to her feet, like an old hen puffing up its feathers to protect her young. "I thought it was Shuangfu. So it was Baigou. What right did he have? I'm going to get to the bottom of this." She turned to go out the door, but Maodan stopped her.

"Mengzi gave him a bloody nose. He started it."

"I don't care. Mengzi didn't hit anyone with a bottle. Pick him up," she said. "We'll carry him over to their house. He can't get away with this." Hantou cast a helpless look at his father.

"What are you yelling about?" Laoshun spouted, sending spittle into his wife's face. "This boy has shamed our ancestors; with a son like that, how do you have the face to go to their house?"

"He's my boy. Don't you tell me I can't find out what gave them the right to do this."

"Why didn't he take it out on me, or on you? Why did he do it only to this no-good bastard? He was born to have the shit beat out of him. I wish he'd hit him harder. Too bad it didn't crack his skull and spill his brains. That would have saved the country a bullet."

"Where did all that hate come from?" his wife roared. "Who are you cursing? Take a minute and ask yourself what kind of father you are. Hantou, go get him the pickaxe. We'll see whose brain he's going to spill. I went through a lot of trouble raising the boy and never laid a finger on him. You think you're being reasonable. Well, you're not."

Laoshun was steaming; his beard quivered. "It's your fault for spoiling him. When I tried to discipline him, he talked back and got away with it. Now see what's happened? He's grown up, and this is the sort of thing he's capable of. Maybe you don't care about losing face, but I do. I know your skin is as thick as the city wall, and I know your guts aren't as clean as you think they are. So don't talk about me, you disgraceful old crone."

"Now, now." Maodan tried to push Laoshun away. "Don't use this as an excuse to bring up something else, all right? Let's all calm down. What happened happened, so there's nothing to talk about."

"Get lost!" she spat at Maodan. "Let him explain how I'm disgraceful. Ask him what I've done. Did I steal stuff, rob people, cheat them, sell my body, what? Tell me. I won't let you off if you don't. I've had enough anyway. You might as well crack my skull while you're at it." She rammed her head into her husband's chest repeatedly.

Poor Hantou did not know what to do, taking a step forward but quickly backing away. He reached out to take his mother's sleeve, for which he was rewarded with a slap. Now he looked even more helpless.

Finally, Huaqiu decisively stepped up and pulled her back by grabbing her arm.

"Let her go, Huaqiu," Laoshun demanded. "Let's see what the old crone can do. What does she think she's doing, acting up like that?

You know what your son has done, so why can't I say something? You think you've done a good job with him, so why couldn't you keep him in line, instead of shaming the ancestors?"

"Let it go, just let it go," Maodan urged. "Everyone take a step back and hold your tongue. You can get past this."

"Are you saying that this is about me only?" she said, stepping forward threateningly. "You're his father, have you done a good job with him? Raising a child without teaching him right from wrong is the father's fault. What did you ever teach him?"

"Me, teach him? Every time I tried you bit my head off. How was I supposed to teach him anything?"

"You call what you do teaching? You threaten to spill his brains and curse him to high heaven. No other father around here deals with his son like you do. Why don't you ever have a nice word to say to him?"

"Nice word? Has he ever listened? Is he a human being? No, he's a beast. Did I ever tell him to go whoring, tell me that?"

Ying'er walked in, took her mother-in-law's hand and tried to pull her back. "Let me go!" she shouted, struggling to break free. "You think you can stroll in here and everything's fine? Has he ever carried out his responsibility as a father? Let go, let go of me. I don't believe he's going to chew me up and spit me out. All my life… all I've taken from him… and he still picks on me, even with the boys grown up. Go ahead, start chewing, if you can."

With Ying'er pulling and Huaqiu pushing from behind, they were able to ease her out of the room and quiet her down.

Mengzi's eyes were shut, his forehead was beaded with sweat. Even he did not know what was worse, what he was feeling in his heart or his injured head.

Laoshun's anger melted away, now that his wife had left the room. He climbed onto the bed and lit his pipe. "What was wrong with the old crone? How could she say all that?" he wondered aloud after a few moments. "How can she say I was irresponsible? What did she mean? Because I haven't found a wife for our son? I can't believe she'd say something like that." He tossed away his tobacco pouch and lowered his head, not saying anything to anyone. The tears came again, but this time he let them flow. No one would know he was crying if it weren't for the choking sound.

The atmosphere had cooled by the time Lingguan walked in. His mother was sobbing in Ying'er's room; his father was on his haunches on the bed, still steaming. He interrupted his cursing by loud puffs on his pipe, like a roasted bean popping in cooling ashes. Maodan was still gesturing, talking about the incident, while Lingguan felt under assault by an evil wind, which swept away all the clarity Meng Eight had granted him.

8

The injury helped Mengzi out of a jam, allowed him to return home after the scandal.

What bothered him most was facing his mother. He felt no sense remorse toward his father, whose tongue-lashing and complaint had helped shed some of his psychological burden; but a shadow settled over his heart when he thought about his mother, and that made him feel close to suicidal. It was harder to cope with than any embarrassment over the incident itself.

He woke up in the morning with a throbbing headache. The first glimpse of daylight included the sight of his mother, her face a study in anguish. Clearly, concern about her son's injury had weakened her feelings about the disgraceful incident itself. A natural exchange followed: She asked him how his head felt and he responded; no embarrassment, nothing forced, and no evasion, as if nothing had happened.

That put him at ease; as a result, his head did not hurt quite as much, and his anger toward Baigou subsided. Calmly, he recalled the details of the quarrel, admitting to himself that he had overreacted. That did not excuse Baigou for smashing a bottle over his head, because it could have killed him. He recalled he'd been first to lose his temper and bloody Baigou's nose. He'd pounded on his friend as if to let off some steam and had come to his senses only when he saw the blood. He'd frozen, giving Baigou the opportunity to pick up a bottle and whack him.

Mengzi was glad he could come home, where he was safe from the elements and could leave the rumors and gossip at the doorstep. He turned over when a particular spot hurt under the pressure, and took a pain pill when his head hurt. Still feeling dizzy, he hovered between sleep and wakefulness. He was even feeling grateful to Baigou. If not for what he'd done, Mengzi would be out there somewhere, wandering like a homeless mutt, not knowing when or if he could go home.

His mother brought him two fried eggs for breakfast. He was dizzy and his head throbbed. When he sat up, he realized he'd been badly hurt. But when he saw the worried look on her face, he smiled—surprised he could do that—and sprawled on a pillow to eat a unique sickbed meal. His mother watched him eat, her eyebrows and lips twitching with each bite.

"I'll be fine," he said. "You don't have to stay with me."

She walked out of the room, the sight of her bony back having a strange emotional impact on him. How painful it must have been to hear what he'd done. He experienced almost crippling remorse. "What kind of person does something like that?"

He lay back down after placing the empty bowl on the edge of the bed, and once the pain caused by that simple motion diminished, he reflected on all that had occurred over the past couple of days. Everything felt like a dream; too much had been packed into two short days, as if many years had gone by. He wondered what Shuangfu's wife was doing at that moment. What would she do even if she did get a divorce? Hard to say. The thought of marrying her had never occurred to him; she was not what he had in mind for a wife, and thought of her only when he felt the urge. Afterward, the attraction no longer existed. Worse than that, when it was over, her hugs and kisses, her wild behavior and passion, repulsed him. She was not for him.

The costs of physical injury and loss of reputation over a woman who meant so little to him was too high. To be sure, he'd never imagined it would reach this point. He had thought that it was between the two of them only; no one else knew, so he could pull up his pants and still act respectably. He would never have done it if he'd known they would be found out. He would rather sleep with Yue'er, if the cost was to be that high. She was pretty, sexy, and a virgin. That would have made the sacrifice worth it—he recalled her seductive glance. But he'd always been afraid of getting her pregnant and ruining his reputation. And yet, he still managed to ruin it by gaining less.

Just let it go. What's done is done. He forced regretful thoughts away, but they reentered his head like rats finding holes. Instead, he focused on recalling how Shuangfu had arrogantly ignored him when they'd met in the village two years before, which was a good reason to avenge the slight. His mood brightened and all the unhappy thoughts vanished, leaving only satisfaction and the pleasure of revenge.

Shuangfu was, after all, a proud man, educated, showy, and rich. There was nothing degrading about bedding his wife; it was like slapping the man on both cheeks, something Mengzi would have loved to do when he saw that arrogant look on his face. What do you have to be so smug about, besides your filthy money? He also believed that what he'd done pleased many of the villagers, who were choking on jealous thoughts of Shuangfu's wealth. Now he had screwed the man's wife in such spectacular fashion that he would have been surprised if it hadn't pleased some of them. He wished he hadn't run away, especially in that disgraceful manner, which made him resent the woman. If she hadn't told him to flee, he wouldn't have. He'd have fought back. A few punches and kicks to the chest and abdomen would have sent Shuangfu to the floor, followed by a vicious stomp with his foot—but not hard enough to do permanent damage. Then, when the defeated man begged for mercy and kowtowed, he'd magnanimously let him off. A gentleman does not bear grudges against a worthless opponent; he would clap his hands, toss his hair, and walk off.

Mengzi was so animated that his headache, which he'd forgotten in the excitement, returned with a vengeance. Along with his return to reality, he realized how foolish he'd been, especially the giddy thought of whipping Shuangfu, who was not the sort to beg for mercy, let alone kowtow. On the contrary, he was a real man, physically and mentally strong, which was why he stood out. In Mengzi's mind, Shuangfu was someone who would not flinch even if a knife were plunged into him.

Mengzi began to get suspicious when he recalled Shuangfu's performance; during the fight he had not seemed particularly aggressive. His punches were measured and lacked power; and he surely could have broken free of his wife's hold on his legs and run after Mengzi if he'd wanted to. Then when Mengzi went back to the house the following morning, there was no sign of overwhelming hostility, which would have been more befitting his ruthless nature. He didn't come after Mengzi after that either, for he was too busy demanding a divorce. That was not normal. Mengzi felt his head throb, the pain swirled like an eddy, but he managed to capture a dangling shred of suspicion, which was: Shuangfu's plan all along was to get a divorce, and Mengzi had helped him achieve his goal.

With that realization, the satisfaction of sleeping with Shuangfu's wife turned to dejection and shame over being duped.

"I smelled his farts," he said to himself. As boys, Beizhu used to get him to smell his hand after passing gas. That was much the same way he felt now, except that this time it had cost him his good name. He was so angry he had a splitting headache. Now he understood that she had seen through Shuangfu's scheme of using the scandal as an excuse to get rid of her. Mengzi had been so proud of himself! What a joke. A real halfwit, as his mother often called him.

Mengzi was so caught up in his thoughts that he did not realize that Lingguan was there by his bed giving him a funny look. Annoyed, he turned his head, suddenly too ashamed to see anyone, as if everyone knew how he'd been the butt of a clever ruse.

No wonder Shuangfu had made a spectacle out of something most people would prefer to keep out of the public eye. He had put on a show of humiliation to convince others that he had every right to renounce his wife, who deserved her punishment. No one in the village would actually blame him for wanting a divorce, that Mengzi had caused the divorce and the breaking up a family. That must have been his plan. The picture was getting clearer, and Mengzi was getting angrier. He grabbed his pillow and choked it, as if it were Shuangfu's neck, and didn't let go till he was exhausted by another sudden wave of pain.

Chapter Eight

1

Laoshun had aged considerably, seemingly overnight, and had lost so much weight that his cheekbones protruded and his eyes were sunken. His workaday clothes hung on him.

The first thing he did that morning was seek out the village sorceress.

Born to the Qi family, she was the second richest person in Shawan. Only fifty years old, her face was deeply lined; her upper lip overlay the lower one, and both were a deep red. As she spoke she lovingly licked those lips, habitually puckering them into a smile. She walked seductively on small feet, hips swaying like willow branches. Word had it that she had suffered a serious illness in her youth, one that had hung on for a full three years with no cure in sight. Then one night a spirit came to her and returned every night just before midnight, when she would yawn three times and shiver, her joints cracking loudly, before she foamed at the mouth and passed out. When that happened, the spirit entered her body and gave her the power to tell fortunes and cure other people's illnesses.

The storyteller said that what entered here body was a sprite, not a spirit. True spirits, like gods, do not come just because they are summoned. And once they come they are not easily dismissed. Easy in, not so easy out. Once, when she was done administering her cure, she said, in an eerie, strange voice that she was from Lantian, Shaanxi, where she'd died of an illness at eighteen before practicing self-cultivation to become a sprite. According to her, she was among the lowest rank of deities, which included celestial deities, immortal deities, earthly deities, human deities and ghostly deities, or sprites. Sprites gained their attainment in the underworld, with no clear image or recognition on the three magical mountains. Though free of the cycle of transmigration, they were nonetheless denied entry to Penglai Island, except to be reborn as humans. Those who practiced self-cultivation were not interested in great enlightenment; instead they sought speedy success, which led to a withered figure with an ashen complexion. Possessed of the mind and consciousness of humans, they had a focused will to attain spirituality, and eventually succeeded in becoming spirits of the underworld, which was why they were enlightened ghosts, but not immortals of the pure yang world. They were called sprites because of their single will, a coalescence of the yin.

When she had time on her hands, she chattered away about the local customs and culture of Lantian, Shaanxi, and sang about its ten most unusual facts: "Their steamed rolls look like pot lids, their noodles are like trouser cords, they squat outside their door to eat, their houses are built in a straight line with no courtyards, their daughters never marry out of town, they eat spicy fried vegetable seeds, and they squat not sit on benches." That was the truth. When an herbal medicine peddler from Shaanxi came to the village one year, he said, "This is bizarre. The woman must be a deity, because she knows about Shaanxi's ten most unusual facts and speaks with an authentic Lantian accent, though she has never been there." So people from near and far crowded into her house after nightfall, and, over the decades, her door sill, crafted from a desert date tree, broke eighteen times from foot traffic.

Nearly every villager in her age group considered the sorceress to be a kind of in-law, a qingjia. She was called in as a protector whenever a village youngster fell ill, and when her services as sorceress were not needed she became the village matchmaker.

"I've been disgraced, Qingjia," Laoshun complained with a sigh. "Raising that boy has brought shame on my family, and it seems pointless to even think of going on."

"It can't be that serious, Qingjia." She puckered her lips. "All young people do foolish things. Besides, it was preordained and could not be avoided."

"Is that so?" Laoshun started at her wide-eyed.

"It's what's known as a karmic hurdle. Sometimes it is out in the open, sometimes not, but it is inescapable. Once he gets past that hurdle, the danger will be over, so you need not worry. When he's married and has a son, by working hard he'll be a new man. Right now, he's like an unbroken stallion."

When Laoshun heard the sorceress talk about karmic hurdles, he was reminded of his own foolish escapades as a young man, and he thought she must be right. Why worry if it's unavoidable?

The sorceress picked her teeth with a bamboo splinter. "I know why you're here," she said. "You want me to find Mengzi a wife, don't you? No problem. We are qingjia, so your business is my business. I'll keep my eyes open and let you know when I find a suitable match. Have you gone out into the desert recently?"

"How could I? I'm about to fall apart over what's happened over the past few days. I haven't been taking care of my hawks, let alone go into the desert. I'll go out and catch some rabbits for you one of these days."

"No hurry. Whenever it's convenient. Tell me what you're looking for. That will make my job easier.

"As long as it's female, the rest is up to you. After dividing up the property, he can be a tiger or a dragon, and I'll be spared anger when I see him. As they say, fathers owe their children a karmic debt, so I'll pay off my debts, and the rest is up to him. People who are aware of what he did consider him to be a no-good shit, while those who don't blame me for not finding him a wife. I don't want that, so go find him someone. It doesn't matter what she's like. I trust your judgment. Too pretty and he'll have trouble keeping her. Not pretty enough and he'll grumble. Someone in between, smart enough and honest enough is best.

2

After leaving the sorceress, Laoshun went to see Meng Eight. The minute he walked in the door he said he needed to borrow some money. "I can manage that," Meng said with a smile, "but I'll have to go to the bank to get it." Laoshun knew he meant fox hunting in the desert. "No problem," Laoshun said, "but it's kind of urgent. If you can get me two thousand, I'll find a way to borrow some more and sell off some grain to pay off my karmic debt to that damned son of mine."

"The time has come," Meng said with a chuckle. "After Mengzi's out the door, it'll be Lingguan's turn. You won't have time to pause in turning your millstone, you old donkey."

"One day at a time," Laoshun replied. "You gather the firewood the mountain makes available. I think time has just about run out for these old bones. The man in charge ought to take pity and give me a chance to rest."

"Not yet. Too early for that," Meng said. "That would let you off too easily. An old cow shits until the day it dies. You still have hard times ahead, first finding daughters-in-law, then getting grandchildren, and you can't wash your hands of any of it. That would be too easy on you."

"I know. I have to keep working while there's still breath in my body. But there are days when I feel like ending it all… it all seems so pointless."

"What kind of bullshit talk is that?" Meng fired back, deadly serious. "You live the best you can. An ignoble life is better than a noble death. Nature spares even a rootless weed. If you end it yourself, you'll be the ghost of a wrongful death and there'll be no place for you. If you don't have much to show for being alive, you can't put yourself in that state after death."

"I hear what you're saying. I'll have to keep going on, like an old cow that suffers all its life, and when it dies, its bones and flesh wind up in people's stomachs. But I ask you, what's the point in living?"

"It's all tied up with destiny," Meng said with another smile, "so deal with it. If eating shit is your fate, shut your eyes and eat it. Don't think too much. Crazy thoughts solve nothing and they drive a man crazy. It's pointless."

"That's what you say, but it doesn't make it any easier. If suffering gives you comfort, fine. But I feel… somehow fouled."

"What do you have to be uncomfortable about? Your son slept with a woman, that's it. He didn't do anything to lose his head over. You suffered no broken limbs, and everyone in your family is doing fine. What else do you want? Go to the hospital in town and take a look. Someone is always dying, with weeping, moaning and groaning, rotting noses, blindness, problems with intestines, liver problems… anything and everything. So what do you want? People always want more, more than they can handle. Be content with what you have, and everything will be fine."

"Sure, I feel better when I compare myself with those people," Laoshun said. "But the problems haven't gone away."

"What problems? What problems could you possibly have? Tell me. They add up to nothing. When you think about it, they're less than nothing. It's like New Year's. Think about it, and it passes. Don't think about it, and it passes. So why waste your time thinking about it? It won't leap from one year to the next just because you think about, nor will it turn back to the Mid-Autumn Festival simply because you don't. New Year's will be there whether you think about it or not. Worry about it, and it passes. Stop worrying about it, and it passes. Either way it makes no difference. When the time to solve a problem arrives, you'll take care of it, but not before, so don't worry yourself sick for nothing. When your son is small, you worry if he'll grow up. A waste of time. He'll grow up whether you worry or not. He sure won't go back into the womb. Then when he grows up, you worry that he's getting old and still not married. Also a waste of time. He's going to get old no matter what you do. So stop worrying about it."

Laoshun wore an unhappy look. "That's easy for you to say, but how do I keep from worrying?"

"How? Do you have to ask? Can worrying bring you wealth? Will it bring your son a wife? Let's say you're worried about having an affair with your daughter-in-law. That won't bring her to your bed. You can't get a grandson by worrying. Can you reach down and pull one out of your daughter-in-law? Of course not. So stop worrying and be content with doing what you have to do. What you should be doing now is borrowing money to find a marriageable girl. Don't worry about anything else. It's like growing watermelons. Spread manure, dig up weeds, irrigate, and it's done. Worrying can't do it. Things turn out the way they're supposed to, and you'll have melons to harvest. Worst case is, you do what you need to do, but still no melons. Even then there's no need to worry. You've poured your heart and soul into it, and what's left is up to Heaven. Nature won't worry. If Heaven is wrong, it will have to worry, so why should you? You foolish old man."

"All right, stinky mouth, you win," Laoshun said with a laugh. "You could talk a sterile mule into having offspring."

"It's not the mouth," Meng replied.

"Then what is it, a sluice gate?"

"It's the heart, not the mouth. You need to know that. It's important to be content with what you have. Don't be greedy. If it's millet soup in your bowl, don't wish it was rabbit, and when it's rabbit, don't sneer at millet soup. Enjoy what you have and don't wish for more. Always wanting more turns you into someone who exploits people, takes advantage of them, schemes and harms them… and that's a life not worth living. It's pointless. The key to life is how you live it. A good heart makes for a good life; a bad heart ensures a life with no value. You've made a big deal out of what Mengzi did, but if it is a big deal, stringing yourself up won't make it less of one. He's a youngster who had a momentary lapse of judgment and did something he shouldn't have done. Who hasn't at one time or another? You? I won't pick at your scabs. You say he's humiliated you, soiled you somehow. So what? You walk around with a face so dirty and smelly that even the Dasha River couldn't wash it clean. But say it's no big deal, and that's what it becomes. You think someone who leads a Confucian life has never messed up? Confucius himself did. The storyteller said that Confucius once had a fling with a woman called Nanzi. You can look it up, he said. That's just how things are. So all this talk about doing away with yourself, what with your 'Ai, the ancestors are so ashamed they would jump off the altar.' What do they have to be ashamed of? Why do they need to jump off the altar? They were humans, too, and I can't believe they were never guilty of whoring… so there's no need for you to yell and scream about Mengzi. Think back to your own youth. That's all you need to do."

Laoshun glared at Meng before laughing. "There isn't another mouth like yours anywhere. You're like a mule in heat, going this way and that, and always in the right. You were the one who was most critical of Mengzi at first, and now this is what you say."

"To you only." Meng smiled. "With the youngsters I say something different. We're getting old, and we've seen and done pretty much everything. It's time for us to take it easy. But I'd never say any of this to them. That would make them think there's nothing wrong with doing something bad. Or they might quit and do nothing but eat and sleep, like pigs. What works for you won't necessarily work for him."

Laoshun was beginning to feel better. What Meng was saying drove away the glum feeling he'd suffered for days. "I'll do what you say, and quit worrying. But I'll still need half of the money from you for Mengzi's wedding. Don't worry, you'll get it back. I wouldn't get four ounces of oil if I melted down my bones, and I couldn't scrape enough hair to fill a plate. I wouldn't have enough to get him a wife if I sold off everything I own."

"You're shameless." Meng said. "She'll call you Papa, not me. Why should I concern myself with things like that."

"I'll make sure she address you nicely. She can call you what you want. Sweetheart, darling, even Papa won't be a problem."

"No, that's your right. I don't want it. Later on, when you reach into her arms to pick up the baby and you touch something nice and soft, don't forget me."

"That's easy. I'll move away so you can reach for the baby and do it."

They shared a hearty laugh. Laoshun looked up and saw the sun. Strange, he was thinking, why haven't I seen the sun over the past few days?

3

Mengzi finally left the house after a difficult week, spent mostly in bed. His injury had healed; all major symptoms now gone, only an occasional stab of pain lingered. From Huaqiu he learned that Shuangfu had left without a divorce. Apparently, the township clerk had not been in his office, so Shuangfu had simply "slinked off," according to Huaqiu. The villagers thought that Shuangfu had beaten Mengzi bloody, until Huaqiu, Maodan, and Baigou disabused them of the "rumor" and they accepted the embellished version that Mengzi had knocked Shuangfu to the ground and had stopped short of stomping on the man's back only because the woman had begged him to. Otherwise, he could have broken the man's back.

"Guess what," Huaqiu said excitedly. "People are saying that the bastard had it coming. So what if he's rich. That doesn't give him the right to abandon his village wife." Thanks to the warm autumn sun and Huaqiu's exaggerated narration, Mengzi was pleased by how things had worked out. The guilt he'd felt for days was on the wane.

Huaqiu grew increasingly animated. "Know when Shuangfu left? Early before sunup. As a cuckold, he could not face the villagers. But someone saw him anyway. Know who? Beizhu. He said Shuangfu's face turned bright red when he saw him, and he immediately handed Beizhu a cigarette—a good one, of course, probably foreign. Beizhu could tell what Shuangfu was thinking. He asked him not to tell anyone he'd left the village so early. But Beizhu told the first person he saw, saying he'd slipped away before dawn, his face red from humiliation. Say what you like, but he left as a cuckold."

Mengzi smiled as he recalled how he had flirted with Fengxiang. Beizhu doesn't know it, he was thinking, but he'd nearly made him a cuckold too. Huaqiu misinterpreted the smile. "That's right," he said. "It makes everyone happy. The arrogant bastard has a little money, so what? The last time he was here he treated everybody but me to a cigarette. The arrogant bastard. I don't smoke, of course, but that's my business. Agree? He wouldn't even look my way. Treated me like a child. Well, fuck him. How much older is he than me? He's got me by a couple of years, that's all. Ambition has nothing to do with age, and a long life is wasted if you have no aspirations. Material things are easy to deal with, but people are impossible to predict. Who knows, I might have a windfall one day, get so rich I'll smoke opium if I want. Who needs his cigarettes anyway?"

Mengzi laughed; Huaqiu's boasts had sounded as if he was ready to take on the world, but in the end all his talk amounted to was a hoped-for windfall. "I agree. Sometimes food will drop right into a blind man's mouth, so who knows, maybe one day an official's hat will drop down on your head. You'll be a township magistrate."

"Township magistrate?" Huaqiu said with a wry laugh. "I might just manage a term as Party Chairman... what's wrong with this country, how come only one chairman? Feels shabby to me. Pump it up to seven or eight, and I'll be one. I won't ask for a salary. Who cares about money anyway?"

Mengzi laughed so hard his head hurt, so he reached up and touched the scar. Huaqiu delighted in seeing Mengzi laugh. "Actually, it doesn't make a damned bit of difference. Chairman or ordinary citizen, they're all the same, just the way whatever you eat ends up the same way. They both have to shit. When it's time to die, you die. So what's so special about the chairmanship? If you've got a bottle, finish it; don't worry if tomorrow there'll only be water. Each day is no more than A.M. and P.M."

"What is it with you?" Mengzi said. "One minute you're going to rule the world, the next you're worse than an ant's grandson."

"Just like everybody else."

Laoshun walked out through the gate, so Huaqiu stopped talking. Laoshun ignored them both as he led his camel out toward the Dasha River.

"Oh, I almost forgot the most important thing." Huaqiu took a fifty-yuan bill out of his pocket and handed it to Mengzi. "Baigou told me to give it to you to buy something good for your health and not be mad at him."

"I don't want his money." Mengzi's face darkened. "Men fight, that's just how it is. Maybe one day I'll crack open his skull, and I won't give him anything."

"That's what he's afraid of." Huaqiu laughed. "He knows he's no match for you, but that won't stop him from using a knife if it comes to that."

"Don't try to scare me with that. It won't work."

"As I see it, you can't put all the blame on him. You got in some good punches."

"Let it go, will you?" Mengzi said as his spirits dropped. "Everything is fine now. It's history. He can keep his money."

"Sure. I told him you wouldn't take it. Everybody knows what you're made of."

4

Lingguan walked out and spotted Mengzi chatting pleasantly with Huaqiu. "What is it with you?" he said to his brother. "After scaring the henhouse with a pole, you think it's all right to be joking with friends."

"You sound mad," Huaqiu said with a laugh. "But are you man enough to use your pole like that? I doubt it. Anyone who can take a bite out of Shuangfu's woman's ass is OK in my book."

"Go bite her yourself," Lingguan said as he gave Huaqiu a shove. "But be careful you don't lose your teeth in the process."

"Too late. Someone's already got his foot in the door."

Lingguan punched Huaqiu in the arm and turned to Mengzi. "You think what you did is no big deal, but Father is furious."

"I know," Mengzi said with a frown, "I know he is. You all want me to look like a penitent, don't you? Well, I can't do it."

"Lingguan means well," Huaqiu said with a smile. "You saw the fire in your father's eyes and those deep toad-like creases in his forehead. He might start croaking one of these days."

"What does he have to croak about? I'm not his punching bag. I'll live as long as I can, but when the day comes that I can't, there are all sorts of ways to end it. I can cut my throat or hang myself."

"Listen to your big talk," Lingguan sneered. "Forget I said anything." He turned and walked off.

When he reached the field he saw Hantou squatting by one of the earth dykes holding his side. "Go home and rest if you don't feel well," Lingguan said. "The rapeseeds won't be yellow for days yet. Besides, we can help."

Ying'er dropped the seeds in her hand and wiped her face with her scarf. "He won't listen to me," she said. "I've said the same thing to him more times than I can count."

"I'm fine," Hantou said. "It hurts no matter where I am, even in bed, so what's the difference?"

"What is it you've got?" Lingguan asked him. "You need to find out. You can't keep taking whatever medicine is handy."

"They've checked, including my liver function, and still don't know. They want me to take a B-scan, but they're too expensive, almost a hundred. What's the point?" He straightened up. "It's better already, a little pain is all. Weird, don't you think, how there's swelling and pain between my ribs?"

"Thumping your side doesn't help," said Lingguan. "Besides, a minor problem can develop into a major one if you don't take care of it right away."

"I've got it all planned." Hantou said. "I'll go ahead and spend the money on a B-scan in a few days, and we'll see. If my time is up, so be it."

"Listen to him. He's always saying gloomy things like that," Ying'er complained. "You need to be upbeat to keep going."

"She's right," Lingguan agreed.

"How's Mengzi?" Hantou asked. "You need to keep your eye on him. Don't let him do something stupid."

"He and Huaqiu were having a great time talking. He looked like he was on top of the world.

"That's enough sarcasm," Hantou said. "Don't push him too hard."

"He gave me hell just a moment ago."

"Why would he do that for no apparent reason unless he wasn't feeling bad?"

"That's what I thought." Lingguan laughed. "I was just wondering why he doesn't seem to care about what happened."

"The more you seem not to care," Ying'er volunteered, "the more you care."

Hantou quietly picked a handful of rapeseeds. "It's really nothing... but doing that to another man's woman. Think about it. It's like a thunderclap on a clear day. How is she going to live if her husband divorces her?"

"He wanted a divorce all along," Lingguan said. "This was just an excuse. They say he wanted to give her lots of money, but she said she wouldn't take it."

"What good is a lot of money?" commented Ying'er. "What matters most to a woman is a man's heart. If they have that, being poor means nothing."

"What doesn't Shuangfu have," Hantou asked. "He's got money, so what else does he need in order to be a loving man?"

"That shows how little you know," Ying'er said. "There aren't words to describe what loving is, but a woman knows. Shuangfu knows only money. Family means nothing to him. She's better off divorcing him than living the life of a grass widow."

Taken aback, Hantou looked unhappy as he yanked out a handful of weeds.

One look at Hantou told Lingguan that he was hurt by her careless comment. "Hey, sounds to me like you're one of those progressive women," he said. "You didn't deserve to be born here. Like a big turtle in a small pond, you don't have the space you need."

Ying'er wiped her sweaty face, looked at Lingguan, and said with a smile, "Maybe so, but only if nothing happens. Shuangfu's wife is a strong woman. I can't imagine what might have happened if it had been another woman."

"Strong?" Hantou nearly shouted. "A shameless..." He didn't finish. He trailed off, and moved forward.

Ying'er's face turned red. She bit her lip and looked first at Hantou, and then at Lingguan. "That's right," Lingguan sounded off. "Men steal objects, women steal men, and they are worse than pigs and dogs." Ying'er quietly reached over and pinched his arm hard.

Chapter Nine

1

During lunch Laoshun's wife said, "Wuzi's illness has gotten worse. He set Goubao's haystack on fire and went around biting women on the lips. Gimpy was so angry he used a whip on the boy."

"No wonder there was a whole bunch of people out there," Lingguan said. "I thought it was another meeting."

"Gimpy is at his wit's end," she said. "He's sold off his grain and whatever else he could sell. The boy has been hospitalized, and has taken piles of medicine, but he's still the same."

"Staying the same would have been good news," Laoshun said. "Because it looks like the more he's treated, the worse he gets. At first he only chased women when his illness flared up. Now... ah, it's like a rope breaks at the thinnest spot. The poorer you are, the more likely you'll come down with something that costs a lot of money."

"I agree," Lingguan said. "Take someone like Shuangfu, healthy as a horse."

The mere mention of Shuangfu rekindled Laoshun's unhappiness, so he snorted but held his tongue.

But Mengzi chose to speak up. "He knows how to take care of himself, the picture of health with all the ginseng and tortoiseshell he consumes. He could scare off any illness."

Lingguan looked at Mengzi and could not keep from laughing.

"What are you laughing about?" Mengzi glared at his brother. "That's the truth."

"Of course it is. I'm laughing at you, the clown."

Hantou glanced at Mengzi and laughed also; he was about to join in, but said nothing after stealing a glance at his father.

With a look at Laoshun, Lingguan's mother changed the subject. "What does Gimpy have to say?"

"What could he say?" Laoshun snapped. "It's in the hands of fate. He could take out one of his ribs, but it wouldn't be worth a damned thing."

"Does your side still hurt?" Hantou's mother asked after a few sips of soup. "Talk of illness always makes me uneasy."

"It's fine now," he said as he patted his side. "It's not serious. The medicine we bought last time seems to have done the trick."

"Don't listen to him" Lingguan erupted. "You were doubled over in pain out in the field this morning."

"Sometimes he curls up like a shrimp it hurts so much," Ying'er said. "How can you say it's fine?"

"Who are you trying to fool?" Hantou's mother paled. "An illness can't be fooled."

"I know how to deal with it," Hantou said with a reassuring smile. "The pain comes in waves, and all I have to do is press against my side to stop it. That works better than any medicine, stops the pain but isn't a cure, like pounding on cold water. Medications don't work."

"No matter what you say, taking medicine is better than doing nothing," his mother said.

"What are you saying?" said Lingguan. "There's hot medicine and there's cold, just like illnesses. If you take hot medicine for a hot disease or cold medicine for a cold one it'll only get worse."

"He's right," Hantou agreed. "My mouth is always dry, and the more I take the medicine, the harder it is… to… you know."

"Don't say things like that while we're eating." Ying'er frowned.

"I didn't say the word shit."

"Enough!" she complained. "You've already said too much."

"You eat your lunch," Mengzi laughed, "and let him say what he wants. He's not shitting in your mouth, so what's the problem?"

Ying'er gave Mengzi a dirty look, but said nothing.

"Just eat, everybody," Lingguan said. "No more gross talk. Anyone who does will get a full chamber pot over his head."

Mengzi laughed so hard he spit out the food in his mouth. Ying'er banged her bowl down on the table, got up, and left.

"Did you see that?" their mother said. "A couple of words and she has trouble eating, like her throat froze up."

"That's true," Laoshun echoed with a smile. "Hei, young men these days. Back when we went to the city to collect animal dung, we rubbed our hands together when we were done and ate whatever we had, not like young folks these days, with their delicate teeth chewing slowly… Actually their cleanliness is all for show. No one has laundry detergent in their gut to keep it clean, do they?"

"There! Now you finally admit it. You were upset before when I said you ate shit," Lingguan's mother said with a smile.

"That's enough dumb talk," Laoshun said. "Eat up. Finish and get on with what you have to do."

"How come what I say is dumb talk," his wife said, "but everyone else spits out pearls of wisdom?"

After lunch, Laoshun went to see Gimpy. A crowd had gathered at his house, where his wife was sitting on a stool by the door sobbing. Wuzi was sitting on the steps, a mysterious, satisfied smile on his face, off in his own world. Gimpy, who was crouching on the *kang*, pipe in hand, did not look up no matter who walked into the house.

"This could happen to anyone," Meng Eight said to console Gimpy. "There's no need to hang your head like this. We're all made of flesh, and only a heartless person would say anything."

"I didn't hear anything," Beizhu joined in. "Everyone knows that Wuzi isn't well."

"That's true." The others voiced their agreement.

"Besides, what could anyone say, since all he did was burn up a haystack," Beizhu said. "What's the big deal? It's just hay, isn't it? If Goubao's unhappy, I'll let him have mine."

"Who said I was unhappy? I never said a single word. There's plenty of kindling for the *kangs* in the winter. I can get some anywhere if I need it. What's the concern?"

"He's right," Beizhu agreed. "Come to my house and take what you want. You can even eat it if you want."

"You eat hay, I don't."

"What else did he do?" Beizhu asked. "Bit some women's lips. So what… they've all been kissed before, haven't they? They aren't virgins, so what are they afraid of? He just bites a little harder, draws a bit of blood. It's nothing serious. We played the kissing prank on his bride on Goubao's wedding day. Mengzi bit her bloody. Did people say anything about that?"

His comment lightened the mood in the room, drawing plenty of laughter.

"Don't you ever shut up?" Goubao complained. "You're like a crazed pig that bites hard and won't let go. Why don't you try to let it go?"

"I won't say anything more about you, how's that?"

Goubao whacked him in the backside and let the matter drop.

"Besides, it's not all Wuzi's fault. Those women should have dealt with it better. He's crazy, but they're not. So he chased them. They have legs, so what's to keep them from running away? He can't bite them if he can't catch them. It's odd, isn't it? I think they want to see what it feels like to be kissed by a virgin."

More laughter.

"You're talking out of both sides of your mouth. You can argue sides of anything," Meng Eight said. "You could even conjure up a few babies with your talk."

"Beizhu! Take your glib talk outside," Gimpy shouted. "I feel bad enough already. This boy is the bane of my existence, and he'd be better off dead. I feel terrible about what he's done to all of you, and I don't want anyone talking behind my back."

Beizhu's lips moved, but nothing came out.

"That'll be enough, Gimpy," Meng said. "Beizhu will say anything, everyone knows that. Whatever he says is like a new mother's fart—no smell."

"I wasn't serious, you know," Beizhu said to Meng, with a friendly punch. "Be nice with what you said; it's not a woman's fart. It can be a dog's fart, a man's, even a pig's, but definitely not a woman's."

The others laughed again. All that talk lessened Beizhu's embarrassment, and Gimpy crouched down again.

"Let's get serious," Laoshun said. "We have to do something about Wuzi's condition. One haystack today, another tomorrow, and before you know it, there won't be any left, and we'll freeze this winter. And the biting has to stop or no one will dare come to our village."

"I've been thinking about the same thing," said Meng Eight. "Let's put our heads together and come up with a solution."

"He needs treatment," Goubao said. "What else is there to say?"

"We're all standing at the well without scoops," Beizhu said. "Treatment? There's nothing Gimpy hasn't already tried."

"That's enough talk," Gimpy looked up and protested. "I can't stand it."

"That's your problem," Meng said. "I've watched the boy grow from playing in the dirt to a full grown man. We're all sad to see him the way he is now, and something has to be done. We need ideas."

"I know what you're getting at," Beizhu said. "I've got no money after paying fines for having too many kids, but I can give something at least, say fifty yuan. Everyone has to chip in; we all give what we can."

"I don't have much," Laoshun said, "but I can kick in a hundred."

Everyone present pledged what they could afford.

"Stop," Gimpy protested. "I appreciate the sentiment, but you'll just be wasting your money. It can't do any good. He goes into the hospital, and he's fine. But he goes off again as soon as he's back home. A waste of money. I've already thrown away several thousand, and he's only getting worse. So it's all in the hands of fate. I'll take whatever comes."

"Don't you worry," Meng Eight said, "you've done the best you could. Now wait till we do the best we can, then we'll see. Heaven will spare those who need it most."

"That's exactly right," Laoshun echoed. "Heaven will do that."

That night, Laoshun and Meng Eight went door-to-door, taking money from those who had it and provisions from those who didn't. They ended up with more than eight hundred. Gimpy refused to take it. "Count it as a loan," Meng said. "Pay us back when you're got it." That convinced him to accept it, and he took his son into town the next day.

2

Laoshun's wife was giving Hantou a talking-to. The pain in his side had returned, and she wanted him to see a doctor, but he refused. Medicines don't work, he claimed. Two prescriptions from Doctor Chen Routou only made it worse.

"You're like the blind cat focusing on a dead rat. Can't you go somewhere else? Try the city. Ying'er says you moaned from the pain in bed last night. You can't put it off. Just look at yourself, your face is all twisted."

"You make it sound horrible," Hantou said.

"It's worth a try," Laoshun spoke up. "If there's a problem, it can be taken care of. And if there isn't, you'll put your mother's mind at ease."

"Let's drop it, can we?"

"They want you to have it checked," Mengzi said impatiently. "So why don't you just go? Do you want them to get down on their knees and beg?"

Hantou held his tongue.

His mother handed Lingguan Baigou's fifty yuan and told him to go with Hantou.

The two brothers took a bus into town, where they registered at the district hospital.

The doctor prescribed a B-scan. When he heard it would cost over thirty yuan, Hantou was dead set against it.

"It won't cure what ails me, and it'll mean I'll have to spend more on medicine, so why not skip the B-scan and simply take the medicine?" That sounded reasonable to Lingguan.

After checking Hantou's pulse and studying his tongue, the doctor knitted his brows in thought before writing a prescription. Hantou's forehead was beaded with sweat as he looked hard into the doctor's narrowed eyes, his lips moving along with the man's eyelids.

"Nothing to worry about," the doctor said. "Liver discomfort caused by indigestion."

Lingguan breathed a sigh of relief; Hantou's facial muscles relaxed.

Lingguan fetched the prescription of two traditional medicines and some packets of liver pills, at a cost of a little over twenty yuan. Pleased with his decision and in high spirits, Hantou could not hold back: "Not bad, huh, only twenty yuan. The exam would have cost thirty or more, and wouldn't have done any good." He smiled.

After stopping for a bowl of beef noodles, they took advantage of the early hour to stroll around town. Hantou took delight in the sights and sounds of the city, which he seldom visited. Obviously, the doctor's assurance that it was nothing serious came as a great relief. As he pointed sights out to his brother, Lingguan was troubled by threads of guilt over his relationship with Ying'er.

Suddenly, at an intersection, they spotted a woman with one hand on her hip as she pointed with the other, flinging harsh words at passing cars. The gist of her shouts was a protest against official tyranny and the oppression of the common people, condemning the people in the cars for exploiting ordinary citizens and predicting a bad end for them. She was awe-inspiring, if slightly mad, vilifying the crestfallen drivers of every passing car that sped past her. Well pleased, she laughed buoyantly, joined by the people around her. She alternated between two facial expressions: fierce scowls for the car drivers and cordial smiles for the people on the street, occasionally exchanging pleasantries with them.

Intrigued, Hantou stopped and watched her for a moment. “Is she crazy?” he asked Lingguan.

“What do you think?” Lingguan replied with a smile.

“Not really, but she doesn’t sound normal either. And if she is, she doesn’t look it.”

“You’re right. Crazy but not mad, sane but a little crazy. She’s a celebrity in town, famous for standing in intersections and railing at drivers.”

“How does she get away with it?”

“Who would interfere? Everyone’s upset with the people driving those cars these days, but most people won’t go public with it. They love the idea of what she’s doing. Notice how the policeman isn’t stopping her?”

Hantou watched the woman and a policeman engaged in a friendly, light-hearted conversation, but she stopped and poured rancor onto the next car that drove by. The car sped by like a panicky beetle. That made Hantou laugh.

“She has guts,” he remarked.

They walked on. “Ma wants us to buy some tins of cypress incense, so let’s go.” He tugged on Lingguan’s sleeve. They asked in a number of shops, but none had what they wanted. "I'm sure we can find some at Haizang Temple," Lingguan said, "but it's not close to here. So let's go see if it's available at the God of Thunder Shrine. We might find some there."

An ancient shrine devoted to prayers for rain, it was built of clay and stood several feet tall, topped by a majestic temple. The grounds were jammed with people, for it was the fifteenth of the lunar month. A number of women were cavorting in dances of sorcery and making strange music. Lingguan, who had seen them before, found nothing unusual in the sight, but to Hantou it was a sinister scene that seemed to make his head swell.

One pair of women dancing opposite one another set up a contrast with one moving gracefully, the other awkwardly. Teacher and student, as if learning opera moves. Mystified, Lingguan asked an elderly man what the dance was about. 'Learning sorcery,' he was told. "How do you teach something like sorcery?" he wondered.

"You're right, of course," the man said. "A sorceress is a woman whose body is possessed by a supernatural being, and that is not something you can teach or learn."

"What kind of being inhabits a woman's body?"

"They're really just spirits, ghosts, what we call sprites," the old man said.

"I call it a form of madness," a young man in a suit commented.

"Some people say that," the old man replied. "But it's strange how some sick people are cured with the magical scorching after medicines fail to work."

"It's all in their heads," the young man said.

"Well, then it's psychotherapy," Lingguan said with a smile. "Some things are hard to explain and you can't treat everything the same way.

Take a crying baby. A month-old baby can't know anything about psychological effects, but strangely it stops crying once you incite a magic incantation."

Hantou quieted his brother by dragging him away.

Lingguan went up and bought two tickets, wanting his brother to see something new and different. As they walked through the gate, the drone of more shamans made Hantou's hair stand on end.

Stone lions fronting the main hall were covered with coins and small bills. Bunches of incense burning in the censers permeated the space with thick smoke, which turned the shamans into shadowy figures. With spooky buzz sounds emanating from hazy shadows, Lingguan felt like a man dream-walking. A woman with a tear-streaked face was praying before an incense burner, banging her head against the floor as she mumbled her prayer, while others burned spirit paper as they droned.

Coins, small bills, steamed rolls and fruit were piled high on the sacrificial table before deities' statues. A shaman was offering small bills to one deity after another. Lingguan tossed some loose change onto the table.

The young man in the suit materialized next to Lingguan and laughed when he saw what he had done. "I never give them money. I haven't committed any crime, so I don't need absolution."

"This is alms giving. In life, some give and some take. Some give away money to save lives while others give up their lives and keep the money," Lingguan replied.

The young man's face darkened.

At a bricked up site for burning spirit money in the southeastern corner of a rear hall, a burning fire was emitting dark smoke. Ashes rose like a small hill, in front of which knelt a few believers. The shamans were displaying their magical skills, either practicing the scorching cure or fulfilling a vow. A young man with delicate features stood out, as he hummed in a girl's voice to offer a magical cure to a married woman. It was strange to see a young man among the older shamans, particularly because he made up chants on the spot and answered questions spontaneously with no need to think. Speaking in rhymes, he was articulate and eloquent, understandably drawing a crowd.

An old woman told the onlookers about the man's background, saying he'd fallen ill while still a student. Nothing worked to cure him until a deity visited him during a ritual and turned him into a shaman himself. "He was too shy at first to do what was expected, but it wasn't up to him. He had to go up to the prayer terrace on the first and the fifteenth each month; otherwise, he would ache all over as if his joints were shattering. Who could live with that kind of punishment?" The old woman sucked in air through her teeth, sounding as if she were in pain.

The shaman's chant sounded familiar to Lingguan, who realized that it was a Liangzhou tune called "Second Young Mistress Is Lovesick." This discovery led to the realization that the shamans around him were mostly singing such Liangzhou tunes as "Brother Wang Herding Sheep," "Flying a Kite," or "Shili Pavilion," except that the old melodies were fitted with new lyrics, like used liquor bottles containing recent brew. Lingguan was pleased by the possibility that they were possessed by Liangzhou's sprites, for why else would they favor these tunes? He had to laugh. Then he noticed an old shaman teaching an off-key Liangzhou tune to a girl with a sallow face, a clear sign that she was spirit "chafing." The term reminded him of crushing a hawk. Much hardship was couched in the single word—chafing. He'd heard it was an excruciating process during which the sprite and the human life force waged a battle that often lasted years. If the human life force won, the possessed would recover; if the sprite had the upper hand, it would control the life force and could take possession of the person any time it wanted.

Lingguan saw his brother craning his neck in the crowd and pushed his way in to see a shaman telling fortune. Instead of divination pamphlets, the woman used her palms and fingers. After a customer told her the year, day, and time of birth, she relied on her fingers and hands before showing her palm and saying something like, "See. Here's where you got your illness. This is a forest, located to the southeast of your house…" She said her palm was a mirror and everything one had done would show up in it, but only those with magical eyes could see it. That was followed by her divination, which she sang in the form of doggerel, unlike the other shamans who used the melody of local tunes. The content sounded quite literary.

"I want my fortune read." Hantou nudged his brother.

"Forget it. It's fruitless. You'll feel good if it's positive, but sad if it isn't."

"Just for fun, how's that? Besides, it's cheap, only two yuan." Hantou revealed his birthday details after the previous customer left. The shaman studied him through half-closed eyes for a while before saying:

"You lost your spirit. Go back home to get it. Do you feel tired all the time? Do you often feel confused and overwhelmed? You can't put on weight no matter what you eat, and you have frequent bad dreams?"

Hantou nodded to everything she said, with a reverent look.

Then she mumbled to herself before adding, "And you have an unspeakable affliction."

"Aiya!" Hantou cried out involuntarily. He glanced at his brother before looking down.

"You have a difficult threshold to cross this year. If you make it, everything will turn out fine, but if not, it's hard to say what will happen."

"Give us a cure, please. We'll pay, of course." Lingguan snickered, fully aware of the shaman's usual trick of scaring customers to relieve them of their money.

"No need to talk to me like that, young man." She gave him a look. "I'm just telling as it is."

"I believe you." Hantou hastened to add. "I do."

"Forget it, I don't feel like saying more." But she chanted a divination: "This karmic trial has been pre-destined/it could be good or bad and no one can avoid it/with a jug of liquor in this vast space between heaven and earth/the mind and body are in separate places, and one is just passing through."

Lingguan's face was white with anger. He was convinced that the woman was mean-spirited, for he'd read something similar to her divination in a fortune-telling book. She had memorized the book before coming to frighten and trick people here, and she punished your refusal to her deception by leading you on with doubts. He took out two yuan, tossed them at the woman, and dragged his brother out of the crowd.

"What did she say? What exactly did she say? What is this about good or bad?" Hantou bombarded his brother with questions, for, with little education, he did not understand what the shaman had said.

"She told you to stay away from liquor. It's good if you don't drink and bad if you do."

"She's right. That's what the doctor told me. She was incredibly accurate. How did she know I'm tired all the time? How did she know I often feel confused and overwhelmed? So accurate, so magically accurate. She said I'd have something like a tough threshold this year."

"It's your spirit. You would fall ill easily if you didn't get it back, but would be fine again once you had it."

Lingguan explained cautiously, knowing that once Hantou understood what the woman had said, he would fall ill even if he had been healthy. What a witch! Lingguan cursed silently as worries began to build up inside. It dawned on him that he was upset precisely because the shaman had pinpointed what worried him most; he had been feeling something terrible would happen in his family. The premonition had been hanging over his head for a while, like a sword suspended in mid air. He always thought of the word cancer whenever someone in his family had a health problem, and the scary term disappeared from his mind only when the person recovered. It was the same with Hantou's illness; he had been tense until they heard the doctor's diagnosis of discomfort in the liver and stomach. He could finally relax, but his heart still felt as if it had been gripped and pinched by something unreal, sometimes light and sometimes heavy. The shaman, that annoying woman, had turned the light to heavy.

The foggy incense smoke dissipated and the eerie chanting subsided once they were out the door. With the sun shining down on him, Lingguan's mind cleared up, and he could even laugh at himself for letting someone like that foul his mood.

The slanting sun meant they mustn't dally, so they bought the incense and got on the bus home.

Their mother scrutinized their expressions when they walked in the door, and relaxed only when she failed to detect anything fearful. "Is everything all right?"

"Everything is fine. The doctor said it wasn't serious, just some discomfort in the liver and stomach," Lingguan said. "A little medication will take care of it. He's not sick."

Ying'er came out of her room. She glanced at Lingguan, with an expectant look. "Did you get what I wanted?" she asked Hantou.

"Aiya! I forgot. Why didn't you remind me this morning. I went to bed and it slipped right out of my mind." Hantou smiled foolishly as he took out the packets of incense. "I did remember the incense Mother wanted. But you can use laundry detergent on your hair. Shampoo is so expensive, and it doesn't do a very good job."

"Fine, fine." Ying'er said. "I told you laundry detergent hurts my scalp and gives me dandruff. You're really something. She spun around and went back inside.

"Actually, I didn't forget," Hantou whispered as he rubbed his head. "I asked around. It cost anywhere from a few yuan to nearly fifty."

Chapter Ten

It was barely light the following morning when Laoshun's raspy voice shattered the calm: "Rise and shine, young masters. Time to get up. You're like a pair of lazy wildcats."

Lingguan woke up with a stuffy feeling. The dreary sound of a broom and the dusty air greeted him as it did the first thing every morning. As he got dressed, he noticed wet spots on his underpants, a reminder of his absurd dream, which he recalled with a distraught shake of his head.

Breakfast was, as usual, potatoes, millet, and flour, plus *mantou*. His heart skipped a beat when he saw Ying'er carry it in. Had she had a similar dream? He stole a careful glance at her; there was nothing out of the ordinary in her appearance. Women are natural actors, he told himself. She looks totally unruffled.

After breakfast, their mother sent Mengzi and Hantou to Lanlan's house to help with the autumn harvest. Their land holdings were large, and Lanlan had to work them alone, since her husband could not be counted on to lift a hand. Every autumn, she worked until she was skin and bones, so her mother sent Mengzi and Hantou over to help out. But there was more she wanted to accomplish this year: she wanted her son Hantou to see a woman in Lanlan's village who had only recently become a shaman, and, she'd heard, one with true powers.

Shortly after Mengzi and Hantou left home, Laoshun told Ying'er to "survey" the desert and pick out spots with dense Artemisia growth, since the price for Artemisia seeds had risen and everyone was heading into the desert.

"That's a good idea," Lingguan's mother said. "You should go too. Take a sheet to carry as much as possible. I'll go with you, if you find a good spot, and we can spend a few serious working days out there."

Lingguan looked over at his mother and blushed when their eyes met. "I haven't seen anyone selling seeds," he grumbled.

"Every bit counts," Laoshun said. "It's better than nothing. With the way things are these days, we'll all have to find ways to earn extra money so we don't have to dine on the wind. Take the goats out to graze if you don't want to pick seeds. I'll go with them."

"The thought of tending the goats makes me sleepy. I can't keep my eyes open once I hear that baa-baa-baa. I'll go. I'll get Huaqiu to go with us."

"This isn't a pheasant hunt, why do you need someone to go with you? You failed to get into college, but you've got your share of quirky ideas."

With an unhappy snort, Lingguan filled a water jug, stuffed a few steamed rolls into a bag, and then picked up a bed sheet, a birch branch, and a scythe before walking out.

He turned to see Ying'er come out of the house, wearing a bold red kerchief. He found that and her bright green clothes jarring. Why dress up in such gaudy colors, like you're going to meet a matchmaker?

Handless Wei rode up on his donkey, the source of his livelihood. The clip-clop of its hooves was proof of its vitality. It was clear, from the way the animal ran and snorted, that Wei had taken very good care of it. He glanced first at Lingguan and then at Ying'er.

"Ah-ha!" he announced suggestively. "I see you're on your way out to the desert. That's a real fine place, warm and comfy—got a sheet with you?"

Unaware of the insinuation, Lingguan waved the sheet in his hand, which drew a belly laugh. "Ah, you have one, that's great. Makes it easy. You won't find a soul out there, ghost or human. Ha-ha. Lots of young men have flings with their sister-in-laws."

"You'd better rein yourself in and not get too attracted to your donkey," Lingguan retorted. "You'll be in serious trouble if you produce a donkey with a human head for your customer."

"Hah. I'm not that good." Wei laughed. "I can always get you to help. Ha-ha."

"Save the best for yourself." Lingguan said, as he watched Wei ride off. He turned back to look at Ying'er, who smiled. His heart skipped a beat.

Once they were in the desert, they ran into some women harvesting desert rice seeds; they laughed and jeered, making fun of Lingguan and Ying'er. He could hold his own with Wei, but was no match for these women, with their brazen comments. Fresh from high school, he was not used to hearing such "slutty words," so he lowered his face, now red, while Ying'er giggled nearby.

The desert rice and Artemisia seeds had been harvested from the shrubs closest to their village, leaving nothing but bits and pieces of wind-blown straw. That was to be expected. Some of the scrubs along the way remained untouched, but "signposts" had been placed around them. These markers were small desert rice plants and Artemisia shrubs that were stuck on sand dunes or between ridges to indicate ownership and to ward off others. It was a well-established convention around the area. Despite the many signposts, Lingguan knew that there was plenty more waiting for him amid the vast expanse of Tengger sand. And yet he was reminded of his father's warning: "If you don't go harvest the seeds now, you'll have nothing left." How strange.

The women headed to their signposts, leaving him and Ying'er on a road that was barely a path. His legs were sore. He knew they were a long way from the dense growth of Artemisia, for the village's tower was still visible from where they stood. Walking in the desert was much harder than on a hard surface; his feet sank into the sand with each step, and the awkward footing exhausted him.

Like a deflated ball, the sun lacked its usual red color and light. Lingguan looked up at the sun while switching the water jug to his left hand and taking a deep breath to regain control of his fitful breathing. But he continued to breathe erratically, like a broken bellows.

His hand felt light all of a sudden, and he knew that Ying'er had taken the jug from him. Tossing down the sheet he'd been holding, he lay down on it and heaved a sigh. Ying'er giggled, calling him a slacker. "Your hips work fine, your legs do not; you walk three steps, and fall a lot. How do you expect to gather Artemisia seeds that way?" Lingguan ignored her and shut his eyes, his legs continuing to throb.

Ying'er smoothed the hair around her temples as she squinted into the distance.

After a brief rest, she said with a sigh, "Let's go. The sun is high, and we won't get there by noon at this pace. We'll spend all day just coming and going, without gathering a single seed. I'll get to work when we reach the spot and you can take a break. If not, your father will curse us."

He sighed again as he got to his feet. His mood darkened when he thought about the prospect of spending his whole life in the desert. During his student days, thoughts of the desert had brought him pleasure, but now that he was in it, he missed the quiet life at school. He could see his future in the life of his father, a fearful thought. Sometimes he wished he'd never gone to school; that way he'd have been happy to muddle through life, like his father, who was easily satisfied; catching a wild rabbit in the desert and stir-frying it cheered him as if it were New Year's. Gnawing on a rabbit bone produced moments of sheer joy and contentment.

"Not even an immortal lives any better than this," he'd say.

But not Lingguan, whose jumbled thoughts usually diluted the taste of rabbit, his hunger not satiated even after stuffing himself.

The sandy ridges were getting higher and the valleys deeper, making the going especially hard. He made little progress with each step. When going downhill, he had to be careful not to let his momentum send him tumbling head over heels. He nearly lost his balance several times, though all that would have meant was a bit of rolling around in the sand. He'd get sand in his mouth, his ears, and his clothes, which didn't bother him. All he cared about was not losing face in front of Ying'er, even though, as a younger relative, face should not have worried him. The "older uncle" was the one who should be concerned about face. As the villagers said, one would rather sleep in the arms of a father-in-law than walk past the older uncle."

Ying'er had an easy gait, but appeared to be taking too much time. She avoided paths with sharp rises and falls, favoring gentle hills in a zigzag pattern and turning with switchbacks down the shaded sides of hollows. He knew that the sand in shaded parts was tightly packed, while the sunny sides were covered with loose wind-blown sand that could swallow his feet up to the ankles. He purposefully ignored the fact, as if waging a fight with himself. He walked straight up and down hills with sharp rises and falls; looking like a snail as he struggled upward and an untamed ox as he rushed downward, he was soon panting hard, like an old cow.

"The shady side is better." She advised. "Take an indirect route along gentle slopes and avoid going straight up and down. Doing that takes longer but it saves energy. People say a switchback route takes thirty days, while a straight line requires a month. That makes sense. It takes about the same time to cover the distance, but my way you won't tire yourself out. Give it a try."

Without replying, Lingguan bent down to take off his shoes, which were filled with sand and very heavy. Banging them against each other, he dumped the sand out and tied the laces together to drape them over his shoulder. The coolness of the sand swiftly spread across his feet.

"I think you ought to put them back on." She advised this time. "The sand is cool now, but it won't take much walking for you to feel bloated. Besides, you won't walk far before the sand will skin your feet."

He forged ahead, stubbornly walking straight up and down the hillocks. He wanted to put a great distance between them to show her he wasn't a weakling. They went on for quite some time like that until he realized that she was never too far behind, no matter how fast he walked. When going downhill, he was able to move far ahead by rushing forward like a mad dog, kicking up sand; but she managed to catch up and remained close behind as they went up a rise.

The sun was high overhead by now, a ghostly orb devoid of its usual bright red glow and heat. Lingguan rushed down a hill and collapsed when he reached another one. Taking the shoes off his shoulder, he rubbed the sand off his feet and put them back on, not because of a fear of bloating, but because of the bone-chilling coolness. The cold seemed to have penetrated his torso and put pressure on his bladder. He sheepishly watched Ying'er walk up slowly, breathing softly.

She dried her sweaty forehead with a corner of her kerchief and then the sides and corners of her mouth. He looked away. She was obviously "making herself up," which was somewhat suggestive out in the desert, where no one was around but the two of them. His heart raced until he heard her say, "All right, let's start here."

He looked around at the sparse groves of Artemisia and desert rice. It was a bleak, lonely scene, with no trace of life—humans, birds, or other animals. The sun seemed to make a noise he could feel, but not hear. Silence pressed in around them, and he felt his heartbeat quicken. Reminded of what Handless Wei had said earlier, he found his breath coming in fast, shallow spurts, and his heart stirring in a very peculiar way. He swallowed hard, and heard Ying'er do the same.

After laying down the sheet and birch branch, he walked over to the Artemisia grove to cut down tips of branches laden with seeds and gently lay them down on the ground.

Holding a gaping sack in one hand, Ying'er pinched off the seeds and threw them in each time she had a handful. A fragrance unique to Artemisia spread in the air.

A small mound of Artemisia boughs formed after a while. He dragged the sheet over and spread it out on the ground before laying down the boughs. Picking up his birch branch, he began beating them with such force that he seemed to be venting or covering something up. A column of dust rose, accompanied by the pounding sounds that broke the silence.

She kept her eyes on him as she pinched off the seeds; he exuded an air of masculine beauty each time he raised the branch. A faint smile spread across her face.

After beating the boughs about hundred times, he put down the birch branch, gently lifted the Artemisia seeds, shook them, and tossed them to the side. He brought another pile of boughs over before taking off his shirt. Then, bare-shouldered, he picked up his birch branch and spit into his hands.

Ying'er laughed. She wondered why he did that. Was it to smooth them or to show off his masculinity? She couldn't figure it out; it was, however, amusing.

The sun was directly above them now, sending down blinding rays. She could sense the heat rising, but with a gentle breeze blowing, it wasn't too hot in the hollow. It was late autumn, when the desert yellows and grass whitens, so the sun was not as sweltering as in the height of summer. Lingguan confidently wielded his birch branch, but shiny dots began to emerge on his forehead and the sides of his nose were filmed with dust. Realizing that she must look the same, she removed her kerchief to wipe her face, which turned out to be fairly clean. After retying her kerchief, she stopped what she was doing to watch him, like the village women appraising a pale-chested college student who was new to farm work.

Beads of sweat rolled down his head; his bare arms were coated with perspiration. Dust and bits of shrubbery settled on him, dirtying his appearance. From the frenzied movement of the birch branch, she could tell that he had switched to deep breathing from the short, sharp intakes of air.

"Take it easy, young scholar. No girl will want to marry you if you ruin your health."

He threw down the branch after several savage poundings. Abandoning all pretense, he was breathing hard as he picked up his shirt to wipe his face and lie on his back to gaze at the clouds through half-opened eyes. Soon a wonderful sensation spread across his body from sand that had been warmed by the sun. Words could not describe how he felt.

She brought over the jug and told him to drink, but he stayed still. Thirst could not make him give up the wonderfully comfortable sensation in his back. When he relaxed with his eyes shut, he felt as if everything disappeared around him, including the sun, the desert and even his body, except for the part touching the hot sand. Language paled in the face of a sensation that was beyond reason; the word comfortable was hardly acceptable.

"Drink some," she urged.

He opened his eyes, rolled to sit up, and took a few drinks. After being exposed to the sun for so long, the water had lost its coolness and gained the smell of its plastic container. He neither wanted nor needed the water, almost as if the soupy potatoes and millet he'd had for breakfast continued to provide his mind and body with the moisture he needed. No wonder the residents of Liangzhou liked to say they grew irritable after three days without the concoction. He smiled as he recalled that. She retrieved the jug and took a few sips without wiping the spot touched by his lips earlier. She smiled at him, which made them both blush.

An awkward silence engulfed them. "Hungry?" she managed to ask. "Have a steamed roll." He said he wasn't hungry, ending the conversation before it got underway.

She unmindfully picked up a pinch of seeds, rubbed them between her fingers, and tossed them from one hand to the other. The husks flew off, leaving behind tiny brown seeds the size of needle tips. She popped them into her mouth and chewed, before spitting out the pulp.

“Isn’t it odd? These things look so ordinary, but a pitch aids in rolling out dough.”

It failed to draw a response from him.

“I hear it’s indispensible in Shaanxi, where noodles turn to a mushy paste without it.”

He remained quiet.

“I hear it’s used to make bread, too. Keeps it fluffy. Have you heard that?”

He merely snorted.

“Back in 1960 this stuff saved lives. They rubbed off the husks, ground the seeds into powder, and stirred it in boiled water. A bowlful went down with a single slurp.”

Without a word in response, he remained lying on the sand, face up, eyes shut. A twig quivering at the corner of his mouth was the only sign that he was awake.

She squinted into the sky, where a black hawk circled, darting here and there among clouds.

Silence reigned once more. The sun was getting brighter, but she did not feel hot. She glanced at Lingguan, then at the hawk above, before fixing her gaze on a rat hole amid Artemisia shrubs. A sigh escaped from between her lips after a moment; she wanted to say something, but decided against it.

With his eyes still shut, Lingguan bit down on the twig, making the exposed end twitch. The noise created by the stillness seemed to be getting to him, too.

After staring at the rat hole for a while, she removed her kerchief and twisted it before stopping to say, without looking at him, "I want to ask you something."

The words were barely out when her head jerked up, as if she had startled herself. She lowered her eyes when she realized he wasn't looking at her.

"I want to ask you something. I, I'm a loose woman, aren't I?"

He did not respond. The twig bounced up and down.

Her face was red by then, her eyes sparkled. She glanced at him before turning to gaze at the expanse before her and biting down on her lip. "Say something."

The bobbing twig came to a halt. His face felt as if it were being roasted. At that moment, his lips were his last line of defense.

Suddenly he felt hot and stuffy, his heart filling with a liquid of some sort. Something, an insect, maybe, crawled down his cheek and made him itch. He reached up to wipe the spot while swallowing hard.

With her head lowered, she continued to wring the kerchief in her hands. The rising and falling of her chest got increasingly noticeable, as a sobbing sound became audible. When she looked up, her face was covered in shiny tears.

"What can I do?" She raised her voice. "I'm a woman. I have to accept my fate. There is only this lifetime, so what do I have to lose?" Her voice was getting raspy and she was no longer the gentle, frail self that could be blown to pieces by the wind.

Lingguan sighed and glanced at the sky, as if searching for something. The gummy feeling in his heart was getting unbearable.

"Actually, Hantou's problem is curable. It's not serious," Lingguan said.

"You—he said he couldn't stand the loss of face and refused to get help. I—I'm only—in my early twenties—life—I have a long life ahead of me."

"I'll talk to him."

"What would he think if you did?"

She blushed, and he felt his body heating up.

"Tell me. What would he think if you talked to him? He'd surely be assuming all sorts of things, now that I've told you about his problem out here in this desert with no one around." She lowered her voice to a whisper; her voice had regained its soft liquid tone, but even softer.

His heart was beating so fast it sounded like a rushing mountain torrent.

"What would he think? What did Handless Wei say a while ago?"

The liquid voice gently brushed against his ears, making him gulp for air. He felt nothing but his racing heart, that and her gentle, liquid voice. His mouth was parched, so he reached out for the jug, but came into contact with a hand that felt as if it were on fire.

There was no telling who grabbed first, but now they were holding hands, both palms moist. She let out a moan while he pressed down on her, and a strange dizziness overtook him when their lips met.

She was sighing softly, emotionally, and rapidly, like a soughing wind. He, on the other hand, was like a flame. His hand reached under her clothes and grabbed her soft, supple, lovely breast.

"Give me a son," she muttered.

The sun shone brightly above them, sobering him up. "Wait. Let me make sure there's no one around." He got to his feet and slapped at his forehead before walking to the top of the rise to look around. Nothing but dunes, the noisy sun, and the roiling sand. By the time he got down, she had bagged the seeds and spread out the sheet.

He felt something explode inside him, the first sensation after entering her, before a surging current swallowed him up.

An intense desire overtook him urgently and swiftly, and then was carried off. The short-lived passion subsided so quickly he didn't have time to savor the indescribable pleasure, and he was left with a sense of loss, emptiness, and dullness. Her impassioned, fiery eyes and enfolding arms troubled him; her attentions frightened and disturbed him. He avoided her fervent eyes and dodged her lips as they moved toward his, and instead got up to pull up his pants.

The bright sunlight put him in a dreamy state, infused with a melancholy from the sand hollow. His mood plummeted when he saw Hantou's image. Wearily, he took off his undershirt and lay down to let the sand comfort him with its scorching heat.

Still in the afterglow of sex, Ying'er smoothed down her clothes and lay down next to him, touching his sweaty bare shoulders, kissing him over and over, and biting his arms affectionately. He was not used to intimate gestures like these.

"No longer interested in me after you've used me, is that it?" she said with a pout. "Men—"

Ignoring her, he rolled over to an Artemisia shrub. She sighed warily as she took the sack of steamed rolls and said, "Would you like one?"

"I'm not hungry."

"You should eat one even if you're not hungry. We'll have to go back to work in little while."

He did not reply.

The hottest time of the day had arrived, so she hung the sheet over a shrub near him.

Touched by her action, he smiled, bringing a smile from her. He accepted the roll from her and took a bite, then picked up the jug and uncapped it.

"Wait. Let me see if the water is warm." She touched the jug. "It's not cold, so you can have some. Don't forget, you can't drink cold water after doing what we did, or you'll fall ill. Your wife would be mad at you if that happened." She tittered.

His mood had improved; now he was keenly aware of her kindness and her beauty, no longer annoyed by the excessive intimacy. He dried his sweat and took a drink of water.

"Take it easy, don't eat too fast," she said after sipping some water. "I'll start on the seeds again. Otherwise, your father would be angry." She continued in Laoshun's icy, unhappy tone of voice, "This is all you two wildcats got after a whole day. What were you doing?" She laughed. "What do you think I should say?"

"Tell him you were sleeping."

"I'll tell him to skin his son, who is no good at real work, but an old hand at indecent things. As they say, a mouse's offspring knows how to burrow, like father like son."

He smiled as he shrank under the shade and watched her quietly.

She wore a stern, focused look, straining not to glance at him; but the more she tried to contain herself, the less convincing was her feigned seriousness. In the end, she smiled, which once again both dizzied Lingguan and awakened feelings of urgent desire.

"Don't look at me like that," she said. "I'm working here."

"Keep working. I'm not stopping you."

"How can I keep at it with you looking at me like that?" she chided with a pout before turning her back to him.

Infatuated, he stared at her back. In his view, Ying'er's backside was her most attractive feature. Smooth and round, it always excited him, nearly made him drool.

His face burned. They had broken down the barrier between them, like poking a hole in a stiff piece of paper; yet he remained bashful, embarrassed to reveal his naked desire. He tore at his hair resentfully.

"That should do it." She gazed at the sun and stopped working. "We won't get home before dark if we linger any longer. Traveling back and forth like this means we spend half a day on the road. It would be so much better to stay overnight out here. What do you say we bring bedding with us tomorrow?"

"Why not? Lots of people spend nights in the desert, but you won't have anyone to come with you. It would have been so much easier if Lanlan still lived at home."

"You can be my companion. Do you dare spend a night with me?"

"Why would that be a problem? I'm willing if you are. There's nothing to be afraid of."

"Ha! Listen to your bravado. I don't think you'd go through with it."

He blushed as he made a pile of the seeds, masking his feelings. She opened the mouth of the sack so he could dump them in easily.

When they were packing up their stuff, Lingguan twisted the cap off the jug.

"Don't pour it out. Better to keep the water. Caution wards off major mistakes." She prompted him to put the cap back on.

"Actually, it's still early," he said as he looked into the sky. "Don't be in such a hurry. Let's not leave right away."

"I think we'd better leave now, so we can take it slow. With the way you are, lazy as a beef cow, you'd fall apart like a puddle of mud if we went too fast."

He took her hand. She gently smacked the back of it and said with a smile, "You have to carry seeds on your back, and I don't want to tire you out. Come night. He went to my parents' place, so he won't back tonight. It won't be any fun if we rush it."

"All right. But you have to sing me a tune."

"Sure. But why stop at a tune? I could give you my heart. But don't just sit there. You can listen and pack at the same time." She started singing:

The tree fern in the moon,
Leaves blown by a spring breeze.
When I think of the road we've traveled,
My heart aches and I cannot leave you behind.

"Did you like it?"

"I did. It was like a heavenly melody. More."

Grass piled on the rocky crag,
Stems on flowers look like sesame stalks
No one in this world is as intimate as us,
We can talk through the night.

Juice from a white radish is sour,
Vinegar mixed with wheat bran is strong.
I'd rather the Emperor's land be mired in chaos
Than have the road between us blocked.

They bantered their way back amid her singing; the return was less taxing than the morning trip, even though he was carrying a sack of seeds on his back. When they walked in the door and he laid down the sack, Laoshun came up to give the sack a kick. Instead of complaining about the quantity, he said, "What did I tell you? There are gold nuggets all over just waiting for you to pick them up."

"Is there a lot of Artemisia out there?" he asked during dinner.

"The shrubs closer to home all had signposts. There's more beyond that, but so far away that a round trip takes half a day. It not only wastes time, the walk is exhausting."

"Spend a few nights there and get as much as you can," Laoshun said. "Take your mother along tomorrow."

"Who's going to cook for you if she comes with us?" Lingguan asked.

"I don't have a donkey's belly, how much can I eat? It's just three meals a day."

Lingguan saw Ying'er wink at him, so he said, "Then I won't go. No family has a man doing woman's work."

"Right, you don't have to go," Laoshun said. "There's an empty seat waiting for you at Liangzhou's municipal government office. The problem is, you aren't good enough. What did you learn at school, except how to stuff yourself with disgusting old phrases? Think it over. Stay if you want. I haven't plowed the plot by the river dam, so you can get a taste of turning dirt clods."

"I won't dare puff myself up if you tell me to go into the desert," Lingguan hastened to reply. Ying'er giggled and made a face at him.

As he hunkered down on the *kang*, monkey-style, Laoshun puffed noisily on his pipe. "Have you fed the pigs, you old crone?" he shouted to his wife. "Make a few flatbreads so you can take a stroll in the desert tomorrow. You'll see some new things while you gather Artemisia seeds."

"Don't you always say you're bored staying home?" his wife

replied from the kitchen. “Why not take this opportunity to go for a stroll yourself?”

“Have you ever seen a man go into the desert with his daughter-in-law?”

“I thought that would be exactly what you hoped for? No one has to warm the *kang* when you’re out in the desert.” They both laughed. Ying’er cleared the table and went into the kitchen.

“I thought you came back with more than half a sack of seeds,” Lingguan’s mother said as she walked into the room. “Who figured there’d be more twigs than seeds?”

“Think about it.” Lingguan said. “It took us five hours to walk there, and after an hour for lunch, we had four hours left. We had to gather these a handful at a time. It’s not like we could just scoop the seeds off of a pile.”

“I was just saying.” His mother laughed. “You do what you can. That’s all.”

“Go get ready,” Laoshun said. “Fill the large water jug. And ask around to see if anyone else wants to go along. You can all watch out for each other. Actually, it doesn’t matter if you personally gather seeds. You can cook and keep them company, be the idle lady of the house.”

“When have I had the chance to be lady of the house?” His wife smiled. “An old cow bears a dozen calves, and that’s all she has time for. I have to keep working as long as there’s breath in my body.”

“You can stay home,” Lingguan said. “If anyone heard what you just said, they’d think we oppress our mother.”

“All right, I won’t say any more.” She returned to her work in the kitchen

Lingguan went to bed and immediately fell asleep. Ying’er waited in vain that night.

2

It was light out when Lingguan was startled awake by the sound of his father calling him. He had been sleeping with Ying'er in his dream. By the time he was up, his father had loaded the camel with water, flour, pots, bowls, and bedding. His mother was feeding the pig, her chatter unsettling so early in the morning. After a quick splash of water on his face, Lingguan squeezed some toothpaste onto his toothbrush and thrust it here and there in his mouth before spitting out a mouthful of foam.

"Do it right if you want to brush your teeth," His mother said. "You're just wasting money the way you spit the toothpaste out before you've even started."

"Can't you tell that Father is just looking for an excuse to lash out? If I don't hurry, it'll be a miracle if he doesn't blow his top."

"Go eat your breakfast," she said. "We'll get on the road once you're done."

Ying'er gave him an unhappy look when she walked in with a bowl of rice. "You had a good night," she whispered. "I on the other hand waited up for you."

"I was completely worn out. I didn't stay up to watch Judge Bao, and had no idea when I fell asleep."

"Are you going to do that again?"

"No. There was the first and second time, but there won't be a third or fourth."

"Is there nothing that can shut your trap?" Laoshun walked in. "Do you know what time it is?"

"I didn't say anything. I just told her I missed Judge Bao last night, that's all." Lingguan said, making Ying'er nervous. She glared at him from behind his father's back, and he knew why; it was almost an admission of guilt to say 'that's all.'"

"And she complained that I was too heavy a sleeper," he added.

Her eyes bulged as Ying'er nervously pointed at Laoshun's back. Lingguan stuck his tongue out. "Hurry and finish," his father said. "What are you waiting for? In the old days, when we went into the desert, we were on the road before the rooster crowed. By this time we were already hard at work."

"Would it kill you not to talk so much?" Lingguan said. "If I don't stop to listen, you complain that everything you say goes in one ear and out the other. If I stop eating, you say that I'm dawdling."

"Okay, fine. I won't say any more. I know you hate listening to what I have to say. Good medicine is always hard to swallow." Laoshun turned to his daughter-in-law. "You hurry up and finish breakfast, too. Your mother said Beizhu and his family are going, so don't make them wait."

Lingguan wolfed down his food and started to pack toiletry items.

"You're not going there on official business, so why take all that? It's a long trip, so take as little as possible."

"But we have the camel," Lingguan replied, eliciting an icy snort from his father.

He led the camel out of its pen, while his mother made sure the pig was fed. "The swill needs to be warmed up first, and don't add too much bran. Don't be wasteful and finish off six month's good food in a few days. If you spoil the pig now, you won't have anything left for it later."

"I know."

"The chickens get a meal of watery feed every day." She continued. "Make sure to lock the gate."

"Are you finished, you old crone?" he said. She ignored him.

"Make sure the broth isn't too thin."

"Go on, get on the road. I'm not your son."

"What about her son?" Lingguan groused. "You complain about Lingguan this and Lingguan that every time you open your mouth. What has Lingguan done to deserve that?"

Ying'er smiled at his outburst; so did their mother.

They walked out and called to their neighbors, Beizhu and Fengxiang, who had talked Yue'er into going along.

"Meng Eight went into the desert again," Beizhu said. "There must be a lot of foxes this year. The desert is overrun by rats."

"There are more rats because the foxes are gone," Lingguan said.

"The abundance of rats attracts the foxes," Beizhu said. "Big Head shot one last night. He was so pleased he couldn't stop grinning." He turned to Lingguan's mother. "You're too old to be messing around with this. Leave the work to them. Aren't you afraid they'll think you're in the way?"

"You're right," Ying'er said. "Why don't you let Baigou go out with his sister-in-law? What are you messing around for?"

"Hey, I didn't say anything about you," Fengxiang said. "You can talk about anyone you want, but keep me out of it."

"What makes you think it was about you?" Ying'er said with a smile. "Only people with an aversion to cold shy from eating watermelon. Baigou has more than one sister-in-law."

"I'm not talking to you anymore. You have a sparrow's mouth, always chattering away," Fengxiang said. "Listen carefully, Lingguan. Pay attention to what our sister-in-law is teaching you."

"That's right," Ying'er said. "Your Sister-in-law, Fengxiang, is teaching you something. Does that make you jealous, Beizhu?"

Lingguan's mother laughed, and so did the others.

They ran into Huaqiu and his mother shortly after they entered the desert. Huaqiu was steadying a water jug on the back of his snorting camel. Water was dripping noisily down the camel's side. Beizhu went up and, after some combined effort, managed to set the jug straight. The two camels, along with eight villagers, continued on.

The sun leaped out from behind the tip of the rise and, with a silent swish, shot high into the sky. The saxaul trees and desert rice took on a white patina from sun's rays that reduced the camels to mere outlines.

Lingguan and Huaqiu led their camels past a high ridge and onto the camel path.

It was less a real path than a way of walking on the sand, a meandering course that lengthened the trip.

The camels, their bells, the early morning sun, saxauls, the shrubs, and the people created a wondrous tableau. Lingguan felt new strength rise inside. He was about to ask Ying'er to sing a tune when he heard Beizhu's loud voice:

Brother Wang herds—the sheep on southern hills—
The sun sets—to the west—hills—the sheep return to the pen—
With hands on the widow sill I look out—
Why—don't—I see—the face of Brother Wang—

It sounded more like shouting than singing, for he'd started at too high a pitch, making the women laugh. "Stop it." Fengxiang said. "That yak voice of yours grates on the camels' ears so much they're about to pee."

"You don't understand," Beizhu argued. "This is a popular singing style these days. The guy who sang 'Little Sis, Don't be Afraid and

Walk On' had a worse voice than I do."

"Then go sing in Beijing," Fengxiang said. "You can get yourself a woman with a bird's nest hairdo if you're good enough."

"Would you be all right with that?" Beizhu asked her.

"The frost hasn't kill off all the men in the world, so you're not so special to me."

"I don't want you to start crying," Beizhu said.

The squabble between the young couple took away Lingguan's emotional reaction to the surroundings. The canvas bag containing his toothbrush and rinsing cup banged against the pot lids draped over the camel's back, making a monotonous sound with each step. Lingguan began to feel a sense of loss as an emptiness rose, like a leather ball that has been pushed down under the water, only to bob up when he wasn't paying attention.

"Aiya! Rats," Huaqiu yelled out. "They're huge and there are hordes of them."

The camels stopped. Lingguan heard loud, chaotic birdcalls, but could not trace the source of the noise. What he saw was a group of rats chasing each other. A rat as big as a cat stood on its hind legs by a dark hole beneath a giant Artemisia shrub. It held its front paws together as if praying; its beady black eyes looked first at the camels and then at the villagers, like a child enjoying the sight of animals. Seven or eight smaller rats were running back and forth, oblivious of the humans as they played; they were the source of the chirping birdcalls.

"Come look at the rats," Huaqiu shouted at the women.

"Aiya! Demonic rats." Yue'er ran over. Disturbed by her footsteps, the frolicking rats stopped and stood up like humans, front paws in the air, as they watched the inexperienced creatures.

The women screeched, sending the rats into a panicky run toward the hole. But they stood up human-like again to look back when they reached the opening. Their eyes, while far from bewitching, were lively enough to leave a deep impression on the villagers. They then scampered inside.

Obviously with a higher level of attainment, the large rat was not frightened by the shrieking women nor goaded into scurrying like its fleeing friends. It would have seemed to be meditating if not for its shiny, shifting dark eyes.

"It's really a demonic rat. A cat would probably lose a fight with a big one like that." Ying'er said.

"No matter how big the rat, it will fear even a frail cat. It's their nature." Lingguan's mother said.

"I heard that a rat changes into a bat after eating salt and vegetable oil," Fengxiang said.

"You're like a dog trying to bite a moving train." Beizhu pooh-poohed her. "You know nothing about science. Bats and rats are two different species. They're not the same, got it? Baby bats come from grown bats, not rats, just like you can't become a mare no matter what you eat. Heh—maybe a female donkey."

"You're an ass," his wife retorted. "So you know science, do you? All you know is how to give a leg to the baby in your sister-in-law's belly."

That made everyone laugh. Lingguan had heard that years earlier Beizhu had tried to get his sister-in-law into bed when his older brother was away from home. Obviously Beizhu had used the excuse that the baby in her belly hadn't gotten a leg yet and might be born a cripple without his help.

Beizhu scratched his head and smiled. Fengxiang gave him an ugly look and continued with a raised voice, "No one would have known that if his sister-in-law hadn't praised him for his contribution." She switched to a different voice, "It's all because of Beizhu's help; otherwise the baby might be a cripple."

The others were now roaring in laughter, except for Yue'er, who blushed at the racy talk and turned her head away.

Finally the huge rat was shaken by their laughter, lost its composure and ran back to the opening, where, like the smaller rats earlier, it turned to look back. Huaqiu took off one of his shoes and shouted, "Damn you!" He threw it, but the rat ran off unharmed.

3

It was noontime when they finally reached a sand hollow with abundant desert rice and Artemisia. By then, both camels and humans were drenched in sweat.

"How should we go about it?" Beizhu asked. "Work together here or each find a spot and gather our own?"

"I think we should find our own, so we won't enjoy chatting so much and forget to work," Ying'er said.

"I think we should work together," Yue'er disagreed. "We'll get bored soon if we work separately."

"I agree. One can cut the shrubs, another can carry them over, and others harvest the seeds," Huaqiu said. "We work harder when we work together and everyone a job to do."

"That sounds good to me," Lingguan's mother said. "No loafing on the job, and everyone gets an equal share of what we get."

They found a relatively solid spot away from the wind, "smooth, even ground," as they called it, and unloaded the camels. After unpacking their bedding and other items, they produced cooking utensils—pots, bowls, spoons and basins—for Lingguan's and Huaqiu's mothers to dig a pit and create an opening for the firewood and a smoke vent around the edge, before heading out to gather kindling in a nearby hollow. Lingguan's mother filled a basin with flour, one ladleful per person, poured in water, and mixed the dough. Back in the time of collectivization, she had often come to the desert to gather desert rice, so she was an old hand at cooking there. Soon, the dough was ready. With her knife she cut it into thin, long strips and rubbed on oil for it to rise. Then she said to Huaqiu's mother, who had just returned from gathering firewood. "Start the fire."

Huaqiu's mother placed a pot on the pit and lit a fire, sending cooking smoke rising from the "smooth, even ground." The smoke reminded Lingguan of a line of ancient poetry: "On the vast desert a single column of smoke rises straight up." He turned to Huaqiu and repeated the line. "But I've never seen smoke rise straight up. It's always puffs or shreds of smoke. Where does that single plume come from?"

"The line was about a windless moment," Huaqiu replied.

"When it's windless, the smoke will just drift downward. It will never rise. In fact, it will fill the area with smoke that makes your eyes water. Who's ever seen smoke rise straight up into the sky?"

"Maybe you need some wind," Huaqiu followed up.

"That's even less likely. With wind, the smoke will drift off. It can't rise up straight." Lingguan would not relent.

"I can't explain it," Huaqiu said. "How do you expect me to know that if you don't? You're the bookworm."

Yue'er and Ying'er walked over from another hollow, each carrying an armload of shrubs.

"You wasted all those years at school, Lingguan," Yue'er said.

"The smoke was from burning wolf dung, not from Artemisia plants. When wolf dung was lit on a windless day, the smoke it produced rose straight into the sky. Haven't you read about wolf-dung smoke in one of your books?"

"You're amazing!" Lingguan said with his eyes fixed on Yue'er. "You're a doctor."

"Sure I am." She laughed. "Don't think you're so smart you can ignore other people."

That comment earned an odd look from Ying'er, who said, "Let's go. They may need firewood in a hurry." Yue'er walked off with a smile.

"Does your sister have a fiancé?" Lingguan asked Beizhu.

"Not yet. She has her eyes set as high as the sky. No one she's met is good enough for her. My mother said she was ruined by the education she received. A girl's heart goes wild once she has some schooling."

"That's true. But for a girl, finding a husband is more important than going to college. She'll have everything she needs once she finds herself a good man."

"That's what my mother says, too. But Yue'er won't have any of that."

"What kind of husband is she looking for?"

"All she's said," Beizhu said, "was that even a dung collector would work if it felt right. Tell me, what did she mean by feeling? You can't see feelings or touch them. There's a line in a song about following your feelings. But how? That's beyond me."

"Of course you wouldn't understand. But feelings are real."

"Then tell me what they are," Beizhu persisted.

"I can't. It wouldn't be feelings if I could put them into words."

"Hey, we're just about ready, but there's no firewood. The noodles will turn to mush if we have to wait for your firewood," Fengxiang shouted to interrupt their conversation, then walked back with them and the firewood they'd gathered.

Ying'er and Yue'er were stretching the dough and pinching off pieces to toss into the pot. Ying'er skillfully produced one piece of dough after another in a seemingly unbroken line, while Yue'er's were uneven, one side thick, the other thin. And the dough was so sticky it stuck to her hand instead of flying into the pot. She didn't know whether to laugh or cry.

"Let me do it, my dear lady, so you won't be laughed at," Lingguan's mother said with a smile when she finished chopping vegetables.

Using that comment as a cue, Yue'er tossed the remaining dough into the pot and sat down on a slope.

"I told you to start learning, but you wouldn't budge, like an animal digging in its heels," Fengxiang said. "Who's going to wait on you when you're married? You can't expect your husband and his family to place you on an altar, can you?"

"Then I won't get married. I'll let Ma take care of me." Yue'er smiled.

"In your dreams," Beizhu said. "I'll tell Ma to find someone for you and throw the two of you out. "

"Be sure to pay attention, Lingguan," Huaqiu's mother said. "Catch her when they throw her out. Where else will you find a smart, pretty wife like her?" They all had a good laugh over that.

Ying'er looked at Lingguan and laughed when she saw that he was blushing.

"He doesn't have that kind of luck," Lingguan's mother said.

"Listen to that, Yue'er," Fengxiang said. "That's your mother-in-law's consent. Now, how about you?"

"He likes women who wear high heels, with permed hair, who sway when they walk, and who speak with a seductive voice," Yue'er said with a glance at Lingguan. "Why would he be interested in me?"

"But you're interested, aren't you?" Fengxiang teased.

"Are you finished?" Yue'er pouted.

Lunch was ready. They fetched their bowls and mugs.

"This is our first meal in the desert, and custom requires that we make it the best we can," Lingguan's mother said. "If you have anything good, bring it out to share. I have rabbit meat here."

"I have fried flatbreads," said Huaqiu's mother.

"I have—" Fengxiang was interrupted by Beizhu, who said, "Boiled potatoes."

"And —" Again she was cut off by her husband, "and desert leeks. That's all."

"That doesn't sound like good food to me," Huaqiu said.

"Not to you, maybe, but to me it does," Beizhu said.

"Hey, stingy one, where's the pheasant?" Fengxiang remarked. "Keeping it for your unborn son?"

"Ah—pheasant." Yue'er clapped her hands.

"I thought you hadn't cooked it yet," Beizhu said with an awkward smile.

"Hadn't cooked it?" his wife said. "Do you think I wanted it to go bad?"

"I thought you hadn't brought it with you," Beizhu said.

"And what, left it at home for the dog?"

"Then maybe you ate it."

"Are you saying I'm a dog sneaking food, keeping everything to myself?" The others laughed. Yue'er and Ying'er laughed so hard they held their bellies and groaned.

The rabbit, pheasant, desert leeks, and other items made a fine meal, based on desert standards. The only imperfection was the sand that had infiltrated the rice.

"Say, who mistook sand for salt?" Beizhu asked.

"You do the cooking if you think you can do better, and we'll see if there's sand in it," his wife said.

"I was just saying."

"People who talk while standing up never have sore backs. You wouldn't be so picky if you actually cooked a meal."

After finishing one bowl of sandy rice, Lingguan poured some water into his bowl.

"You shouldn't drink water right after a meal. It'll cause indigestion," Ying'er cautioned, drawing a smile from Beizhu.

When Huaqiu asked him what he was smiling about, Beizhu said, "Look how she's treating her brother-in-law." He then mimicked her: "You shouldn't drink water right after a meal. It will cause indigestion."

Huaqiu laughed. Ying'er turned to Fengxiang, "Do something about him, won't you? He has a one-track mind. That's all he thinks about. He's twisted."

"He's beyond my control." Fengxiang smiled. "And the emperor's too. You need to be nice to your little brother-in-law, but I haven't heard you say anything so caring to your husband." She turned to Lingguan's mother, "You haven't either, have you, Auntie?"

Lingguan's mother responded with a silent smile. Her face red, Ying'er pointed at Fengxiang, "You two are a good match, a pair of twisted minds that think of nothing else."

"What exactly?" Fengxiang was smiling. "Tell me, what am I thinking? Not what you think. How strange that you think you know what I'm thinking."

Ying'er was blushing. "That's enough," Lingguan's mother said with a smile. Stop chattering and finish your lunch. We have work to do."

4

They finished their meal and passed out work assignments at about two in the afternoon: The three men would be responsible for cutting the tops off the Artemisia shrubs; Ying'er, Fengxiang and Yue'er would handpick some of the seeds after carrying the tops over to the canvas sheet, where Lingguan's and Huaquiu's mothers would beat the shrubs with their birch branch. They got down to work, and the sand hollow was soon a hub of activity. While waiting for the men to cut more shrubs, Lingguan's and Huaqiu's mothers joined the young women in handpicking seeds. As they worked, they chatted about trivial matters and gossiped about the neighbors, nothing especially memorable, but the amiable back and forth created the desired scene.

Ying'er and Yue'er were not talking. Yue'er, who was still thinking about the earlier conversation, smiled at the recollection and stole glances at Lingguan, who was a ways off, cutting down shrubs. Ying'er was bothered by feelings of jealousy. She had felt a hint of animosity toward Yue'er when they first entered the desert, unsettled by her youth and beauty. Not the type to wear her emotions on her sleeves, she was an expert in hiding what was on her mind. Except for an occasional moment of intense feeling, she rarely lost control. Her natural disposition was dominated by an ease, not that of women of easy virtue, but a tender serenity. Since becoming Hantou's wife, she had suppressed this part of herself, busy with life in general and household chores, though it manifested itself if the occasion was right.

At such moments, she could tolerate everything but a pretty young girl who posed a threat. Now that she was aware of her own hostility toward Yue'er, she treated the girl cordially—on the surface. Not merely masking her heart's desire, she truly felt that it was unbecoming to harbor animosity toward a nice girl like Yue'er.

"Go get some of the branches so we can starting beating," Lingguan's mother said.

Fengxiang and Yue'er went over, picked up the branches the men had cut, and lay them on the canvas. The two older women beat them noisily, sending fine dust into the air. Yue'er ran away, as if from a raging fire.

"Look at our hygenic girl," Huaqiu shouted. "Hang your feet from your shoulders if you want to avoid dust or dirt."

"Hygenic?" Beizhu said. "Not without detergent inside to wash herself clean."

"Forgot to brush your teeth this morning, didn't you?" Yue'er said to her brother. "Since you don't mind dirt, how about rolling in the mud like a pig?"

"Sure, if you will."

"Don't listen to him," Ying'er said. "He has a foul mouth."

"Lingguan's mouth smells good, doesn't it?" Beizhu mocked. "But, you know, it's strange. I've never put my mouth on yours, so how do you know mine stinks?"

"Go scratch his lips bloody, Ying'er," Fengxiang said with a laugh. "Or stuff his mouth with camel dung."

They all looked up at the mention of camels. They weren't there.

"The camels are gone," Lingguan said, obviously concerned.

"Camels aren't donkeys," Beizhu said. "They don't run off so easily. They'll be back once they've filled their bellies."

Not reassured, Lingguan climbed a high ridge to look around, and there they were, rummaging for food in a hollow. Theirs was the farthest away, looking like a tiny yellow dot.

"Our camel has strayed too far. I'm going to bring it back," Lingguan said.

"Do your work and forget about the camel. It'll return once it has something in its stomach," his mother said to put his mind at ease. "It won't go missing."

He was breathless from rushing up the hill, and his heart was racing, almost panic-like. So he sat down to catch his breath. Gazing into the distance, he saw ridges higher than the ones near them. Watery mist hovered above the sandy surface and flickered in the sunlight. In shady spots, the sand was inky black, while that under direct sunlight was a burnt yellow, a stark contrast in colors. What drew his attention were black hawks in the cloudless sky, creating a scene all to themselves. They spread their wings and glided leisurely, reminding him how wretched his life was.

"Come on down, Lingguan," his mother shouted. "You might catch cold up there in the wind."

"Don't worry, I'm not sweating," he shouted back.

"Look at him," his mother remarked to Huaqiu's mother. "He's almost twenty, and I still have to worry about him."

"They're all the same. Huaqiu too. People say a boy becomes a man at eighteen, but not these two."

"Get down here and carry your share of the load. I'm doing all the work," Beizhu said.

Lingguan came down feet first, sending sand cascading ahead of him like water.

It didn't take long to clear out the new growth in the hollow, as well as the older shrubs. "Let's move to another spot," Lingguan said.

"Forget it." Beizhu looked up at the sun. "Moving around wastes time. We'll wait till tomorrow to move. Let's go cut some in the hollow over there. We have enough people to bring the branches back. We're going over to that hollow," he called out to the women.

"Go ahead," Lingguan's mother said. "You can chat, but don't stop working. Moving slow is fine, stopping isn't. The work will get done if your hands keep at it long enough."

"We know that," Lingguan said. "You're always saying that. It makes my scalp itch."

"Good birds never let anyone ruffle their feathers." His mother laughed. "You're on your own, don't forget that."

The men walked down a hollow just to the east of where they'd been working, where Artemisia grew in profusion, their thick branches, all from this year's growth, loaded with seeds, and easy to cut. Beizhu was happy, but not Huaqiu. "There's too much here. We'll never finish."

"Listen to you," Beizhu said. "Anyone else would be worried there isn't enough, but there's too much for you. Are you here as a new bridegroom?"

"The more the better, I know that. But I'm shocked to see such massive growth."

"Don't think too much. One branch down is one branch less, and one *jin* of seeds gathered is one less *jin* to pick," Lingguan said. "You may think our mothers nag us too much, but some of the things they say make sense. Speed isn't a problem as long as you don't stop working. The work gets done if your hands keep at it long enough. That works for everything we do, doesn't it, whether we're cutting Artemisia branches or studying."

"I'm glad you understand. But enough talk. We've got work to do," Beizhu said.

"Now that there's no one around, you have to be honest with me." Beizhu swung his scythe and asked Lingguan, "Have you done it with Ying'er yet?"

"Can't you talk about something else?" Lingguan picked up an Artemisia branch to smack Beizhu with.

"What else is there? You live a lifetime for nothing but keeping yourself fed, clothed, and wedded. What's there to talk about when you've got enough to eat and wear? What else? Now tell me the truth. Did you do it?"

"You tell me first if you've done it."

"I have. Remember that talk about giving the baby a leg?"

"Did that really happen?" Was your sister-in-law really that stupid?"

"Shit. She wasn't stupid. I was just joking with her and never expected her to take it serious. Women. You can never tell about them. What she says is never the same as what she thinks. Her pants were untied and I put my tool there, but, with her hands on my butt, she kept saying, 'No, no.' What do you think that meant? This is what books call, a 'half-hearted rejection.' You think she's stupid but maybe she knows more than you. It was about giving the baby a leg, and it didn't make her look too bad, so we did it."

"Not stupid?" Lingguan gently added his branch to the pile. "If she wasn't stupid, why did she tell people about it? And what about praising you?"

"Come on. Where would she get the nerve to tell? I was the one who told. Big Head Sun, that ass, promised not to tell anyone but he has such a loose tongue that he told someone, who told others, until it was public knowledge."

"That wasn't very smart. How could you tell anyone something like that? How will your sister-in-law face the world after that?"

"I didn't want to. We were drinking, and they were all talking about what they'd done. Everyone but me. They laughed at me, whooping it up and mocking me, saying what a disgrace I was and how I was in my late twenties and still a babe in the woods. Think about it. How could I keep my mouth shut? Besides, everyone agreed not to tell."

"What did Meng Eight say about you the other day?" Lingguan laughed, smacking Beizhu on the butt with a branch he'd picked up. "Hmm, oh, yes. You can't take the heat from hot noodles, buckling too easily under pressure."

"Well, I told people what he did. Guess what that was. Ha. One day, when he was out irrigating the field, he pushed Handless Wei's wife to the ground and had his way with her. She struggled at first, calling him a mule, but guess what happened then? Heh, she put her arms around him and wouldn't let go, asking him to do it again." Beizhu looked around and lowered his voice. "Wei's tool doesn't work so well, and his woman didn't know any better until Big Head Sun showed her a good time."

"What do you mean, not so well? Too small?" Huaqiu asked.

"That's no problem. A man's build doesn't matter if he can do the work, and the size of his dick is no concern as long as he can get it hard. Wei's is like a stump and barely hard enough to get in the door. That's what his wife told Big Head."

"And you repeated that to others?" Lingguan asked.

"I didn't say anything about his tool not working well, but I did tell people what she did. Well, she came to my house and scratched my face bloody. Wei gave me a savage slap, saying he'd castrate me if I told lies about his wife again. That ass, what an ingrate."

"Shush. The women are here," Huaqiu said.

"What were you two talking about?' Ying'er asked when she walked down into the hollow with the other two young women.

"We were talking about a young man getting intimate with his sister-in-law. Make sure to tell Lingguan to keep his mouth shut. He shouldn't have told anyone. Hantou would beat the shit out of you if he knew about it," Beizhu said.

Ying'er paled, but quickly recovered. "Is that so? I want to know what he said. Was it to make a leg or a hand?"

"A leg and a hand."

"It must be maddening to be married to someone like that," Ying'er said to Fengxiang. "That mouth of his is always spewing something filthy. He probably only behaves himself when he's sleeping."

"He's worse when he's in bed. He talks even more, smuttier, just disgusting."

"Ai. He ruined you. You were such a nice girl, but you became a tramp after marrying him."

"I have a trashy mouth, but I'm chaste inside," Fengxiang said, "while you're chaste on the outside, but have a dirty mind. You don't look at your little brother-in-law in the daytime, but who knows what you do at night? Tell us, Lingguan, have you sucked on her breasts?"

"Yes I have, and now I want to suck on yours." Lingguan decided to be brazen about it. "Do you want me to?"

"Sure," Fengxiang laughed. "Let's swap, you and Beizhu. Otherwise, he'd be so jealous he'd turned sour inside. Come on." She pretended to unbutton her blouse, making him blush.

Lingguan breathed a sigh of relief after the three women, still giggling, took their bundles of branches back over the ridge.

"Aiya, Beizhu. Your wife has a sharper tongue than you have." Huaqiu laughed.

"Of course. She's already had a man inside her. Women are full of contradictions. They can be chaste, so calm and serene, but when they let themselves go, they can be wild and lewd. Fengxiang has a trashy mouth, but deep down she's not like that all, so don't get any ideas."

"Who knows? Every man thinks his wife is pure and that other men's wives are sluts. That's self-deception, the so-called Ah-Q mentality, but you wouldn't know," Lingguan said.

"Of course I know. I saw it in a movie. It's about that worthless man who tried to sleep with a widow, but got a whipping instead, isn't it? That ass was hopeless. Why did he have to kneel down before a woman? You'll be nothing to her once you do that. He should have just gone ahead and done it. Push her down, rip her pants off, and put his tool in, and that's that. Of curse, she'd yell, struggle, and curse, but once she has a taste of it, he won't be able to pry her hands off him. That ass, simply worthless."

"It isn't always like that," Huaqiu said. "You have to have feelings for each other."

"Feelings?" Beizhu said quizically. "A woman's heart is like a dog's, and whoever has her body can have it."

"If that's the case, then why would a woman report to the police after she's raped?" Huaqiu refused to agree.

"Hah." Beizhu said with exaggeration. "What rape? You've never had a woman, I'm sure of that. You can try all you want, but can't get it in unless she lets you. So you won't get close if she fights back. I don't believe rape is possible. Seriously. Think about it. That thing can't find its target during the first time and she'll have to guide you in. Keep working. You can listen to me, but don't stop cutting the branches."

"So there's no such thing as rape, is that what you're saying?"

"Sure there is. A girl in Xixiang was raped and she reported it. The police asked her, 'Why didn't you run away?' Guess what she said? She said, 'I couldn't. It would have fallen out if I'd run. Hah—"

Lingguan laughed, so did Huaqiu.

"Let's keep at it. It'll be dark soon, and it's cooled off enough for us to work."

The sun had migrated behind a towering ridge to the west, taking a great deal of light from the hollow. Puffs of red clouds floated above them. Breezy wind blew over their sweaty bodies, cooling them off, like being doused with water.

The three young women came back for another load of branches.

"We'll be making dinner now," Ying'er said as they were leaving. "Mother said you can continue cutting here, but we'll be back for them tomorrow. She said to cut as much you can, but take it slow." She glanced at Lingguan before walking off.

5

It was completely dark when they finished another sand-infused meal. Nighttime brought cool air. Their sweat dried quickly, turning their clothes icy, like armor.

After tethering the camels, Beizhu and Huaqiu brought over a pile of seedless branches to light a bonfire, giving the desert a different kind of vitality. The flames burned off a sense of desolation and loneliness brought on by the descent of night. A smile returned to Yue'er's face. Huaqiu, Lingguan, Ying'er, and Fengxiang crowded around the fire, followed by the two older women after they washed and put away the dishes.

Though Yue'er had been to the desert before, this was her first overnight stay. The bonfire instilled in her a novel sense of excitement; she jumped around like a child, tossing firewood onto the fire. Soon the flames were several meters high, and the two older women laughed as they backed away.

"That's enough," Huaqui's mother said. "Save the firewood. We just need a little heat to keep us warm. The night is long. What would we do if we burned it all?"

"There's more than enough," Huaqiu said. "Firewood is one thing the desert has plenty of."

"Go ahead, waste the wood," Beizhu countered. "When it's all gone, you'll gather more, not me. But watch out for the snakes and rats when you're out there. Don't let them slither up your pant legs."

Yue'er shrieked at the mention of snakes.

"I've been to the desert countless times, but I've never seen a snake," Fengxiang said. "There are lots of rats though."

"Rats are scary too," Yue'er said.

"Who says there are no snakes?" said Beizhu. "I saw a king rat snake last year when I came here to gather seeds. It made a shu-shu sound as it slithered into a rat's nest."

"How come I didn't see it?" Fengxiang asked.

"Just because you've never seen one doesn't mean they don't exist here. You've never seen a wild rabbit, but Mengzi and his father are always bringing dead ones home."

She said nothing.

"So what do I do?" Yue'er was shaking in fear.

"What do you do?" Lingguan joined in. "There's nothing to fear. Just use your scythe and cut them in half."

"Would you really do that?" Beizhu asked. "Snakes have

supernatural powers. If you cut one in half it'll come back for revenge."

"Even after it's dead?" Ying'er asked.

"Hei, they don't die that easily." Beizhu said dramatically. "Magpies can patch a snake up by tying a knot and the two halves will grow back together, and then it will follow the smell of the person who hurt it. Once it finds him, it will… bite Lingguan and kill him."

"Liar." Ying'er laughed, along with others.

"Hah, why would I lie to you? He'd die before you knew it. When you woke up in the morning you'd see, Aiya, he's turned black and purple. His head would have swelled to the size of a flowerpot, his eyes staring and his teeth bared. Ah, then he'd snatch you away."

"I'm not afraid." Ying'er was still laughing.

"Watch your mouth, Beizhu," Lingguan's mother complained. "Don't keep saying unlucky things like that."

"I was just joking. Don't take me seriously." Beizhu grabbed one of Lingguan's ears and jerked it, imitating villagers who do that when they utter inauspicious words around children. "Donkey ear, donkey ear, make sure that you don't hear." Lingguan's mother laughed despite herself.

"Are there really snakes?" Yue'er asked Lingguan's mother.

"Yes there are, over there, deep in the desert. But they're all right; they're beneficial, because they eat rats and they don't bite people."

"It wouldn't have to bite. Just seeing it would scare me to death." Yue'er shuddered.

"Don't be afraid," Fengxiang said. "Those things slither away when they see people. Actually, everything fears people, who dominate the world. People will eat anything and everything. They're the world's worst creatures."

The fire slowly died down as they talked.

"You forget to add firewood when it's necessary, and add too much when there's no need," Huaqui's mother chided Yue'er, who quickly brought over an armload of firewood to send the fire burning bright again.

Fengxiang retrieved a dozen or so potatoes and buried them in the fire, after pushing some embers aside.

"What time is it? Is it bedtime?" Ying'er asked.

"It's still early," Beizhu said. "To me it feels like it's barely dark out."

"I worked hard today, and I'm a sleepy."

"Every one worked hard. You young people fare worse than us old folks, "Lingguan's mother said. "That's not sleepiness; it's laziness. The more you sleep the sleepier you get and the lazier you are. But go spread out the bedding and go to bed if you want."

"I won't then. I'll stay up a little later since you and Huaqiu's mother are still up. What would I be if I went to bed before you?" Ying'er finished with an imperceptible sigh.

6

At that instant, Lingguan, who'd gone to relieve himself in nearby hollow with a flashlight, shouted, "Hurry, Beizhu. Come, quick. There's a hedgehog."

"Catch it." Beizhu jumped up. "Don't let it run away or flee into its nest."

"It won't," Lingguan said. "It's rolled into a ball. Bring a rope."

With a shout, Beizhu ran to his camel and rummaged through the saddlebags.

Huaqiu ran up and kicked the hedgehog, forcing the creature to roll up tighter, fighting off the attack with its natural armored defense. Protecting his hand with the sleeve of his shirt, he tried to pick it up, but let out a yelp of pain. The balled hedgehog rolled down to the slope as Huaqiu shook his injured hand.

"Aiya, it ran away," Huaqiu yelled as he ran down after it.

Beizhu snatched the flashlight from Lingguan and searched the area carefully, but failed to find the hedgehog. "What a screw-up," he complained. "Two young men have let a little hedgehog run away. How do you expect to protect your wives in the future?"

"I had my eyes on it," Huaqiu said. "Lingguan was the one who lost it."

"That's because it rolled down the slope." Lingguan took back his flashlight.

"Forget it," Beizhu said. "I can't find it, so you won't either. It's the same color as the sand and hard to see even in broad daylight. Besides, it may have gotten into a rat's nest."

"I don't think so," Lingguan said. "We rushed down here as soon as it rolled away."

"But which way did it go? East? West? North? South? It has excellent night vision and can disappear down a rat's hole before you even see its shadow."

"They ball up and tuck their heads in, so what would good would excellent night vision do?" Lingguan said. "We can find it."

"Then go ahead," Beizhu said. "I'm not going to waste energy looking for it."

"Will you eat it if we catch it?" Huaqiu asked.

"No, I won't." Beizhu shook his head and walked off.

Lingguan and Huaqiu made a careful search of the area, but came up empty. "Forget it. Let's head back," Huaqiu said.

"Beizhu will laugh at us," Lingguan said.

"Hey, there it is!" Huaqiu shouted.

Lingguan looked closely and could see that an Artemisia plant on the downslope had blocked the hedgehog's progress. "No wonder it didn't get away. It couldn't roll all the way down."

"Run up and get Beizhu to bring a rope," Huaqiu said.

"No." Lingguan said. "I'll come up with something; otherwise, he'll take the credit for finding it."

"But it'll get away while you're trying to come up with something."

"No, it won't." Lingguan assured him as he took off his shirt, bent down, and slowly nudged the balled creature into it. He told Huaqiu to go back and tell the others they couldn't find it.

Beizhu puffed himself up before Huaqiu even had time to feign a defeated look as he returned to the bonfire. "Hah! If you'd listen to your elders once in a while, you wouldn't mess things up. I told you you wouldn't find it. But you wouldn't listen, so after all that looking, in the end what did you get? Wasted effort. Are you ready to concede?"

"You're a prophet," Huaqiu said. "You'd have taken the credit if we'd found it—but you did say you wouldn't eat any."

Beizhu snorted and barely managed to say "Of course" when Lingguan walked up and dumped the hedgehog down next to the fire. "Of course… but you see, I told you it ran down a rat hole. That's where you found it, wasn't it?"

"No, it wasn't in a rat hole."

"Then it had to be in a sand pit. It's the same color as the sand, so it's hard to spot. No wonder the sand felt spongy under my feet. I figure it was a sand pit."

"No, not there either."

The others laughed. Yue'er, who was laughing the hardest, pounded the sandy ground and squealed gleefully. Lingguan's mother pointed to her son, but was laughing too hard to utter a word.

"Of course it wouldn't be in a hole or a pit," Beizhu said with a dry laugh, so it had to be at the bottom of hollow? It couldn't roll uphill." His confidence restored by this logic, he looked around and continued. "It was in the hollow, wasn't it? It had to be. I'll walk on my hands if it was anywhere else."

"Ah." Lingguan smiled. "Well, it was somewhere else."

"It was on a slope, blocked by an Artemisia shrub," Huaqiu said.

The women were by now doubled over with laughter. Holding her belly, Fengxiang could barely catch her breath, while Ying'er, lost her serene composure and shrieked, with her arms wrapped around Yue'er.

"Aiyo—go on—walk on your hands." Yue'er laughed and pointed at Beizhu.

Tossing off his hat, Beizhu bent down, did a handstand, and began walking around the bonfire.

His startled audience stopped laughing. After circling the bonfire once, Beizhu asked Lingguan and Huaqiu smugly,

"Can you do that? Come on, give it a try."

"We can't," Lingguan said.

"Of course you can't." Beizhu said firmly. "All you know is minor skills, like catching hedgehogs. What's the big deal about that? Even a blind man could do that. It rolls into ball when it sees people. I could catch one with my hands tied behind my back. Believe me? Well? No? Then I'll show you."

"I believe you," Lingguan smiled. "You eat the hedgehog you catch with your hands tied behind your back, and we'll eat this one. How does that sound?"

"I said I don't want any, and I meant it. They have a strong odor.

Besides, hedgehogs feed on insects, and that's gross."

"So you don't want any?" Lingguan asked.

"No, I don't."

"How do we cook it?" Huaqiu nudged the animal with a stick.

"Cook it?" Ying'er asked. "It's never done anything to you, so why do you want to cook it?"

"So we can eat it. Why would we have gone through all that trouble if we hadn't planned to eat it?"

"Don't cook it alive," Huaqiu's mother said. "Get some water and drown it first."

"Why?" Beizhu asked. "Just stab it with a pointed stick. That'll take care of it."

"No, I'll drown it," Huaqiu said. He rummaged though his saddlebags and came up with a water basin. He returned with the water and picked up the hedgehog, but Lingguan stopped him before he dropped it into the basin. "You're really going to drown it? Let it go. Why take a life for that little bit of meat? It doesn't make sense. Let it go."

"He's right," Ying'er echoed. It'd be a shame to kill it."

"You don't have to eat any of it if you don't want," Huaqiu said. "But this creature was created for us to eat. Why would that be a shame?" He dropped the hedgehog into the basin and pressed it down with a stick; the surface of the water bubbled.

"Now you've ruined a half basin of water," Lingguan's mother said.

"I didn't ruin it," Huaqiu said. "I'll save it to wash my face tomorrow morning. We all have to do that." He unhooked a small knife from his key chain and fished out the hedgehog, which spread out, its spineless belly exposed. "Who's going to help me skin it?"

"I will," Beizhu said.

"Get out of here." Huaqiu smiled. "I won't give you any even if you ask for it."

"Who wants it?" Beizhu said awkwardly. "I was just offering my help. I figure you'll be clumsy and puncture its guts. That would be disgusting."

"I won't do that, don't worry. You can help me, Lingguan."

With a sigh and a shake of his head, Lingguan walked up and exposed the creature's head. "Add some firewood, Yue'er."

Huaqiu removed the guts and tossed them into the fire, which sizzled.

"Isn't there a better place to toss that stuff?" Yue'er frowned. "It stinks."

"You don't understand. This is called cremation." Huaqiu laughed. "You have to do something for a creature if you want to eat its meat." He handed the flashlight to his mother and asked her to get him the seasonings and some five-spice powder.

"Get them yourself," his mother said with a smile.

"I'm too clumsy." Huaqiu returned her smile. "Aren't you afraid I'll spill the powder all over? I'll get it if you think it's safe."

"I'll get it." His mother took the flashlight and walked over to the saddlebags.

"You came well prepared," Lingguan's mother said. "It looks like you planned to enjoy some wild game out here."

"Ignore him," Huaqiu's mother said. "I haven't seen any five-spice powder."

Lingguan helped Huaqiu add Sichuan pepper, salt, and other seasonings to some flour, which they mixed thoroughly before stuffing it inside the hedgehog's abdomen.

"Hold it, while I get some wire," Huaqiu said to Lingguan. He took the flashlight from his mother and returned with a piece of wire to wrap around the creature and prevent the stuffing to spill out. Then he placed the hedgehog among the embers.

"What a shame we don't have five-spice powder. A pinch would make it much better."

His mother flipped him a baked potato. He tossed it from hand to hand, but was in no hurry to eat it. Instead he went on and on about the hedgehog's aroma. "Heh, its fat will slowly dissolve and seep into the stuffing. The fragrance will linger in your head."

"Can't you shut that traps of even with a potato?" his mother said. "How many hedgehogs have you eaten so far?"

7

After finishing the potato, Huaqiu retrieved the hedgehog with a forked branch and poured the stuffing into a bowl after unfastening the wire. An intoxicating aroma quickly permeated the area, drawing comments from everyone.

"Huaqiu, I never expected you to know how to do this," Beizhu complimented him.

"Of course you didn't. But I'm still not giving you any."

"Who said I want any? I've had so much I'm tired of it."

Lingguan's mother nodded after tasting the fragrant stuffing. Huaqiu's mother and Fengxiang both tasted it and had the same reaction. Ying'er refused to try it.

"This is wild game," Lingguan's mother said. "Try some while you can. You won't have a chance later."

So Ying'er tried it, and so did Yue'er. In the meantime, Lingguan poked Huaqiu and pointed at Beizhu.

"Beizhu is a man of his word." Huaqiu said loudly. "He said he wouldn't eat it even if we gave him a piece."

"And I won't. I ate too many potatoes earlier and I'm stuffed. I couldn't stand the sight of any more food."

"Let him be," Fengxiang said to Huaqiu with a smile. "That'll take care of his problem."

"What problem? All I said was I didn't want any."

Now it was time to eat. Hedgehog meat is unusual in that it sticks to the skin; the uninitiated see no meat, only skin and gusts when it's opened up. But skin is veined with rolls of meat. Stripping a hedgehog is like unraveling a ball of yarn; the meat falls away in strips. Huaqiu removed strips of meat and handed them to the two older women; neither Ying'er nor Yue'er would touch it.

"No?" Huaqiu said. "You might regret it. Hedgehog meat works magic on your skin. Just a few bites makes it nice and soft."

"Really?" Yue'er asked.

"I'm not a beauty expert," he said, "but I know it's fattening. And it's true that it makes babies' skin soft."

"Then I'll try some," Yue'er said. Ying'er remained unmoved.

Lingguan's mother nudged him and signaled with her eyes for him to offer some to Beizhu. Lingguan did the same.

"No matter what, Beizhu, you ought to taste this. Some people would say you're a man of your word who refused to eat, but there are some who might think we kept you from eating any. We know you're a man of your word, so come have some."

"I meant what I said," Beizhu said. "I said I wouldn't have any, so I won't. I'm not like you Huaqiu, who goes back on his word and boasts shamelessly, a real tongue-wagger."

"Listen to him," Huaqiu said to Lingguan. "He's gone on the

offense."

"That's not the right tone," Lingguan said.

"Do you really not want any, Beizhu?"

"Of course not."

"But it's so good." Huaqiu took a bite and smacked his lips. "Was it good, Ma?"

"It was."

"Did it taste wonderful, Auntie?"

"It did."

"How about you, young sister-in-law?"

"It was delicious."

"Fragrant and delicious," Huaqiu boasted.

"Really?" Beizhu said. "Give me a slice so I can have a sniff. I'm not going to eat it; I just want to smell it."

Huaqiu laughingly peeled a stripe the size of a matchstick and handed to Beizhu, who put it up to his nose and sniffed deeply.

"Aiya!" Beizhu shouted. "How did you open its belly and strip the meat? How come I keep smelling something stinky?"

"Nonsense," Huaqiu said.

"I mean it. Take a sniff if you don't believe me."

It smelled fine to Huaqiu, who cast a dubious glance at Lingguan, who knew that Beizhu was playing a trick. "Beizhu is a fox and the meat is grapes," he said.

"You'd better watch out, Beizhu." Huaqiu laughed. "If you pop off like that again, I'll smear your face and make you look like Judge Bao."

"If he keeps at it, you'll make him look like an ass," Fengxiang joined in. "I had some too, Beizhu, so try not to be so disgusting."

"I mean well, but no one appreciates me," Beizhu protested. "Think about it. How many hedgehogs has Huaqiu stripped before? This time he worked with little light, and when he wasn't careful he punctured the intestines—bam—the shit spilled into the meat. Of course it would stink."

"Would you stop it, Beizhu?" Lingguan's mother said.

"Let him say what he wants," Fengxiang said. "The shit he spews won't make it into our mouths at least."

Yue'er had a pained look as she covered her mouth with her hand. Ying'er put her hands over her ears.

Holding the hedgehog, Huaqiu looked at Lingguan, not sure whether to laugh or cry.

"Seriously, why wouldn't it stink?" Beizhu persisted. "What did it eat? It ate dung beetles and blind rats. What's a dung beetle, you ask. That black insect that crawls and rolls over disgusting animal droppings. Hedgehogs eat at night, so this one had just filled its belly, and you caught it before it could return to its den. Heh, think about it. It didn't have a chance to chew and digest the dung beetles' heads, legs, and the shit in their bellies, so everything spilled into the meat. It's too dark to see clearly. Now you took a bite and she had a taste, and you all said it was delicious. Well, to me it's disgusting."

Yue'er threw up noisily.

The two older women were also looking uncomfortable, one frowning, while the other rubbed her chest.

"You really do talk through your ass," Fengxiang cursed with a laugh. "Stop being disgusting, will you? I had some too, you know."

Huaqiu looked at the creature before glancing at Beizhu, as if unsure if it was clean or not.

That tickled Beizhu.

"Don't listen to him," Lingguan said. "Actually, it couldn't have been cleaner. And it smells wonderful, not at all like shit. He was trying to gross everyone out because he couldn't have any. I personally have never enjoyed such fragrant hedgehog."

"That's for sure," Beizhu continued with a smile. "Of course not. Who else could manage to put dung beetles and rat meat in their bellies but Huaqiu and Lingguan?"

Yue'er was by then dry heaving. Looking at the suffering girl, Ying'er congratulated herself for staying away from the meat. She'd have been the first to throw up if she hadn't.

"Would you stop it, Beizhu?" Huaqiu complained loudly. "Take a bite if you want. I'm not having any."

"You see? He knows what he did. Why else would he stop eating? Now you're giving it to me? You think I've never seen hedgehog before? Why would I eat something so filthy?"

"That ass ruined my appetite." Huaqiu handed the creature to Lingguan. "Here, you can have it."

"Go ahead, eat it." Lingguan tossed the animal to Beizhu. "Happy now?"

"Not me." Beizhu guffawed. "But it would be a waste if no one wants it. Maybe Huaqiu punctured the intestines and the dung beetles are in the meat, but luckily he stuffed it with flour and seasonings. See how the stuffing soaked up everything, including the dirty little dung beetles. So, hah, I'm sure the meat is clean."

Now Ying'er threw up, because she had tasted the stuffing.

"You're all so delicate." Fengxiang smiled. "This guy's filthy mouth is always spewing dirty stuff like that. I'd be reduced to skin and bones if I were like you."

Beizhu grinned as he pulled off strips, tilted his head back, and dropped them into his gaping mouth. He chewed a few times and smacked his lips. "You know, it does smell great and tastes good. You don't need to tell me that Huaqiu is good at this. It smells great."

"Be careful," Huaqiu said. "Don't swallow any of the *zhazha* and the rats."

"I couldn't. They were all mixed into the stuffing that went into your bellies."

The others didn't know whether to cry or laugh.

After a while they began to show signs of fatigue. Yue'er looked at her watch and said, "It's way past ten. Time for bed."

"You stay put. I'll make a warm bed for you," Beizhu offered, as he scraped embers to the side and spread the heated sand with a stick to mix with the sand near the fire. Then he laid down a felt blanket and cotton bedding before placing a long stick of firewood to mark the boundary between men and women, with Huaqiu and his mother next to each other in the middle to form a buffer zone. Soon the toasty heat would penetrate the felt blanket and provide them with comfort and warmth.

8

Even submerged in the tranquility and coolness of a desert night, Lingguan could not sleep. Nocturnal air spread gently, sending the tenderness of the desert seeping into every pore, as if it could cleanse one's insides. He heard it flow like water. It was uncommonly dark, which made the sky appear eerily high and the brightly sparkling stars unreal. The flickering starlight seemed to clamor; he wished there were an off-switch so he could render the night solid darkness.

When he wasn't looking at the stars the night was much quieter. He heard virtually no sound, only the faint noise of night air as it brushed past his ears. It was stillness typical of the great desert that villagers called the sea of death, a quiet devoid of sound, yet with a surging life force. There was hushed power in stillness that made him aware of his own insignificance. Poets had sung the praises of a moonlit desert, and "Smooth Sand under a Night Moon" was included in the eight notable scenic sites of Liangzhou; but he had deep affection for the desert cloaked in a nocturnal curtain. The night sky obscured its vastness, hid its enormity, and blotted out its menace, leaving only its most realistic essence, which was ordinary and yet mysterious. The desert looked truly boundless with its vastness masked, more immense with its magnitude concealed, and therefore more alluring.

Lingguan got dressed and walked up a rise, from which the vista was beyond his ability to see; he savored the enigmatic tranquility and solitude. Movements of the night currents were more noticeable, though they never developed into a wind. He felt the currents stroke him tenderly, but it was his "spirit" not his skin that received the caresses. Devoid of thought and form, he felt nothing but pleasure and coolness; it was a pleasure derived from the intoxication of body and mind and a coolness that was transparent and unadulterated. Little by little, the pleasure dissipated, and then so did the coolness, and he entered into a state of total oblivion.

A long time later, or perhaps instantaneously, he heard a sound that oozed instead of erupted from the dark night, and therefore was a sound of nature. The emergence of the sound imbued the desert night with a unique charm. After a brief respite, it awoke, which was manifested not in impatient churning, but in a composed smile. It was composure that originated in enlightenment, in liberation from worry, in knowledge from understanding the past and apprehending the future. As a result, the desert looked simple and yet imposing, unaffected and enigmatic, broad and level, all encompassing.

Amid the sounds of nature, foxes woke up, as did rats and wild rabbits. Everything in the universe was contented, wherever it might be, following the trajectory of its existence and fulfilling its predestined lot.

He was immersed in the state for a long, long time. The night grew late. Orion, what the villagers called the "three stars," had shifted to the west, but Lingguan was not sleepy. Rather, he felt unusually energized; his mind was calm and focused, so much so that he did not sense Ying'er, who had stood behind him for a long time before he heard her soft sigh.

He knew it was her without turning to look. Only she could emit that gentle airy sound, for she was always coming and going lithely, working nimbly, smiling gracefully.

"You can't sleep either?" he asked her.

"I can, but I don't feel like it."

He sighed as he folded her into his arms wordlessly, as if she too had been under the spell of a tranquil peace. He held back his questions, for at a moment like this, words were superfluous.

"I read a phrase in a book," she said after a long silence. "'A beautiful mistake.'"

"What?"

"You and me."

He shuddered, owing partly to the tranquility, but also to the desert and the people in it on this quiet night. An agitation in his chest woke up something that had long been buried in the great desert's yellow sand.

"Was I wrong, Ying'er?" His eyes were moist.

"If it's a beautiful mistake, then—it's worth being wrong for the rest of our lives."

"But I—but Hantou—my own brother—" He sighed, but did not

finish, for fear of ruining the atmosphere.

"Don't talk about that—let's—let me sing you a tune." The words were pulled from her heart, as threads:

A blacksmith struck the iron to make a nail,
A tinkerman made a scale.
Little brother shows his true heart,
Little sister will have no regard for her life.

A ladder leads up to the sky,
To pluck from it a good star.
I'll die with you if you want to die,
I'll be with you forever if you don't.

The knife that kills me, the basin to catch my blood,
The heart of this little sister will never feel remorse.
With a cleaver in your hand to take my head,
I'll sleep next to you even drenched in blood.

It was getting cold. The night air began to blow, a dry, cold, bone-chilling desert wind. They held each other tight.

"I wish we could die like this," he said.

"Me, too." Ying'er echoed. "I want to tell you something. I'm with child, our child. My period stopped after our first time together."

Oh, my! His body shook.

Chapter Eleven

1

Shortly after returning from gathering Artemisia seeds, Lingguan's mother was once again fretting about Lanlan. To her, children were like the fingers of her hands and were tied to her heart; each of them was precious. Lanlan, who lived with her in-laws in the neighboring village, worried her most. After adding two rabbits to two boxes of biscuits and two canned goods from the village shop, she had Mengzi ride her to the outskirt of their in-laws' village on the back of his bicycle. She then told him to go home, while she walked alone to their house.

She had long known that her in-laws were worse off than her own family, but the sight of the crumbling gate saddened her nonetheless. Her heart ached when she thought about her daughter, a flower of a girl, living in a place like that.

"Aiyo, come in, dear Qingjia. Come in, have a seat. What wind blew you to us today?" Lanlan's mother-in-law greeted her warmly.

"North, south, east, and west," Lingguan's mother said with a smile.

"I keep telling Bai Fu to invite you over. Now that the autumn harvest is in, we have nothing to do; so it's an ideal time for you to visit and take a breather. We'll have a nice, friendly chat, now that you're here. That's wonderful, just wonderful. How is Ying'er doing? Oh, I know, with in-laws like you, I have nothing to worry about." The woman was hitting all the right notes.

Lingguan's mother just smiled. She was not particularly articulate to begin with, and Lanlan's mother-in-law had her thoroughly tongue-tied. Facing a silver-tongued woman whose words flowed freely, like pouring out walnuts out of a jar, Laoshun's wife could not get a word in edgewise; so she kept quiet and let the woman carry on, responding only with facial expressions.

"Aiyo. I sure miss you. I tell people I don't know what good karma I have to deserve such a wonderful in-law. You're so wise and so kind. I keep telling Bai Fu to go see his mother-in-law, but the little rascal is a real lazybones. He just says, 'My mother-in-law is no different than my own mother, so why bother with all the niceties?' I have to agree with him. Before the marriages, we were two separate families. but now we're one. Don't you agree? We mustn't be like strangers."

"You're right, of course. Where's that little girl of mine?"

"She's out in the field, but she'll be home soon. Just some light work, building up ridges. I told her I'd do it, but she said she could do it faster. Light work, that's all. She won't be long."

Laoshun's wife was unnerved by the woman's thin lips, which seemed to move at lighting speed; she was also discomfited her affectionate and solicitous attitude, which was the main reason she had always felt a distance between them. She sensed something phony about Lanlan's mother-in-law, and the insincerity, even a shred of it, made her uneasy. Besides, she was sure her daughter was no match for a mother-in-law with such a clever tongue, who could talk up a storm. That made Lanlan's mother unhappy, but for the moment she was obliged to say,

"My little girl has a lot to learn, and you mustn't spoil her."

"Aiyo. What are you talking about, dear Qingjia?" She drew out the exclamation. "I always say we're old and set in our ways, so there's nothing we can do. But young people have their whole lives ahead of them. If we spoil them and let them develop bad habits, it will affect them for the rest of their life. Don't you agree, dear Qingjia?"

"You're so right," Lingguan's mother said, though she didn't mean it. I know my own daughter, she said to herself, and she has no bad habits. You're the one who should rein in that son of yours. "You're right. We indulge the children with nothing but love. We want only the best for the children."

"Right you are." The woman laid out a plate of steamed rolls and poured water. "Have a bite to tide you over for now."

"I'm not hungry." Laoshun's wife declined the offer.

"Don't say that, dear Qingjia. We're not strangers, so there's no need to lie, unless, that is, you're afraid the rolls are undercooked. You don't want to get sick or you think I might have put rat poison in them. Is that it? Try them, even just one." The woman broke a roll in two and stuffed one half into her guest's hand. She had no choice but to take it.

"Yum. This is so good."

"I'm so glad that you found it edible. They're not very good, but at least they're fully cooked. I'm no match for you, dear Qingjia. You make rolls that taste like bread. If only you'd taught your girl half your skills. Are you following a tradition of passing down family secrets to sons but not daughters? Ha-ha."

Laoshun's wife was pleased at first, since she was naturally proud of her kitchen skills, but she heard something else in the woman's comment. Was she praising my skill or complaining about my failure to bring up my daughter properly? Lanlan was not as good at making rolls as her mother, but she wasn't bad. She might cut a corner or two and probably did not spend enough time kneading the dough, but that was the only difference. Her kitchen skills were certainly better than her mother-in-law claimed. Laoshun's wife chewed a small piece of the roll and mulled over the comment, but got nowhere, so she laughed dryly and took a sip of water. As if sensing the guest's displeasure, Lanlan's mother-in-law said,

"Aiyo. You know me. A mouth like a knife, but a heart like tofu. I always say what's on my mind, and I guess I've said something to make you unhappy. Actually, your daughter is my daughter too, so we don't have to say one thing to each other and another thing behind each other's back."

"You're right." Laoshun's wife brightened up, realizing that she was being petty. "You're right, of course. You go ahead, teach her however you feel necessary."

"Sure. And you do the same with Ying'er. Parents are all the same; we want our children to have a good life, don't we? We teach them as long as they listen, but can do nothing if they won't. They can be dragons or tigers, it's up to them. Wouldn't you agree, dear Qingjia?"

Her heart skipped a beat. "Did that ingrate daughter of mine do something to make you unhappy?"

"Aiyo, listen to you. What are you talking about? As her mother-in-law, I know better than to be upset with youngsters. Wouldn't you agree, dear Qingjia? Besides, I didn't do anything to make her complain about me, did I? I'm still strong enough to work, but when I get old and useless, I'll have to let my son and daughter-in-law do whatever they want with me. They could feed me to the dogs or push me into a pit. Wouldn't you agree, dear Qingjia?"

Even more convinced that her daughter had done something to displease her in-laws, Laoshun's wife laid what was left of the roll on the table and said,

"Tell me what's bothering you, dear Qingjia. Tell me everything, don't hold back. I know that girl of mine has a temper and doesn't always say the right thing. She must have said something to offend you. But you're tolerant enough not to be bothered by that, and that's because you're such a nice person. Please tell me what she's done. I gave birth to her and raised her, no matter what, and she can't fight back if I beat her or talk back if I scold her. Don't hide anything from me."

"Aiyo. You're making too big a deal, dear Qingjia. She's not that bad. But, being young, she has yet to learn to be a member of society, so it's only natural for her to have problems. Actually, they're not serious. Those who understand will do things for her own good, but those who don't will say I'm being petty or finding fault. Wouldn't you agree, dear Qingjia?"

"Please tell me, dear Qingjia. I'm no stranger. If you think I'm worthy, then let's be frank with each other and share what's on our minds. I won't force you if you disagree. I know what my daughter is like; she doesn't have a gate covering her mouth, so sometimes she can't avoid offending people."

"Actually, it's really nothing. Just has a minor problem—she's a bit on the lazy side. She sleeps in and snores away until the sun is at the tip of the poplar tree. Think about it, dear Qingjia. I have breakfast ready, but I can't be expected to take the food in and feed her, can I? So I gave her and my son a piece of my mind. Since then, I have seen improvement."

"You did the right thing. If she's lazy you need to stop that. If a young donkey or a pony can be trained, a girl surely can. You did the right thing, dear Qingjia, you did."

A smile escaped the woman's pursed lips as she said, "Aiya, dear Qingjia. I'm happy you're so understanding. If only my daughter-in-law could be half sensible as you. It—there's—well, she actually didn't say anything to offend me; it's just the way she walks, storming around. I could close my eyes and not see her, and everything would be fine. But we live in such close quarters, you can't ask me to turn a blind eyes forever, can you? You see, dear Qingjia."

"She does have that problem. She sometimes stormed by me in the past. Don't worry, dear Qingjia, I'll talk to her."

"It doesn't matter whether you talk to her or not, dear Qingjia. It doesn't bother me. No one outside this house will know as long as I don't tell anyone. We don't air our dirty laundry, do we? But some things cannot be dealt with that way. People will talk even if I don't, and stir up rumors—don't get angry, dear Qingjia."

"I won't. I promise."

"Take visiting neighbors for instance. What do you think people would say about a young woman going to this house and that house all the time? Sensible people will say it's simply too hard for young people to stay at home, but others will surely gossip and say her mother hasn't taught her anything. It would upset you to hear what they say. I told them my qingjia is a scrupulous woman who knows proper behavior, and I refused to allow them to badmouth you. You see, dear Qingjia."

Laoshun's wife felt her face burning hot. She was angry, but tried not to show it. "Tell me what's on your mind. I don't believe that damn girl—"

"Aiyo, dear Qingjia. I don't want you to think I'm a gossip. I hate people who talk about others behind their backs. I'm pouring my heart out to you simply because we get along so well."

"Yes, I know."

"Now try to see it my way. It upsets me when my daughter-in-law goes to our neighbors' homes and banters and laughs with the young men there. I don't mind people criticizing me, but I don't want them talking about you. You see. And she hums and sings all day long about love and romance. Don't you see? She's not an actress or a singer, so why does she do that? People laugh at her. These are trivial matters, of course, and they can talk all they want; I could care less if they laugh their heads off. But there are other matters that can't be taken so lightly. She's always chirping away with other young women, and what am I supposed to do when their mothers-in-law come to see me about it? I can say nothing, dear Qingjia, but everyone knows she's my daughter-in-law. If I say something, she's unhappy. I don't want you to think I'm not a good mother-in-law or that I'm always wrangling with youngsters over trivial matters."

Laoshun's wife was too incensed to say anything. That shameless girl. She has made her entire family lose face. This has been a humbling visit. She heaved a sigh.

"Look at you, dear Qingjia. You're upset, aren't you? Ai! It's all because we get along so well. I shouldn't have told you that; really, I should have kept my mouth shut. See how upset I've made you."

Laoshun's wife managed a forced smile. "What do you mean?

Don't say that. We're a family, so we can tell each other everything. Don't be like that."

"You're so right. That's what I think too. No matter how you look at it, we're a family, right? A daughter-in-law is the same as a daughter to me—no, a daughter-in-law is more important. Which is why I put up with it as much as I can, pretend I didn't see something when possible, and shut my eyes when I can't stand it. I put up with it when she spends money without asking me or eats treats behind my back. But there are some things I cannot abide. Like when she talks someone into giving her a pair of stinky shoes. Try to see it my way. We aren't so poor that she can't afford shoes. Whatever she wants to wear, she need only tell me, and I'll trade in grain or sell the house to get it for her. Why does she have to swindle someone out of a pair of shoes? You see, dear Qingjia."

"That shameless girl." Laoshun's wife was on the verge of tears. She was so angry that, no matter how hard she tried, she could not hold them back. "What a shameless girl." She was sobbing now.

"Aiyo! Dear Qingjia, my dear Qingjia. Why are you—it's my fault—I'm so sorry, dear Qingjia. I—I should have kept my mouth shut. But I can't help it; I just feel like pouring my heart out when I see you. Don't be upset, dear Qingjia."

"It's not your fault, dear Qingjia." Laoshun's wife dried her eyes. "I'd have been in the dark if you hadn't told me. I wish I had broken her back the day she was born. It would have been better if I'd fed her to the dogs than lose face like this."

2

"Hey, Mama's here." Lanlan was elated to see her mother.

"You finished your work?" Laoshun's wife forced a smile, as she didn't want to lash out at her daughter the moment she saw her.

"No, it'll take another day to finish."

Laoshun's wife could see that Lanlan was visibly thinner. Her face was ghostly pale, with protruding cheekbones and sunken cheeks. With an aching heart, she glanced at the qingjia, who, she saw, was breaking off a piece of the roll that had been offered to her. Perhaps she had been too busy pouring her heart out to recall that it was intended to tide Lanlan's mother over.

"Be careful." Lanlan's mother pointed to her bulging belly. "You know your limits."

"It's all right. I read somewhere that a pregnant woman needs exercise," Lanlan said.

Her mother sighed. "You've lost weight."

"Oh, she prefers a nice figure over good health," her mother-in-law interjected. "Her appearance is more important than the baby inside her."

With a look at her mother-in-law, Lanlan was about to say something, but changed her mind. Instead she asked her mother, "How's everyone at home? Hantou had pains around his ribcage when I was back home the other day. Is he better now?"

"He's much better. The doctor gave him a prescription and said it isn't serious."

Lanlan's father-in-law walked in with her daughter, Yindi, while they were talking. He was a well-known "big talker," but his talkativeness was reserved for "big business." He did not deign to engage in small talk with women, "people with long hair and short sight." He walked out after a brief greeting. Lanlan's mother-in-law went into the kitchen after telling Lanlan to keep her mother company. She pulled the girl over and gave her several eager kisses, as if she wanted to eat the girl up.

"Where's Bai Fu?"

"Bai Fu? Who knows? Father and son are always up to no good. Senior runs around all day, making big deals on antiques or steel products, but we never see any money from his frantic transactions. Junior plays mahjong, cards or other games, and that's all he does. A few days ago he even pinched the money from selling a pig and lost it all." Lanlan's eyes glistened as she talked.

"Your father and I are to blame." Her mother looked down with a sigh. "We weren't thinking straight when we pushed you into this hell hole. Ai. Back then—"

"It's all right, Mama." Lanlan dried her eyes. "That's his only problem; he's fine in every other way, and he works like an ox. What more do we want from a farmhand? Besides, he can change, and everything will be fine when he does."

Her mother merely breathed a sigh.

"Hei, tell me, is he a prick or what?" The oath came from the yard. Lanlan said, "He's home." Before she finished, a powerfully built man walked in.

"That ass—Oh, Lanlan's mother is here. You see, that prick cheats, so no wonder I lose every time. That prick, hei—he's no good."

"Then stop playing," Lanlan said. "Why play cards with someone like that?"

"What? I can't let him off so easily. I haven't won enough yet. Hei, that prick. I was so mad I grabbed him and slapped him around. Know what happened after that? He couldn't cheat any more, and I won." He took out a handful of crumpled bills.

Lanlan's mother glanced at her. With an unhappy laugh, she turned to her husband. "Enough about that. Let's talk about something else"

"I deserve some credit, don't I?" Bai Fu laughed heartily. "You're always saying I give my money away. Well, I won this time." He walked out and soon they heard him boasting in the kitchen.

"A man like that—" her mother smiled sadly. "If we'd known he's like that—hei—"

"You haven't seen what he's like when he loses," Lanlan said. "He smashes things or throws them around—but it's not too bad. Don't worry about it, Mama."

"At least we were lucky to get a good girl like Ying'er. Otherwise, we'd die filled with regret. I wish your husband was half as good as Hantou."

"He's only human and can't be perfect. Don't you worry about it. I'm used to it. I mean it, Mama. I'm used to it. I hardly notice anything now. When I first came—I wanted to die." Her eyes were filled with tears again.

"You've suffered so much. Really suffered, Lanlan. I should have done better by you."

"It's nothing, really. Except—"

Lanlan's father-in-law walked in searching for something. "You must laugh at us for raising a son like that," he said to Lanlan's mother. That's just how he is. He's never up to anything good, and if we say a single word about it, all hell breaks loose."

"He's still young. He'll learn and he'll be better in a few years."

"Hah! A few years? Once I leave for the other world, I won't care what he does." The man fumed as he walked out to do whatever he was doing.

"They fight every day, back and forth over the smallest matter. She can outtalk him, but he's got his fists, so there's never a winner or a loser," Lanlan said with a smile.

"What's an old couple like them still fighting over? That's no good." Her mother forced herself to smile too.

"It's like they wouldn't know what to do if they didn't fight. Maybe arguing can be addictive. Maybe they feel an itch in the throat if they let a single day pass without a fight."

Mother and daughter laughed over the comment, a rare light-hearted moment for them both. Lanlan's mother took out a kerchief and unfolded it until a small white sack came into view. Inside was a red purse containing ten yuan. "Your papa gave me this to buy medicine for my headache, but I couldn't bring myself to spend it. I saved it for you to buy something for your needlework."

"I feel bad enough for not being able to offer you anything. How can I take your money, Mama?"

"Take it, and keep it in a safe place. Don't let them see it."

Lanlan took the money and put it in an inside pocket.

"Come take out the food, Lanlan," her mother-in-law called to her. Lanlan went into the kitchen, where Bai Fu was in front of the stove smoothing out the dirty money he'd won, still prattling about the game. Lanlan picked up chopsticks, the spice bowl, and other condiments, and carried them into the other room.

"I'm really sorry, dear Qingjia." Lanlan's mother-in-law said as she came out with two bowls of noodles. "I didn't have time to put something better together, and besides, unlike your family, we don't have everything we'd like, so I can only offer you some mushy noodles. But mushy noodles are all we have, and you can eat as much as you want, dear Qingjia. I'll feel better if you try a few bowls."

"No need to worry. We're just like you," Lingguan's mother said. "This is fine, really."

3

"Bai Fu, go with your mother to build the ridges, Lanlan's father-in-law said after lunch. "Give your wife and her mother a chance to chat. They don't get to see each other often, so we'll let them talk."

Still exuberant from winning earlier that day, Bai Fu readily agreed.

"That sounds good," his wife said. "You two stay here and talk while we go work in the field. You don't mind, do you, dear Qingjia? I'd like to keep you company, but I want to give you some privacy. With us around, you surely wouldn't enjoy the visit as much."

"What are you talking about? We don't have much to say to each other. I raised her from the time she was no bigger than my shoe, so I know her inside out, including every rib in her body, so there's not much to talk about. But I should let you go on with your work. You need well-built ridges for the winter floods."

Mother and son walked out a moment later, and the father went out with Yindi in a little handcart.

Now that they were alone, a sudden quiet descended in the room. The girl's mother studied her, while she avoided looking at her mother.

"I want to ask you something, Lanlan, and you have to be honest with me."

"Go ahead. I have nothing to hide from you."

"Do you not get along with your mother-in-law?"

"Not really. She's my mother-in-law, that's all. Like all mothers-in-law."

"Do you quarrel?"

"A few times when I first came here, but not after I learned how to deal with her. Why? Did she say something to you?"

"No, I'm just curious. But try to get up a little earlier."

"How early does it have to be? I get up, make breakfast, sweep the yard, and feed the pig before everyone else is up."

"Good. Keep doing that. You're the youngest in the family, so you ought to get up before them. They've toiled for most of their lives and it's time for them to take it easy. Oh, and don't go over to the neighbors' all the time, unless it's for something important."

"I don't do that. Sometimes I go next door to watch television. That terrible set of ours broke, and since we don't have the money to fix it, I go next door. I don't do that very often, once every ten days or two weeks. Why? Have you been hearing complaints?"

"No. But people will talk if you go to their houses too often. You won't mind, but the in-laws won't be able to take it, you see. You must think about them. Besides, you can't help but chat with neighbors when you're at their house. Sensible people won't have a problem with that, but others might say you're flirting with the men and that something must be going on. I know what my own daughter is like, of course, but not everyone does. Don't you agree?'

"Mama." Lanlan looked up. "Why don't you tell me what's bothering you? What else did she say about me? You can tell me."

"She's all right." Her mother sighed. "You just have to be more careful. Come home when you feel like eating something special, and I'll make it for you. If you want something, just tell me and I'll buy it for you. Don't touch their stuff and give them an excuse to talk about you. That feels like lashes across the face."

"You don't have to say any more. I know. That witch must have told you I stole their food and used their money." Lanlan began to cry. "This isn't the first time the witch has smeared me in front of other people. When I was pregnant, I had a craving for fried eggs, so

I cooked and ate one. Now she says I stole her food. Tell me, which pregnant woman doesn't have cravings? Some crave something sour while others love sweets. I just felt like having a fried egg. I only ate one, Mama, but the witch complained about me indirectly for two weeks. She ought to have forgiven me for having a miscarriage, shouldn't she? I drank some cold water. What's wrong with that? I felt like hanging myself I was so angry. And the money? When Fifth Granny needed to buy some medicine for a headache, she didn't have any—she's on the public dole—and asked if I'd lend it to her. I didn't have any, but I spotted a one-yuan bill on the table, so I gave it to her. That's all, but the witch told people behind my back that I stole her money. Tell me, Mama, what kind of mother-in-law is she? I may not be worth much, but surely more than one yuan." By then Lanlan was sobbing.

Her mother, now in tears, felt as if she'd swallowed a fly when she recalled the warm smile on the mother-in-law's face.

"She also complains that I like to visit neighbors to gossip and flirt with other men, and that I tricked someone into giving me their stinky old shoes. Everyone in the village has heard that. Visiting neighbors to gossip? How would I do that? All I ever did was watch television at Xiulan's house when her husband wasn't home, so what could have I done? Later I decided to visit neighbors precisely because of what she'd said about me. She can jabber away with other men while I'm not allowed to say a word to anyone. If someone asks me a question, I have to answer, don't I? But she said I was bantering with this one and flirting with that one. She was the one gossiping and spreading rumors. Is that grown-up behavior? Xiulan did give me a pair of shoes, a new pair she'd just bought, but were too small for her. I gave her a headscarf in return. But the witch said I disgraced her family when

I tricked someone into giving me her stinky old shoes. What's so disgraceful about exchanging a headscarf for a pair of shoes?"

Her mother's head was buzzing. She was speechless.

"She even egged on her son to get him to beat me, saying a whipped wife is submissive the way well kneaded dough tastes good. She's a horrible woman. It's like she's upset when Bai Fu is nice to me, so she tries to find fault with me and is happy only when he beats me. I commit a sin even when my father-in-law looks at me. He has eyes, so what can I do if he wants to look at me? I can't gouge out his eyes, can I? I have to serve him food, don't I? If I don't, she says I was badly brought up, but if I do, she still has something to say. Have you ever seen anyone like that?

"That's nothing. The worst is—ai." Lanlan dried her tears. "What's strange is why I keep having stillborn babies. Every one is born dead, one after another. The one who had gotten Grannie Qi's blessing was the only who lived a bit longer, but only for a few days. Mama, could it be my fate not to have a son? I'd just as soon be dead, if not for Yindi. But that heartless man yells and beats me, saying I don't want him to have a son to continue the family line. I shouldn't talk about all this, Mama. I don't want you to worry. I'm married into their family, so all you and Pa can do is cry with me when you know what's going on here. I wouldn't have said a word if you hadn't brought it up today. It's pointless anyway."

Lanlan's mother wanted to console her daughter, but could think of nothing to say; she could only shed more tears. The woman not only abused her daughter, but also humiliated and deceived her. It sent a chill to her heart when she realized that her own daughter lived among such people.

"Tell me everything, Lanlan. Let it all out and you'll feel better.

Don't hold it in or you'll be sick

"There's nothing else, Mama." As if waking up, Lanlan opened her eyes wide and dried her tears. "Really, nothing more. In any case, I'm actually doing better than most daughters-in-law, and that's true. I have enough to fill my belly and clothes on my back. There's a woman on the production team who doesn't even have enough to eat. It's really all right, except that I feel terrible sometimes. But I'm used to it, now that I've learned to put up with it. Don't worry about me."

Knowing that her daughter said all this to make her feel better, Lanlan's mother felt even worse; tears streamed down, as if a dam had broken. Lanlan did her best to console her, but only ended up crying along with her mother. Mother and daughter wrapped their arms around each other.

4

Lanlan's mother had a revised view of her in-laws after learning the truth. Naturally, she did not try to explain away her daughter's so-called flaws, since that would only lead to an argument. Worse yet, someone might say the wrong thing when emotions were high. She had married her daughter into their family and that was where Lanlan belonged now; as a mother, she could only shed tears with the girl if her mother-in-law yelled at her or hit her. Lanlan's mother was not going to be like some parents, who raised hell at their in-laws' house over trivial matters; that would not only not solve any problem, but could ruin the relationship, which in turn would only worsen daughter's situation in her new family.

It was about time for the mother-in-law to return from the field, and what worried Lanlan's mother was how to face her. The woman was no fool, and would have expected Lanlan to tell her mother everything; knowing the truth was out would would make her feel awkward. Lanlan's mother worried about how the woman would deal with the tricky situation.

She needn't have worried. The moment the mother-in-law walked in the door, a warm smile blossomed on her face as usual, an unadulterated natural smile, as if she had never had anything bad to say about her daughter-in-law. The smile was accompanied by an earnest greeting that came out effortlessly, "Aiyo, dear Qingjia." Her joyful tone made Lanlan's mother sense her own pettiness.

After dinner, Lanlan's mother-in-law told Bai Fu to kill a chicken for Lanlan to make a plate of quick-fried chicken before frying the rabbits brought by Lanlan's mother. She even sent her son to the village shop to buy a bottle of liquor. She planned for all three of them to sit with the young couple around a table to exchange toasts and enjoy the meat.

Lanlan's mother felt the dark shadows in her heart lifted by the actions of her qingjia. Lanlan's face also brightened, thanks to her mother-in-law's decision to kill a chicken. Now Lanlan's mother had a change of heart—her daughter's situation was better than she'd thought, and her mother-in-law wasn't so bad. Her mood now lightened by the cordial hospitality, she felt bad that they had killed a chicken for her sake.

"Aiya, dear Qingjia. You didn't have to do that. I'm no stranger, you know, so there was really no need."

"What are you talking about, my dear Qingjia? We're kinfolk, and you don't visit us often enough, so we must enjoy ourselves and each other's company," the woman said with a smile and what appeared to be unalloyed sincerity.

The reply completely erased the ugly image Lanlan's mother had created that afternoon. Which family doesn't have problems? Even your teeth get into a fight with your tongue sometimes, she thought.

"Come have some while it's hot." The mother-in-law urged when Lanlan brought out a steaming plate of quick-fried chicken. She picked up a drumstick for Lanlan's mother.

The gesture made Lanlan's mother smile as she thought back to her anger after hearing what Lanlan said. Maybe she too easily fooled by a smiling face, but at the moment, the joyful family gathering softened her heart.

"Come, have some, dear Qingjia." The woman continued her invitation in earnest, while picking out tender pieces and laying them on the side of the plate facing Lanlan's mother. It was a silent declaration that the meat was reserved for the qingjia, and no one else was permitted to touch it.

Knowing she could not possible eat all that herself, Lanlan's mother spread the pile around and said, "Come, have some, everyone. I don't have a donkey's stomach. I can't eat all this."

But the other woman pushed the pieces together again, making it hard to spread them out. So Lanlan's mother served her daughter's father-in-law, her daughter, and then her son-in-law, with a determined look that said she would not quit till she had her way.

"You don't have to do that. They have hands."

Obviously moved by her mother-in-law's genial treatment of her mother, Lanlan picked up a piece of chicken with her chopsticks and offered it to her mother-in-law. "Have a piece, Mother. You should take a lead when you want others to eat." Her mother-in-law accepted the piece without protest, took a bite and smeared her lips with grease; her face glistened with an oily sheen, as if to gloat over the fact that she had a good daughter-in-law, while others did not.

Everything seems fine between us, Lanlan's mother cheered herself silently. Thinking back to her qingjia's complaints and her daughter's explanations, she realized that the bones of contention were trivial matters, like getting up late in the morning, or visiting neighbors too frequently. Why had she reacted so strongly, as if the sky were falling? That was utterly unnecessary. No wonder Lanlan's father was always saying she fell apart under the slightest pressure.

The father-in-law and his son were focused on the food; the older man chose chicken feet and wings, the way of a good host, unlike the young man, who, with a hungry look, nearly obliterated all the tender pieces his mother had picked out for his mother-in-law. He was crunching loudly on the bones, and his lips and scraggly stubble were covered in grease. When Lanlan's mother offered him the tender pieces in front of her, he wolfed them down unabashedly.

Lanlan's mother did not touch her chopsticks when her daughter brought in the rabbit meat. "This is for you. I've had so much rabbit my head aches when I see it."

The mother-in-law knew that Lanlan's mother was saying that for her benefit, but it was also clear that Lanlan's mother often ate rabbit, so she refrained from urging her to eat some. "The rabbit isn't cooked right," she said. "It's dark and overcooked. The rabbit meat I had before was nice and white."

"Oh, that would be domestic rabbits." Lanlan's mother said with a smile. "Wild rabbits are all like this; their meat turns dark when it's fried, but it has a wonderful smell and taste. They eat grass, so their meat is so much more fragrant than from raised rabbits."

"Hmm, it does smell wonderful."

Still with a greedy look, Bai Fu completely abandoned his table manners; he was so fond of wild rabbit meat he ate until grease was dripping down his face. Even his father shed the refined airs of a host. Lanlan's mother smiled when she noticed the shockingly ill table manners of both father and son.

When they were done with the rabbit, Bai Fu's mother told him to pour for his mother-in-law, so they could have a toast. After a few rounds, she said to Lanlan's mother, "I want to make sure you have enough to eat and drink. Otherwise I'd feel terrible."

"I've had plenty of both." Lanlan's mother smiled.

"I'm someone with a good heart but a sharp tongue," the woman said after downing several cups. "So it's inevitable I'll say something to offend you, but you mustn't take it to heart. Like they say, a generous person forgives the small-minded ones."

"What are you talking about, dear Qingjia? I much prefer straightforward people, who say what's on their minds. I can't stand those who're always beating around the bush and never come to the point. I know what you're like; otherwise we would not have become in-laws." Lanlan's mother surprised herself by the ease with which she uttered the words. They came out naturally and effortlessly, and replete with sincerity.

"I have a flaw, I know. I'm petty, and I let trivial matters bother me too much. They can have me tied up in knots. If only I had half your temperament," Lanlan's mother added.

"That's not true. I have my flaws, too. I can't keep anything to myself and I say whatever is on my mind, so I offend people easily without meaning to. That doesn't bother people who know me, who just say I'm not the crafty type. But those who don't know me often mistake my attitude as difficult to get along with."

"That's all right, honestly," Lanlan's mother said to follow her lead. "It's best to say what's on your mind, like pouring walnuts out of a jar. If you keep things to yourself, they will fester and could ruin your health. That's where my flaw is; I lose my appetite over a trifle. You see, that's why I'm skinny as a rail."

"That has its upside, though. You know how older folks can spend lots of money without losing a bit of weight."

"What do you mean? It's better to be on the heavy side. A strong body can fend off diseases. Me, I wheeze and cough whenever I catch a cold."

The two women carried on with their mutual compliments, boring the men so much they went to bed after a few more drinks, while the women chatted away until midnight.

She's not so bad, Lanlan's mother said to herself later as she lay in bed, enlightened by a new view of the woman, who turned out to be worse than she'd hoped for, but better than her daughter claimed.

Chapter Twelve

1

Lanlan's mother returned home two days later, despite her qingjia's efforts to have her stay longer. She was concerned about her pigs and chickens, and most of all, Hantou's illness, a dark shadow that wouldn't go away. A young man on Lanlan's production team had recently died of stomach cancer; it had started out as a stomachache and he had put up with it as long as he could. When he was taken to the hospital, they discovered that his stomach was filled with cauliflower-like cancer growths, and he died shortly thereafter. If it had been discovered earlier, she heard people say, removing part of the stomach could have saved him, but it was too late. When she heard about it, her scalp turned numb. She could almost see Hantou rolling in bed from pain. She could not bring herself to wonder what he had, as if he'd get whatever illness she thought of. It took a great deal of effort not to associate Hantou with that illness, but his twisted face seemed to forever flash before her eyes.

"Ah, the lady of the house is back?" her husband, who was cleaning his handcart in the yard, said with a smile when she walked in. "I was wondering if you'd eaten too much to move, but you still look like a skinny monkey. How come? Hey, Bai Fu is here too."

Laoshun's wife handed a bag of a new breed of soybeans to Bai Fu before he left. "Only someone like you, who was a pig in his previous life, would be talking about food all the time," she said. "Where's Hantou?"

"At the well."

"Any better?"

"He said the medicine seemed to be working."

Her mind finally at ease, she told Laoshun about Lanlan and her mother-in-law.

"That's so typical of you women, always getting upset over something trivial, like one yuan, an egg, or a pair of shoes." He laughed. "And the more you folks with your long hair and short sight worry about things like that, the more worries you have."

"What important matters have you thinking about then?" she chided. "Probably your handcart or animals' reins, things like that. What else is on your mind? Are you focused on government policies or world affairs? No, people like us are caught up only in trivial matters. What else could we be thinking about?"

"All right, go ahead and ponder your trivial matters." Laoshun laughed again. "I wasn't talking about you, anyway. I was talking about that qingjia of ours, so why are you getting all hot and bothered?"

"You're mocking me again. If you could only be a mother-in-law yourself. Nothing gets done if you put things off, but if you do what you're supposed to do, there are bound to be minor arguments and major fights."

"You said it yourself," Laoshun said. "So why get upset with Lanlan's mother-in-law? Try putting yourself in her shoes. Besides, you're a mother-in-law, too."

"I didn't say anything bad about her. I'm just telling you what happened. And I'm not upset."

Fengxiang and Ying'er walked in, talking and giggling. They clammed up the minute they saw Laoshun's wife.

"Why didn't you spend a few more days there, Mother?" Ying'er asked.

Convinced that the two young women were talking about her, Laoshun's wife was unhappy, so she said curtly, "I was born to a life of hardship. I can't stay there and do nothing, so I came back to suffer in case someone wants to talk about me behind my back."

Fengxiang and Ying'er exchanged a look.

"You're imagining things. Who has the time to talk about you?"

"You never know. All kinds of birds nest in a vast forest. There are always people who like to stir up trouble."

"I'm here to borrow a cart. I didn't say anything bad to Ying'er," Fengxiang said.

"You don't have to say anything. I wasn't talking about you," Laoshun's wife said tersely. "If you've never done anything shameful, you don't have to worry about what people say."

"I just cleaned it," Laoshun said. "You can take it with you, and not a word about 'borrowing.'"

Fengxiang walked off wordlessly with the cart.

"Listen to you. Must you say everything that's on your mind?" he criticized his wife. "What were you getting at?"

"She really wasn't talking about you," Ying'er said. "She just told me about her fight with Beizhu's mother."

Laoshun's wife realized she'd been unfair, but she had to find a way out. "See? You were talking about someone, weren't you? A long leg gets covered with more dew and a big mouth stirs up trouble."

"You're so right." Laoshun smiled. "But don't hold the mirror up to others only; you ought to look at yourself sometimes."

She glared at her husband and walked into the kitchen.

"Fengxiang asked me to help her with the potatoes, Mother," Ying'er said after a pause. "She's near term and doesn't want to hurt the baby. She can't pull a cart alone."

"Go, then," Laoshun's wife said from the kitchen.

Ying'er turned and walked out. She had wanted to ask about her family, but it was obviously not the right moment.

2

Ying'er went into the field.

Fengxiang's family reported a bumper crop of potatoes that year; the harvested root vegetable, all large and evenly formed, made the field look white from a distance. Fengxiang and Ying'er spent the whole morning digging and praising the potatoes; both had been raised on the staple, to which they had a special attachment. The sight of such fine potatoes lifted their spirits, and they talked and laughed all morning; but when they went to Ying'er's house to get a cart, her mother-in-law received them tersely.

"Don't let her get to you," Ying'er said to her friend as they loaded the cart. "That's just how she is,"

"I know what she's like. Mothers-in-law are all the same," Fengxiang said. "I know all the twists and turns in their guts. They say whatever they please. Who care about them?"

"That's right. Just pretend you didn't hear them."

"What she just said was nothing. Beizhu's mother was really mean when I was first married into their family. She smashed plates and bowls if I ever got up even a few minutes late. She was a shrew, a tigress, that one, but she's better now. People aren't all that different, and that includes mothers-in-law. Be bold and act like they do, and they won't be able to do a thing about it; they might even be afraid of you. Forget that and you'll get a typical mother-in-law who picks on the weak and cowers before the strong."

Ying'er cast a glance at Fengxiang without responding.

"Don't you think it's weird that she flies into a rage whenever my man is nice to me? She really does. I was wearing some new clothes once, and guess what happened? The two of them—mother and daughter—refused to look at me. That was okay by me, but they spun around and walked off. So I said, be careful, don't twist your butts so much, they might break."

"They were just jealous." Ying'er laughed. "Think about it. She went through all the trouble raising her son, and now he's completely devoted to you. How could she not be jealous? The nicer he is to you, the angrier she'll be."

"You may be right." Fengxiang laughed too. "But a man had to have a wife; that's a custom passed down from the beginning of human history. He can't spend his whole life with his mother, can he?"

"Just watch yourself and you'll do fine. Try not to be too affectionate in front of her."

"What are you talking about?" Fengxiang said. "We never do

that. You know what he's like. No, that man of mine isn't the type. He hardly ever looks at me. Men are like that. They're only nice to you when they want you-know-what. Don't you agree?'

"Maybe," Ying'er said. "I'm not a man, so I don't know what they're thinking. In any case—eh, what can I say?"

"Aiyo! Don't act so prim and proper with me. I know what it's all about. Quiet men and flashy women are best in bed. Hantou is gentle as a lamb, but who knows if he turns into a wolf in bed? It's your fault for being so pretty. If I were a man, I'd want to gobble you up."

"Stop that," Ying'er said. "Please, let's talk about something else."

Fengxiang studied her. "Why are you acting so bashful? The rice is cooked and the girl has become a woman, so what's there to be shy about? In the end, the you-know-what is just—tee-hee."

"I really don't want to talk about it." Ying'er was blushing. "Tell me how you managed as a daughter-in-law."

"It wasn't easy, I'll tell you that. After nearly eight years I got to the point where I could barely stand it, and things didn't get better until we divided up the household."

"Was it really that bad?"

"Of course it was. She was always giving me a hard time for the smallest thing. So in the end I fought back. I showed her respect, but she refused to be nice to me, so what was the point in being respectful? Eventually, I yelled back when she yelled at me, and we were even. I had nothing to fear. I was ready to fight it out. I'm no longer afraid of her. Sure, I got a beating now and then. That no-good husband of mine cared too much about losing face, so he hit me whenever I fought with his mother, and he could be brutal too. Once I was laid up in bed for several days, but I didn't mind. I couldn't get up so I stayed in bed and slept, not doing any work, even when the wheat was about to rot in the field in June. Finally, things improved a bit. I didn't yell if she didn't, and I was ten times as nice as her whenever she treated me better. But I'd bring a gun to that knife fight. It worked. She stopped being a shrew, except to curse me indirectly or storm past me once in a while. Isn't that weird, though? Why would she rather I showed her no respect?"

"That is strange." Ying'er smiled. "A woman in the production team in my parents' village said the same thing about her mother-in-law."

"But I cured her! Would you believe it? In the past, all hell would break out if I dared to spend a few extra minutes in bed. She'd raise a stink that could send chickens flying and dogs leaping over walls. I made breakfast, swept the yard, and cleaned the kitchen every morning, while she stayed in bed until I asked her to get up for breakfast. Now that we've divided up the household, she has to do all the work herself. We live separately and do our own chores. She lorded it over me for nearly eight years, but she can't do that any more."

"I thought you were the happy-go-lucky type. I never saw you as a schemer."

"Schemer? I'm a simple girl who says what's on her mind. But I notice things even if I don't seem to care. Once she bought some tomatoes and shouted when she walked into the yard, 'Yue'er, have a tomato.' I was cleaning vegetables in the kitchen. She didn't say a word, just looked my way. It was only a tomato, right? Why should I care about eating a tomato? So later I went out and traded for two bushels of wheat and took one to her. Her face turned red as she said reluctantly 'Aiyo, we already have some of that.' Hei, of course they did. Who doesn't? So I said, 'I bought too much and we can't finish it. It'd be a waste to feed it to the pigs.'"

"You're terrible." Ying'er laughed. "Calling her a pig."

"And there's more. Once, Baigou bought some cured meat. 'Aiyo,' she said, acting all phony, 'you paid for it and could have eaten it privately without telling me. You don't have to share it.' I was furious when she said that, because I knew what she was getting at. Back when I was pregnant I had a craving for cured meat. I didn't have any money of my own, so I asked that no-good man to buy a little. He wanted to share it with his mother, but I said no, because with so many people in the family, no one would get a real mouthful. So we didn't share it. But that stupid daughter of mine blabbed, "Grandma, we had some meat-meat." My mother-in-law never forgot that, which was why she said what she said that day. Just think. After we divided up the household, I brought her things when I didn't have to, so there was no need for her to get upset if I didn't. Agree?"

"Of course. All these disputes are over piddling matters. There's no need to let them bother you, is there? Why fuss over every little thing?"

"You're right, of course." Fengxiang curled her lip. "But she's the petty one. There's so much more. Things improved after we moved, but not much. Any time she sees me chatting with someone, she makes a sarcastic remark, like your mother-in-law did just now, because she thought I was talking about her. What a joke. I have better things to do than talk about her. Why would I do that? Because my teeth itch?"

Ying'er smiled. Isn't that what you're doing now, talking about her? Just a thought.

"Even if we're talking about her, it would have to be because she'd done something to deserve it, wouldn't it?" Fengxiang said, as if she could read Ying'er's mind. "If you stand straight, you'll never have a crooked shadow. What's she afraid of?"

3

Ying'er ducked into the kitchen to help her mother-in-law with dinner.

"Do they have big potatoes?" she asked Ying'er.

"Yes, they do."

"Of course they do." Her mother-in-law said with a bite. "They fertilized the field with sesame husks. We'd have gotten even bigger ones if we'd done that."

"Then we'll do that next year." Ying'er smiled. "Their potatoes were large and evenly formed, not many small ones."

"Next year? That's easy for you to say. Where do we get the money? Mengzi and Lingguan aren't yet married, and Hantou's not well. Every dose of his medicine costs several yuan."

Ying'er wanted to say that a good potato crop would fetch several times more than the cost of sesame husks, but decided not to, given her mother-in-law's lukewarm response.

"She's not someone you should spend too much time with."

"But she asked me to help. She couldn't pull a load of potatoes all by herself. Father agreed."

"The old man is no good either. But I didn't say you couldn't go. Of course you should help her out, but, but don't gossip about other people. She has a piece of foot-binding cloth on her tongue and can spin ten stories for every one of yours. Everyone in the village knows that, and I don't want her turning you into someone like her."

"I didn't say anything, and she – she didn't either. Besides, I'm not stupid. No one can lead me astray."

"You never know. You learn how to be good from good people, and you attack the river gods if you're with the dragon king. As time goes by, you gradually pickup bad habits, and once that happens, it's hard to change."

"I know."

"She has so many problems. Beizhu's mother cries whenever she talks about her. She thinks no one's good enough for her, as if she were perfect. But she's not. I don't even like the way she looks. And then there's that mouth of hers; she's always talking about something or someone to anyone she runs into. She stirs up trouble among neighbors when she tells people how the Zhang's cat killed the Li's dog. Should her mother-in-law try to rein her in? She lost that right when they divided up the household. But if she doesn't even try, people will say that so-and-so's daughter-in-law is acting like this and that. So she does all the talking while her in-laws get all the blame."

Ying'er knew Fengxiang liked to visit neighbors and gossip. Of course people would talk about her after she did it too often. On the other hand, she said what was on her mind. Most people in the village knew what she was like, and she had a good relationship with them. She didn't stir trouble, contrary to what Ying'er's mother-in-law had claimed.

"Besides, you can't be a pheasant with you head under a shrub and leaving your tail feathers exposed. Just look at that house of theirs, a pigsty, a real pigsty, run by a slovenly, lazy woman."

"She's cleaned it up now."

"That's now." Her mother-in-law raised her voice. "You never saw what it was before. You could hardly bring yourself to walk in there. Torn shirts, worn shorts, stinky soles, and smelly socks were strewn all over the place. The awful smell came at you the moment you walked in."

When was this? Ying'er wondered.

"Let's not talk about that and focus on the—well, who's her

provider? Their grown-up son, right? So why does she act so high and mighty? If she's wearing new clothes and no one pays her any attention, there's no problem. But if someone does, then she prances around proudly, and that's something she should avoid. She's like a beggar who cannot save food for the next day."

Laoshun walked in and his face darkened when he got a sense of what his wife was saying. "Are you still at that? You're always complaining about this person or criticizing that one, as if you're a world beater."

"Don't be so superior." She gave him an ugly look. "One of these days, when I get the chance, I'll be talking about you, so your daughter-in-law will know what you're really like."

"Go ahead, talk away." He laughed. "I'm not some frightened little three-year old."

"Really? You're not afraid? Then I'm going to tell her. I'll start with the ladder—"

"Oh, shit!" He fled the kitchen, and she doubled over laughing, finally erasing the angry look on her face. If only she'd laugh like that more often, Ying'er was thinking.

Mengzi and Lingguan came home with several rabbits when dinner was about ready. Ying'er felt her heart fill with happiness when she heard Lingguan's voice.

4

Late that night the sounds of a door being smashed and a dog barking erupted from Beizhu's yard. Laoshun's wife nudged him awake.

"Listen to that. A thief, you think?"

"Coming in through the front door?"

"Then what is it?"

"It could be Beizhu coming home after a card game."

"Their dog wouldn't bark at him."

"Aiya! This could be bad," he said with a frown when hit by a realization. "It could be the family planning people. The team leader said the township has been stepping up their arrests and that the city government has sent out several vans."

She turned on the light and quickly got dressed. "I'll go take a look. I hope they don't take Fengxiang; she'll surely get the knife if they grab her."

"That's quite likely, since she's had two babies already."

She ran out, still working on her buttons.

Soon she ran back inside with Fengxiang in tow. The younger woman was wearing only a vest and a pair of wool pants, both covered in dirt. Laoshun's wife stomped her feet and turned around in the room, her eyes darting here and there.

"Now what? Where can she hide?"

She opened a large wardrobe, but it was filled with cotton batting and some worn blankets, no place to hide a woman. Someone shouted from outside and banged on their door. Now she was in full panic mode. She stomped her feet again, and then took Fengxiang to their bed and pushed her under the blanket.

"Where are you hiding her?" the team leader yelled the moment he was in the room.

"Who? I just woke up. I have no idea who you're talking about," Laoshun's wife said.

"She has to be hiding here," a young man said. "I heard their door open."

"That was me. I went out because I thought a thief was in our yard."

The group searched every room before entering the old couple's bedroom.

"I asked the old crone to use some moxa on my head, but she wouldn't do it." Laoshun was complaining about a headache and about his wife. "My head's about to explode from the pain."

"Could you be hiding Fengxiang under the blanket?" Big Head asked with a smile. "How does it feel, you dirty old man?"

"Go ask your father," Laoshun replied with a groan. "How the hell would I know?"

"Let's go," Big Head said amid rowdy laughter. "We'll search somewhere else."

"It looks like there are two heads under the blanket," The young man said.

"He can't be sleeping with his daughter-in-law," Big Head said to cover for them.

"Says who? Go ask your daughter-in-law," Laoshun said with a smile, making others laugh again. The young man walked up to the bed and grabbed a corner of the blanket. Laoshun paled. "What do you think you're doing? he demanded as he held the blanket down. "I'm sweating in here, and I'll come after you if I catch a cold."

"Fine with me."

Fengxiang jumped out from under the covers, shrieking with despair, and ran out the door before anyone could react. The young man managed to pull off part of her torn vest, and they all gave chase.

"I have to hand it to you." Big Head burst out laughing. "Sleeping openly with your nephew's wife in your arms like that."

Laoshun grunted as he covered his naked body and his head with the blanket, leaving Big Head to laugh his way out.

"What now? What are we going to do now?"

"Would you stop that?" Laoshun stuck his head out from under the covers. "What to do? What to do? How am I going to face the world when people hear about this?"

"What are you afraid of? An upright man doesn't fear a crooked shadow."

"Horseshit! Couldn't you have found a better place to hide her than under our blanket? I'll be ashamed to face people now. And it's all your fault, you old crone."

"My fault? You shouldn't have let her in if you didn't want to, but no, you lifted the blanket up high for her to slip under it. And you didn't even make yourself decent; we could all see the black hair down there. Stop complaining. I could tell it was just what you wanted. Am I right? You have such shifty eyes, there's no need to pretend to be an innocent bystander. I didn't say anything about you, so why complain about me? Who knows what was going on under the covers? It looked like there was only person there. How do you explain that?" She demanded indignantly.

"Oh, please." He was getting angry. "Did I go out and drag her into our house? Did I?" He threw a shoe at her, but it missed and broke the mirror on the wardrobe.

"What was that?" Hantou raced in.

"They're arresting women with too many kids," she said after a quick glance at her husband. "They were after Fengxiang. Go see if she got away." Hantou did as he was told.

Knowing she had to leave her husband alone, Laoshun's wife sat by the window, her mind going back to the scene after the blanket was lifted. He really did get what he wanted—hei, what made me think of hiding her like that? She wondered.

"You surprised me with that crazy idea of yours," Laoshun said with a chuckle.

"What are you laughing about?" Her anger flared up again. "Why are you so happy? Go ahead if you're dying for a tender young morsel. Wash your face and shave, and you'll look young enough to have fun with one.

"Look at you, old crone." He was laughing out loud now. "I didn't come up with the idea. You forced me into it. So why complain about me? You're really—hei." He stopped laughing and frowned. "The whole village will know about it before the night's over. Tell me, how am I supposed to face them?"

Hantou walked in. "She got away," he said. "She gave them the slip. They had to leave with nothing to show for their effort. Big Head said his hands were tied and wants me to tell you not to treat him as a puffed-up traitor."

"Go back to bed. It's still early." Hantou's mother breathed a sigh of relief when she heard Fengxiang was out of danger. Hantou left. She wrapped herself in the blanket and lay on her side as thoughts flashed through her head and jealousy festered in her heart. Laoshun smiled secretly when he knew what she was thinking from her heavy breathing.

Early the next morning she went to Beizhu's house, where she spotted a ladder against the back wall when she entered the yard, and knew how Fengxiang had gotten away. Beizhu was still in bed, tired out from the commotion the night before, while their older daughter was mixing pig slop.

"Where's your Mama?" Laoshun's wife rubbed the little girl's head. She looked over at her father without replying. Beizhu woke up and said with a yawn, “She’s gone to a place no one knows about. Hei, they almost got her. I hear they dragged one woman off to induce labor, and it turned out to be a boy. She lost her mind when they let her go.”

“Then you must make sure no one knows where she is.”

“No one knows.” Beizhu yawned again.

A donkey brayed somewhere. Laoshun’s wife walked out and saw a black donkey sticking its head out of the stable. It must be hungry. She went up to check; sure enough, the trough was empty. She hoisted a basket over her shoulder, went into the storage shed for some hay, and came back to fill the trough.

When Ying’er came out of their house with a bucket to feed the pigs, she gazed at her mother-in-law, who knew what she was thinking, and said, “Everything’s fine.”

“I don’t understand why she doesn’t have her tubes tied,” Lingguan said at breakfast. “The government is after them, and they have to be on guard all the time. What kind of life is that?”

“Everyone wants a son. It’s no problem when you’re young, but you’ll need someone to care for you when you’re old,” Laoshun said.

“And someone to hold the filial banner at your funeral and burn spirit money at New Year’s and holidays,” his wife added.

“Why worry about all that?” Mengzi blurted out with a laugh. “Get drunk today, and don’t worry about having nothing but water the next day.”

“He’s right. Everything ends when you die and you won’t feel a thing,” Lingguan joined in.

“Says who? Your soul will feel it,” their mother argued. “Besides, you get to keep the spirit money your offspring burns, and no one can take it away.”

“You’re getting more mystifying all the time.” Mengzi said it with a smile.

"It's the truth. Grannie Shaman said if you draw a circle around the ashes when you burn spirit money, no ghosts but your ancestors can cross the line. Like the circle drawn by the Monkey King on TV."

"Ha! The offspring become monkeys," Mengzi said, "but how do the ghosts of people without offspring live?"

"How?" Their mother said. "As wandering ghosts, roaming the streets until they bump into someone with weak vital energy. Then they cause health problems that will get the person to burn spirit money for them."

"Sounds great to me," Lingguan said with a laugh. "A ghost can become a millionaire by bumping into lots of people. It sure beats hiding out and sneaking around to have a son when alive."

Their mother blinked. She felt like saying something, but in the end decided not to. Ying'er just smiled.

"That's not how to look at it," their father said. "You know what people will say if you don't have a son? They'll say you're heirless because you're immoral or wicked."

"But aren't you always saying that sons are people to whom you owed money in your previous life? Then why does everyone hope for a son?" Lingguan asked.

"That's not how to look at it either. What's the purpose of life if not to have a son to bring you a grandson? Why stay in this world if you don't do that? You've made the trip in vain."

"What's the point of having a son to bring you a grandson?" Lingguan persisted.

Ignoring him, their father continued, "If you don't have a son, people will insult you when you get into an argument. You can ignore them, but girls aren't as good as boys when it comes to working in the field, are they? Take irrigating the field, for example. A boy can be sent out in the middle of the night without a worry, but you can't do that with a girl. That's why people say ten perfect daughters can't compare with one blind son."

"Aiyo. That means there's no point for us to exist," Ying'er said. "Might as well feed girls to the dogs the moment they're born."

"She has a point," their mother said. "That's why a family can't live without a mother. A cow can have ten calves, and every one of them relies upon her for everything. You men think you're so much better, so Ying'er and I won't do anything for a few days, and you'll see how it feels. You won't say these heartless things once you've suffered for a few days."

"That's no way to look at it." Laoshun said. "A chicken pecks and a pig roots. Everyone is good for something."

"Ha, that's right," their mother said. "So how is a blind son better than ten perfect daughters? Let the blind son have a few kids, and we'll see how he does."

"Ma sounds so enlightened, so why don't you talk Lanlan into tying off her tubes." Lingguan said.

"That won't do. She wants a boy so much she's just about run out of ideas," their mother said.

"See what I mean? Boys are more precious," their father said, making everyone laugh.

"I wonder what's happening at Lanlan's." Their mother sighed. "She's worried sick. She doesn't think she can hold her head up without a son."

Lingguan glanced at Ying'er and blushed when their eyes met.

Chapter Thirteen

1

People say that Liangzhou is an unusual place, known for its coincidences. At noon one day Bai Fu showed up on a donkey with his daughter, Yindi. After greeting his in-laws, he put his daughter down and went to see Handless Wei. Laoshun's wife picked up the little girl, cooing the whole time.

Goubao showed up at Wei's house on Bai Fu's heels. He and Bai Fu often gambled together.

"What are you looking for, Bai Fu?" Goubao asked.

"A mule."

"Stay with a donkey. Getting a mule from a horse is as easy as planting onions in the mud, but getting a mule from a donkey is like panning gold in the sand."

“Onion or gold, I don’t care. If others can manage, why can’t I?”

“Did Fengxiang get away?” Wei asked.

“They almost caught her,” Goubao said. “Be careful, Bai Fu. They’re stepping up their arrests. If they catch one, they toss her into their van and lay her an operating table, where a knife is waiting. I hear they’ve warned the township head that he’ll lose his job if they don’t get serious. I also hear that several vans were sent down from the city.”

“I’ll bow to my fate if we get caught, but we’ll keep trying if they don’t catch us. We have to have one with something between his legs,” Bai Fu said.

Wei walked out to bring in his stud horse, which neighed excitedly at the sight of Bai Fu’s donkey, making the donkey drool and smack its lips with the same excitement.

“This animal isn’t stupid.” Wei laughed. “It didn’t do anything all morning two days ago, when Baldy Wang brought over his donkey. It was scrawny and skittish. When the horse was finally ready, it kicked and brayed, and we tried over and over but could not get the horse to do its job. Look at it now. The horse knows you got a handsome donkey there and I don’t have to be the matchmaker.”

“There’s no comparison.” Bai Fu was mightily pleased by the comment. “Look at the hair on my donkey, black and glossy. It looks like a thoroughbred.”

The horse and the donkey were touching lips.

Wei tied the donkey’s tail to one side, while the horse neighed loud and long, then stood up and laid its front hooves on the donkey’s back.

Soon the donkey’s rump began to tremble. “Success,” Wei exclaimed. “It’s going to work. Just look at them—hey, it’s going to pee. Pinch its midsection, right there, and pinch hard. Don’t let that happen, or all our work will be for nothing.”

Bai Fu kept pinching the donkey's midsection, forcing the animal to give up its desire to pee.

Goubao walked up, untied the donkey's tail and gave it a pat on the rear. "Looks like the horse did a good job, so maybe it will work. If it fails, the donkey will lose its appetite and its fat. Isn't that weird? Even an animal loves doing it. It doesn't fill your stomach and won't keep you warm, but you can't get by without it. We humans are worse, of course, and some people have lost their heads over it."

"Heaven has its reason for all creations," Wei said. "Unlike that shaman mother of yours. She's always mumbling things no one can understand."

"Don't say that," Goubao said with a stern look. "My mother is the latest in a long tradition, and she doesn't make stuff up. She has a book called *Peach Blossom Magic*, or something like that. It was passed down from the Peach Lady in the Zhou dynasty. Lord Zhou's divinations were no match for the Peach Lady's prayer rites. He was an expert in hexagram divination and could foresee disasters, but all that vanished once she performed her prayer rite. He once divined that a young man would die in three days; the man would be hit by a rock and buried under the rubble, and could not escape his fate. Being a filial son, he did not want his mother to suffer, so he sneaked out of the house, hoping to die away from home. When his mother found out, she went to the Peach Lady for help. The Lady drew a magic tally and told her to burn it on the third night while calling out her son's name in front of the stove. It was pouring rain that night and so the son took shelter in a brick kiln. When he heard his mother calling out urgently to him, he emerged from the kiln just before—crack, it collapsed. He was saved. If not for the Peach Lady, he would have died. Lord Zhou finally realized that the Peach Lady had higher spiritual attainment and more magical powers than he did."

"I'd heard that Grannie Shaman had many powers, but I didn't realize there was such a long tradition," Bai Fu said with a surprised look.

"She does have that power. I've seen the book, made of the same yellow paper as spirit money, with all sorts of strange-looking magic tallies. They give me the creeps."

"The harmful *qi* that hexes you, is that real?"

"Of course it is. Last year a man from the city who was a *qigong* adept said this all made sense. Take people born in the year of the goat. You notice that every woman in our village born in the year of goat has had a tough life, don't you? There are even a few widows. I heard that the constellation controlling that year has a lot of harmful *qi*. So do people born in that year. For men it's not a problem, but it's terrible for women, who have more magnetic fields. Think about it. It would be strange if she didn't hex someone to death somewhere along the line."

The color drained from Bai Fu's face. "A fortuneteller came by one day," he managed to respond, "and she said that my daughter has lots of harmful *qi* and that she could hex someone. She could be the cause of the baby boys' deaths—I didn't want to believe her—but the girl was born in the year of goat."

"Do you mean Yindi? That's what my mother said too," Goubao blurted out. But, sensing that was the wrong thing to say, quickly added, "I didn't believe it though."

"What did she say? What did your mother say?" Bai Fu persisted.

"We really shouldn't buy those outlandish ideas."

"Don't be cruel, tell me. How can you stand by and watch me become heirless? Just tell me what she said, that's all. That'll give me a chance to find a solution and have someone hold a prayer rite. So tell me, what did she say?"

"Actually she didn't say much—just—but—actually—just the hexing part, hexing brothers as a child and then a husband when she grows up. She didn't say anything else, nothing else, really."

Ignoring Goubao, Bai Fu squatted on a small mound of dirt with his head down and spoke again after a long pause: "I knew something wasn't right. How could that happen over and over? I knew there had to be a cause." He exhaled deeply when finished.

"She did say that, but, but what can I say? Just ignore it and you'll be okay."

Bai Fu remained as motionless as a rock for a moment before standing up and, without a word to his friend, shook his head and walked off with his donkey.

2

"Rubbish." Laoshun's face darkened when he heard what Bai Fu told him. "I don't believe a word of that. What kind of harmful *qi* can such a pretty, clever little girl have? How is she supposed to hex someone? I don't want to hear any more crazy nonsense and irresponsible talk from you."

"I didn't make it up. Grannie Qi said the same thing."

"Her? What is she? A demon, that's what. A woman in her late fifties who still has bright red lips and wriggles her hips when she walks, trying to look as if she had a willowy waist. She can't have anything nice to say. Even her farts are toxic."

"What are you saying?" His wife laughed. "She doesn't use lipstick, she was born with red lips. And how do wriggling hips affect what she says? Beizhu doesn't wriggle when he walks, but you can't trust a word he says."

"I don't care. Just don't any of you give me any more that nonsense." Laoshun seethed.

"What does it mean to hex?" Yindi looked at her father and then at her grandfather before turning to her grandmother.

"Little children should be seen and not heard." Her grandmother patted her.

"I'm just asking. What's a hex, Grandma. Tell me, please." The girl grabbed her grandmother's hand and shook it.

"Hexing, well—it means—hacking a human figure out of a block of wood. See?"

"Then I hacked my little brother. I did." Yindi clapped and laughed. "I'll hack out another one, Daddy. I'll hack one out for you."

"Would you stop that? Stop already." Bai Fu pulled a long face, grabbed the girl, and spanked her. She cried. Laoshun's wife grabbed Bai Fu's hand and yelled angrily, "You're heartless, cruel and heartless."

"If you're trying to show off your authority, do it outside." Laoshun shoved Bai Fu away and picked up his granddaughter.

"You heard what she said. It was terrible." Bai Fu was red in the face.

"What did she say? I didn't hear anything. She's a child. What does she know? Would you dig up chicken shit if that's what she did?"

"Be a good girl." Laoshun's wife wrapped her arms around the girl and comforted her until she stopped crying. Not understanding why her father had spanked her, Yindi sneaked a look at him with her pretty, limpid eyes.

"Don't say those things again, all right." Laoshun's wife said to the girl.

"Daddy said I hacked out a little brother. So why can't I hack another one?"

"I told you to stop," Bai Fu demanded, raising his hand. Yindi shut up and buried her head in her grandmother's arms.

"Don't listen to what you don't like to hear." Laoshun glared at his son-in-law. "And stop getting so worked up over nothing."

With an angry snort, Bai Fu glared at his daughter and crouched down on the edge of the *kang*, where he snatched Laoshun's pipe, wiped it off, and took a few furious puffs.

"It's superstition," Laoshun said. "Don't dismiss it out of hand but don't believe it completely. That's the best way to deal with superstition. You have to believe some, like which is an auspicious day and which isn't, or offering sacrifice to the deities. But you can't apply the same set of beliefs to everything; otherwise, you'll back yourself to a corner. You shouldn't believe everything you hear and then act on it."

Bai Fu continued to puff angrily without responding, a display of his distress and contempt. Sensing the younger man's reaction, Laoshun changed his tune: "Come with Grandpa, Yindi." She walked out with Laoshun with a final backward glance at her father.

Laoshun's wife picked at a kernel of rice stuck to her lapel and looked up at Bai Fu. "Did Grannie really shaman say that?"

"It wasn't her, it was Goubao." Bai Fu exhaled audibly.

"Is there a remedy?" She stared into his eyes as if trying to draw one out.

"I don't know. I didn't ask. She was the one who gave us the magic tally and found us a solution the last time. The baby wasn't stillborn, but it died after a few days, a little better than the first one."

"I know all about that. You go ask her if there's an effective remedy."

Bai Fu spat, wound the tobacco pouch around the pipe, and tossed it down before getting down from the *kang*. He stood lost in thought before heaving a long sigh.

"What's the matter now?" Lingguan asked as he walked in and noticed the looks on their faces.

"Just the man I want to see." As if roused from a dream, Bai Fu said. "You have more education than me. Have you read anything about hexing people or harmful *qi*?"

"Hexing people?" asked a puzzled Lingguan.

"Yes. Like someone was hexed by someone else. Have you read anything about that in your books?" Lingguan's mother looked at him with nervous expectation.

"Why do you want to know?" Lingguan laughed. "I didn't come across anything like that in my books—but I once attended a lecture about *qigong*. The master said it was real and that everyone has a magnetic field of some kind. It's different for everyone. If they mesh with others, they can even cure diseases, but if not, they can interfere with each other and cause illness."

"So you can really hex someone then?" Bai Fu asked in a trembling voice, as beads of sweat oozed on his forehead.

"Don't get hung up on that. That's what he said, but who knows if it's true. Since you can't see it or touch it, it's hard to say. But I have to admit that sometimes it does seem to make sense. I feel fine when I'm with some people, but terrible with others, whether I know them or not. So I suppose this field must be there. I even heard there's an infrared camera that can capture a person's magnetic field." He stopped when he noticed the color draining from the faces of his brother-in-law and his mother, who, in particular, seemed to have suddenly gotten a few years older.

"So that means it's true," Bai Fu murmured as if in a dream.

"What? What's happened?" Lingguan asked.

"Grannie Shaman said Yindi can hex people," His mother said with a bitter smile. "The babies died because she hexed them."

"Oh, that? I thought something terrible had happened." Lingguan laughed. "That's utter nonsense. You can't take it seriously."

"But the woman who came by said the same thing." His mother would not concede.

"Lingguan shook his head. "Don't believe things like that. You're born with your own destiny. How could a little girl change that? It's ridiculous when you think about it."

"But didn't you just say something about a field?" His mother looked up at Bai Fu, whose forehead was bathed in sweat.

"A field? That was what the man said. But who knows if it's true? And what if it is? If everyone has one, how can it hex others? That's laughable." Lingguan knew he sounded less convincing as he went on, so he decided not to expound further on the field and changed the subject. "You can't really believe those *qigong* masters. Few of them are for real. Most just want to cheat you out of your money. One even said he'd tied mosquitoes' tubes with his thoughts, and that none of the mosquitoes in the world can produce offspring. Who would believe something like that?" He saw that the mention of offspring produced a grim look on Bai Fu's face. Slightly panicked, Lingguan forgot what he'd planned to say.

"I don't believe it either." His forced the words out between her teeth. "A little girl like that couldn't possibly change what has been preordained by the Heavens."

Bai Fu remained silent, lost in thought, his forehead dry now, though his face was still a steely gray.

3

"What can I say?" After a belch with a strong garlic smell, Grannie Shaman Qi glanced at Bai Fu, who was staring at her like a cancer patient looking into the eyes of a medical specialist. She stopped, like the blind storyteller when he felt an urge to relieve himself just as he reached the point in his story where a knife slices down on the head of the protagonist. Bai Fu felt as if cats were scratching his heart. She was enormously pleased with the effect. "Goubao—" She called out to her son. "Take eighty cents to the Lin Family Shop to pay for the box of tissue paper I took earlier." Then she picked at the dirt under her fingernails, using a needle with such care and focus that it took nearly two minutes per nail. Bai Fu thought he would have a nervous breakdown.

"Tell me, please." He could manage only a few words.

"It's really hard to say." She finally looked at him again. "You can believe it, but it's illusive, and you can't see or touch it. No one has ever seen a scar or a mark on the body of someone hexed to death. But if you don't believe it, how do you explain all the people who died after being hexed? Haven't you noticed that most of the widows were born in the year of the goat?"

"What I meant was—"

"Stop right there. I know what you want to say. Children are the same; they actually carry more harmful *qi*, which is why ghosts are afraid of them and sometimes turn into deadly fireballs. Those with special vision can see it. You see, when someone is about to be hexed, there will be a force like a whirlwind, really strong—but I don't talk about this often. People who understand believe me, while those who don't say I'm a dangerous fraud." She stopped, pursed her lips, and released another garlicky belch.

"Take those struggle sessions, for example. They said I defrauded people out of their money, but the ones who struggled against me eventually came to me to beg for help. Like Huang the Beard, who's dead now. He really did bully me, but he had to come beg for help, dripping in yellow pus. It was disgusting, with not an unblemished spot on his body. He had to beg for my help, and he was fine after I got his soul back. Guess what I'd done to him? I'd sent his soul into a thorny bush. No wonder he was dripping in yellow pus. How could he not be? He could not have fought back. You see, he'd struggled against me—when the session was over and we came back, he hemmed and hawed when he saw me. I was so mad I decided to send his soul off. And in the end he had to come begging. Ha!" Grannie Shaman Qi forgot her plan to string Bai Fu along, for she was now completely preoccupied with her own recollections.

He had heard the story many times before, but pretended it was his first, his expression changing from surprise to delight following the development of the tale.

"I can't be intimidated so easily. I don't bully others easily either, but I will surely fight back if cornered. There's another person—I won't mention his name, and don't tell anyone else about this—but back when I was at the farming co-op, he took me into a field and forced himself on me. I was so mad I sent his soul into a large water-formed hollow and smashed it with a rock. Of course, he had no idea what was happening, except that he went home with glazed eyes. He died within six months. They never found out why, and I never told anyone. So don't go blabbing, please."

Bai Fu nodded and mumbled a promise he wouldn't, though he had to laugh, since he'd heard this story, which she'd "never told anyone else," many times. Yet, he treated her with respect, for he believed her story. So did the villagers, who knew who the unnamed person was. He had died under suspicious circumstances; before his demise, he'd roamed the village as if he'd lost his soul before curling up and freezing to death in the hollow. Everyone said it was punishment meted out by Grannie Shaman.

"What's a soul?" she asked. Bai Fu was like a student who can't answer a teacher's question. He had no idea what a soul was; fortunately, she had not expected a response.

"A soul is a soul," she said, to which Bai Fu feigned sudden enlightenment.

"Humans have three elements in their souls and seven in their spirits. See?"

He did not dare say he did, but he couldn't say no. Realizing she did not expect a response, he regained his composure. She pursed her lips, a habit he only now noticed. Her lips were red to begin with, and glowed when she pursed them. She then cast an unwitting look at him, which made his heart race.

"Red, orange, yellow, green, blue, indigo, and purple. Seven of them, all on shoulders. The red one has a tendency to fall off; a light scare will send it dropping to the ground, just like a human. You resemble your spirit, so you will get sick. I can't tell you how many spirits I've collected. The lives I've saved are as numerous as goat droppings. I should get some credit, if not reward, for my hard work."

"Sure, right." Bai Fu's mouth was dry. "But—can you help me with my problem?"

She stopped abruptly and gazed on him till he felt eerily discomfited. Exhaling after a long pause, she said, "Of course I can. Did you actually think I couldn't? I can do anything."

"Then you must help me, please." He felt like getting down on his knees. "Nothing has worked, and I don't know what to do. I've even felt like ending my life—I didn't know the cause—who could have known—"

"You've come to the right person. To be honest, I'm the only one who can do it. The others—they can do nothing." She sneered. "My remedy works every time, without fail, and with everyone. If it doesn't work, then there's no need to see anyone else, just accept your fate." She wore a curious smile.

"This isn't much, Ganma." He referred to her as a surrogate mother as he took out fifty yuan and laid it on the table. "But I'll bring you a substantial thank-you gift once it's done."

"Why are you treating me this way? Take it away. We are nearly related, so I can't take your money. Please, take it away.' She pushed the money toward him.

"You must take it, Ganma; or it won't work." He pushed her hands away and nudged the money back again. "This isn't for you, but for the deities."

"When you put it that way, I have to accept it. I'll keep it for you to buy incense or something for the deities," she said solemnly. "Just this once. I'll only take your money this one time and help you out only once. If it works, that's a blessing from the deities; if not, it's your lot in life. But my remedy is very powerful and works for anyone not predestined to be heirless. I'm giving this powerful remedy to you only, no one else." She went on to tell him what it was. "Bury seven peach wood stakes in the center of the yard, hide seven new needles under the door sill of your bedroom, and hang a peach wood bow and willow arrow over the door. Then place a sharp object by the pillow of your pregnant wife to ward off evil."

Tears streamed down his face when he heard the remedy. "It's all over. I'm done for. That's the end of it. That's exactly what you told me to do last year." He sobbed.

4

Bai Fu walked in the door in a daze. The look on his face made his mother-in-law feel as if her world was falling apart.

"It's all over. I'm done for," he said. "What's the point in living?"

"What did she say?"

"What did she say? She went on and on before giving me the most powerful remedy, which turned out to be the same one she gave me last year. If it was so powerful, it would have done the trick last year and we wouldn't have go through it again this year."

"I thought it was something terrible." She breathed a sigh of relief. "The world is big enough that there have to be better shamans than her. We'll seek help from someone else since her remedy doesn't work. Don't be upset and don't give up."

"She said something else too."

"What did she say?"

"Do you remember that white fox? The trapped one?"

How could she forget? It was back when Lanlan was first married. Bai Fu and Hantou had set a trap where foxes frequently came for water. One morning, when the gate was open, they saw a white fox leaning against it, caught in the trap; its leg was broken and it had tears in its eyes. Bai Fu killed it with a club. Laoshun gave him a serious tongue-lashing. "A white fox is a thousand years old and a black one ten thousand. This fox had enough self-cultivation that it knew to seek out whoever set the trap. It's extraordinary. Even someone who eats shit would not have done what you did."

"Grannie Shaman said her remedy would have worked if Yindi hadn't been able to hex it. Grannie could not overpower her. She also said that a little girl who can sing and dance and is concerned only about her appearance at such a young age must have been a fox in her previous life. I suspect that Yindi was the white fox coming to exact revenge in this life. Otherwise, why would every boy die right after it was born?"

"Shut your trap," she said. "I can't believe a sweet little girl like her was a fox."

"Foxes are clever, smarter than humans. Haven't you seen how pretty the TV Snake Demon is? And you've seen that the fox fairy in Ordination of the Gods is smarter than us."

She shot him an angry look while trying to find a response, but something else occurred to her, and she lost her composure. Sitting down on the edge of the *kang*, she was unable to utter a word.

Not until Hantou, Ying'er, and Lingguan returned from the field did she finally emerge from the dream-like state and go into the kitchen. Seeing the strange look on his brother-in-law's face, Lingguan realized that he was fixated on the earlier topic, but he pretended not to know that.

"What's happened?"

Bai Fu let out a long sigh and lowered his head after a look at Lingguan.

"Come on, spit it out. You'll make yourself sick if you hold it in," Hantou said.

"It's all over. Grannie Shaman can't do anything about it. She said—and I suspected as much—that in her previous life Yindi was that white fox—the one I clubbed to death that year."

Lingguan, who was drinking water, spewed out it out, but managed to say with a laugh, "I thought it was something really bad. Turns out you're worried about something totally unfounded."

"I thought it was something terrible. It gave me such a fright I broke out in a cold sweat. Turns out—" Hantou was laughing too.

"What do you mean?" Bai Fu said unhappily. "How can you all think this is nothing? Ever since she was born, we've been having stillborn babies. Don't you find that odd? If she was the white fox, then it will be a miracle if I don't end up with no son at all."

"That's ridiculous. You must be possessed. What can this possibly have to do with the fox?" Lingguan jeered.

"I agree," Hantou echoed. She's such a sweet child I'd rather believe she's a fairy reincarnate."

Bai Fu looked at them one after the other and said nothing more.

Laoshun walked in with Yindi and blew his top when his wife related what had been said. "He's a shithead. His mind is closed off. When he needs to use his head, you couldn't get it to open even if you hammered it a dozen times. With nonsense like this he backs himself into a dead end. Fox—rubbish." He wanted to say more, present some facts, and reason with his son-in-law, but unfortunately he didn't know how to refute the young man's claim. So with a snort, he went in and crouched on the edge of the *kang*.

"If you're like every human who lives on the five grains," he said to no one in particular, "then you have to talk like one. Say what you should and seal your lips about what you shouldn't, so you won't confuse yourself. Whether you should have clubbed it or not, the fox is dead, so leave it alone and don't lay any blame on it. How many foxes do you think Meng Eight has killed by now? Which one has ever been reborn? Or maybe the fox owed you a life and returned to pay it back.

It could then be reborn as a human."

"That's true," Bai Fu said. "That's what Grannie Shaman said too, and that was why it was reborn — to be — a human."

"Enough!" Laoshun roared. "Stop that crap. I don't want to hear any more of that."

"You'd better go get a physical exam," Lingguan offered. "There's a cause for every problem. Maybe it's some kind infection. I saw on TV that there's a hospital with too many new-born babies dying, and a checkup showed it was caused by infection."

"That's a good idea." Hantou agreed. "And don't be suspecting this and blaming that all the time."

"Exam? She and I have been checked and we're both fine, but the baby is in there now, and we can't check it out," Bai Fu said.

Laoshun's wife called him over quietly after dinner. "I'm afraid that what Bai Fu says is true. I did have a dream the night he killed the white fox. In it I saw the fox sobbing at our gate. It cried for a while before rushing into Lanlan's arms like a whirlwind and then disappeared — later, she had Yindi."

"Would you stop that nonsense about dreams?" Laoshun shot her an angry look. "Keep your lips sealed and don't let that blockhead hear you."

When he went out with the goats, Laoshun could not stop thinking about this whole business, and in his mind's eyes his granddaughter took on the look of a fox, with a pointed mouth and slender cheeks. But he took Yindi along, and had to laugh at his own foolishness when he saw the adorable girl's lively face. "Is it fun in the desert?" he asked her.

"Yes, lots of fun."

"Do you like foxes?"

"Yes, I do."

"Aren't you afraid of them?"

"Why should I be? They're really lovely. I liked one the moment I saw it."

"You've seen one before?"

"Yes. Uncle Meng shot one with a pointed mouth and red fur. It was so pretty. People are mean – Grandpa, why did he shoot a fox that didn't do anything to him?"

"Its pelt is worth a lot of money."

"So he wouldn't shoot it if it didn't have pelt?"

"Of course. What would be the point?"

"So would I be shot if I had a pelt?"

Laoshun was startled. Is she really a fox fairy? He looked down to see the girl smiling innocently. Her guileless face made him ashamed of his thought.

5

Laoshun handed Gimpy Five some water and a steamed roll he'd brought from home.

"No, thanks. I have my own."

"How can you eat those hard, knobby things? They'll ruin your stomach."

"That's my lot in life, and I consider myself lucky to have even these. I'd be wasting food if I fed them to the livestock. Besides, we don't have enough, so I couldn't even feed them to the animals."

"Come to my house and get some of ours."

"No, thanks. I'll make do and take it one day at a time. If I borrow too much and can't pay it back, people will still be cursing me when I kick my legs out straight one day. "

"Who wants you to pay it back? Just come and take however much you need. We all run into a tight spot now and then," Laoshun said while snatching the moldy bun from his friend and tossing it to the goats.

"I wonder if Wuzi will get better this time." Laoshun sighed.

"I figure his mother ought to be back by now. We can't afford it any longer, whether he gets better or not. It's his good fortune if he gets better; if not, there's nothing more we can do. We've sold what we could—wood, grain, and trees. What comes next and last would be to sell our pot for scrap. We've borrowed a few thousand yuan already and did our best, so it's up to Heaven now."

"He should be better, since he's been there for quite a while," Laoshun said.

"He is better than before. But the doctor said that for a complete recovery he'd have to go through several series of treatments. Where would we get the money? He did look better when he took his medicine, a small handful of tablets. He's better when he takes them, but they make him sleepy, and once the effects of the medicine wear off, the symptoms return and he can't stop talking. I tell you, it's hard."

"Won't all those pills ruin his stomach?" Laoshun asked as he looked at Yindi, who was picking berries from buckthorns.

"That's what everyone says, but—Chinese herbal medicine is so expensive—in any case, it's up Heaven now. We can only do so much."

Laoshun felt a chill rise inside when he thought of his son, Hantou. "Heaven is blind, piling on more pain for the suffering people, while giving good health to corrupt officials and evil-doers, the ones we see on TV receiving prison sentences."

"You're absolutely right," Gimpy Five said. "But there's nothing we can do. We have to keep on living, so we take what's given us.

Death is the only thing that counts."

"What are you talking about? Heaven spares those who have nowhere left to go. Just put up with it, and sooner or later something good will happen."

"That's what I think, too. But sometimes nothing works, no matter how hard I try. With all this suffering, tell me, what's the point of living?"

"A sand baby, Grandpa!" Yindi called out.

"Let it be, and don't shout," Laoshun said.

"But it's eating an insect."

"Let it eat then. Don't worry about it."

"But the insect was crying, calling for help."

"Well, go ahead and save its life."

"I still have to tend these goats at my age, and after a day out I'm like a dead pig," Gimpy said. "But I have to do it. No matter what, the little bit I earn is some help to the family—it's better than nothing."

"The amount should go up this year, don't you think?" said Laoshun. "Now it's still five *fen* per goat. The price for everything else has gone sky high, so five *fen* is nothing."

"Not really," Gimpy said. "Five *fen* is a little better than nothing. If we ask for more, they may just go ahead and slaughter the goats, and we won't even have the five *fen*."

"You're right," Laoshun said. "None of us common folk have money; the officials are the rich ones. They get richer and even worry about how to spend their money, while we're so poor we can't keep a fart between our cheeks. The world's gone crazy."

"It can go crazy all it wants and none of our worries are going to change it. One day lived is one day earned. We'll think about what to do when we can't go on any longer. We can use a knife, take a rope, or swallow poison, all easy remedies."

"There you go again. The sky won't fall when common people can't go on any more."

"A fox, Grandpa!" Yindi shouted.

"Where?" Laoshun cried out in surprise. He looked where she was pointing, but saw nothing but a vast expanse of yellow sand. No fox. "I don't see anything. Her eyes are playing tricks on her."

"I didn't see anything, either." Gimpy Five said.

"A big fox, it's white. It's staring at me with its big, shiny eyes."

"Stop the nonsense."

"It's not nonsense," Yindi insisted. "But it ran off, so we can't see it any more."

"That's odd." Gimpy Five glanced at Laoshun. "How come I couldn't see it?"

Laoshun gave the girl a dark look before turning to say to Gimpy Five, "Her eyes played tricks on her."

"No, my eyes are fine. Really. It was a big fox," she argued, waved her little hands.

"Little kids have good eyes, so maybe she saw a fox fairy," Gimpy Five said.

Laoshun squinted into the distance and replied with a sigh, "What fox fairy? It's all made up."

"No, you're wrong. It's true," Gimpy Five said. "They know everything. They even howl at the moon on the first and fifteenth of each lunar month. Dogs do that too. That dog of ours did it, like a demon, so I killed it. Then Wuzi got sick. All the shamans I talked to said it was that dog's spirit messing with him. It's strange, though, because he howled each time he started acting up and sounded exactly like that dog howling. Really strange."

Yindi ran over and handed some berries to her grandfather.

"Good girl. She's too young to know so much." Gimpy Five rubbed Yindi's head.

"Kids these days all like that. We knew nothing at their age," Laoshun said.

Putting a few berries into her grandfather's mouth, Yindi asked him if they were sweet or sour. "Why does a fox have such nice fur, Grandpa? If it didn't, then people wouldn't shoot it, would they?"

"That's a strange question." Gimpy Five laughed. "What would it wear then?"

"Wear clothes, like us."

"Who's going to give it clothes?" Gimpy Five asked.

"Me." The girl thumbed her lapel. "I'll give it all I have on."

"What does a fox eat?" She asked.

"Insects, or rats. Whatever it can find."

"So it picks on smaller creatures too. That's not nice."

"Of course it does. Otherwise it would starve to death." Gimpy Five laughed.

The girl knitted her brows, deep in thought, before saying, "I know, give it some steamed rolls so it won't eat rats."

"But if it didn't eat rats, they would run wild, getting bigger than a donkey. There would be more of them than grasshoppers, and they'd eat up our crops. And when there's nothing left, they'd eat us. They could bite off half a little girl like you." Yindi cried out in fright and burrowed her head in Laoshun's arms, making the two old men laugh.

"So, should a fox eat rats or not?" Gimpy Five asked.

"Yes." Yindi nodded.

"It's interesting how the world is set up. Everything has its place. People shoot foxes that eat rats that eat insects that eat dirt that eventually eats us up. Weird, isn't it?"

"Sure. And it's predetermined by Heaven. It's like parts of our body, each with its function. You can't do anything with one missing."

"I wonder if Heaven really exists. Everything on earth is so well organized, it must. But then why is there so much injustice in the world? Why doesn't Heaven do something about that? Why are the bad people always in power? The money-grubbers, the cheats, the scammers, and all those people without a conscience live the good life. The good die young, while the bad live forever. So is Heaven blind or does it simply not exist?"

"Why worry about that. We only live a few decades so it's pointless to think about things like that. We live whether it exists or not and live the way we do whether it sees well or is blind," said Laoshun.

They lamented and commiserated until the sun set and they called in their goats to head home. The setting sun lit up the sand dunes, the goatherds, and the trees. Hearing the goats' bleats, Gimpy Five began to sing at the top of his lungs:

The sun sets in the west—the goats—return to the pen—
Black-headed—lambs—are attacked by wolves—
Girl—girl—stand to the side—
Don't—mess up—Brother—Wang's—herd—

Yindi laughed at Gimpy Five's hoarse voice. Laoshun joined her, shaking his head. When he finished, Gimpy Five seemed to be reminded of something as his last note disappeared into a deep valley like a falling pebble.

6

Bai Fu woke up grim-faced. "Pointless, totally pointless. Life isn't worth living," he grumbled.

"What's the matter now?" his mother-in-law asked.

"Nothing. I dreamed—that—Yindi's mother gave birth to a plump little boy. I've heard that dreams are the opposite of reality. Since I had a boy in my dream, we'll probably wind up with another girl in real life."

"You don't know how to interpret dreams, so stop that, will you?" said Lingguan.

"Do you know how?"

"Of course. The plump little boy represents a petty man, which means you have a small-minded person stirring up trouble behind you, which could lead to a dispute."

"Can't you say something nice?" his mother asked. "Whether a dream is good or bad depends on the tone of the person interpreting it."

"Say, Mother has become a grannie shaman. Listen to her," Ying'er said with a smile. "She sounds so believable."

"Damn!" Bai Fu blurted out. "Lingguan's toxic mouth has ruined my dream. What do I do now? What if I really have a dispute with someone? Lingguan, you and I will have the argument now and fulfill the dream."

"Sure. We can even fight if you want," Lingguan said in jest. "With the way things are these days, everyone has something to gripe about, so we all need opportunities to vent once in a while."

"I recall that my second brother mentioned a way to offset a bad dream," Lingguan's mother said.

"What is it?" Bai Fu asked.

"What's your hurry?" Mengzi said. "Let her finish. You don't start eating till the food cools."

Ying'er was by now doubled over laughing. Bai Fu thumped Mengzi on the back.

"It's simple. After you get up in morning, walk out of the house with a bowl of fresh water right at the moment the sun rises. Draw a cross on the ground with your left middle finger, step on the cross, turn to the left three times, and spew a mouthful of water three times. Then turn to the right and do the same thing. There. Now you can make bad omens positive."

Bai Fu complained that she should have told him earlier, to which his mother-in-law responded with a laugh before saying, "You're as lazy as a pig and won't get out of bed until the sun burns your backside. So don't blame me."

"I have a solution," Yindi piped up, her innocent eyes opened wide.

"What does a child like you know?" Bai Fu's face turned grim.

"You give me a beating, and that will be the same as having a fight with someone, won't it?" She made everyone laugh, so she added, "I mean it. Daddy can give me a beating, and he doesn't have to be really mad either."

"Get away from me," he said. "I get upset just looking at you, so shut up."

"Don't you shout like that in front of me!" Laoshun shot him an angry look. "I like my little granddaughter. And you, all you ingrates here, you aren't worth even one of her toes. Which one of you has ever massaged my back, tell me that? Which one of you has ever brought me water? She's a little girl, but one who knows a lot."

Bai Fu's Adam's apple hopped up and down.

"Enough," Laoshun's wife protested. "Flapping your lips so early in the morning, with that non-stop chatter of yours. Go fetch some water if you have too much energy."

Ying'er went out to bring in some bowls.

"Time for breakfast. Let's eat and stop arguing. It's like leading a cat to drink just to have something to do," Mengzi said as he picked up a bowl and took a sip. "Aiya! I burned my throat. Why did you make it so hot?"

"Know who you are talking to in the future. This is retribution for your impudence," Ying'er said lightheartedly.

"Just stir some wheat bran in cool water for him from now on. That way he won't complain so much," Lingguan said. She smiled at his comment.

"Why are you just now having breakfast?" Goubao walked in and hollered. "Don't you even look at the clock?"

Ying'er's mother-in-law told her to prepare a bowl for Goubao, but he declined,

"No, no need. I had my breakfast so long ago it's probably already on its way out."

Ying'er set down her bowl with a frown and covered her mouth with a handkerchief.

"That's disgusting," Laoshun said unhappily.

"We'll turn our chamber pot upside down and cover him with loose stool if he doesn't stop," Mengzi said, making Ying'er run out, rubbing her chest with one hand and covering her mouth with the other. Goubao laughed. A smiling Mengzi winked.

"Don't mind him," Laoshun's wife said. "He can say what he wants. You just eat your breakfast, and don't let him get to you."

Goubao stopped laughing and signaled Bai Fu with his eyes to go outside. Bai Fu followed him out.

Soon the family heard the sounds of an argument. "Who's raising a stink so early in the morning?" Laoshun said. His wife walked into the yard and cocked her ear to listen. "That sounds like Bai Fu. Go take a look, and hurry. It could be the family planning people. Go tell the idiot to hold back and not provoke any of them."

Laoshun tossed his pipe onto the *kang* and ran out, followed by Mengzi and Lingguan.

They saw Goubao and Bai Fu in a tangle, grabbing at each other's hair. "So I said you're going to be heirless, what are you going to do about it?" Goubao was shouting. "Can you pinch off my tool and skin me alive?"

"You think you're better than me just because you have a son, don't you?" Bai Fu said. "Well, he's not going to live long, not past eighteen."

Goubao's fist came down hard on Bai Fu's face, making him scream as he swung wildly.

"What's this all about?" Laoshun raced up to them.

Goubao stopped and backed off, panting as he said, "Listen to this—he said I didn't pay him when I lost at cards. I did, but he insists I didn't."

"How much could it be? Just consider it money spent on medicine, can't you? You're related, you can't get into a fight over that." Laoshun glared at his son-in-law.

"You—ask him—what else did he say?" Bai Fu was also breathing hard.

"What else did I say? You kept saying I didn't pay you, so what else could I do? I swore to show my innocence."

"Swore to show your innocence? More like trying to put a curse on me."

"What did you say, anyway?" Laoshun asked Goubao.

"I said he'd end up with no son if I hadn't paid him, and he got mad at me."

"You were mocking me." Bai Fu gnashed his teeth. "You have your sons, so you think you can fly up into the sky or disappear into the ground if you want, don't you?"

"I really didn't mean it that way," Goubao said to Laoshun.

Laoshun's face darkened. Ignoring the younger man, he starred daggers at his son-in-law. After a long pause, he said to Goubao, "I'm not deaf. I heard every word you said. You're no good either. So what if he doesn't have a son now? They're not sterile. You think you have sons? Well they're not yours until they're as tall as a wall."

The insinuation was not lost on Goubao, who decided not to get angry at the sight of Mengzi and Lingguan nearby. He swallowed and said, "Forget it. I don't want to talk to you people." He walked off, but turned back after a few steps, "Let me make it clear. I did pay you back."

"Get out of here. I don't want your damned money," Bai Fu roared. "You can cheat me, and the money will pay for your medicine."

Goubao walked off wordlessly and said to the gawkers before he'd gone too far, "Hei! He wouldn't let me get a word in. Don't waste your energy getting mad at me. Use it on top of your woman? Did you all hear that? Be careful dealing with him from now on."

"Hey you! Come back here." Bai Fu shouted, pointing his finger at Goubao.

"What?" Goubao shouted back. "So you can sink your teeth in me?"

7

"Did you hear that? This time he went too far." Bai Fu continued to mutter long after they were back inside.

"That's okay," Laoshun said. "Let him say what he wants."

"But I recall, he did pay you," Laoshun's wife said. "You must have forgotten. Think hard. It was that time you went to drink with Beizhu at his house."

Bai Fu knitted his brows in concentration. "So what? It's no big deal whether he paid me or not. But that ass, what he said went too far."

"No big deal?" Mengzi smiled. "Then what were you fighting over?"

"It wasn't about that," Bai Fu replied stiffly. "It was what he said. Heirless? No offspring. He was clearly—"

"He says that all the time. He's always swearing on this and vowing to do that. That's all. It's a habit of his, and he can't change it," Lingguan said playfully.

"But he said I can't have a son because I did something morally wrong."

"Did he really say that?" Laoshun asked. "Then why didn't you knock out those dog teeth of his? What an ass. He ought to think about his karma."

"Let him say what he wants." Laoshun's wife said. "You can't sew up his lips, can you? Good hands stay away from shit stink. You beat him, and he'll just play dead."

Bai Fu snorted and said, "Let him. I'd just as soon be dead, anyway, so I'll kill all his sons and cut off his family line first—"

"You call yourself a man," Laoshun's mother glared at him, "and can't even deal with a minor problem like this. Let him say what he wants. Lanlan can give you another child. Giving birth isn't all that different from a hen laying an egg."

With a grim look, Bai Fu sat wordlessly for a long time before exhaling noisily.

In the meantime, Yindi held her breath and shrank into Ying'er's arms; she stole a look at her father before lowering her eyes. "Are you afraid of something?" Ying'er whispered to the girl, who merely touched her lips to Ying'er's face. "Don't be. He had a fight, but you had nothing to do with it." Yindi squeezed her aunt's hand.

"On the other hand, we need to think of something. Why are you having so much trouble keeping a baby?" Laoshun's wife said. "There has to be a reason."

"We've done everything we could think of," Laoshun said.

"Back home we have a new shaman—Ying'er, it's the woman with a crooked neck—Bai Fu said. "She's so good she even knows things about people who come from far away to see her."

"What deity does she worship?" Laoshun's wife asked him.

"She's all-knowing. She can even tell you if you have a mole."

"Then go see her so you can put your mind at ease. I told Hantou to ask another shaman, but—"

"Did that do any good?" Hantou asked. "You keep coming up with problems, but it's all in your head."

"He's right," Laoshun said to his wife, "Every time you go see a shaman, male or female, you always say it will make you feel better, but how many have you seen, and are you feeling any better? I don't think your mind is ever at ease, though you've spent enough money trying."

His wife snorted without responding.

"I'll ask my mother to see if the woman worships a real deity," Ying'er said after a moment's hesitation. "I have something to find out, too, so we can see if she's for real."

"What do you want to find out?" Laoshun's wife laughed. "Is something bothering you?"

"Stop that." Ying'er poked her mother-in-law in the ribs and the two women had a laughing fit.

"That sounds all right to me," Laoshun's wife said. "We don't have much to do these days, so I'll go with Ying'er."

"Bad idea," her husband said. "With the two of you gone, who's going to cook for us and feed the pigs?"

"Aiyo. Will you starve without us?" his wife teased.

"No sweat," Mengzi said with a smile. "I can't cook, but I know how to make paste."

"Right," Lingguan said approvingly. "One bowl of paste down the gullet to seal the intestines will keep our bellies full for days."

"All right then," said Laoshun. "You two can go. We're not cooks, but we know how to slaughter a goat. We'll boil some mutton and eat it with our hands."

"Go ahead, you can eat whatever you want." His wife laughed. "You can kill a cow or a goat. I'm not a child, so you can't fool me."

But she changed her mind after lunch, saying she felt uneasy, worried that something bad might happen at home. She'd wait a few days. Ying'er figured that was probably because she didn't have anything decent to wear. So she left with her brother for their parents' house.

8

Ying'er came back with instructions from the shaman to offer a sacrifice to the deities in their house, saying they were disturbed and that the kitchen god was restless. They had to do something to appease them. Laoshun's wife sent Mengzi to see her second brother, a gaunt man with a severely receding hairline that left a broad expanse of scalp on top, but a profuse growth of hair on the sides, giving him an unusual look. Laoshun did not think much of this brother-in-law, particularly his affected mysterious air. Mengzi, on the other hand, trusted his maternal uncle explicitly and sought his help or advice whenever something came up.

After learning the reason behind Mengzi's visit, the uncle executed a divination with his fingers before saying, "The family deities are disturbed and the kitchen god is unhappy, so a sacrifice is in order. Generally speaking, it's best to do it once a year so they'll protect you. But last year—last year there was a problem."

"What was it?" Mengzi asked.

"Something didn't go right during the offering. You forgot the spiritual tablets after the worship and didn't burn them until a day later. We've done this more than a hundred times and nothing like this has ever happened before. Isn't that strange?"

"So the sacrifice was futile," Mengzi said.

"Yes. We failed to send off the evil demons. And there's more. You have to wait until the deities are gone before casting the vinegar stones to expel the ghosts. Think about it. The deities would surely be unhappy if you cast the stones before they left. They might even mete out a minor punishment."

"Hei!" Mengzi slapped his thigh. "Mother asked you to perform the rite precisely because she was worried the others might not do a good job, but you—"

"It wasn't up to me. It had to happen, and it did. I wouldn't have forgotten to burn the tablets no matter how addled I was. We invited the deities in but forgot to send them off, before casting the ghosts out along with vinegar stone—it wasn't really our fault. What had to happen happened. That's all."

Mengzi sighed with an unhappy look, but did not complain.

"Don't tell your father. Who knows what he might say. We'll do a good job this year. I found a date, the twentieth day of the last lunar month. The kitchen god returns to Heaven on the twenty-third, so he'll put in a good word for your family after the sacrifice on the twentieth."

He wrote out a list of items for the young man to prepare:

A white rooster, three catties of mutton, ten grams of scarlet solvent, three feet of red cloth, thirty sheets of yellow paper, and ten sheets each for five other colors.

Laoshun's wife made the starter for the dough to steam rolls for the worship.

Obviously, they should have done that earlier, for the sow that was about to give birth stopped eating and drinking around noontime. It was a large sow, a fine specimen, and all the piglets had already been spoken for. Laoshun immediately sent Lingguan to summon Veterinarian Huang, but he did not arrive until an hour later, and hemmed and hawed, without coming up with an answer when Laoshun asked him if the sow would be all right. Laoshun recalled that a sow ended up dying when Huang said it would be fine, and another pig ran wild when he said it was in grave danger. So he decided not to press the man. Huang produced a syringe and a capsule. Laoshun saw that it was Gentamicin, the man's habitual antibiotic, so he asked what exactly was wrong with the sow. Why use the same antibiotic each time?

"Does that mean you don't want me to give it a shot?"

"No, that's not what I meant," Laoshun said. Huang went ahead.

They saw no improvement after repeated shots; the sow turned its nose up at its dinner, a fragrant meal with added wheat bran. Laoshun's wife was ready to rip out her heart to feed the sow, the corners of her mouth twitching each time the pig grunted. She'd done a rough count: if the sow had ten piglets, each would fetch seventy yuan, seven hundred altogether; besides, it weighed at least six hundred catties and would be worth more than a thousand yuan. It was their lifeline; how would they survive if something were to happen to the sow? She was relying on the sow's belly to get Lingguan and Mengzi each a wife; the piglets would even pay for their electricity. Heaven, please help us, she muttered over and over. But instead of eating, the sow just grunted like a spoiled child, not caring how its owner's lips twitched from all her muttering. She was on the verge of total despair.

When dusk descended, she walked in listlessly with a bucket and fell after tripping over a small stool by the gate, bruising her forehead.

The sow began to shriek later that night, as if it were being stabbed. Convinced that someone had come to steal their pig, Laoshun threw on something and ran out pant-less. His wife was frightened out of her wits and called out urgently for her sons to get dressed. They went out and found the pig howling at the sky, its cries seemingly loud enough to stop floating clouds. Laoshun asked for a flashlight, with which he examined the ground. There was a pool of blood. "She's about to have her piglets," he muttered as he stood up cheerfully, only to hear women's laughter behind him.

"You'd better not stand up," Mengzi said to him in a loud voice. "Unless you want to show off what you've got."

Laoshun recalled that he hadn't put on his pants, so he quickly squatted down and shouted, "Who told you to come out? What good do you think you can do?"

Ying'er ran into the yard, while Laoshun's wife said, "Shame on you, old man. You could have put your stuff away, at least, and should never have shone your flashlight on it. Were you afraid we couldn't see it clearly enough?"

"No one told you two to come out here. I just wanted to see if we had a thief."

"It's okay," Mengzi said with a laugh. "I don't think she got a good look – she wouldn't have cared even if she had." Lingguan nudged him while trying to hold in his own laugh.

"Watch your mouth. Don't make fun of your father," their mother chided.

The two young men went back to bed, while Laoshun, still not fully dressed, stayed at the pen to watch over the sow with his wife to make sure it didn't crush its own babies, a common occurrence. It had given birth the year before at midnight with no one around; in the morning they found three piglets crushed to death beneath her. Several hundred yuan was lost, and Laoshun's wife bemoaned the loss for a year.

He turned off the flashlight to save the battery, plunging them into shivering cold darkness. "I'm going to get myself a pair of eyeglasses after selling the piglets this time, no matter what. Big Head has promised to sell me his for a hundred and twenty."

"Aiyo – I see you want to puff yourself up. How are we going to pay the electricity bill, or for the boys' weddings? And we need money for New Year's. Eyeglasses can't bring us anything to eat or wear, so why do you want them?"

"Why?" Laoshun snorted. "Why do you think? Everyone has a pair but me. We have three young masters and have spent all these years waiting for them to grow up. What do we have now that they're fully-grown? I can't even get a pair of eyeglasses?"

"Aiyo. Big Head shows off because he has money. He's worked himself to death all these years as a team leader. But you, you ought to know what you're worth."

"I don't care. I'm going to get the glasses tomorrow."

"Do what you want. I'll come to you when I need money."

A long time passed before it started to light up outside. The sow kept grunting, but no piglets. Laoshun saw droppings in the blood when he took a closer look at the ground. "Aiya!" He yelled out. "It's shitting blood. The sow is shitting blood."

Laoshun's wife ran into the yard and managed to get her stiff tongue to work as she shouted, "Mengzi—Mengzi—hurry, go get Huang."

"What's the problem now?" Mengzi jumped off the *kang* and parted the curtain.

"The sow is shitting blood."

"Hei." Mengzi shouted back at his mother. "Are you trying to scare me to death? I thought something had happened to Father." He dressed and left for the veterinary clinic.

Huang took his time, as usual. The sun was high in the sky when he came into the village, big belly out in front. As if seeing her savior, Laoshun's wife was so nervous her hands shook, but she could not get a word out. Huang examined the blood on the ground and shook his head, making her dizzy in the process. Laoshun stood by helplessly. "Can you save it?" He asked the veterinarian, who replied, "I'll try."

"What do you mean, try? Give it a shot if you can save it, but no shot if you can't. Its meat will be inedible once you do," Laoshun said.

"The meat? Food is all you think of," his wife shrieked. "There's nothing to try. Give it a shot. I won't stand for any objection."

"You'd better think it over. If you want, I'll give it a shot, or I'll do nothing if you decide against it. It's hard to say how this will turn out; it may get better, but there's nothing I can do if it doesn't."

"Forget it, then." Laoshun said. "You can't save it; you can't even cure a cold. It's shitting blood and that's a big problem. We'll slaughter the sow and get something out of her." Lingguan and Mengzi agreed with their father.

"No!" Laoshun's wife said. "You think it's easy raising a sow? We need to try to save it as long as it's breathing. Whatever's necessary." She bared her teeth at her husband and said, "And you, I don't want to hear anything more from you."

Laoshun lowered his eyes, his sons kept their mouths shut. Huang brought out his kit and gave the sow a shot of penicillin, after which Laoshun's wife invited him into the house and told Ying'er to fry a couple of eggs.

9

Huang was smoking his pipe after finishing the eggs, when they heard a scream from outside. It sounded like the sow, but with feeling and a note of despair; it couldn't be her. The veterinarian was puzzled, but the color quickly drained from Laoshun's face, for he could tell it was his wife wailing. Quickly he wound the tobacco pouch around his pipe, jumped down off the *kang*, and ran out the door.

The dying sow released a pool of blood. It was breathing its last when Laoshun ran up, and stopped moving after a few shallow breaths. Laoshun's wife howled as she tugged at the sow, as if in disbelief. It hadn't stiffened yet, and its flesh jiggled with her hand movements, sending clusters of fleas bouncing around. Afraid the insects would hop onto his mother, Lingguan walked over to pull her to her feet.

She was bawling so loud that a crowd quickly formed, so embarrassing Mengzi that he tried to stop her, but she wouldn't listen. Instead she continued to sob and howl, her face streaked with tears, irritating Mengzi, who said loudly,

"What's there to cry about? It's just a pig, so stop making a scene. It's disgraceful."

She lowered her voice, making a choking sound, but soon was wailing again.

Mengzi wanted to scold her again, but held his tongue when he saw Lingguan glaring at him. She continued to bawl, drawing tears from a few old women and from Ying'er, intensifying the dreary sadness in the pen.

Laoshun stood by the pig with a dejected look; something sticky gripped his heart as he was engulfed by an emotion bordering on despair. With the death of the sow one of the family's sources of income was gone. Hantou too was frowning.

"It's all right." Huang came over and gave the dead sow a few kicks.

"What do you mean all right? The sow is dead," Laoshun said angrily. He was intentionally rude to the veterinarian, wondering if the shot had killed it.

"What I meant was, the meat is still edible if you let the blood out," he said with a magnanimous smile.

Mengzi plunged a knife into the sow's throat. Not a drop of blood appeared when he removed the knife, so he stomped on the sow's belly, and bloody bubbles gurgled out from the knife cut.

"Forget it," Laoshun said.

"You can eat the meat, don't worry," Huang said. "I didn't inject it with poison—New Year's is just around the corner."

Laoshun frowned and wavered before finally telling Hantou to borrow a large wok to scald the pig bristles.

"No," Lingguan demanded. "We can't eat this pork."

"Why not?" Mengzi asked.

“We don’t know what it had. Do you? It was shitting blood. It could have been an infectious disease, we just don’t know. Our health is more important than eating a little pork, don’t you think?”

“I think it’s okay to eat,” Mengzi said, before quickly changing his mind. He rubbed his neck. “I recall reading somewhere that you shouldn’t eat the meat from a sick animal. We should think about it. Eat it or not?”

“I say you can—but think it over, it’s up to you—several hundred catties of pork isn’t that big a big deal.” Huang softened his tone.

“I say no.” Lingguan was relentless. “Pork is not as important as our health. Let’s bury it.”

“What are you saying?” Laoshun said, clearly angry. “I’ll eat it if you won’t. It’s just a dead pig. There’s nothing to fear. Go borrow the wok and get a fire going.”

Laoshun’s wife could not stop crying. She forced herself to weep silently, but sobs continued to escape from her mouth. A pig. A sow with piglets in its belly. She would rue any day a chicken went missing, let alone a pig. Her world was falling apart.

Hantou and Huaqiu returned with a large wok. Beizhu came to dig a large pit in a pile of manure to set up the wok.

“Fuck,” Laoshun cursed. “Why do terrible things keep happening to us?”

“Heaven is blind,” said Gimpy Five.

“That’s so true,” the onlookers echoed.

“Is Wuzi better now?” Laoshun asked Gimpy Five.

“I wish. Always that foolish smile.” Gimpy Five sighed.

“Still raising hell?”

“Not any more, at least. But he just sits there, with that foolish smile, staring straight ahead.”

"He should probably keep seeing doctors."

"We can't afford it." A shadow fell across Gimpy Five's face.

Ying'er emptied two buckets of boiled water into the wok. Mengzi tied the hooves together, front and back, and, with Beizhu and a couple of the others, lifted up the pig and lowered it into the wok, where it bobbed up and down in the water. Gimpy Five scraped the animal's skin with a spade, exposing a patch of starkly white skin, after which the young men began the debristling.

"Our two young masters are old enough to get married, but we have no savings." Laoshun squinted at the pig, which was looking whiter by the minute. "Now our pig is dead. Isn't Heaven—ai!"

The cleaned pig was strung up on a date tree, where it swayed in the air. Everyone said it was a shame that such a well-built sow had to die. Mengzi brought up a pot of cold water and splashed on the pig to stiffen the fine hairs and make the scraping job easier. Then Beizhu slit open the belly; a bunch of children behind him clamored for the bladder. They backed off when he yelled at them but quickly crowded up again.

"What about the intestines?" Beizhu asked Laoshun.

"Throw them away," Lingguan said before his father could answer. "The pig was sick, it was shitting blood."

"Give them to me," Gimpy said. "You're just going to throw them away, anyway."

"No," Lingguan insisted. "It was a diseased animal, with blood all over the place."

"I'm not afraid. It won't kill me. I won't die, because I haven't suffered enough yet. Actually, I'd be better off dead, but that won't happen." Gimpy laughed heartily but not for long; he lowered his head and quietly dried tears stealing out from the corners of his eyes.

"Forget it. We'll give you some pork," Lingguan said. "The intestines aren't for anyone – we really have no idea what disease it had."

"I don't want any pork, but it's up to you. I'll take the innards if you want to give them to me; if not, I won't take anything," he said softly.

"All right, you can have them." Beizhu retrieved the innards and hung them from a fork in the date tree. "They're all yours."

Lingguan gave in with a sigh.

10

Laoshun's wife was still crying when her younger brother came the following morning to perform the sacrificial offering to the deities. Her eyes were red and puffy from sobbing through the night, and nothing anyone said could stop her. After comparing his situation with that of Gimpy Five, Laoshun realized that he was doing worse than some but better than others, which made him feel better until his wife's non-stop crying reawakened his unhappiness. He tossed and turned the whole night.

"Good!" The uncle said the moment he heard about the dead pig, making Lingguan exchange looks with his brothers. Their uncle explained: one, the sow died the day before the worship, an obvious indication that the pig had offered itself up to the deities, and that they would be surely be pleased. Second, money spent meant disaster averted. Now that they had lost money on the sow, they would enjoy peace and good health, for the pig had taken their potential problems with it.

Laoshun had always been dubious of his brother-in-law's abilities, because the younger man appeared to be a dabbler in the area of divination; but this time he was reassured by what he heard. His wife, on the other hand, maintained an unshakable belief in her brother, a semi-deity in her eyes, but his rationalization on this day failed to alleviate the heaviness in her heart. Everything he said seemed abstract and vague, whether the deities were pleased or not, whether the disaster had been taken away by the sow, or whether they would enjoy peace and good health. In contrast, the sow's death was a real, tangible, and consequential loss to her. She saw the dead pig before her eyes all the time, its large, white body pressing down on her until her heart trembled under its weight. What her younger brother had said had no effect on her heart, which was marinated in grief. Instead of lowering her voice, she cried even louder, now that she had a new audience for her grief, with an increased frequency of nose blowing.

"What are you howling about?" Laoshun said irritably. "Can you cry the pig back? If you could, I'd improve your air intake for you to cry for three whole days. If not, stop your sniveling now."

"Why shouldn't I cry over the dead pig?" She dried her tears.

"All right. Go ahead and howl as much you want, since it pleases the deities. I say we forget the worship, and just let you cry," he said. She lowered her voice at the mention of worship and went into the kitchen to prepare the sacrificial offerings.

Following their uncle's instructions, Mengzi went to the Dasha River and brought back a vinegar stone deity—a smooth, round, dark green stone that was impervious to fire. Soon their uncle's frequent partner in deity worship, arrived. He wrote the sacrificial incantation while their uncle created spirit tablets. Hantou borrowed two dippers, which he filled with wheat before placing them on the sacrificial table. He then got a handful of needle grass, pinched off both ends, stripped the thick outer layer, pasted the spirit tablets onto the stalks, and set them in the dippers, as instructed.

In the dipper to the left were eight tablets and five colored banners: a green banner for the eastern *zhen* sphere, representing nine essences for the spring deity; a red banner for the southern *li* sphere, with three essences for the summer deity; a white banner for the western *dui* sphere, with seven essences for the autumn deity; and a black banner for the northern *kan* sphere, with five essences for the winter deity. In one dipper were placed four tablets: one for the *yuan* sphere, with twelve essences for earth, with the Yellow Emperor as the deity in charge (yellow banner); one for the five deities for the east, west, south, north, and center, the earthen god, and the dragon deity; one for the local earth god; and one for that year's guardian deity.

To the left of the left dipper were placed three tablets: one for the deity guarding the door, one for the deity in charge of the pasture and herds, and one for the horse deity. To its right were two tablets for the kitchen god and the Northern Dipper deity of longevity and disaster avoidance. In the middle were two tablets, one for the Lord of Medicine for illness elimination, and one dedicated to the family's ancestors, for the deity in charge of scholarly honors.

There was also a special tablet with the inscription "In the Chen Family/ Members of three generations," "Spirit tablet for Great great grandparents."

After the tablets were in their proper places, Laoshun went down to their family plot for some dirt. Following his brother-in-law's strict instruction, he faced northwest, burned three sheets of yellow paper, kowtowed three times, and scooped up some dirt. When he returned, he put the dirt in a plate and placed it before the tablets. In the middle of the plate was an egg for the Earth God, who was fond of eggs cooked in distilled sorghum liquor.

Now the space before the tablets was replete with such offerings as steamed rolls, noodles, rice, water, liquor infused with chicken blood, walnuts, and dates.

Darkness had fallen. Their uncle's frequent partner in deity worship stood beside the altar and announced in a queer voice:

"Be quiet—stand still—take up what you're in charge of—main worshipers take your positions—other worshipers take your positions—"

Following his instructions, Laoshun and Hantou, led by the uncle, who was the main worshipper, presented incense sticks, sprinkled sacrificial liquor, burned spirit money, and offered the blood-infused liquor. Mengzi was in charge of the sacrificial mutton. After this part of the rite was over, the man began to recite the incantation he'd composed earlier:

> *...Oh, Spirit, you control the Big Dipper, which sends its light throughout the universe. You protect the people and provide them with longevity. You are omniscient, fair and impartial. Calamities are inevitable in the lives of humans, fortune, good and ill, are registered in the stars. Here now is your faithful follower, Chen Shun, who is seeking peace and good health. For several years, the stars have not been aligned. His eldest son falls ill, the animals in the house are not thriving, and nothing is going right. So here now, he is offering this sacrificial incantation to seek protection from the deities for them to bestow their boundless blessing.*

With looks of supreme probity, Laoshun and Hantou followed the uncle's lead in sprinkling the sacrificial liquor, kowtowing, and burning the tablets. Lingguan followed by setting off firecrackers before

Mengzi removed the mutton.

"Offer worship for happiness," the main worshipper intoned.

"Offer worship for happiness," the others echoed.

"Disaster averted."

"Averted."

As Laoshun's family performed common worship, they only offered sacrifice to fifteen deities. The rite given this time was repeated twelve times and required twelve sacrificial texts, since offers were made to two deities together several times, and the three generations of family members required their own incantation. Each deity was in charge of a particular matter, to which the worshippers sought different favors, so a new incantation was needed for each.

We offer sacrifice to the deities of the five directions and ask them to give us their blessings, drive away pestilence and disease, and send the evil spirits and demons back to their places. We ask that the five elements not fight each other, but work together harmoniously, that the five fortunes prosper, the five grains thrive, and that peace reigns in the land in all five directions.

We offer sacrifice to our ancestors, and ask them to ensure peace over the three lifetimes and good fortune throughout the family, and to bestow felicities and dispel illness.

We offer sacrifice to the Lord of Medicine and ask for his prescriptions to expel disease and for his magical formulae to fend off pestilence.

We offer sacrifice to the deities in charge of livestock, and ask them to protect the animals from falling ill from their feed and to give them nothing but good health.

We offer sacrifice to the Kitchen God, and ask him to give us blessed water and to prevent fire in the house.

We offer sacrifice to the earthen god, and ask him to rid the land of evil miasmas, to ensure the proper functions of the four seasons, and to help us maintain good health and longevity by fending off diseases.

We offer sacrifice to the deities guarding the door, and ask them to let in blessings and admit only filial offspring.

We offer sacrifice to our three generations of ancestors, and ask them to protect the family members and bring everyone boundless happiness and good health.

After the sacrificial offerings were made to the deities and the tablets were burned, the spirit money was reduced to a mound of ashes. Candles flickered amid a fog of black smoke, and the room was now shrouded in a gloomy darkness. Needle grass continued to burn in the mound of ashes, as did the egg cooked in sorghum liquor for the Earth God. Blue flames cast an eerie glow to accompany the crackling sounds and an unpleasant smell of something charred. Walking behind the uncle, Laoshun and Hantou carried ashes, paper and wheat stalks to send off the deities, and five colorful banners out the door to where Laoshun had scooped out dirt. The ashes were poured and the paper and wheat stalks set on fire. The uncle knelt to recite a prayer: "One changes into ten, ten changes into a hundred, a hundred changes into a thousand, a thousand changes into ten thousand—what's burned is not money for first or the fifteenth of the month, but is money from Chen Shun's family to thank the deities for averting disasters—seeking blessing from the deities for peace and good health, for people to thrive, for the animals to stay healthy, and everything to go smoothly." He kowtowed when he finished.

11

Custom required the casting off of the vinegar stone after a sacrifice. During the worship, the door deity and gate guard also came down to enjoy the feast, leaving the gate and doors wide open for wandering ghosts and homeless spirits to sneak in among the deities and three generations of family members. That seldom presented a problem, since the door deity and gate guard were on duty, and could distinguish family members from wandering ghosts; they let the former pass and blocked the latter. Naturally, the door deity could do nothing if an ill-behaved family member brought wandering ghosts home to cause trouble, like a security guard who is unable to stop strangers coming in with residents.

The vinegar stone had its own deity, which also must be invited. Its whereabouts was unknown, so when its presence was required, a worshiper would simply go down to the riverbank to find a round, dark green stone, kneel before it, and kowtow to ask its blessing. That made it the vinegar stone deity, which was rumored to be mighty enough to intimidate both deities and ghosts. When it arrived, all members of the family and wandering ghosts, as well as the deities who refused to leave the feast and overstayed their welcome after the worship, scurried away.

Laoshun, who was in charge of the vinegar stone, added some human hair to a metal ladle and poured in a dash of vinegar before dropping in the burning red stone. A sour smell of burned hair, along with sizzling steam, permeated the room. He became unusually nimble, as he dashed into the room and leaped onto the *kang*, where he jumped up and down, thrusting the odoriferous ladle with its rising white steam into every corner. Then he stormed into another room after dabbing the doorsill with vinegar.

Once the vinegar stone was out, Mengzi shut the door to prevent wandering ghosts from sneaking back inside.

Lingguan took care of the last round of fireworks, which soared into the evening sky, where they exploded loudly and dispersed the heavy smell of gunpowder, forcing the ghosts that were chased out of the room to leave the yard.

What interested him most was not the process of casting the vinegar stone, but the overall atmosphere, for the psychological effects of the unique rite surprised him. A mysterious aura was created out of the fog of steam, the acrid smell, the person who whirled in and out of rooms, and the sizzles of the hot stone's contact with vinegar. They combined to excite his emotion in a strange way. The wandering ghosts were expelled, bad luck was sent off, and disaster was averted, leaving behind good fortune, cleanliness, and happiness.

Followed by a sense of peace and serenity.

He could feel it almost viscerally. The gloomy eeriness before casting the vinegar stone had been replaced by a refreshing brightness, and he felt a palpable vitality, mentally and physically.

His mother and Ying'er were busy frying the chicken made headless during the sacrificial rite, while his father, after sending off the vinegar stone deity, got onto the *kang* and lay there contentedly, as if he had accomplished something profound.

"The metal ladle is called a deity-simmering ladle," the uncle's partner expounded. "The stone represents the heads of ghosts and demons, who would be terrified to see the head of one of their own, along with its hair, simmering in the ladle. They would flee, panic-stricken. Ha-ha—at least that's what our ancestors used to say."

"Vinegar can dispel evil spirits. All things malevolent are afraid of vinegar. Hey," Laoshun's brother-in-law said as he slapped his thigh, "Where's the vinegar? What happened to the vinegar from the ladle? Go find it and bring it over. That's good stuff. A sip of it will make everything right, and all our children will be disease-free."

Mengzi retrieved the vinegar. His uncle took the first sip, followed by the others, who complained that it was too sour. Mengzi's uncle told him to take it to the kitchen for the women to have a sip.

"I read in a book that vinegar kills germs," Lingguan said. "Spraying it in the house when the flu is going around can prevent the spread of germs. Maybe that's what's behind the casting off a vinegar stone."

"Book?" His uncle responded. "What you get in books is nothing but rubbish to explain the inexplicable with scientific nonsense. Something that needs no explanation to be clear gets confusing the more you try to explain it. Expelling ghosts is just that—expel ghosts, and drive off evil spirits, yes, drive off evil spirits. Once they are expelled and driven off, people's health will be restored and peace will return to the house. That's all there is. There's no need to explain anything. The more you rely on science, the less scientific you actually become."

"That's true," the other man echoed. "Ghosts are just ghosts, and they're the same whether you call them bio-feedback or electromagnetic waves. It's bio-feedback to the scientists, but ghosts to us, just like our mountain taros are potatoes to other people. They're exactly the same. And that nonsense about dispelling superstition? Bullshit."

Laoshun cracked a smile. He was always the first to smile on such occasions, whether he understood what was going on or not.

"Some things are hard to explain," the man continued. "Take the human life span for instance. Those who know about science and nutrition may well be the ones who die young. Look at my grannie. What do you think she eats? Potato and millet soup all her life—a half pot of water, a handful of millet, plus some chopped potatoes. No need to worry about nutrition or vitamins, and she's still alive at age ninety."

"You're right," Lingguan said. "No one can be sure about these things. The more you talk about science, the more likely you'll get sick. Have you noticed that young people who know science are dropping like flies? I hear there's a place called Zhongguancun in Beijing where their young scientists are dying off. The human life span is still a mystery."

"The northern dipper is in charge of life, and the southern one death," his uncle said with a smile. "Can't you see the words on the tablet? 'Deity for the Northern Dipper in charge of longevity and averting disaster.' You see, it's in charge of life because it can save you from calamity and prolong your life."

"There was once a filial son, who was still tilling the land at the end of his life," the other man revealed to them. "Lü Dongbin, one of the eight immortals, appeared before him as a Taoist monk to enlighten him. When the man saw the Taoist from a distance, he tossed away his whip and ran up to Lü. 'I only have this much money on me, Grandpa,' he said. 'Wait here while I go home to get some more for you?' Lü said, 'You'll be dead by noon tomorrow, so why are you still tilling the field?' The man burst out crying from the news, so Lü said to him, 'there will be two old men playing Chinese chess on Mount Hua at midnight tonight. Take a jug of liquor up there, but don't say anything; just kneel to the side, refilling their cups when they're empty. Then you beg the one sitting on the north side to extend your life when they empty your jug. They will owe you for that, so he will surely do so.' Well, the man went up to the mountain, and indeed there were two old men playing chess, so he knelt down, poured liquor, and later begged for longevity. The old man railed at Lü for meddling with his business, but he had no choice but to change the young man's life span from nineteen to ninety-nine. Ha! That's how we know that the Northern Dipper is in charge of life and the southern one death."

"That's what everyone says, but no one can prove it, can they?" Laoshun asked jovially. He sent Lingguan into the kitchen to see if the chicken was ready.

"Everything is real if you believe it and unreal if you don't," the man said.

"Never mind who's in charge of life or death," Laoshun said when Lingguan brought in the chicken. "Let's enjoy ourselves. Each new day on earth lets us eat for another day. We eat and drink our fill until the one in charge stops us. We'll worry about that when the day comes."

They all laughed before washing their hands and sitting down to enjoy the spread.

12

They had to avoid visitors for the next three days, according to custom. Laoshun went out and hung a piece of red cloth on the gate.

One reason was to avoid trouble by not allowing the spirits of family members to bring in non-family ghosts. Each family gate had a guard, who would let in the spirits of deceased family members, yet could not stop troublemakers from bringing in evil spirits. It explained why the spirits of family members were usually the culprits when an outside ghost harmed a living member. When sacrificial offerings were made to the ancestors during holidays, it was to ask them to protect their descendants, drive away evil spirits, and, most of all, not let in troublesome outside ghosts. The spirits of the ancestors were invited when offerings were made to the various deities, at which time outside ghosts could sneak in, so the vinegar stone was cast to send all spirits, good and bad, away. The red cloth on the gate would also block evil spirits, even if the gate guard could not keep out family members.

Another reason was to block a particular class of outsiders, the yin—women, to be precise. Women were burdened by the dirtiest, most inauspicious thing—menstrual blood, and should be avoided by all cost. The red cloth served to tell visitors to come another day.

The house was quiet. Mengzi, who liked to be in the middle of any action, was getting bored; he listlessly flipped through martial arts novels, while racking his brain to find an excuse to go out, when he heard someone call from outside.

Mengzi saw his sister, Lanlan, and her husband, along with the donkey Bai Fu had brought to their village. Laoshun had a hard time deciding when Mengzi asked him if he should open the door for them, since they had to avoid all outsiders for three days. Lanlan was a woman, a very pregnant one, no less, which meant she had far too much yin. Besides, Bai Fu coming with the donkey could only mean that the insemination had not work and he was coming to see Wei again. Laoshun knew how important it was to offer the sacrifice to the deities; he had heard that in the ancient times people had to fast and bathe before the rite. He was hesitating when his wife spoke up, "Open the door and let them in. They're not outsiders. We can't forbid entry to our own family members."

Mengzi went out and opened the gate for them. Laoshun's heart sank at the sight of his very pregnant daughter coming through the gate. The sacrifice was wasted, he said to himself. He grunted a response to Lanlan's greeting before walking outside, but turned after a few steps to say to Bai Fu:

"Didn't it work last time?" It hadn't, as he'd suspected, so he told Bai Fu to come along.

After a few days of rest, the stud horse whinnied the moment it was let out, putting its masculine airs on full display by kicking and snorting, shattering the relative quiet at Wei's house. It reared up when it saw Bai Fu's fetching donkey, trying to rest its hooves on the donkey's back. The donkey smacked its lips and drooled.

Wei jerked at the reins to stop the horse from losing control and wasting its energy.

"You have to work harder this time and get it done right," Laoshun said. "That way he won't have to keep coming back."

"If you're in such a hurry, do it yourself," Wei said lightheartedly.

"Not me. Someone who neuters cats doesn't castrate pigs. This is the job you were born for," Laoshun said as laughter erupted behind him. It was Wuzi. Gimpy Five had told Laoshun that his son was doing better since his discharge from the hospital; the young man had stopped chasing women and rarely acted up at night.

"What are you laughing at, Wuzi?" Laoshun asked. Wuzi silently watched the donkey. Laoshun thought that something wasn't quite right in the young man's eyes, but he couldn't tell exactly what, so he said, half in jest, "You want a woman too, don't you?" He ignored Wuzi and turned to watch Wei.

Wei was trying to guide the overeager stud horse to channel simple animal desire into a force for reproduction. It was a simple but complex process. Simple because all he had to do was to straighten the throbbing object for it to rub the right place; complex because some of females in the animal world feign resistance, jumping and leaping so much that a stud has trouble getting the job done. This required Wei's patience and guidance. He did his best to arouse the animal and awaken its natural instinct. Strangely, however, there are donkeys and horses that treasure chastity, like humans. Such animals like fight off male advances, sometimes punishing them with their hooves—they will kick back until all desire has left the stud horse, destroying their confidence. At such a moment, Wei had to work hard to increase the stud horse's mettle and get it to start over. Stabilizing the female by putting it in a special wooden cage, helped the stud horse do its job with no resistance from the female. Though the act was akin to rape, Wei had no qualms; for him, it might be ugly, but its purpose was noble, since it was for reproduction, not simply to satisfy an animal's sexual urges.

Bai Fu's donkey was three years old, and yet to bear offspring; in fact, it would have been completely oblivious to what was happening if not for the previous visit. The stud horse must have been too rough the first time and frightened her, for she seemed surprised when the horse put its hooves on her back, and she kicked out.

Suddenly Wuzi screamed.

The horse hesitated, but was obviously more aroused by the resisting donkey—humans clearly do not have a monopoly on teasing. It could tell that the donkey was not entirely opposed to the act, but was too cautious to make any sudden move. "Jump—jump," Wei yelled, but his horse simply circled the donkey, snorting and whinnying.

Finally it reared up and laid its hooves on the donkey's back. To everyone's surprise, the donkey accepted what was to happen and put up no more fight; soon it was moving its lips, apparently enjoying what was happening.

Wuzi, who had stopped laughing, stared at the stud horse as if in a trance; his face was red, his nostrils flared, and he was breathing hard and fast. His eyes were a frightening red, as if bloodshot. Then he screamed again; it did not sound human, was as if he wanted to expel something churning in his chest. His face was twisted into an expression of either extreme pain or ultimate ecstasy, while his eyes had the glaring look of an angry beast.

Wuzi turned his gaze to Lanlan, who was walking up with Lingguan, and pounced.

"Wuzi – Wuzi!" Laoshun shouted as he flung the reins away.

Lanlan did not have time to react before Wuzi's arms encircled her and he began to bite her lips. He was really biting her, making her cry out in a terrifying way, as he pushed her up against a wall thrust his hips into her over and over.

She tried to fight him off, but her strength left her; she was paralyzed from the sudden fright. He, on the other hand, seemed to become more powerful and easily overcame the little fight she put up.

"Hey!" Laoshun shouted as he slapped Wuzi. Wuzi pushed him away.

Lanlan managed to avoid his foul mouth when he was distracted; she shrieked as she tried to evade his red, contorted face, which he then pressed up to her over and over.

Bai Fu threw himself on Wuzi and tore at his hair to drag him off his wife. It hurt enough that Wuzi let go. Lanlan ran in through the gate.

It took Laoshun, Bai Fu, and Wei together to overpower Wuzi, who then turned docile, like a deflated balloon. He was smiling, but at no one in particular, just smiling foolishly and vacuously, a vacant look in his eyes. "He's beyond saving," Laoshun said as he and Lingguan walked the boy home.

Surprisingly, though, Gimpy did not appear to be shocked. "Animal!" he cursed his son perfunctorily before heaving a sigh, taking out his pipe, and squatting down to smoke. Wuzi was dazed but still smiling, so tranquil and focused he looked like a maiden thinking about her lover. No trace of his earlier bestial act remained.

"It's all right," Laoshun said to Gimpy. "It's really nothing. He's not right in the head."

Gimpy responded only with another sigh.

"He can't help it. It's an illness—he should be in the hospital."

"That's up to Heaven," Gimpy said.

Lingguan could tell from Wuzi's dazed smile that he was happy. He must be savoring something, Lingguan thought. But what? Was he recalling a romance from the past or reveling in imagined pleasure? Either way, he sure did look happy. His trance-like smile was scary and bewitching at the same time.

Suddenly the smile vanished and a red light shot out of his eyes. His nostrils flared, his breathing turned heavy and fast. Lingguan followed the direction of his gaze, and saw Huilanzi, Big Head's wife, talking to Wuzi's mother at the door.

Wuzi let out a strange cry and pounced. Huilanzi was pushed to the floor before she could react.

"What a karmic curse," Wuzi's mother shouted. "Hurry, old man."

Gimpy Five raced out, took down a leather whip from a post, and used it on his son.

Wuzi screeched and, his face twisted from excitement or pain, turned to face his father; but he jerked his head back and gnawed at the woman's face, his body quaking the whole time.

The whip cracked, making a muffled noise each time.

Shouting shrilly, either to scold her son or stop her husband, his mother jumped back and forth, like a hen spreading its wings to protect its chicks.

Laoshun grabbed the whip. "That's enough, Gimpy."

"That animal. What a beast. An animal that has humiliated us."

Throwing down his whip, Gimpy Five strode up and grabbed a tuft of his son's hair to slap him.

Laoshun and Lingguan dragged Wuzi off Huilanzi, whose lips were bleeding. She was shaking all over, her face a ghostly white.

Wuzi screamed, either from excitement or as a protest. With his eyes still on a cowering Huilanzi, he continued to display his animal intent—eyes red, nostrils flared.

"Animal! Beast!" Gimpy Five paced the yard.

"How am I supposed to face the world now?" Huilanzi was crying. "How?"

"Please, I beg you," Wuzi's mother took the woman's hand and sobbed, "take pity on this old woman, won't you?"

"Don't cry," Laoshun said to Huilanzi. "He's not well, and you know it. Besides, this isn't the first time someone has bitten your lips, is it? On your wedding night, you had your lips bitten badly by frisky men in the bridal chamber, and no one saw you shed a tear. Why act like a virgin now that you're married?"

"It's easy for you to say," the woman replied. "Let him bite you and we'll see how you feel."

"Would he do that? I actually would like to know what it feels like to be bitten, but I don't think he cares for my stubbled face. He bit you because he likes your pretty lips." Laoshun smiled.

With her hand over her mouth, Huilanzi walked inside, looked at herself in the mirror, and left with the kitchen steamer she'd come for.

13

When Laoshun got home, his wife told him Lanlan wasn't feeling well after Wuzi pressed down on her. It might have hurt the baby, so she'd sent Mengzi to ask the doctor to come take a look at her. "She'll probably be all right," the doctor told Laoshun after checking her pulse and writing out a prescription.

Laoshun was troubled by the doctor's tone, which sounded too much like that of the veterinarian's. Probably? What exactly did that mean? Probably this, but also probably that; she was probably going to be all right or she was probably not. He handed a cigarette to the doctor, who then said, "She'll be fine." That eased Laoshun's concern.

But the long list of ingredients in the prescription put him on edge again. The death of the sow meant lessened income, the sacrifice had cost money, and now they had to pay for their daughter's medicine. What lousy luck. A sense of dejection, now compounded by unhappiness, spread like flowing water to foul his mood, which prompted him to say to his wife crossly, "How did it harm the baby? Would you stop talking nonsense?"

"Her belly hurts." His wife looked put out, clearly annoyed by his tone of voice.

"She's delicate, isn't she? Her head aches, she's running a fever, her belly hurts, or she can't shit. How do you know it's the baby? She was born into a poor family, so she has to be tough. But she's delicate, like the young mistress in a rich family. Is that it? Back then, you were out in the field with a hoe the day after you had a baby, and I didn't see anything wrong with your—but we're spoiling her."

"You have a point. Why are young people these days so delicate? They've been spoiled." His wife looked into his eyes cautiously and said timidly, "Should we get Grannie Shaman Qi to do something for her?"

"Nonsense!" Laoshun roared. "Enough of that nonsense already. All you know is Grannie Shaman."

"What I meant was, the sow's death was puzzling, and so was what happened today. Just think, how did Wuzi suddenly—it just feels weird to me—besides—"

"Besides what?" Laoshun raged. "Would you stop getting all these crazy ideas? What could happen now?"

"All right," she said, her face red with anger, "I won't say anything. I'll shut up, and you can deal with it if something goes wrong."

Bai Fu left with his donkey after lunch without Lanlan and their daughter. Laoshun worried that Lanlan might really have suffered some harm, which could become a cause for complaint with Bai Fu, but he couldn't send her home. All he could do was vent privately.

14

Lanlan began to cry when she sat down with Ying'er. She managed to stop long enough to say the village officials were pressing them to pay a fine of five thousand yuan to avoid induced labor. Her mother-in-law, Ying'er's mother, sent her home for help and to borrow the money. Laoshun was livid.

"What? Borrow money from me? I have nothing left but this sack of bones."

Lanlan started sobbing again, and Ying'er cried with her.

Yindi slowly walked up to Ying'er and dried her aunt's tears with her hand, making Ying'er, with her arms around the girl, cry even harder. Laoshun's wife dried her own tears and berated her husband, "It's fine that you don't have money, but do you have to talk to her like that? She doesn't come home often, and you shout at her when she's back. It's bad enough that others bully her, but can't she enjoy a little peace and comfort when she's home with us?"

Her complaint shut Laoshun up.

"Go ahead and cry," she consoled her daughter. "You'll feel better after a good cry. Don't hold it in or it'll make you sick."

Lanlan dried her tears. "It's not that I didn't know how hard life is for you; it's just that we have no way out. Otherwise, I wouldn't have been able to bring myself to ask."

Laoshun heaved a sigh.

With her arms still around Yindi, Ying'er forced a smile. "Can you still sing the songs I taught you?" she asked the girl.

"Yes, I can. 'Pretty flowers sprouting atop grass and reeds/I send gentleman away, and the world is wonderful.'"

"What else?"

"Young sister married to a faraway place/she can't come back and I can't go see her. Tears drip to the chest and chills a sparrow when it drinks. Tears fall into a donkey trough and the sparrow sings."

"That's nice." Tears flowed again when Ying'er heard the child's sweet voice.

"I know what my brother's like," she said to Lanlan. "He likes to be flattered and he won't take advice if it goes against what he wants. He's even gotten into fights with my parents. So I know life has been hard for you."

"What's the point of talking about that now?" Lanlan replied with a wan smile. "But isn't it the same for you? I know that brother of mine; he's as boring as a block of gnarled elm, and you don't know how to express your emotions to him."

"Go on, get out of here," Ying'er pushed her away.

"But he has a good heart. Whenever I pouted as a kid and ignored him, he'd rub his head, turn round and round, tugging at his ears and scratching his cheeks, wishing he could open his heart to me," Lanlan said, to which Ying'er made a non-committal noise, her face suddenly reddened, as if reminded of something.

"Don't pick on him," Lanlan said with a tug on Ying'er's ear. "Don't drop my brother if you see an oily smooth-talker with a smiling, handsome face one day."

"Would you stop that?" Ying'er laughed. "You're the one who needs to watch out. Don't flirt with those slackers on the production team until you lose control."

Lanlan blushed and studied her sister-in-law for a while. "I'm not like you."

"I miss you so much," Yindi said sweetly, as she took Ying'er's hand.

"I miss my little niece, too." Ying'er gave the girl a kiss.

"I have so much to tell you," Yindi said.

"Does Yindi have secrets now? Here." Ying'er cocked her ear toward the girl. "Tell me."

"I don't want them to hear." The girl shook her head and led Ying'er out the door.

"I bought a cloth doll." Yindi looked around and then whispered, "It's for the little brother in Mama's belly."

"My, you're so grown up." Ying'er laughed. "Where did you get the money?"

"I got some from you last time, and also from Uncle Mengzi, Uncle Lingguan, and Grandma. The doll has a long, white, pointed beard, and a really red body. I like it a lot, but I won't play with it. I'm afraid I'll ruin it."

"Don't worry. Play with it, and I'll buy a bigger one if you ruin it." Ying'er kissed her cheek.

"No, that one is for my little brother. I really want a little brother.

Mama does too. She asked me, 'Yindi, what will Mama have this time?' I pretended I was a little boy peeing, and she laughed."

A warm current rose in Ying'er's heart. She bent down to wrap her arms around the little girl. "My little niece is the best. She's like a grown-up."

"Little brother is better. Daddy said a boy can grow up to take care of the family. A girl will belong to somebody else's family no matter how good she is. Ten best girls can't compare to a blind boy. Wouldn't it wonderful if I could be a boy?"

"He's talking nonsense. Yindi is the best; you're so smart and so sweet. If the boy turns out to be stupid, the parents might die in anger. I prefer a smart girl like you."

"Don't say that." She pushed Ying'er away and said with a somber look, "What you said could turn the little brother in Mama's belly into a little sister."

Ying'er laughed and said, "All right. I won't say that."

"I really don't understand." Yindi cocked her head and thought with a frown. "Daddy said I've hacked the little brothers to death. But I didn't."

"That's nonsense." Ying'er's face darkened. "Did he really say that?"

"Yes, he did. At first, I thought I could hack another one for him if I could. So I told him and he slapped me. He hit me so hard I couldn't think and fire went up in my eyes. It really hurt."

"That was terrible of him." Ying'er knitted her brow. "You're such a good girl, he ought to spoil you. How could he bring himself to hit you? He's a block of gnarly elm. Tell me, Yindi, do you hate your Daddy?"

"No." She shook her head. "Of course not. But why did he hit me?"

"Why?" Ying'er held the girl's face and gently rubbed her head. "Because he's stupid. You did nothing wrong. But don't say another word about hacking this and that, all right?"

Yindi said all right, but added, "Will be all right if I tell him I won't hack my little brother?"

"No." Ying'er pretended to be upset. "Don't say anything, not a word about hacking. Do you hear me?"

Yindi looked at her aunt in total incomprehension for a while before nodding.

"All right, my little niece." Ying'er kissed the girl on the cheek. "I'm going back inside. Do you have anything else to say to me?"

"Auntie Ying'er, Mama said Uncle is sick." The girl took another look around before whispering. "Do you need money? I know how to get some."

"How?"

"Grandma has money." Yindi pressed her lips to her aunt's ear. "Lots and lots of money, in her pillow case. Not coins, but bills. I'll bring you some."

"No. Don't do that. Or your Daddy will really beat you."

"I'm not afraid. I'll pay it back when I grow up. I'll grow up, make enough money and pay him back."

Ying'er felt her nose ache. "My good niece. You're such a good person, but I can't take it."

"I'll get some for you. I'm not afraid."

"No, I really don't want it. I'll borrow it from Mama if I need money."

"That won't work. Grandma won't lend it to you," Yindi insisted. "Last time Mama needed money, Grandma said, 'Where would I find any money? We're so poor we can barely get by.' I know she was lying.

But Daddy said we can't touch the money because it was to pay some fee."

"Is it the fine for violating family planning?"

"Yes, that's it."

"That's the money to get you a little brother, Yindi. What would happen if they came for him after you gave me money?"

The girl stopped to think. With her head cocked, she began to cry when she couldn't think of a way out.

With her arms still around the girl, Ying'er let her cry for a while before drying her tears. She forced a smile.

"It's all right, don't worry. Your uncle will get better soon."

"I'm worried sick," Yindi stomped her feet. "It really worries me."

Ying'er picked her up and laid her face again the girl's cheek as they walked out the gate, both in tears.

"What are we going to do?" Yindi said. "Wouldn't it be great if I could be a pig? You could sell me and get some money."

"I'm not worried." Ying'er was sobbing. "I'm—I'm just—my dear niece, I'm touched by what you say, and no amount of money can match a good heart."

"Whose heart? How much could it sell for?"

"It's priceless." Ying'er laughed despite herself. "And no one can pay enough for it. I'd be so happy if I could have a smart, good girl like you."

"Wrong again. It should be a boy."

"All right, a boy then." Ying'er laughed again. "In fact, my little Yindi is better than ten good boys. Much better." She couldn't stop kissing Yindi, embarrassing the girl so much her face reddened.

15

Laoshun finally spoke late that night when Lanlan was half asleep. His voice sounded hollow, as if he were talking in his sleep, when he called his daughter's name. "I shouldn't have blown up like that. But we can't sell any grain, no matter what, or we'd have to sew our mouths shut this year. I hope you understand the difficult situation I'm in."

"I know," Lanlan said. "It's all right, really. You need to eat."

"See, now you're pouting. I know you're upset with me. I haven't done right by you, but what choice did I have? Now that it's come to this—"

"You're talking nonsense again, Father. No one is blaming you. I don't, I mean it."

"It doesn't really matter whether you do or not." Laoshun sighed. "We all need to be flexible to get by. Life ends when you shut your eyes for the last time.

"I know, so please don't feel too bad. It's all right, really."

"I can't think of anything to help you out. I scrimped and saved, and have a little. Not much, just over two hundred. You take it. No one knows about it. It was for emergency use in case we couldn't come up with money, but yours is an emergency. So you take it; it's not much, but at least it's something. Beyond that you'll have to think of something else, because I really have no other way to help you."

"Aiyo. You sneaky old man, saving up for yourself." Lanlan's mother laughed, to their surprise. "You have a scheme cooking, is that it?"

Laoshun remained silent for a long while before finally letting out a long sigh.

"I've got it all worked out now. It's finally clear to me," Lanlan said. "We can't pay anyway, but even if we could, we won't. Five thousand. I get scared just thinking about it. A dead pig isn't afraid of scalding water. They can do what they want. It's no big deal if they arrest me. No matter what happens I'll make do. I hear prisoners are given meat a few times a week." She laughed.

"You're right about the dead pig and scalding water." Laoshun mulled her comment over. "What could they possibly do to you? They'll have to keep you alive, won't they?"

"Yes."

They fell silent before Laoshun started up again. "Actually, I didn't save up much. I was just saying that to make you feel better."

"Aiyo. You can't take that back." Lanlan's mother laughed again. "Give me the money. It's getting cold and I need a new coat. My old one is too far gone, both the inner and outer layers little more than rags. I look like a plucked chicken in that coat."

"Ai, I should've kept my mouth shut. But I let it slip and now you know everything. But to be frank, I think we need to put the money aside. With all these people in our family, what if we have an emergency one day? Who would we go to for help?"

"Stop with the jinxes, will you?" his wife said. "We don't need the trouble."

"I'm not saying that—this—I'm saying—when—if—there's an emergency."

The more Laoshun explained, the more unsettled she felt, as if trouble would visit them for sure.

"Mama really does need a new coat," said Lanlan. "You've been wearing that lumpy thing for how many years? Now that you have sons who are grownup, you ought to think about how it would make them look, if nothing else. You should dress a little better."

"That's easy for you to say. Don't think I wouldn't like some new things, but how am I supposed to get them? I could sell one of my ribs, but no one would want it. Forget it. I'm halfway into the ground already, and all I need is something to keep me covered. You young people are the ones who need to dress better. How about this? Buy some fabric tomorrow with Father's money and ask Huahua to make something for you. She's a good seamstress and she'll do if for nothing."

"Oh, no, not me. I don't want anything. I have plenty to wear. It wasn't easy to save up a little, and I can't take it. That'd be like cutting out of piece of his heart." Lanlan giggled.

"Take it and do something for yourself," Laoshun said. "I talk about money all the time, but I'm not tightfisted when it comes to you and your brothers."

"Forget it. I don't want it. You sounded uneasy about it anyway."

"I agree," Lanlan's mother said. "Everyone knows you're a tightwad."

"Hei, so you're not? You're the generous one?" Laoshun laughed. "What would you have lived on all these years if I hadn't been a tightwad? The wind? Back when we were in the farming co-op, two of us were working, with four kids at home. You'd have been fed to the dogs if I hadn't been a tightwad."

"I'd rather have been fed to the dogs," Lanlan commented.

"It's so much better now," her mother said. "You think life is hard for you, but that's nothing compared with what we had to go through as kids. We didn't even have a blanket, just a big fur coat. We were frozen stiff when my father left early in the morning to work for the landlord. We had nothing to eat, and hunger made our eyes glaze over."

"No need to go back that far," Laoshun said. "Just look at a few years ago, when we were with the farming co-op. It was tough going.

We couldn't fill our bellies after a year of hard work. It's better now. At least we have enough to eat. What else do we want?"

"You're always talking about food. Do we live to eat?" Lanlan said.

"Aiyo," her mother exclaimed. "What else do you live for? Clothes, of course. As the saying goes, one's whole life is for nothing but food, clothes, and a wife."

"Then it's better to be reborn as a pig," Lanlan said with a laugh.

"Don't compare us with pigs," Laoshun said. "All they do is eat, drink, and sleep. They have it made, no worries. I'd like to be a pig in my next life, if not for the butcher's knife."

"Listen to you. You want to be a pig. Do you think it's easy to be reborn a pig? You need enough karmic merits from your previous life. You'll have to keep suffering and just be who you are. If not, maybe you'll be reborn as a cow and toil away yet another life. Then, when you die, you'll be slaughtered and wind up in people's stomachs. They'll even cook your bones to get every drop of oil you've got."

"Ooo, that sounds just terrible." Laoshun said, making his daughter laugh.

"In my view, we owe our cows so much. I heard that Heaven had originally planned for cows to have a two-layered coffin for a magnificent funeral, but humans misheard and thought Heaven was talking about two-level cooking, and that's how cows ended up in a pot and on our dining table."

"That's nonsense," Laoshun disagreed. "Don't we cook and eat goats?"

"I also heard that cows are Bodhisattvas incarnate and are here to serve humans, like plow the fields and supply us with milk," his wife said. "They even give us their bodies when they die."

"That's what we're told, but who knows? What does retribution mean these days anyway? Why are evildoers the ones in power? The rich make money by cheating, scamming, and scheming, while law-abiding people suffer in poverty," Laoshun said.

"And, mostly it's the good people who are afflicted with strange illnesses," Lanlan said. "How do you explain that?"

"Is Heaven blind?"

"Hush, don't say that," His wife chided. "We don't live only one lifetime. People who have accumulated enough karmic merits in one life deserve to have a better life the next time. But you have to suffer the consequences in your next incarnation if you do evil in this life."

"That's what people say, but who can be sure? In any case, in today's world, the honest people always suffer. Does that mean that they all did something terrible in their previous life?" Laoshun asked.

"I don't know," his wife said. "That's just what I heard."

"That's enough." He turned and heaved an unhappy sigh. "Let's get some sleep. The more we talk the more upset it makes me."

Chapter Fourteen

1

Snow fell heavily on the third day of the lunar year, the first snowfall of winter, and the temperature dropped precipitously.

Naturally, the farmers preferred snowy days. As the world outside their windows was blanketed in white, they could sit or lie on their heated *kangs*, catching up on sleep or conversing as they sipped tea and cracked watermelon seeds. Words can hardly describe the lazy, carefree pleasure.

But not Bai Fu, who came to visit his in-laws. He woke up in a bad mood, after dreaming that his wife had given birth—to a boy. He even experienced the sensation of touching the pointed little treasure, until a white fox ran up and snatched the baby away. He woke up screaming, even waking Lanlan. "What's wrong?" It took him a while to mutter, "A fox—"

"What fox?"

"A fox snatched our boy away—the one in your belly." His throat was parched.

"Your ass was exposed, that's all." She laughed.

He closed his eyes to think about the dream. Suddenly he realized that the fox in his dream was none other than the one he'd killed a few years earlier. He shuddered. "Do you remember the fox I killed that year?" he asked her.

"What about it?"

"It was a white fox. People say a white fox lives a thousand years and a black one ten thousand. That one must have been a demon by then. I killed it, so don't you think it would want to get back at me?"

"What do you mean?" Lanlan tensed.

"Grannie Shaman told me the two dead boys were hexed to death." He sighed.

"By who?" She asked, wide-eyed.

"Who else could it be?" He looked at Yindi, who was fast asleep, her face a bright red. "Someone in our house, so who do you think?" He tore at his hair with a long sigh.

"Do you mean—Yindi?" She hesitated to say the name.

"Who else?" Bai Fu fumed. "Just think, since she came, both of the baby boys died at birth. And there's more. You'll recall that she was born after I killed the fox. Haven't you heard the blind storyteller tell the tale of Fan Lihua, the woman warrior, who helped her husband, Xue Pinggui, vanquish the enemy in the West? When she killed one of her opponents, Su Baotong, he slipped into her belly and was reborn as Xue Gang, who caused so much trouble that the Emperor beheaded everyone in the Xue household. Hundreds of Xue family members were gone, and Su got his revenge."

"That has nothing to do with Yindi," Lanlan said. "She's such a sweet little girl. How could she be a fox reincarnate? No. I don't believe it."

"Why not?" Bai Fu was getting angry. "Do you think I'd say bad things about my own daughter, a clever little girl, unlike you or me, who both have brains like blocks of gnarled elm? Just think about all those songs she memorized after hearing them once. Can you think of a single child in the village who's as smart as her?"

"So that's your proof? Tell me then. Is my father smart? How about my mother? Lingguan is smart, so what was he in his previous life? I want you to stop this nonsense."

"Lingguan's brain is no damn good." He glared at her. "He couldn't learn how to yoke an ox to plow the field after three days. If he's so smart, he should have gotten into college, but he didn't. Your parents wasted a decade supporting him, and he went through baskets of food in the process. Yindi isn't like him."

"What did I do?" Yindi awoke and sat up. "What did I do?"

"Go back to sleep," Bai Fu yelled, scaring the girl back under the blanket. Lanlan mumbled with her arm around her daughter, "My Yindi is such a sweet girl." She patted Yindi's backside and said to Bai Fu, "I don't want to hear any more of your ideas, so don't bring them up again."

"What are you yelling and screaming like that for in the first month of the year?" Lanlan's mother walked in to say. "Sleep in if you want. If not, go watch people play cards."

Pulling a long face, Bai Fu shot Lanlan an angry look as he covered his head. What he'd seen in his dream reappeared before his eyes.

He was sure his wife was carrying a baby boy.

The signs were all there: one, she craved sour food. Sour meant male and spicy signaled female. Two, she entered a room with her left foot first. Left was male, right was female. Three, he'd stolen a radish from someone's field on the night of the autumn festival. It was smooth, with no cracks, but had a pointed tip, which was nearly identical to the little pecker on the baby boy he'd wanted all these years. Four, when he'd gone to Lake Leitai in the tenth lunar month, a shaman had told him that he would surely have a boy this year, but that the baby might not live long. Someone would hex him. He had been so frightened that his tongue seemed to have shriveled up like dry potato skin, and had spent fifty yuan to buy a remedy—putting a knife under his wife's pillow and having her wear a stomacher made of red cloth that had been used in a sacrifice to the deities.

And yet he still had a terrible dream.

"I did all I was supposed to do, including the red cloth," he mused dejectedly, "so why did I still have that dream? That's damned scary." His wife whispered something to Yindi, and they both laughed. The shrill noise bored into his ears. Pushing the blanket to the side, he shouted, "What's so damn funny? Go outside if you want to laugh."

"You can leave if you don't want to hear us laugh. No one's stopping you. Father left long ago. The sun would already be up, except it's not a clear day."

Bai Fu balled his fists and could barely stop from hitting her, but they were in her parents' house, so he had to hold back. All thoughts of sleep vanished, so he got dressed, washed up, and walked out into a snowy world, suffused in a blinding light. Snowflakes hung on trees; an icy wind seemed to blow right through him. He wrapped his coat around him and crunched through the snow to Beizhu's house.

The place was buzzing with noise from all the people on the *kang* playing cards. Mengzi was yelling, "Take it. Don't worry, just take it. It's a great card. What are you waiting for?" Goubao wore a strange look at the sight of Bai Fu. He seemed to be smiling or mocking him. Bai Fu took it as mockery; he felt like slugging Goubao. His wrath spread to Mengzi: How could he hang out with Goubao?

It was New Year's, so the people from family planning were taking a break, giving Fengxiang the opportunity to come home. She was sitting on the edge of the *kang*, sewing a shoe sole. As she worked, she drew a hempen thread all the way through again and again, creating a rustling sound that seemed to rise above the din in the room. She gestured to a stool by her feet with her chin when she noticed the look on Bai Fu's face.

"I hear Lanlan's pregnancy suffered a setback. Is she all right?"

"She's fine."

"That lunatic really bites," Fengxiang said. He smiled when he saw marks on her lips, erasing the unhappiness that had been building up all morning.

"I hear they're going to be arresting people again after the holiday," she whispered after a quick glance around the room. "Be careful. Maybe she should hide somewhere. I heard that nine women in Gaogou were caught and dragged onto an operating table. They couldn't do anything about it." Bai Fu merely snorted.

Laughter erupted among the card players; Mengzi could be heard saying, "What the hell did you do?" Mengzi said to Beizhu. "I knew he had two sets of fish—three in a row of the same suit—but you didn't believe me and insisted on taking it. You fell into his trap."

"Bullshit," Beizhu said. "You told me to take it. I didn't want to."

"You had such a good hand you had to take it. You'd have won the hand if he hadn't had two sets of fish."

"See how they are? Their chatter makes my scalp itch." Fengxiang gestured at the crowd with her lips. "Turn it down, will you?" she shouted. "You'll have to go play in the yard if you don't."

"You can go out to the yard if you don't like it," Mengzi said.

"This is my house. Don't you dare tell me what to do."

"I'll get Wuzi to bite off your tongue if you don't stop yelling at us," Mengzi said.

Fengxiang smacked him on the back with the shoe sole she was sewing. With an exaggerated cry, Mengzi said, "Hitting me means you want to kiss me and cursing me means you love me. Be careful, Beizhu might get jealous."

"Then I'm really going to kiss you," she wisecracked as she hit him even harder, sending him moaning to a corner of the *kang*.

"I wish Wuzi would bite off those lips of hers," Beizhu said before turning to Bai Fu. "She jabbers and nags all day long, making my head spin. Don't you want to play? Come on up. I'm done for the day. I'd have to give them my wife if I lost again."

"Hear that?" Goubao said to Fengxiang. "You'll be up if he loses again. That would be easy for you of course. Just loosen your trouser cord and the money will roll in."

"No problem. You can lick it if you want. Name it and I'll do it." Everyone laughed.

"You go ahead and play," Bai Fu said. "I'm not in the mood."

"What's your worry? There's wine today, so drink. Tomorrow, only water. I know what's bothering you. You're hoping for a son. You'll get one if it's in the cards and won't if it's not. Life goes on."

"He's right. This is the way to live. You should take it easy once in a while," Goubao said with a glance at Bai Fu.

The glance was obviously a sign of reconciliation, but Bai Fu still could not forgive Goubao, so he ignored him and said to Beizhu instead, “I’ve got things to do.”

“What do you need to do? Heaven says today is a day of rest.”

“Go up and play,” Fengxiang urged. “It’s just a game, not gambling, so why worry?”

“No, not today. I really have got something to do.” Bai Fu waved and walked out.

2

A cold wind splashed against him, washing away what remained of the din he’d carried with him from Beizhu’s house. The vast whiteness on the ground stung his eyes; the sky was a dusty gray, with swirling snowflakes. Bai Fu enjoyed walking in snow, for only at such moments did he feel strong. At other times, he felt coarse somehow.

He walked on, and before long the dream resurfaced in his mind. It was terrible. It had become a hex, ruining his mood the moment he thought about it.

A black dog leaped out from an alley and startled him. Two more dogs, one white and one spotted, emerged behind it and, like young men chasing girls, ran off spiritedly. Bai Fu was left with a sense of loss. How wonderful it would if he could be like a dog, carefree and footloose, while he dragged his feet, in no mood to move faster, let alone run wild.

Huaqiu walked up. “What are you doing?” he asked when he saw the look on Bai Fu’s face. “Praying?”

Bai Fu smiled without replying.

“Come on, let’s go play cards.”

“They’re playing at Beizhu’s house,” Bai Fu said. Then, recalling his dream, he said, “You’re better educated than I am. Can you tell me what dreams are all about?”

“What’s up? You dream when your ass is exposed, you know that.”

“Be serious,” Bai Fu said.

“I’ve heard that what you think about during the day shows up in your dreams at night. You dream about what’s on your mind.”

“Have you ever read any books about dreams?”

“Books?” Huaqiu laughed and pointed at Grannie Shaman’s house. “She knows how to interpret dreams. She has an answer for everything. Me? I can make things up, but don’t take me seriously.” Huaqiu walked off toward Beizhu’s house. He’s right, Bai Fu said to himself. Why didn’t I think of that?

Grannie Shaman Qi was leaning up against her *kang*, cracking melon seeds. An old woman, a visiting relative, was with her.

“Come on up,” Qi said when he walked in. “Up here. The *kang* is nice and toasty.”

“That’s all right, Ganma, I’m not cold.” Bai Fu stomped the snow off his feet. She offered him a handful of melon seeds; he accepted the seeds but kept them in his hand, as he listened to the women talk. Soon his hands were sweating , soaking the melon seeds.

It took him a while to realize that they were talking about a matchmaking deal. It was a boring topic, but seemed to consume all their energy and concentration. Back and forth, they kept it up, forgetting about him. Bai Fu forced himself to listen patiently until at one point he became engrossed in the narrative. He admired Grannie Shaman for her ability to make a simple matter so interesting, and in such vivid language.

“You want to talk to me? Tell me what it is.” She turned. “I know you wouldn’t come to see an old lady like me for nothing.”

Bai Fu was so immersed in their conversation that he'd forgotten all about himself. He froze at her question. Yes, why was he here? He racked his brain until he recalled his dream. "Nothing. I had a dream."

"I thought it was something serious." She laughed. "Everyone dreams."

"But it was a strange dream." Bai Fu went on to tell her about the dream and the white fox he'd killed years before.

"A white fox lives a thousand year and a black one ten thousand," the visitor said. "You shouldn't have killed it. It was an immortal fairy after years of self-cultivation."

"See? I told you back then you'd committed a crime." The shaman turned to the old woman. "None of his baby boys have survived."

"You really shouldn't have killed it. It was an immortal fairy, and you should have shown it respect instead."

"That's what everyone says. But there's nothing I can do about it now. Its bones have turned to ashes. Why am I supposed to do?" Bai Fu's face fell. "I'll have to take whatever comes my way."

The women exchanged a wordless look. Feeling utterly grim, he furrowed his brow and stammered his suspicion: "I think—the girl, Yindi—she was the fox."

"Look at him." Qi smiled broadly. "He's so anxious nothing is impossible for him." She turned to the old woman again, "But that girl of his is awfully clever. She's very young, but she can do just about anything, from paper cutting to singing popular tunes, and her lovely face has a nice glow. But she sometimes does have the bewitching air of a fox." The old woman laughed. "Maybe she was a fox," she said with a little laugh.

"Don't laugh. It's true. Something isn't right with the girl. We haven't kept any of the baby boys alive since she was born. And I keep dreaming about her having a fox tail."

"Don't let your imagination run wild," the old woman said. "So what if she's a fox incarnate? What will happen will eventually happen. But that dream of yours is worrisome, so you ought to do something about it."

"That's true," the shaman echoed. "You must find a way to fix your problem."

"What can I do?" Bai Fu asked mournfully. "I've done everything I can think of. You tried a few remedies before, but nothing has worked, absolutely nothing."

"Then why are you here?" The shaman's face darkened. "I may not have the gift, but I didn't go to you to offer my help, did I? You should stop coming here."

"Oh—what I meant was—" Bai Fu's face paled. "It actually did work. The first one was stillborn, but after you performed a rite, the next one lived for a month."

"You see? It did work," the old woman said.

"But—" Bai Fu stopped.

"Let me tell you." Her face set, Shaman Qi said with her eyes half open, "I've used my Peach Blossom Magic a hundred times, and it worked ninety-nine times. Yours was the only exception. Why? Because it was hexed. You should know that. That's all I'm going to say now, and don't come see me again. You're wasting your time."

"Ganma." Startled, Bai Fu clasped his hands and bowed tearfully.

"It really isn't going to work," Shaman Qi said coldly. "We're related, so I have to be honest with you. My attainment isn't as high as your daughter's. She's coming for what you owed her; I'm only human and can only do what is humanly possible. I have no more remedies for you. I mean it. You should go home now."

“Do you want me to die, Ganma?” Bai Fu dried his tears, choked with sobs. “I will if you refuse to help me.” He got down on his knees and banged his head loudly on the floor. Shaman Qi closed her eyes and ignored him.

“Get up.” The old woman said. “A grown man should not be doing that. I’ve heard that thousand-year-old foxes fear nothing but a neutered white dog. That’s what people say, so go find one and see.”

“Where am I supposed to find a dog like that?” Bai Fu whined woefully.

3

“Rubbish!” Meng Eight was laughing before Bai Fu finished. “Your ass was exposed and you had a dream. That’s all. There’s no need to cry your heart out and go on like this. A thousand-year old white fox and a ten-thousand-year-old black fox? That’s something people made up. I once saw a den of black foxes; the young pups were all black. Do you think they’d really lived for ten thousand years already? Total nonsense. They were black simply because their parents were black. They lived for a few decades at most. I don’t believe they live for ten thousand years. But enlightened foxes do live longer. They practice self-cultivation, worshipping the moon on the first and the fifteenth day of every lunar month. They manage to prolong their lives once they reach a certain realm and can transform themselves into pretty girls. I heard that a fox like that fears thunder more than anything. Sooner or later it will suffer a burst of thunder and reach attainment if it manages to survive.

“Of course it fears a neutered white dog, the way a mouse, no matter how big it is, always runs away from a cat. It’s their nature. A neutered white dog has strong negative *qi*, and a mighty fox loses its power when faced with a dog like that. That's what I've heard from old folks but, to be sure, no one has ever seen a thousand-year-old fox. A fox is lucky to live for a few years these days. One hunter's eyes are sharper than the one before him and gives chase when he spots fox prints. They can't live long however they try. If they can't even control their own fate, how can they exact revenge on someone?

"I heard some old folks mention an old Manchu in Liangzhou, an official in the yamen who had a neutered white dog. One day a hunter came to borrow his dog, saying he'd located a thousand-year-old white fox but couldn't take it down. He'd seen where the fox was, but it vanished the moment he raised his musket. He'd heard from a Taoist priest that a thousand-year-old white fox feared a neutered white dog, so he wanted to borrow the old Manchu's. The official agreed to lend him the dog.

"That night a white-bearded old man came to see the old Manchu, asking him not to lend out his dog. The Manchu said, 'All right, I won't. I'll take it to the yamen.' The old man left after eating a bowl of millet noodles. The Manchu tied the dog out back and had his family tell the hunter that he'd taken the dog to the yamen. Ai, the fox was meant to meet its demise. When the hunter came and heard the dog barking out back, he managed to get it out over the fence. The dog pounced on the white fox when they reached a graveyard. It had yet to digest the millet noodles completely when the hunter cut open its belly. Turns out the fox had been transformed into the white-bearded old man.

"Later the white fox came back for revenge and wrought havoc in the Manchu's family, causing deaths and stamping out their fortune. He deserved the punishment for not carrying out his promise. Ai! I shouldn't be telling you this. Bai Fu, Bai Fu! What's wrong? Why is your face so white? Don't take this to heart. It's just idle talk, pure nonsense. Why are we talking about this? Hey—Bai Fu, what's wrong? Bai Fu—Bai Fu—"

4

Yindi was beaming, because Bai Fu, who had always been cross with her, was suddenly very nice. With a chirpy laugh, she sang in her child's voice, "Pretty flowers sprouting atop grass and reeds/I send gentleman away, and the world is wonderful." She had no idea what a gentleman was, but that did not dampen her spirits. She was brimming with such happiness she nearly blurted out to her father about saving money to buy a doll for her little brother.

Daddy can be so nice, even nicer than Mama, when he wants to be, Yindi said to herself. All Mama does is put her arms around me and rock back and forth when she teaches me songs. But Daddy carried me on his shoulder to the Lin Family Shop to buy me something to eat.

"What would you like, Yindi?" He asked her. She was afraid to reply, but he persisted until she found the courage to say, "Instant noodles."

"Say, you have good taste. What else? What else would you like?" She was stumped, for she couldn't think of anything more delicious than instant noodles.

"All right, then. You shall have some instant noodles and enjoy yourself." He took out two yuan and bought three packages.

She finished one. It tasted so good the aroma lingered in her head, and she was tempted to ask for the second package. But she could not bring herself to seem greedy—Mama's usual complaint about Daddy.

Why? She wanted to save one for the little brother in Mama's belly and the last one for Mama, who simply looked at Daddy instead of eating it.

"My, my, it appears that the sun is rising in the West today."

"Why are you looking at me?" he asked her. "Are you feeling bad about me giving the girl something good to eat?"

"Now you're acting like a real father." She stared at him for a while before telling Yindi to give the pack to Grandpa. He took it, poured hot water over the noodles, and wolfed it down. Yindi could not comprehend why Mama had turned down the noodles. They were so tasty. She was a fool. But Yindi was happy that Grandpa ate them, because he was too thin. Grandpa was always thinking about big business deals, exhausting him so much he never gained weight. He was a meat lover. He was always asking for meat, and when he did, Grandma would frown and say, "Become a leopard cat in your next life and you can eat all you want."

"Did you win?" Yindi heard her mother ask.

"I just want her to have something nice to eat." Daddy snorted. "Why all the fuss?"

"That's strange. You never showed her any affection before. Have you finally learned how to be a good father?"

He even carried her on his shoulder to a big store in the township town and bought her a pretty dress, a beautiful dress with blue flowers and white dots. Yindi wanted to save the dress for the little boy, but Daddy told her to put it on, so she did. Little Brother, don't be mad at me, she said silently. You'll have even better things to wear. I'm sure Daddy will buy them for you. This was her first pretty dress, so the village children crowded around and touched it with their dirty hands. She dodged left and right, but still got some dirt on it. Daddy will be mad at me, she thought, but it was all right, because he wasn't looking at her.

Yindi wondered why he was looking so grim. She wanted him to smile, but he wouldn't, so she kept quiet. He tried to make her laugh when he saw her face, but, strangely, he stopped smiling and began to sigh once she laughed.

She could not forget what he'd said about her "hacking" the little brothers, even though she couldn't understand how she'd done it. Was that like carving a block of wood? But she couldn't recall picking up a knife or a pair of scissors, because the moment she touched one, Mama always snatched it away so she wouldn't hurt herself. She did not have the courage to ask him, though she desperately wanted to know, so she asked Mama, Auntie Ying'er, and Grandma, who told her, "Little girls shouldn't ask so many questions."

It was clear to her, however, that "hacking" made Daddy mad, though she did not know why. He had deep lines on his forehead, and she wondered if he had been "hacked."

Yindi loved making him smile, but he fought it. His face muscles twitched when he bought her the dress, and she knew it was his way of smiling. How do I make him happy? She wondered. How about a little tune? Every time she heard a tune, she was so happy she felt like jumping and laughing. Maybe he was the same.

So she started—

The sesame in the sesame plot, the sand in the sand lot.
Brother Wang found a flowery handkerchief,
Let me have it, or not, good grief.
You ride a donkey and I ride a horse.
We ride to uncle's house.
On uncle's door are two flowers.

That was her favorite tune, taught to her by Auntie Ying'er. The children in the village loved it, and every time she sang she drew a large circle of them around her. But not her father, she realized, for his face darkened every time she started singing, and he would look at her in a funny way. He didn't like it, she could tell, even if he didn't say anything.

Strange. It's such a wonderful song. Why doesn't he like to hear me sing it? Didn't I sing it well? Maybe. Her voice had been hoarse over the past few days, so she sounded raspy when she talked. Dear voice, she said, please get better so I can sing Daddy a crisp tune and make him smile.

How do I cheer him up? she wondered silently.

"What will your Mama have this time, Yindi?" She recalled Grandma asking one day.

"This time—she will have this—this—" She made a gesture of little boy peeing.

"Children tell the truth," Grandma smiled and said to Yindi's father. Yindi realized that he liked to hear such things when she saw him smile, so she kept making the gesture with the same phrase. But he scowled and said, "Stop it. That's enough. You're annoying me." So she stopped. She did not understand why he was unhappy when she said the same thing with the same gesture.

Yindi desperately wanted him to be happy, but there was nothing she could do. She wondered what went on inside his head and why he always looked grim and worried that keeping everything to himself might make him sick. To make him happy, she told him about the cloth doll, but only the muscles on his face twitched; he was not smiling.

What should she do?

She went through everything in her mind until her head hurt before recalling that he seemed happy only when he played mahjong—and won, of course. But Mama did not like him to play. Mama's face clouded over when he went out to play, and she criticized him when he came home, which always made him angry. Sometimes he hit her when he was upset; at other times he wouldn't say anything, but pull a blanket over his head and sleep for a long time. Yindi did not want to see his unhappy face, but didn't like it when he slept for a long time either, because then she had to keep quiet, tiptoeing around so as not to disturb him. At moments like these he was like a powder keg that would explode from even the tiniest spark. When that happened, he'd turn on everyone, including his parents.

Mama was wrong; she shouldn't have criticized him, Yindi said to herself. Mahjong was his only hobby, so what was the problem? Let him play as long as it makes him happy. Everyone likes playing games, her too; she liked hide-and-seek, foot bag, eagle catching chicks, and playing house. Her favorite game was sitting across from her mother playing patty-cake and singing:

Beat a gong, make the dough, when Uncle comes we roll out the noodles,
What kind of food do we roll out? We roll out bright red bean noodles.
White flour is too good and dark flour would make him laugh at us.
A hen lays eggs, so we can't kill it; a rooster crow and has to be kept.

How about a duck, but it flies up to the haystacks,
And lays eggs to hatch a nest of old monks.
One on the back and one over the shoulder, crosses a ditch and sprains an ankle
But there are still over a dozen back at home.

It was her favorite pastime, and Mama laughed like a little girl when they played it. Obviously, her father had his favorite game too, so he should go play as long as it made him happy. He might fall ill with nothing to cheer him up. But she knew why Mama didn't like it; he lost too often, and that was bad, because it made him so grim. But he won sometimes, and when that happened, he was nicer than Mama; he would put his arms around Yindi or lift her over his head and call out, "Yindi, Yindi." He'd even kiss her face, his beard tickling her cheeks.

So at one point she made up her mind to hide some of the gifts from Uncle Lingguan, Auntie Ying'er, Grandpa and Grandma over New Year's, and stop giving it all to Mama. Instead, she'd put the money in her black jar and hide it under the wardrobe. When Daddy was bored or didn't have money to play mahjong, she would secretly take a handful out and give it to him, so he could play. The thought made Yindi smile. He would be so happy he would lift her over his head, like when he won money. He would say, "Aiyo, my Yindi is all grown up now." He would kiss her face.

Yindi smiled so happily at the image that she was nearly in tears.

So she said to her mother, "Daddy likes to play mahjong, Mama, so let him go play. He's bored and he'll get sick if he doesn't." Mama took Yindi into her arms and said, "Good little girl, you're too young to understand. It isn't just a game. It's a bottomless pit that could end up swallowing you, Grandpa and Grandma, me, even our house and everything in it."

Yindi didn't believe her, of course. Where was the pit when he played? She asked if the pit was like the round hole on her headscarf, but Mama said no. "You're too young; you'll know when you grow up," her mother said.

Despite her refusal to believe the scary things her mother said, Yindi knew her father needed money to play. Maybe the money she saved would not be enough; she convinced herself that she'd make lots of money when she grew up, and then Daddy could play all he wanted. She recalled her uncles talking about an Uncle Shuangfu, who had as much money as leaves on the trees. That was amazing! So she asked her mother if the pit could be filled with the money Uncle Shuangfu had, and that made her mother laugh.

"Where did you hear that, crazy little girl? Of course Shuangfu has enough money to fill a pit like that."

"I'll make as much money as Uncle Shuangfu when I grow up, and Daddy can play all he wants, day or night. But—I want him to lose."

"Why is that?"

"If he wins, other kids' Daddies would be unhappy."

"Aiyo, my Yindi looks like a little girl, but thinks like an adult." Her mother drew her into her arms.

Yindi began to fret after that. When would she grow up? When would she make lots of money like Uncle Shuangfu for Daddy to play and be happy?

5

"Come, Yindi. Let's go somewhere that's fun," Bai Fu whispered to his daughter one day when the sun was inching slightly to the west. The girl hopped like a sparrow and clapped her hands. Maybe Mama had told him about her growing up and making money for him, and that had made him so happy he was taking her to a fun place. Yindi wanted to ask her mother if it was all right, but Daddy had sent her shopping in town. Mama is a tattletale and can't keep a secret. Bad Mama, I won't tell you anything from now on. Bad Mama.

But she was happy to go out with her father.

It was freezing. Clean white snow lay in the shaded side of the sand hollow. Yindi liked snow and the sound of her feet crunching on a snowy ground; she loved building a snowman with her mother. They used a carrot for the nose, one so long it made her mother laugh. Mama would pinch her nose and said, "Grow—grow longer," trying to make Yindi's nose as long as the snowman's. Yindi was frightened at first, and kept checking the mirror to see if she had grown a strange looking nose. One night, it did. Aiya, it kept growing and growing until it was as tall as the big poplar tree, but the tip continued to shoot up. She was so scared she screamed, but then Mama woke her up. It was just a dream. When she told her grandma the next morning, Grandma said, "Don't listen to that witch." Grandma called Mama a witch behind her back, but Yindi never breathed a word to her mother. I won't be a tattletale, Yindi thought.

What would Daddy and me do? Best was a snow fight, a game she played with the village children. Make a snowball and hurl it, bang—it burst. Then her hands would be frozen red, so would her little face. Steam rose when she breathed, one puff after another, looking like Grandpa smoking. Sometimes she put a stick in her mouth to imitate him smoking, then bent at the waist and coughed—hei—one small column of white steam—hei—another column, making Grandpa roar laughing.

The snow in the hollow wasn't thick enough to make a snowman or have a snow fight, but she remained in high spirits, since she was out with her father. But why does he have that wooden look on his face? And he keeps sighing, over and over. She wondered why he wasn't laughing, like Mama? Mama looked like Yindi when she laughed, and sometimes she would roll atop the *kang*, holding her belly. Her father never laughed like that. Mama loved to joke, but that only made

Daddy angry, which usually led Mama to sing "The spring breeze is insensitive and stirs the heart of a youth." Mama sang the line so often that Yindi knew them by heart.

"Am I a good daddy, Yindi?" Bai Fu asked.

Yindi gazed up at her father, who looked down at her in a strange way. He'd never looked at her like that before. Why did he ask me that. Why does he have to ask? Of course he's a good daddy. There's no bad daddy, is there? He had beaten her and screamed at her, but he was her father, after all. Like Grandma said all the time, family is family, like broken bones that are always attached by sinews.

"Of course you're a good daddy."

"Do you hate Daddy?" he asked, still looking at her strangely. His eyes were moist, as if he'd been crying.

Why did he ask me that? She tossed her head. Has Mama been a tattletale again? Yindi had said to her mother that she hated Daddy last time he hit her mother. Bad Mama, why couldn't you keep that between us?

"I did, last time, when you whipped Mama and left bloody marks on her. I was so scared. Don't hit Mama again, Daddy. She's always crying secretly. You can hit me when you're upset. Smack my bottom as much as you want. It's soft and can take all the spanking. But you can't hit other spots. No one would make money for you if you hit other spots and caused a problem." It took a lot of effort to stop from blurting out her plan to make as much money as Uncle Shuangfu.

"All right, my little girl. I promise I'll never hit Mama again. But sometimes Daddy can't help it. I was born this way, with a terrible temper, and I can't always control myself. But Daddy has a good heart – my little girl, do you believe me? Daddy has a good heart."

"Of course Daddy has a good heart. Otherwise, how could you

be a Daddy?" she said childishly. "Mama said it wasn't easy raising me. She said I was like a tiny mouse when I was born. That's strange. How would I have looked like a tiny mouse? I don't believe that. Bad Mama. She has a big mouth."

Bai Fu's hands flew up to cover his face as he squatted down on the sand. They had reached the desert without knowing it. His shoulders convulsed.

"What's wrong, Daddy?" Yindi was frightened. "What's happened, Daddy—Daddy!"

He jumped to his feet, his eyes moist. He kept wiping his eyes, but more tears came, until his face was streaking wet.

"What's the matter, Daddy?" She was about to cry herself.

"There was—a bug—in my eye."

"Aiya! That's terrible. I got one in my eye once. It felt awful and made my eye hurt. I couldn't stop crying. But Mama licked my eye until it was better. It felt really good. Here, Daddy I'll lick your eye for you." Yindi spat a few times. "Mama said to spit out the dirty stuff in my mouth before licking. Here, Daddy. You'll feel better."

"No, it's all right." Bai Fu swayed before he managed to steady himself. "Do you want to spend more time here? We'll go home if you don't."

"I do. Why aren't there any insects, Daddy?"

"They only come out in the summer."

"When will summer be here? Grandpa Shun said rats eat insects, foxes eat rats, and humans hunt foxes. Daddy, why do people hunt foxes? They're such nice animals."

"There's nothing good about them. They are—troublemakers. Come here. If you want to spend more time here, I'll carry you." A grim look returned to his face.

Seeing Yindi's face turning red from the cold, he took off his jacket to cover her before hoisting her onto his back and striding into the desert.

6

Yindi was delighted.

She felt as high as the sky on her father's back, and saw a very bright, very white sun, like an ice platter. There were also gauzy puffs of clouds, just like Mama's tattered white scarf. She was very fond of the scarf, which she held up and ran, so it would billow behind her. She was sad when Grandpa later tied it to the donkey's halter.

Reminded of the scarf by the puffy clouds, Yindi abruptly realized she'd done something wrong again. She should not have asked for instant noodles. They tasted awfully good, but hadn't lasted long and she was hungry again when they were gone. It was a waste of money. She should have asked Daddy to buy a scarf, either a red one or a white one. Mama liked white, while Yindi preferred red, but white would be best. A white scarf would serve two purposes: neckwear for Mama and a toy for Yindi, who could make it billow. Filled with remorse, Yindi wanted to ask her father when he would buy her something good to eat again. The next time she wouldn't ask for instant noodles, no matter how much she wanted them, or how good they smelled. She'd ask for a scarf. It had been a long time since Mama had worn a scarf, and she would be happy to have a new one; she would smile so much her eyes would be as round as circles, like pigeon droppings.

Yet she could not bring herself to ask her father for anything; she recalled one of Grandma's favorite sayings: A greedy person is like a snake trying to swallow an elephant. I should have known better.

Daddy didn't even want to spend money to buy socks but she was so greedy she was thinking about a scarf not long after eating instant noodles.

All around them enormous mountains of sand reached into the sky, making the sun seem so much lower, lower than when they first entered the desert. When her father was climbing one of the dunes, she looked back at the path behind them. Ai, she could see their village, though not clearly, and the houses were no bigger than matchboxes.

She also spotted chimneys with plumes of black smoke. Those houses are just like Grandpa, who does nothing but smoke. He can blow smoke rings, some big and some little, but all looking so nice. When he blows big ones, his lips form a circle and his eyes bulge, with his mouth wide open; he holds his breath while his tongue moves, and big smoke rings fly out of his mouth and into the air. Little rings are even better. He takes a puff and, with his lips barely open, taps his cheek with his finger to send tiny rings leaping out. It was great fun. But he had been busy with his "big business deals" lately and looked unhappy when he wasn't busy, so Yindi knew better than to pester him.

The chimneys looked clumsy, so they probably did not know how to blow smoke rings. See, the smoke just rose straight into the air. But that was fun too, and reminded her of a tune Auntie Ying'er had taught her: Smoke from the chimney rises into the sky/water in the Yellow River is good for washing a red carpet/lay down a red carpet for Seventh Girl to dance."

Suddenly her father's body teetered. I'm too heavy for Daddy, she thought.

"Put me down, Daddy. I'll walk on my own."

"Just sit tight, little girl. This is the first time I've ever carried you on my back." He coughed. "Do you like it?"

"Of course I do." Daddy seemed very tall, so tall he was as high as the sky. He had broad shoulders and great strength, better than the sky. She knew it was good to be strong, for she'd heard people say how he could work like an ox. That was utter nonsense to her, because an ox does not have her father's strength. Could it pull a cart piled high and run up a steep slope? Definitely not. How could slow, dead-eyed oxen be her father's match?

But great strength is not always good, it occurred to her. When he hit Mama, Daddy could grab her, like a hawk preying on a chick, toss her around, and smack her. She had no defense, and at times like that, Yindi wished that her father were weak, and uttered a silent prayer: Please take Daddy's strength from him and make him as powerless as a chicken. But no one ever listened to her prayers.

She swayed on her father's solid shoulders, her curious eyes scanning the rolling dunes, the blue sky, and the specks of desert plants dotting the sand hills and hollows. It made her so happy. But a feeling that something wasn't quite right quickly followed her delight; her enjoyment could tire her father out.

"Put me down, Daddy." She wiggled to get down.

"Why? Don't you like it?" He sounded subdued.

"I do. But you'll get tired."

"I'm not tired, little one. I haven't treated you well. It's not your fault; it's just that you – forget it. Remember what I'm going to say, little one – don't hate me."

Yindi was confused. She wondered why he was saying all these strange things. All he'd done was slap and spank her once in a while, and those no longer hurt. So she said:

"You bought me instant noodles, Daddy. Don't you remember? You're really nice – it's just – from now on – don't hit Mama again.

Please?"

"From now on? All right. I promise. I won't hit her again."

7

The sun was suspended above the tallest dune, painting Yindi with bright red rays of light.

Bai Fu put Yindi down, his eyes filling with sweat from his forehead. Yindi wondered how eyes could sweat. She recalled a phrase her mother often used, "Sweat drips from the eyes and callouses form in the palms." Daddy is tired from carrying me.

But where are we? She rubbed her numbed backside and cocked her head to look around. Sand dunes, sand hollows, sand shrubs, Artemisia, and many other things whose names she did not know. Eventually she recalled that she had once come here with Grandpa Shun and his goats. What did he call this place? Yes, he called it the desert. But she also recalled another name Uncle Lingguan had used. She had no idea why there were two names; adults did things differently and children should not ask too many questions. Who cared what they called this place?

Spring had just arrived, and it was still cold, turning her face red and her feet numb; her hand hurt from the firm grip of her father's hand. But she was in high spirits. It was fun to play in the desert, unlike her village, with so much dirt it was impossible to keep her nice clothes clean. Here she could roll in the sand without soiling her clothes. The new dress her father had bought her was already looking a bit grubby from the village kids' dirty hands. The desert was a wonderful place; she couldn't soil her clothes even if she wanted to. Yindi loved the place.

"It's getting dark, Yindi. Are you afraid?" Bai Fu squatted in a sand hollow. "Do you want to stay here to play or go home with Daddy? You decide."

"I want to stay to play. Look, Daddy. There's a crescent moon. Grandpa Shun said foxes bow to a crescent moon, like kowtowing, pang-pang, over and over. He also said a fox will turn into a young girl after bowing for hundreds of years. A pretty young girl. I wonder if she'd be as pretty as Auntie Ying'er."

Bai Fu stared at his daughter with such a strange look she had to avoid his gaze fearfully. Did I say something wrong again? I didn't say anything about hacking a little brother, so why is he upset? Bai Fu turned and muttered to himself:

"It looks like it's her fate. It's not entirely my fault."

He got to his feet, walked down into a sand hollow, and returned with a pile of strange looking things. Long like cucumbers, they were vaguely familiar.

"What are they, Daddy?" she asked, but immediately recalled seeing them when she'd come out here with Grandpa Shun and his goats. Calling them "sandy donkey dicks," he had picked one up and crumbled it to show the sand inside.

"Gold," Bai Fu said.

"What is gold?"

"Gold? What is gold?" Bai Fu frowned for a moment before answering, "Gold is gold, worth more than money. A pinch the size of your finger can get you a big pile of money."

"More than Uncle Shuangfu's money?"

"Of course." He gave her another funny look. "You know about Shuangfu?"

She laughed. Should she tell him about her plan of growing up and making more money than Uncle Shuangfu? About having enough money for Daddy to gamble with? He would be angry when he lost, but other kids' young masters would be upset if he won. This was too hard. What should she do?

"Crazy girl." Bai Fu did not persist.

Yindi cheered up; he'd called her that when he won and given her a peck on the cheek. But this time he didn't kiss her; instead he stared at the pile of gold. How much money could they fetch, she wondered. Maybe she didn't have to wait until she grew up. Why would Daddy complain about a lack of money if these were all gold? She was puzzled, so she said, "Grandpa Shun called them sandy donkey dicks."

Bai Fu was startled. He looked around before giving her another funny look.

"These—they—of course they're called sandy donkey dicks, but they're gold." He picked one up and snapped it in two, then picked through its contents to extract a tiny, shiny speck the size of a pinhead. "See, this is gold. When we take it home, we soak it in water and sift out the sand, and this is what's left. A tiny pinch from here and another tiny pinch from there, and soon we'll have a handful, which we put into a ladle and hold it over a fire to make a big chunk of gold."

Yindi was convinced. She had once seen someone make an aluminum pot, and it had been just as what Daddy said. A chunk of aluminum was placed in a metal pan over a fire. It turned into a pool of shiny water, which was then poured into a mold to produce an aluminum pot.

Now Mama would not have to worry about money ever again, nor would Grandpa and Grandma, Auntie Ying'er, and so many other people. She didn't have to grow up either. All she had to do was come here for the sticks every day and carry them home to soak in water, sift, and turn into money. The prospect had her lost in a trance before she suddenly said, "You're terrible, Daddy."

Bai Fu's face blanched at the startling accusation as he looked around again.

"Why didn't you—bring this up earlier? With so much gold, Grandpa's hair wouldn't have turned white from worry."

"This—I—" Not knowing what to say, he just stared at his daughter foolishly.

The girl frowned, deep in thought, before breaking out in a big smile. 'I know. Ginseng babies."

"What are ginseng babies?"

"These are just like ginseng babies. Auntie Ying'er told me about them. No one can catch them because they vanish when you try. Only good kids can see them."

Bai Fu was speechless. It took him a while to recover. "A clever little devil." He sighed. "You're a clever little devil—how do you know so much. Hei—amazing."

"I'll be the good kid then. Will they die if I catch them? Don't be a bad guy, Daddy."

"Of course not. They're so lonely here. See, it's cold here—eh—we take them home and wash the dirt off them. They'll be real pretty." Bai Fu shook his head ruefully, mumbling to himself, his eyes on the sun above the hill.

"Did you bring any red thread?" Yindi asked.

"What for?"

"To tie around the sticks so they won't vanish. You see, ginseng babies can't run away with a red thread around them. That's what Auntie Ying'er said. I'm sure these golden babies are the same."

"All right, I'll go get some red threads. You stay here to watch them and make sure they don't run away. All right?" Bai Fu suddenly howled.

"I'm no good. I'm horrible—but go to a good family in your next life."

"I didn't say I wouldn't stay to watch them." Frightened, Yindi looked at her father cautiously and said. "Don't worry, Daddy. I—I won't go anywhere."

8

Night arrived.

The bright red rays of light above the hill were swallowed up by the night; the air turned into cold water spreading and flowing all around, and soon Yindi was trembling in the chill. Daddy had walked off with his warm coat. She had insisted on it, so he put it on after frowning over her suggestion. Her teeth were clattering now, but she was comforted by the idea that her father was warm. He's a good Daddy; he bought me instant noodles. They were delicious and I'll always remember how they smelled. She smiled at the recollection, though it was harder to do that now, for her jaws were growing stiff.

The crescent moon hung in the sky, like a disc of ice. She gazed at it, wondering if it was like her, waiting for its Daddy to return; it had waited for a long time, and was crying because its Daddy never came back. Look, the stars are its tears. Poor crescent moon. It cried so much it made many stars. Why did Auntie Ying'er say that the number of stars in the sky depends on the number of people on earth? Maybe she was right. Auntie Ying'er never lied to her, so she always believed what her auntie said. So, which star is Mama, which is Uncle Lingguan, and which is Auntie Ying'er? Grandpa and Grandma have to be old stars.

When a star grows old, it will sprout a beard. So, a bad-luck comet could be a star with a beard. Grandma was always calling her mother a bad-luck comet. Grandma, Yindi said silently, you're the bad-luck comet. She smiled at the thought.

She began to name the stars. This is Mama, that one is Uncle Lingguan, that is Auntie Ying'er, and that's Grandpa Shun. But then the stars began to move and blurred her sight. Why are you running like that? Are you visiting neighbors? Yes! When someone goes to visit a friend, his star will move; the stars in the sky will be a mess if they're all on the move.

Her mind was briefly occupied with the stars, but soon returned to the cold air. Her feet were numb, so she stomped around; she was freezing, so she jumped up and down while saying to herself, Daddy will be back soon, so don't worry. He's a fast walker. She could almost see him taking big strides toward her.

9

Yindi's mood brightened when she looked down at the gold at her feet. Her father had found so much that they'd get a pile of gold when they took the sticks home to soak and sift in water. She was sure her mother would be happy. I'm sure Daddy brought me here because I'm a good kid. Didn't the bad man use a good kid to help him catch ginseng babies? Yindi felt a pang of guilt toward the gold babies. I'm sure they're just like the ginseng babies. Will it hurt them when they're put over a fire? It will. She recalled a spark that had once singed her hand; it had hurt for days. The memory made her feel sorry for the gold. We shouldn't put them over a fire, she thought. We'll just sell them as they are. It's all right if we get less money, as long as they don't suffer.

The wind picked up, howling as it took her breath away. She trembled and tightened her coat around her, but that did nothing to warm her up. Tears welled in her eyes, and it took a great effort not to cry out loud. Wiping her eyes, she looked around for shelter from the wind, but changed her mind when she thought that the gold babies might run away. Would they? Hard to say. She realized that she was harboring bad intentions and getting greedy. They would run off when they knew what would happen to them, and that would make her father unhappy. When he was mad, he would cover his head and sleep, hit her mother, or yell at Grandma. Please don't be upset, gold babies, Yindi said. I'm not a good person, but, but we're friends, so won't you please help me. She saw the gold babies nod and smile, and she laughed.

"We're good friends, aren't we?" She thought.

Her father was still nowhere in sight.

Bad Daddy.

She was nearly frozen stiff. Her face felt prickly, her hands were frozen numb, and her body felt like an ice bar. She brought her hands up to her mouth to blow on them, but they were still cold. I'm turning into an ice bar, she said to herself, and was reminded of the ice bar vendor by the village school. She had yet to try the white, yellow, and red frozen treats. She wondered what they tasted like; her head hurt from trying to conjure up the taste. Then it occurred to her that they must taste like her hands. Since they had turned into ice bars, it would be the same as eating one if she sucked on her hands.

Daddy, bad Daddy. Look, I'm eating an ice bar. Don't you want one?

A strange noise came from somewhere, like the cry of an animal. The wind, gustier now, pelted her face with specks of sand. She was scared, as she recalled Auntie Ying'er's story about the wolf pretending to be a grandma. Yindi was terrified of the grandma-wolf. Auntie had said that the grandma-wolf drank human blood, gulping it down like slurping potato millet. It also ate human fingers, crunching away like chewing broad beans. So scary. Yindi had seen fox pelts, but never a wolf. She wondered if grandma-wolf was just like a fox. If it was, then she wouldn't be afraid; and yet she was. Her scalp turned numb at the thought of grandma-wolf gnawing on her fingers. Well, my fingers have already turned into ice bars, so they'll break your teeth. She felt like laughing when she imagined what the wolf would look like with broken teeth. She opened her mouth, and let out a cry instead of a laugh. The sound of herself crying terrified her.

"Mama—" She cried, and immediately wondered why she was calling for her mother when she was waiting for her father's return.

"Mama—Mama—" Her puzzlement notwithstanding, she could not stop from crying out for her mother. Soon she was bawling, and the sound echoed in the hollows until it seemed to fill the space all around her.

Some time later an even gustier wind swept over her, raining sand on her face, and swallowing up the sound of her crying. Moving her lips soundlessly, she covered her eyes; the grains of sand were like dirt clods numbing he face; but the pain was gone. She bit her fingers; they did not hurt either, as if they had turned into real ice bars. Well, now I have no fear of grandma-wolf. Go ahead, bite me if you want to crack your teeth. You probably never tasted an ice bar either. Come on, try it. She sucked on a finger to show the wolf, and made herself laugh, a real laugh this time.

Bad Daddy still isn't here.

The crescent moon was gone and the sky was darker than the blackened bottom of Grandma's pot. The heavenly dog must have eaten the moon, she said to herself, recalling a frequent phrase of her grandma's. What was a heavenly dog? Yindi had no idea, but she thought it might be just like a wolf, which was like a dog, according to Grandma. Yindi loved Pup, a lovely black and white dog. It wagged its tag when it saw Yindi and licked her feet with its long, red tongue, which tickled. Maybe the heavenly dog was the grandma-wolf, who bit off the moon when it didn't want to break its teeth gnawing on her fingers. Yindi giggled at her own explanation.

She looked around but could see nothing in the darkness; there was only sand and wind, darkness and bitter cold. Her dread of grandma-wolf was gone, replaced by a fear of ghosts, which frightened her most, though she did not know what a ghost was. The earlier noise must have come from a ghost, she told herself. Grandma-wolf wouldn't cry like that; it would change itself into a grannie and call out with a smile, "Yindi—Yindi—open the door." It would not have dared to be so loud, for that would expose its true self; nor would it dare to turn around to show its tail. Yindi had learned all about a grandma-wolf from her auntie. It must have been a ghost, she was convinced now, and could feel her hair standing up.

"Woo-hoo." The ghost was crying again.

Yindi cried too. She couldn't help it. She hadn't wanted to, but she couldn't stop her mouth from crying. She had no control over her mouth so she let it open and wail. "Mama," Yindi wailed, also uncontrollably. She had meant to call out to her father, but her mouth had a mind of its own. "Mama," she called out, driving away her fear of ghost in the process.

The crescent moon poked its head out. The wind died down, but felt colder than before. Apparently the chill had driven away the ghost, for its sound grew indistinct until it faded away. But her father had yet to reappear. Yindi was so frozen stiff she no longer felt cold, and that seemed fine. She looked around again but it was all a blur, as the sand soaked up the faint glow from the crescent moon before it reached the ground.

"Bad Daddy must have fallen asleep and forgotten about me." She knew her father was a heavy sleeper, because her mother was always calling him a sleepyhead.

Yindi began to doze off when she thought of her father sleeping in, but she shook her head to keep awake. Bad Daddy, sleepyhead. Don't fall asleep on the road though; you'd freeze without a blanket. If you catch a cold, you'll cough, and your nose will run like flowing water. Bad Daddy, sleepyhead.

Out of the blue, she giggled, an involuntary act that frightened her; Grandpa Shun had told her that laughing in the desert in winter meant the person would die soon. She didn't really know what it meant to die, except that it was definitely not good, because a lot of people cried when someone died in her village. Shaking her head with great effort, Yindi wanted to say, I don't want to die, Mama, but nothing came out of her mouth, which seemed to have frozen stiff. She pinched her face without feeling anything. I'm not going to die, Mama, she said to herself. I'm not, Mama. She could not keep from giggling.

As uncontrollable giggles continued to escape from her mouth, she fixed her eyes on the gold babies and told them, "Don't run around. Are you cold? Don't worry. You've got me." She strained to squat down, unbuttoned her coat with great effort, and struggled to pick up the gold babies one by one. Cradling them like her mother with her arms around her, she drew her coat together to hold them tightly.

"Now you won't be cold."

Like an enormous net, heavy drowsiness slowly descended and

shrouded her.

Yet her giggling continued, spreading far and wide eerily, like the bleat of a wild rabbit.

10

Villagers found her bluish corpse in a sand hollow when they came to collect desert rice seeds the next day. They were confused by the sight of the little girl holding sandy donkey dicks in her arms, with her unbuttoned coat wrapped around them.

"She was possessed. An evil spirit must have a cast spell on her," one of them said.

"Yes. I heard that Baldy Wang from Shawan even ate muddy silt, and said as he ate, 'Aiya, such nice long noodles, dear Qingjia,' another one said. "He was possessed, too."

All hell broke loose at Bai Fu's house.

Lanlan looked at her husband with an eerie smile.

"Why are you looking at me like that?" Bai Fu was thrown off balance. "The day before yesterday, I went out for a drink. You don't believe me? Go ask Routou—how would I know where she went?"

Lanlan kept smiling; then she stopped, just sitting on the *kang* like a statue. Some time passed before she let out a heartrending cry, "Yindi—" She began to howl shrilly and banged her head against the wall over and over.

Suddenly she stopped, and got down off the *kang*, and mechanically put on her shoes. With the same eerie smile, she looked at Bai Fu.

"What are you going to do?" He avoided her eyes nervously. "Do you want to kill me, is that it?"

She fixed her gaze on her husband for a while before turning to look at the table with the same strange expression. Then, with a loud shriek, she threw herself at the table and rammed her belly into one of its corners.

Lanlan passed out with a scream.

She miscarried that night.

Chapter Fifteen

1

Hantou did not think much about the lump he found near his ribcage and forgot all about it once the pain subsided. But it flared up again the next day during mealtime. "This is strange. I've got a lump here," he said.

"Wipe it with your spit first thing in the morning," his father told him. "Spit can take care of all skin problems."

"It's not on the skin. It feels like it's growing underneath. And it hurts, a dull pain that comes and goes."

"You get what you fear most," his mother said with a sense of dread. "Your old problem hasn't gone away, and now you have a new one."

"They're the same," Hantou said with a smile. "I think it was caused by this lump. No wonder it hurt so much. How can a lump inside your body not hurt? When I had that abscess on my neck, it hurt so much I could hardly open my eyes until it burst."

"Are you saying that the lump is in your abdomen?" His mother sucked in air.

"I guess so. It's where I get that pain, by my ribcage. I wouldn't have taken the medicine if I'd known it was just a lump. I'd just let the pus build up and wait till it bursts. It was a waste of money."

She told him to take off his shirt and show her the spot. She pressed down a few times, and so did Laoshun, causing Hantou enough pain that he cracked his mouth and sucked in cold air.

"When did this start?" his mother asked.

"I felt it last night. I think it's ready to pop. I hear it hurts when the pus is forming. It hurt really bad a while ago when I was out plowing the field."

"It's not ready yet. It'll be soft and tender when it's ready to pop, but this feels hard. Once it bursts, you'll feel so much better."

Lingguan walked up and pressed down on the spot. His heart skipped a beat, but he forced himself not to draw any ominous conclusion. "You should go see a doctor, even if it's just an abscess."

"Another waste of money," Hantou said.

"It's not. You spend whatever's necessary. I'll go to the city with you tomorrow."

"The city?" Hantou raised his voice. "No way. With bus fare and lunch, it would cost a fortune. Forget it. I'll go see a doctor at the township clinic."

"Those pigs who eat rotten potatoes—you know who I mean, the officials—know nothing," Laoshun said. "If money has to be spent, then it must be used for the right reason. Go see a doctor in the city."

Mengzi finished his breakfast distractedly and, tossing his bowl aside, said listlessly, "Don't make a mountain out of a molehill. It's just a lump, isn't it? Wait till it's ready to pop, get a syringe to suck the pus out, and everything will be fine. Why get worked up over nothing?" He took out some money and said. "Here are my winnings. From that ass Baigou." He tossed it down on the table with an ingratiating look at his father.

"You're an idiot," their mother said. He just cheated you, but you're friends again?"

"That was no big deal. I don't bear grudges. All he did was open a gash in my head."

"Well, well," Laoshun snorted. "You'll remember it when he spills your brains."

"Watch your mouth," their mother chided. "Parents' words can be prophetic."

"Was it something I said that got him whipped? It was his fault, don't blame me."

"He's my young master, and yours too."

"Come on, that's enough," Lingguan said. "You're all getting off the track. Let's focus on the matter at hand."

"He's right," Mengzi said. "And don't bring up young master this and young master that all the time. We haven't done anything to be someone's young master."

"You be quiet." Their mother glared at Mengzi. "Go out and sell a sack of wheat."

"We don't have much. We'll have to tie up our throats if we keeping selling off the grain," Laoshun complained.

"Okay, if we don't sell, why don't you try to pawn your ribs?"

"Don't sell any grain," Hantou cut in. "The medicine is useless. Hundreds of yuan haven't done me a bit of good."

"I didn't say you shouldn't go see a doctor in the city. I'm just telling your mother to take out her private stash."

"Private stash? Sure, I have that," she said. "A thick stash on my heel, but no one wants it."

That night Laoshun lay in bed and sighed. His wife could not sleep either.

"I suspect the boy's problem is more serious," he said, and she sat up.

"Don't frighten me. There's a spot on my body that's been twitching for the past few days, and I'm feeling uneasy. What you just said is enough to scare me witless."

"It wouldn't be a big deal if it were a lump on the skin, but inside, it—it might require surgery."

She let out a cry. "That would cost a fortune."

"We'd have to spend it." He sighed again. "We'll scrape together what we have. And then there are the two boys who need to get married at some point. Ai. My heart sinks every time I think about it."

"The boy's illness has me so worried my heart is tied up in knots. As for the other two boys, well, they'll get married even if we have to take this house apart and sell the land, or borrow money and put ourselves in debt. No family waits until they've saved up enough. We'll borrow money and pay it back little by little. But the boy's illness really worries me."

"You can worry yourself sick, but it won't do any good. What will happen will happen. Worrying doesn't make sense, but how do you stop? My heart is in my throat all the time, you know. Hei. We've been poor all our lives, but that's all right and we can get by if we're healthy. A lifetime passes no matter how you live your life. But Heaven doesn't want to allow us to make do. It creates so many problems you can't live in peace."

"Yes," she agreed. "I don't think I've ever had a day free of concerns. When the kids were little, we constantly worried about where our next meal would come from. When we had food to feed them, we had to find ways to clothe them. Now that they're grown, we have to find them wives and think about grandchildren. There's also Lanlan to worry about; I get depressed just thinking about her. And there's more. Someone's always getting sick, a headache here, a fever there. How can anyone live in peace?"

"I know. In all these years we've never had a joyful moment. Day after day, worry about this and fret over that. What's the point of life, when you think about?"

"What point could there be?" she said. "We're supposed to muddle through life, so that's what we'll do, whether we're able to make something out of it or not. When a day is over, that means we've muddled through a morning and an afternoon. When our life is over, we've muddled enough to earn four boards for a coffin."

After an emotional sigh, Laoshun got up to smoke. All was quiet but for dogs barking somewhere in the distance. "Let's stop talking about it," he said. "The more we talk, the greater our worries. Let's just muddle through the days, one at a time." He tossed down his pipe and crawled back under the covers without another word. He tossed and turned for most of the night.

2

Lingguan, Mengzi, and Ying'er went into the field to break up dirt clods the next morning. Later that day, Wuzi set another fire, but Hantou spotted it and put it out. Wuzi ran off. Hantou turned over the burned wheat stalks carefully to make sure no embers were left smoldering when Maodan strutted over, humming a tune in the peculiar voice of his:

Looking ahead—a gobi desert —
Looking behind—the Jiayu Pass
On either side are two mountain ranges high—
Raising my head—to see patches of the sky—

"Aiya, Hantou. You're just like your name—blockhead!" Maodan jeered when he saw Hantou. "I can't believe you're hanging out here. You actually let your wife go into the field with Lingguan? You'd better watch out. Cotton catches fire when a flame touches it. Be careful he doesn't add a leg with her."

Hantou ignored him and focused on turning over the stalks.

"You don't believe me? I've seen them with my own eyes having an intimate chat. They were nearly in each other's arms. Birds land in pairs. Ai, but not you and your wife."

"Shut your stinking mouth," Hantou said in a low voice, his face dark with anger.

"Aiyo. I know my mouth stinks, but not Lingguan's. He has bright red lips to show off his gleaming white teeth. Aren't you worried that they might, you know?" Hantou's retort only made Maodan want to tease him more.

"Stop it." Hantou looked up and, with a squint, spat out, "Shut up."

"What are you afraid of? Young men are always involved with their sisters-in-law. It's no big deal, is it? It's like leaving a hole in the ground after you pull up a turnip."

"You prick." With a low roar, Hantou tossed down the shovel, pushed Maodan to the ground and slapped him over and over. "Shut up. You shut up, I said!"

"I was just joking." Maodan squealed like a butchered pig. "Can't you take a joke? Aiyo, don't take me seriously. No good deed goes unpunished, you know."

Hantou did not stop until he'd given Maodan over a dozen slaps. His cheeks red and badly swollen, Maodan sat up with his hands over his face, "Shit, Hantou. I can't believe you actually hit me. I can't fucking believe it. I was just joking?"

Still wearing a scowl, Hantou looked down and snorted angrily.

Lingguan and the others were startled when they returned and heard Maodan's screeches and saw the remains of the burned stalks.

"Hey, Lingguan. I was just joking with your brother, and he actually hit me. He can't take a joke."

"Like what?"

"I just said—" Hantou roared and pounced again before Maodan barely got three words out. But this time Maodan was prepared and hopped off like a rabbit. "I just said—" Maodan repeated. Hantou picked up his shovel and threw it at him. Maodan jumped to dodge the shovel, which ended up cutting down a sapling. He blanched at the sight, too frightened to jest any more. He fled, but they could still hear him after he'd disappeared behind:

"Looking ahead—a gobi desert —"

3

Hantou was beset by jumbled emotions when he looked at Lingguan and Ying'er from a spot behind them. With a sigh, he lay down on the wheat stalks, holding his head as he thought about his affliction. In his mind, Ying'er was a fleeting shadow, not a real person, forever beyond his reach. The same impression surfaced whenever he thought about her, saw her, or touched her; he was plagued by the feeling that she would fly away one day, like a balloon slowly disappearing into a clear, blue sky. He felt unworthy of her, and it wasn't just because of his problem. Everything about her seemed so agreeable; she was gentle, calm, and lovely, always gliding around quietly, as if she had no worries, no temper, not even any concrete form. During the many embarrassing and shameful moments in his life with her, she always comforted him in a voice so soft and tender it seemed otherworldly. There was never a hint of complaint and she never sighed, but her soothing comfort often gave rise to sadness in him, for he knew that he held no attraction for her. He was sure of that, as he was aware of how dumb and inarticulate he was; he even walked in a clumsy way, devoid of carefree grace. Hantou was envious of his younger brother for the confident, airy way he walked, but he could not carry himself like that, as if he hadn't been given the gene to appear natural and at ease. In the past, he'd secretly imitated Lingguan, but blushed after taking a few steps.

I can't do it. I was born a block of gnarly elm, he conceded, feeling even worse about himself.

Hantou was convinced that Ying'er was too good for him, just as his sister Lanlan was too good for Bai Fu, a conviction that weighed heavily on him. He knew he'd let his sister down as a brother and he was not much a husband to his wife. Sometimes he felt that he was less than human, and he regretted not putting up strong enough objections to his parents' proposal of exchanging daughters. Back then, he had already sensed it wasn't a good match, but he was smitten by the girl with big eyes framed by long lashes and a lovely nose that seemed carved from jade. It was true. The mere thought of her took his breath away. On their wedding day, he kept asking himself if it was really happening. He wasn't dreaming, was he? He'd even bitten his tongue; it hurt enough to tell him it was true, but it felt like a dream once he stopped. Enveloped in a dreamy, surreal sensation, he ended up embarrassing himself, and that led to anguish.

During their first three nights together, he could not bring himself to touch Ying'er, who was wrapped in a blanket as they lay in bed. He simply couldn't, even after mustering all the strength and mental energy he possessed. When he heard her sigh on the first night, he immediately suspected that she was sighing over her marriage to a loser. He couldn't blame her. Made even more cautious by his speculation, he held his breath and maintained the same punishing position in bed, afraid he'd frighten her if he rolled over.

He finally touched her on the fourth day, but only after bantering jests from Beizhu and his friends during the day. Beizhu had asked him if his new wife had cried out. Hantou had no idea what he meant, so Beizhu told him that a woman cried out in bed when she had a good time. Beizhu told him to ask her if it felt so good she couldn't tell even her mother. Beizhu said his woman cried out on their first night, saying she was dying and yet was in Heaven, which made him wonder if she was used goods.

"She didn't cry out? Then you must not have done a good job. If you had, she'd have cried even if she didn't want to. Ha, that's what a man looks for in bed. It's like screwing a corpse if she doesn't."

That night Hantou found, to his surprise, that Ying'er undressed without turning off the light. On previous nights, she had waited until the light was off to take off her clothes. On this night, she seemed natural as she took off her blouse, pants, and undershirt, before getting into bed wearing only a sleeveless top and a pair of red panties. He thought she gave him a look, but quickly decided that she might not have. Then she turned off the light before letting out the same emotional sigh.

He felt his heart ram against his chest noisily, while all he could see before his eyes was red, the color of her panties. Oddly though, it was that color, not her nakedness, which excited him; he felt it go straight to his heart before roiling in his abdomen and making his blood boil.

Again and again, he reached out, but always drew his hand back, feeling himself on the verge of a nervous breakdown. His heart pounded, and a loud noise roared in his ears. He was suffocating. He backed away again and again, loathing himself each time; inch by inch he reached out to her, the miniscule progress nearly sapping his energy. Each time he mustered the courage to reach out, he retreated, wasting his energy with nothing to show for it. He was exhausted by the arduous struggle. On that quiet and yet deafening fourth night, he reached out and backed off, his heart in his throat, until midnight, when he finally touched her blanket, which had been next to him all along, but somehow unreachable.

She neither moved away nor responded to his action; in fact there was no reaction from her at all. But now that he'd poked open the proverbial sheet of paper separating them, he moved over and slipped under her blanket. He was surprised but happy to feel her arms around him.

Hantou never knew when the disorder took hold of him. He nearly collapsed the moment he came into contact with her searing body, as if his blood were boiling; his body fell apart when it touched hers. He crumbled, and his passion and happiness, even his self-worth, disintegrated. Covered in sweat, his mouth was dry, and he was so exhausted he could not even move off her when he heard her breathing hard under his weight.

Heaven! He remembered himself calling out.

He fell apart completely, irretrievably, failing to take control of the territory that was his to occupy. He couldn't, despite the passion he felt inside. And little by little, even that deserted him.

Hantou kept probing the cause of his disorder, but came up with nothing. He wondered if he was too old or if he'd been in too much of a hurry that night. But the most plausible cause had to be the summer day ten years before when he'd saved a girl from the Dasha River. He still recalled that he had been sweating, and when he jumped into the icy cold water it felt as if many things had entered his body. The most vivid sensation was of a freezing insect worming its way up to his waist through the soles of his feet. Since then he'd been plagued by a sore back, had difficulty urinating, and was often cold. The symptoms never completely left him.

A teardrop rolled out of the corner of his eye at some point, cooling him as it slid down his cheek. He tried to put these thoughts out of his mind. The sky was blue, so blue that it seemed to be a vast, empty, high canopy. Clouds galloped past his eyes, like goats racing toward a river to relieve their dying thirst. After watching the clouds for a while he felt better

Life stinks, he said to himself.

His mother was calling him to lunch. He got up with a throbbing head. The sun hung above, shining noisily down on him.

4

Over lunch, Hantou told everyone about Wuzi setting another fire, drawing emotional responses from Laoshun and Mengzi, who commented on everyone's good luck that it was spotted before the house caught fire. Lingguan, on the other hand, was in a foul mood over the fight between his brother and Maodan; he suspected that Maodan must have said something about him and Ying'er. Maodan, who had no interest in driving a wedge between the brothers, was just being himself, a jester who enjoyed teasing people. Hantou acted uncharacteristically cheerful at the lunch table, playing up the Wuzi incident, as if he could care less about the spat he'd had with Maodan. But it had truly bothered him, though he hid his feelings. Lingguan was able to guess the reason behind the spat, which in turn unsettled him and put him in a bad mood.

When lunch was over, Laoshun sent Mengzi to borrow some money while Lingguan and Ying'er were sent by their mother out into the field to break dirt clods. "I'm no donkey," Lingguan shot back. "Just what do you think you are?" His father said, "You'd better accept your lot in life." In no mood to argue with his father, Lingguan walked out the door with a hammer.

The afternoon sun on this early spring day was a fireball, bombarding Lingguan with so many bright rays his head was buzzing, while the world around him seemed filled with noise. Gazing into the distance at the stripped fields and the shiny yellow sand ridges, he was overwhelmed by a profound sadness over the thought of spending the rest of his life like a donkey turning a millstone. His so-called ideals and aspirations had turned into mocking haloes on the screen of his memory, after Fate hurled him onto this field. Flinging his hammer aside, he lay down on the ground and shut his eyes, releasing his gloomy thoughts with a gush of tears.

"Go home to bed if that's what you want," Ying'er said. "Don't pretend you're here to work." He quickly dried his eyes.

His mood lightened considerably at the sight of her smiling face, for she had become the solace to his desolation. But his mood soured when he recalled the spat between Maodan and his brother. "Do you know what Maodan said to Hantou?"

"He can say what he wants. I don't want to know."

"He must have said something about us."

"Let him say what he wants. I don't care if that big mouth of his rots off from talking about other people." She smiled. "Why? Have you done something you shouldn't have?"

He sighed, unable to cast off his guilt feelings. Worse yet, it seemed that everyone in his family knew what was happening, but had decided to keep it a secret. He felt as if all eyes were on him.

"Actually, you're as upright as an idol, aren't you? So what are you afraid of?" She shot him a look. "You have nothing to fear if you've done nothing shameful. So I ask you, do you have something to hide?" She fixed a stern gaze on him.

Lingguan sighed again.

"Tell me. You're a grown man, don't cower like a turtle."

With his arms wrapped around his head, he crouched down.

"Quit loafing. Look at you, acting like a shameless hooligan. Why don't you just say, 'Go ahead, kill me, I don't care.'"

Her comment was so outrageous he nearly laughed despite his gloomy mood. "Spare me, won't you?"

"What did I do? Trap you, beat you, curse you, what? Come on, tell me."

"Aiyo! Aunty dear. You're usually so quiet that no one could guess that you have such a sharp tongue. Now you're showing your true colors. Have you seen a movie called Painted Skin? A demon turns into a beautiful woman by putting on human skin."

"Is that right? That's me, I guess. So you think I might be a beautiful woman."

"Not might be, but are beautiful. Just think. How can you not be beautiful with a painted mask?"

Her smile quickly turned into a frown. "That's really what you think, is it? You really believe I'm just a mask, don't you? What you're saying is that I wear one to be a real woman. You consider me a flighty, immoral woman, don't you?" Her voice grew fainter with each question, until she could barely finish. "No wonder—" She was nearly crying.

Lingguan lost his composure as he realized that, like him, she would feel guilty no matter how she seemed on the surface. The last thing she wanted was to be a loose woman in people's eyes. Like him, she was carrying a heavy emotional burden.

"Look at you. I was joking, but you took it so seriously." He tried to sound lighthearted. "Don't be like that. You said I was an upright idol, but then you took my joke seriously. How am I going to talk to you in the future, dear Aunty?"

"The future—will there really be a future?" she said softly, but with the hint of a smile. "You do think I'm that kind of woman, don't you? Am I really? No wonder—"

"Come on, no one is saying that about you. You are smart, sensible, and pure, perfection personified. Does that work for you?" he said in jest.

"You're mocking me again." She blushed. "You're making fun of me with those words; you're actually saying I'm not kind, smart, sensible, or pure. And you're right. I shouldn't have debased myself for you. Men are all the same; only what they can't have is good enough for them."

He didn't know how to respond.

"So I'll be smart, kind, sensible, and pure as long as I spend the rest of my life with a block of wood. Is that what you think?" She was choking on tears.

With panicky eyes, he looked around and saw someone working in a distant field. All he could do was pace like a caged animal.

"Don't pretend to be so nice, trying to make me feel better." She dried her tears. "I know I'm nothing in your eyes, worse than an insect. I know you're a real gentleman and that you're in love with Yue'er. I'm not surprised. She's a swan and I'm a hen; she's a magical herb and I'm a common daisy. It's only natural, of course. You two have grown up together and were childhood sweethearts, while me, I'm just a lowly feather blown over by a whirlwind."

"Listen to you." He smiled unhappily. "What are you talking about? That's utter nonsense, totally groundless."

"Groundless? You think I didn't notice? No wonder—"

He was beset by a host of conflicting thoughts. He could tell she was in love with him, which should have pleased him, but it was so awkward. Now he was afraid, fearful that they would be stuck in a quagmire, unable to retreat. It could wind up as a terrible, embarrassing, exasperating mess. Her jealous words might as well have been an open declaration of her feelings for him, which made him even more discomfited.

"Actually, you can tell me everything on your mind. No need to be evasive. I know what you're thinking anyway. Go ahead, tell me." She gave him a sad look.

"What do you want me to say?"

"Whatever you want. It's your heart and your mouth."

"Enough already." He laughed. "I was just joking, don't take it so seriously. You're hopeless, you know."

She cast him another glance before drying her tears and smiling tensely. "You can say anything you want, painted mask or demon. I don't care. You can think of me however you like. I can't bore into your heart and fill it with my own thoughts. I have no say over what my hearts wants." She sighed and her eyes were moist again.

"Enough, that's enough already," he said. "Look at you. There you go again."

"Actually, there is a true heart in every woman, but it's hidden deep inside and rarely reveals itself. To possess the true heart is to have love. Haven't you seen in movies when couples have a lover's spat? They can't help themselves."

"Do you mean a woman's true heart is to make her lover unhappy?" He glanced at her. "Or wrongly accuse the person of something, or be emotionally unstable?"

"Hard to say." She smiled again. "Didn't I just say it's not up to me? If it were, then it wouldn't be a true heart. I was a big fan of Dream of the Red Chamber at school. I couldn't put it down. My parents wouldn't allow me to read it, so I held a flashlight under my blanket. Lin Daiyu is always pouting; that's the true heart of a woman, while her rival, Xue Baochai, doesn't have one."

"That's strange. My head hurts each time I open that novel, but you actually enjoyed it. I don't get it."

"That's because you weren't born with the intelligence to appreciate it. A bucket made of willow is too heavy to be picked up with a pine wood pole. You have a block of gnarled elm for a brain." She smiled.

"I'd rather have a block of gnarled elm for a brain. It's simpler that way. Life is tiring enough as it is, and would be impossibly tiring if your moodiness and feelings had to be considered. We're just life forms that last a few decades, so why not take the easy route?"

"But that's precisely why we must take life seriously. Otherwise, you'd live those decades in vain and waste a whole lifetime."

"You have a point there."

She fell silent and, with a squint, gazed into the distance. A soft sigh escaped from between her lips. Aware of what was on her mind, he wanted to say something to make her feel better, but could not find the right words. He decided to ignore her.

Lingguan hammered at the dirt silently. He was soon sweating. "Don't think too much. It's not good for you," he said when he saw she was still lost in thought.

"You don't have to think, of course, because you don't have a heart."

"Isn't it better not to have a heart? It saves a lot of trouble. What do you gain even if you think everything through? Love and affection are illusory and unreal."

"Is that really how you look at it?"

"Sure. But—I've read somewhere that love breeds worry and causes fear. Without love, there would be no irritation."

"That's true. I got through all the years easily without understanding much in the past, but now that I know what's going on, every day seems as long as a year. You're right, I should stop thinking so much. I should just take life one day at a time."

"Yes. It's meaningless to overthink everything."

"To you, of course. It's no longer meaningless when you get what you want; it's only meaningful when you can look but can't touch." With a stomp of her foot, she went back to work.

"There you go again. It was you who brought this up, and now you're upset with my response."

"Did you mean what you said?"

"Did you? Have you been joking all along?"

"Of course." She laughed. "I was just testing you. What's called drawing a snake out of its hole."

"You're the snake. A snake beauty." Lingguan was reminded of their argument over painted masks. Seemingly in high spirits, she began to sing:

The dark stone ridge, the sound of an ax,
With my feet on a peony tree
A longing not on my mind,
But in my bones.

A black cat perches on a wall
I become a dog guarding the door
My paws hook onto the wall's edge,
I become your hands, Elder Brother.

A suspended bridge made of rotting wood
I become the road people walk on
I become a gold mountain for you to lean on
How could you be a melting mound of snow?

5

Lingguan went into town with his brother the next day. He took Hantou to a district hospital, where they saw an elderly doctor who shook his head after touching Hantou's ribcage. He could offer nothing concrete when Lingguan pressed him.

"Please don't hold back," Hantou said to the doctor. "At worst it's cancer. It's no big deal even so. You can die at eighty or at age one. At least I've lived."

"I like your positive attitude." The doctor smiled. "But it may not be as bad as you think. It's hard to say actually until you get an ultrasound."

"How much would that cost?"

"Not too much. Under fifty."

"Aiyo! It's gone up again," Hantou exclaimed.

"How much have you spent so far?" The doctor asked.

"A scary sum. Several hundred, at least."

"Has it worked?"

"I felt better when I wasn't taking the medicine." Hantou fumed. "Now, after all that, I've got a lump inside me."

"Taking medicine without determining the cause doesn't work," the doctor said. "You'd have been fine by now if you'd had an ultrasound."

Regretting not getting an examination earlier, Hantou fell silent and went to pay.

"Who is he?" The doctor asked Lingguan.

"My older brother."

"His illness could be serious." The doctor looked squarely into Lingguan's eyes.

"What does he have anyway?" Lingguan was frightened.

"There are three possibilities. One, liver cancer, two, cirrhosis of the liver, and three, liver parasites. Has he ever been out on a grassland?"

"No."

"Well, that could mean trouble. Parasites would be best, since that can be taken care of with surgery. But if it's something else, then it could be really bad. Is he a big drinker?"

"He doesn't drink."

"Maybe it's nothing, then." Lingguan's ashen face spurred the doctor into adopting a comforting tone. "Go get an ultrasound. We'll know what it is once we have the image."

"It could be parasites," the doctor reported after studying the ultrasound image. "A lot of people have the same problem from eating infected pork." He touched Hantou's rib area again and continued in a firmer tone, "It has to be that. The lump would not be so regular and smooth if it were cancer. Besides, you're so young and you don't drink, it shouldn't be cancer."

Lingguan's mind was finally put at ease, and Hantou smiled.

"You were right. I should have had an ultrasound earlier and gotten a prescription to get rid of the parasites. That would have saved lot of money, as well as pain and suffering."

The doctor and his nurse laughed at Hantou's words.

"It's not as easy that easy," the doctor said. "You think you can get rid of parasites with some pills?"

"Then what should I do?"

"DDT." The doctor said, looking serious. "Kill the host to eliminate the parasites."

"So you try to save the host after the parasites are dead?" Hantou gasped.

"What's the point of that? We just bury the body."

"I thought you were serious." Hantou laughed when he realized that the doctor was pulling his leg. "I believed every word you said."

The doctor patted him on the shoulder and said, "No one has

invented medicine to get rid of liver parasites. You need surgery."

"Don't try to scare me." Hantou blanched. "I believe everything you say."

"I'm telling you the truth. Think about it. The parasites are in your liver, so how do we get them out without surgery?"

"Then—how much—how much will that cost?" Hantou asked with trembling lips.

"Three to four thousand, I think. That should do it."

"What!" Hantou cried out in shock. "Why must you keep scaring me? How much do you think I'd fetch if I sold myself?"

"This isn't a business deal." The doctor smiled. "That's my estimate. It may not be that much or maybe more, if you need blood."

"Let's go." Ashen-faced, Hantou turned to his brother. "Let's get out of here. This is a terrible place. I feel like I'm dreaming, and I'll lose my mind if I stay a minute longer."

"Is there something he can take for now?" Lingguan asked.

"No need. Medicine won't work for this condition."

Lingguan led a dazed Hantou out of the hospital.

"I'm done for," Hantou muttered once they were outside.

"What are you talking about? It's not that serious. I was scared at first. Not even the gods can help you if it's cancer, so you're lucky to have parasites."

"I'd rather have cancer and just die. But now—think about it—so much money. Where are we going to get it?"

"Don't worry so much. You didn't try to get this, did you? We'll spend however much we have to, so stop worrying. It's pointless and won't bring in any money."

Hantou stopped to rest against a roadside railing; with a miserable look on his face, he remained silent for some time before finally saying,

"I'd rather get hit by a car and end it all, so Mother and Father won't have to worry about me. Death is better than this."

"How can you talk like that? Do you think they'd breathe a sigh of relief once you were dead? It hasn't been easy to see you grow into an adult, and you haven't started paying them back yet, so no more of that ridiculous talk."

"How can I go home and face them? What bad luck to have a worthless son like me."

"Come on. Stop with the nonsense, will you? It doesn't do any good."

Hantou sat there silently, looking wretched.

"It could have been worse; at least it's curable. If not, we'd just be throwing our money away. What could be worse than giving up both, your life and our money? Look at people who are paralyzed; they're half alive and yet they keep going. Put yourself in their place. At least what you have isn't that bad.

"Life or death, it doesn't bother me," Hantou said with a sigh. "What worries me is the money. Three to four thousand! Mother and Father will be sick when they hear that."

"They're not like you, so easily scared." Lingguan smiled again. "They've been through a lot. Back in 1960, many, many people died, but they made it through. So this isn't going to scare them."

Lingguan tried his best, but could not talk Hantou out of his gloom, "My god, three to four thousand!" he kept saying."

6

Their father said nothing as he listened to Lingguan's account; their mother wore a pained expression. Hantou looked at his father and then at his mother before lowering his head, as if he'd done a shameful thing.

"He'll be fine after the surgery," Lingguan stressed. "It's not a major operation, so he'll be fine."

Laoshun was puffing furiously, trying hard to keep the sound down. "We don't really mind spending the money," his wife made clear." As long as we're around there'll be money."

Her strained effort to show she was taking it well told Lingguan that she did mind spending the money. Hantou, who seemed to sense the same implication, dropped his head even lower. "It's not a big problem," Lingguan maintained. Just liver parasites. They can be removed with a scalpel."

"It's a terrible disease." Laoshun blew out a smoke ring. "I've heard they'll come back if they're not completely removed."

"That means it's really serious!" Their mother cried out in alarm.

"Why wouldn't they remove it completely? Something like that—as long as there's no puncture—" Lingguan tried to assure her.

"Forget it. No surgerty for me." Hantou finally spoke up after hemming and hawking, "Worst case, I die. I'm not afraid."

"Would you stop saying things like that, my dear ancestor?" Their mother said. "Do you think it was easy to raise you to adulthood?"

His face reddening, Hantou sputtered, "If they don't do a clean job—it would be worse than death."

"Why wouldn't they do a clean job?" Lingguan asked, raising his voice. "It's not major surgery. They can even work on human brains now, so your—" Hantou lowered his head again with no objection.

"We'll do what we have to, even if it costs us everything we have," Laoshun said. "Heaven has it planned out for you, so you must go through with it. You can't fight it."

"Whatever we do can't get us much," their mother said. "I can feel the fear eating me up inside just thinking about it."

"You can die from a burst bladder, but no one has ever died from frost."

His wife sighed, the sound prompting Hantou to raise his head nervously. He looked down again after a quick glance. The house was quiet, except for their father's smoking.

Mengzi walked in, looking lively, but froze at the pall in the room. He nudged Lingguan. "Is it cancer?" His voice wasn't low enough to escape the others' ears. Color drained from their mother's face, but she could only point at her second son, unable to utter a word.

"Nothing but farts come out of that mouth of yours," Laoshun growled.

"I was just asking. What did I do? I wouldn't have bothered to ask if it had been anyone else."

"Shut your trap." Lingguan shoved him away. "Can't you find a better way to ask? It's liver parasites—there are parasites in his liver."

"Is it curable?"

"Of course, it is. Surgery will do the job."

"Then why are you all looking like someone just died? I thought it was—well, something serious. Just go ahead with the surgery and everything will be fine."

"That's easy for you to say. It'll cost three or four thousand yuan," their mother said.

"Three or four thousand? What's the problem? There are always ways to get money while we're around." Mengzi said.

"I know what you're like," his father said. "You talk big but accomplish nothing. So be real and tell us the truth. How much can you scrounge up?"

"Don't push me, all right? Tell me how much you need, and I'll get it."

"Good." Laoshun smiled. "You sound like you know something. Here's what I think. We'll see how much we can get by selling off some grain, and you'll find a way to borrow enough to make up the difference. Can you get at least five hundred? Don't worry, I'll pay it back in one year, two at the most. We can pay it back with the next harvest. Will that work?"

"Sure, no problem." Mengzi said casually.

"Two or three years—" Their mother breathed a sigh. "Even if we could pay it back in two or three years, what about Mengzi and Lingguan's marriages?" Laoshun's face fell at her comment, but Mengzi said, "I'll take what comes my way. At worst, I'll be a bachelor my whole life. Like they say, tie the kitchen god to my legs and I can eat wherever I am. Find Lingguan a wife if he wants one. That should do it."

"No, not me either. What's the point of getting married the way things are now?" Lingguan offered with a smile.

"See? Neither of us wants to get married, so there's nothing for you two to worry about." Mengzi smiled to match his brother.

Hantou wept. He tried to subdue it, but it still came out like a lowing cow, effectively shutting up everyone in the room.

"Does it hurt?" his mother asked urgently. "Go get some pain pills, Lingguan. He can take three."

Hantou was nearly bawling now, frightening their mother so much she circled the room. Finally she squatted down and blew at his ribs, as if the spot had been burned.

"I'm useless," Hantou sobbed. "I'd rather die than—death is better."

"Stop the nonsense." Their mother was about to break down. "Watch what you say. You can eat what you want, but be careful with words. Did we say anything bad?"

Lingguan felt his nose ache. He heaved a sigh.

"I thought you were crying because it hurt too much," Mengzi said. "You scared me. What's so good about dying? A grown man like you shouldn't be talking about death. And stop crying all the time. Are you a man or what? It's disgusting."

"Get out of here," Laoshun roared at his second son. "What can you do besides talk?"

Mengzi shrugged his shoulders. With a wink to Lingguan, he whispered, "I can borrow the money."

"We didn't say anything, and you didn't get sick on purpose." Laoshun said to his first son. "Now that you're not well, we'll have it taken care of. That's all."

Hantou dried his tears silently and stared at the floor. From time to time, he choked up audibly.

7

Ying'er was awakened by Hantou's sobbing later that night. It was pitch black, and his weeping fell on her like a darkness that was blacker than the night.

"Does it hurt a lot?" She nudged him, and he stopped crying. The ensuing silence was finally broken when he asked her, "Why are you still awake?"

"I just woke up. Does it hurt a lot? I'll get your pills."

"No, it doesn't hurt." He sighed. "I just feel terrible. I'm worthless and I'd rather die."

"Don't say that. Sickness is beyond our control."

"Three or four thousand yuan. That's half of what it would take to get Mengzi a wife. I really feel like dying when I think about that."

"Please don't say that."

"It's true. And if something happens to me, make sure you have plans."

"Enough of that already." She sounded upset. "Go to sleep."

"I mean it. The road ahead is dark. If I—you should have plans."

"I'm really getting angry. Why are you saying these things?"

"I feel—I'm not good enough for you. I have a block of gnarled elm for a brain. I'm not clever and quick like—like the others. You could have done better."

"Have I ever said anything?"

"What I meant was—" He paused and then started up again. "In case I—if you—leave home—be sure—to pay back—my medical expenses—several thousand—"

Ying'er angrily tossed the blanket to the side and said, "Are you quite finished?"

"No more. I won't say any more. I feel my head is all messed up. I've wanted to say, wanted to tell you this, but of course I shouldn't."

"You're a grown man, but your heart is smaller than sparrow's. A minor illness, and you act like the sky is falling. And you say you want to die. We eat the five grains, so naturally we get sick. We take whatever illness comes our way. But not you, you're always talking about death. You have to be stronger than that."

"I'm just worried about the money, with our tight money situation."

"As long as we're around there's a way to get money. When you're cured, the two of us will do what we have to do to pay it back, even if we have to turn ourselves into beasts of burden," Ying'er said. But

Hantou did not respond.

Their mother sent Ying'er home after breakfast the next morning, telling her to invite her parents over to talk about Hantou's hospitalization. The surgery was no small matter, and etiquette required that the in-laws to be notified. To be sure, their mother was also hoping for some help from them. Hantou was, after all, their son-in-law, a half son, and they ought to offer some assistance.

Ying'er heard what had happened to Yindi the moment she entered her parents' village.

She fell as if the sky had fallen on her.

8

Laoshun and his wife discussed selling the grain and raising money after Ying'er left. He wanted to keep enough to last the family for a year and sell the rest, which he estimated could fetch one to two thousand. Her idea was to start getting loans first and selling just enough grain to make up the difference.

"The price is so low now we'd lose a lot if we sold it all. Besides, we haven't seen a drop of rain for a while," she said.

Deep down he agreed with her, but he still had to say, "Who's going to lend us money? These days, people treasure those colorful bits of paper like their own eyeballs."

"You're always bragging about this and that, but what have you got to show for it?" he demanded from Mengzi. "Go on, go out and get some loans. You, too, Lingguan. Go see your gang and borrow however much they can lend you. Gather enough crumbs of dough and you can make a big pancake. We'll keep the little grain we have if we can help it. It'd be too late to regret the decision if we have a drought next year."

After Mengzi and Lingguan left, Laoshun went to see Meng Eight. "Heaven is blind," he said upon hearing the news.

"That's true. A rope breaks at the weakest part."

"I don't have much. I just sold two fox pelts, but I already spent some of the money. I have about four hundred left. Here, take it. The poor have to help each other. Just take it and forget about considering it a loan."

"Next year's harvest—" Laoshun said, but Meng cut him off, "I won't have any of that. It's not my money anyway; it belongs to the desert, and I just happened to be there to pick it up. Anyone can have it. I'll go get some more when I run out. What's there to fear when we have a big bank like that?"

Laoshun reminded himself to give Meng his fur coat for a winter hunt.

He stopped by the team leader's house. Big Head was out. Huilanzi yelped when she heard him. "We have some money, but it's a CD in the bank, and we can't withdraw any yet." Laoshun told her it was all right and walked out. After visiting a few families, all of which offered a small amount, he came home with a little under seven hundred.

Hantou was squatting by wheat stacked at the gate, looking dejected, head down. Laoshun knew his son was feeling wretched, but he didn't want to be too direct. "Go to bed if you're tired." Hantou dried his eyes with his sleeve and tried to smile. That looked worse than when he was crying. Laoshun's heart ached as he walked out through the gate.

Lingguan was able to scrounge up two hundred from old schoolmates, but Mengzi's trip was a bust. From Mengzi's dispirited look, Lingguan knew his brother had returned empty-handed. He laughed. Mengzi knew why and laughed with him.

"Two hundred is better than nothing." Their father took the money from Lingguan and held his hand out to Mengzi. He knew why his son was looking sheepish, but he thought he should at least have gotten something, if not the five hundred he'd expected.

"Baigou lost everything he had."

"Baigou, Baigou. You're always talking about Baigou. What about your other good buddies?"

"Beizhu needs the money to pay the family planning fine."

"You're better than anyone with your boast and bravado, but you're damned worthless when it comes to important matters." Laoshun said with a sneer.

Mengzi slinked out of the door. Lingguan caught with him. "Have you asked Shuangfu's wife?"

Mengzi slapped his forehead. "You're right. Why didn't I think of her?"

"She's always using you, so now she ought help you out when you need her."

"Get out of here. There's nothing going on between us."

"Forget it, then." Lingguan winked at his brother.

"That doesn't mean I can't ask her." Mengzi ran off.

He soon returned with a swagger and wordlessly tossed down a stack of new bills. Laoshun smiled after one look at his son. "So, you weren't just bragging."

"I'm damned worthless when it comes to important matters," Mengzi said with feigned indifference. Their father laughed dryly, but then scowled.

"Was I wrong? You buckle under pressure, that's all."

Mengzi smiled; so did his father.

Big Head Sun, the team leader, showed up after lunch with a hundred yuan. Saying he was unhappy with what his wife had said, he added that there were other ways to get money, even if theirs was in a CD. "Let me know if you're still short. It's to save a life, so we must do everything we can."

Laoshun counted the money and it came up to over fifteen hundred, a lot less than the three or four thousand estimated by the doctor.

9

Two days later, Ying'er returned with her father, whom everyone called "Big Talk," and two hundred yuan. He was always setting his eyes on big business deals, but never made enough to make his effort worthwhile, squandering the little money his wife managed to earn from raising pigs and selling beans in the meantime. Her mother raged against him, but he merely put on a show of magnanimity, and continued his pursuit of big business deals.

Ying'er, whose eyes were swollen from crying over her beloved niece, begged her father not to mention the little girl. Afraid that her parents-in-law would be devastated, she wanted to wait until Hantou was better. Big Talk promised and tried to make Laoshun feel better.

"It's no big deal, dear in-law. Everyone gets into a jam once in a while, and we all have to find a way out."

"I'm not too worried. People get sick. We eat five grains and get a hundred different illnesses. It's my wife; she frets all day long, sadness written all over her face."

"Women are like that," Big Talk said. "A child to them is a piece of their own flesh, and they can't help but dote on them. In fact, everyone loves their children, but that's not going to solve any problems. Wouldn't it be great if moan and groan could sigh an illness away? But it can't, so what's the point of sighing?"

"You're right," Hantou's mother said. "I don't want to sigh, but I can't help it. My mind is crowded with crazy thoughts, and I sense nothing but doom and gloom. Worries grip my heart and tie it up in knots. Of course I can't be like you; you men are so carefree, never worrying about the next meal as long as your bellies are full now."

"It's better to be carefree. How else can you survive in times like these? You could die of worrying." Big Talk handed the money to Laoshun. "It's not much, so don't laugh. Every family is strapped for cash. We want to help and this is the best we can do. We should have tried to come up with more, but we have problems of our own—"

"What do you mean, laugh? Everyone has to tighten their belts, but I thought your family decided to hold out and not pay the fine," Laoshun's wife said.

"It's something else—" He changed the subject when he heard Ying'er cough. "I have a big business deal on the way. If it works out, a few thousand yuan won't be a problem."

Laoshun's wife knew he was all talk, that nothing of his ever materialized, but she had to go along. "You have talent, I have to say that. What kind of deal is it?"

"Nickel. Someone wants to buy three hundred tons of nickel."

"But where do you get it?" Laoshun asked as he puffed on his pipe.

"I know someone in Jinchang in charge of nickel supplies. When I saw him recently, he promised to let me have some of it. If this works out, I can easily rake in several hundred thousand. Three or four thousand will be no big deal then." Big Talk lowered his voice and asked Laoshun, "Would you like to buy some uranium?"

"No need," Laoshun said, thinking he heard him says something about oil. "We grow our own seeds to make cooking oil."

"It's not cooking oil. Uranium." Big Talk laughed. "For making an

A-Bomb, it's from Russia. A kilo cost several hundred thousand."

Laoshun studied his in-law for a while before realizing the man wasn't joking, so he said, "That's for the government to deal with. We private citizens have no use for that."

"I didn't think so either."

It took Laoshun all his willpower to keep from laughing out loud. His in-law made him want to laugh despite himself, for each time they met, the man was talking up some scheme. Once it was steel, and then antiques. All big business deals, of course. Now it was nickel and uranium, both with the potential of making eye-popping profits. Laoshun cradled his pipe and puffed away while his in-law continued blowing smoke.

Big Talk finally returned to the matter at hand. "Liver parasites aren't serious. Not life threatening, anyway."

"That's true. But money is still hard to come by. We borrowed some to go with what we had, but we're still short."

"How much did the doctor say?" Big Talk asked.

"Three to four thousand."

"How much have you got now?"

"A little over two thousand."

"That's good enough for the time being. I know how it works. You don't have to pay at all at once. You give them five hundred first and pay more when that's used up. With what you have now, you can go ahead with the surgery while trying to come up with more in the meantime. The treatment must not be delayed."

"Really? We don't have to pay the whole amount at one time?" Laoshun was dubious.

"Trust me. I did that last time when one of my buddies was hospitalized."

"We don't have to worry, if that's the case." Laoshun was relieved. "We'll send him to the hospital now and think of something later. As a last resort, we still have the grain."

Mengzi brought his maternal uncle over an hour later to discuss the details of Hantou's hospitalization.

Chapter Sixteen

1

The drought was getting worse.

The sun turned violently harsh, emitting faintly visible rays of white light to scorch the ocean of sand, wilt the wheat seedlings, and bake exposed skin till it was a reddish black. Absorbing all the sunlight, the sand ocean was a deeper yellow than ever and now a backdrop highlighting an azure sky that looked more like a piece of silk ablaze in blue flames that licked indiscriminately at everything on the ground.

It was the time for wheat seedlings to sprout.

Heaven was blind.

Laoshun complained that Heaven was blind, but complain was all he could do. Heaven was blind. They could reap a decent harvest if it spared a bit of rain; there would be some consolation, even though the little amount of income would go directly to pay taxes and fees. Who wouldn't experience contentment at the sight of storage bins bursting at the seams? To be sure, it would not take long for them to empty out again, but they would still supply momentary satisfaction, like sweet dreams. Dreams are not real, of course, but what does remain real forever anyway? Mountains of gold and silver, power to rule the world, children, houses, land and everything else turns to nothing when one closes one's eyes for the last time. Being alive is just having a long dream and what one encounters in life are short dreams, such as the annual harvest. Better to have dreams than not to have them, and good dreams are always preferable to bad ones. Laoshun had heard a Taoist priest chant the Sutra to Guide the Dead often enough to understand all this.

Naturally Heaven deserved to be cursed.

Looking at the wheat seedlings drooping under the merciless sun, Laoshun's heart convulsed over his distress. He had been hoping to pay all their debts with what would rise out of the field. Blind Heaven was killing them. He looked up into the sky and sighed before saying to Beizhu, who was pulling up wild oat stalks.

"What's the point? They're turning into weeds."

"We have to plant crops next year, don't we? These wild oats are strange. See how the wheat seedlings are drying up in the sun, but these still look so full of life."

"Of course. They're like us humans. The worst no-good rascals thrive better than anyone else. Heaven has gone stupid. The Yellow River ran dry just when we needed to water our fields. Hei—Heaven meant to kill us and there's nothing we can do about it."

"When is Hantou having his surgery?" Meng Eight asked Laoshun.

"He's already in the hospital, but the doctors say they need to observe him for a while, so we don't know when he'll have it. The surgeons will drag it out until who knows when if we don't hand them something under the table. At least we have Lingguan's old classmate—enough of that. Let's not talk about him."

"It's not that serious, so have Lingguan stay with him," Meng said, as he looked up into the sky before turning his gaze to the wheat seedlings. "What are you doing, Beizhu? Have you forgotten what I said a couple of years ago? I said it's terrible the way people waste food, and that Heaven would punish us. Now see what's happening? I heard that the Yellow River dried up. Who's ever heard of that happening before?"

"You're right," Beizhu said. "That's unimaginable."

"Even if the Yellow River wasn't dry and we had electricity, that doesn't mean you should waste food. When you go into the city, the sewers are a place for noodles, steamed buns, pork, anything you can think of. That really saddens me. In ancient times white flour rained down from the heavens, and double tassels grew on each wheat stalk. People had so much to eat they wiped their asses with steamed buns. Heaven was so enraged it turned the flour into snow and removed one of the tassels. The people were punished for their sins. Heaven can commit sins, but when we commit evil deeds, we're doomed. There's nothing you can do if Heaven wants you dead. Heaven can find ways to punish us, even if we have electricity and water. Once back in the Republican Era, I forgot which year it was, we had an unusually abundant harvest. One day a dark cloud flew over and landed on the wheat fields. Aiya, it was a swarm of locusts, blanketing the field and blotting out the sky, as they crunched away until, in no time, there was nothing left to harvest. You see, Heaven can always find a way if it wants you to perish. In 1960, we ate anything we could find, anything but shit. We couldn't have eaten that even if we'd wanted to. Where do you find shit when people have nothing to eat? But now, people waste food whenever there's a good harvest. Heaven would surely be blind if it didn't mete out some punishment. Those who take good care of their clothes always have something to wear, and those who cherish food never go hungry. If you don't, you can't even eat shit, let alone grain."

"You're right," Laoshun said. "Remember 1958? The wheat rotted in the fields. So naturally we starved in 1960."

"We brought all this on ourselves," Meng said. "Things are better now, actually. Wait a few years and see what happens next. We're just experiencing a shortage of electricity, but we still have water. In a few years, even the water will run dry. You don't believe me? Take a look at the well they're drilling. Back in the old days, water gushed out when we drilled. Now the water level has fallen a hundred meters. Who knows if it will turn into a dry hole in a few years? No one can say."

"Ai!" Beizhu cried out. "Stop saying things like that, Old Master Meng. You're scaring me. I'm happy to muddle through life, because the more I know, the worse I feel. One day lived is another day earned. We drink when we have liquor and don't worry if tomorrow we have nothing but water. The road ahead is dark. I don't know when my time will come, so why trouble myself with all these thoughts?"

"A man has to take the long view." Meng snorted as he glared at the young man. "It's women who care only about what's in front of them."

"What's the use of taking the long view?" Beizhu retorted. "With the ways things are, we have trouble making it through each day, so I don't need to look into the future. Look around you. All these lizards and bedbugs are sucking us dry. Why take the long view? And now even Heaven's against us. Tell me, what's the point of living? What's the use of a long view? We've gotten away with something if our throats aren't under the knife. What long view?" Beizhu finished with a long sigh.

With a wooden look, Meng sighed and said, "You've got a point. As you say, one day lived is another day earned. We'll start to worry when we can't make it through the day." He tugged on a few blades of wheat grass, making a brittle rustling noise.

2

Suddenly they heard an angry exchange; Huaquiu's mother was having another fight with Baldy Wang's wife. Laoshun thought it must have something to do with the ridges between their fields, a long-standing dispute. One accused the other of over-planting, while the other claimed the ridges had been secretly trimmed to gain an inch of land; both claimed innocence, and yet a foot-wide ridge had been narrowed to the point that they had trouble walking it to water their crops. So they fought all the time. Laoshun had no interest in mediating, but Meng walked over to them.

"What's going on? What are you doing? Get some rest if you have nothing to do, and stop arguing."

Laoshun turned to head back. He'd been irritated for days. The land had to produce enough for all the things he needed, but Heaven refused to stick its leg in your trousers, so naturally he was in a bad mood. The crops were hopeless. The seedlings would turn into dry weeds in a few days, he thought, but at least they were the cows' favorite.

The women continued to argue, like dogs that look tame when they're not chained, but with a leash around their necks, they snarl and puff themselves up. Meng's intervention was the chain; now they looked like rabid dogs, flinging ugly words at each other, holding nothing back. Laoshun frowned. The world's gone mad, he said to himself, truly mad. Things are different now. Heaven has gone mad and so have the people. A few years back, they had lived in peace, even though they'd been poor. Now it was hopeless. Those in power had turned into greedy ants and crazy lice, all intent upon sucking the peasants' blood; those without power were poisonous spiders confined in a bottle where they bit and stung each other, fighting over something as trivial as oat bran. It was pointless.

Were we affected by Heaven's madness, or did Heaven turn crazy because of us? He had no idea; maybe both. Laoshun recalled lines sung by the blind storyteller, "There's good weather for the crops when the country's on the right path; there are filial sons and fine grandsons when a family is on the right path." Obviously, wind and rain were connected to the people; Heaven turned wicked after the people did, and the people's discontent brought on Heaven' wrath. What the ancients said made sense. People were so wicked, so evil that, with the many unreasonable things happening, it's no wonder Heaven has shed some of its reason.

Leaving the field, he got on a dirt path and was immediately assailed by a burnt smell, now that the green had left the seedlings. The drought had seeped into the air and into the blood. In fact, Laoshun could feel himself drying up inside; he was agitated and irritable, like a powder keg that a tiny spark could set off.

"Laoshun!" Handless Wei rode over on his donkey and shouted amid the clip-clop of his ride. "Only one acre. Have you heard?"

"What do you mean, one acre?"

"We're allowed to water only one acre to save enough for food. There's not much water left in the reservoir, so each family can irrigate a single acre. We'll repeat that after this round if there's water left; if not, that's the end of it."

"Is Big Head here?"

"Yes. He's called a meeting for all men. Well, we'll water one acre and tie our throats shut."

"One acre? That won't give us enough grain to fill the gaps between our teeth."

"You can drink milk," Wei said with a laugh.

"What do you mean?"

"Your daughter-in-law's breast milk." Wei squeezed the donkey's sides with his knees and the animal took off running.

"You can drink your donkey's milk," Laoshun shouted after him.

Laoshun shook his head and smiled unhappily. Why do these people enjoy joking about daughters-in-law so much? When a group of old men get together, they joke about each other and their daughters-in-law, as if they had nothing better to do in their dotage than fantasize about their sons' wives. He had no idea if anyone he knew had done that, but not him; he never would. For one thing, his daughter-in-law was like a daughter to him. Besides, he was too tired to think about things like that. His mind was always crammed full, and he was busy just running around. When his heart was taken over by mundane matters, there was no room for that stuff. Laoshun remained hopeful, even though he knew that there wasn't enough water in the reservoir to irrigate much land. One acre watered meant one acre of crops saved, no matter what; they could stir-fry the wheat if they didn't have enough to make steamed rolls. There's nothing else to do, he said to himself. Nothing when facing miserly Heaven.

3

Big Head Sun's house was packed with village men, all clamoring and shouting as if they were having an argument. Sun's voice rose above the others:

"Go talk to them if you think you're better than me. I can't do it."

"Hey, we've always been at the end of the water line," Baigou shouted back. "I'm not going to let that happen again. I'll fight if necessary. With so little water, one stole a little here, another took some extra there, and by the time it reached us we got less than a trickle of piss. How are we supposed to water our field with that?"

"He's right," Baldy Wang echoed. "We pay forty yuan to water an acre of land. So why do other villages get the water ahead of us?"

The other men shouted their agreement; the pot was boiling over.

"Go talk to the people at the Water Management Bureau if you want," Big Head shot back. "Why yell at me? I'll tell you the truth. I'm tried of wearing this hat. Whoever wants it can have my job. I don't want to be your team leader anymore."

"You can't quit at a time like this," Beizhu said.

"He's right," Maodan agreed. "A midwife can't run off the moment she sees the baby's head."

"It's easy for you to say," Big Head spat. "You think it's a cushy job, don't you? I'm always begging those people for this and that, but it never works. Things have changed, and reason doesn't work any more. Do you know what works? The people in Nangou send up chickens, goats, even money to the people in charge. What have we given? And you people complain whenever I need to collect a bit of money now and then. You're a bunch of skinflints who you want to be at the front of water line. You're like a widow dreaming of a dick."

"Hey!" Beizhu said. "Are you calling us widows? I don't believe those people at the Water Bureau have hearts of stone. They won't sit by and watch our crops become hay."

"You think only you have real crops, and everybody else is just raising weeds, don't you?" Big Head said with a sneer. "Or do you think only you need to eat, and the rest of us can live on the wind? When there's a line, some have to be in front and others at the rear. That's what they'll say if you argue with them. You can sue if you want."

"Right, we'll sue," Maodan yelled. "I don't believe we don't have a case."

"On what grounds?" Big Head said. "What have they done wrong? They didn't phone Heaven and ask it to send down less rain or suck up the water in the reservoir. What are you going to complain about?"

"He's right," Laoshun said. "We'll be at the end of the line, which will be all right if enough water is released. If we're not careful and provoke them, they may do something underhanded, and we'll be worse off. The drought is so bad the ditches are all cracked. Do you know how much water they soak up along the way? What can you say, even if we get less water?"

"There's something we can do, of course." Big Head said. " Spend the money. With a drought like this and without electricity, we have to pin our hopes on that little bit of water in the reservoir. If someone gets more, then someone else has to get less. It's obvious; you get the short end of the stick if you don't cough up the money."

"So we have to treat them to a feast again." Baldy Wang sighed.

"Yes," Big Head said. "And we have to do a good job of it. It makes a difference whether you treat them more or less often, earlier or later."

"He's right," Laoshun said. "As long as they go for it—so how much for each of us, ten, twenty cents?"

"Cents?" Big Head laughed. "Are you kidding? We're not talking about your sister-in-law, who'd favor you for a few cents. Eight hundred or a thousand still won't be enough."

Every one yelped at the amount, filling the room with the sound of air sucking between teeth.

"We might as well all out if we're going to do it," Big Head said. "We can't spend money and still wind up looking like cheapskates. We have to put up enough. So, five yuan per person for now. Wheat will do if you don't have the cash, but no money, no water. I have to spell it out for you now. You may not like the sound of it, but I have to say all this up front. Be frank with me if you have any issues; don't tell me everything is fine to my face and complain about me behind my back. I don't want any unfair accusations."

4

Laoshun walked out of Big Head's house with a heavy heart after the meeting. He ran into some old friends along the way, but was in no mood for conversation. He was oblivious to the loose soil, and soon his pants legs were covered in white dust. The air was thick with a burnt odor, which made his heart sink even further when he smelled it; there seemed to be a rock in his chest, making his breaths short and shallow.

Someone was screaming in a sad, plaintive way. Laoshun knew it was Wuzi.

Wuzi had gotten worse, pouncing on any woman in sight if he wasn't shackled. He would pull down her pants and bite through her lips.

Laoshun walked into Gimpy Five's house.

Wuzi's hands were a bloody mess from the metal chain around them, but he still looked solid and robust. There was a strange red glow on his face, giving him the air of a bull, which is exactly what he sounded like.

Gimpy Five was smoking in the shade under the eaves, seemingly unaffected by his son's howls. He moved over wordlessly when he saw Laoshun walk in. Laoshun crouched by the steps. "They're collecting money again," he said, but drew no response from Gimpy Five, who didn't take a puff of his pipe for a while, and when he did, no smoke came out, despite the hiss between his teeth.

"We're finished," Gimpy said after another a smokeless puff.

"You're right."

They fell silent, and Gimpy stopped smoking altogether. Wuzi howled and broke the silence, calling out the same thing.

"See that." Gimpy glanced at his own son. "He's hopeless."

"With what he has, maybe he'll be cured once he's married."

"Who would marry him?" Gimpy said woodenly. "Tell me. Who would send his daughter into this pit?"

Laoshun sighed.

Gimpy Five refilled his pipe and flicked on his lighter, but his hand shook so badly the flame flickered by the bowl of his pipe a moment before lighting the tobacco. He drew on his pipe quickly, and, through puffs of smoke, looked at his wife, who was busy in the kitchen. "We can't go on like this," he murmured.

"Come on, let's go find a quiet place to talk."

Gimpy Five got to his feet.

They walked out the gate into an open field by a sand hill, a dune conquered by plants and rendered immobile. It was overgrown with needle grass and Artemisia. Gimpy Five sat down on the sandy ground and said, "I've been thinking for a long time, but I can't bring myself to do anything about it. It's futile. No one dares come near our family. What a curse."

"Yes," Laoshun said, without understanding what his friend meant. Then a thought struck him: "What are you planning to do?"

"Think about it—what a—" Without looking at Laoshun, Gimpy stopped as he drew his pipe across the sand. Laoshun snatched the pipe away to rub the sand off.

Gimpy wore an impassive look as a breeze brushed his scalp, which seemed to have equal parts of hair, dirt, and bits of wheat stalks.

He's suffered enough over the years, Laoshun said to himself.

"I'll tell you straight." Gimpy raised his voice, a rare occurrence for him. "I can't keep that curse of a son around any longer. If I do, it will be—hei."

"What are you mean?" Laoshun was shocked by what he was thinking.

"What do I mean? It's hopeless, utterly hopeless. He's done enough harm to us, to everyone. Think about it. He's smashed people's windows, set haystacks on fire, chased after women. He's done everything. I won't be able to face the world if I don't do something about it."

"How?"

"Take care of him," Gimpy said with a squint.

"You're his father, you're not an animal. How could you think of something like that? That would be a huge disgrace to your ancestors. You're not digging up chicken droppings. You can't do that, not even think about it."

"What else can I do? Tell me, what else can I do? We've spent so much on his illness. What else is there? We have nothing to look forward to. It's his bad luck to have been born into this pit of poverty."

"But—he's your flesh and blood, no matter what. He's your only son, the only way to continue the family line."

"What family line?" Gimpy Five smiled bitterly. "That curse of a son has caused so much trouble in the village. I have to work and eat, so I can't guard him all day. Who knows what else he might do if he ran out when I wasn't paying attention? I heard that with the way he is now, he wouldn't be responsible even if he killed someone. What else can I do if—not—"

"You can't." Laoshun knitted his brows. "Stop those crazy thoughts, and let Heaven decide, all right?"

"Heaven? Hei-hei." Gimpy Five laughed dryly as murky tears streamed down his face. "What is Heaven? Tell me, what is it? I've spent my whole life invoking Heaven this and Heaven that, but I've yet to see it open its eyes. Does anyone really know if there's a Heaven? If there is, then why, why are we powerless people always the ones who suffer? Let Heaven decide, you say? What could it do anyway?"

Laoshun's heart ached at the sight of tears on his friend's face.

"And, and the people in the village suffer too. They've suffered enough, taking whatever they could and enduring what they couldn't. I'd be a man with no conscience if I let them suffer more at the hands of my crazy son." Gimpy Five paused. "I'd accept my punishment after I took care of him, go to jail, even take a bullet. I'd die with a clear conscience, unlike now, when I have to keep apologizing to people."

Laoshun filled Gimpy Five's pipe and puffed away with a frown. They remained motionless for a long time.

5

A dejected Laoshun sat on the edge of the *kang* when he got home; he felt a chill rising up his back when he recalled the conversation with Gimpy Five. Taking a life is a serious matter, he thought. He's running out of options, but still a human life is invaluable. Laoshun decided that he'd try to talk his friend around the next time he saw him. Let Heaven decide. Laoshun himself was losing faith in Heaven, but he had to tell Gimpy Five to leave it up to fate.

The urgent matter of money collection occupied him once he put thoughts of Gimpy Five aside. Based on Big Head's calculation, Laoshun's family had to pony up thirty yuan, which was no small amount. Who knew what other fees they'd have to pay after this. They could, not, however, sell the grain. In the midst of a drought, they would have no harvest without rain. So what else could he do? Their pigs weren't old enough. Then there was the big tree. Handless Wei had asked about it several times, but Laoshun was reluctant to sell it; he wanted to save it for himself. When you lived past the age of fifty, you had to be prepared for the inevitable end. He refused to accept the possibility that he wouldn't even have four boards to make a coffin after a lifetime of hardship. He simply couldn't sell the tree, good timber for coffin boards. Though it was only a poplar, in his eyes it was good wood. Laoshun had looked at coffins in the shop, and they were flimsy, small and devoid of respectability. He wanted to make one himself, with thick boards and a handsome look. After saving and scrimping on everything his whole life, he had no intention of skimping on this final matter. The tree stays, he told himself.

Someone was raising a stink nearby. He saw that it was his wife. This had been happening too often lately; something had gotten into her and turned her into a scold. He usually ignored her, considering women unworthy of his attention—he didn't think they knew much, that they had long hair but short vision. She was a woman after all; he let her prattle on, but wondered what he'd done to incur her wrath this time. Normally she had her reason to roar, such as his smelly feet or oversleeping.

"See what you've done? You can wash them this time." She was pointing at the mud on his pants.

"Oh, that. I thought it was something serious." He gave her a forgiving smile as he thumped his pants legs and sent dust flying.

"Go over to the door. Go over there. Don't get the furniture dusty." She frowned.

He noticed that she was glaring at him. Another storm was on its way, he was sure, so he quickly changed the subject, "The team is collecting money again."

"What?" That got her attention. "More money? Don't scare me like that."

"Why would I do that? It's tribute to the Water Tigers, the men in charge of water."

"What are we going to do?" Her face darkened. "Is this ever going to end? What do we do?" She couldn't stop muttering.

"We can't touch the grain; that's for sure. With this weather, we don't know if we have enough to live on next year."

She frowned and sighed She had no answers.

Mengzi returned a while later, complaining loudly before he was even in the house. "What's the world come to? Robbing people in broad daylight. It's extortion."

"Who?"

"Who else? He's built a house and hired a guard charging four yuan each time. Believe it or not, four yuan! Four crisp bills."

"Don't go through there."

"Don't go through there? They've dug up the old road, repair work, they said. So I had to take the new road in Wunan, the so-called superhighway. It took only three days for the road surface to start melting, and cars got stuck. What the hell kind of road is that? Guess what the sign says? 'Road Repairs Done with a Loan/To Be Paid off by Toll Charges.' How much did they collect last time? Nearly a hundred per car, and trucks paid by tonnage. Even the government cadres had their pay docked. Collective contribution to repair the road, they told us. Schoolteachers fumed every time road repair was mentioned. Where did the money go? How come they needed a loan this time? And why couldn't they have done a better job? The surface is cracking everywhere. It'd be a miracle if the money didn't wind up in the pockets of corrupt officials. Those monsters are like hornets that draw blood with each sting. And we're their camels, their victims. No, that's not right. They aren't hornets; they're bedbugs."

"Enough, already." Laoshun waved him off with a frown. "Would you stop your obnoxious prattle? They're born with stingers and you're born to be stung. What's the use of yelling and screaming like that? Just take good care of that mouth of yours and let them do what they want. Did Baigou give you any money?"

"What money? Everyone wants the same job, and three-wheelers are everywhere, like ants. I collected only a few bags of beans after three days and that cost me eight yuan—We haven't figured out to divide it up. He agreed to pay me ten yuan a day, but now I think it was just empty talk. It's clear to me he couldn't even afford the diesel fuel, so I can't ask him for anything."

"All right." Laoshun waved him off again with an angry look. "I asked a simple question and got a long-winded answer. Stop going with him if you can't make any money. Go pull oat sprouts in the field."

"All we're getting is hay in this sun. So what's the point?"

"What? What will you eat next year if they fall to the ground, the wind?"

"Why take it out on me?" Mengzi's face reddened, as he mumbled softly. "I've barely caught my breath after running around all day."

"For that you get credit? Tell me what you've done. You're a lazy ass who keeps stopping to pee in a field. You were afraid I'd send you to work if you stayed home, so you sneaked out. Now you want credit for whatever you did." Laoshun was getting hot under the collar; his spittle was flying.

"Are you done yet?" Laoshun's wife asked him. "The way you two go at each other people would think you were gamecocks in your previous lives. Save your energy and go out and work the field."

"Stop sticking your nose in," Laoshun berated his wife. "All these young masters of yours care about is food, not work. They're as tall as they're ever going to be, but all they have on their shoulders is a bowl with chaff, no brains. If people want to drink your blood, you have to give them at least a little, and stop always coming to your old man." He shot Mengzi an angry look.

"What do you mean?" Mengzi stiffed his neck, unwilling to concede. "Are you saying I did nothing? I wasn't out sightseeing on that three-wheeler. What else do you want me to do? With a foreman like that, I barely made enough to feed myself; a year of hard work and I've been unable to save a thing. So tell me, what else do you want me to do? Steal? Rob?"

Laoshun glared at his son, who glared back; feeling the anger building in his chest, Laoshun told himself it was pretty much over. "Ingrate," he cursed his son, wishing he could club him into submission. But he knew that Mengzi would snatch the club away and snap it in two. He was getting old and had lost his authority. The sadness of a fading hero sneaked up on him, but was overwhelmed by deep-seated gloom. He felt like bashing his head against the wall and spilling his brains. But all he managed was to pound his head with his fists, over and over, with so much force he saw stars.

6

Lingguan sensed that something was amiss the moment he returned from town and walked in the door. Father was scowling, so was Mengzi. He did not want to ask why, for he knew that could set off a fight; instead he signaled to his brother to come out with him. Before they were out the door, he heard his father shout,

"Where are you going? Go get your scoop and sell it."

"What are we selling?" Lingguan was confused.

"What else is there but those handfuls of monkey food?" Laoshun shouted back. "Nobody wants these dry bones of mine."

Lingguan dragged Mengzi over to a corner, where his brother fumed, "I'm his punching bag."

"So what?" Lingguan said. "How else can he vent, if not by taking things out on us? You can't blame him. With all our problems, it's enough to get on anyone's nerves. Are they collecting money again?"

"We just pay up when they collect. It's not my doing. Go scream at the people who want our money. Monks don't eat meat, but they beat a leather drum. He picks on me no matter what I do, but I'm not an alms bowl, and he can't bang on it whenever he wants."

"Be patient with him. Words can't hurt, so let him rant," Lingguan said.

"I don't mind it if he hits me. He can do that when he feels like it, but I can't stand how he sets off like that. It makes my head hurt when a grown man nags me like a gossipy old woman."

"That's just how old folks are."

Lingguan found some sacks while Mengzi got an old washbasin and took it into the storeroom, where they filled the sacks with wheat. Plumes of dust permeated the room. Lingguan frowned and turned his head to the side. Mengzi dumped the wheat carelessly, as if releasing anger, and spilled grain all over the floor.

Their father came in after they'd filled one sack and had started a second. "How many do you plan to fill?" he barked angrily. "You're going to ruin the family. What'll we eat if you sell off every last kernel?"

"You didn't tell us how many sacks." Lingguan grumbled.

"Just fill enough to fetch thirty yuan. We need the rest to keep us going." Laoshun fumed when he spotted the grain on the floor. Staring wide-eyed, he flew into another rage, "How can you two young masters waste food like that? You're intent upon ruining this family."

"All right," Lingguan said. "We didn't spill it outside. Every kernel is still in here. We'll sweep it up to feed the chickens."

"How nice of you to say that," Laoshun spat out. "Listen to you. You sound as if you've saved up tons of grain."

"So we can't go on living if we don't save up tons of grain, is that what you're saying?" Lingguan murmured. Mengzi, wearing a dark look, jumped off the grain bin and walked out. Lingguan found a rope to tie up the sack, but his father pushed him aside, undid the knot, squatted down, and, grunting, picked up the sack and climbed into the bin. He poured the contents back until there was about half a sack left;

then he weighed it on the scale after testing its heft. He took out a few handfuls and re-tied the sack.

"Enough," he said. "Fifty *jin* should be enough. We have to be careful. This weather is going to do us in. Whoever heard of the Yellow River drying up? It's weird, I tell you." He sounded calmer by now, as if he hadn't yelled at anyone moments earlier.

Lingguan knew his father was muttering to signal a peace offering, which he did after every family quarrel. Never admitting he was wrong or apologizing, he conceded by mumbling something inconsequential; if he didn't do that, then he believed he was in the right or his feelings had been hurt.

Without a word, Lingguan walked out with the sack and called out to his brother, so he wouldn't get into another fight with their father.

"I'm not going." Mengzi said angrily. "It's a disgrace. If we're going to sell a few kernels we may as well tell people we're so poor we can't pony up thirty yuan."

"What? You think this is disgraceful?" Laoshun said from inside. "Then find a way out. Everyone thinks I've raised able young masters, but what are they good for? Nothing, except to argue with me."

"There you go again," Lingguan said. "All right. I'll go and you can stay home. There's nothing disgraceful about it to me."

"Why not? When did you see a family sell grain a bushel at a time? At least it should be a whole sack," Mengzi said softly, unaware that his father had come up behind him.

"What do you mean? You think it's too little? I say it's already too much. If there's not enough, go load up a whole cartful. That should make you look good, but what would you eat after that? You can't pluck your pubic hair to make a beard for your face, but it would hurt like hell." Laoshun sounded noticeably less ill humored.

The change in their father's tone of voice wasn't lost on Mengzi, who tugged at Lingguan to stop him from loading a bicycle with the sack. "All right. I'll see what I can do. We'll sell the grain if I can't." He left, and Laoshun smiled. "That's right. He's grown up, so he ought to able to share the burden." He squatted on the edge of the steps and puffed on his pipe.

Mengzi was gone a long time; the dejected look on his face told Lingguan he hadn't be able to borrow any money. Sure enough, he was cursing Baigou for not being a real pal. Laoshun's face darkened again, but he didn't say a word and continued to puff on his pipe noisily.

"They need money, too." Lingguan left with the sack.

The township flourmill was jammed with people who thronged to the site because it offered one cent more than the grain station. The villagers greeted each other, joking, laughing, and mocking in a light, cheerful tone. Ever since they'd been given their share of land to farm, they had less to do with each other and fewer chances to meet up, so they were given to bantering when they did. The older ones joked about fooling with daughters-in-law while the younger ones asked each other how many times they did it a night. In the end, however, they all looked up at the sky and complained about Heaven's blindness.

Lingguan handed his father the money after he got home from selling the grain. Laoshun took the money and rushed over to Big Head's house, while Mengzi crinkled his nose and said, "You see that? He curses up and down every time we have to pay some fee or other, and yet he's always eager to hand over the money."

"Everyone in Liangzhou is like that. They talk big and don't follow through. But you can't blame him. With a weather like this, the seedlings will turn into hay for the cows if we don't get any water soon."

Big Head was squatting on his *kang* slurping potato millet. He raised his bowl when he saw Laoshun. "Another bowl," he shouted. Laoshun shook his head. "No, no need. I ate just before I came over."

Huilanzi came in with a bowl and pushed it into Laoshun's hand. "Here, have some. Walk through the door, have some more."

Laoshun replied with a smile, "I wasn't born with a donkey's belly or a horse's stomach." But he took the bowl, hunkered down, and began slurping his favorite food, gooey, mushy, with a wonderful feel in the mouth. He was done in no time and stopped Huilanzi from refilling his bowl as he wiped his lips. "We can't live without this monkey grain. Life is losing its flavor day by day," he said.

"What flavor would you like? We muddle through life and take whatever comes our way, that's all," Big Head said, twirling his bowl on the *kang*; when it rolled toward the edge, he reached out, steadied it, and sighed.

"Well, keep your money for now." Big Head continued. "There's been a change. The people at the Water Bureau said they would release the water on two conditions. One, no water to any village that owes money, even if there's only one person in a given village. Two, well, the cost is going up again. Ten more yuan per acre and fifty per person, and we have to make up the difference. They said it was a city government decision. We have to pay up or no water."

Laoshun felt a loud buzz in his head, and everything went dark. Fifty per person. That meant three hundred for his family. Damn it, that would finish them off. They'd have to close off their throats. His mouth went dry and his parched tongue stuck to the roof of his mouth. "That'll be the end of me," he managed to say.

"I've checked. It was an order from above," Big Head explained. "The township government decided to let the co-op give loans to those who don't have the money. File the paperwork and the money will be sent directly to the township office. In the fall when the harvest comes in, the people will go to the co-op, instead of the grain collection station, and will get paid there after repaying their loan."

"That's like looting during a fire," Laoshun said. "We're already so poor we're standing at the well without a water scoop. Are they trying to kill us? What has the world come to?" He couldn't go on; with a grunt, he lowered his head and frowned.

"I haven't had a chance to tell people about it. I wonder what hell they're going to raise when I do. These days, being a team leader is no job for any man. I'm just an errand boy, getting people to pay their grain tax, carrying out family planning, and so on. Each job requires so much running around my soles are worn thin. I'm everyone's punching bag. Whenever those higher up want to collect a fee, everyone turns on me, as if I were filling my money belt. Damn. I'm not on the charity dole, so why do I continue to take it? I'm going to quit after this year and not even an eight-man sedan chair could bring me out to be the team leader next year." Big Head laughed drily.

"I've heard you say that a hundred times," Laoshun sneered. "You say it every year, but then you agree to be the team leader again every year. At least you're the leader. As they say, better to be a chicken's head than a cow's tail. Let's forget everything else and focus on visits from guests. You get to eat and drink until your face turns red. And that's our life's blood. We don't even get to drink piss."

"Come on," Big Head said with a laugh. "Your back doesn't hurt when you're standing straight. Do you think I enjoy that little food and drink I get? Everyone curses me for eating with those wolves. It makes me so uncomfortable I get indigestion. Do you really think I like people to criticize me behind my back? A tongue can ruin a man. I'll feel a lot better when I can toss away this hat and eat soupy millet and drink plain water like everybody else."

"All right. You can talk now that you've eaten." Laoshun softened his tone and continued, "but we can't do without people like you. We need someone to take care of things for us. There are people like you in the movies. They worked for the Japanese invaders and the Chinese. What are they called again, something like a peace-preservation association chair?"

"Old fart. Is that what you're calling me?" Big Head roared. "Then our government, what is it?"

Laoshun's mood darkened when he thought of the rising water fee. He felt weighted down, and there was nothing to laugh about. I'd rather die, he said to himself.

"I'm wondering what to do." Big Head stopped laughing. "Everyone will come after me when I give them the news, like I'm trying to make life difficult for them."

"Think about how the world is now," Laoshun said. "Why does Heaven make it so hard on us common people? Why won't it send down some rain? They can't raise the fee if we don't need the water, can they? Now our lives are in their hands, so there's nothing we can do but let them have their way."

"Wake up," Big Head said snidely. "Do you think they try to squeeze you dry only when there's no rain? They've just found a good excuse this time, that's all. Don't think they wouldn't come up with something else if it was raining. When a wolf wants to devour a lamb, it can always find a reason. There hasn't been a shortage of excuses in recent years, has there? One day they tell us to buy energy-saving transformers, the next day it's some fee or tax. If not this excuse, there'll be others. They can always find something."

"It's terrible being peasants." Laoshun shook his head and sighed.

"It's the same for everyone at a time like this. The city folks fare worse than us, believe it or not. Forget those who are laid off, since they can't fill their bellies. Even the officials have it tough. Repairing the city gate one day, and collecting money to build a superhighway the next. Do this, do that, and everything costs money. They're like kids making other kids smell their farts. I heard that just a few miles of highway cost hundreds of thousands. A pile of money as big as a house, and what did it get us? When you drive over it, the road buckles and muddy water bubbles up. Where's the money? Where did all that money go? It makes no difference to a wolf whether you're a skinny goat or a fat lamb. It will gobble you up."

Beizhu and Baigou walked in. "Here." Beizhu flapped the bills in his hand. "Give this to them, so they can get sick and buy medicine."

Big Head winked at Laoshun, who sighed and said. "Don't shame your ancestors. They don't care about that little money. They go after hundreds of yuan. The water fee is going up."

"How much?" Beizhu asked wide-eyed.

"Fifty. Fifty per person."

"Is that true, Big Head?" Beizhu raised his voice.

"Of course it is," Big Head replied with a bitter smile.

Beizhu froze, his blank gaze switching from Baigou to Laoshun and then to Big Head. He flung his money on the floor and said, "Fuck it. We're going to starve. It's all over. The world is hopeless."

"The cat under your blanket bites your dick," Baigou cursed. "If they're so good, why don't they bleed the foreigners? Why are they doing this to us common people?"

They all heaved a sigh. "I have only my blood left to sell." Beizhu frowned. "There's nothing else I can do. I could scrape the meat off my bones, and couldn't get more than two or three hundred."

"They're giving everyone a loan. You can pay them back with the next harvest," Big Head said.

Beizhu relaxed, but then blew up again. "A loan? With the high interest rate they'll charge? No. I won't pay. They can have me if they want."

"No?" Big Head smiled coldly. "They won't give us a drop of water if just one person in a village refuses to pay. No matter how you look at it, they're a rock and you're a blade of grass; they can crush you, and you can't do anything about it."

"This is it," Baigou said with a stomp of his foot. "I won't take it any more."

"What won't you take?" Big Head sneered at him. "You get to keep that puny life of yours if you do, but if you don't, you'll end up with a bullet in the head. Can you fight an atomic bomb? You'll have to accept your fate."

"Accept—fate—" Laoshun mumbled.

Chapter Seventeen

1

The days before his surgery were the worst that Hantou had ever experienced.

One of the causes was the frightening cost—more than forty yuan a day—for the hospital. Doctors annoyed him, for they were always prescribing drips of one sort of another. In his view they, the medications and the shots, were a total waste of money, since they could not rid his liver of the parasites. Infusing an IV bag amounted to drinking his parents' blood each time.

The other cause was that the day for the operation had to yet to be determined. The doctors kept telling him that they needed to observe him carefully. Observe? What was there to observe? In addition to three ultrasounds, he'd also had a chest X-ray, a liver function test and an EKG, all of which he considered doctors' tricks to make more money. His problem was with the growing lump in his liver, not with his head or chest. Why did they have to perform all those other tests? Why pick a poor man like him for their scam?

There was one other patient in his hospital ward with the same problem as Hantou—liver parasites. One end of a tube had been inserted in the man's rib area, the other end connected to a bottle containing red liquid. He walked with a bent back, baring his teeth and holding the IV bottle in one hand. Hantou heard that whoever came into contact with the liquid in the bottle would be afflicted with the same disease, so the man was treated like the carrier of plague. Hantou felt terrible at the thought that he would end up like the man, and yet he couldn't wait for that to happen, for every day in the hospital meant more money spent.

"Be careful not to touch the liquid in the bottle," Hantou said to Lingguan with a smile about the only topic that let him pretend to be cheerful.

"Are you afraid?" Lingguan asked.

"I'm like a whipped gecko. I have to go through with it, afraid or not." Hantou did his best to look unconcerned, but glum soon overtook him again.

Finding the smell in the room unbearable, he dragged Lingguan outside after he finished a bag of IV fluid. But he wanted to go back inside once they were on the street, as he thought of the empty bed they'd paid for; he wanted to spend as much time on that bed as possible in order to get his money's worth.

"Let's walk around some more. That will cheer you up," Lingguan said. "Even a healthy person would get sick being cooped up in that room all day. Besides, you'll have to stay in for a while once you've had your operation."

"But when will that be?" Hantou sighed. "More than forty yuan a day. It scares me just thinking about it. They're going to operate sooner or later, so why waste money sitting around waiting? Can't you talk to your classmate about moving it up?"

"I've talked to him more times than I can count, but it's no use. They have their procedures to follow, and everyone has to be put under observation for several days. Besides, they do your operation on Saturdays, so we'll have to wait. But I'll go talk to them again in a day or two."

"Wait? How much longer?" Hantou scowled. "The little money we have will be gone before the surgery. This is a scam. Why did they have to run all those tests? Having liver parasites is a clear-cut condition; open me up and take them out. But they make it so complicated. Oh, and I hear it requires gifts. Without them they won't schedule the surgery."

"Don't worry about that." Lingguan laughed. "I'll take care of everything."

"So, you gave them gifts already?"

"Just take good care of yourself and don't worry about that, all right?"

"Take care? Take good care? I take good care and the lump gets bigger every day. It's no big deal, since it'll burst when it gets too big. But the money. How are we going to pay it back?"

"As long as we're still around, there'll always be money. We'll shoot a few foxes and catch some rabbits once you've recovered. We'll find a way to pay."

"It's my debt, and I don't want any of you to pay it for me. I'll ask Father to divide up the family property when I get out. I'll settle my debt while you and Mengzi can save up to get married. I'm not going to become a burden to you."

"This is no time to talk about that," Lingguan said.

"I feel terrible if I don't. I've wanted to say this for days, but I couldn't. Now that I have, I feel so much better." Hantou exhaled softly.

They reached a busy street. All the vehicles and pedestrians made Hantou's head swim. The sun was hazy, not bright and clear, like the countryside. Feeling like a sleepwalker, Hantou would have preferred to return to the hospital for a nap, but he did not want to disappoint his brother, so he tagged along dreamily. When they reached a square with a bronze statue, Hantou gazed up at the horse rearing up over him.

"They say it was this horse that sucked up all the water in Xiying Reservoir and caused our drought. Is that true?"

"Who knows?" Lingguan said. "People say all sorts of things about this horse. The positive ones have the horse eating Yongchang's grass and leaving droppings in Wuwei to enrich the soil there. I heard that people in Yongchang carved a stone ox with long horns to butt up against this horse. So who can say which story is true?"

"It's weird though. To me the horse looks like it's falling over."

"Me too. The city has spent too much on the horse for it to do that. We'd have to pony up more money to fix it if it fell."

"Then it can't fall," Hantou said.

"That's right." They laughed at the way they were talking, as if they had a say in such important matters.

Hantou said he wanted to have his picture taken. "It'll be my first ever. It could come in handy one day."

"Sure, go ahead." Lingguan studied his brother, who smiled back at him. "But don't think any bad thoughts."

"I'm not." Hantou wondered if his brother was hiding something from him. His heart sank at the suspicion, but he managed a forced smile as he entered a photo studio to have a picture taken with his brother.

"Since we're here, I may as well have one taken alone. Maybe it'll come in handy." Hantou stole a glance at his brother. He was relieved to note nothing unusual on Lingguan's face.

2

Lingguan's head seemed to swell once they were back in the hospital room. The medicinal smell was unbearable, not to mention the mix of other odors. Six beds crowded into the tiny room, each occupied by a patient and accompanied by a family member. He was so nauseous from the foul breath exhaled by the twelve people in the room that he left soon after arriving, leaving Hantou behind.

As for Hantou, once he was off the streets and back in the room, he felt reassured, like a bird returning to its nest. No more street noise, no more chaotic crowds; he felt comforted in his bed, but that was a fleeting impression. It did not take long for him feel unnerved again, as thoughts of the expense returned. Low self-regard made him avoid looking at the other people, and he was so flattered when someone asked him a casual question that he responded with a grateful smile.

The liver patient, with his bottle and tube, was the last one Hantou wanted to see. It frightened him to imagine that he would look like that, but he envied the man's luck—his surgery had been performed on his fourth day in the hospital. He was reminded of the worried look on his parents' faces.

One of the patients had "chill symptoms." Hantou had no idea what that meant. An old man told him the patient had swollen testicles. A businessman from Huangcheng had a broken leg, the innocent victim of a fight between two herders over a piece of grassland. The fifth patient had appendicitis, and the last was the old man who told him about the chill symptoms; he had an unusual problem, a kidney stone.

Hantou considered himself to be the unluckiest one.

3

Laoshun brought two chickens along and told Lingguan to give them to the doctor. Lingguan went to see his old schoolmate with the chickens. "Is this a greeting or a gift? Chickens are fine as a way of saying hello to a doctor," he explained when he saw the puzzled look on Lingguan's face, "but they won't cut it as real gifts."

"Right, I see," Lingguan said. "We'll let them be a hello. But what should we get as real gifts?"

"Don't buy anything," his friend said. "Give money. You don't know what he needs, so money works best."

"How much do you think would be right?"

"The more the better, of course." His friend smiled. "There's no right or wrong amount. I know you don't have much, but you must have four or five hundred."

"Aiya, that's a lot." Lingguan sighed

"A lot?" His friend shook his head. "That's nothing. Everything would be behind you if they'd scheduled the surgery a few days ago. Every patient wants to get this over with as soon as possible, so they're fighting to see who gives the most money." His friend took him and his "glad-to-meet-you" gift of chickens to the doctor's house.

"Well, we'll have to find the money for the gift." Laoshun sucked air through his teeth when Lingguan told him what his friend had said.

"We'll do whatever's necessary. Your brother's health comes first. I'll go home to sell more grain."

"Let's wait and see," Lingguan said. "We don't have to pay it all at once. Five hundred at a time. That way we'll have time to sell the grain if we come up short. We've already paid five hundred twice, and I have a few thousand left. We'll see how it goes and sell more grain if we need more."

Laoshun mulled it over and agreed with his son's idea. After a moment, he said "I think I'll go borrow some more and keep the grain for the time being. We'll sell only in an emergency. Just spend what you need to spend. Don't hold back. We have to deal with your brother's illness." Lingguan promised he would.

Laoshun returned to their village. He saw that Ying'er had dark circles under her eyes, while Mengzi looked the same, as if nothing had happened in their family. Pleased to notice that she had lost weight, Laoshun saw that as a sign that she had a heart; Mengzi, in contrast, irked him, so he barked at his son, "You have to share the burden. I can't take care of everything. Go scare up a few hundred. We have to send gifts to those donkeys."

"What donkeys?" Mengzi asked.

"The doctors."

"What for?" Mengzi's eyes were ready to pop.

"What for?" Laoshun said coldly, "Nothing, except he's been there several days, and they haven't set a date for the surgery, saying they need to observe him longer. He'll never get it if we don't give them something. The money has to be spent, there's no way around it."

Mengzi alternated between gritting his teeth and staring wide-eyed, until he realized that neither was working. "I've asked everyone I could ask," he said. "We'll sell the grain if we have to."

"Sell?" Laoshun smirked. "That's all you know, isn't it? What will you eat when all the grain is gone? The wind? With a drought like this, it's clear we're in for hard times. So go out and see how much you can borrow. Every cent helps."

Mengzi's Adam's apple rolled up and down, but not a word came out.

Still squatting on the edge of the *kang*, Laoshun smoked, his brow tightly knit as he went over a list of the people he could ask for a loan. His wife fixed her gaze on his mouth, moving her lips each time a puff of smoke escaped from between his. She wanted to ask him something, but could not muster the courage to do so.

Ying'er moved about quietly, looking shy and apologetic, afraid to look the old couple in the eye, as if she'd been the cause of Hantou's illness.

"You make a pancake out of little bits of flour." Laoshun blew out a smoke ring, wound up his tobacco pouch, and jumped off the *kang*. "Ask anyone you see. One yuan is fine, even a few cents is better than nothing. We'll see how much we can put together."

"Yes," his wife said. "Every family runs into hard times, and the kind-hearted ones will help us out."

"I'm not going to do it," Mengzi said.

"Then you can go eat shit." Laoshun shot daggers at his son.

"I won't go door to door begging, but I'll get you eighty or a hundred."

"All right," Laoshun said.

The old couple set out after lunch, Laoshun starting from the east end of the village, his wife from the west. Going door to door, they told the same story and repeated their request. Hantou's surgery was critical, and everyone in the village did their best to help out. They managed to borrow a little over eight hundred and fifty yuan by the end of the day, while Mengzi turned up with eighty-two. Laoshun told his son to record the amount they'd borrowed from every family. He had a terrible memory, but this time he had an unerring recollection of the amount each family had given.

Laoshun told Mengzi to take the money to his brothers the next day, but the young man said he wanted to go earn some money. Reminded that Mengzi wasn't often reliable, Laoshun was worried that the money wasn't in good hands, so he took the bus and went to the city himself.

4

Hantou was being given another IV drip when Laoshun entered his hospital room. The patient with a kidney stone was groaning in pain. Lingguan told his father that the old man had had his surgery, but had suffered for nothing, since the doctor could not find the stone. He had poked all over his kidney, but no stone. His face a ghostly white, the old man continued to moan while calling the surgeon a shit-eating doctor.

"That's enough. Drop it, will you?" The patient with "chill symptoms" complained. "Consider yourself lucky; at least he didn't cut out one of your kidneys and throw it away. Did you know that someone with bone cancer on his left leg had his right leg amputated?"

"That's true. I read it in the paper," a man from Huangcheng echoed. "There was also a cadre with cancer in the left lung, but who lost his right one during an operation. That's the end of him. And then there was a girl with appendicitis who had her uterus taken out."

Laoshun blanched at the stories and took Lingguan out into the deserted hallway. "Did you hear that? With the way things are, I guess we have to spend the money."

"We did, we spent what was needed," Lingguan said.

"How much?" Laoshun asked urgently.

"Five hundred, to the head surgeon. We were supposed to treat those working with him to a meal, but the head surgeon said he'd talk to them on our behalf."

"Take them to a meal if you have to. We have to spend the money," Laoshun insisted.

'We can't afford it." Lingguan laughed derisively. "It would cost hundreds."

Stunned by that fact, Laoshun stared slack-jawed and nearly forgot to breathe.

"Nine hundred." Laoshun handed his son a packet wrapped in newspaper. "We managed to save the grain for now."

"It's better not to keep too much money with me here." Lingguan gave the packet back to his father. "We'll keep the money at home, but we probably should get larger bills at the bank. Small bills and loose change looks terrible."

"Why would it look terrible? Small bills are money too."

"I know. But it would be hard for them to handle."

Laoshun put the packet back into a used bag.

The three of them left the hospital and went to a diner after Hantou was done with the IV drip. "You go ahead and get something to eat. I just had some of the *mantou* I brought with me," Laoshun told his sons.

"We won't go broke over a meal. You've skimped all your life, and for what? I don't see you getting rich because of it," Lingguan chided his father.

"He's right," Hantou agreed. "You've traveled a long way to come here. Of course you have to get something to eat. I don't eat much, just a few bites. Otherwise, I feel bloated and uncomfortable."

"Eat as much as you can. Food is what keeps us alive," Laoshun said, "and the five grains give us energy. Don't try to save money."

"I really can't eat too much. It's unpleasant," Hantou said.

Laoshun felt his heart sink when he looked into his son's sallow face. Lingguan ordered three bowls of fried noodles.

"Is the lump still growing?" Laoshun asked.

"It is," Hantou said. "Like a balloon. It was eight millimeters in the first ultrasound, but it grew to fifteen millimeters in the second one. I guess it must be close to twenty by now."

"It's mealtime," Lingguan jumped in when he noticed the dark look on his silent father. "Let's not talk about that."

"I'm going to have the surgery soon, so it can grow as fast as it wants. A scalpel will take care of it."

"That's right." Lingguan looked over at their father, who was preoccupied. He sat quietly for a while before finally putting a few noodles into his mouth.

They took a walk when they finished.

"Why don't you go back to the hospital? What's the point of walking around without any money in our pockets?" Laoshun said to his sons as he headed toward the bus station. His heart was heavy, a pall was crushing down on his head, and all the people out on the street seemed not exist, as his mind was occupied with his son's unhealthy look.

He spotted a skinny fortuneteller who was expounding on deities. Laoshun stopped to listen; he was tempted to have his own fortune told when he saw a man nodding his head at the results. He extended his hand to the old man, who waved and said, "I don't read palms. I work with the time of birth, your 'ba zi.'" He explained what that was when he saw that Laoshun did not understand; his explanation that it was the eight characters of his birth—the year, month, day, and hour—only confounded Laoshun more.

"I only know I was born in the year of ox, on the eighteenth day of the first lunar month. I don't know what year it was or what hour. With the way we live, who has time to know all that. My parents didn't tell me either."

"That's all right." The fortune-teller smiled. "We won't use your ba zi then. I'll check your horoscope for the year." He tapped his right thumb on each of Laoshun's knuckles and said, "There's a white tiger in your horoscope, which means that things will not go well in your family. You have to spend a good deal of money, and there may be cause for worries and fears."

"You're so right." Laoshun nodded. "My son is in the hospital."

"Money is no big deal, compared with the possibility of death."

A loud noise went off in Laoshun's head. "You can't be serious!"

"That is what your horoscope provides," the old man said somberly.

"Is there any way around it?"

"Hmm—" The old man stroked his beard, while Laoshun took out his pile of filthy bills and picked out five one-yuan notes. The fortuneteller shook his head after one look at Laoshun and the money in his hands. "Forget it. You look like a decent man. I won't charge you anything. Keep your money, so you won't go hungry."

"Money is no object as long as his life can be saved." Laoshun laid the bills on the man's stand. "I'd give you an ox if I had to."

"All right, then." The man smiled and told him what to do: gather a pinch of flour from seven families, or from seven people, mix it to make a white tiger, take it to a place due West, and burn seven sheets of yellow money.

"What is yellow money?" Laoshun asked.

"Gold."

"Gold?"

The man smiled and took out a stack of yellow paper printed with strange-looking red patterns. He counted out seven and handed them to Laoshun, who asked the price. "Don't worry about it. You can have them for nothing. It will save you time looking for them."

A warm feeling spread through Laoshun's heart. He was about to get down on his knees to kowtow, but the old man had turned his attention to someone beside Laoshun, so Laoshun quietly backed out. With his newfound faith, he felt the worry over the debts and Hantou's illness begin to lessen.

He was now finally able to look around him: passersby rushing around, the racket of mahjong tiles at tea stands, a blind storyteller's hoarse voice competing with notes from his three-string lute, and so on. Everything felt far away, as if from a different world. Everyone looked happy, while he was mired in misery. He couldn't wait for Hantou to get better, so his mood could finally lighten up. You cannot be happy when you're worried. When Hantou was better, his thoughts continued, then he'd worry about finding Mengzi and Lingguan wives. Lanlan had yet to have a son. It seemed to him that he was surrounded by so many worries that they crowded into his mind whenever they found an opening. Now he knew that for the rest of his life he would never be totally happy or completely carefree. So just move on, he told himself. Everything is predestined and I was born to suffer. So I will suffer.

He was still dejected on the bus. He took a seat in the back, a quiet corner for his troubled heart and jumbled mind.

Recalling what the fortuneteller had told him, he was happy that his memory did not fail him this time. A pinch of flour from seven families or seven people to form a white tiger, due West, and gold paper. His heart nearly stopped at the thought that he might have left the sheets behind during his hurried retreat or lost them out of carelessness. He checked his pockets and found them alongside the money. He did a quick count; there were seven, but one was missing a corner. He wished he'd been more careful and had it replaced; on second thought, he realized he was being greedy. The fortuneteller had given them to him for nothing, so what if one of them was missing a corner? In the human world, bills with missing corners are still legal tender, so the same should go for the deities and spirits in the other world. Feeling more at ease, Laoshun carefully refolded the sheets, wrapped them in a handkerchief, and put them back in the same pocket. He exhaled with assurance when he touched the spot and felt the bulge.

Concern over the paper was immediately replaced by his worries over Hantou's illness. His heart began to beat almost audibly when he recalled Hantou talk about the fast-growing lump. How could his illness develop that way? Maodan's father had had the same ailment but his lump hadn't grown so much. Could it be—that scary illness? Laoshun could not bring himself to say the word, for even just the thought seemed to bring the sky crashing down on him. Nothing was sadder than for gray haired parents to send off their young children. He could not let his thoughts go any further. Damn it. Heaven is truly blind. It should've picked me and let the youngster have a good life.

On the other hand, the doctor did say it was parasites and had ordered an ultra-something, so he had to be right. The doctor wasn't someone who begged out on the street, and then there was the machine. He had heard that it came from overseas, made by those clever foreign devils who also created machines that show everything inside a person. With a machine from the foreign devils, the diagnosis had to be accurate—as long as it wasn't that dreaded illness. Now he actually hoped it was liver parasites.

The bus engine chugged into action, and Laoshun heard a buzz in his head. He was a bit nauseous as the bus began to move, but that was just an old affliction.

5

Laoshun's wife went to seven families that evening to ask for a pinch of flour from each to make a white tiger; that seemed to be the way to go, even though the fortuneteller had said a pinch from seven different people would also work. She had seen plenty cats, but never a tiger, so she based her flour tiger on the image of a cat, but after a great deal of effort produced a figure that bore little resemblance to a real tiger. She went west with it and stopped after taking a hundred steps, and then burned the seven yellow sheets.

She felt somewhat heartened after completing the rite, but could not stop fretting over the possibility that her lack of artistry to recreate a tiger with flour dough could affect the efficacy. When she mentioned her worry to Laoshun, he blew up:

"Just consider it a white tiger and stop worrying, will you?"

His outburst only made her even more anxious, which led to a terrible dream that night; the white tiger came and took Hantou away. Strangely, however, it looked real in her dream, like a white cat, only a hundred times bigger.

She was covered in a cold sweat when she woke up. Laoshun was snoring next to her, making her wonder if he even had a heart. How could he sleep like that when his son was in the hospital? But if he tossed and turned all night, of course, she'd be concerned that he could worry himself sick. He was smacking his lips amid his snores, raising a racket that grated on her ears. After nudging him a few times but failing to wake him up, she took the drastic measure of pinching his ears, which eventually managed to rouse him.

"I was gnawing on a delicious pig's foot. It smelled wonderful. What's the matter with you? It's the middle of the night." He yawned and licked his lips.

"Go buy one if you want."

"Costs too much. At least eight yuan."

"I had an awful dream."

"What about?"

"Hantou was snatched away by the white tiger."

"Would you stop thinking about that?" He lost his temper. "I finally manage to put it out of my dreams and feel a little better, and now that mouth of yours—"

"The white tiger looked like a big cat."

"A cat?" Laoshun relaxed. "A cat is like the fairy lady who brings people babies. Don't you remember when you were pregnant with Lingguan—?"

"Yes. A cat ran into my arms. But why was a cat bringing me a baby? I already had my tubes tied."

"You're still young at heart and you sound like you want another one." Laoshun had a good laugh. "My head aches worrying about these three young masters, and you want more."

"Shush. It looked like a white cat, but I know it was a tiger."

He was quiet for a long time, giving her the impression that the silence and dark night were pressing down on her, when he suddenly spoke up,

"A good dream."

"A good one?"

"Yes. The blind storyteller once said that tigers represent people special in your life. When you dream about a tiger, it means you will meet the person who can help you. Xue Rengui, the great warrior general, was a white tiger incarnate. If a tiger snatched Hantou away, that must mean that someone will save him. Who could it be? Ah, yes. It has to be the old fortuneteller. I'm sure it's him. Just think, he didn't ask for money when he gave me the seven sheets of paper. Not a cent. He had to be that special person."

"But didn't you give him five yuan?"

"I did, but I insisted. He didn't want it, so I left the money there."

"I'm glad we have someone special. We certainly need the help."

He smacked his lips again, as if savoring the pig's foot in his dream. Then he got up for his pipe and squatted on the edge of the *kang* to smoke. The heavy smell of tobacco spread in the air.

"Why are you doing that?" she complained. "You won't give me a breath of fresh air even at midnight. Aren't you afraid of getting sick?"

He inhaled, held the smoke in his mouth for a while, and then slowly exhaled, once it had seeped into his pores. "Why? You want to know why?" he replied slowly. "This is the sixth grain. I can do without the five grains but this is my only vice. It's better to die from smoking than from worries." He blew hard on the mouthpiece, as if to chase away the gloom in his heart.

"You have it all figured out, don't you? You have your sixth grain, but what about me? I toil away all day long, and what have I got?"

"You can smoke." Laoshun said lightly. "It doesn't cost much. A few *jin* of wheat gets you half of a sack, which will last you a whole year, unlike cigarettes. I hear that the cigarettes Shuangfu smokes cost eighty cents apiece."

"Me smoke? Do you mean it? Well, if I do, I'm going to smoke the eighty-cent ones and smoke this family to ruins."

"Sure, go ahead." He laughed. "So what if the family is ruined? We can't get any poorer than we are not. If that happens, I guess we won't be able to afford pants."

"Don't think that won't happen," she said. "Just look at the way the world is. Everything is in chaos, everyone's running around busy over nothing, and officials want to suck the people's blood. They even try to squeeze old bones likes ours. You just wait and see; there'll be more hardship ahead."

"That's true. The crops die all too often. Think about it. Isn't it weird that fine wheat seedlings die in patches, big patches."

"Lingguan said it had something to do with fertilizer. It happens when too much is used."

Laoshun blew out a smoke ring; a red spark arced in the air and landed in a corner. "But we have to use fertilizer. Crops are like people, they're greedy."

"Well, then we'll just have to suffer." She sighed. "But we won't be the only ones. It will happen to all the other families too."

"You're right. We won't be alone. The taller ones will prop it up when the sky falls, so there's no need to be afraid. Heaven won't kill rootless grass, and it has to leave us a way out, don't you think? Actually, what if we don't have a way out? Worst case, we all die. It's not that hard; just close your eyes and you won't know a thing."

"How do you know?" She objected. "Your soul hangs around when your body dies, and it will still suffer. You're poor when alive and you're a destitute ghost after you die."

"Maybe not. We're poor, but at least we have three sons, and we'll do fine if they burn spirit money for us on holidays. We'll fare better than the childless lonely ghosts."

"What do mean? If Heaven really wants to eliminate us, our sons won't even be able to afford a pair of pants. How could they afford spirit money?"

"You're right," Laoshun agreed. "No one offered anything to their ancestors in 1960. Our chests caved in and pressed up against our spines. Our mouths stank. Who could be bothered with ancestors when you're like that?"

"Life is really futile." She sighed. "I'd hoped Lingguan would make it into college and get a good job, so we could have a taste of good life, but he didn't. Our two young masters are getting older, we haven't saved up enough to find them wives, and now Hantou—"

"Drop it. Let's not talk about that." Laoshun grumbled. "I'm scared enough without having to think about it, so don't start in. We'll muddle through for as long as possible. We'll survive a few more days if we can, and if not, a knife or rope, take your pick. Kick your legs out one last time and that's that. Worst case, you become a headless wandering ghost. Once that happens, there's no need to worry about suffering or anything else. Everything will be fine. Like they say, a monk recites his own temple's sutras. Don't worry so much and don't think too far ahead, all right?"

She responded with a sigh. Laoshun's pipe crackled, unusually loud, until dawn.

6

After a night of worries, Laoshun's wife went to see Grannie Shaman Qi after breakfast. Her dream had not seemed to be a good one, but she was afraid to explore it further with her husband, fearful that it would only make him grumble more. Hantou's illness had turned her into a bird that has barely escaped a hunter's arrow, and now she lived with a sense of impending doom. Her heart hung in perpetual suspension, and she felt ungrounded, which was why she wanted to know what Grannie Shaman had to say. She knew how to read dreams.

After hearing Laoshun's wife out, Qi insisted that it was a good dream, offering the same interpretation as Laoshun's, that a special person was helping Hantou out. A warm, comforting calm washed over Laoshun's wife.

"I'm glad you came to see me first thing in the morning," Qi said. "Actually, the person who interprets a dream determines the nature of that dream. If the person is positive, it will be a good dream, and if not, it will be bad. Even a wonderful dream can be ruined if you relate your dream to someone who only puts a negative spin on it."

"We're so lucky to have you," Laoshun's wife said with a smile.

"Years ago there was a Master Kang in Shuangcheng's Yang'ergou." She tightened her red lips before continuing: "The night before the provincial examination he dreamed about two coffins and woke up at the third watch—the only time a dream has critical importance—and heard a hen crow. They were both unlucky signs, so he decided not to go to the capital. But his mother said it was clearly a good dream. Two coffins sounds like two coffers; the hen takes over when the rooster does not crow, and the family's fame and fortune will surely grow. He went and passed the exam."

"Aiya!" Laoshun's wife feigned a look of surprise. In fact, she had heard the same story many times before, but she pretended it was a first for her. "You're amazing. You've been to so many places and seen so much more than any of us."

The woman tightened her lips again, a clear sign that she was pleased by the flattery. "There was another scholar in the same village who also dreamed about two coffins and told his wife about it. She said it was a bad dream, for the coffins were meant for husband and wife. Hei, her words were God's ears. Her husband ran into highwaymen on his way to the capital and they cut off his head. She hanged herself when the news came. That shows that the person interpreting a dream determines the nature of that dream."

"You are so right." Laoshun's wife concurred. "We are lucky to have you." What interested her was the nature of her own dream. At home she'd often mentioned the kinds of things that Qi had just told her, but now she waited until the shaman was finished before asking about Hantou's illness.

"I can't tell you," Qi said. "I need to investigate but I cannot do that until the deity's visit. We need to find the cause, whether something filthy has latched onto him, his karmic connection has been damaged, or the feng shui is bad. Maybe there are issues with ancestor graves, or something else. Once we find that out, we can try to fix it. Then we'll know for sure. But now I'm just like you."

"What are you saying? How can you be just like us? You're almost an immortal, while we're not much better than animals, except that we can talk and have no tails."

"Hei, hei." Qi laughed. "Don't demean yourself like that."

"I'm not. If we were animals, we'd have no worries and would have to do nothing but work in the fields. I've worked as hard as a donkey. Or look at pigs. They sleep after they eat and eat after they sleep, a better life than we have. What's so good being a human? Look at me. I'm old before I know what's what. I worried about my sons not making it into adulthood, and now that they're grown-ups, they aren't good for much. The younger two aren't married, and now Hantou—well I'd be happy to take his illness. No matter what, I've lived long enough, but the children must have a longer life!" Her eyes were moist.

"It's fate." Qi tried to console her. "So don't worry so much about it. Heaven looks after the worthy ones. He'll recover once you've spent what you need to spend. We're only human, and there bound to be problems in life. Life is hard. A baby cries the moment it arrives in this world. Have you ever seen one smile? That's why I say life is hard. A bloody little mess cries when it lands here because it knows it faces hard times ahead, but it has to keep on going."

"You're right, of course." Laoshun's wife dried her tears. "We have to keep going and take what Heaven hands us. As long as Heaven keeps handing it down, I can take it. You will look out for us if we miss something, won't you? We live in the same place. A distant relative cannot compare with a close neighbor, and a close neighbor isn't as good as the one across the street. We're so lucky to have you."

"Listen to you. What are you saying? Your problems are my problems. Besides, I've liked Hantou ever since he was a little boy. Even then, he was well behaved and sensible. He blushed when he talked, like a girl, unlike those rabble-raising rascals who show no respect for their elders. Come back tonight and I'll try to find the root of your problem. It may turn out to be nothing. Headaches, fever, and aches and pains are unavoidable over a lifetime. This is a karmic crisis that he has to pass through, and he'll be fine once it's over."

Finally relieved of her apprehension and worries over the dream, Laoshun's wife felt so much better on her way home. She smiled when she saw her husband, who asked, "Where have you been off gossiping so early in the morning."

"Everything is going to be fine. I mean it." She ignored his disagreeable tone. "Grannie Shaman said it was a good dream, just as you said."

Laoshun knew why she'd been out so early. He was piqued that she ran over to see the shaman for the smallest problem, but smiled when he learned what Qi had said about her dream. "Of course it was. That's what I said."

Mengzi walked into the room and stretched lazily as he said to his father:

"Huaqiu and the others are going to the salt lake to buy salt tomorrow, and they asked me to go with them."

"What for?"

"So we can have salt. They're going to take some flour and other thing to swap for salt. A few loads of salt will fetch some money back here. We can't let ourselves be buried in debt."

"Sounds good." The hint of a smile appeared on Laoshun's face. "You're old enough now to share our burdens. I can't be the only one shouldering responsibilities."

"Then I'll go ahead." Mengzi turned to leave.

"But be careful." Laoshun stopped him. "It's government salt, after all, so you must listen to the people there. Don't let them get you into trouble."

"I won't. We'll give them money if that's what they want, and that should take care of it. Besides, Huaqiu and the others know these people. They offered a few *mantou* last time, and were given a load of salt. This time Huaqiu told me to take some rabbits along."

"Go catch them yourself. It's getting harder. "But give it a try. I've been preoccupied with other matters over the past few days and have neglected the hawks. They'll soon forget how to hunt if they're away from the desert too long."

"Forgetting how to hunt would have been the least of your problems; they'd have starved already if not for me."

"What do you want, a pat on the back? Where would you be if not for me?" Laoshun asked.

Mengzi took a hawk and went into the desert with Huaqiu after breakfast. They caught a few rabbits and left the following morning with their camels to transport salt from the desert salt lake.

7

Lingguan took a break from the hospital to go home. He was surprised to see his mother had lost so much weight that she seemed a different person.

It was village women's busiest time of year, weeding and pulling up oat stalks, sweating profusely under a scorching sun. Unquestioned conventions dictated that these were women's jobs, so the men had the free time to loaf and shoot the breeze. To be sure, some women talked or forced their men into coming to the field to pull oats, turning these men into objects of comparison for the other women. But those women's husbands always showed their contempt for their henpecked fellow villagers.

She blanched when she saw Lingguan walk in, but could not find the courage to ask why he was home.

"Nothing's wrong." He assured her. "The surgery is set for this Saturday."

"Why did they drag it out so long?" Laoshun asked.

"That's the day they operate on infectious cases," Lingguan replied. "We shouldn't complain. At least they've found a slot for us."

"How many times did you have to give them something?" his

father asked.

"Twice. Five hundred each time. They asked for more yesterday, but I haven't paid them yet."

"So much has been spent already, before the operation," his mother said. "How much more will we have to spend after that?"

"Most of the money is spent before the operation. An ultrasound alone had to be done three times, costing thirty to forty yuan each time. But what can we do? The actual procedure doesn't cost that much."

"It's not right to have to pay for all that, but we'll do it. We have no say where illness is concerned," Laoshun said.

"Where's his wife?" Lingguan asked.

"She's in the kitchen," his mother replied. "She's lost weight. She doesn't eat enough, and has become sallow and gaunt."

"I don't feel like eating much myself. Food doesn't taste good," Lingguan said. "I feel a pressure in my chest that makes me restless. Hantou asked me to give her something." He went into the kitchen.

Ying'er was rolling out dough. She blushed when she saw him, but the color soon receded.

"The surgery is set for Saturday, and he'll be fine once it's over Lingguan said."

She cast him a wordless glance before lowering her head, sending teardrops falling onto the dough.

"It's nothing, really. It's minor surgery."

Ying'er dried her tears with her sleeve and, still not saying a word, went back to work. "Are you going back today?" she asked after a long pause.

"Yes."

"I'll go with you. He's my husband, after all."

"There's no place for you to sleep."

"It's just one night. I won't sleep, how's that? They must have a place to sit."

"It's not up to me. Go ask Mother. You can go if she lets you." He took out a bottle of lotion and handed it to her. "From him to you."

"How much did it cost?"

"More than ten yuan."

"Oh!" she cried out. "I can't believe he'd spend so much on me."

"He said it's been hard on you over the years. All the city girls use this."

Ying'er was startled by the comment; her eyes reddening, she quickly turned to remove a pot lid.

"She wants to see Hantou," Lingguan said to his mother when she walked in.

"So do I. I feel like I haven't seen him for ages."

"So it's okay if I go?" Ying'er asked.

"Why not? I've wanted to go, but I can't bring myself to spend the money."

"It isn't much," Lingguan said. "The bus fare is only a few yuan, and the food is cheap."

"I'll take food with me," Ying'er said.

"I was just talking," Laoshun's wife said. "Make sure you eat something. Just don't buy anything you don't have to."

"*Mantou* are better. I have trouble eating in those filthy restaurants," Ying'er said as she turned to cut the dough into noodle strips.

"Of course we have to save money," Lingguan's mother told him. "But don't scrimp on food. Spend what you have to."

"I know," Lingguan laughed. "I'm not like you; I don't value money more than my life. When you go into the city, you won't even buy a fried cake even if you're about to faint from hunger."

"You young scoundrel," his mother scolded jokingly. "When you kids were growing up, we couldn't even afford a pair of pants after filling your bellies. Now you use that to mock me. Ingrate!"

She then tugged at Lingguan's sleeve for him to go out with her. "Make sure to keep your eyes open." She whispered once they were outside. "Leave them alone when they're together, all right?"

"What do you mean?" He laughed. "There are a dozen people in one room. I can leave them alone, but I can't ask the others to do the same."

"Just let them talk about whatever they want." His mother glared at him. "Do you have a block of gnarled elm for a brain?"

"I know. I know." He smiled.

8

After lunch, Ying'er packed up some changes of clothes for Hantou and made a few of his favorite fried cakes before walking out the door with Lingguan. When they neared the village entrance, they saw Beizhu and his friends teasing Maodan.

"Nonsense." Maodan was giggling, unable to come up with anything else to say.

Lingguan laughed, while Ying'er walked on, her face reddened.

"What are you laughing about, Lingguan?" Maodan blurted out. "Run to catch up. Your sister-in-law can hardly wait."

With that, Maodan shifted the butt of the others' teasing to Lingguan.

"Yes, hurry and catch up," one of the others said.

"Just look at how she walks. So sexy."

Ying'er kept walking; her face turned a bright red, as she knew they were about to say something unsavory.

"What are you waiting for, Lingguan?" Maodan was relentless. "Go on. Put your arms around the girl and give her a kiss; then a block of ice will melt with a hiss."

"Right. Hurry up. Red, smooth lips and lovely, seductive eyes; beneath reddish purple underwear a body goes limp," taunting them with lyrics from a folk tune.

"Look, she can hardly wait. She's so weak from pining for you she can't blow out the lamp; ashes from the wick are falling all over the place."

"Hey, Lingguan. Your sister-in-law was the 'Queen of Folk Songs.' Ask her to sing us a song. Like this one, 'Willow saplings line the Yellow River/They will soon grow into towering trees/Counting the days on my fingers/Waiting to be naked with you soon.'"

Laughing and jeering, they quoted from popular tunes that were getting more and more blatantly suggestive.

Lingguan quickened his steps to get away, knowing it was useless to talk back.

"Look at him. Lingguan turns into a mad dog when he's chasing his sister-in-law."

"I bet he wishes he could knock the sun out of the sky."

"Why? It's much more fun doing it in broad daylight."

The Dasha River and a sand hollow separated their village from the highway. Once they were in the hollow, Ying'er turned and, with an imperceptible smile, asked Lingguan, "What did they say?"

"I didn't catch any of it. Did you?"

"I was walking so fast I only caught some chatter. I couldn't make out a word."

"Really?" Lingguan chided, then looked into her eyes. She held his gaze, but her face slowly reddened; suddenly, she bit her lip and began to weep.

"Look at you." Lingguan was alarmed. "I didn't do anything. Why are you crying?"

She lowered her head to dry her tears, but they kept coming, until her face was wet. Lingguan worried about what people would accuse him of if anyone happened to walk by. He looked around, and was relieved to see that they were alone.

No longer just shedding silent tears, Ying'er was sobbing audibly by then. He tried to get her to keep moving, but she fell into his arms instead. Lingguan failed to nudge her away, while her lips were all over his face and streaked it with her tears.

"Hey!" he cried out. "Can't you pick a better spot? What if someone sees us—?"

"I don't care," she said in mid sob. "The worst that can happen is we die."

"All right," he said gently as he kissed her, before pushing her away. She let go and, drying her tears, stared into his eyes as if in a trance.

Emotionally stirred up by the gaze, he made sure no one was around before lifting up her face and kissing her. She sighed contentedly, rousing him so much that he smothered her with kisses.

"Will it be all right?" he whispered.

"Here?" she murmured. "Too many people pass by."

He was breathing hard as he pointed to a nearby ridge. "It's more secluded over there." Wordlessly she followed him up to the ridge and rolled down the slope behind him. "In broad daylight—" she said cautiously.

"Don't they say it's more fun doing it in broad daylight?" Lingguan said, but suddenly Hantou's face barged into his mind. I'm no damned good! he said to himself, but he was too weak to suppress his surging desire. His mind and body had been steeped in anxiety and agitation for days, and now Ying'er had appeared like a cool breeze, turning him into a hungry beast with no self-control.

When they had finished, Lingguan's passion spent, he felt himself drowning in self-reproach. He tore at his hair and said, "I'm no damned good!" She blanched, as she knew what he was referring to, and her hands froze in mid movement of smoothing out her clothes. "I'm no damned good!" He said again while banging his forehead with his fist over and over.

She sat up. "It's my fault," she said quietly. "Don't blame yourself. Let me accept the retribution and punishment. Don't be hard on yourself."

"I knew—I shouldn't—" He kept hitting his forehead. "But I can't—I can't help it—let's go."

They retraced their steps up the ridge, where they saw Big Head walking, pigeon-toed, down below. Thrown into a panic, Lingguan wanted to back away, but Sun had already spotted them. "Just tell him we were here to catch a rabbit," she whispered. Big Head's voice rang in the hollow before she'd finished.

"Hey, Lingguan, what sort of fun were you having with your sister-in-law?"

"Hei—we saw a rabbit, one with a bad leg. We chased it, but it got away."

"Really? You weren't catching those two rabbits of hers, were you?" Big Head laughed.

"You think everyone is like you, don't you?" Lingguan quickly changed the subject. "Have you seen the bus?"

"It just went over to the Dragon King Temple. It'll be here soon."

"We nearly missed it," Lingguan said, but immediately realized that betrayed a guilty conscience.

"What's your hurry? There'll be another one soon." Big Head laughed again. "Take your time catching those rabbits of hers."

"You go ahead if that's what you're thinking," Lingguan said.

"Did you hear that?" Sun turned to Ying'er. "He gave me permission. How about you?"

"Sure." Ying'er decided to go along. "You can have a taste so long as you call me Mother."

With a shout, Sun pounced with open arms, as she giggled and ran off.

"Oh, no." Lingguan slapped his forehead after they were back on the road. He explained to a startled Ying'er, "I didn't smooth out the sand. What if he and saw—"

She chuckled. "Don't worry. Who has time to go check? And so what if he found out?'

"Why do the gentlest women often tend to be most daring?" he whispered, to which she answered, "Of course. Have you ever tried to push a ball down into water? The more you push down, the higher it leaps back at you."

He felt a stir when he looked at her lively, lovely face.

She began singing a folk tune softly, with tears brimming in her eyes, yet smiling at him with infatuation, as if trying to drink him in—

A parrot perch made by a blacksmith,
A hawk rests on the perch.
With so many people around it's hard to exchange a word,
But our hearts can speak to each other.

A lamp hidden in the Lanzhou pagoda,
A treasured urn in Labrang Temple.
I long for you, heart and soul,
Until my eyes are ruined from crying.

After a wonderful dream at midnight,
I wake up to find myself in my bed with flowered sheets.
Surprised to see you are nowhere,
Tears flow freely to soak the kang.

9

The moment he saw Hantou, Lingguan was flooded with self-reproach, like surging water. "I'm no damned good, a true beast," he mumbled silently.

Hantou was rail thin. Lingguan hadn't realized until now how gaunt his brother had become, almost skeletal, in fact, and with a frightening yellow pallor. His face was covered in spots, but not enough to hide the sallow tone. Lingguan's heart ached for his brother, and his self-condemnation intensified.

Hantou was delighted that his wife could be with him at a moment like this. With no intent to hide his excitement, he smiled broadly to show how pleased he was and how lucky he felt. That made his cheekbones look higher than usual, his eyes sunk deep in their sockets.

Obviously unprepared, Ying'er was startled to see how he'd changed. He had never looked less attractive. At the instant, he felt like a total stranger to her, as if she'd never shared a bed with him. But her sympathetic nature gave rise to an unusual tenderness and brought tears, as she condemned herself for what she'd done earlier with Lingguan.

Too moved by her tears to know what to do, Hantou rubbed his hands and looked at his brother as if asking for help. Lingguan's eyes were downcast; he was still mired in self-reproof. Hantou turned anxious. "This place—I, I don't have anything for you to eat."

"I'll go buy some fruit," Lingguan said and walked out.

"Who's she?" One of the other patients asked Hantou, who said, "She's my wife."

"Ah! You've got a beautiful wife."

"I know. That's what everyone says." He was smiling. "They all say she's a pretty flower stuck in a pile of cow dung."

"Who says that?" she pouted, which made him laugh.

Lingguan walked in with some fruit. When Hantou took them out to wash them, she looked at Lingguan, who shook his head and gave her a bitter smile tinged with self-reproach. She smiled too, but with the implication that what had happened had happened, and there was no needed to dwell on it. That did nothing to dispel his guilt feelings.

Hantou walked in with a handful of newly washed fruit. He put them on a table before going for a handkerchief. "There's no need to dry them," Ying'er said, "Really." But he insisted on doing so until Lingguan said, "You'll only get them dirty if you do."

Ying'er picked one out for Hantou, who said, "Not for me. I have them all the time."

"Come on, have one. We know what you're like. What do you eat all the time, air?" Ying'er said. Hantou laughed gently as he accepted the fruit from her. He took a small bite and chewed for the longest time before swallowing.

"Does it hurt?" she asked.

"About the same. But I feel bloated. It's uncomfortable. That thing is still growing."

"It's all right. The operation will take care of it."

"You're right." Hantou echoed. "The operation will take care of it. I'm getting anxious cooped up here. This is no place to be; even a healthy person will get sick after a while."

10

Mengzi returned from the salt lake with several bags of salt, looking mightily smug, like a proud donkey. He started crowing about his accomplishment the moment he walked in the door: "Look, Ma. Four hundred *jin*, to be exact. Four hundred! What did it cost us? A few rabbits. Are you happy now, treating me like a prodigal son that will ruin the family? See this? You can't complain anymore."

"All right." His mother laughed. "But it's just some salt. There's no need to go on like that. It's not like you found gold nuggets on the road."

"What's wrong with salt?" Mengzi snorted. "This is money. We'll trade it for wheat and sell the wheat for real money."

"You sure picked a good time to go. Your older brother is in the hospital, and Lingguan had to run around taking care of everything."

"Has he had his operation?"

"It's scheduled for this Saturday. He's reduced to skin and bones."

"That's no problem. When he's out, I'll catch some rabbits for him. A few good meals will put some meat back on his bones."

"What are you going to catch the rabbits with? We've been too busy to care for the hawks. Your father is going to release them tonight. He's fed them with bloody meat for several days to restore their wild nature."

"That's good. It's time for the hawks to return to the mountains. We're late this year. In the past we released them in early spring," Mengzi said as he walked over to a perch and smoothed his hawk's feathers. The hawk cried softly. "Well, you're going back to the mountains. We don't have anything good to feed you, and you haven't shed your old feathers. See how ragged you are. Go back, find yourself a wife, and raise a baby hawk. Return with your baby after White Dew. But you're too old to work. You can't take the cold, and I'm not sure you'll survive the winter."

"Out with it if you want a wife yourself. Don't use the hawk as your pretense." Ying'er, who had returned alone, said with a smile.

"What are you talking about?" Mengzi said. "What's so good about having a wife? A wife is like handcuffs and kids are like shackles. It's so much better the way I am now. I come and go as I please. So carefree."

"You're carefree, indeed." His mother said. "But be careful not to cause me trouble, since you have no wife to rein you in."

"What do you mean? What kind of trouble have I caused you?"

Ying'er smiled. Mengzi blushed, realizing that she was thinking about what had gone on between him and Shuangfu's wife. His mother smiled too.

"I'm glad you don't. Everyone knows that Mengzi is a simple fellow who won't make a sound even if you hit him with a hammer."

Ying'er laughed, making him blush. "I'm glad you know that about me," he said.

"Stop trying to be clever," his mother said. "Finish what you have to do and go into the city. Have you talked about how to divide up the salt?"

"There's no need to talk about it." Mengzi said. "You keep what you bring back. I was worried that our camel couldn't bear too much weight, so I didn't load enough."

"That's all right," she said. "How much would be enough? We've managed all these years without salt, haven't we? We'll be happy if it can supplement our income and make life a bit easier on us. No one should expect to get rich this way."

"Go ahead and trade with anyone who wants our salt." Mengzi kicked at the sacks of salt under the eaves. "One *jin* of grain for two *jin* of salt. I'll make another round in a few days. This is better than taking on part-time work with a bad boss."

"That's the right thing to do." His mother said. "If you've got a belly to fill you have to be willing to work for it."

"I know that. I hate it when you nag like that."

After giving the hawks a good meal at dusk, Laoshun and Mengzi swatted them with willow branches, making the birds screech and fly up to the trees. Their wild nature would be reawakened when the night was over, and they would return to Qilan Mountains to procreate. As aging hawks with flimsy feathers and diminished strength, they would likely not make it through the winter. Their children, the so-called hawks of the year, would take their place.

11

The sun shone brightly overhead, true to its reputation as a ball of fire. Laoshun decided to give up thinking when he felt that his brain was baked dry. There was no point in thinking about anything, so why bother? Just muddle through life. Drink your fill when there's liquor today and don't worry if you have only water tomorrow. Water is fine, too, so no need to worry. If there's water to mix in with millet, life can go on. Potatoes and millet is just like that: a pot of water, a handful of millet, a few potatoes, and some flour. Generations in his family had survived on that staple, as had all the residents of Liangzhou. They wanted nothing more than that to get them through the day. If they made it, fine; if they didn't, well that was okay too. So many had died of starvation in 1960, when the sand hollows brimmed with bodies, but no one had complained. It was fate. No one had thought of getting guns or knives, except for showoffs like Baigou. Naturally, it was best to keep going, but so what if you stopped breathing? Being a ghost wasn't all that bad.

Laoshun felt that his mind had not been working so well in recent days. Once your anger reaches its limit, he told himself, you stop stewing, and once your worries reach their limit, you stop worrying. If the sky falls, the tallest ones would prop it up, so what was he worrying about? Why be anxious? Why curse? Why complain? There were so many who lived off the land and then were claimed by the land. There were many who were so oppressed they could not even hold back a fart. And there were many whose bones were squeezed dry, leaving behind not a single drop of grease. They survived, so why couldn't Laoshun? What was he angry about? Anger can ruin a person's health. Futile, life was truly futile. No matter what a person says, you keep going as long as there's something in the pot. Why be angry? You keep going even when there's nothing left in the pot. One day at a time, and when that becomes impossible, you close your eyes, kick out your legs for the last time, and you're beyond the cycle of suffering. Ha-ha. Laoshun laughed; he tried to sound carefree, but failed. His heavy heart and hoarse voice aside, that laugh sent a string of unseemly tears sliding out of his feckless eyes.

He recalled a writer, a good man, who had come to his house to collect local folk songs. He thought that the writer was a good man because he hadn't put on airs and treated the villagers with respect; he'd also smoked a pipe and eaten potato millet with them. He kept saying that the people in Liangzhou had unparalleled capacity for suffering and injustice, since there had never been an uprising in their history; they preferred to hang themselves over rising up against the government, even when they ran out of options for survival. Laoshun understood most of what the man said, but had wondered why one must rise up against the government. If he had enough, he ate his fill; if not, he ate less. If possible he'd live longer; if not, he'd die. What was the point of an uprising? It was a concept beyond his ability to comprehend and accept, for it usually led to execution. To Laoshun anyone who was executed was a criminal. It was nothing to die of hunger, but being executed brought too great a shame to the ancestors. Besides, Laoshun and the villagers had yet to reach the point where they could not add millet to their pots, except, of course, in 1960. No one would think of anything unlawful as long as they had potatoes and millet to slurp. There were those who were dissatisfied with reality, but Laoshun found them contemptible; they were beasts, like animals that spilled their guts, debased animals incapable of reproduction, people with evil intentions, born to disgraced parents and bred in the wild.

The writer also mentioned sand babies, saying they might be members of the lizard family. Laoshun did not know if the man was right. He did know that the sand babies looked like, but were not, scorpions because of short legs that were too weak to support their bodies. Yet they moved fast, and had a special ability, that of self-mutilation. When cornered, they gave up their tails rather than bite an attacker. Luckily, it did not take long for the wound to heal and the tail to grow back. They seemed to enjoy a happy life. Laoshun would never understand why the writer had said the Liangzhou people were like the sand babies.

The blistering sun shone down noisily. He felt an enormous irritating heat wave surging between heaven and earth. It was the sand babies' favorite weather. A group of them were chasing each other around his feet. One of them looked up at him curiously, almost as if it were mocking him. A stomp of his foot sent it scurrying away to a small hole, where it stopped, turned around, and made a face.

That's rubbish, he said to himself. How could we be like the sand babies? They never worry about their next meal and live a carefree life, with no one to bully or exploit them. He was filled with envy as he looked at the frolicking creatures, which were running back and forth, chasing each other, on the sand under a hot sun. Quite a few of them were looking at him, making him wonder if it was curiosity, pity, or something else in their eyes. So he stared back. They had childlike eyes that were kind, pure, and devoid of the guile typical of grown-ups.

After looking at them for a while, he had a sense that he was surrounded by sand babies, while he himself had disappeared, and yet the weightiness of being human continued to press down on him. Wouldn't it be nice to be a sand baby? he thought.

A dull pain began to spread around his back, so he straightened up as he wiped the sweat off his face. Now he was aware of his own foolishness. What's wrong with me? Why do I think it would be good to be a sand baby? He shook his head at himself. I'm too old to think clearly. Yet he had to envy the creatures when he recalled the fees he needed to pay.

"Hey. Are you stealing my seedlings?" He recognized the voice as belonging to Meng Eight without looking. Laoshun knew that the jocular greeting required a similar reply, but he was not in the mood, so he just looked up and smiled at his friend.

Meng could tell what was on his mind. "You're worrying about the water fee, aren't you? Well, stop worrying. Get a loan, that should take care of it. Don't worry so much. Someone from the co-op has arrived; he's at Big Head's house now. So take out a loan from the co-op and see what happens next if you find you can't pay it back. I don't believe they'd make you pay with your life. A day lived is a day earned. Even Heaven spares the rootless grass, so it has to give you a way out."

12

"Time for a meeting." Big Head's voice boomed in the village after dinner. "All men must attend."

"Listen to that. He plans to put another nail in our coffin," Laoshun said.

"We'll be hexed to death by our debts," his wife said. "Actually the loan is what will hex us. The interest alone is enough to put the fear of death in me."

"What are you worrying about? We won't be the only ones," Mengzi said. "If everyone else takes out a loan, we can too."

That was what Laoshun would have said, but now he had to object, since it had come out of Mengzi's mouth, not his. "That's easy for you to say. Once we get the loan, the repayment will still have to be scraped off of me. Which one of you young masters might be concerned about something like that?"

Seeing Mengzi's face turn red, Laoshun's wife knew her son was about to talk back to his father, so she signaled him with her eyes, but it was either too late or ineffective.

"When did I scrape anything off of you? We take out a loan and then pay it back after we sell the grain. You aren't the only one who works in the field, you know. Would it make you happy if I said you were? We're like beasts of burden, but you take all the credit and treat us like freeloaders."

Laoshun knew his son was right, but he could not bring himself to admit it, for that would be a loss of paternal authority. He wanted to rebuke his son, but could not find a good reason, so he turned to his wife. "See how he acts when his old man can still work. He'll probably eat us alive when I can't work any longer. I'd have no say in anything."

"Say what you should and not what you shouldn't." She glared at him. "The harvest didn't come in from your hard work alone. So stop saying you're always having things scraped off of you. You should be ashamed of yourself for saying that."

"All right." He laughed. "The young masters are all grown up now. From now on, I'll go sun myself by the south wall after every meal and leave everything to you."

"That's fine with me," Mengzi said. "What have you done but complain about this and gripe about that? Just eat your own food and take care of yourself. I don't believe the earth will stop moving without you."

"Great. I've raised a young master who can take charge. That will save me a lot of work." Laoshun looked at his son with a hint of a smile. "You attend tonight's meeting."

"Sure." Mengzi left with a sulky look.

The sun had already set, but it was still stifling hot. Outside on an earthen berm, bare-chested men were eating dinner, while children kicked up dirt as they jumped rope nearby. Unconcerned, the men kept eating, stopping only to talk. Mengzi overheard that they were talking about the rising cost of water. Uninterested in joining the conversation, he walked over to Baigou's house.

Baigou was drinking with some village youths; Mengzi recognized one of them, a man from Nanzhuang who was always getting into fights. The others looked familiar, but he couldn't recall their names. Baigou, whose eyes were bloodshot, did not bother to make the introductions; he merely thrust a cup of liquor into Mengzi's hands. It had a nice fiery taste. Mengzi liked it so much he downed the whole cup.

"Damn!" Baigou was slurring his words. "No guts, no glory. Would you do it, Mengzi? I'm—going to— these days, only people with guts manage to eat their fill. Timid people will starve to death. So would you?" His eyes were so red they seemed ready to spew blood.

"Do what?"

"What else?" Baigou gritted his teeth, bulging the muscles on his cheeks. "What else is there? Business deals with no investment, like the highwaymen on Mt. Liang."

Mengzi was shocked. He was known for his courage, but something like that had never occurred to him. "You're drunk, Baigou. You can eat whatever you want, but you can't do whatever you like."

Looking at Mengzi out of the corner of his eye, Baigou tried to shove him out. "Get out of here. What do you mean, I can't do whatever I like? Who says? Officials do that, so why can't I? So will you do it? If you will, we'll do it together and we'll get to eat and drink the good stuff together. If not, to hell with you."

"You've had too much to drink, Baigou." Mengzi said with a smile. "I'm through talking to you."

A skinny man glanced at Mengzi with an imperceptible smile while pushing Baigou's hands away "Don't listen to him, he's drunk."

"Who's drunk?" Baigou yelled. "Don't worry. Mengzi is a real pal who won't sell us out even if it cost him his life. The way the world is now, there's no need to watch your every step."

"Enough." The skinny man's face darkened as he smacked Baigou on the shoulder. "No more nonsense, all right? We're going to leave if you keep spewing this rubbish. That little bit of liquor and you're raving like that, like we were really planning to do something."

"Don't worry, he won't tell. Mengzi is a real pal."

"Baigou!" The skinny man shouted.

"Let him talk." Mengzi smiled. "That's just how he is. He's always talking about killing someone. Drunken words are like farting in your sleep. Just let him talk."

"You're right, of course." A smile finally emerged on the man's face.

"I have to go to a meeting." Mengzi disentangled himself and headed toward Big Head's house, trailed by Baigou's shouts: "Who farts in his sleep? I'm really going to do it; mark my word. If they chop my head off, it'll just leave a bowl-size scar." Angry bravado.

Mengzi could tell that they were planning something big, but not because of how Baigou was shouting; he was just being himself. Instead, he sensed the truth of Baigou's outburst from how strongly the skinny man strained to conceal their plan. Mengzi felt like doing something himself; something inside was galvanizing him into shouting, leaping, even wielding a knife.

A steady din emerged from Big Head's house when Mengzi arrived. Everyone who had heard about the fee hike was loudly "screwing someone's mother." Their collective shouts lasted only a while before turning into sighs; newcomers picked up the slack and raised new shouts. Finally Big Head banged on a table.

"Why curse me? Did I raise the fee? Go scream at City Hall if you've got the guts."

Big Head pointed to a man in a Western suit once the complaints died down.

"This is Director Fu from the co-op. If you need money, apply for a loan from him today. If you've got the money, then hand it over. Everyone knows that the crops are dying in the sun, so say only what must be said. Save your idle farts for later."

"What's an idle fart?" Beizhu snorted. "Reservoir water came from the heavens. Did the government pay the heavens for it? If not, what gives them the right to hike the fee? We were just talking, but you call that idle farts."

"He's right." Echoes of Beizhu's sentiment rose up. "He's so right."

"Let's not waste time talking about that." Big Head waved them off. "I don't care if it's idle farts or not, but it's no idle matter that we won't get water without paying. Actually, the city leadership is worried sick too. Direction Fu just told me that the City Party Secretary and mayor have gone up to Big Buddha Mountain to pray for rain. They burned spirit money and got down on their knees to kowtow to Heaven. Who do you think they did that for? For us, the peasants, of course. We can't blame them for no electricity, can we? They didn't pack up the electricity and walk off with it. The matter at hand today is collecting the fee, because the crops wait for no man."

The villagers quieted down, their reasons behind the complaints wiped away by the news of the city leadership praying for rain.

"Out of deep concern, the leadership ordered the agriculture bank to lend as much as needed and do whatever is necessary to save the crops." Director Fu was all smiles.

"Why is the fee amount going up?" Handless Wei asked.

"That's out of my hands. I'm only in charge of loans and payment collection." Fu turned to Big Head. "Shall we start?"

"Hurry up and get your loans, or else go home and get the money. No one in the village will get water if there's even one missing payment. Don't let a single mouse turd ruin the pot."

The villagers held their collective breath, as if they were putting their fingerprints on contract to sell themselves.

"I'll borrow five hundred." Mengzi said after a quick calculation. Three hundred will go to pay for the water while the remaining two hundred will come in handy if Hantou needs more for his surgery.

"You'll only need three hundred for the six people in your family. No need for any more," Big Head said. "The co-op will give you a loan for the water and nothing else. Is that right, Director Fu?"

"Money is tight." Fu nodded. "Borrow just enough to pay the water fee." He handed a form to Mengzi and showed him how to fill it out. "There," he said when it was filled out. "You can go now. Next."

"Where's the money? I filled out the form, so when do I get the money?"

"Did you think they'd actually give you money?" Big Head sniggered. "It will be transferred directly to the Water Bureau. You'd spend it all if we gave it to you, and we couldn't do a thing about that. The government knows how to stop peasants like you from scheming."

Taken aback, Mengzi blinked, unable to utter a word.

"I've seen officials cheating the people, but not the other way around," Beizhu laughed coldly. "Now you're afraid of us. That's funny. Real funny."

"Nothing funny here. A peasant should be contented with millet gruel," Big Head said. "Now who's next?" Goubao stepped up.

13

Mengzi walked out, feeling a mixture of disappointment and humiliation—disappointment because his plan to borrow two hundred extra was foiled, and humiliation because he did not even touch the money after taking out a loan. But soon his forgetful nature took over, and his emotions quickly left behind in the dust he kicked up.

A lonely white moon hung in the sky, a sign of the beautiful night to come and no time to go to bed early. Usually he would be playing cards with Baigou or shooting the breeze with Beizhu, but tonight Beizhu was still at Big Head's chaotic house getting a loan. Baigou was drunk, and, like the dark character in *The Water Margin* who was always saying he'd "kill his way into the capital to take over the government," was ready to bring his broad axe down on something or someone. It would surely feel good, but Mengzi knew he couldn't do it. He was Mengzi, the ferocious one, but not ferocious enough to lose sight of reality. He knew this was not a night to be at Baigou's house.

So where to go? On such a quiet night, his heart felt empty. It was never easy to sit through a night, especially a long one, and he dreaded the prospect of tossing and turning in bed.

There was no better place than Shuangfu's house, he concluded, though it wasn't without problems. He had made himself scarce since the incident. People were aware that he was implicated in Shuangfu's plan to divorce his wife, for which he considered himself responsible. He felt inevitable pangs of guilt, though he flaunted his conquest when joking with his male friends. No matter how he looked at it, he did climb up on her *kang*, thus becoming the excuse for Shuangfu's demand; though he might have found another cause without him, Mengzi had made it easy for Shuangfu to achieve his goal. Mengzi felt terrible when he recalled her lonely figure—strangely, she appeared lonely in his mind.

What would have happened if I hadn't slept with her that night? Maybe Shuangfu would not have asked for a divorce. If so, then what?" The answer was, she'd still be a straw widow, which meant she would likely have an affair, which meant the man would be caught, and divorce would still be the only possible outcome. Mengzi felt better about himself after coming up with this reasoning.

Maybe that's what people mean by fate, he said to himself.

He had run into her a few times since then and she had hurried away with her head down each time. He wondered if she hated him, though she did not really mean that much to him; he couldn't even recall her name, though he remembered her telling him once. She had always been "Shuangfu's wife," and he did not know what to call her now, since he could not and did not care to recall her name. She had only been in his thoughts and his life when he felt the urge to get into her bed. He forgot about her once he climbed off the *kang*.

He was going to her house on this night because he truly wanted to know how she was doing. She always came to mind when boredom was too much to bear; he did not think it was wrong to feel that way about her, since to him, women were good for cooking, sewing, and untying her pants. That was all.

The light was on at her house, but he no longer felt the same kind of excitement as before. To him, she was like a book he'd read and could go back to when he had nothing better to do; but the sense of novelty and the thrill were gone. Suddenly he heard a man's voice; it was Huaqiu, who was laughing and talking. Mengzi did not hear her voice, although he imagined she was probably laughing soundlessly.

His head seemed to swell, as complex emotions rose up. What did he feel? Disgust? Humiliation? Surprise? Maybe all of the above, or none of the above. She hadn't promised him anything, and yet he felt deceived.

The door was flung open, splashing light on Mengzi and revealing her in the doorway with a basin in her hands. She stopped at the sight of him, but soon a smile emerged at the corners of her mouth, while Huaqiu's smile froze on his face.

"My father told me to come borrow some money," Huaqiu muttered.

Bullshit. Mengzi cursed inwardly. Your father was getting a loan at Big Head's house. He smiled without replying, rattling Huaqiu even more; his lips moved, but no words came out.

"Are you afraid of him?" She cast Huaqiu a glance. "Just tell him you want to sleep with me. What are you afraid of? He wanted to. So, are you both afraid? I'm not. You don't want to lose face, but I don't care. What is face? It's worse than a rag. You can toss it away when you no longer want it."

Huaqiu looked first at the woman and then at Mengzi; he appeared to be about to say something, but instead sidled out the door. She laughed, seeing that Mengzi could not stay, but could not leave either, as if he were rooted to the spot.

"You see, this is what men are like," she said with a contemptuous glance. She laughed until there were tears in her eyes, which unnerved Mengzi, who could not stand to see a woman cry. What would people say if they saw her crying like that? After standing there for a few awkward moments, he realized that the best thing for him to do was leave.

He was relieved when he reached the main road and rounded the corner. No one would know where he'd been now. Then again, why had he been afraid that people would know? he wondered. He'd been exposed like the lice on a bald man's head. Sometimes he felt the urge to do whatever he felt like, but could not shake off the feeling that he might have ulterior motives. Mengzi hated himself for not having had the courage to openly say, "I want to sleep with you," when the woman taunted him.

Seeing two dark shapes coming toward him, Mengzi coughed loudly, like whistling through the graveyard to show he wasn't afraid, which actually had the opposite effect. The cough was filled with conviction but lacked confidence.

"Who's that?" one of the shapes asked. Mengzi heard the phlegmy voice of Maodan.

"It's me," he answered in a loud voice.

"Who's me?" Maodan asked.

"Stop asking. It's Mengzi." That was Gimpy Five's voice. When they got closer, Mengzi saw that Gimpy was leading a donkey cart. He also saw something writhing on the cart and he detected the strong smell of liquor.

"Everything's fine," Maodan said. "We're taking Wuzi to see a doctor. Honest—we're taking him to a doctor—he'd run off—if we didn't tie him down—hard to manage."

"That's enough," Gimpy Five bellowed.

Mengzi finally saw Wuzi, who was tied up on the cart, also the source of the smell of liquor. "That's the truth. He has to see a doctor, or he'll just get worse."

The donkey snorted loudly as it clip-clopped along. Mengzi turned to walk off, but hurried footsteps caught up with him. "Mengzi." It was Gimpy Five. "Don't tell anyone you saw us, please," he whispered.

Gimpy's beard tickled the Mengzi's face. He grunted his agreement and backed away. The old man repeated his request before running off to catch up with the cart.

With the sounds of hurried footsteps ringing in his ears, Mengzi knew that something was up.

14

"What kind rubbish are you spewing now? You'd better shut your trap," Laoshun snapped at Mengzi the following morning, when he mentioned his nighttime encounter with Gimpy Five. But then Laoshun sat blankly for a while before he sighed and softened his tone: "Don't bring it up again, something like this." He sighed in mid sentence.

"What's the matter now?" Lingguan's mother asked.

"Not you, too. You're a woman." Laoshun shot her a look and stood up on shaky legs as if he'd suddenly aged a decade.

He walked out to the gate. The sun was a white ball, so pale it looked nothing like a morning sun. Another day hot enough to kill a donkey. Oblivious to the heat, Laoshun felt he'd entered a different world, where everything was a blur. Confused, he felt himself enveloped in a bleak sadness. Not missing the implication of what Mengzi had told him, he wanted to go see Gimpy Five.

The street was getting crowded, but he felt separated from the crowds by a great distance. Handless Wei was laughing as he walked by with his donkey, followed by someone named Genxi, rope and stake in hand, leading a goat-sized young donkey, and Huaqiu's mother carrying two buckets of water over her shoulder. He heard Huilanzi's soft voice as she fed their pigs. Goats bleated along the way as they were being let out, barely containing their excitement. Everything looked real and yet appeared illusory to him.

What's he doing now? Laoshun asked himself. Gimpy Five's wooden look appeared before his eyes. He could not imagine any changes on that impassive face. Maybe he looked the same, a man who would never change, even if the sky were to fall. Maybe Gimpy was sitting on hunches smoking on the *kang*, motionless as a rock. But not his wife, who cried easily and often. She would be hoarse from sobbing and choking on tears; how could she not be crying?

Laoshun did hear someone crying, and thought it must be Gimpy Five's wife. But he looked around and saw that it was coming from Baldy Wang's house. A crowd had formed, and was chattering away at the gate. Goubao walked up to Laoshun.

"What'as the world come to? he complained. "This is outrageous, stealing pigs."

Laoshun learned that someone had carried Baldy Wang's big fat pig off on a three-wheeler the night before.

"See there. When your luck is lousy, even your farts hit the back of your feet. Baldy Wang is so poor he has practically nothing to eat but the northwestern wind. He pinned his hopes on that pig, and now, it's all over for him. His wife tried to hang herself over the family tragedy, but they managed to save her. Think about that, hei." Goubao said.

Laoshun frowned, annoyed by Goubao's dry laugh. Baldy Wang has lost a pig, Why were you making that sound? This he said to himself. He walked off with a disdainful snort.

Baldy Wang's wife was still wailing as if they'd lost a son. Sprawled on the ground, she was covered in mud, her face streaked with dirt and tears. Fengxiang, who had returned only two days before, after a miscarriage, was drying her own tears while talking to Baldy's wife. His spittle flying, Beizhu cursed:

"That thief is rotten. Why couldn't he steal something else? Why their pig, after all their hard work to raise it."

"That's true," exclaimed a chorus of onlookers.

"What's the world come to? They'll probably steal bundled wheat out in the fields next," someone said.

"You said it!"

"People are getting more and more wicked."

"That's true. That's so true."

Baldy Wang squatted on bricks by his gate, seemingly beyond feelings. Big Head and other neighbors squatted nearby silently, as if to see who had the stoniest look.

"That's enough," Meng Eight said to talk the woman around. "You can stop crying now. What's lost is lost. Crying isn't going to bring it back. Just consider it money for the thief to pay his medical bills."

"He's right," Beizhu said. "Or money for his coffin. Besides, lost money can ward off potential disaster."

She refused to listen and continued to cry.

"That's easy for you to say," Fengxiang said, giving Beizhu a look. "Do you know how hard it is to raise a pig? You have to scrounge for all the food you feed it, everything from corncobs to proper grain. Pigs provide what they use for clothing, school expenses, daily necessities, everything. People who don't have to bend their backs to talk don't know a thing about back pain."

That only made the woman cry harder. In addition to howling, Baldy's wife now began to smack the ground with her hands, sending dust flying.

With a displeased grunt, Beizhu stomped his feet and said to Fengxiang, "Fine. The pig is gone and all is lost. Why don't you tell her to go try hanging herself again? She didn't succeed last time, but she can keep trying until she does."

Realizing that what she'd said was out of line, Fengxiang tried to smooth it over: "He's right. It's gone, and crying won't bring it back. If you get sick from crying, you'll have to spend even more and that will make it a worse tragedy. Whoever stole your pig will see his hands rot off, his family will die, and—"

"You don't even know how to curse. Here, I'll show you." Beizhu laughed and started to hum a tune in a nasal voice:

If an official stole my pig, he'd fall off his private car.
If a Taoist monk stole my pig, he'd have a trumpet between his cheeks.
If a Buddhist monk stole my pig, his bald pate stick in a donkey trough.
If a young girl stole my pig, she'd marry a man with a limp dick.
If a young man stole my pig, he'd marry a stone woman.

The neighbors laughed, which lightened the atmosphere and made Beizhu so pleased with himself that he continued with even less savory lines that incurred tittering curses from the women.

But the gloom did not leave Baldy Wang's face. Sensing that his wisecracks were inappropriate, Beizhu changed the subject. "Aiya! We nearly forgot the most important thing. We have to report the theft at the police station."

"And when we catch that thief, we'll beat the shit out of him," Huilanzi said.

"What's the point?" Goubao said with a contemptuous laugh. "The missing pig is worth maybe five or six hundred yuan. But when those lords and masters come down to investigate, they have to eat and drink, and a few meals will use up the money we could get back for the pig. In the end, we'll have nothing, and the investigation will be a total waste of time."

"He's right," said Laoshun. "When Niu Three at the Dragon King Temple lost a tape recorder, he reported the theft, and wound up spending enough to buy three new tape recorders. The investigators came up with less than a pubic hair."

"I have to agree with you," Beizhu said. "They're champions in browbeating ordinary people and complete idiots in solving crimes."

"Besides, one would rather die of poverty than curse Heaven, and die of an injustice than rely on the government," Laoshun said.

"We have to be more careful from now on, with thieves so blatant they'll steal a pig. We have to form a night patrol, or one of us could be next," Meng Eight said slowly.

"But thieves don't follow a schedule or announce where they'll hit next. This isn't a small village, and patrols can't cover every spot—but it's better than nothing."

"We'll do the best we can," Meng said. "Teams with two or three men patrolling through the night. A thief can't sneak off with a pig without making noise. This requires some serious planning. We need to do it right."

Mengzi alone recalled the scheme Baigou was cooking up with his friends. Could it be them, he asked himself. The villagers would suffer more if they were the ones in "that line of work."

15

Maodan ran in nervously when Laoshun's family was having dinner.

"Let me fill a bowl for you," Laoshun's wife said.

"I can't." Maodan waved her off. "My tongue is frightened stiff."

"What happened?" Laoshun asked, but the young man just hemmed and hawed.

"Out with it. Does it have to do with last night?" Mengzi asked, earning a glare from Maodan, but he went on. "We're not a bunch of strangers." That earned him a look from his father, so he corrected himself, "We're not strangers."

With a miserable groan, Maodan held his head in his hands and hunkered down, but quickly stood up again. "So fast," he said. "Just think."

"What was so fast?" Laoshun asked him.

"The police. They went straight to Gimpy Five's house when they got to our village." Maodan's face was a ghostly white. With trembling lips, he got down on his knees in front of Mengzi.

"Just look at you." Mengzi jumped up, as if dodging sparks from a charcoal fire. "What do you think you're doing? Spit it out, and get up."

"I tell you, I didn't want to go, but Gimpy Five dragged me along." Maodan refused to get up. "I didn't care about his hundred yuan, but he insisted. He promised he wouldn't rat on me and that no one would know, no one but you, since you saw us. No one will know if you don't say anything."

"What's going on?" Laoshun said. "Get up."

The young man finally stood up. Laoshun's wife brought over a chair for him.

"What happened?" Laoshun asked him. "Tell us."

"Wuzi's dead." Maodan was choking up.

They fell silent. Mengzi looked at his father, who looked at his wife, but no one said a word. The pressure in the room was becoming unbearable when Maodan said tearfully, "I'll tell you the truth. When we were taking him to see a doctor, he stopped to pee and fell off the cliff."

Silence returned. No one responded. Maodan was sucking air

between his teeth.

"He's dead, and that's that." Laoshun finally said hoarsely, as if he needed a drink of water. "There's nothing else anyone can do, I know that."

"He fell, he did. I didn't push him."

"No one said you did." Laoshun sighed and wiped his eyes. "That boy had suffered enough, so it's all right. An early death brings early liberation, so now he can be reborn to a better place. It's no one's fault. He should not have been born in the pit of poverty. Then he had that terrible condition. It's no one's fault."

"You're right." Maodan looked somewhat relieved. "It's really no one's fault. It was his fate. No one did him any harm."

Laoshun's wife began to sob, making Maodan panic again. He glanced at Laoshun, then at Mengzi, and finally at Laoshun's wife, looking like a baby animal that has fallen into a trap. "But—

"But—" he repeated. "But—" he couldn't finish.

"Damn him—" Maodan changed the subject. "I didn't want to go, but he begged me, pleaded, over and over. I had no choice. It wasn't for the hundred yuan—"

"You shithead," Laoshun growled. "Would you stop talking about money? He fell and that's that. Forget about the money."

"Right," Maodan said. "It wasn't about money. I didn't care about the money. Besides, we agreed on a hundred, but I haven't seen a cent."

"A real shit." Laoshun shook his head. "Keep that trap of yours under lock and key, and not another word about money. Otherwise, people will know what you've done."

As if a light had gone on in his head, Maodan appeared to understand what Laoshun was saying, but he shook his head again. "Of course I won't. But Gimpy Five—would he—go back on his word?"

"You're a real shit." Laoshun blew up. "Just keep your mouth shut, will you? You beg us not to tell, but you're the one with the loose tongue. You can't keep a fart from escaping your backside. You must have a craving for a bullet in the head."

"I won't say a word, all right?" Maodan was frightened. "I'll be a mute, pretending my lips were glued together. How's that? Honest, I didn't really care about that hundred yuan. I mean it. Let that be money count as my medicine."

"Why are you going on like this if you really don't care?" Mengzi said.

"Can't I even talk?" Maodan said. "It was a hundred yuan, no matter what you say. Just thinking about it makes me—"

"It takes all kinds." Laoshun sneered. "Get out of here. I can't stand the sight of you, you and that stinking trap that can't hold a sound in. At a time like this, you should be looking for a rock to stuff your mouth shut."

Maodan tucked his neck in and, blinking rapidly, wanted to say something, but had trouble getting the words out. With some considerable effort, he finally found his voice: "If you promise not to tell, I'll split the hundred with you, fifty-fifty."

"Get out!" Laoshun roared, his face an angry red. He took off a shoe and flung it at Maodan, but it flew over his head and hit the wall. Maodan was startled, but quickly recovered and bounded out the door.

16

A wind blew up.

It was a wind unique to the desert, scorching hot, raging mad, and wreaking havoc. Sand flew everywhere, the small village shook, and the sun shrank back to hide in mid sky where it was a pinpoint of dim light.

The villagers were out in the wind, because Gimpy Five was being taken away by a wailing police van.

He had confessed immediately.

According to Beizhu, the police had come to investigate after someone recognized a dead body as the madman from Shawan. To everyone's surprise, Gimpy Five had admitted that he'd done it to "rid the people of a pest" the moment the police walked in.

"I committed no crime," he'd said calmly.

But they had to take him away.

Undaunted by the wind, Gimpy Five kept his eyes nearly shut and his back as straight as he could; with his beard and hair fluttering in the wind, his impassive face had the look of someone going willingly to his death. The policemen, unused to the wind and sand of the desert, kept raising their arms as if to fend it off.

Laoshun's heart was heavy, not simply because of Wuzi's death, but also because of Gimpy Five in police custody.

"Will he pay with his life?"

He didn't know. Of course he didn't. Laoshun was ignorant of the law, but he did know the principle that one paid money to settle a debt and paid with one's life for a life taken. The issue was, would Gimpy Five have to pay with his life for taking the life of someone like Wuzi, who had been a danger to the villagers? Laoshun did not know. His mind was a jumble of thoughts, like swirling yellow dust.

The white van was covered in dust, but still dazzled white in the yellow surroundings. To Laoshun, white, the color of mourning, did not bode well. Maybe he'll never come back, he told himself as he looked at his friend, who wore no expression. One of the policemen was talking to Big Head. The policeman terrified Laoshun, who, strangely, felt his legs give way whenever he saw someone from the government. Wuzi's mother was wailing loudly and muttering something, but it was impossible to tell whether she was crying for her son's death or her husband's arrest. Several village women were helping her up.

That woman is bound to suffer more, Laoshun thought.

Laoshun knew that Big Head was begging the policeman for leniency for Gimpy Five, so typical of Big Head; the team leader could maintain his composure and continue to be a big head when dealing with government agents. After listening to him for a while, the policeman, a fat one, waved his hands, as if shooing away flies that were bothering him.

The fat policeman pushed Big Head out of his way and prodded Gimpy, who then stumbled toward the frighteningly white police van.

A gust of wind peppered them with sand pebbles. To Laoshun the sand felt like whips lashing at his face. The policeman, clearly affected also, raised his arm to block the wind and sand; Gimpy Five, however, stood blankly by the van door, motionless in the howling wind and whipping sand.

Once the wind died down, the fat policeman pulled the van door open. Gimpy hesitated, unsure of how to get in properly, his stony face now showing a hint of unease. He surveyed the new interior before looking down at his exposed toes in beat-up cloth shoes. As if afraid to soil the van, he scraped his feet on the sand before reaching out to steady himself against the door. At that moment Laoshun saw a pair of shiny metal rings on his wrists, connected by a metal chain; those, he knew, were handcuffs, or what the villagers jokingly called Roman watches. A heartfelt pity rose from deep inside Laoshun at the sight of his friend attached to such a frightening object.

After getting into the van with difficulty, Gimpy Five returned to his blank self. His upper body tipped slightly forward as he sat on the edge of the seat, as if afraid he might crush the padding. The policeman jumped in and nudged Gimpy to the middle.

The white van drove off, siren wailing, the villagers looking on silently. Wuzi's mother was still howling, her voice starting to get hoarse. Someone sighed, and that became contagious; everyone began sighing.

"Gimpy Five is a good man," Beizhu said.

"He is," the others agreed.

"They shouldn't have arrested him," Beizhu continued, and the others echoed his sentiment.

"You're all standing around passing gas," Big Head said, sounding angry. "I didn't see any of you do anything just now."

Meng Eight got to his feet and headed silently out of the village, swaying as he walked on unsteady feet, like a sleepwalker.

Chapter Eighteen

1

Hantou's surgery, twenty-one days into his hospital stay, resulted in a diagnosis of cancer. The lump by his ribcage was smooth because of the membrane around it. Stupefied by the news, Lingguan turned numb; his tongue went dry.

"What?" he asked in disbelief.

"A malignant tumor on his liver, about the size of a small melon." The doctor watched him carefully.

"How long—does he have?"

"Hard to say, but not long. There's bleeding in the chest and a massive hemorrhage is likely."

"Does he know?"

"Not yet. He's still sedated."

"Did you remove it?" Lingguan felt his strength leave him, as a din echoed inside.

"I couldn't. I just sewed him back up. You need to pay five yuan for the tissue sample." The doctor pointed at a lump of flesh bobbing in a jar.

Lingguan rummaged through his pockets and brought out a handful of small bills. "Are these all right?"

"Sure. As long as it's money."

Lingguan's hands were shaking so badly he couldn't be sure he had the right amount after counting it several times. The doctor took the bills and counted them quickly before they disappeared into his pocket.

"Please, don't tell—the others—especially my parents—I'm the only one to know. Please?"

"Of course. Get your folks ready. They'll be bringing him down soon."

Lingguan walked back to the hallway, zombie-like, and leaned up against a wall, feeling himself go limp. One thought stood out amid the buzz in his head: What if Mother found out? His heart ached when he thought of her wrinkled face marked by years of pain and suffering.

Then another thought: he wished Hantou would die quickly. Liver cancer was the king of all cancers. Someone in their village had it, and his screams from the pain, like a lowing cow, had sliced at the villagers' hearts for months. Instant death would be better than suffering like that. Moreover, Lingguan shuddered at the thought of the despair Hantou would feel once he knew; that would be worse than death.

Everything felt like a bad dream—if only it were.

Could the diagnosis be wrong? Lingguan perked up, as if given a shot in the arm. It was possible. That would be wonderful. He mustered up the energy to walk back to the hall and wait for the doctor to come out.

"Be ready. Get some more people over here to lift him onto the bed. He'll be down any moment."

With great effort, Lingguan managed to ask, "Could it have been misdiagnosed, Doctor?"

"Unlikely." The doctor looked at him and continued in a firm voice, "Besides, there's the tissue sample, and we'll know when we get the test result."

"Could he have another operation if the result comes out negative?"

"We'll wait and see." The doctor smiled faintly.

Lingguan felt a bud of hope sprout in his heart.

He went downstairs, where his father greeted him.

"Did he have the operation?"

"Yes, he did." Lingguan's heart skipped a beat when he looked into his father's murky eyes, but he forced a smile.

"Good, that's good." Laoshun exhaled. "As long as it's over."

Lingguan's mouth was bone dry and his throat felt as parched as leather being cured under a searing sun. He wanted to swallow to smooth the itchiness, but his tongue was numb and devoid of moisture. He sighed when he thought of his mother.

"Tell me the truth." Laoshun blanched. "Is it really bad?"

"No." Lingguan smiled. He knew he'd put on a convincing performance when he saw the color slowly return to his father's face.

"Good, as long as it's not bad," Laoshun muttered, as if in a trance, before blurting out, "Do you have all the help you need?"

"I think so," Lingguan said. "There's also the nurse."

The door to the operating theater opened.

Hantou was lying on a gurney, his chest exposed. He was awake; his eyes were sunken and his lips colorless on a face that was frighteningly yellow. What Lingguan found most shocking was how such drastic changes could occur in only a couple of hours. My dear brother, do you know what you have? Lingguan cried out silently.

Hantou moaned.

Laoshun rushed up to him.

"Step back." The doctor tried to wave Laoshun back. "Try to bear it, Hantou," he said. "Do your best."

"Get back, I said," the doctor said impatiently. They pushed the gurney into an elevator. Lingguan and his father raced down the stairs.

Hantou moaned when they walked into his room. "They operated on me without a shot. When the knife first went on, aiyo; it hurt like hell."

"Did you give him a gift? The one in charge of anesthesia?" A ward mate asked.

"We had to give him one, too?" Lingguan asked.

"Of course. No wonder—no wonder." The man shook his head and sighed.

Looking at Hantou's bandaged and tubed belly and then at his sallow face, Lingguan's heart ached terribly. Hantou would not have had to suffer through the operation if they'd known what he had. Someone once told Lingguan that an ultrasound can tell the difference between an infected liver and cancer. In other words, the doctors had lied to them, for money, most likely. But deep down, Lingguan knew that Hantou would have had the operation even if they had known; his family would be appeased and would give up only after the surgery. He shuddered when he thought about how the doctor had made a seven-inch incision on Hantou's belly without anesthesia.

"Aren't they afraid patients will sue them if they skip it?" Lingguan asked.

"The doctor would never admit it. He'd say the patient had reacted slowly. I hear there's some scientific basis for that; anesthesia has little effects on those who drink a lot."

"My brother doesn't drink."

"That's terrible." Laoshun sighed and looked at Lingguan, who knew his father was reproaching him for his incompetence, which had caused Hantou's suffering.

2

Lingguan was on the verge of a nervous breakdown.

Hantou's moans were like a blade sawing through Lingguan's heart; it pained him to see sweat oozing from his brother's gaunt, pallid face.

Does he know? Lingguan examined Hantou's face, but failed to detect any sign. Maybe he doesn't, but he'll realize that the lump is still there. Lingguan tensed at the thought. If— The earlier thought reared its head. If he'd died on the operating table, it would've been so much better; he'd have died without being aware of the truth.

With his eyes fixed on Hantou, the corners of Laoshun's mouth twitched, as if trying to transfer the pain from his son to himself. Lingguan looked at his father, who wore the hint of smile, as if to say, "I'm glad the surgery is over."

If he only knew— Lingguan could not bear to finish the thought.

A nurse came in with a syringe. With great effort, Lingguan and his father managed to turn Hantou onto his side. Lingguan followed the nurse out.

"Please keep it a secret. No one must know what he has."

"I know," she said.

That night Lingguan spread out bedding on a borrowed army cot and placed a blanket in the middle for him and his father to sit on. The room had a terrible smell, but what Lingguan found unbearable were his brother's moans, which grated against every nerve in his body. Soon he was on the verge of a nervous breakdown, so he walked out and sat on a heating vent in the hallway, the window open to bathe his head in a cool night breeze.

Laoshun, obviously also unable to stand the torment in the room, came out with his pipe. Smoking was not allowed in the hospital, but he managed to sneak in a few puffs late at night. He knew the acrid tobacco smoke could irritate the patient's throat, making him cough and pull at his wound, so he shut the door and blew the foul smelling smoke through the open window.

Lingguan noticed that his father had lost weight. He had seldom looked into his father's face, which seemed unchanged; tan and rife with wrinkles, with a few scraggly whiskers that gave him a coarse appearance. It was a common face, the kind Lingguan would trouble picking out in a crowd. Father had always been gaunt, burdened with the look of someone who had been through many hardships. His once healthy glow was gone, replaced by a wizened, steely gray.

"I don't mind being poor, as long as no one is sick in the family," Laoshun said emotionally after a few puffs.

Every time his father breathed a sigh of relief and said "I'm glad the surgery is over," Lingguan felt like crying. But he could not; he had to force a smile. Once, when his smile was not authentic enough, his father was put on alert: "Are you sure everything's all right?"

Lingguan had to quickly say, "Everything's fine. Why wouldn't it be?" He had to rearrange his face so that his smile could put his father's mind at ease.

He knew he couldn't hide it from him forever, but he wanted to drag it out as long as possible, which meant that he alone would have to shoulder all the pain and pressure. If Mengzi were around, he might share the truth, so the two brothers could cry together, comfort each other and plan the next step. But Mengzi was at home, waiting for water to save the crops and their future. Lingguan felt alone and helpless. This was the first really big event in his life, as his father had been the one who'd taken care of everything. He'd been a tall tree, sheltering Lingguan all these years, which was why he staggered under this sudden blow, and the disaster sent him into a daze.

What he had been hoping for was a misdiagnosis.

It was now the only bright spot in the darkness of his life. He repeated the same question to the doctor, who answered without hesitation, "Normally, no."

"Normally no, but there could be an exception, couldn't there?"

"Not this time."

"Why not?"

"We opened him up. The cancer has grown to the size of small melon. You'll know once you get the test results."

"What if it's not cancer? Can you operate on him again?"

"We'll wait and see."

"He's so young. How could he get that kind of illness?"

"Age has nothing to do with it. In fact, the younger the patient, the worse it is. The cancer cells can multiple very fast."

"But he's only in his twenties."

"I've had one as young as six."

Lingguan resented the doctor's reply. His world was falling apart, but the doctor sounded like he was enjoying himself at Lingguan's expense, taking delight in his misery. Otherwise he would not be looking at Lingguan like that, as if checking his ability to bear up under pressure. Why was he doing that?

"I'll take whatever Heaven doles out to me; if it can give it, I can take it." That was one of his father's favorite comments, but Hantou was only in his twenties and had yet to live life to the fullest. Lingguan turned into a tight knot when he was reminded that his brother had weeks, maybe even just days to live.

As if he were losing his grip, Lingguan roamed the other rooms, hoping to find someone else with liver cancer, which might to make him feel better. But there were only sagging stomachs, hepatitis, gastric bleeding, kidney inflammation, and the like. Those weren't real illness. None was as serious as Hantou's terrifying affliction.

People are always saying the good will be rewarded and the evil-doers will be punished. Then why would a decent man like Hantou get this horrible disease?

Lingguan recalled that he had studied Hantou's palm before he was hospitalized; he had a long, thick, deep lifeline, straight with no split. "You'll be fine," he'd said. "See, your lifeline is so long." Hantou had smiled foolishly, "You're right. I know I'll come out alive." Remembering the scene, Lingguan cursed himself. Nonsense. To him palm reading was rubbish, totally worthless.

The deserted hallway was quiet late at night. Alone in the silence, Lingguan let his thoughts run wild, cursing one moment, crying another, followed by prayers. Recalling a monk who'd once said that all wishes will be granted if one sincerely begs the Guanyin Bodhisattva, he put his palms together to pray for the Bodhisattva "to remove Hantou's cancer and restore good health to him." He repeated his prayer, wishing he could pluck out his heart to offer to the deity. At some point, he thought he saw colorful clouds in the sky, where, amid

Buddhist music, Guanyin Bodhisattva stood on a lotus-shaped cloud and sprinkled purifying water from a willow branch over Hantou . His prayer finished, Lingguan went back inside, only to hear his brother moaning in pain, as the cancer obviously never stopped growing.

Lingguan was wasting away fast.

3

His mother and Lanlan came to see Hantou. Lingguan nearly wept when he saw his mother; he turned around to dry his tears, silently calling out, Mama, poor Mama. Do you know he has only weeks left? But he put on a smile when he turned back to face her. She wasn't smiling, nor did she have her husband's happy look over the surgery. Instead, she looked pained, the muscles on her face twitching as she sucked in air, as if she had been the one undergoing surgery. As she held Hantou's hands, she was soon sweating, seemingly having exhausted her strength trying to help him fend off the pain.

"I'm fine," Hantou said to his mother with a wan smile.

Lingguan glanced at his brother with watchful eyes. Does he know the lump is still there? He didn't spot anything unusual in Hantou's face; the smile was genuine, not faked. Lingguan was relieved.

Lanlan wept silently.

Their mother pulled back the blanket to check on the surgical wound; it was covered by a small square of gauze that failed to conceal the bulge underneath. She sucked in more air and touched the spot gently, but then her hand froze in mid air as she turned to face Lingguan, whose heart was racing.

"Why does it still bulge like that?"

Lingguan was caught totally off guard.

"It's swollen," Hantou said. "It's from the operation."

She looked him in the eye. "It's all right, isn't it?"

"Of course it is, he said. "That happens to everyone who has an operation. The swelling has to go down before I can leave." She finally exhaled.

Lingguan washed an apple for her. He would never forget how she ate it, sort of gnawing at it, like a mouse. She was going through the motions, with nothing to show for her effort. With her eyes still on her son, she nibbled slowly, over and over, but failed to take any but the smallest bite. She did not cry, for she knew that was unlucky. Once long ago, when one of her children was ill, Grannie Shaman Qi had told her that a god of tears had jinxed the child, so she tried hard not to cry before them.

Lingguan felt a dull ache when he looked at his mother, who seemed to be gnawing on his heart, not the apple. She stopped abruptly, the apple suspended by her mouth. A long time passed before she turned to Lingguan and then to her husband, searching their faces gravely, as if trying to ferret out the truth.

"He's all right, isn't he?" she asked softly.

"Of course he is. Why do you think he wouldn't be?" Laoshun said almost scornfully.

She fixed her gaze on him and exhaled slowly before going back to nibble on the apple, her eyes now trained on Hantou's pallid face.

"Look at us." A young woman staying with one of the patients spoke up. "We were scared at first, but he got better after the surgery. He's leaving tomorrow."

"Really?" Laoshun's wife smiled. "You were scared, too."

"Sure. It felt like the sky was falling on us."

"That's understandable." Laoshun's wife heaved a sigh. "I felt like my mind was in a fog and my heart was tied up in a knots. I was worried, but now everything's fine."

"That's right," the man with a wormy infection of the liver joined in. "At least he had his surgery. The old man who was discharged a few days ago had his, but when the doctors couldn't find any kidney stones, they sewed him up. But the stone showed up in an X-ray. How about that? The old man was beside himself with anger; he cursed the doctors, but it was useless, of course. He wasted his money and would have to pay again for another operation. No matter how you look at it, we both had our operations. Everything's fine once you have that; at least you don't need another one. The pain is beyond human."

"You're right." Laoshun's wife was feeling more talkative. "No matter what, he had his operation, and that counts for everything. Money is nothing, as long as he's fine." Finally she took a real bite.

With a nearly inaudible sigh, Lingguan walked out of the room and saw Director Wang of Internal Medicine and Hantou's surgeon, Director Hou, talking in the hallway.

"I sent them away," the fat Director Wang said. "Told them we couldn't operate. Ke-ke." It was a self-satisfied laugh.

"Good," Hou said, "It was filled with pus. Disgusting. I'm glad you sent them off." The two laughed gleefully. Lingguan felt sick at heart. They were not what people called angels in white.

A slightly awkward look appeared on Hou's face when he noticed Lingguan's eyes on him, but he quickly resumed his indifferent expression. "Ah, I have the test results. It's liver cancer. Primary liver cancer." His eyes were gauging how the patient's family would take the bad news, but his tone seemed to be saying, "See. I was dead on, wasn't I?"

Lingguan walked into the nearby nurses' station. No one was

there, so he took his brother's chart to read the test result: "Liver cancer—cellular cancer in the liver—partial necrosis—signs of internal bleeding."

"Partial necrosis?" He felt renewed hope. "Could that lead to total necrosis?"

His heart racing, he hurried into the doctor's office and said, "I just read the chart. It says there's partial necrosis. Could the cancer cells all die out later?"

"Don't be so naïve, young man," the doctor said. "Those cells can't be eliminated. When one cell dies, a hundred more grow to replace it. We don't call it a malignant tumor for no reason."

Lingguan backed out to lean against the door weakly; inside the room the young woman was comforting his mother. He wished Hantou would vanish without a trace, to spare their mother the agony of seeing his dead body.

"With what he has, it's pointless to stay here any longer. Better to go home," the doctor said to Lingguan.

"You're kicking us out?" he demanded angrily. "Is that it?"

"It's not like that, young man," the doctor said. "That's not what I meant. He should go home and rest, or he could undergo radiotherapy or chemotherapy."

"Radiotherapy or chemotherapy. Will that help?"

"Hard to say. In his case, maybe he'd get better and maybe he'd die quicker. Based upon what I've seen, neither therapy will do much good in cases like his and will be a waste of money. Talk to him and convince him to go home in a few days."

Lingguan went back inside; his mother did not look as distraught as before. Apparently, the young woman had managed to set his mother's mind at ease, and he felt immense gratitude toward that simple-looking farm girl.

Lingguan's mother led him outside when there was a pause in the conversation and told him about Yindi's death. Lanlan had just told her, she added. Her eyes were sunken on her stony face, and she shuddered as she related the incident, but she did not cry. Lingguan's face fell; he was shaking all over, but could not utter a word.

She sighed and told him to keep it from Hantou until he got better. She also wanted him to find the time to talk to his sister. "She nearly died. The doctor said she could have bled out. The girl has had such a tough life, and now she has nothing to look forward to."

"That hothead." She wanted him to talk to Mengzi too. "When he heard about Yindi, he took a knife to go see Bai Fu. Luckily someone tipped Bai Fu off, and he went into hiding, sparing us some big trouble. Ai. These young men. What can you do about them?"

She went silent for a while before adding, "The sky is crashing down on us."

Chapter Nineteen

1

Mengzi went to Shuangfu's house after dinner; all that pent-up energy needed an outlet. With a body like a piece of white jade, Shuangfu's wife could help him cool off.

She was making the bed when he arrived, but she carried on and ignored him.

"Hey, it's only been a few days since I saw you, and you've already got yourself someone new," Mengzi said, but she continued to ignore him. He walked in and looked around. The girl wasn't home; he knew she was out playing somewhere, so he put his arms around Shuangfu's wife from behind and began feeling her up.

"Are you heartless or what?" she spoke up. "You can still be in the mood when your brother is in the hospital."

"That's no big deal. They're just opening a tiny hole in his belly. I'd still be doing this tonight even if I was to be beheaded tomorrow."

"You really are heartless," she replied, though with a laugh.

"What's the point of having a heart?" He said. "It's useless. It's out of our hands, whether it's a blessing or a misfortune, and calamities are unavoidable. So don't worry so much, it can't help." He moved her over to the *kang* and they kissed.

"The girl will be back," she said, so he quickly let go. She locked the door and then came back to let him have his way with her.

"Aiyo. I couldn't wait to see you," he said when they were finished, still breathing hard. "I thought about nothing but you when I went into the desert."

She got up to open the door before combing her hair at the mirror. "The girl is old enough now, and we can't go on like this. He sent a message saying we should get a divorce to avoid gossip. I keep the girl, and he said he'd give me a one-time settlement of two hundred thousand and then five hundred each month for child support. I sent my response back to tell him I didn't want a cent from him. He can come back to file the paper when he's free. But he should notify the man at the township office this time to make sure he doesn't make the trip in vain."

"Two hundred thousand! Why in the world did you turn that down?"

"Money over face, is that it?" She scowled at him. "Do you know what the money is? It's spit, his spit in my face. I'd sooner be a garbage scavenger than take his dirty money. Even if I were at the end of my rope, I refuse to believe that I couldn't feed myself."

"You're really something." He gave her a sober glance. "I didn't know you had it in you."

"When did you learn flattery?" She smiled. "I want to tell you something. When Huaqiu came that time, it really was to borrow money. You saw how his face turned red when I teased him, so don't you dare treat me as a slut who would untie her pants for any man who comes along."

"I know." Mengzi smiled too. "You're the chaste Wang Baochuan, who slept with quite a few men during her eighteen years of waiting for her husband to return.

"Go on, wag your tongue." She pinched him. "What can I say about you? You only care about yourself and are incapable of thinking of others. I'll be a straw widow forever."

"What do you mean, a straw widow?" Mengzi grinned. "How can you say that even before tying your pants back up?"

"You think that's all a woman wants, don't you? I know you think I'm a loose woman. Now I want you to tell me the truth. Are we for real or what?"

Mengzi knew what she was hinting at, but the idea of marrying her never occurred to him. He thought of her only when the flame of desire flared up. Once the fire died out, he noticed the age difference. "But—my father would never agree."

"What's that?" She turned her back to him. "Your father wouldn't agree? Did he give his consent when you climbed on top of me the first time? Huh? Did he give his consent when you and that no-good Shuangfu got into a fight? Now he might object, is that it? Everyone knows that Mengzi is the most obedient son in the village."

"Don't turn on old friend. Don't forget you're still Shuangfu's wife. Isn't it a bit premature to talk about this? When the time comes, it won't matter whether he agrees or not. All right?"

"It really doesn't matter what you decide. I'm not going to

shamelessly hang on to you. The divorce didn't go through last time because the township clerk was away. I told him to come back for it whenever he wants. That has nothing to do with you. I've thought it through and I want to go ahead with it. Money is nothing but colored paper. I don't want to be a straw widow just so I could have some of his. I don't care if you don't want to marry me. The frost hasn't killed off all the men in the world. Besides, it really doesn't matter which one, since you're all the same. I can see it clearly now; in the end, men are nothing but a dick, and I shouldn't treat them as real humans. They work best when I treat them as dicks, and when I don't, well…"

"Listen to you. What did I say? Did I say I don't want to marry you? You can treat me however you like. I'll marry you. Will that work for you now?" Mengzi kept his eyes on her, surprised to see how she'd suddenly turned into a stranger. He was amazed by all the things she'd just said. What a woman.

"Actually, I don't think you're heartless." She sighed. "But have you ever given this any thought? The girl is old enough to know what goes on here, and I can't keep carrying on with you or I'll look horrible in her eyes. Something has to be done. In fact, I know what's on your mind. You're a young rooster, while this would be my second marriage."

"Young rooster?" He laughed. "I broke eggs before you did."

She smiled, fixing her bewitching eyes on him.

"Say what you want. I'll go tell my father as soon as your divorce goes through, how's that?"

"No hurry. Actually, I just want everything out in the open so I'll know what's what. You're a man; I believe you and everything you said. But, remember, the frost didn't kill off all the men in the world."

Her daughter came in and walked right out again with a pout when she saw him.

"Stupid girl, no manners at all. What happened to her schooling?"

"That's all right." Mengzi smiled. "I'll take care of her attitude when I become her stepfather. A good whipping will change that."

"Don't you dare—" She had to laugh.

"But—you should take what he wants to give you. No need to turn it down."

"You're like all the rest!" She spat out. "I'll be frank with you. I don't want a cent of his stinking money. I came with nothing and I'll leave with nothing. I'm not even going to take the clothes he bought me. I have backbone, and I refused to believe that I can't have a decent life without him."

"What I meant was, you worked hard and should be rewarded," Mengzi said sheepishly. "He didn't earn that money on his own, so why should he keep it all?"

She snickered, but did not respond.

"Besides, why let him off so easily—"

"Enough." She crinkled her nose and kept her eyes nearly shut to show her disgust, as if he'd suddenly turned into something foul. "I know what kind of shitty idea you have in that head of yours. You want me to be a rich widow, don't you? Forget it, Mengzi. I was wrong about you. I thought you were an upright man with guts, but in fact you're a worthless shit. Get out. From now on, you go your way and I'll go mine. I still have my hands and I can work; even if I couldn't, I know a way out, either by knife or by rope. I'm not going to debase myself. No way." She picked up a feather duster and dusted the *kang*.

"Get out. I'm sleepy and am going to bed."

2

The cool water, with its roaring vitality, had finally come, as they had hoped.

Every man and woman in the village got into action to guard the water from thieves; shovels in hands, they had the impressive airs of republican guards. The sun was a singeing ball of fire, looking less like the sun and more like the mad Wuzi, spraying its heat to dry out the little moisture on faces that were turning dark red or burnt yellow, and made them all appear dazed. Only an urgent matter like watering the field could lift them out of their stupefied state.

Wearing a blackened, tattered straw hat, Laoshun squatted on a ridge by the sluice gate, mind and energy focused on smoking his pipe. The rushing water sounded cool, but he could not rid himself of a baffling agitation. The invisible thread tying his throat snapped at the arrival of water, but oddly, the good news failed to alleviate his agitation.

Maodan walked up with a shovel and a smile, a common sight on his face. He smiled so often it was almost a mask.

"Have you heard? Gimpy Five was on TV." He squatted down beside Laoshun, who frowned without replying. Of course he'd heard; that was the cause of his foul mood. He'd also heard that Gimpy Five had been interviewed by a journalist on TV news and had justified in what he'd done, convinced that he'd rid the village of a great harm. There was no mention of a prison sentence on TV. Since hearing about the interview, Laoshun could not stop thinking about his old friend, and Wuzi, who ceased to be a menace in Laoshun's eyes. Instead, he now recalled some of the amusing things Wuzi had done as a boy, such as peeing while he walked, like a cow, or running wild as a happy mule, or scooping up dirt to make so-called *mantou*, and so on. Now the boy was dead, gone just like that, and not from a debilitating illness. Laoshun's heart ached.

"TV." Maodan was smiling.

Frowning again, Laoshun did not bother to respond. His pipe had gone out. Baking in the sun, he could not feel the coolness of the water flowing in his heart.

"He actually made it onto TV. Impressive," Maodan added.

Laoshun jumped to his feet, and, snorting angrily, walked down off the ridge and stumbled his way home. He sent Mengzi out to water the field.

With a shovel over his shoulder, Mengzi spent some time chatting with Baigou and his friends, who were guarding the water before heading out to their plots.

"What took you so long?" Maodan shouted from a distance. "The water's already reached your field."

"Really?" Mengzi was startled.

"Of course. Would I lie?"

Mengzi ran back to the house to tell his father before running back.

He realized that Maodan had tricked him as soon as he reached their plot, but it was close enough. So he put his shovel down to wait.

"Where'd that irresponsible old man of yours get off to, Mengzi?" Goubao shouted off in the distance. "We agreed to guard the water together, but I haven't seen hide nor tail of him."

"Why are you screaming like that? It's not like he told you to bring a load of coal back from Jiutiao Ridge, or anything. Would it kill you to do it alone?"

"You should talk. The sun's turned my head to mush. I'm bored to death with no one to talk to."

"Take a few bites of grass and give your teeth something to do,"

Mengzi shouted back with a laugh.

"Tell your father to go eat the grass himself," Goubao said.

When Laoshun showed up with a shovel a while later, he looked at Mengzi when he saw that water was flowing several plots over. Mengzi thought his father was about to yell at him, but all he did was sigh.

"The dyke is leaking!" Maodan shouted.

Sure enough. Water was running through a hole in the dyke. Goubao shoveled dirt into the hole, and then pounded it in to seal it.

"You should focus on watering your field instead of standing around bullshitting," Maodan said.

"How come you don't look worried, Maodan?" Goubao replied. "Don't you know that Gimpy Five was on TV? He's going to, but you won't get off scot-free."

Maodan paled and looked over at Mengzi. "I thought you agreed not to tell anyone?"

"Don't blame me, I didn't say anything."

Maodan looked at Laoshun, who snorted, his face grim.

"It was you who blabbed," Goubao said. "You ran around telling people what you and Gimpy Five did. You're like a little donkey that's frightened by its own farts. Don't blame other people. Everyone knows what you did."

Maodan was speechless for a moment, before a sound escaped his throat. "I'm not afraid. Beheading just leaves a bowl-sized scar."

"You're not afraid? So why do you look like that?" Goubao smiled.

"I didn't do anything. Even if I'd been the one who flipped the cart over, Gimpy Five told me to do it. He said he'd take responsibility. So it has nothing to do with me."

"Says who? Wuzi wouldn't have gone over the cliff if you hadn't flipped the cart," Goubao taunted. "You owe him a life, no matter what you say."

"You know, it's strange." Maodan scrunched his neck down, looked behind him, and stuck out his tongue. "I get this feeling that he's following me with his tongue hanging out. Isn't that weird? He didn't hang himself, so why would he stick his tongue out like that? I see his face with my eyes open and closed."

"Look! He's right behind you," Goubao said. Maodan let out a startled cry and ran off, trailed by Goubao's delighted laughter.

3

It was nearly dusk when water finally reached Laoshun's field. Clouds to the west were painted in streaks of white and red; the sun, hovering above the hills, was bursting with visible rays of lights, as if venting its anger. The villagers called the phenomenon "fire clouds," and expected that the next day would be cloudy, if it occurred in the morning, and sunny, if it occurred in the evening. They were looking at another hot day that would bake the donkeys to death. But at least they got some water; even though each family was allowed to save only one acre, it was better than nothing.

Laoshun could breathe easy now that the water was flowing into his field, as if it would be there forever. He thought he could hear the crops chattering happily as they drank it up. They were dying of thirst, he was sure. He felt the same tender affection for the seedlings as for his sons; no, he had more feelings for the crops. He could yell at his sons and order them around, but he'd never done that to crops. He felt a cool, limpid delight course through his body, as if he were the one drinking the water. Such a rare cool sensation, such an uncommon sense of lightness. Squatting at one end of his plot, he was hypnotized by the sight of seedlings swaying in the water rushing onto his field. Only at this moment could he put Gimpy Five and Wuzi out of his mind and forget everything that had been troubling him.

Dusk was deepening all around him, driving the daytime summer heat into the ditches. Night air quivered, like water, refreshing and silky, as if a tongue were licking his exposed skin. Watering the field was enjoyable work, especially at night. Normally, Laoshun felt that his mind and body were steeping in the fluid of worries, and the sun and dust only added fuel to his annoyance.

It was better at night.

Darkness and tranquility blotted out the source of his agitation, while the sound of water and the coolness it brought washed away his anxieties. With croaking frogs and chirping insects, Nature was at its best when showing off its extraordinary beauty on a peaceful night. The beauty always seemed to seep into his heart, imbuing him with a crystallized relief.

He was reminded of a phrase Lingguan once used, something called "Smooth sand under a night moon," one of the eight scenic spots of Liangzhou, about the enchanting sight of moonlight splashing down on the desert. Rubbish. The idle literary type always liked went on and on about banal subjects like that. Laoshun refused to believe that moonlight on the sand was a pretty sight, but how could he, since he'd never seen it? It appeared to him that he hadn't seen the moon for a long time; he was sure of that. So he looked up to see a tiny hook, a worm-like object in the sky. After gazing at it for while, he had to say it did seem nice. Dark shadows teemed beneath its faint light. Mengzi was off walking around with a lantern, which swayed with his movements and created ribbons of light. A wondrous pleasure washed over Laoshun. He had to agree with Lingguan; maybe the sight of smooth sand under a night moon could be a pleasing sight at times.

Laoshun breathed in deeply, filling his chest with evening air infused with the fragrance of young seedlings. It felt absolutely wonderful, intoxicatingly marvelous. He was nearly melting in the night air, the refreshing sensation, the trickling water, and the sliver of hooked moon. He took a puff on his pipe and let the smoke circulate in his chest until his body was soaked in the delightful essence of the tobacco. Add to that the fact that Hantou had had his surgery, water had come, and he had found himself in a rare good mood. Dogs were barking in the distance. He could tell that one of them was Baldy Wang's mangy dog, a skinny creature that looked like a lean fox. It had a cowardly bark, like timid villagers when they're talking to an official, diffident and devoid of confidence. The other one was an old mountain dog belonging to Meng Eight, barking like a real man; it wasn't loud, but sounded like rumbling thunder. Even the barking dogs sounded lovely to Laoshun, better than any crooning women on TV.

Mengzi walked up with his lantern, making the wheat stalks rustle as he stumbled along. "It's dry. The water seeped into the soil completely and after all this time only a small section was watered." His voice spread into the night before reverberating in the field like pebbles, creating ripples on the surface of water.

Of course, Laoshun thought happily. In addition to the drought, the soil was fertile, so there had to be seepage. This was a former graveyard, under which lay countless strong men and charming women who gave their blood, flesh, and bones to the land. As if mixed with oil, the soil was tar black and had a wonderful feel; it kept the water in, unlike land that soaked it up quickly, but dried up as soon as the sun was out, so the crops wilted like hay when there was a drought.

We have a natural treasure here, Laoshun said to himself.

4

Laoshun went home after watering the field. Lanlan was back. He was distressed at the sight of her sitting on the *kang* with her mother, both of them crying. Without a word, he frowned and took out his pipe, and was reminded of Yindi, a smart, lovely little girl who had died so tragically. The sun turned into a black lump when he thought of his granddaughter.

How he wished he could slice that bastard up with ten thousand cuts.

And now Lanlan had become another worry for him. Before she was married, he'd hoped to find her a good family so she wouldn't suffer. After she was married, he worried constantly that her in-laws would abuse her. Sons were so much easier; they could get a wife as long as they came up with the money. If it worked out, they would be husband and wife for years; if not, just get some people to intervene, split the family into two, and they each start out again with their own lives, no need to worry about how the other one lives. Laoshun had been on tenterhooks ever since Lanlan married Bai Fu, a hotheaded gambler who could make any woman suffer, no matter how clever she was.

Was it simply her fate?

He'd once heard Grannie Shaman Qi say that Lanlan was not destined for a good life because she had been born at the unluckiest time of the day. Laoshun had been outraged by the comment. He'd heard of the importance of saying the right thing; for instance, the toad became a spiritual creature only after receiving *qi* from the God of Thunder. The same held true for interpreting dreams; a dream portended something terrible if anyone called it a nightmare. Maybe it was the same for one's destiny. He had been terribly upset when he heard what Qi had said about his daughter, but he managed to suppress his anger and merely said, "Really? Ha-ha. I don't believe such things." Yet what she'd said had stayed with him, like a fly he could not shoo away.

Looking at Lanlan's haggard face, he asked himself if his daughter was indeed fated for a life of suffering. Or could she have been jinxed by Qi's foul mouth? Hard to say. One simply cannot tell about certain things, such as Lanlan's fate. But suffer or be jinxed, nothing could be changed now that she was someone's wife. It would be pointless for him to say or do anything; he was like a pig or a sheep on a butcher's block, unable to escape the knife whether it shrieks or not.

"That prick Bai Fu will get a taste of my knife one of these days," Mengzi fumed.

Laoshun shot him a look, but Mengzi breathed noisily and ignored it. Another hothead, Laoshun said silently. Sure, that would feel good, but what would he get in the end? A bullet in the head, while his sister would be a widow, a bad outcome all the way around. A person's tongue and teeth get into a fight every once in a while. A couple sleeps in the same bed, but since no one can tell what the other person is thinking, squabbles are inevitable. How would it look if she got her family involved in an insignificant dispute? Laoshun would not want to appear willful, raising hell whenever their daughter had a minor complaint. That would be shameful.

"I've made up my mind, I'm not staying with him." Lanlan was sobbing.

Nonsense! Laoshun grumbled internally, with a severe look at Lanlan, who was drying her eyes with her sleeve. In the past, she had always checked his expression when she made that sort of explorative comment, but not this time. She may have really made up her mind. Laoshun's heart fluttered. It would be a great loss of face, and you can't make that decision by yourself, he wanted to say, but did not. He hoped it was simply an angry outburst. Couples have arguments. His marriage was a good example. He and his wife fought five days after their wedding ceremony and had wanted to get a divorce; over the next three decades, they'd never stopped talking about a divorce, and yet had produced four children together. No harm done if it was a casual comment; otherwise, it could spell trouble. She would be smearing black marks on her parents' faces, and people would say she was "raised by an ass or sired by a horse."

"Go ahead, get a divorce," Mengzi said. "He's worse than a pig or a dog anyway."

Laoshun looked at his son before shifting his gaze to his wife, who continued to sob. The woman is hopeless. How can she not say a word in response? Was she egging their daughter on? Maybe. Her favorite word was "divorce," which she'd uttered softly at first but grew louder and determined after they had children. To be sure, Laoshun had said the same thing himself, since their children had kept his wife around, like every other married woman with kids, sort of like an animal out in the pasture. Tie a rope to a wild animal's foreleg, leaving enough length for it to graze but not long enough for it to look up. It will bang its head each time it takes a step forward, and can never manage to escape. Children were a woman's rope. No matter how clever she may be, the rope would keep her tethered to the ground. Which was why Laoshun had always been able to say in a firm voice, "Sure, we can get a divorce." But Lanlan, after Yindi's death—his heart ached at the thought of the little girl—would have nothing to tie her down. The prick Bai Fu lost his head when he gambled and hit her, unlike Laoshun, who had a good heart despite his tendency to complain. When he beat his wife, Laoshun knew to use the sole of a shoe and only hit her backside. He could not tell if Lanlan had really made up her mind this time. Everyone makes mistakes. As a young man, Laoshun had gambled and beaten his wife—what man didn't?—but he had mellowed over the years.

"Freshly ground flour is best, girl." Laoshun said slowly. "Don't bring up divorce so easily. Bai Fu has his flaws, but who doesn't? Every couple fights once in a while. Besides, he's not entirely worthless; he has his virtues. Take fieldwork, for example. He works like an ox, and few men can beat him on that. Girl, don't underestimate him. No one's perfect."

"My mind is made up this time," Lanlan was still sobbing.

"Ai. Don't be so extreme." Laoshun shook his head and continued, "You should never be too extreme in word or deed. Rain from the sky flows into the ground; after a quarrel, a couple's hearts always turn around. Like I said, Bai Fu does have his flaws, like overreacting to the slightest provocation, but young men are all like that. He'll be better once he gets older. Big Head beat his wife all the time when he was young, even using a whip or a rope sometimes. Take a look at them now. They have a bunch of kids and get along just fine. It's hard to put up with some of these things, I know. That's why the Chinese character for 'restraint' is a knife over a heart. So put with him and make do for the time being; it will get better, girl."

"Enough, Father, that's enough." Lanlan dried her tears and frowned. "You've said that so many times I have callouses on my ears. Make do, make do. That's all you can say. Do you know what I've had to put up with? The whole family bullies me. They gang up on me whenever they don't like what I do. The old witch is the worst; she uses every possible excuse to scold me. I can't ever talk to a man, or she'll say I'm trying to seduce him. If he asks me a question, I have to reply, don't I? I can't keep my mouth shut all the time. But if I don't, all hell breaks loose. The woman curses me while her son hits me. Tell me, how am I supposed to keep making do with that? And now Yindi has died under such suspicious circumstances—my Yindi—if I keep making do, you'd better be prepared to come collect my body one of these days."

Stunned, Laoshun glanced at his daughter and then at his wife. They wore the same dazed look. He heaved a sigh and said, "What will you do if you don't want to make do with him? Human life only lasts a few decades, and we'll be reduced to a pile of bones in the blink of an eye. It will be over before you know it. You could turn the world upside down, but what would you gain except disgrace? A tree needs its bark, and a human needs face to go on."

Mengzi jumped to his feet and walked into the next room, slamming the door behind him. Sensing the mutinous intent in his son's action, Laoshun did his best to suppress his anger.

"Life is hard, Girl." Laoshun's wife dried her tears. "What do you expect your parents to say? Grownups in a family are like the rock pressing down on the pickle vat. We have to deal with whatever happens. What do you want us to say?"

The old crone, Laoshun cursed silently. She sounded as if she agreed with the girl's plan, but could not support openly her, because the grownups had to deal with whatever happened. Women! They never take the long view. What kind of man could she get after a divorce? Do you know what people would say about you? Use your head. "This goes beyond whether we deal with it or not," he said. "I'll be frank with you. I don't want you to get a divorce. If you keep going, the road ahead can only get broader. Even a cow or horse can be turned around. I don't believe Bai Fu has gnarled elm for brains. Keep trying to talk him around, and sooner or later he'll change. A reformed prodigal is worth more than gold, as they say."

"Try to talk him around, is that what you said?" replied Lanlan. "He wouldn't be all that bad if he'd listen, but it doesn't work that way with him. He curses and hits me when I barely start."

"She's right," his wife agreed. "You know very well what a hothead he is. Anything can set him off. When he's having one of his angry fits, not even his parents can talk him around. So how do you expect him to listen to Lanlan?"

Laoshun's temper flared. "Stop adding fuel to fire. Don't you have something else to do? You've talked about divorce for years, but we're still here."

"Aiyo. Venting your ill temper on me, are you? Go show the world how brave you are." Her face was red with anger. "I raised the girl; she's my flesh and blood, and she's dear to me, if not to you. I never cursed or hit her when she was home, and now that she's become their punching bag, you don't care."

"You should have kept her home to live her life out as a spinster. If you don't want them to do or say anything to her, why did you marry her off in the first place?"

"She'd have fared better being a spinster at home."

"Enough. Would you two stop fighting?" Lanlan dried her tears again. "I feel it all bottled up inside if I don't tell you, but you get into a fight when I do. What kind of life is this? I hear nothing but people arguing wherever I go. Death would be better than this."

5

Lanlan's mind was set this time.

It was getting late. Her father's snores troubled her. She resented his being so heartless. Nothing, including terrible events in his daughter's life, could keep him awake. She knew he was not the sensitive type. Years earlier, when they had no rice left in the cupboard, he was able to sleep through the night, as he did when her mother was having a baby. In her mother's words, he was the lucky one; with nothing to trouble his heart, he enjoyed good health. But not that good, since he easily caught colds. Her mother said that someone like him would never get indigestion. Lanlan knew that anyone whose throat was blocked could starve to death in a barrel of rice. She'd prefer an insensitive father than for him to suffer a horrible illness. Yet, she was hurt by his attitude. On the other hand, she'd feel even worse if he was too worried about her to eat or sleep.

Mother was quiet, though Lanlan sensed that she was likely awake. She knew her mother did not want her to know she could not sleep. She was thoughtful that way. Mother had lost weight until she was skin and bones. Her heart must have shattered over her and Hantou. Lanlan's heart ached; she wished she hadn't told her mother about her worries, but there was no one else to talk to. The wide world had so many people, but Lanlan's tiny world had few. Being able to cry in her mother's arms was a source of great contentment.

Through the open window, she could see the lonely, emaciated crescent moon, and that reminded her of how she seemed suspended in a bottomless dark night. She sighed and quietly curled up, afraid to disturb her mother, but the blanket rustled like a mountain crashing down. A similar sound came from her mother's side, equally soft. In a corner somewhere, mice were gnawing on something amid squeaked conversations. Lanlan envied them, whether it was a couple or just friends. She and Bai Fu had nothing to say to each other. Silence and quarrels constituted their most common forms of communication; the silence between husband and wife was the result of mutual, intense disgust. She lost all desire to speak when she was with him. She knew more than anyone what he was like, and full understanding of someone's worth removes all desire to converse.

Lanlan had friends, young married women in the village she could have talked to, but only when she was first married. Later, when she and Bai Fu argued, her mother-in-law blamed those women for being bad models. In her nasty voice she railed against them out on the street like a circus performer. Lanlan lost her friends one by one; they kept her at arm's length whenever they saw her.

She sighed to release pent-up emotions, which had bothered her for a long time. Her heart felt as if it had been filled with something that made her nauseous, though she could not rid herself of it.

That had gone on for a very long time.

The mice couple was still chatting away, and Father continued to snort. Mother made no noise, almost as if she had stopped breathing. Yet, Lanlan felt Mother's eyes on her, deep like dried-up wells, instilling so much pain in her that her heart quaked.

It had been several years since they'd last rebuilt the *kang*, and the odor of animal droppings seeped into the night air, bored into her pores, and clouded her mind. She felt as if she were suffocating. She was out of tune with the world around her—always tense, annoyed for no reason, and so agitated she felt like tearing at her chest. Nothing looked right to her; everything was out of kilter.

What's the point of going on this way? She thought. The path of her life was a transparent passageway, and she could see from one end to other. It was devoid of joy or pleasure. All she had were constant arguments with her mother-in-law and fights, verbal and physical, with her husband. Yindi, her only source of happiness in life, was gone—

it was a painful spot in her soul she could not bear to touch. Her father wanted her to put up with it and make do. He said life was short, and that those who fought turned into a pile of bones, as did those who endured the hardship. In her mind there was no difference between putting up with life and waiting to die. To endure hardship was nothing but silently accepting what life doled out to her and waiting for the day when she became a pile of bones.

Lanlan refused to do that.

She could not bear to reflect on the dreams of her youth. Everything, those dreams, those aspirations and goals, were long gone, vanished like passing clouds and scattered smoke. The wedding ceremony was the demarcation point of her life.

Her happiness was like the frost on roof tiles, which became vapor all too easily; helplessness and a lack of choices were impossible to change; they kept inching toward her, like the mound of sand at the village entrance.

Why not end the marriage?

The idea startled her at first. In her mind, divorce was more mortifying than walking naked on the street. A real steed accepts only one saddle and a virtuous woman stays with one husband. As far as she knew, a woman got divorced usually because she had made unforgiveable mistakes or had irreparable defects, such as adultery or childlessness. She drove the notion away every time it popped up, but it came back with a greater force, like pushing a ball deep into water. Eventually, she decided to do nothing about it and just let it rise.

But then she started taking it seriously.

With a different perspective, she fantasized about life after a divorce. A crack opened up in the oppressive sky over her head, to let in refreshing air and bright light. Divorce still sounded scary, especially when she thought about village gossip. She could even see in her mind's eye the odd looks they'd give her, but divorce was seductive, when compared with the passage of life that led straight to a pile of bones. Especially for Lanlan, who had never wanted a boring, monotonous life.

Life lost its pleasure when you followed a preset course and pace. The field, the yard, the kitchen stove, and the toilet were transformed into a gigantic rut in the mill, while she became the mule that turned the stone round and round. She seemed to have traveled far, but she opened her eyes to see herself walking in a circle on a preset track. The only change was the fading of the rosy glow on her face. She refused to head to the end of her life like that.

But she never brought up divorce, naturally, because her marriage was the result of an exchange. Lanlan knew that the moment she asked for a divorce, her mother-in-law would force Ying'er to do the same. For the sake of Hantou, Lanlan knew she had to put up with everything.

She was disappointed in her father's reaction and response, but she knew he was simply old-fashioned. He was getting old. He could help her out now, but not forever; she had only herself to count on in the end.

But this time her mind was set. She could never again share a bed with the man who "murdered" her daughter.

6

The sight of her mother-in-laws' gate provoked an intense loathing in Lanlan; she wished she didn't have to walk into that yard again, where everything was oppressive. The house looked irretrievably ugly to her every time she walked in, with its peeling walls, a back fence darkened by smoke from heating fires under the *kang*, and that long-handled wooden shovel. Her mother-in-law used that shovel to fill the *kang* in winter, in and out, exuding the aggressive nature typical of a shrew. That shovel always reminded Lanlan of her mother-in-law's large face, big as a silver platter, and her beady eyes. When they argued, a red glow shone on that face, while the eyes seemed sharper than a knife, causing Lanlan to tremble in fear.

Despite Bai Fu's beatings, Lanlan feared her mother-in-law most, the type of woman who was generally called a Dragon Lady, or Woman Warrior in popular fiction. From between her thin lips could emerge expressions that could make people blush, but she knew how to deal with people, plying them with perfunctory chitchat. With a honey jar for a mouth and a pincushion for a head, she would gossip with anyone about anyone. Soon after Lanlan married into the family, the villagers knew what she was like, and some of the older women were surprised. "Oh, she looks so sweet, but she's actually like that, is she?" In response to comments like that, her mother-in-law would prattle on:

"A keen eye can tell genuine gold and silver, but not what lies under a person's skin. You can only see the surface, not what's inside someone's heart. I thought she was a coral tree, but she turned out to be a red willow stump. I'd rather my son remain a bachelor if I'd known she was such rotten goods; I would not want him to suffer. He hasn't had a peaceful day since that slutty woman came through our door."

The villagers might believe what she'd said about Lanlan, but they knew she was lying about Bai Fu suffering, for they were all aware what he was like.

Her mother-in-law was sweeping the yard when Lanlan walked in. The woman glanced at her and spit, wielding the broom with a savage force to shroud Lanlan in a cloud of dust. That was a common trick to show displeasure, and she did it all the time. She would sweep chicken droppings and other trash toward Lanlan, pretending not to notice her daughter-in-law walking by. Lanlan could fume, but not say a word. If she even tried, the woman would throw the broom down and shriek:

"Who do you think you are? You don't like dirt? Too bad you weren't born in the city. You should have been born into a wealthy family. Too bad you weren't. You were born to be a maidservant, so don't try acting like a young mistress. That bit of dirt won't kill you. Peasants get dirt on them all the time; we are born in dirt, we grow up in dirt, and in the end claimed by dirt. Go live in the city if you don't like dirt. You have your eyes on the sky, but you're not destined for anything better than this."

Besides tirades like this, her mother-in-law had other devices that Lanlan had not encountered elsewhere. One was "bolting off." The notion of "bolting" was unique to Liangzhou, and its full meaning could only be grasped when used with another common Liangzhou expression, "thundering and blaring." "Thundering and blaring while bolting off" meant spinning around when she saw you and showing you her back, as she clomped away. So she thundered and blared off: she clomped off with exaggerated, mechanical movements in every part of her body, her attention to minute details meant to demonstrate her disgust and displeasure. She knew full well that silence was more powerful than words at moments like this. This was a strategy that worked exceptionally well for her. Since they lived together and ran into each other all the time, she could use it on Lanlan any time she wanted, and Lanlan could not protest when that happened. It would have seemed unreasonable to complain that her mother-in-law would not talk to her or walked too fast. All this made life oppressive.

If that weren't enough, her mother-in-law had another tactic: spitting. She spat often when she saw Lanlan. Liangzhou people believed that being spat on by a woman portended terrible luck. If it happened to a man, he could grab her by the hair and kick the life out of her, all with the support of public opinion: "Serves her right. She shouldn't have spit at you." But not Lanlan. So eventually she learned to adopt the strategy of "an eye for an eye." Bai Fu gave her a savage beating the first time she fought back, and she was laid up for three days. He slapped her the second time she spat at his mother and only glared at her the third time. By the fourth time, Lanlan had earned the right to spit. She spat back when her mother-in-law spat at her, which greatly reducing the woman's dominance.

Now with her mind made up, Lanlan was undisturbed by the dust flying at her and, without trying to avoid it, walked straight through the yard into her room. She was greeted by the stench of Bai Fu's feet. He was still asleep; he could sleep until noon when he didn't have to work in the field. Snores escaped from his open mouth. He had accumulated an excess of fluids in his throat, where nauseating sounds erupted as air passed through. She could not believe that this was her husband. What a nightmare. Her mood lightened at the thought that the marriage would soon be ended. But her heart sank, as if weighed down by a boulder, when she was reminded of all the unpleasantness that would surely follow a showdown. The last thing she wanted was for her mother-in-law to punish Lanlan's family by forcing Ying'er to do the same. The fleeting good feelings vanished.

A cloud of dust flew in through the open door. The powerful draft and the sound of the broom hitting the ground told Lanlan that her mother-in-law was sweeping the dust at her door. Loathing rose inside her, Lanlan smacked the door, abruptly ceasing the sound of the broom. She could almost see the woman's beady eyes glaring at her door. Maybe she'd flare up now. Her mother-in-law usually complained if

Lanlan carelessly banged a pot lid against a bowl, treating every noise she made as an act of defiance. An argument usually ensued. Lanlan waited for her mother-in-law to blow up; she hoped that would happen, for it would provide her with a legitimate reason to bring up the divorce.

The sound of the broom rose again. Obviously, the woman was not in the mood for a fight on this day. The house had long felt like a powder keg, where the slightest spark could create an explosion. What puzzled her was why it didn't happen this time. Somewhat disappointed, she picked up a rag to wipe the unsightly dust off the large armoire. It was part of her dowry, the only object in the house that was dear to her heart. She looked at herself at the mirror and saw dark circles under her eyes; sadness overwhelmed her when she saw how haggard she'd gotten. The best years of her life were over, and she had trouble believing, let alone accepting that.

Bai Fu mumbled something, rolled over and opened his eyes; he snorted when he saw her.

7

No argument followed Lanlan's announced plan to seek a divorce. The room was eerily quiet, as if they'd been waiting for her to bring it up. The silence dragged on. With his beard quivering, her father-in-law brought out his tobacco pouch with a trembling hand. His hand shook shamefully as it pinched and twisted the tobacco, but missed the bowl again and again. Bai Fu stared at her coldly, the muscles on his face twitching scarily.

"I've been prepared to die for a while now. My life for yours."

"What's the big deal, son? Go ahead, get a divorce. There are plenty of girls in the world for you to choose from." Her mother-in-law sounded tough, but her eyes betrayed a hint of weariness. Usually the woman was like a fully inflated ball, bouncing right back when you pushed her down. But on this day, the ball was punctured by Lanlan's demand.

Naturally, Lanlan knew what her decision meant to the family; she felt a measure of satisfaction when she intuitively grasped the truth behind her mother-in-law's forced nonchalance. Normally, as truculent as a wolf or a tiger, this time Lanlan noticed that she gave her husband a look, obviously unhappy with his performance.

"Sure," she said with a strained laugh. "Go ahead. But don't think you can get off easily. We're going to drag it out until the donkey dies and the saddle rots."

"You can drag it out all you want, and the outcome will be the same," Lanlan said with a smirk. "The Bai family does not rule the world. There's always the district court if it doesn't work out at the township office, and if that doesn't work, there are courts above it. I don't believe I'll be denied a place to make my case."

"You damned well think you've got a case, don't you?" Bai Fu kicked a white rooster that was pecking by his feet out into the yard, where loud cackles erupted.

Sensibly, she held her tongue, for she knew what would happen next. Bai Fu fixed his furious eyes on her, a clear sign that his anger was building, and that all he needed was an excuse to use his fists on her. Lanlan wanted very much to explain her reasons, but in this family, reason always lost out to clenched fists.

"What do you think you're doing?" Bai Fu's mother shot him a look. "Vent your anger where it belongs. That rooster didn't do anything."

Sensing the woman's intention to incite her son, Lanlan wished she could talk back, but anything she said now would be the spark that set off the explosion. The frightened rooster was still crowing in the yard; a dog was barking. A tractor rumbled by, shaking up everything, including the newspaper keeping down the dust on the rooftop. All the noise cramming into Lanlan's head nearly suffocated her.

Her father-in-law jammed his fingers through his dirty, straw-like hair, and began to cry; he began by sobbing, but soon he was howling like a cow. Lanlan was unnerved. She had anticipated the likely outcome of her demand—a beating from Bai Fu—but had never expected the old man to cry. In her eyes, he was the only decent member of the family. Surprised that he would lose control of himself like that, she felt a loud buzz in her head. He was wailing without tears, yet to her it sounded as if he were mumbling curses at Heaven, at earth, at everything.

"Life stinks." It was the only phrase she heard clearly.

Her mother-in-law did not know what to do about her husband's loss of self-control, except to glare at him, vainly wishing he could act like a man. In her view, they lost a great deal of face when Lanlan made her demand, and the most powerful counterattack was indifference. She would liked to have kicked Lanlan out like throwing away a worn shoe, so everyone would know she was cast out of their house. Then she could buy her son an even prettier wife. But it takes a knife to take a life; she could sell everything they had, and still not have enough to pay the exorbitant cost of another wife. Her head hurt just thinking about it. Besides, her son had never lived up to her expectations. If you raise a pig, you know its nature; she knew very well what people thought of Bai Fu. All these depressing thoughts made it impossible for her to do what she really wanted. She was resentful, and would not allow the slut to have her way. A woman who had wanted to outdo everyone all her life, she simply could not bring herself to admit defeat to a young woman. Her husband's sobs fueled her anger. Worthless man. Losing face was worse than anything. She wanted to level him with curses.

She knew that he was crying not purely over Lanlan's demand. Things had not been going well for them in recent years. Their son, a great disappointment, was addicted to gambling, and had such lousy luck that their doorsill was nearly worn down by creditors. Then there was Yindi—all this was enough to make her lose heart. Her husband was always saying that life stinks, owing to all his pent-up frustrations, so naturally he needed an outlet, which on this day was weeping. The problem for her was his bad timing; he should not have cried before that slut, and definitely not right after she demanded a divorce. Finally, she could hold back not longer, and screamed at her husband, "That's enough. What are you crying for? Nothing is worse than losing face."

He stopped after a few more howls. Then he seemed glued to the spot, staring blankly and shedding silent tears. Bai Fu gritted his teeth and balled his fists, getting ready to release his anger. Lanlan felt strangely calm. She too knew that her father-in-law cried not simply because he did not want the divorce to go through. So much had happened in the family in recent years that her demand was like the last straw. She felt her heart soften. She was not someone who flinched under a verbal or physical assault, but she lost her resolve when treated to a smiling face and kinds words, let alone tears. She was about to give up.

Bai Fu chose that moment to jump to his feet. Lanlan did not have time to react before she felt her face burn with a numbness, followed by excruciating pain on her scalp that soon spread to the rest of her body, legs, eventually all over.

He began his usual exercise.

Normally his mother stepped in when he beat Lanlan, but not this time. She might not have wanted to ruin a piece of property in the past, since it would cost them money to repair the damage. Now that their daughter-in-law wanted to leave, she deserved to be beaten more than anything else.

Bai Fu was doing his best; thumping Lanlan back down each time she got up. She felt a loud ringing in her ears, her nose was bleeding, and pains were shooting throughout her body. It felt to her as if a large platter had settled over her head, heavy and stifling, making her dizzy.

Onlookers had formed a wall around them.

In the past Lanlan would rather be beaten to death than run away, for she had not wanted to be a laughingstock among village women. It was different today, now that she had made up her mind. Face no longer meant anything to her; instead, she wanted as many people as possible to know what Bai Fu was like. In addition to having enough witnesses at court, she also wanted them to see for themselves that she had asked for a divorce in order to survive.

Chapter Twenty

1

The villagers were going to appeal to higher officials to lower the grain tax. Big Head had summoned people from more than a dozen villages, each family required to send at least two people.

"They want to fight the tax, so let them fight." Laoshun gave Mengzi a warning look. "You be careful and keep your mouth shut. I don't want you to be arrested."

After slurping down the hot potato and millet slurry, Laoshun and Mengzi walked outside and saw a crowd at the village entrance, where three-wheelers, tractors, and walking tractors formed a long line. Laoshun saw that the villagers were unusually animated, as if they were on their way not to see a higher official, but to enjoy an opera performance. Women were dressed in their best. Big Head was busy running around, assigning people to various vehicles.

Maodan and other youngsters brought over bundles of wilted wheat shoots and tossed them onto the vehicles. It was real wheat grass; the tassels lacked berries, because they dried up when they were still green; they were a favorite of the farm animals. The villagers tied the sprouts into small bunches to hang on the vehicles, like flags of protest. They were talking and laughing, nudging and slapping one another, disregarding the solemnity required of such visits. Likewise, the young women were checking out each other's attire, tugging at lapels and stomping their feet while secretly watching others' reactions to their new clothes. Old men were cursing corrupt officials, complaining about heartless Heaven, and lamenting the loss of crops. Yet none of that kept them from smiling, since they were able to eat their fill regardless of what was going on. In earlier days, they put on New Year's Festivals on empty stomachs. Back then, hunger had made their wives and children cry, and yet they'd danced, swaying their hips and beating their waist drums so loudly that the hills shook, masking the rumbling in their bellies. Cheerful smiles had blossomed on their faces, where sweat rolled down to wash off the dirt. Hunger had meant nothing to them. Now they had millet, potatoes, corn, and more to fill their bellies. They weren't afraid. Worst case, they lost their lives.

Such gatherings were rare these days. It was good to have their own assigned plots to till, but the new system created distances between people. Back in the days of collective farming, they had worked together in the fields and held constant meetings, both of which admittedly meant less individual freedom, but made life interesting. Now, they worked on their own plots at their own pace and were too preoccupied to meet up. This was the first time they'd come together toward a single goal in a long time.

Big Head made a few things clear to them: One, they must focus on what they were going to do and not cause any trouble. Two, they must not steal or loot. There would be lots of nice things at the city government office, even treasures like gold or silver; they could look but not touch. Three, no one was allowed to leave before it was time to go. Nothing would work if they started walking out one by one. The law breaks down in the face of the masses. They would be fine as a large group, but when some slip away, those who remain will suffer.

Laoshun was directed to Huaqiu's three-wheeler. He felt lightheaded; everything seemed unreal. Dust swirled and the lonely sun looked pale, not a red sunbeam in sight. The noise from the people around him swept him up in eddies of sound. Yes, he was being swept up; he felt coerced, though no one had actually forced him to go. It was clear to him that they would fail; individuals never outwit the government. If things got out of hand, they might even be put in jail, which would constitute a great disgrace to the family.

The motorcade began to move. Columns of dust dragons rose up from under the tires and into the faces of passengers in the vehicles behind. Women shrieked, dismayed to see their new clothes soiled so quickly. Laoshun laughed. It's what you deserve, he said to himself. He found these shrill women unbearable. What do you think you're going to the city to do? Watch an opera? Window shop? He looked down at his drab, dust-covered clothes; they didn't look bad to him. He did not mind the dust, would not have refused to jump down and roll around on the ground if necessary. He smiled smugly as he glanced at the young people screeching and brushing the dust off.

He felt dizzy when they reached the city. Everything, it seemed, was screaming, moving, and rushing at him. How peculiar. Pedestrians flowed down the streets like water; some were jabbering away, some were laughing, and some were expressionless, but they all looked the same to him. Their faces were a ghostly blur. He'd heard that the mark of a ghost's face was the lack of a chin. In his eyes, none of the city folks out on the streets had chins, an impression formed from memory after his return home. He had wanted to see if the city folks had chins, but had forgotten to check once he was in town; all he could feel was the dizziness, which made the city leap and shout in his mind.

Huaqiu drove like a maniac, seemingly intent on hitting the vehicle in front of him. The people on the streets looked crazy too; like frantic ants, those riding bicycles shot this way and that, as if riding crazed donkeys. Frightened out of his wits, Laoshun could not bear to look ahead, so he turned to the side, only to see the pedestrians looking at them with eye-popping mania, like gaping at rare animals. Laoshun wondered why, until he realized that they were drawn to the bundles of wheat shoots swaying like banners and the long rows of vehicles, like a writhing dragon. With over a hundred vehicles on the street, it was an impressive sight.

Everyone fell silent once they were in the city; it took on the feel of a funeral procession. The young men stopped bantering. The women wetted handkerchiefs with their saliva to wipe their dusty faces clean, unwittingly removing the cream they'd applied earlier that morning and exposing either dark or pale skin underneath. Most of them wore serious faces, but their eyes betrayed their curiosity, or shyness and trepidation. Laoshun wondered if they felt as dizzy as he did. He'd already asked Fengxiang, who had said, "No, I don't feel dizzy. I'm just tired. The city roads are so hard I turn into a sickly camel after walking around all day." All day? How could they walk all day? Laoshun found that hard to believe. What's there to see? You can't even find a toilet. He'd heard of an old villager who'd done his business on a street corner when he failed to find a toilet. When a city resident walked by, he'd covered it up with his straw hat, telling the man that he'd caught a thrush. He said he was going to buy a cage, and asked the man to keep the hat down. After a while, the man could wait no longer, and reached down to catch the bird; instead he got a handful of human waste. Villagers were fond of stories that demeaned city folks. Laoshun had to laugh. He did not believe that they could be that stupid; the man had to have smelled it and would not have reached down to grab anything. On the other hand, the old villager did find a clever way out of a fine. It was a shame he had to lose the straw hat, but leaving it behind was better than being caught and fined. Besides, city folks were so mean they deserved to have their hands soiled.

Everyone out on the street stopped to gawk at the strange procession; they were pointing and talking among themselves. Apparently they knew why the villagers were there. Laoshun had heard that Nanxiang had sent their people over a few days earlier, and that they had nearly pushed the mayor's car into a ditch. They had not been as impressive as Laoshun's village, with at least two members from every family showing up. Laoshun was pleased with their display of force. He had always been intimidated when he came into the city, but not on this day. He did not like the police. There were always a few at any given intersection, where they—in his mind they all looked the same—screamed at visitors from the countryside like ill-tempered fathers screaming at ill-behaved sons. Damn them. Why were they shouting like that? Just because of that yellow uniform? They think they're superior, don't they? Me, I get to sleep in as late as I want. Can you do that? I can feed my potatoes to the pigs if I want, can you? Bullies. Laoshun laughed at his thoughts. These people actually deserve some sympathy. Out on the street every day even with a hot sun baking their backs. It's tough on them. They could freeze to death in the winter or die of heat stroke in the summer, and that's so sad. Laoshun decided to forgive their screams and overweening attitude. But they were well behaved on this day. We know you banned motor vehicles in the city, but we're coming in today. Do you dare stop us? Go ahead and try. We'll trample all over you and turn you into pulp. Hei. You'll be meat patties. Laoshun thought smugly, and yet he felt a chill on his back and lost his swagger when a policeman looked at him while they were crossing a street.

"He represents the law, after all," Laoshun muttered.

The municipal government office was located on East Street, with an oversized entrance, which threw Laoshun completely off. Well, this was a government office, the city yamen, so it needed to be big. Unlike villagers' gate used by donkeys and other farm animals, this one had to allow cars to go through. The cars all looked the same to him, since he had no knowledge of car makes, except for a description people used—grand. He once heard a ditty from Beizhu: "A worker peasant works harder than his peer/making three hundred thousand in a year/he buys a tortoise shell/so a jackass sits in the rear." Three hundred thousand was an unfathomable figure to Laoshun. Three hundred thousand? He could dwell on that until his head was spinning, but he still could not figure out how much that was; maybe it could fill up a room. Then why would anyone spend a roomful of money on a car? In the old days, the township magistrate traveled in a sedan chair carried by four or eight carriers; how many would it take to carry a car? The thought angered Laoshun, who felt gleefully vindicated when the three-wheeler rammed through the entrance.

The compound was packed with people, more onlookers than protesters, all raising an incredible racket. For some reason Laoshun thought they had suddenly shrunken, like ants; the building was even grander than its entrance. It did not look all that impressive from a distance, but the people became ant-like once they got closer. He was too awestruck to make a sound. Those who had arrived before him, however, were clamoring. He heard Baigou yell, "Trash it. Trash the damned place." No one took up his suggestion.

Vehicles poured through the entrance and unloaded their human cargo. Obviously all first-time visitors, the villagers looked around, visibly awed by the building. Country bumpkins, Laoshun said silently. A real eye-opener, isn't it? He smiled, as if the villagers had dared to enter the courtyard only with his permission.

The crowd carried him along into the building's lobby. Laying his eyes on walls so white and floors so shinny, he could not help but look around, his head swinging back and forth, like everyone else, as if they were on a city hall tour.

"Come out here!" Baigou was shouting. "Come out, you corrupt officials!" No one emerged, and many of the villagers were outraged. "Fuck you and your mothers. Come out here!"

Still no one appeared.

They went up the stairs and saw a large room with an open door. "This is the city government office," Laoshun heard Huaqiu mumble.

A fat man was on the phone, the sight of whom further enraged the villagers, for they realized that all the employees were gone. They had wasted their impressive display of village power. Baigou threw the bundle of wheat he was carrying at the fat man; the others followed suit, and soon the man was almost buried under a haystack.

"What is this?" He looked around angrily. "What do you think you're doing?"

"Where are the others? Why did they all run away?" Baigou

demanded.

"No one works on Sunday." The man laughed. "Didn't you know that?"

That hit Laoshun like a bolt out of the blue. You shit-eating idiot! he cursed Big Head. How could he have forgotten to check the day? Why didn't he use his head? A sense of loss and emptiness overtook him. The others must have been feeling the same way, for they exchanged panicky looks. They were like soldiers ready to do battle, only to discover that their opponents were nowhere in sight.

"He could be lying," Baigou muttered.

"He's right." Huaqiu jabbed his finger at a calendar. "Look. Today is a Sunday."

How stupid could he be? Laoshun said to himself. But I can't blame him. Sunday means nothing to peasants. This thing called Sunday is meant for others, not us. We get up to work when the sun rises and go home to rest when it sets. Every day is a workday and every day is Sunday.

After the commotion died down, Baigou said, "Where does the mayor live? We'll go to his house and we'll see if he can crawl up a donkey's ass and hide."

"Right, let's go," the others shouted their agreement.

"He'll be here soon," the fat man said. "I just called him, and he said he'll be here right away." The villagers quieted down to wait for the mayor.

But those outside kept crowding in, and in no time the spacious office was packed. The newcomers were still shouting, and their anger persisted. Baigou jumped onto a desk, cracking the glass desktop in the process. "Get down," the fat man said. "This isn't your bedroom. A sheet of glass like that cost nearly a hundred."

"Get down," Laoshun said when he heard the cost. "Stop breaking things." But Baigou would not listen; instead he grabbed a handful of wheat stalks and let them drift down like a fairy lady sprinkling flowers.

2

Suddenly some of the villagers rushed out, saying the deputy mayor in charge of agriculture was in the lobby. Laoshun, who had never met the man, had once asked Big Head what he was like. "Like anyone else," Big Head had said. Of course the mayor was like anyone else. He heard a man shout, as he followed the crowd down the stairs.

"What are you doing here? Is this an insurrection? Don't you understand the law? You must have your township head report concerns and problems. You can't just show up here to raise hell. Go home now. All of you."

Laoshun was alarmed. This could be serious. What if they were shot as rioters?

"Beat that jackass," Baigou shouted. "Who is he anyway?"

"That's the deputy mayor," someone near Laoshun said, which frightened him. Deputy Mayor. What if he calls in the police?

"Beat the bastard. Our crops died in the drought. What have you done about that?" Baigou shouted.

"Yes, beat him," many villagers shouted in unison, including Laoshun, who yelled, though in a softer voice. He's right. Our crops are dead and we still have to pay grain tax. You're taking our lifeline away from us and still you have the nerve to shout at us. His indignation spurred him to shout, "Beat him up."

The shouts were deafening. Those behind surged forward, taking

Laoshun along. The man didn't know who Laoshun was, so he'd be off the hook even if they crushed the man to death. With that rationalization, Laoshun doubled his effort to push forward along with the others. The lobby was in total chaos. The wave-like crowd bolted this way and then darted that way.

"Enough. Stop!" Someone was shouting himself hoarse. "Let the deputy mayor speak."

Laoshun saw someone shouting from the second floor. It was their township head, now looking pale, but still recognizable.

"Be civil. Let's talk things over," he said. "Or someone is going to get killed."

"Quiet down," Big Head shouted. "Let him talk. We'll hear what he has to say."

Finally, the villagers hushed.

Deflated, the deputy mayor was sweating and puffing, as if on the verge of total collapse. Someone nearby shouted, "Get back. Get back and let the deputy mayor make a call and talk this over with the mayor."

"Yes, move back and let him make the call," another hoarse voice shouted. The crowd parted to let the man through, but he ducked out of the lobby, jumped into a car, and drove off.

"Shit," Baigou grumbled. "He ran away." The incensed crowd was shouting again. "Come back." "Don't run away." "Go hide up a donkey's ass if you can."

"He's probably calling the cops." Goubao said, sending a panic through crowd. Laoshun tensed up. His backbone crumpled at the mere sight of those men in caps. The others around him must have felt the same, for many of them looked apprehensive and frightened as their eyes darted this way and that. A few even left the lobby, likely to flee the scene. Laoshun was afraid too, but he did not want to run away yet. If the sky fell the tallest people will prop it up. Besides, he did not believe that the police would shoot their way in. Even if they did, he wouldn't be the only one getting hit. With all the people around him, many of them would be shot, and that made it all right for him to take a bullet himself. And there was more; this was not the old society, when weapons had been used liberally on the people. Laoshun sadly recalled the deputy mayor's distressed look. The man clearly wanted to do the right thing, with no intention to ruin the country or cause the people's suffering. The villagers had been too harsh on him.

"We're not afraid. Worst case, we lose our lives," Big Head announced.

"Right. I don't believe the police can bite off our dicks and skin us alive."

"Let them bite if they want. We have plenty of dicks among us."

"The law breaks down in the face of the masses. They can't put us all in jail. Where are they going to find the space? Even if we were put in jail, they'd have to feed us. We'd get to save some food. That's even better."

"I hear they get to eat meat twice a week at the labor reform farm. That's the life of a carefree immortal."

"Gimpy Five has gotten fat. He's put on weight after a few months in jai. So I'm not afraid."

The anxious look disappeared. A few of the old men were smacking their lips, as if savoring the food at the reform farm. Laoshun had to laugh. How could anyone not look forward to meat twice a week? He thought fondly of meat the rabbit hawks would supply upon their return around White Dew, and drooled at the thought. He'd die a happy man if he got to eat meat twice a week. Nothing would be better than that.

They were reassured after pumping up each other's courage. They continued to wait, like staying by a rabbit hole, certain that the prey would appear. They could lie down on the smooth, shiny floor and take a nap to outwait the mayor, hoping he hadn't managed to hide up a donkey's ass. They had brought food with them.

Noontime arrived. The sun felt harsher to Laoshun in the city than it did back home. In the countryside the sun might be scorching, but breezes brought cool relief. Here, with so many tall buildings to keep the breeze out, the yard felt like it could bake a donkey to death. Luckily, the lobby was big enough to accommodate a few hundred people, who could also spill out into the staircases if necessary. Those who could not squeeze into the lobby had gone off to find cool spots on their own. Either sitting up or lying down, they took out their *mantou* and water and began to eat.

The miserable-looking township head ran around talking to the villagers, his position now precarious owing to his failure to quell the unrest in a timely fashion. The poor man, Laoshun said to himself. It isn't easy being an official. He's always bossing people around, but now he's in big trouble. Ha! What happened to your cockiness? Your domineering air? Obviously he was powerless when the villagers banded together. Like they say, even ants can topple the Taihang Mountains. They had nothing to fear when they were united, but it wasn't easy; they were like sand that can form a ball with water, but falls apart once the water dries up. It was hopeless. Someone always caves in, losing his backbone when yelled at, and this small number of people did not amount to much. It was futile. Individuals can never outwit the government; peasants will always be peasants, fated to live off the land. It's hopeless.

The villagers began to curse again after a fruitless wait for someone in charge; like a chorus of curses, they were saying all sorts of unsavory things, especially the women. Women from the countryside excelled and outclassed their urban counterparts, since every one of them was a verbal woman warrior. Each with her own style, now they were all showing off their repertoire, venting unjust suffering at the hands of their husbands and parents-in-law. It sounded as if someone had poked at a sparrow's nest, their chirps and chatter converging to form a whirlwind of sounds in the government compound. The mayor obviously has a tough job, Laoshun thought. As the saying goes, it's hard to please the masses, since a hundred people have a hundred demands. It's hard to do his job and still make every one happy. Reminded of the deputy mayor's sweaty face and exhausted look, Laoshun felt a pang of guilt. He abhorred overweening officials, but hated even more to see someone embarrassed. His heart softened.

He looked around, and all he could see were bobbing heads with dusty, gaunt faces. An imposing platform with a large base that grew narrower at each ascending level stood like a pagoda in a corner of the lobby. The flowerpot on top was the only one left on any of the levels; they had to have been moved away, their spots claimed by young women, who carried on blithely amid the clamor. They were cracking melon seeds and chatting among themselves. The staircase, strewn with wheat stalks, was taken up by village men, most of whom were smoking Russian Mohe tobacco and filling the lobby with pungent smoke. The space along the railings on the stairs to the second floor was crowded with people who were cursing, horsing around, gawking, or chatting happily with villagers they rarely saw.

"They tricked us," Baigou shouted. "They pulled a fast one on us. The jackass mayor ran away."

"It's all right. The monk can run away, but not the temple."

"Right. He can't hide up a donkey's ass."

Laughter erupted as they echoed the comment. "He can't hide up a donkey's ass."

3

The mayor arrived when the sun was slanting westward. Its intensity lessened as did the anger of the villagers, most of them by then lying around or sitting down. They had exhausted their repertoire of curses; their fury eased off with every dirty word out of their mouths. And now the mayor was here, the real one this time; unlike the one who'd fled, a mere deputy, this one was really in charge. Many of the villagers stood up when they heard of the mayor's arrival.

He did not come by car, which was a good move. It would have been outrageous if he had, not when the villagers' crops had wilted in the drought. That was how they would look at it; they would be upset and curse him. So he was smart. As a result, most in the crowd did not know he was the mayor when he walked in.

He was taller than average, but without the haughty, bullying air that could come with a height like that. He was also thin, but pleasantly so; that was another positive feature, since it meant he was not a glutton. He was smiling, genuine and not forced, his eyes as round as pigeon droppings. His teeth were white, a pleasing sight. These days, few government representatives smiled at peasants; people working in the township office and the water bureau, even an electrician scowled at villagers, treating them with disdain. The peasants were so used to that they were surprised to see the mayor smiling, at them, no less. It was a flattering smile, one they found almost hard to believe. Laoshun even felt a warm current spread through his heart.

"I'd like to offer my apologies. First, I had a meeting, so I couldn't come earlier."

Delayed by a meeting, not avoiding them. Meetings were so important it would have been all right if he hadn't shown at all, let alone come late. To Laoshun, meetings topped everything else in the world, and his heart melted at the mayor's smile. He did not know how the others felt, but he couldn't help feeling soft and gentle.

"Second, I haven't done my job as your mayor, and have caused your crops to dry up."

So he knew that our crops died? The mayor actually knew about it? Laoshun was touched. It's good that he knew. He even said he hasn't done a good job. Hei. Laoshun was almost feeling guilty. There was a drought; it wasn't his fault. So why was he saying he hadn't done his job? Well, that was enough for Laoshun, who was pleased to hear the mayor's words, and didn't mind the hardship any more. He was now apologetic that a peasant like him had caused the mayor to reproach himself, a sentiment obviously shared by the others, who were saying among themselves:

"He's a good mayor."

"He treats us like human beings."

"He smiles at us."

"Unlike that other one, that ass, unfit to be a mayor."

"The meeting I attended was about the drought. We're trying to find a way…"

That compounded Laoshun's guilt feelings. The mayor had been worrying about the peasants; he was working on a solution; he attended a meeting; he was the mayor, a high official, and he was trying to find a solution for the peasants. And yet they cursed him, using all sorts of language. Fine sounding words made Laoshun nervous, especially from such a high official. He had no idea how high a position the mayor occupied, except that it was way up there. Big Head was already overbearing, always on his high horse, but he cowered in front of the township head, like a mouse with a cat, which, Laoshun had heard, was exactly how the township head acted before the mayor. What was a township head? A local overlord, the regional emperor. No wonder Laoshun felt bad about making a high official like the mayor apologize to them.

"Please feel free to bring up any issues you have."

Of course there were issues. Laoshun had a lot to say, but not just now. Someone spoke up in a confrontational tone, "Why don't you pay more for our grain? The price of wheat doesn't go up, but the costs for water and fertilizer skyrocket."

"He's right." Many villagers shouted their agreement.

"We'll convey your sentiment to higher authority. You have my word," the mayor said with a smile, defusing the tension.

"We want the first round of water," someone from a neighboring village said, meaning to be the first to water their field when the water was released.

"We want the first round, too."

"Us too." A clamor erupted in the hushed lobby.

"All right," a man who looked like a cadre said. "One at a time. You, you go first." He pointed to a young man not from Laoshun's village.

"Our village never gets the first round of water. We're always last. No more. We pay the same fee for the water and the construction of the reservoir, so why don't we ever get to be the first? Is it because the women in our village never sell their asses?"

The mayor frowned, but quickly laughed. "All right. You want to be the first to water your field for once, is that right?" He turned to the cadre. "Write it down. And tell the water bureau to set it up for them."

"We want to be the first, too." the others began shouting even before the mayor had finished. "So do we."

"Take that down." The mayor waved. "Write it all down." He took out a notebook and started writing as well.

Laoshun was touched by the man's gesture. How could he not be, when the mayor was willing to take care of matters like theirs? Those at the water bureau were like ferocious tigers, unlike the mayor. See, he smiles when he talks, his gleaming white teeth sending rays of light straight into Laoshun's chest to brighten his heart.

"I have something to say." Baigou raised his hand and started when the mayor nodded. "I want to say, Mr. Mayor, that you ought to rein in those people at the water bureau. When they come down to our production team, they won't smoke if our cigarettes aren't the best and won't drink if our liquor isn't good enough for them. They only eat the skin when we offered them chicken—"

"Really?" The mayor raised his eyebrows. "Write that down and start an investigation. Find whoever it is that only eats chicken skin and fire him."

The cadre nodded as he took notes, while the mayor scribbled something in his notebook with a furious look before spitting out his order: "I want him fired."

"I have something to say, too." Big Head jumped in. "I have a tough job as team leader. I have to see to everything, implementing family planning and getting all the shit from the villagers, running around to bring water to the field. It's a tough job."

"You're the team leader?" The mayor had a severe look on his face.

"Yes."

"Are you a Party member?"

"Yes, I am."

"Did you bring all these people here today?"

Big Head looked at the mayor and then at the people around him. He was quiet, but Baigou spoke up for him, "He didn't. We came here on our own."

"Have you brought any of this to my attention?"

"No—I haven't." Big Head evaded the man's eyes.

"No?" The mayor demanded in a dangerous tone. "You have never once brought up the villagers' problems with me. Then you're not doing your job, are you? You sound as if you're overworked and underappreciated. Is that right? Go home and write a letter of resignation and turn it in to the township office. And," the mayor turned to the cadre, "I want you to conduct an investigation to see if he's one of the organizers. If he is, report that to the Party for appropriate punishment."

Laoshun's heart raced. The mayor looked like a nice man, but he could be scary when he lost his temper. Big Head was sweating, his face drained of color. Laoshun knew that the position of team leader had fringe benefits; it was a tough work, but a cushy job. Big Head was clearly cowed by the mayor. Suits him well.

"Are there any more village cadres here?" The mayor's eyes swept the crowd. "Come up here now. You can quit if the job is too hard and demanding. I'll accept your resignation right here." The lobby fell as silent as a deserted graveyard. "Let me sum up what you've said, and you let me know if I've got it right." He turned to the villagers, all smiles again. "One, the price for the grain is too low and the fees for water and fertilizer are too high. We'll let our superiors know about this. Two, some people would like to be the first to water their fields. I'll make sure the water bureau settles the order fairly. Three, the cadres at the water bureau are out of line in their conduct. We'll investigate and mete out proper punishment, either by removing them from their positions or from the Party."

"I'm grateful for your visit today," he continued with a smile. "I consider myself personally responsible for all the problems you're having. We'll take care of whatever we can quickly, but," he paused and shot Big Head another searing look. "there are some with ulterior motives, especially the cadres and Party members. They have decided not to report problems and the views of the masses; instead of trying to finding a solution, they instigate the masses into disorderly conduct. We and the Public Security Office will get to the bottom of this and see that they are properly punished, either bringing them to justice or firing them. Any other problems?" He repeated the question three times, but got no response; he took another look at Big Head, who was busy wiping his sweaty forehead.

"Very well, then. That's all for today," said the mayor. "I have another meeting to attend. Before I go, I'd like to thank you all for your support and for watching over my job performance."

The villagers parted to let him walk out with a big grin.

They stood around blankly, wordlessly, and soundlessly, until Big Head roared:

"Fuck him and his mother. What are you waiting for? Let's go home."

The villagers picked up their things and crowded out of the lobby.

"Shit," Huaqiu yelled at some point on the way home. "We forgot to ask for a lower grain tax."

"Fuck," the other echoed. "How could we have forgotten the reason we came?"

Chapter Twenty-One

1

Lingguan decided to tell his father about Hantou's condition. There would be a funeral in the end, and he couldn't hide it from him forever. Besides, he was worried that his parents would fall apart if they did not have time to prepare for the worst; it would be better if they were told gradually. During Laoshun's last trip to see Hantou, Lingguan had led his father into the hallway one night, but Laoshun had turned pale before he'd even opened his mouth, so all he said was, "There are some complications, but the doctor said it isn't life-threatening."

Laoshun sat blankly for a while before taking out his pipe, but he put it back after a few puffs. His eyes, dry as a gobi desert at first, began to glisten, and soon he could not dry his tears fast enough. Before long, his face was wet with them.

"It's all right," Lingguan said. He did not like to see his father cry and hated even more the blank look before the tears came. "It's all right, really. The doctor said it isn't life-threatening."

"Don't lie to me." Laoshun dried his tears and mumbled, as if to himself, "The boy is done for." He began to sob.

"Careful." Lingguan hurried over to shut the door. "Don't let him hear you."

Laoshun covered his mouth to muffle his sobs. "He's done for," he repeated.

Lingguan decided there was no point in hiding the truth at this point; Father could sob all he wanted as long as Hantou did not hear him. He'd read once that crying is good for one's health, as it relieves pain and eliminates harmful elements in the body.

No longer sobbing as hard, Laoshun fixed his sunken eyes on the floor for a while before muttering, as if in a dream, "Heaven is blind."

"Yes."

"What's that song you sing, 'A Good Man Has a Good Life.' Then how did he get this? It would kill your mother if she knew. Don't tell her. We have to hide it from her for as long as we can."

"I know."

Laoshun sighed and shed silent tears. Visitors walking by glanced at Laoshun, then at Lingguan, who looked back at them, and they walked off silently. Laoshun took out his pipe and stroked it over and over before trying to take a puff without adding tobacco. Eventually he put the pipe back into his pocket, got up, and walked into the doctors duty office.

"Tell me the truth, Doctor. Can you save my son? If you can, I'll sell the land and do whatever is necessary."

Dr. Hou, who was on night shift that day, could not recall who

Laoshun's son was, but he remembered when he saw Lingguan walk up next to Laoshun. Hou looked at Lingguan, who nodded back at him.

"It's hard to say with what he has—but—to tell you the truth—with an illness like this—the younger the patient, the more aggressive it is. Maybe there could be a miracle."

"So, you can't do anything for him here?" Laoshun asked in an extraordinarily calm tone, with his eyes on the doctor's face.

"You could say that."

"How long does he have?"

"Hard to say. He could suffer a massive hemorrhage—but a few weeks at most."

The last phrase destroyed Laoshun's calm demeanor; he collapsed onto the chair and began to sob.

"This is where the doctors do their work." Noticing the frown on the doctor's face, Lingguan tugged at his father's sleeve.

"So what?" Laoshun shook off his arm. "I don't care. Why should I care when my son is so sick?" The doctors ignored him and concentrated on what they were doing.

He finally regained his composure after sobbing for a while. Wiping his face with his sleeve, he opened his mouth to ask a question, but decided against it and got up to walk out. Lingguan saw he was staggering, as if he'd suddenly aged a decade or more.

With his eyes shut, Hantou was quiet after receiving a shot of morphine. Laoshun sat on a stool by the bed to stare blankly at his son; soon tears were streaming down again despite himself. He quickly dried his eyes with his sleeve, but a noise escaped his throat from his effort to stop crying. Lingguan tugged at his sleeve again, afraid that Hantou might choose that moment to open his eyes. He wanted his father to go outside to cry, but Laoshun would not move; luckily,

Hantou did not wake up.

Mengzi and Ying'er arrived at noon, bringing Laoshun's favorite food, roasted potatoes. He had no appetite. After talking about what had happened in the village, Mengzi stopped; he was puzzled by Lingguan's apparent lack of interest. Lingguan signaled for him to follow him out.

"Is it really bad?" Mengzi whispered when they left the area.

"Liver Cancer." Lingguan nodded and heaved a long sigh.

Mengzi staggered under the shock, staring wide-eyed for a while before saying, "Oh no! Can it be cured? If so, we'll sell everything; we'll send him to Beijing, even to America. We have to save him no matter how much it cost."

Lingguan, who was choking on tears, could only shake his head.

"Why?" Mengzi was crying. "Why did he have to get the illness? He's such a good man; he's never hurt a soul. Why do the evil people get to live? Why him? Why?"

"Don't tell Mother," Lingguan said softly. "And not Ying'er." He squatted down on the stairs to cry silently, drawing the attention of passersby.

Mengzi stared blankly with a grim face. He looked up abruptly and roared:

"Fuck you!"

Lingguan stood up and took out a handkerchief to wipe his face before handing it to Mengzi. They walked back inside. Ying'er was feeding Hantou something from a can. His face was flushed; obviously embarrassed by the rare moment of intimacy, he stopped eating when he saw his brothers. Ying'er put the can away while Hantou pointed at his bedside cabinet. "There are apples in there."

She took one out and handed it to Mengzi, who fixed his eyes on

Hantou and quickly took a bite when he felt his nose ache.

Ying'er looked over at Laoshun, then Hantou, and then at Lingguan, obviously trying to read something in their faces. The wrinkles on Laoshun's face and his dark dark skin seemed as placid as the earth; Hantou was moaning, his eyes shut, but softly, to show that the pain was bearable. The cheerful smile on Lingguan's relaxed face looked phony to her; she could not say why, only that it didn't feel right.

Finally she saw something on Mengzi's face. He smiled when he saw she was looking at him and then broadened the smile, probably because he knew it was forced. It had the opposite effect, and he knew it, so he lowered his head to gnaw at the apple.

It was clear to her that they did not want her to know something, which could only mean that Hantou's illness was serious. Her heart thumped violently. What exactly did he have? She wanted to ask, but was afraid to know; she sighed softly.

Noting her reaction, Lingguan glared at Mengzi, who smiled back apologetically. We should tell her now; she'll know sooner or later anyway, he said to himself. Better to tell the truth now than to keep her in dark. He tilted his chin slightly at her.

"What exactly does he have?" She could hardly wait until they were outside.

"It's not too bad." He had a change of heart when his gaze fell on her pale face.

"I'll hate you for the rest of my life if you lie to me now. I have to know, even if it's catastrophic."

Lingguan hesitated and sighed before saying, "It's—it doesn't look good."

"What is it?"

"Cirrhosis of the liver, but it's not too serious." He stammered. "It's in the early stage. Not easy to cure, but not fatal either."

"Really? Is it really not fatal?"

"Really. But it'll be expensive."

"As long as it's not fatal." She sighed. "It doesn't matter how much; we'll spend it. I'll work like a dog if necessary. We'll find a way to pay off the debt."

Laoshun and Ying'er left for home that afternoon, leaving Hantou in the care of the two brothers. Over the following days, Lingguan ran around in the day, getting a second opinion on Hantou's biopsy at another hospital in the city and searching for supplies of pethidine for after Hantou was discharged. He knew that the worst part of his brother's illness wasn't dying but the pain; he'd heard it could be impossibly painful. Bucinnazine would be useless; only pethidine offered relief. But it was a substance under strict control in the city because drug addicts preferred it. Sometimes he turned up empty-handed after searching for days.

Hantou never asked about his condition; he moaned, but seldom said anything. The only thing he brought up with Lingguan was his request to leave the hospital in a new set of clothes. He wanted to look his best, he said. By then, Lingguan was secretly preparing for his brother's funeral, and had already bought cloth shoes, pants, cotton knit shirts and pants. He needed an excuse to make a jacket for Hantou, whose request gave him what he needed. Lingguan wondered if Hantou knew how ill he was and that the request was meant to have his own funeral clothes ready. But he seemed calm when he wasn't moaning; his face was devoid of expressions except for muscles that twitched from the pain. One night, however, Lingguan woke up and thought he saw, in the hospital lights, traces of tears on Hantou's face. Hantou dried his tears, moaned and said, "Go find the nurse to give me shot."

The lump seemed to have disappeared, but that was because his abdomen had turned into a solid mass. When Lingguan touched it, it felt hard as a rock. Hantou often tapped his belly, with the same placid expression; he appeared convinced by the doctor's explanation that his surgical wound was infected and would be better soon. He had even given that explanation to their father to make him feel better. Most of the time, however, he was silent, as if his illness had taken him into a new realm.

What worried Lingguan most was the pain typical of liver cancer, which frightened so many people. After doing his best, he managed to get hold of a few doses of pethidine, but they would only last several hours and wouldn't be much help after Hantou was back home, and bucinnazine, though easy to find, had no effect on his pain. Lingguan knew that day would come, and he feared the pain more than death. Death was inevitable, so it made no difference to him whether it came early or not, but pain was different; his gums hurt when he thought about the pain, as if there were a visible demon laying in wait, ready to pounce on Hantou and tear him into pieces.

Worse yet, he wondered how their mother could stand to hear Hantou scream from pain. Often the people who hear the cries of pain seem to suffer more than the patients themselves. Mother would lose her mind, she would. She would spin around and tear at her chest when she was worried, shouting helplessly; it was a sight he could not bear to witness. He was at his wits' end.

Then an idea occurred to him: keep Hantou away from home. He could either have him spend a few more days in the hospital, until the fateful day arrived, or he could rent a room in the outskirts of the city for Hantou to stay under the pretense of further treatment. The first option was out of the question, for they had been repeatedly asked to leave, and, besides, they could not afford the exorbitant cost. The second option was doable and he went so far as to rent a room, but his father vetoed that when he told him.

"No. We cannot let him die a wandering ghost away from home."

2

Laoshun and Ying'er got back just in time to see the township grain tax team carrying sacks of grain out of their house. The team was made up of dozens of collectors, including members of the police force, bureau of justice and the court, in addition to the cadres from the township office. They were all crowded into their yard.

"We'll pay. But my son is in the hospital and we have to take care of him first. Can't you wait?" Laoshun's wife pleaded, but the fat township chief shoved her aside to let two young men in.

"You have to pay."

"The price of fertilizer keeps going up, but you didn't do a thing about that. This is robbery." She was shouting. "We never said we wouldn't pay. I told you my son is in the hospital and we have to take care of him first. When he's out, we'll turn in every last kernel."

"So if he stays in the hospital, you'll never pay, is that it?" the township chief said.

Laoshun felt the blood rush to his head. Fuck you and your mother. How can you act like that when my son is dying? I'll show you. He tore at one of the young men's jacket, and the sack fell to the ground, spilling its contents of corn.

"What do you think you're doing? Interfering with official

business. Arrest him." A policeman walked up with a menacing air.

"That's all right, don't be upset." Big Head stepped in to keep the situation from escalating. His son is very ill, so he's in a terrible mood."

"Move away, Big Head," Laoshun shouted. "I'm not afraid. He could swallow me up and shit me out, and I wouldn't give a damn. Shoot me if you want. You lawless bandits."

"You think I wouldn't? I'll arrest you if you refuse to pay. What law are you talking about? Pay your tax and no one can touch you; be a filial son and you have nothing to fear from Heaven. That's how it's always been."

"We've done everything we could for you people," the deputy township chief said in a gentler tone. "You should be grateful and stop causing a scene."

"You think you're in charge, don't you?" a young cadre said. "The government's in charge, and the Party, not you people."

"Cannibals, you're all cannibals." Laoshun shouted tearfully.

"Are you going to pay or aren't you? If you don't, your family will lose everything," the policeman said.

"That's what you people want." Sneering from frustration and anger, Laoshun picked up a shovel. "Fuck you, fuck all your ancestors. Come on. I'm no rabbit, but you know that rabbits bite when they're cornered. I'm not afraid. One of my sons is about to die, but I have two more. Go ahead, kill us all. Fuck you and your mother. Come on, kill me. I've had enough of this shitty life anyway."

"What did you say?" Laoshun's wife charged at him. "What's happening to Hantou? Is he all right?"

"I won't hide it from you any longer." He threw down the shovel and began to sob. "I'll tell you everything. We have to take what

Heaven doles out to us. Hantou has cancer and he only has days to live."

She let out a despairing shriek and keeled over.

The cadres looked at each other. "Come on," one of them said, "let's go to someone else's house." They crowded out of the yard.

"Don't blame us," said the township chief. "We're not heartless, and this isn't easy on us either. The municipal government is breathing down our necks and we have no way out."

"He's right," a young cadre said. "We're humans too. We know that life is tough on the peasants, but what can we do? It's our job and we have to do it."

"Take it with you, take everything," Laoshun said between sobs. "We'd rather die of hunger than owe you a single kernel. I'll take it over tomorrow, so don't worry. You'll have every kernel that I owe." He pinched his wife on the spot between her nose and upper lip. She came to after a moment. Ying'er was crying so hard she had to put her hands on the wall to support herself.

"Bandits," Beizhu shouted after the cadres. "You're all bandits."

"Where were you when we didn't have water for our fields? And where were you when we couldn't afford the fertilizer?" Meng Eight shouted after them. "But you show up when you want our grain."

Laoshun and his wife sat down in the yard and continued to cry. He was as loud as a lowing cow, while she shed silent tears and muttered mindlessly to herself.

"Didn't they say it was parasites? How did it turn into that scary thing? How?" Ying'er ran into her room and cried herself hoarse on the *kang*.

Stunned by the news, Beizhu and the others stood still in the yard and sighed. Then he walked over to help Laoshun up. "Don't cry anymore. You have to take care of yourself."

"Let him cry, Beizhu," Meng said. "He'll feel better after a good cry. The way the world is, the damned heavens – let him cry. Don't try to stop him." He too was choking on tears and soon began to sob, followed by Beizhu's wife, Huaqiu's mother, and neighborhood women.

"This is it," Laoshun's wife cried and mumbled. "This is it for us."

"Enough. That's enough," said Laoshun through his sobs. "We'll take what heaven doles out to us. We can and we will." He dried his eyes with his sleeve, thumped the dirt off his clothes, and went to lead their camel cart out of the shed, picking up a scoop on the way.

"What are you doing?" Meng asked him.

"Don't pay them," Beizhu said loudly. "Don't. At worst, you die. The price for wheat is much higher on the free market. They pay only half of that. It's like robbery."

"I'm going to do it," Laoshun said. "I'll pay. It's better than letting them humiliate us. At most, we'll have less to eat, so we'll just tighten our belts."

"This is no way to live," Meng said. "We'll see the end soon."

"Don't worry," replied Laoshun. "We'll keep going if we can, and if not, it will be the end of us. We won't be missing anything. We'll just be ghosts. Come on, woman, get up and help me carry this."

"Come on." Beizhu turned to Baigou. "Let's help. We'll carry it for you."

Laoshun's wife stood up and dried her face with her sleeve. She swayed, seemingly about to topple over, but managed to steady herself. Tears continued to flow and she was choked with sobs. She tried to force herself to stop crying. Her face wet with tears, she began picking up the spilled kernels of corn and putting them back in the sack.

Laoshun led his camel over to yoke it to the cart, while Beizhu and Baigou loaded the cart for him. With a shout, Laoshun set off for the grain station, followed by his wife, who paused constantly to dry her tears.

3

Laoshun's wife felt that she was falling apart.

She was completely drained after clenching her teeth and carrying the heavy scoop up to the grain mound. Collapsing on the cart as it bumped along, she thought she was dying, not an unwelcome thought at that moment. It would feel so good to die then and there, for her nightmare would be over. She lacked the strength to go on. Her throat was dry, her head felt heavy, and she could hardly breathe. It would be good to suffocate; she'd prefer to die like that. But the jolting cart felt too real, as did the noise made by the bumping movements and the camel's snorts. She was the only unreal one, a puff of air, a column of smoke, or a specter of condensed sorrow and despair.

Her eyes were dry from the bitter tears as she headed home in a daze. The tiny dot of a sun had set, but it wasn't yet completely dark. She would rather be in darkness like death, but there was still a faint yellow glow all around, like the graveyard in *Strange Tales* on television, or like paper aged after being soaked in water. A bleak, turbid color with a desolate feel. The sky had fallen, but it was still up there. If it had, she'd have felt better.

Hantou, a decent boy who was dependable as a camel, was dying. The thought lashed her constantly; lightning flashed across an inky sky when she least expected it. Death had been a distant, abstract concept, but now it was on its way, drawing closer and closer to their family, about to land on her precious boy. She could not believe it, she simply couldn't. Ever since Hantou was hospitalized, that blurry and yet distinct word had bored into her heart like a crow returning to its nest at dusk. She had done her best to avoid it, keeping it at arm's length and averting her eyes, but it was still coming, surely on its way. Flapping its jet-black wings, it stirred up a sinister wind and grew so large it blotted out her sky.

She wept, crying herself hoarse, as the whip continued to lash at her heart. Laoshun sounded far away, as if from a different realm, when he offered comforting words and called out to their camel. Her son also seemed far away; only the dark whip flogging her soul was close by.

Her son was dying. He'd barely made into adulthood, and now he was going to die. She did her best to avoid the word death, but it kept hurtling toward her heart, like a stone that has just been fished out of water. The illness, that illness, how could her son have gotten it? People were always saying that the good are rewarded, and the evil meet with a bad end. So why did Hantou get that illness? Why, damn it, why? Why hadn't an evildoer gotten it instead? Why not those corrupt officials? I wouldn't mind getting it myself, she thought. I'm in my fifties now, and I've lived long enough. But not my son, he's barely an adult; he's hardly a grownup.

"Enough. It'll be all right. Stop crying," Laoshun said.

Enough? All right? How could it be all right when her son was that sick? She resented Laoshun for his lack of feeling. But she did not complain; she just continued to cry, a heart-wrenching wail. My son has that disease—that horrible illness—he's cruel to tell me not to cry.

She wondered if she and her husband had done something for which their son was paying retribution. People were always saying that retribution can be immediate and can be meted out on oneself or manifested in the children. Could that be true? She looked back on her life, but found nothing particularly bad. Granted, she had killed a few chickens, but butchers were all flush with money, weren't they? She had done a few unsavory things, but who hadn't? Why didn't Heaven exact revenge on those who scheme and lay out traps to cheat, deceive, and ruin others? Damn you, Heaven!

It was late, but they were wide-awake. She cried, fell into a silent blankness, and then mumbled to herself. Laoshun kept puffing on his pipe, having shed all the tears he had, though he still felt being strangled by grief. He could not think of a thing to say to make her feel better, except to complain about the unfairness and reassert the need to accept fate.

The pig was squealing, reminded her to feed the hungry animal, so she struggled to get up.

It was pitch black outside. After mixing the food, she walked into darkness, where, like a blind woman, she groped along with her hand on the wall and shuffled out the gate. She still could not see anything, and it took her a while to finally adjust to the darkness to see a small path stretching out before her like a gray blot.

A watery breeze blew over and cleared her head. Everything just now, everything in the dark night, felt like a dream to her. Did Hantou really have that disease? That was almost impossible to believe. Maybe it was a dream. She wished it were, but it wasn't. Her husband crying felt like a dream and real at the same time. A cruel reality. How wonderful if it all turned out to be false, but it was real, immutably real. It was their fate.

Was it really fate though? She could not bring herself to believe that.

And yet she could not keep thinking; her thoughts were deathly, like a dagger in her heart. Her son, who had barely grown into manhood, could just fall ill like that, an incurable disease. Heaven was blind.

The cool breeze roused her from her addled state, but also reawaken her pain, plunging her into the abyss of despair. Her face felt chilled from the tears. She lost control and began to wail again.

4

The hospital suspended Hantou's medications. The nurse came in the morning to set up IV drips for every patient in the room but him. Doctor Hou told Lingguan that their account had been settled. A scowling Lingguan left without a word and went to tell his brother that his wound had healed and the doctor said he could go home.

The wound did look better, a fresh scab that looked like a red snake. Hantou seemed to believe the explanation.

"That's great. I can't wait. I'll go crazy if I spend another day here." He tried to smile to show his eagerness to leave, but because of the pain, he managed only to move his lips.

He put on the new clothes—the set he'd asked for. His eyes had sunk deep into the sockets, his cheekbones protruded, and he was skin and bones. The lump, on the other hand, looked unusually prominent, as if he had hidden a basketball under his shirt, while the spots on his sallow face were particularly noticeable. The blue shirt helped his appearance, but the color tended to highlight his sickly face.

Mengzi went out to hire a three-wheeler as Lingguan continued his search for pethidine. The head nurse had promised to give them two boxes of the painkiller, but now she indifferently offered an excuse: "The account has been settled."

Lingguan was outraged. She laughed coldly,

"What do you expect? I wouldn't even if I could. The rules say these shots can only be administered in the hospital."

"Really? I wish you a long life." Lingguan managed a cold retort, but tears gushed the moment he walked out the nurse's office. What had happened to the world and the people in it? She had no compassion, no feelings. Hantou's illness was a huge catastrophe to his family, but nothing to the doctors; Hantou was a medical specimen and a paying customer.

That was all.

An impossible task suddenly landed on his shoulder—where to find enough of the painkiller, especially now that the head nurse had broken her promise. Pain was worse than death, but controls over the dispensing of pethidine were tighter than ever.

Lingguan's head ached. Hantou's life was beyond saving now, so relieving him of the pain was the only thing he could do. "Don't worry, my dear brother. I'll do everything I can to get more painkiller, so you won't suffer too much."

Lingguan dried his tears when he saw Mengzi in the corridor. Mengzi could not know about the hospital's decision to force them to leave. He was easily provoked into rash actions, and Hantou would suffer if he got into a fight with the medical staff.

The two brothers packed up to leave. The general surgery department had yet to send the bill to the accounting office for in-patients. "Come back in a few days," the bookkeeper said icily.

Everything was cold and impersonal. White walls, expressionless people, trees with bare branches, leaves gnawed away by insects, and hard floors that hurt the feet. Good riddance to the lousy place, teeming with death and inhumanity, with its nauseating odor. Lingguan hoped he'd never have to come back, not ever.

They followed the vehicle's slow progress into a headwind. Hantou had one hand on his abdomen and gripped the handrail with the other. A dazzling sun shone down. Lingguan wondered what his brother was thinking and feeling at that moment. Was he calm or just numb? Lingguan knew that this was Hantou's last time out on Liangzhou's streets, the thought of which nearly broke his heart.

The three-wheeler rolled along slowly in a world bustling with people and action. Noise rose all around them: the shrieking horns of cars, listless shouts from vendors, eager calls from young men offering rides on their motor scooters. Everything was near and yet far, as if the world had abandoned them. The people out on the street looked happy, while on this lonely vehicle sat a man who had been sentenced to death.

Lingguan walked along in a dreamy state; Mengzi telling the rider to take it slow, and Hantou's face twisted in pain from the jolting motion both felt like something out of a dreamscape. Sunlight was magnified and yet hazy. Nothing felt real, only the pain in his heart, so sharp and clear it would be etched in his memory forever.

"I want to visit the Temple of Confucius." Hantou said. "I've never seen it."

The Temple of Confucius? Lingguan studied his brother's sallow face, which was still twisted from pain. What for? Lingguan wondered. Maybe he was aware of his condition, but if so, how could he remain so calm? Why hasn't he asked for details on his sickness? Lingguan took another look at Hantou, who was staring at the street with eyes as unfathomable as a deep well. He could be obstinately clinging to worldly desire or indifferently holding himself aloof from everything around him. Lingguan could not tell. Maybe his illness and hospitalization had transported him into a different realm.

"What's there to see?" asked Mengzi.

"I just want to stretch my legs," Hantou said casually. "I was bored out of my skull after all that time in the hospital."

"Sure, let's go." Lingguan told the driver to head over to the Temple, while asking himself why his poorly educated brother had chosen the temple dedicated to scholars to visit. He had never been there, which was a perfectly sound reason, but there were other places he had never visited, like the Drum and Bell Tower, Haizang Temple, and so on. Why the Temple of Confucius? Maybe he wished he'd been a better student.

After leaving Mengzi at the gate to watch their belongings, galloping Lingguan walked in with Hantou. It was a fine place to be. The bronze horse at the entrance held Hantou's attention for quite some time. Lingguan heard him sigh softly. Hantou stared at the dark pine and cypress trees for a while before going into a room with calligraphy and paintings, where he stopped and gazed raptly at every scroll. Lingguan realized that he was greedily savoring art, his mouth hanging slack, like a child at a circus.

"So real," he mumbled as he pointed to a portrait of someone from the late Qing period; he swallowed two painkillers and slowly moved along.

They entered another display room. Lingguan decided not to offer any explanations, and his brother, looking at the works silently and diligently, asked no questions. The room showcased Liangzhou historical relics, and he knew that everything was new to Hantou; wooden figurines, wooden carts and horses, rusty knives, stone axes, porcelain vases, armor like spring beds, cloth paintings, and Buddhist statutes, were all uniquely wonderful. He stood in front of giant bronze figures so long that Lingguan thought his brother might be praying, mistaking them as Buddha statues.

"Let's go," Hantou said.

He smiled when they got home, a genuine smile, though brief as a meteor.

Their mother ran out from the kitchen and smiled when she saw Hantou. "Good." Her eyes were moist as she repeated, "Good." It was impossible to know whether she was saying it was good that he was home or that he'd been restored to a good condition. Lingguan felt his heart tighten. "How can I tell her the truth? This could be the death of her." He gazed over at his father, who wore his usual stony look. Lingguan tried to decipher the look; was it numbness, despair, or resignation? None of the above or all of the above? His father was darker and bonier than ever.

"Just look at him!" their mother said.

They went inside. After folding a blanket in half to lay on the *kang*, she then dragged over another blanket, which she propped against the wall. Laoshun and Hantou's brothers helped him up onto the *kang*. Lingguan had thought their mother would ask Hantou if he felt better, but she didn't. Instead she stared at her son, the tears gushing so fast she could not keep her face dry.

5

The days after his brother came home felt to Lingguan like a bad dream in which everything seemed frighteningly surreal. He did not recall ever seeing the sun during those days, as a dull grayness pervaded the space between the earth and the sky. Their mother hardly ever stopped crying, carrying on with the household chores tearfully, smiling only when she was with Hantou. Lingguan could not bear to see her smile like that, for teardrops swirled in her eyes as she smiled and rolled down her cheeks when she let down her guard. She would hurriedly wipe off the tears and put on a broader, even less attractive smile. It was a good thing Hantou rarely look at them, since he usually had his eyes shut and faced the wall when he opened them. He moaned when the pain was unbearable; Lingguan would give him a painkiller, after which Hantou would shut his eyes again or turn to face the wall.

The chaos in Lingguan's head gave rise to that grayness. Everything looked shadowy gray, as atoms of despair and pain permeated every corner of the house. The end was hopelessly clear—death. The patient and his family were waiting for the same thing, the inevitable arrival of the Angel of Death.

He knew that his brother had only weeks, maybe only days, to live, according to the doctor. Everything lost its meaning, life would burst like a bubble when death arrived. Days or weeks were but an instant in the river of life, and a man's life was nothing but a spray of water that passed fleetingly down the long river of history. When facing the inevitable end, decades weren't all that different from weeks. Hantou had been given a death sentence, while the others in their family had received a stay of execution, a term that could not be reduced further. That was all.

Recalling Hantou's fight with Maodan, Lingguan was convinced that his brother would have avoided it if he'd known his life would be over soon. The eternal concern of death rendered all old scores meaningless, like soap bubbles. A man would be able to see beyond many worldly matters and refuse to fight over petty profits if he could sense that death was never far away; he would not be obsessed with transient fame and wealth, since nothing was permanent. Only death was real.

The realization was disheartening to Lingguan, and yet it managed to dull the pain brought on by his brother's illness and pending death. Everything changed in his eyes, now revealing its illusory, transitory and ugly side. He recalled how, during his childhood, Beizhu had held his fist for him to smell a flower, but it had turned out to be an awful stench. "Grabbing at a fart," he thought. That was how he felt about life. What was the point? It was totally meaningless. His parents were the very manifestation of life's difficulties. As children, they had to worry about where the next meal would come from and whether or not they had enough clothing; when they got older they needed to be married, and when they were married, they wanted a son, whom they must work hard to raise; once the son was old enough, they had to find him a wife, who was expected to give them a grandson, and so on. And in the end you worried about four boards for a coffin. Life controlled you as if you were on a tether and called out to you like a magic towel. You chased after it diligently until the day you kicked out your legs and shut your eyes one last time. It was all over, just like that. One windy day when he was little, he saw a pack of dogs chasing a bobbing pig bladder the village children had blown up. One of them caught it and, pop, it broke, leaving a fetid stench. Humans weren't all that different from the dogs, but at least the dogs got a leftover pig's bladder. Humans have nothing in the end.

His heart hardened somewhat when he was reminded that everyone, including his parents, Mengzi and Ying'er, would be gone eventually. Tables would rot, trees would wither, and pigs would become manure that transforms into nutrients for the crops. Everything was the same and nothing was real.

Their mother had aged, her wrinkled forehead erasing all signs of her youth. Ying'er would grow old too, and the glow on her face would no longer be as red as a peach blossom. He too was walking closer toward his grave, having grown up from a tiny baby with a little exposed pecker. Every passing day took him one step closer to death. "It's pointless," he said to himself.

His mind was addled, the notion of death crowding out every other thought.

In addition to giving Hantou shots, he continued his frantic search for pethidine. During those days, his life was filled with a benumbed despair, interrupted only by the temporary elation over finding another dose of the painkiller.

He was hopelessly despondent.

One night when Hantou was moaning in agony, Lingguan had an appalling thought—stop his suffering, since the end would be the same. Relieving him of pain would be a compassionate act. What would they do when Bucinnazine no longer worked and they ran out of pethidine? Lingguan knew he wouldn't be able to face that. He went to see his high schoolmate and pleaded with him until the schoolmate told him to inject Hantou with several doses of pethidine at once if it came to that.

More than once the thought of ending it all for his brother occurred to him. Stop the nightmare then and there, for his brother, for his parents, and for everyone else. But the thought was always followed by self-inflicted condemnation for his lack of humanity.

He was disoriented; gray was all he could see. The smell of death surrounded him. He was mentally and physically exhausted in this never-ending nightmare.

Hantou was quiet, all but the moans and the occasional explanation to their mother that the protrusion was caused by infection in the surgical wound. He did not know that she already knew what he had.

Just as back in the hospital, he never discussed his illness with anyone, nor did he ask any questions. The doctor had said Hantou did not know the severity of his situation because he was barely conscious. Lingguan did not believe him, for Hantou was too calm, unlike other cancer patients, who were usually restless, complaining and blaming others, sometimes even getting hysterical. Hantou was unperturbed, at least on the surface; he had little to say, did not sigh much, and gave no meaningful hints or instructions about later. He seemed perfectly calm.

Lingguan gave him shots at regular intervals, one to ease the pain and one to reduce the swelling, though the latter was bogus. Then for two days in a row, he stopped the pointless shot for inflammation reduction, telling his brother that he was giving him a combined dose for both the pain and the swelling. "You're all lying to me," was how Hantou reacted. He did not talk to anyone for days after that.

Money flowed out like water. Their father sold his favorite black mule, even though it hurt him to do so. Lingguan gathered up what he'd bought for Hantou's funeral and handed it over to their mother. She cried when she laid her eyes on items usually reserved for old people, as if she was convinced that her son would die only after being reminded by what she saw. Then, tearfully, she put it all away in the cleanest and safest spot in the house, fearing that someone might soil the best clothes her son would ever wear.

Everyone in the family was exhausted. Dispirited and seemingly ready to keel over, their father began to snort the moment he leaned up against a wall. Their mother was skin and bones, walking on unsteady feet, as if braving a headwind. Mengzi was doing better, well behaved, like a changed man. As instructed by their mother, Ying'er stayed away from the room she shared with Hantou; she was expecting, and their mother did not want the aura of a pregnant woman to jinx Hantou.

Lingguan could tell that their mother still harbored unrealistic hopes.

Everyone in the village came to see Hantou, each bringing a gift of two catties of refined sugar and a couple of canned goods, as gratifying as anything Hantou's parents had experienced since the onset of his illness. It showed they were well respected. The visitors all did their best to console Laoshun's wife, who wept with them all. Staring at the visitors though tear-filled eyes, as if seeking their help, she repeatedly asked:

"What am I going to do? Ai—" She looked like a helpless little girl.

"It'll be all right." They offered the same words each time. "Heaven has eyes. A good man like Hantou will surely get better. He will."

She would sigh with relief, as if she'd received a promise from Heaven.

The string of visitors discomfited Hantou, who seemed angry at himself over the trouble he'd caused their neighbors. He would struggle to sit up when a visitor came in, nearly out of breath, and leaned against the blanket. The lump was getting bigger, spreading from his rib area up to his chest and down to his lower abdomen. His belly was now as hard as a rock, which for him became a second private area; he would cover his belly with a blanket or his clothes each time he sat up. But no one could spend more than a few minutes with him, not with him gasping for air. Unwilling to make him suffer even more, they offered a few words of compassion before saying good-bye and going into the kitchen to comfort his mother, who continued her teary muttering:

"What am I going to do?"

They offered a few more words of sympathy and left.

Maodan's visit mattered most to Hantou, who smiled at his friend, a genuine, sincere smile. He waved for Maodan to come closer and held his friend's hands wordlessly. Maodan smiled foolishly, but didn't say anything. Lingguan knew they'd made up. They really had, that was obvious. He also saw Hantou heave a long sigh and, racked by exhaustion, shut his eyes. A teardrop rolled out of the corner of each eye and down the cheek. He licked it off when it reached his lips.

That was the only time since leaving the hospital that Lingguan had seen his brother cry.

6

For days Hantou's mother's eyes dry, her voice was hoarse, and her head buzzed, as if a swarm of bees had taken up residence there. Something seemed to have sucked her energy dry, and fatigue had seeped into every pore; she felt she would crumple to the ground like an empty sack if she loosened up just a bit.

She did not know what cancer was, but knew it was synonymous with death. She couldn't get away from that "life snatcher," which constantly stole into her mind and tormented her so much she wished that she herself were dead. Her lack of medical knowledge did not prevent her from seeing that her son was going downhill fast and that the layer of fat under his skin had turned into a thin membrane. He was reduced to a skeleton, his bones sticking out so much that every one was discernible; the insolent lump had taken over most of his abdomen. The word that she was afraid to think of was stealthily closing in on her son.

Despair. Helplessness. Incapacitating powerlessness. Heartrending despondency.

Bottle gourds, watermelons, carrots, tomatoes. She even told

Lingguan to buy two cases of carrot juice despite its eye-popping cost at nearly two yuan per bottle. Huaqiu had read in Reference News that it had cured someone's cancer. They had to get some.

When she heard that the Guanyin Bodhisattva granted everyone's wish from those in pain, she prayed like a madwoman, begging the compassionate savior to save her suffering son or to take her in his stead. She pleaded so much and so often that her lips were callused. But Hantou was fading, and the lump continued to grow at an alarming rate. Not a sliver of light appeared in the dark sky over her head.

Her son, who had barely made it to adulthood. Her precious boy, her life, her everything. She prayed and pleaded, but received neither answer nor hope. All she could do besides cry was shed more tears; she felt nothing but sorrow, pain, and desperation. Surrounded by her family, she nevertheless felt utterly alone, sunken in lonely despair and desperately lonely. All the words she mumbled were directed at herself, for no one could see what went on in her heart, no one. No one could ever understand how much it hurt and how deep the wound in her heart was. She hated her husband, who could still squat there smoking expressionlessly when their son was dying. She wanted him to cry, even though she knew that his blank look was more alarming than tears; she wanted him to cry, to beat his chest and stomp his feet, to put his arms around her and wail with her. But he did none of those. Mengzi was flipping through his dog-eared books. His brother was moaning next to him and yet he continued to leaf through the pages. Did his love for his brother mean less than a few sheets of paper?

Lingguan had lost a great deal of weight, the poor boy. She couldn't imagine how they would manage without him, but to her he appeared to be going through the motions. He wasn't trying hard enough. She wanted him to find a way, to think of something, anything, but he didn't. He just kept administering painkiller shots, not serious enough about his brother's illness, and waiting—ah, the terrifying thing.

She dried her tears and looked up at the sky. Despite the sun and clouds, it felt overcast to her. The sun was blinding, but she could see no light. Heaven, are you really going to end it all? Is it true that even a deity can't save him? Guanyin Bodhisattva, ah, Guanyin, can't you do something? Heaven. He's so young.

She knew she shouldn't have complained about Lingguan. He had said he'd sell his flesh or his blood to save his brother, even if there was just a glimmer of hope. She believed him. Yet she could not bear to sit and watch her oldest son die. They had to spend money, even though they knew it wouldn't help; at least it would make her feel better. They couldn't try to save money when her son was at death's door. What for? She would be happy to sell the house and everything in it.

She regretted making Hantou marry Ying'er, who hadn't been born in the best year for Hantou's horoscope. But he couldn't have remained a bachelor all his life. Besides, Grannie Shaman Qi had performed a rite to avert possible calamities. Seven embroidering needles were buried in the newlywed's room, weren't they? The bridal sedan came through the gate facing east, didn't it? Water was carried into the wedding chamber first, followed by fire, wasn't it? A white rooster's head was lopped off when the bride walked through the gate, wasn't it? So why—why—she recalled that Ying'er was having her period that day. A bad omen; she had jinxed him. A bride carries harmful energy into the marriage and, with that, could only be even more lethal.

She decided to ask Grannie Shaman Qi to perform another rite, based on the puzzling question of why a liver infection had turned into cancer. Maybe another rite would change the liver cancer into a curable illness.

The rite was the only straw remaining in the sea of suffering. She felt an impulse surging inside and a fire burning in her belly; it was the fire of hope, the fire of life. Her life would exhaust itself when it died out, leaving only an empty shell behind.

Laoshun lowered his head to smoke when she told him her decision. Mengzi looked at Hantou with an open mouth, while Hantou faced the wall wordlessly, an enigma to the others.

Surprisingly Lingguan agreed enthusiastically.

He had done everything he could, and felt no regret on an intellectual level. He agreed simply because he didn't want their mother to live with a shred of regret and remorse, so he supported her decision despite his doubt about the effectiveness of these rites in curing cancer. "We should take such things with a grain of salt, but it's better to believe than to doubt."

"How much?" Laoshun asked after puffing on his pipe.

"A hundred should be enough to cover everything, shouldn't it?" Lingguan asked.

Laoshun puffed away noisily without responding.

7

After several days of frantic preparation, they finally gathered every item that Shaman Qi had told Goubao to write down for them:

Three hundred sheets each of red, white, yellow, blue, and black paper, two catties of mutton, two catties of liquor, one white rooster, a pinch of flour from one hundred family each, three plates of steamed rolls, a peach branch, one hundred sheets of yellow paper money, one hundred sheets of white paper money, seven pebbles of different colors, and a straw avatar.

Grannie Qi's plan was to find a substitute for Hantou and rid him of his illness.

She seldom used this formula. The Hall in the underworld had got the number for the person in question and he must report to them, so now she would perform a rite and save his life by sending a substitute along. In their village a few people had had their lives saved through this method, and they reinforced the faith that Laoshun's wife had in Shaman Qi's formula. Beizhu's father, for instance, had recovered from coughing up blood clots. To Laoshun's wife, coughing up blood was much more serious than Hantou's illness, and she found consolation in the case of Beizhu's father.

Finally the sun finished its daily rotation and went down behind the mountains, followed by the night curtain. The village was quiet; gone were conversations at the village entrance. Even the dogs fervently chasing each other's tails went back home. In the sky the crescent moon was a tiny flake, like a worm that is frozen stiff. Everything was shrouded in white, the village, the field, the mountains – and the heart of everyone in Laoshun's family.

After sending Mengzi to summon Grannie Shaman Qi, Laoshun's wife went inside and sat down on the *kang* to look at Hantou, who lay facing the wall. Motherly concern rose up when she noticed that his hair had been mussed by his pillow and that the skin on one side of his face was stretched taught by his protruding cheekbone. Lingguan had been her favorite, but Hantou's illness had elevated him above anyone else. Now he was her happiness, her sense of well-being, even her life. "Why couldn't it be me?" She asked herself. In her constant fantasy, she reached over to pull out Hantou's illness and stuff it into her own chest. She would have done it long ago if she could, without hesitation.

Only a mother has the comprehensive meaning of "son." Son, my son, she muttered constantly. She kept repeating the two words at moments when she could not stop crying, as if it were a potent incantation to ease her suffering. At moments like this, "my son" referred only to Hantou, the son she had raised for over two decades, now laid low by illness.

Hantou was reticent, never complaining or fighting over anything, which now made her regret not treating him better in the past. She hadn't realized it until he fell ill. Mengzi and Lingguan had always been given the best clothes the family could afford because they were going to school, an important reason for preferential treatment. Hantou, who dropped out of school, naturally had no need for nice clothes. Mengzi and Lingguan ate better, for the same reason. Studying drained their mental energy, so they needed more nutrition. Hantou had never complained. She had ignored him for the longest time and hadn't noticed her partiality until he got that awful disease. Her heart ached every time she recalled the unfair treatment. Son! My son! She wished she could cut out a slice of her heart to compensate him. Son. My son. I'll make it up to you when you're better—Heaven is not blind.

Son. My son. Her heart nearly broke as she called out to him.

She frequently looked at him like that, which brought her so much pain because she must confront her son's deterioration, suffering, and moans. And yet it made her happy to suffer, and she greedily savored it. She sat down on the bed to be with him whenever she had a free moment. The corners of her mouth twitched when he moaned. Convinced that her presence reduced his suffering, she strained and exhausted herself to fight off the pain on his behalf. She was afraid he could not withstand the pain alone if she left the room. In her eyes, pain was a bucket of water, which was an easier load for two people to carry. She was often drenched in sweat from the agony, but she was happy to do that; it was painful yet blissful at the same time.

Hantou was going to roll over. She took off her shoes and climbed onto the bed to help him. Gently she smoothed his skin made red and wrinkled by the blanket, rubbed his hands, and blew softly on the horrible bed sore on his backside. In addition to suffering for him vicariously, she did all this happily and willingly, diligently and carefully. Like a child eager for praise from her teacher for doing good, she looked at him, hoping to detect from his expression that she had done enough to ease his suffering a bit. But no. Her effort amounted to a glass of water, while the excruciating pain from cancer was a burning cartload of firewood. Not once did he look comfortable and free of pain. He frowned, instead, because he wasn't used to such intimate gestures as a caress from his mother, and he was sorry to have caused her trouble. Which made her even less sure of herself.

"It's all right. Grannie Qi said Heaven has eyes. Remember Beizhu's father? He was so sick, but Grannie helped him recover."

Hantou shut his eyes wordlessly, responding to her comment by breathing audibly. It was a unique way of breathing typical of cancer patients, as if something oppressive were forcing him to exhale sharply with strained, short bursts of air. Her face muscles twitched each time he made that soft explosive sound.

8

Grannie Shaman Qi arrived, greeted like a savior by Laoshun's wife, who walked up to Hantou and said, "Ganma is here to see you, Hantou." He kept his eyes closed without responding. With a wave of her hand, Qi sat down on a sofa and accepted a cigarette from

Lingguan. "Everything ready?"

"Yes," his mother said. "It's all set."

"You shouldn't have had any trouble finding everything except the flour from a hundred families. It will work if you get a pinch from a hundred people. The others are easy."

"We went to a hundred families, three villages in total." Laoshun's wife said.

"That's best, of course." Qi took a puff of her cigarette and looked at Hantou with her eyes half closed. Laoshun's wife stared at the shaman's eyes, trying to find hope and reassurance in them, but Qi shifted her gaze away.

"Take that down." Qi pointed at a portrait of Chairman Mao. "That's the spot for your ancestors; with that god standing there, they won't dare to come."

Laoshun told Mengzi to remove the portrait.

Qi told Laoshun to divide the three hundred sheets of colored paper into ten piles each. With concentration, he struggled to count them out clumsily, so Lingguan took over and quickly got the job done.

"How about the soupy rice? Is it ready?" Qi asked.

"It is. We have everything ready," their mother said.

"Let's begin then. The sooner the better." Qi tossed away the cigarette butt and told Mengzi to bring over the table and lay out plates, each containing fifteen *mantou* that took up most of the space. Qi then told them to lay out an incense burner, liquor infused with rooster blood, candles, mutton and other sacrificial offerings. She chanted as she lit incense sticks and the candles, and burned the paper.

Her rite was simple, reaching directly for the goal without the need to inscribe spiritual tablets or reciting prayer. After burning the incense and paper, she got up on the *kang* with a pile of the five-color paper to wave over Hantou.

"Burn it off and burn it away." She intoned. "Burn it off if it was caused by a living being—"

"Burn it off," Laoshun and his wife repeated after her.

"Burn it away if it was caused by the dead."

"Burn it away."

"Three souls and seven spirits return to the body."

"Return to the body."

"Three souls and seven spirits enter into the bones."

"Enter into the bones."

"Burn it off, all filth and anything vile."

"Burn it off."

"Burn it away, all filth and anything vile."

"Burn it away."

"Burn it down, the lump in the abdomen."

"Burn it down."

"Burn it away, the illness in him."

"Burn it away."

"Burn and make him healthy; burn and bring him comfort and wellness."

"Comfort and Wellness."

"Roll over." Qi said as she put the paper away. Lingguan and Mengzi helped their brother roll over for the shaman to repeat her earlier actions and incantation with another pile of paper.

Laoshun's wife knew the rite well, for she had done it for her children when they were sick. She also knew that what Grannie Shaman Qi was doing differed, because Qi had the "force." Laoshun's wife did not know what the force was, but it meant something divine in her understanding. She saw hope each time she heard the paper rap as Shaman Qi repeatedly tapped the pile at Hantou's body. Glancing at her son's face again and again, she could not detect any noticeable sign of sorrow or happiness, but there was something else. It was impossible to say what it was, however, except that it was complex, with an irrefutable hint of hope, something new to his usual calm, slightly dazed expression. She also saw an occasional expression of gratitude in his eyes when he looked at the shaman. It had to be gratitude. Hantou had unwavering faith in Ganma Qi; Laoshun's wife understood the meaning behind his gaze.

The rapping of the paper and Qi's peculiar style of cryptic intonation lent the room a mysterious feel. The candles flickered; called longevity lamps, they must be kept burning until the rite was over, but the flames seemed forever ready to go out in the current caused by fluttering colored paper. She felt her heart tethered to the quivering flames. Her mind was finally at ease when she made Mengzi and Lingguan stand between Qi and the table to block the current.

After she had made use of all ten piles of colored paper, Shaman Qi took up the peach branch to gently beat Hantou's body and chanted:

In my hand is true incense that burns my palm;
The peach branch comes from a boundless source.
One will be given to Celestial Master Zhang;
One will stay with the deity of longevity.
And there is one more to stay behind,
In the human world to fight deities and demons.
Firstly it strikes at spirits of family members and wandering ghosts;
Secondly it strikes at evil spirits and erring deities.
Thirdly it strikes at spirits caused by bloody death,
Fourthly it strikes at ghosts of wrongful death seeking redress.

Fifthly it strikes at all five directions and five spirits,
Sixthly, it strikes at the temple judges in the underworld.
Seven strikes, seven killings, nails in the karmic coffin
Eighthly it strikes at the demonic evil spirits and filth
Three thousand bronze clubs strike out first,
Followed by three thousand iron cudgels on the heel.
The bones and veins are smashed and pulverized,
Turning into dust motes by the platform of white lotus.

She continued to beat and chant in her cryptic tone for a while before climbing down off the *kang*. She told Laoshun's wife to hold Hantou's undershirt and crawl under the table on his behalf, and then she walked out to the yard, where she chanted before the straw figure and offered the liquor. As Hantou's substitute, it was entrusted with the mission of taking away his suffering and all possible misdeeds and reporting to the underworld. Qi burned a large stack of spirit money for the figure, intoning as she did, "What's burning here isn't for the first of the month, what's burning here isn't for the fifteenth of the month, what's burning here is money to ransom Hantou's life. One turns into ten, ten into a hundred, a hundred turns into a thousand, a thousand turns into ten thousand, ten thousand turns into a multitude."

When she was done, she told Mengzi and Lingguan to take the colored paper, yellow and white spirit money, a dough tiger made of flour from a hundred families, and the avatar to burn at the crossroad.

9

Hantou closed his dry eyes shortly after Qi left. His head was throbbing, as was his abdomen, where the pain was dulled after a shot of pethidine and bearable if he gritted his teeth. Now his mind wandered and hovered between reality and a dream world. He was tired, bone-tired but couldn't sleep. He was wide-awake, from complete depletion of energy and total exhaustion; he was so awake he was in a fog, a nightmare where he could think rationally but could not shake it off. The haziness felt like a dream, but for the actual pain and the lump in his abdomen. Everything was real.

It had been a long time. He felt he'd been sick for ages, so far back in time that he couldn't recall the time when he wasn't. Memories of healthy days receded into swirls of yellow fog, as if covered in dust. Life had been wonderful back then; he hadn't known at the time how wonderful it was. He finally appreciated good health when he no longer had it. Good health was bliss.

Everything was gone, everything.

Distant scenes flickered in his mind, all blurry, as if they were exhausted, too. He could barely make them out in the haze: he was a little boy stealing fruit from a tree, fighting over a carrot with Baigou, getting married, scuffling with Maodan—the scenes were fading, receding far away. All he had left was the pain in his abdomen.

He was tired, tired beyond words. Exhaustion, nothing but exhaustion. His heart was barely beating; he felt it too was struggling. His breathing had become faint, almost like a thin thread that could break at any point and at any time; he had to strain and use caution to let it out. There was blockage in his windpipe, interfering with his normal breathing and making an aspirated sound with each breath.

Death, like a sword suspended above his head, could come down on him at any moment, but he had no time to be afraid; he just wished it hadn't come so soon. He had yet to enjoy a full life, and now he had to leave. He recalled a phrase commonly intoned by ritual masters,

"No one knows who you were when you're born, and you don't know who you'll become after you die." That was so true. He was still in the dark about life and himself, but it was time to go. He did not want to; he wanted to live a bit longer. He had yet to gain an identity; he had wasted his life. He hadn't done what he should have. He'd run out of time. What if he'd known he would die so early in life? He was sure he'd have lived differently, but how? He had no idea. But he was certain he'd have gone to shool. He'd lived his life in vain. He'd done nothing, leaving nothing behind like a fly flitting across a void.

Suddenly the sky fell and the ground gave away under his feet, with explosions going off all around him. Rocks and heavy objects rained down and buried him. His body felt unusually heavy, flattening out his breathing. Boulders pressed down on every pore in his body, oppressively heavy. Dense, heavy, weighty. The ground pressed up and the sky pushed down. Huge rocks fell like rain. Like a nightmare, a waking nightmare. Terror-stricken, he wanted to shout, to scream, and moan, but failed to make a sound.

Some time later, all the heavy objects were gone. His mind and body exploded and filled the sky with light. Shards of broken glass in the air were refracted in sunlight, flashing noisily; light was everywhere, undulating light like waves of water. The light was flowing, flickering, clamoring, ray chasing ray, raising a racket, like a gleaming surface of water, like countless flying birds of light, noisy and rowdy, bursting, exploding, multiplying, sweeping off. Everything was moving fast, impossibly bright and shiny.

His limbs tingled as if electrified. Bits of metal filled the veins of his body. His heart was a powerful magnet and was crushed and pushed by all the shreds it had attracted and accumulated, until it broke into pieces and slowly turned into flying glowworms. They fluttered, playfully and noisily, doing a dance of life, before slowly gathering together and turning into a bright light.

It was the light of life, with a faint, fluttering, tender, bright flame in the quiet void of emptiness. Everything disappeared. What had existed between heaven and earth, objects, and pain all dissolved in the serene nothingness. Only the light continued to flicker, bringing a sense of tranquility and detachment.

Suddenly the light went out.

10

"Hurry. Hantou's hands are getting cold," his mother shouted.

The rest of the family put down their bowls and ran to the *kang*. Hantou's eyes were losing focus. His mother wailed, "Heavens. How am I going to go on?"

"Don't let your tears fall on the boy." Laoshun shoved her away. "Hurry, bring the clothes."

His wife collapsed and howled, banging her head on the floor. Fengxiang, who had been alerted by her cry, came in and tried to pull her up.

"Get his clothes," Laoshun roared.

"Pull down his lids and keep your hands on them." Laoshun told Lingguan.

Lingguan pulled down his brother's upper lids to cover the terrifying, unfocused eyes. Tears burst out, as he was engulfed by regret over not giving Hantou more pethidine to ease his pain; afraid that he might run out, he had been conserving it, and now had eleven left.

He'd have given Hantou more shots so he wouldn't suffer so much if he'd known his brother would be gone so soon.

Lingguan was beside himself with remorse.

Death had finally arrived. Lingguan was alerted to many of his mistakes by its arrival: he should have spent more time talking to his brother, he should have asked if he had any requests, he should have been by his side more often. Now, separated by death, he would never see his brother again.

He removed his hands to see that his brother's lids were shut one last time. Hantou looked calm, dispassionate. A detached look after forgoing everything in this world, a calm after a raging storm.

His eyes blurred as hot tears rolled down his cheeks.

"Don't let your tears fall on him," Laoshun said.

Lingguan dried his tears. They'd all been told that a corpse turns into the living dead if touched by the tears of a living person. How scary was that! If it were true, he'd prefer his brother to be one of the living dead; Hantou would always be his brother, no matter how scary. It would be so much better than not seeing him ever again.

Their mother brought out the funeral clothes, commonly called longevity garments for old folks. Hantou had to wear them, even though he was only in his twenties.

As the last gift from the living to the dead, the clothes were brand new, never before worn. Hantou would depart for another world dressed in them, something he could have never hoped to wear when alive.

It requires some skill to dress someone who is no longer alive. Mengzi held up Hantou's limp head. The discolored, bulging abdomen formed a sharp contrast with his bony, protruding ribcage, giving him a freakish look. Laoshun guided his feet one by one into the cotton pants and outer pants.

His wife continued to wail, her hoarse voice brimming with despair. She had known this was coming, but could not accept the cruel end; in the past, death always happened in others' houses, and she had sighed emotionally when she talked about it. Now it was tied to her son. Her world collapsed, and she could only cry, beat her breast, and bang her head on the floor in extreme grief.

Humans are pitiable like that.

Ying'er had also cried herself hoarse; she no longer had to avoid him now that he was gone, so she came to see him one more time. To her his death had come suddenly; he'd been alive when she'd seen him the previous time, but now he was a corpse. Chaos seemed to have broken out in the room, and all she heard was people crying. For a while she thought she was dreaming.

"Go get a car." Laoshun told Lingguan.

Lingguan dried his tears and walked out.

They had agreed upon cremation. An earth mound would just bring back the sorrow all over again if they opted for burial. Besides, Hantou was so young that cremation would ensure a clean end and prevent any future mischief. Cost was another concern. They had about exhausted all they had, and a burial would have required up to a thousand yuan.

"What are you doing?" Laoshun's wife pounced on Lingguan. "What are you going to do? I'll kill myself right here if you have him taken away. I will."

"All right. We won't," Lingguan said.

"I don't care how you do it, but you must get him a coffin. I'll kill myself if you don't." She was bawling hysterically.

Lingguan went into the city. It was quieter now that he was away from the noise at home, but everything still felt like a dream. He was dizzy, his mind a jumble of thoughts, still reproaching himself for not giving his brother more shots and making him suffer. The streets, bustling with people, only made him feel lonelier; his grief, like a thick fog, cut him off from the world.

Hantou was dead. His brother, the quiet camel-like brother was dead. Lingguan began to tear up again when he recalled how helpless Hantou had looked at the school entrance when he brought noodles for him. He had let his brother down.

"He'd have been so happy if I'd passed the exam."

Lingguan regretted not studying harder to get into college to make Hantou happy. He regretted not spending enough time talking to his brother. But it was too late now. Death had created an insurmountable wall; he was on one side, his brother on the other.

He decided on his own to buy a coffin. To be sure he'd have preferred cremation, which would save the impoverished family unnecessary expense. Besides, cremation or burial really made no difference.

The most important task ahead was how to go on. When one died, everything was over, and that was the same whether one was buried or cremated. But his mother's hysterical bawling kept ringing in his ears; he did not want her to live out her life with regret. So he made a quick calculation; burial would cost three hundred more than cremation if they did not go in for an elaborate funeral. Three hundred—or maybe a bit more—would buy her peace of mind. It was worth it.

When he returned with the hired truck carrying the coffin, Hantou had been carried outside and placed under a canopy by the gate. Their yard was thronged with people. His mother, who was howling inside, stormed out when she heard the sound of the truck. She pushed away anyone who tried to stop her and sprawled across her son's body. When Meng Eight and other neighbors restrained her, she screamed shrilly:

"I'll kill myself if anyone dares take him away."

Lingguan pushed his way up and walked up to her.

"No cremation, Mother. I brought back a coffin."

"Don't lie to me. I'll kill myself, Lingguan, if you take him away."

"I won't. I promise. Look. The coffin is on the truck."

She walked out the gate to look at the coffin before falling to the ground in tears.

The neighbors were surprised to see the coffin, but no one said anything; they merely looked displeased. Hantou was young and childless, which disqualified him for a coffin, though Laoshun's wife used the baby Ying'er was carrying as justification. The villagers preferred cremation, a safer option, so the sight of a coffin unnerved them.

"It's better this way." Laoshun sounded relieved. "The old crone was losing her grip and would surely kill me if we cremated the boy."

"Actually it won't cost too much more," Lingguan told him. "The fee for cremation and the price of an urn are high, so in the end they're about the same."

The villagers could not object now that the coffin had been brought back.

Hantou's bulging belly was conspicuous. When the yellow paper covering was blown away, his grim face was exposed, but he looked calm, with a barely detectable expression of enduring pain. He almost seemed to be smiling if one did not look too closely; it was as if he were saying, "It's good to be dead." Lingguan stood quietly before his brother; it was good to be dead, he had to agree. It was good to be dead at least to Hantou, who had suffered for months. "He's finally free," Lingguan said to himself, but grief returned when he once again realized that he would never see Hantou again. He couldn't bring himself to imagine what life would be like without Hantou.

Meng Eight started the ritual of encoffining to prevent animals like dogs and cats from doing harm to the body. Village men carefully picked up the blanket and sheets under Hantou to lift him into the coffin. Laoshun's wife dried her tears and sobbed as she brought out a new silk blanket. Part of Ying'er's dowry, it had never been used. Laoshun wanted to say something, but stopped after glancing at Meng Eight.

Mengzi had brought back a talisman from a Taoist priest. It was a piece of paper with the inscription, "Place on the metal plow to chase away evils spirits/The god of thunder has shown its face to scare off deities and ghosts." Meng pasted it on a plow that had been brought into the yard for that purpose. Then he tied a big white rooster to the plow before placing it behind the coffin to prevent the corpse from becoming one of the undead.

"The priest said that three days from now would be an auspicious date, and no preparation is needed. He'll bring two people over to play music. It's a favor to us, no charge," Mengzi said.

"We can't forgo all preparations. We should at least make paper cranes and some wreaths. It would look terrible without anything," Meng Eight said.

"You're right," Laoshun said. "Please do what you think is right. I've completely lost my head." Then, drained of energy, he slid to the ground against the wall.

11

Laoshun's wife woke up before the rooster crowed. Her parched throat hurt as if on fire. A sticky film covered her eyes, and she had to strain to keep them open and focused. Everything from the day before came back to her when she searched for the reasons behind the changes in her throat and eyes.

"Hantou?" She shuddered, seized by paralyzing grief once again.

She got down off the *kang* and groped around to find her shoes before walking out. The yard was lit up, making it impossible for her to miss the bright red coffin. A heaviness assaulted her chest and she began to tear up again. Hantou—her Hantou was in the wooden box. He was dead. Her heart shattered as she struggled to recall the true meaning of death.

Forcing herself not to look at the coffin, she raced across the yard and into the kitchen. Suddenly, she felt Hantou's eyes chasing her in the dark night, as if he had something to say to her, so she turned to take another look at that jarring object. She felt aggrieved for her son—still so young—sleeping in there, but her sorrow was alleviated somewhat by the thought that he at least had a coffin. Cremation was out of the question for her; she couldn't stand the thought of putting her son through the fire.

She turned on the kitchen light and stoked the stove. The noodle dough for Hantou's funeral, which had been shaped the day before, had risen. She scooped out some dough and added to the starter. Her body felt heavy, and she ached all over. Hantou's face kept flashing before her eyes, and the tears returned, blurring her eyes and rolling down her cheek to fall on the dough. Her son was gone and life had lost its meaning.

She wished she could smash her head against the coffin and kill herself.

Hantou had been a timid boy everyone had picked on. Now he was going to the underworld alone, and how could she be sure that the evil ghosts down there wouldn't pick on him too? The thought was unbearable. She wanted to go with him.

She wailed again, no longer able to hold back. She rubbed her floured hands and tossed the under-kneaded dough to the counter so she could sit down by the stove to cry. Trying to control herself in order not to wake the others up, she could not stop, but at least her voice was so hoarse it was little more than a whisper.

The heaviness in her chest eased up a little after a while. She remained where she was, staring into the void, before drying her tears and going back to the dough, which she kneaded between sobs.

When the dough was ready, she sat down by the stove to stare again. Memories of Hantou flashed through her mind, each bringing renewed regret. Hantou loved pan-fried flatbreads, but she hadn't made it for him more than a few times. She'd have made one every day for him if she'd known he'd be gone so soon. Hantou loved tomatoes, but she'd never once had Lingguan buy some for him in the city.

Her mind moved from his favorite food to his dream object, a walking tractor; he'd wanted one to plow the field, thresh the grain, or start a work sideline. She recalled that he'd once touched Goubao's machine and gotten a tongue-lashing from his friend. "What's the big deal? I'll give you a new one if I break yours," Hantou had said, to which Goubao had replied, "I'd be able to buy an airplane if you could afford a tractor."

She sighed at the memory. Her son had been looked down upon; she shouldn't have let that happen. If she'd known he would die so young, she'd have done her best, worked herself to death, to get him a tractor. The worst was going into debt… her son had never had a chance to gain respect before he died.

Her heart was aching, tied up in knots.

"Make one." A light went on in her head. "Yes, we'll make one. Make a paper tractor for the boy. He never looked impressive, not even for a day, while alive, but he will now."

It was light out when the clan members began arriving. It was a small funeral, with no banquet for the mourners, so they didn't have to borrow tables, stools, bowls or plates. They had little to do, unlike at a funeral for old folks, which was considered a happy event, when they could eat and drink in high spirits. Hantou died young, and it was inappropriate to play finger guessing games, drink, and joke, so the yard felt quiet and dreary.

Laoshun's wife told Meng Eight, the lead rite performer, about the tractor. He wasn't too keen until hearing her explanation. "You two make a paper tractor," he called to Beizhu and Huaqiu.

"We've never done one before," Beizhu said.

"Now's a good time to learn. Get some sunflower stalks, needle grass, and willow branches, and copy a real one."

After Beizhu and Huaqiu left, Meng got some of the performers who were good at paper figurines to make a paper crane and wreaths. The crane, for calling to the soul, was an indispensible funeral item.

Lanlan arrived as Meng was giving orders. She said she'd dreamed that their house had collapsed. "A crumbling wall signals the death of a relative, a falling tree the death of a neighbor, a collapsing house a death in the family." It was a well-known saying for dream interpretation, so she was worried sick when she woke up and hurried home.

Lanlan had been closest to Hantou, who'd grown up with her and taken care of her. She fell to the floor and wailed the moment she walked in, which had her mother crying again, along with the neighborhood women who came to help.

Sounds of weeping filled the yard.

12

When they were picking up the coffin Lingguan noticed the sun was bright red, a rare sight. It sneaked into his heart, as the funeral neared its end, order was returning, and peace and quiet was about to be restored.

The dazzling bright red sun shone down on the crooked desert date tree in the yard, casting its twisted shadow on the door. Hantou was on his way on this brilliant day. Their mother's hoarse, anguished cry was heartbreaking to hear.

A big fire continued to burn from wreaths and paper money at the gate, its flames dimmed by the sunlight but its roaring sounds audible above all else. Shreds of charred paper and ashes flew into the sky and then slowly drifted down to the ground.

Every one was rushing about. The rite performers were gathering up poles and other items for the departure of the coffin; the Taoist priests were getting ready to leave, except for one to take care of the remaining rites. Laoshun hurried to stuff *mantou* in a cup Hantou had used and put it in the coffin as his last meal in this world.

Meng Eight took away the pillow under Hantou's head to prevent him from bringing illness to the living, as dictated by local custom. His mother, still wailing, brought out everything Hantou had ever worn to place in the coffin. Meng took them from her and told someone to cut off the metal buttons, following the Shawan taboo that the dead will turn into a demon after contact with metal objects.

His mother insisted on looking at her son one more time, which required her to wipe off her tears and stop crying, but she couldn't. Meng was adamant, and told one of the performers to drag her away, so that her tears wouldn't fall on the dead to give him the possibility of harming the living.

Beizhu cut off the metal buttons and handed the clothes to Laoshun.

Meng removed the coffin lid. Lingguan looked at his brother, whose sallow face was relaxed, as if asleep. The only sign of his former suffering was the protruding front teeth biting down on his lip, seemingly still in pain.

Meng asked Laoshun for Hantou's clothing. "Why don't we keep them for the living? Whatever we put in there will just rot and turn into ashes."

"That's fine. Actually some of the fabric doesn't rot very easily, and I've heard that the soul can't be reincarnated until the clothing has completely decomposed. We're doing it for Hantou's sake." Meng replaced the lid and took a hammer to pound in the nails.

The remaining priest recited the *Sutra to Point the Way*, the last ceremony before the coffin departed for the graveyard.

"The sun has set in the West and the moon is rising in the East. Summer is gone and winter is here. Sakyamuni Buddha presides over heaven and earth, while Lao Tzu brewed longevity elixir and made immortality pills, but neither could evade the soul-snatcher. Zhuge Liang was magical at predictions but could not avoid dying at Wuzhangyuan. Shi Chong was as rich as an emperor, with troves of gold and silver, but could not buy another day in this world. No one knows who you are when you come and don't know who'll you be when you go... Three cups of liquor are offered to the dead soul to deliver him from the life that is a dream."

Lingguan's heart stirred, as sentiments over the vicissitude of life came at him like a rising tide. It was true that no on can evade the soul-snatcher. Hantou was leaving before everyone else, who would follow him sooner or later, and a hundred years of long life was evanescent as a bubble. Death was regrettable and life should be rejoiced, and that was what life and death were all about. Nothing lasts forever, parents, brothers, sisters, spouses, friends, even the radiant red sun.

The most important thing was how to live.

The pallbearers got into action. They were all married, men in the real sense of the word. A virgin bachelor, even if he were eighty years old, would not be qualified for the task. They shouted cadence at each other as they picked up the coffin, placed it on two side-by-side benches, and tied poles of various lengths to it. The coffin creaked and groaned as the coir ropes shackled it.

Hantou's mother stormed out; she was howling, but not a sound emerged from her open mouth. Several village women tried to block her, but she broke through and threw herself onto the coffin to bang her head against it.

They could not tie a piece of white cloth, called a "tow-line," to the family's eternal regret. It would have been tied to the coffin on one end and held by the deceased's son by the other, but that was an honor enjoyed exclusively by those who left heirs. Many people exhausted their means and took great pains to violate family planning law just so they could have a son to tow the family line when they died.

Maodan held Hantou's portrait in his arms, the one taken after he fell ill; Hantou looked gaunt, but his eyes were filled with longing. What had he longed for? Life? Going to school? It would not have occurred to him that death could spring on him so quickly, or he might have lived differently.

The villagers were all sad over Hantou's premature death, and none of them could see the helpless longing in his eyes.

The coffin left the yard and materialized before Lingguan's eyes, like a racing train, or death, unstoppable. He would never forget the scene.

All of them breathing hard, the pallbearers continued shouting cadence, as if they carried Mount Tai on their shoulders.

Throngs of villagers lined the street Hantou would take; they were there to see him off. Every family along the way lit a fire by their gate, to ward off evil spirits and stop wandering ghosts from sneaking into their houses, as local custom dictated. But on this day it felt more like a farewell ceremony. Like a gun salute for fallen comrades.

The coffin moved quickly down a street shrouded in smoke on its way to the graveyard. Dust motes kicked up by the pallbearers blended with the foggy smoke, creating a surreal image. Lingguan followed close behind, like a sleepwalker, proceeding mechanically, holding the paper tractor.

He had been in such crowds before, seeing off other families' coffins as they went down the street. Now it was their turn to watch his family. Later he would be in the crowd again, seeing one of the onlookers on this day off to the final destination of life.

Village women, Fengxiang, Huaqiu's mother, Huilanzi, and others, were wiping their eyes. Lingguan was touched.

Maodan had dug a pit, a gaping mouth that would soon swallow Hantou up and eventually turned him into nothing. The coffin stopped by the pit. Beizhu removed the poles and placed a coir rope on each end of the coffin for the pallbearers to lower the coffin into the grave. Meng used a red cotton string to make sure the coffin was straight and even, following another custom to ward off evil spirits. Once the string served its purpose, it was torn into small pieces for the mourners to fasten to one of their buttons.

"Hantou's life is over," Beizhu said emotionally.

Lingguan could only weep silently.

Hantou was gone. The brother who had smiled at him dimly was dead; he would never see him again. He could not imagine what life would be like without Hantou, a thought that gripped his heart like an invisible iron hand.

The mourners took turns shoveling dirt into the grave; it was the last rite for Hantou, and no one was allowed to make a sound. One would shovel in a bit, toss the shovel to the ground, and another would come up to take over. Reminded by Meng not to let his tears fall on the dirt, Lingguan dried his eyes and walked up to pick up the shovel Beizhu had put down. He worked mechanically, still like a sleepwalker.

He was burying Hantou. He'd experienced the entire process of a healthy life's slow decline toward eventual death; he had stayed with him every day and now he was burying him with his own hands.

Lingguan felt he had lived a whole life cycle, with all its trials and tribulations.

The dirt that had been dug up had all been shoveled back into the grave, but the pit wasn't completely filled, to the puzzlement of the mourners. There should be a mound on the site after they put back the dirt and a coffin. But no, the grave had yet to be completely filled.

Based on the theory of geomancy, that was an unlucky spot. In the past, people would often dig a square pit of about two meters on all side, take some dirt, rub it into powder and sprinkled into the pit. They would check it the next day. The spot would be auspicious if the powdery dirt formed a mound and unlucky if the mound collapsed into itself.

An unlucky spot. Hantou was buried in an unpropitious spot. A geomancer was heard to say that Hantou's descendent – the baby in Ying'er's belly – would have a tough life.

Lingguan naturally did not believe a word of it.

13

Huaqiu's wedding was the next major event in the village following Hantou's death.

The grumpy old man eventually found his way to Huaqiu's door, followed by his daughter, heavily pregnant and sobbing. Every one winked when they learned of Huaqiu's romantic escapade in the desert, saying they had underestimated the young man's talent. Other men could had trouble finding a wife, even with money, but not him; the woman had come to his home on her own.

According to Maodan, who had taken it upon himself to be the villager reporter, the old man was a hard-nose and said the moment he walked in the door:

"The rice is cooked and the girl has become a woman. I'm giving her away today, and you will marry at once. Don't make the family lose face."

A reluctant Huaqiu hemmed and hawed; the old man's face darkened. "This old goat pelt for your young lamb's wool." He planned to fight it out with Huaqiu.

"Hei," said Maodan, "Huaqiu was acting like a dead donkey that didn't care if a wolf bit him. The old man had backbone and courage, a real man. He pulled a long face, spat on the floor, got to his feet and took his daughter by the hand. 'Let's go,' the old man said to the girl. 'I know where I can have our case heard.' Aiya, that was when Huaqiu lost his cool."

His report sent the villagers into laughing fits.

They laughed even louder over the wedding negotiations. At first the greedy old man demanded ten thousand. Huaqiu was so stunned his tongue shrank all the way down into his throat. Seeing that it was beyond his ability, the old man reduced the amount to eight thousand. Huaqiu responded by knitting his brows and saying, "Sure. I'll find a job in the city and make four thousand a year. Maybe I can come up with eight thousand after two years." The father was staggered. Two years? Hell, by then his grandson would be two years old. Maodan laughed dramatically at this point in his narration before going on. The father cut it down to four thousand, and Huaqiu offered to work in the city for one year. So now down to two thousand, then one, reducing the length of time Huaqiu needed for the job. In the end, the old man looked at his daughter's big belly and shouted unhappily, "You're shameless! You've punched me in the gut, and I have to take it. Just consider I raised you for nothing. Marry her in two weeks." Maodan told the villagers that Meng Eight really reamed his grandson out when he learned about it. "It wasn't easy for them to raise the girl," Meng said and went around the village, managing to borrow three thousand; he wrapped the money in red paper and gave it to the old man. Even with that, Huaqiu's wife was still the most affordable one in the village. Most people had to spend eight to ten thousand. Huaqiu's father was so pleased his smiling eyes turned round like pigeon droppings. Huaqiiu, on the other hand, wore a glum look and abruptly aged a great deal. His wedding night turned out to be a rowdy affair. The groom's father slaughtered a pig and a goat, and bought fifty *jin* of beef. Every family sent one member to the banquet, as dictated by village custom. The village men drank until their faces turned bright red, and, following the usual practice, painted the groom's father's face, put a cloth donkey blinder around his neck, placed a basket made of needle grass on his back, and led him around the room. It was a joking proclamation: look at the dirty old man who had his eyes on his new daughter-in-law.

The prank made everyone guffaw, startling crows in the tree and making the women double over laughing. Even Laoshun, who was reminded of Hantou and saddened by the wedding, had to give in and laugh.

Mengzi joined in the bridal chamber pranks, as usual, seemingly unaffected by Hantou's death. In fact, he and Baigou were the worst, both taking part in the favorite antic of Shawan men, "A pigeon carrying fortune in its beak." The new bride holds one end of a cigarette in her mouth for the prankster to catch the other end in his lips; the bride passed if their lips touched without dropping the cigarette. Then she had to call a prankster guye, meaning husband, with an added description demanded by each prankster, such as "Guye loved me," "Guye waited for me," "I leave the door open for you, Guye," or "Come on, Guye." They had endless gags to fill the night with fun and laughter. Mengzi had a crowning performance: his unruly teeth bit the bride so much she kept calling him "Stinky Guye."

But Meng intervened, stopping Baigou and his friends from trying out even worse pranks. The villagers didn't have all the fun they had hoped to have, but still they laughed themselves silly that night.

The festivity of Huaqiu's wedding wiped out the sadness brought on by Hantou's death.

14

Lingguan found himself in a state of crisis.

The dead need nothing, but take away half the family fortune. The house looked empty with Hantou gone; everything lost its original appearance, replaced by a dull sadness. His mother continued to sob and Ying'er dried tears, both trying to hold back and not cry out loud, which, on the contrary, was more heartbreaking than if they had been wailing.

Lingguan still couldn't believe his brother was gone. When he was inside, he kept expecting Hantou to walk in any moment, and when he was outside, he thought Hantou could come out right away. When a bird called, he wondered if it was a messenger from Heaven to tell him that Hantou was still alive and had crawled out of his grave. As he squatted on the southern loess hill, he had the illusion that his mother would come with a smile to tell him, "Your brother has come back alive."

But it was just that, an illusion.

It was only Hantou's shadow that stayed alive and floated before his eyes.

He dreamed about his brother often, though.

In the dream, Lingguan, aware of Hantou's death, was surprised to find him alive. Surprised and delighted, he would run up to his brother, but Hantou always avoided him with a grim look on a dark face, unsmiling and quiet, and frowning. Lingguan was heartbroken. But at least Hantou was alive in his dream. He was glad, and wouldn't have minded if Hantou were to stab him, as long as he wasn't dead.

Waking from a dream like that was the worst; every familiar object repulsed him, untouchable spots that reminded him of a reality he could not accept.

He had been avoiding that reality for days, and did his best to ignore it. It was a thorn, and even accidental contact would cause shooting pains in his heart. It always felt like a staggering blow when he thought about Hantou's guileless smile when he'd come to the city with noodles for him, about how Hantou had worked as a laborer to provide for his education, and about many others scenes that were long forgotten but now caused agonizing pangs. He froze and then began tearing at his own hair, cursing himself with clenched teeth.

"I'm no good. I'm a beast. No, I'm worse than a beast. A lamb kneels at its mother to suckle and a crow repays its mother's for rearing it; all the creatures in the wild know gratitude, but you, what you have done? Older brother is like a father, and what he's done for you is as high as a mountain. But you, you're worst than an animal."

His head felt as if stuffed with wool, a tangled, expanding mess that was driving him out of his mind. His throat was dry and his ears rang. Spasms struck his heart when he thought of Hantou's grim face avoiding him, and he was suffocating.

"No wonder he avoided me. No wonder he had a dark look on his face. No wonder he refused to say a single word before his death. He must have known. It's so obvious, like lice on a bald man's head. She—she's pregnant now. Mother told her not to go see Hantou, didn't she? Mother didn't want her to jinx him. No wonder. You're a bastard, Lingguan."

He was so ashamed when he recalled what he had done with Ying'er in the sand hollow when Hantou was in the hospital. He had smiled as he fell in love with her and listened to her singing. He was worse than a dog or a pig. Think about it. What are you then? How do you continue to live? Why—why don't you go kill yourself?

It would have made him feel better if he could take a knife, like a samurai, and cut himself open; he would take out his heart and offer it as a sacrifice to Hantou. If only he could bring out his ungrateful coils to form the word for "remorse." But would that soothe his conscience? Could it help him regain enough self-esteem? Everything in the room seemed to be reproaching him, reminding him of his sin.

But what he found most difficult to think about was Ying'er.

Every "romantic" recollection was a scorpion gnawing at him, evidence of his sin. He feared her, could not bring himself to look at her, and did his best to avoid her.

Obviously, she'd been avoiding him also.

She spent her days in the room she'd shared with Hantou. She sobbed until she was hoarse and could hardly catch her breath. Was it possible that she was feeling the torment of her soul? His partner in sin.

Lingguan could almost see her face, which was now impossibly sallow. It was a scab on his heart, a trigger for self-reproach, and the dark cloud over his mental sky.

Worse yet, her pregnancy was approaching full term.

A new life would soon be born.

It was the sorest spot for him, a punishing reality, an unavoidable cruelty, an eternal nightmare, an unforgiveable sin.

He wondered if ghosts really did exist. He sincerely hoped so, for then he would be able to see his poor brother and offer him repentance; he would ask for his brother's forgiveness, and invite him to open his heart to let the blood wash away his sin. But could his sin be cleansed?

Maybe he should simply be sent to hell, where he'd burn until he turned to ashes that dispersed in the wind. Or be cut by thousands of knives, gnawed on by millions of poisonous insects until they destroyed his sinful body and soul. He wished his filthy self would vanish, leaving not a figment of his repugnance behind.

But nothing could be done now.

His existence became a burden.

He tried to hold back and put up with everything; he couldn't stop shivering.

Each time he shivered, he saw all the people he knew, which only added weight to his chest: Yindi, Lanlan, Wuzi, Gimpy Five, Maodan, Bai Fu and other living "dead." Like him, they were turning round and round in a giant mill, as if in a dream.

He wished he could rouse himself with a few shouts. But he knew he wouldn't hear a thing, not even an echo. Soon he would be affected by those around him and sluggish like them, and when that happened, he, the sinner, would be so used to his sin that he'd become just another collection of cells engaged in mediocrity. It would be worse than going under a bloody knife.

Lingguan began to ponder how he would live out the rest of his life.

The villagers came to the conclusion that he was crushed by Hantou's death. He was often seen lost in thought on the loess hill, his glazed eyes fixed on something. He walked around stiffly, like a sleepwalker.

One crimson evening, a whirlwind blew over a blood red sun in a sky with lead-like clouds that looked about to drop to the ground. Gray shadows were cast on a lonely sand dune, where a solitary figure stumbled along. The dust kicked up by his feet was like gossamer fog and turned him into an indistinct, spectral shadow. That was Lingguan.

The evening sun, like a large bloody orb, perched gingerly on the tip of a distant mountain, providing a bleeding backdrop for him. His shadow grew longer on the sand as the sun continued to descend, and merged with shadows on the horizon at some point to spread out like water. Little by little, an evening mist fell with the dust and, like a large wok, covered him up in the hazy black desert.

The villagers in Shawan thought they heard shrill calls from a wild animal or a large bird in the east that night; it went on for a long time. It actually sounded very much like a pent-up man's shout.

The next day Lingguan was gone.

No one was sure what happened to him. Someone said he went to

Shenzhen to see a schoolmate but failed, so he got a cane and begged on the street. It was a sad sight. Another said he went to the south and worked in a feedlot where he was secretly learning a skill. Yet another said he did odd jobs at a museum while studying some language with a specialist. The language had a strange name, Xixia-ese. But, according to a profiteer who often traveled into the desert, he heard that someone from Liangzhou had died recently at Pig's Belly Well in the heart of the desert. The body was tossed into a sand hollow and gnawed out of shape by foxes, reduced to a pile of bones. The man even said he'd seen the bones and wondered if it could be Lingguan.

In any case, there was no shortage of sightings and tales.

Laoshun had too much to do to listen to the gossip. White Dew would arrive soon, and the rabbit hawks would be coming down again. He had bought a large bundle of cotton thread, and his time was taken up by weaving nets. Besides, Ying'er had just given birth to a chubby little boy, who now filled the large void from Hantou's death and brought him and his wife enough daily matters to keep them busy. More importantly, he and his wife had faith in their son; they believed he'd left for a wider world and knew he'd be back one day; Lingguan would come home no matter how far he'd traveled.

He left because he wanted to return.

Ying'er was their only cause for concern. Day and night she sat blankly, softly singing a tune known to every villager in Shawan—

The log-carrying pole is broken,
Drops of clear water fall to the ground.
Soiling my body and turning it black,
You left, walking down a broad, open road.

图书在版编目（CIP）数据

大漠祭 = Desert Rites：英文 / 雪漠著；葛浩文，林丽君译. —北京：中国大百科全书出版社，2018.9

ISBN 978-7-5202-0342-5

Ⅰ. ①大… Ⅱ. ①雪… ②葛… ③林… Ⅲ. ①长篇小说-中国-当代-英文 Ⅳ. ①I247.5

中国版本图书馆CIP数据核字（2018）第199109号

出 版 人　刘国辉
特约编审　阿去克
策划编辑　李默耘
责任编辑　姚常龄
特约编辑　刘　琦　王人龙
英文校对　石学亮
责任印制　邹景峰　李宝丰
装帧设计　U-BOOK
出版发行　中国大百科全书出版社
地　　址　北京阜成门北大街 17 号
邮　　编　100037
网　　址　http://www.ecph.com.cn
电　　话　010-88390739
印　　刷　北京汇瑞嘉合文化发展有限公司
开　　本　880 毫米 ×1230 毫米　1/32
字　　数　500 千字
印　　张　23.5
版　　次　2018 年 9 月第 1 版第 1 次印刷
定　　价　132.00 元